PRAISE FOR CATHERINE COULTER'S
FBI THRILLER SERIES

"Fast-paced." —*People*

"This terrific thriller will drag you into its chilling web of terror and not let go until the last paragraph . . . A ripping good read."
—*The San Francisco Examiner*

"A good storyteller . . . Coulter always keeps the pace brisk."
—*Fort Worth Star-Telegram*

"With possible blackmail, intra-judiciary rivalries, and personal peccadilloes, there's more than enough intrigue—and suspects—for full court standing in this snappy page-turner . . . A zesty read." —*Book Page*

"Twisted villains . . . intriguing escapism . . . The latest in the series featuring likable married FBI agents Lacey Sherlock and Dillon Savich."
—*Lansing* (MI) *State Journal*

"Coulter takes readers on a chilling and suspenseful ride . . . taut, fast-paced, hard to put down." —*Cedar Rapids Gazette*

"The perfect suspense thriller, loaded with plenty of action."
—*The Best Reviews*

"The newest installment in Coulter's FBI series delivers . . . a fast-moving investigation, a mind-bending mystery . . . The mystery at the heart . . . is intriguing and the pacing is brisk." —*Publishers Weekly*

"Fast-paced, romantic . . . Coulter gets better and more cinematic with each of her suspenseful FBI adventures." —*Booklist*

THE
BEGINNING

CATHERINE COULTER

BERKLEY BOOKS, NEW YORK

THE BERKLEY PUBLISHING GROUP
Published by the Penguin Group
Penguin Group (USA) Inc.
375 Hudson Street, New York, New York 10014, USA
Penguin Group (Canada), 90 Eglinton Avenue East, Suite 700, Toronto, Ontario M4P 2Y3, Canada
(a division of Pearson Penguin Canada Inc.)
Penguin Books Ltd., 80 Strand, London WC2R 0RL, England
Penguin Group Ireland, 25 St. Stephen's Green, Dublin 2, Ireland (a division of Penguin Books Ltd.)
Penguin Group (Australia), 250 Camberwell Road, Camberwell, Victoria 3124, Australia
(a division of Pearson Australia Group Pty. Ltd.)
Penguin Books India Pvt. Ltd., 11 Community Centre, Panchsheel Park, New Delhi—110 017, India
Penguin Group (NZ), Cnr. Airborne and Rosedale Roads, Albany, Auckland 1310, New Zealand
(a division of Pearson New Zealand Ltd.)
Penguin Books (South Africa) (Pty.) Ltd., 24 Sturdee Avenue, Rosebank, Johannesburg 2196,
South Africa

Penguin Books Ltd., Registered Offices: 80 Strand, London WC2R 0RL, England

This is a work of fiction. Names, characters, places, and incidents either are the product of the author's imagination or are used fictitiously, and any resemblance to actual persons, living or dead, business establishments, events, or locales is entirely coincidental. The publisher does not have any control over and does not assume any responsibility for author or third-party websites or their content.

PRINTING HISTORY
Berkley trade paperback one-volume edition / September 2005

Berkley trade paperback ISBN: 0-425-20551-7

This book has been catalogued with the Library of Congress.

PRINTED IN THE UNITED STATES OF AMERICA

10 9 8 7 6 5 4 3 2 1

CONTENTS

THE COVE

ACKNOWLEDGMENTS

To my creative and talented sister, Diane Coulter, who said to me, "Let me tell you about this little town on the coast of Oregon called The Cove." And thus *The Cove* was born.

To my assistant, Karen Evans, who snits without fear of death, and with charm.

And finally to my husband, Anton, partner and confidant, who manages to keep everything in proper perspective.

ONE

Someone was watching her. She tugged on the black wig, flattening it against her ears, and quickly put on another coat of deep red lipstick, holding the mirror up so she could see behind her.

The young Marine saw her face in the mirror and grinned at her. She jumped as if she'd been shot. *Just stop it. He's harmless, he's only flirting.* He couldn't be more than eighteen, his head all shaved, his cheeks as smooth as hers. She tilted the mirror to see more. The woman sitting beside him was reading a Dick Francis novel. In the seat behind them a young couple were leaning into each other, asleep.

The seat in front of her was empty. The Greyhound driver was whistling Eric Clapton's "Tears in Heaven," a song that always twisted up her insides. The only one who seemed to notice her was that young Marine, who'd gotten on at the last stop in Portland. He was probably going home to see his eighteen-year-old girlfriend. He wasn't after her, surely, but someone was. She wouldn't be fooled again. They'd taught her so much. No, she'd never be fooled again.

She put the mirror back into her purse and fastened the flap. She stared at her fingers, at the white line where the wedding ring had been until three days ago. She'd tried to pull it off for the past six months but hadn't managed to do it. She had been too out of it even to fasten the Velcro on her sneakers—when they allowed her sneakers—much less work off a tight ring.

Soon, she thought, soon she would be safe. Her mother would be safe too. Oh, God, Noelle—sobbing in the middle of the night when she didn't know anyone could hear her. But without her there, they couldn't do a thing to Noelle. Odd how she rarely thought of Noelle as her mother anymore, not like she had ten years before, when Noelle had listened to all her teenage problems, taken her shopping, driven her to her soccer games. So much they'd done together. Before. Yes, before that night when she'd seen her father slam his fist into her mother's chest and she'd heard the cracking of ribs.

She'd run in, screaming at him to leave her mother alone, and jumped on his back. He was so surprised, so shocked, that he didn't strike her. He shook her off, turned, and shouted down at her, "Mind your own business, Susan! This doesn't concern you." She stared at him, all the fear and hatred she felt for him at that moment clear on her face.

"Doesn't concern me? She's my mother, you bastard. Don't you dare hit her again!"

He looked calm, but she wasn't fooled; she saw the pulse pounding madly in his neck. "It was her fault, Susan. Mind your own damned business. Do you hear me? It was her fault." He took a step toward her mother, his fist raised. She picked up the Waterford carafe off his desk, yelling, "Touch her and I'll bash your head in."

He was panting now, turning swiftly to face her again, no more calm expression to fool her. His face was distorted with rage. "Bitch! Damned interfering little bitch! I'll make you pay for this, Susan. No one goes against me, particularly a spoiled little girl who's never done a thing in her life except spend her father's money." He didn't hit Noelle again. He looked at both of them with naked fury, then strode out of the house, slamming the door behind him.

"Yeah, right," she said and very carefully and slowly set the Waterford carafe down before she dropped it.

She wanted to call an ambulance but her mother wouldn't allow it. "You can't," she said, her voice as cracked as her ribs. "You can't, Sally. Your father would be ruined if anyone believed us. I can't allow that to happen."

"He deserves to be ruined," Sally said, but she obeyed. She was only sixteen years old, home for the weekend from her private girls' school in Laurelberg, Virginia. Why wouldn't they be believed?

"No, dearest," her mother whispered, the pain bowing her in on herself. "No. Get me that blue bottle of pills in the medicine cabinet. Hurry, Sally. The blue bottle."

As she watched her mother swallow three of the pills, groaning as she did so, she realized the pills were there because her father had struck her mother before. Deep down, Sally knew it. She hated herself because she'd never asked, never said a word.

That night her mother became Noelle, and the next week Sally left her girls' school and moved back to her parents' home in Washington, D.C., in hopes of protecting her mother. She read everything she could find on abuse—not that it helped.

That was ten years ago, though sometimes it seemed like last week. Noelle had stayed with her husband, refusing to seek counseling, refusing to read any of the books Sally brought her. It made no sense to Sally, but she'd stayed as close as possible, until she'd met Scott Brainerd at the Whistler exhibition at the National Gallery of Art and married him two months later.

She didn't want to think about Scott or about her father now. Despite her vigilance, she knew her father had hit Noelle whenever she happened to be gone from the house. She'd seen the bruises her mother had tried to hide from her, seen her walking carefully, like an old woman. Once he broke her mother's arm, but Noelle refused to go to the hospital, to the doctor, and ordered Susan to keep quiet. Her father just looked at her, daring her, and she did nothing. Nothing.

Her fingers rubbed unconsciously over the white line where the ring had been. She could remember the past so clearly—her first day at school, when she was on the seesaw and a little boy pointed, laughing that he saw her panties.

It was just the past week that was a near blank in her mind. The week her father had been killed. The whole week was like a very long dream that had almost dissolved into nothing more than an occasional wisp of memory with the coming of the morning.

Sally knew she'd been at her parents' house that night, but she couldn't remember anything more, at least nothing she could grasp—just vague shadows that blurred, then faded in and out. But they didn't know that. They wanted her badly, she'd realized that soon enough. If they couldn't use her to prove that Noelle had killed her husband, why, then they'd take her and prove that she'd killed her father. Why not? Other children had murdered their fathers. Although there were plenty of times she'd wanted to, she didn't believe she'd killed him.

On the other hand, she simply didn't know. It was all a blank, locked tightly away in her brain. She knew she was capable of killing that bastard, but had she? There were many people who could have wanted her father dead. Perhaps they'd found out she'd been there after all. Yes, that was it. She'd been a witness and they knew it. She probably had been. She just didn't remember.

She had to stay focused on the present. She looked out the Greyhound window at the small town the bus was going through. Ugly gray exhaust spewed out the back of the bus. She bet the locals loved that.

They were driving along Highway 101 southwest. Another half hour, she thought, just thirty more minutes, and she wouldn't have to worry anymore, at least for a while. She would take any safe time she could get. Soon she wouldn't have to be afraid of anyone who chanced to look at her. No one knew about her aunt, no one.

She was terrified the young Marine would get off after her when she stepped down from the bus at the junction of highways 101 and 101A. But he didn't. No one did. She stood there with her one small bag, staring at the young Marine, who'd turned around in his seat and was looking back at her. She tamped down on her fear. He'd only wanted to flirt, not hurt her. She thought he had lousy taste in women. She watched for cars, but none were coming from either direction.

She walked west along Highway 101A to The Cove. Highway 101A didn't go east.

"YES?"

She stared at the woman she'd seen once in her life when she was no more than seven years old. She looked like a hippie, a colorful scarf wrapped around her long, curling, dark hair, huge gold hoops dangling from her ears, her skirt ankle-length and painted all in dark blues and browns. She was wearing blue sneakers. Her face was strong, her cheekbones high and prominent, her chin sharp, her eyes dark and intelligent. Actually, she was the most beautiful woman Sally had ever seen.

"Aunt Amabel?"

"What did you say?" Amabel stared at the young woman who stood on her front doorstep, a young woman who didn't look cheap with all that makeup she'd piled on her face, just exhausted and sickly pale. And frightened. Then, of course, she knew. She had known deep down that she would come. Yes, she'd known, but it still shook her.

"I'm Sally," she said and pulled off the black wig and took out half a dozen hairpins. Thick, waving dark blond hair tumbled down to her shoulders. "Maybe you called me Susan? Not many people do anymore."

The woman was shaking her head back and forth, those dazzling earrings slapping against her neck. "It's really you, Sally?" She rocked back on her heels.

"Yes."

"Oh, my," Amabel said and quickly pulled her niece against her, hugged her tightly, then pushed her back to look at her. "Oh, my goodness. I've been so worried. I finally heard the news about your papa, but I didn't know if I should call Noelle. You know how she is. I was going to call her tonight when the rates go down, but you're here, Sally. I guess I hoped you'd come to me. What's happened? Is your mama all right?"

"Noelle is fine, I think," Sally said. "I didn't know where else to go, so I came here. Can I stay here, Aunt Amabel, for a little while? Just until I can think of something, make some plans?"

"Of course you can. Look at that black wig and all that makeup on your face. Why, baby?"

The endearment undid her. She'd not cried, not once, until now, until this woman she didn't really know called her "baby." Her aunt's hands were stroking her back, her voice was low and soothing. "It's all right, lovey. I promise you, everything will be all right now. Come in, Sally, and I'll take care of you. That's what I told your mama when I first saw you. You were the cutest little thing, so skinny, your arms and legs wobbly like a colt's, and the biggest smile I'd ever seen. I wanted to take care of you then. You'll be safe here. Come on, baby."

The damnable tears wouldn't stop. They kept dripping down her face, ruining the god-awful thick black mascara. She even tasted it, and when she swiped her hand over her face it came away with black streaks.

"I look like a circus clown," she said, swallowing hard to stop the tears, to smile, to make herself smile. She took out the green-colored contacts. With the crying, they hurt.

"No, you look like a little girl trying on her mama's makeup. That's right, take out those ugly contacts. Ah, now you've got your pretty blue eyes again. Come to the kitchen and I'll make you some tea. I always put a drop of brandy in mine. It wouldn't hurt you one little bit. How old are you now, Sally?"

"Twenty-six, I think."

"What do you mean, you think?" her aunt said, cocking her head to one side, making the gold hoop earring hang straight down almost to her shoulder.

Sally couldn't tell her that though she thought her birthday had come and gone in that place, she couldn't seem to see the day in her mind, couldn't dredge up anyone saying anything to her, not that she could imagine it anyway. She couldn't even remember if her father had been there. She prayed he hadn't. She couldn't tell Amabel about that, she just couldn't. She shook her head, smiled, and said, not lying well, "It was just a way of speaking, Aunt Amabel. I'd love some tea and a drop of brandy."

Amabel sat her niece down in the kitchen at her old pine table that had three magazines under one leg to keep it steady. At least she'd made cushions for the wooden seats so they were comfortable. She put the kettle on the gas burner and turned it on. "There," she said. "That won't take too long."

Sally watched her put a Lipton tea bag into each cup and pour in the brandy. Amabel said, "I always pour the brandy in first. It soaks into the tea bag and makes the flavor stronger. Brandy's expensive and I've got to make it last. This bottle"—she lifted the Christian Brothers—"is going on its third month. Not bad. You'll see, you'll like it."

"No one followed me, Aunt Amabel. I was really careful. I imagine you know that everyone is after me. But I managed to get away. As far as I know, no one knows about you. Noelle never told a soul. Only Father knew about you, and he's dead."

Amabel nodded. Sally sat quietly, watching her move around the small kitchen, each action smooth and efficient. She was graceful, this aunt of hers in her hippie clothes. She looked at those strong hands, the long fingers, the short, buffed nails painted an awesome bright red. Amabel was an artist, she remembered that now. She couldn't see any resemblance at all to Noelle, Amabel's younger sister. Amabel was dark as a gypsy, while Noelle was blond and fair-complexioned, blue-eyed, and soft as a pillow.

Like me, Sally thought. But Sally wasn't soft anymore. She was hard as a brick.

She waited, expecting Amabel to whip out a deck of cards and tell her fortune. She wondered why none of Noelle's family ever spoke of Amabel. What had she done that was so terrible?

Her fingers rubbed over the white band where the ring had been. She said as she looked around the old kitchen with its ancient refrigerator and porcelain sink, "You don't mind that I'm here, Aunt Amabel?"

"Call me Amabel, honey, that'll be fine. I don't mind at all. Both of us will protect your mama. As for you, why, I don't think you could hurt that little bug that's scurrying across the kitchen floor."

Sally shook her head, got out of her seat, and squashed the bug beneath her heel. She sat down again. "I want you to see me as I really am," she said.

Amabel only shrugged, turned back to the stove when the teakettle whistled, and poured the water into the teacups. She said, not turning around, "Things happen to people, change them. Take your mama. Everyone always protected your mama, including me. Why wouldn't her daughter do the same? You are protecting her, aren't you, Sally?"

She handed Sally her cup of tea. She pulled the tea bag back and forth, making the tea darker and darker. Finally, she lifted the bag and placed it carefully on the saucer. She'd swished that tea bag just the way her mother always had when she'd been young. She took a drink, held the brandied tea in her mouth a moment, then swallowed. The tea was wonderful, thick, rich, and sinful. She felt less on edge almost immediately. That brandy was something. Surely she'd be safe here. Surely Amabel would take her in for a little while until she figured out what to do.

She imagined her aunt wanted to hear everything, but she wasn't pushing. Sally was immensely grateful for that.

"I've often wondered what kind of woman you'd become," Amabel said. "Looks to me like you've become a fine one. This mess—and that's what it is—it will pass. Everything will be resolved, you'll see." She was silent a moment, remembering the affection she'd felt for the little girl, that bone-deep desire to keep her close, to hug her until she squeaked. It surprised her that it was still there. She didn't like it, nor did she want it.

"Careful of leaning on that end of the table, Sally. Purn Davies wanted to fix it for me, but I wouldn't let him." She knew Sally wasn't hearing her, but it didn't matter, Amabel was just making noise until Sally got some of that brandy in her belly.

"This tea's something else, Amabel. Strange, but good." She took another drink, then another. She felt warmth pooling in her stomach. She realized she hadn't felt this warm in more than five days.

"You might as well tell me now, Sally. You came here so you could protect your mama, didn't you, baby?"

Sally took another big drink of the tea. What could she say? She said nothing.

"Did your mama kill your papa?"

Sally set down her cup and stared into it, wishing she knew the truth of things, but that night was as murky in her mind as the tea in the bottom of her cup. "I don't know," she said finally. "I just don't know, but they think I do. They think I'm either protecting Noelle or running because I did it. They're trying to find me. I didn't want to take a chance, so that's why I'm here."

Was she lying? Amabel didn't say anything. She merely smiled at her niece, who looked exhausted, her face white and pinched, her lovely blue eyes as faded and worn as an old dress. She was too thin; her sweater and slacks hung on her. In that moment her niece looked very old, as if she had seen too much of the wicked side of life. Well, it was too bad, but there was more wickedness in the world than anyone cared to admit.

She said quietly as she stared down into her teacup, "If your mama did kill her husband, I'll bet the bastard deserved it."

TWO

Sally nearly dropped her cup. She set it carefully down. "You knew?"

"Sure. All of us did. The first time I ever got to see you was when she brought you home. I was passing through. That's all our folks ever wanted me to do—pass through and not say much or show my face much, particularly to all their friends. Anyway, your mama showed up. She was running away from him, she said. She also said she'd never go back. She was bruised. She cried all the time.

"But her resolve didn't last long. He called her two nights later and she flew back home the next day, with you all wrapped in a blanket. You weren't even a year old then. She wouldn't talk about it to me. I never could understand why a woman would let herself be beaten whenever a man decided he wanted to do it."

"I couldn't either. I tried, Aunt Amabel. I really tried, but she wouldn't listen. What did my grandparents say?"

Amabel shrugged, thinking of her horrified father, staring at beautiful Noelle, wondering what the devil he would do if the press got wind of the juicy story that his son-in-law, Amory St. John, was a wife beater. And their mother, shrinking away from her daughter as if she had some sort of vile disease. She hadn't cared either. She just didn't want the press to find out because it would hurt the family's reputation.

"They aren't what you'd call real warm parents, Sally. They pretended not to believe that your papa beat your mama. They looked at Noelle, saw all those bruises, and denied all of it. They told her she shouldn't tell lies like that. Your mama was a real mess, arguing with them, pleading with them to help her.

"But then he called, and your mama acted like nothing had ever happened. You know what, Sally? My parents were mighty relieved when she left. She would have been a loser, a failure, a millstone around their necks if she'd left your father. She was special, a daughter to be proud of, when she was with him. Do you ever see your grandparents?"

"Three times a year. Oh, Aunt Amabel, I hated him. But now—"

"Now you're afraid the police are looking for you. Don't worry, baby. No one would know you in that disguise."

He would, Sally thought. In a flash. "I hope not," she said. "Do you think I should keep wearing the black wig here?"

"No, I wouldn't worry. You're my niece, nothing more, nothing less. No one watches TV except for Thelma Nettro, who owns the bed-and-breakfast, and she's so old I don't even know if she can see the screen. She can hear, though. I know that for a fact.

"No, don't bother with the wig—and leave those contacts in a drawer. Not to worry. We'll use your married name. Here you'll be Sally Brainerd."

"I can't use that name anymore, Amabel."

"All right then. We'll use your maiden name—Sally St. John. No, don't worry that anyone would ever tie you to your dead papa. Like I said, no one here pays any attention to what goes on outside the town limits. As for anyone else, why, no one ever comes here—"

"Except for people who want to eat the World's Greatest Ice Cream. I like the sign out at the junction with that huge chocolate ice cream cone painted on it. You can see it a mile away, and by the time you get to it, your mouth is watering. You painted the sign, didn't you, Amabel?"

"I sure did. And you're right. People tell us they see that sign and by the time they get to the junction their car turns itself toward The Cove. It's Helen Keaton's recipe, handed down from her granny. The ice cream shop used to be the chapel in the front of Ralph Keaton's mortuary. We all decided that since we have Reverend Vorhees's church, we didn't need Ralph's little chapel too." She paused, looking into a memory, and smiled. "In the beginning we stored the ice cream in caskets packed full of ice. It took every freezer in every refrigerator in this town to make that much ice."

"I can't wait to try it. Goodness, I remember when the town wasn't much of anything—back when I came here that one time. Do you remember? I was just a little kid."

"I remember. You were adorable."

Sally smiled, a very small smile, but it was a beginning. She shook her head, saying, "I remember this place used to be so ramshackle and down at the heels—no paint on any of the houses, boards hanging off some of the buildings. And there were potholes in the street as deep as I was tall. But now the town looks wonderful, so charming and clean and pristine."

"Well, you're right. We've had lots of good changes. We all put our heads together, and that's when Helen Keaton spoke up about her granny's ice cream recipe. That Fourth of July—goodness, it will be four years this July—was when we opened the World's Greatest Ice Cream Shop. I'll never forget how the men all pooh-poohed the idea, said it wouldn't amount to anything. Well, we sure showed them."

"I'd say so. If the World's Greatest Ice Cream Shop is the reason the town's so beautiful now, maybe Helen Keaton should run for president."

"Maybe so. Would you like a ham sandwich, baby?"

A ham sandwich, Sally thought. "With mayonnaise? Real mayonnaise, not the fat-free stuff?"

"Real mayonnaise."

"White bread and not fourteen-vitamin seven-grain whole wheat?"

"Cheap white bread."

"That sounds wonderful, Amabel. You're sure no one will recognize me?"

"Not a soul."

They watched a small, very grainy black-and-white TV while Sally ate her sandwich. Within five minutes, the story was on the national news broadcast.

"Former Naval Commander Amory Davidson St. John was buried today at Arlington National Cemetery. His widow, Noelle St. John, was accompanied by her son-in-law, Scott Brainerd, a lawyer who had worked closely with Amory St. John, the senior legal counsel for TransCon International. Her daughter, Susan St. John Brainerd, was not present.

"We go now to Police Commissioner Howard Duzman, who is working closely with the FBI on this high-profile investigation."

Amabel didn't know much of anything about Scott Brainerd. She had never met him, had never spoken to him until she had called Noelle and he answered the phone, identified himself, and asked who she was. And she'd told him. Why not? She'd asked him to have Noelle call her back. But Noelle hadn't called her—not that Amabel had expected her to. If Noelle's life depended on it, well, that would be different. She would be on the phone like a shot. But she hadn't called her this time. Amabel wondered if Noelle would realize that Sally could be here. Would that make her call? She didn't know. Actually, now it didn't matter.

She reached out her hand and covered her niece's thin fingers with hers. She saw where there had once been a ring, but it was gone now, leaving just a pale white mark in its place. She wondered for a moment if she should tell Sally that she'd spoken to her husband. No, not yet. Maybe never. Let the girl rest for a while. Hopefully there would be time, but Amabel didn't know. Actually, if she could, she would get rid of Sally this very minute, get her away from here before . . . No, she wouldn't think about that. She didn't really have a choice.

Everything would work out. Besides, what would it matter if Scott Brainerd did find out his wife was hiding out here? So she said nothing, just held Sally's hand in hers.

"I'm awfully tired, Amabel."

"I'll bet you are, baby. I'll just bet you are."

Amabel tucked her in like she was her little girl in the small second bedroom. The room was quiet, so very quiet. She was asleep within minutes. In a few more minutes she was twisted in the covers, moaning.

THERE was so much daylight in that room, all of it pouring through the wide windows that gave onto an immaculate lawn stretching a good hundred yards to the edge of a copse of thick oak trees. The two men led her in, shoving her forward, nearly knocking her to her knees. They put their hands on her shoulders, forcing her to sit in front of his desk. He was smiling at her. He didn't say a word until they'd left, quietly closing the door behind them.

He steepled his fingers. "You look pathetic, Sally, in those gray sweats. And just look at your hair, all stringy, and no makeup on your face, not even a touch of lipstick in honor of coming to see me. Next time I'll have to ask them to do something with you before bringing you to me."

She heard every word, felt the hurt that every word intended, but the comprehension quickly died, and she only shrugged, a tiny movement because it was so much work to make her shoulders rise and fall to produce a shrug.

"You've been with me now for nearly a week and you're not a bit better, Sally. You're still delusional, paranoid. If you're too stupid to understand what those words mean, why, then, let me get more basic with you. You're crazy, Sally, just plain crazy, and you'll stay that way. No cure for you. Now, since I've got to look at you for a while longer, why don't you at least say something, maybe even sing a little song, maybe a song you used to sing in the shower. Yes, I know you always sang in the shower. How about it?"

Oddly, even though the comprehension didn't remain long in her brain, the viciousness of the words, the utter cruelty of them, hung on. She managed to rise, lean forward, and spit in his face.

He lunged around his desk as he swiped his hand over his face. He jerked her to her feet and slapped her hard, sending her reeling to the floor.

The door to his office flew open, and the two men who'd brought her came banging through.

They were worried about him?

She heard him say, "She spit on me and then attacked me. Bring me three milligrams of Haldol. No pill this time. That should calm our poor little girl down."

No. She knew that if they gave her any more of that stuff she'd die. She knew it, knew it. She staggered to her feet. She ran to those wide windows. She heard shouts behind her. She dove through the glass. For an instant she was flying, white shards of glass falling from her, letting her soar higher and higher above that beautiful lawn, flying away from the horror of this place, the horror of him. Then she wasn't flying anymore. She heard screams and knew it was she who was screaming. Then she felt the pain drag at her, pulling her down, down, until there was blackness and beautiful nothingness.

BUT the screaming went on. That wasn't right. She was unconscious, no longer screaming.

Another scream jerked her awake. Sally reared up in bed, straining to hear those screams. They'd been here, in The Cove, in Amabel's house, not in her dream back there. She didn't move, just waited, waited. A cat? No, it was human, a cry of pain, she knew it was. She'd heard enough cries of pain in the last year.

Who? Amabel? She didn't want to move, but she made herself slip out from under the three blankets Amabel had piled on top of her at nine o'clock the previous evening. It was freezing in the small guest room and black as the bottom of a witch's cauldron. Sally didn't have a bathrobe, only her long Lanz flannel nightgown. Scott had hated her nightgowns, he hated—no, forget Scott. He truly didn't matter, hadn't mattered in a very long time.

The room was very dark. She made her way to the door and gently shoved it open. The narrow hallway was just as dark. She waited, waited longer, not wanting to hear that cry again, but knowing she would. It was a cry of pain. Perhaps there had been surprise in it. She couldn't be sure now. She waited. It was just a matter of time. She walked in her sock feet toward Amabel's bedroom.

She stumbled when she heard another cry, her hip hitting a table. This cry came from outside. She was sure of it. It wasn't Amabel; thank God, she was safe. Amabel would know what to do.

What was it? She rubbed her hip as she set the table against the wall again.

Suddenly Amabel's bedroom door flew open. "What's going on? Is that you, Sally?"

"Yes, Amabel," she whispered. "I heard someone cry out and thought it was you. What is it?"

"I didn't hear a thing," Amabel said. "Go back to bed, dear. You're exhausted. It's probably the leftovers of a bad dream. Look at you, you're white as the woodwork. You did have a nightmare, didn't you?"

Sally nodded because it was the truth. But those screams had lasted, had gone on and on. They'd not been part of the dream, the dream that was a memory she hated, but that always came in her sleep when she was helpless against it.

"Go to bed. You poor baby, you're shivering like a leaf. Go back to bed. Hurry now."

"But I heard it twice, Amabel. I thought it was you, but it's not. It's coming from outside the house."

"No, baby, there's nothing out there. You're so tired, so much has happened in the past few days I'm surprised you haven't heard the Rolling Stones bawling at the top of their lungs. There's nothing, Sally. It was a nightmare, nothing more. Don't forget, this is The Cove, dear. Nothing ever happens here. If you did hear something, why, it was only the wind. The wind off the ocean can whine like a person. You'll learn that soon enough. You didn't hear anything. Trust me. Go back to bed."

Sally went back to bed. She lay stiff and waiting, so cold she wondered whether the tears would freeze on her face if she cried. She could have sworn that she heard a door quietly open and close, but she didn't have the guts to go see.

She would relax, then stiffen again, waiting to hear that awful cry. But there weren't any more cries. Maybe Amabel was right. She was exhausted; she had been dreaming and it had been hideous and so very real. Maybe she was paranoid or psychotic or schizophrenic. They had called her all those things for six months. She wondered—if she saw the person actually cry out would that be a delusion? A fabrication of her mind? Probably. No, she wouldn't think about that time. It made her hurt too much. She fell asleep again near dawn.

It was a dreamless sleep this time.

THREE

James Railey Quinlan had more energy than he'd had twenty minutes before. His body was humming with it. That was because she was here. He
was sure of it now, he could feel her here. He'd always had these feelings—
more than intuition. The feelings came to him suddenly, and he had always
followed them, ever since he was a kid. The time or two he hadn't, he'd gotten himself into big trouble. Now he was out on a very long limb, and if he
was wrong he'd pay for it. But he wasn't wrong. He could feel her presence
in this very charming and well-manicured little town.

Dreadful little place, he thought, so perfect, like a Hollywood set, like
Teresa's hometown. He remembered having the same reaction, feeling the
same vague distaste when he'd traveled to that small town in Ohio to marry
Teresa Raglan, daughter of the local judge.

He pulled his gray Buick Regal into a well-marked parking place in
front of the World's Greatest Ice Cream Shop. There were two large plate-
glass windows painted all around with bright blue trim. He could see small
circular tables inside, with old-fashioned white wrought-iron chairs. Behind the counter an older woman was talking to a man while she scooped
chocolate ice cream out of a carton set down into the counter. The front of
the shop was painted a pristine white. It was a quaint little place, just like
the rest of the town, but for some reason he didn't like the looks of it.

He stepped out of the sedan and looked around. Next to the ice cream
shop was a small general store with a sign out front in ornate type that
could have come straight out of Victorian times: PURN DAVIES: YOU WANT
IT—I SELL IT.

On the other side of the ice cream shop was a small clothing store that
looked elegant and expensive, with that peculiar Carmel-like look that the
rest of the buildings had. It was called Intimate Deceptions—a name that
for James conjured up images of black lace against a white sheet or white
skin.

The sidewalks looked brand new and the road was nicely blacktopped.
No ruts anywhere to hold rain puddles.

All the parking spots were marked with thick white lines. Not a faded line in the bunch. He'd seen newer houses on the drive in, apparently all built very recently. In town there was a hardware store, a small Safeway barely large enough to support the sign, a dry cleaners, a one-hour-photo place, a McDonald's with a very discreet golden arch.

A prosperous, quaint little town that was perfect.

He slipped his keys into his jacket pocket. First thing he needed was a place to stay. He spotted a sign reading THELMA'S BED AND BREAKFAST right across the street. Nothing fancy about that sign or title. He pulled his black travel bag out of the back seat and walked over to Thelma's big white Victorian gingerbread house with its deep porch that encircled the entire house. He hoped he could get a room up in one of those circular towers.

For an old house, it was in immaculate shape. The white of the clapboard gleamed, and the pale blue and yellow trim around the windows and on cornices seemed to be fresh. The wide wooden porch planks didn't groan beneath his weight. The boards were new, the railing solid oak and sturdy.

He announced himself as James Quinlan to a smiling lady in her late fifties whom he found standing behind the antique walnut counter in the front hall. She was wearing an apron that had lots of flour on it. He explained he was looking for a room, preferably one in the tower. At the sound of an ancient cackle, he turned and saw a robust old lady rocking back and forth in an antique chair in the doorway of the huge living room. She was holding what appeared to be a diary in front of her nose with one hand, and in the other she held a fountain pen. Every few seconds she wet the tip of the fountain pen with her tongue, a habit that left her with a big black circle on the tip of her tongue.

"Ma'am," he said, and nodded toward the old lady. "I sure hope that ink isn't poisonous."

"It wouldn't kill her even if it was," the lady behind the counter said. "She's surely built up an immunity by now. Thelma's been at that diary of hers with that black ink on her tongue ever since she and her husband first moved to The Cove back in the 1940s."

The old lady cackled again, then called out, "I'm Thelma Nettro. You don't have a wife, boy?"

"That's a bold question, ma'am, even for an old lady."

Thelma ignored him. "So what are you doing in The Cove? You come here for the World's Greatest Ice Cream?"

"I saw that sign. I'll be sure to try it later."

"Have the peach. Helen just made it up last week. It's dandy. So if you aren't here for ice cream, then why are you here?"

Here goes, he thought. "I'm a private detective, ma'am. My client's parents disappeared around this area some three and a half years ago. The cops never got anywhere. The son hired me to find out what happened to them."

"Old folk?"

"Yeah, they'd been driving all over the U.S. in a Winnebago. The Winnebago was found in a used car lot up in Spokane. Looked to be foul play, but nobody could ever find anything out."

"So why are you here in The Cove? Nothing ever happens here, nothing at all. I remember telling my husband, Bobby—he died of pneumonia just after Eisenhower was reelected in 1956—that this little town had never known a heyday, but it kept going anyhow. Do you know what happened then? Well, I'll tell you. This banker from Portland bought up lots of coastal land and built vacation cottages. He built the two-laner off Highway 101 and ran it right to the ocean." Thelma stopped, licked the end of her fountain pen, and sighed. "Then in the 1960s, everything began to fall apart, everyone upped and left, got bored with our town, I suppose. So, you see, it doesn't make any sense for you to stay here."

"I'm using your town as a sort of central point. I'll search out from here. Perhaps you remember these old folk coming through, ma'am—"

"My name's Thelma, I told you that. There's lots of ma'ams in this world, but only one me, and I'm Thelma Nettro. Doc Spiver pronounced me deader than a bat some years ago, but he was wrong. Oh, Lordy, you should have seen the look on Ralph Keaton's face when he had me all ready to lay out in that funeral home of his. I near to scared the toenails off him when I sat up and demanded to know what he was doing. Ah, yes, that was something. He was so scared he went shouting for Reverend Hal Vorhees to protect him. You can call me Thelma, boy."

"Maybe you remember these old folk, Thelma. The man was Harve Jensen, and his wife's name was Marge. A nice older couple, according to their son. The son did say they had a real fondness for ice cream." Why not, he thought. Stir the pot a bit. Be specific, it made you more believable. Besides, everyone liked ice cream. He'd have to try it.

"Harve and Marge Jensen," Thelma repeated, rocking harder now, her veined and spotted old hands clenching and unclenching on the arms of the chair. "Can't say I remember any old folk like that. Driving a Winnebago, you say? You go over and try one of Helen's peach ice cream cones."

"Soon I will. I like the sign out there at the junction of 101 and 101A. The artist really got that brown color to look just like rich chocolate ice cream. Yeah, they were driving a Winnebago."

"It's brought us lots of folk, that sign. The state bureaucrats wanted us to take it down, but one of our locals—Gus Eisner—knew the governor's cousin, and he fixed it. We pay the state three hundred dollars a year to keep the sign there. Amabel repaints it every year in July, sort of an anniversary, since that's when we first opened. Purn Davies told her the chocolate paint she used for the ice cream was too dark, but we all ignored him. He wanted to marry Amabel after her husband died, but she wouldn't have anything to do with him. He still isn't over it. Pretty tacky, huh?"

"I'd say so," Quinlan said.

"You tell Amabel that you think her chocolate is perfect. That'll please her."

Amabel, he thought. Amabel Perdy. She was her aunt.

The stocky gray-haired woman behind the counter cleared her throat. She smiled at him when he turned back to her.

"What did you say, Martha? Speak up. You know I can't hear you."

Not likely, James thought. The old relic probably heard everything within three miles of town.

"And stop fiddling with those pearls. You've already broken them more times than I can count."

Martha's pearls did look a bit ratty, he thought.

"Martha, what do you want?"

"I need to check Mr. Quinlan in, Thelma. And I've got to finish baking that chocolate decadence cake before I go to lunch with Mr. Drapper. But I want to get Mr. Quinlan settled first."

"Well, do it, don't just stand there wringing your hands. You watch yourself with Ed Drapper, Martha. He's a fast one, that boy is. I noticed yesterday that you're getting liver spots, Martha. I heard you got liver spots if you'd had too much sex when you were younger. You watch what you do with Ed Drapper. Oh, yes, don't forget to put walnuts in that chocolate decadence cake. I love walnuts."

James turned to Martha, such a sweet-looking lady, with stiff gray hair, impressive bosom and glasses perched on the end of her nose. She was tucking her hands in her pockets, hiding those liver spots.

James laughed and said, knowing the old lady was listening, "She's a terror, isn't she?"

"She's more than a terror, Mr. Quinlan," Martha said in a whisper. "She's a lot more. Poor Ed Drapper is sixty-three years old." She raised her voice. "No, Thelma, I won't forget the walnuts."

"A mere lad," James said and smiled at Martha, who didn't look as if she'd ever had any sex in her life. She was tugging on those pearls again.

When she left him in the tower room, which gave him a panoramic view of the ocean, he walked to the window and stared out, not at the ocean that gleamed like a brilliant blue jewel beneath the full afternoon sun but at the people below. Across the street, right in front of Purn Davies's store, he saw four old geezers pull out chairs and arrange them around an oak barrel that had to be as old as James's grandfather. One of the men pulled out a deck of cards. James had a feeling he was looking at a long-standing ritual. One of the men arranged his cards, then spat off the sidewalk. Another one hooked his gnarly old fingers beneath his suspenders and leaned back in the chair. Yes, James thought, a ritual of many years. He wondered if one of them was Purn Davies, the one who'd criticized Amabel's chocolate because she'd refused to marry him. Was one of them Reverend Hal Vorhees? No, surely a reverend wouldn't be sitting there spitting and playing cards.

It didn't matter. He'd find out soon enough who everybody was. So there'd be no doubt in anybody's mind about why he was here, he would talk to this group too about Harve and Marge Jensen. He'd talk to everyone he ran into. No one would suspect a thing.

He would bet his next paycheck that those old geezers saw everything that went on in this town, including a runaway woman who happened to be the daughter of a big-time lawyer who had not only gotten himself murdered but who'd also been involved in some very bad business. A woman who also happened to be Amabel Perdy's niece.

James wished Amory St. John hadn't gotten himself knocked off, at least not until the FBI had finally nailed him for selling arms to terrorist nations.

He turned from the window and frowned. He realized he hadn't cared at all about Harve and Marge Jensen until ancient Thelma Nettro, who'd been pronounced dead by Doc Spiver but had risen from the table and scared Ralph Keaton witless, had lied to him.

Investigating the fate of the Jensens had been a cover that one of the assistants happened to find for him to use. It was a believable cover, she'd told him, because the couple really had mysteriously disappeared along a stretch of highway that included The Cove.

But why had the old lady lied? What reason could she possibly have? Now he was curious. Too bad he didn't have time. He thrived on mystery. And he was the best of the best, at least that was what Teresa had told him in bed time and again before she'd run away with a mail bomber he himself had hunted down and arrested, only to have her defend him and get him off on a technicality.

He hung up his slacks and his shirts, laid his underwear in the top drawer of the beautiful antique dresser. He walked into the bathroom to lay out his toiletries and was pleasantly surprised. It was huge, all pink-veined marble, and totally modernized, right down to the water-saver toilet. The tub was huge and was curtained off so he could take a shower if he preferred.

Old Thelma Nettro was obviously a hedonist. No claw-footed tubs for her. He wondered how the devil she could make enough money off this place to modernize the bathrooms like this. As far as he could tell, he was the only guest.

There was one restaurant in The Cove, a pretentious little cafe called the Hinterlands that had beautiful red and white tulips in its window boxes. Unlike the rest of the buildings that lined Main Street, the Hinterlands forked off to one side, faced the ocean, and looked painfully charming with its bricked walkway and gables, which, he was certain, had been added merely for decoration.

They served cod and bass. Nothing else, only cod and bass—fried, baked, poached, broiled. James hated all kinds of fish. He ate everything the small salad bar had to offer and knew he was going to have to live at the Safeway deli. But the Safeway was so small he doubted it even had a deli.

The waitress, an older woman decked out in a Swiss Miss outfit that laced up her chest and swept the floor, said, "Oh, it's fish this week. Zeke can't do more than one thing at a time. He says it confounds him. Next Monday you come in and we'll have something else. How about some mashed potatoes with all those greens?"

He nodded to Martha and Ed Drapper, who were evidently enjoying their fried cod, cole slaw, and mashed potatoes. She gave him a brilliant smile. He wondered if she recognized him. She wasn't wearing her glasses. Her left hand was playing with her pearls.

After lunch, as James walked toward the four old men playing cards around the barrel, he saw at least half a dozen cars parked out in front of the World's Greatest Ice Cream Shop. Popular place. Had the place been here when Harve and Marge came through? Yeah, sure it had. That's when old Thelma's rheumy eyes had twitched and her old hands had clenched big time. He might as well get to know the locals before he tracked down Susan St. John Brainerd.

He wasn't quite certain yet what he was going to do with her when he found her. The truth, he thought. All he wanted was the truth from her. And he'd get it. He usually did. Then maybe he'd work on the other mystery. If there was another mystery.

TEN minutes later James walked into the World's Greatest Ice Cream Shop thinking that those four old men weren't any better liars than Thelma Nettro. Unlike Thelma, they hadn't said a word, just shook their heads sorrowfully as they looked at each other. One of them had spat after he repeated Harve's name. That one was Purn Davies. The old man leaning back in the chair had said he'd always fancied having a Winnebago. His name was Gus Eisner. Another one of the men said Gus could fix anything on wheels and kept them all running. The other old man wouldn't meet his eyes. He couldn't remember the names of those last two.

It was telling, their behavior. Whatever had happened to Harve and Marge Jensen, everyone he'd met so far knew about it. He was looking forward to trying the World's Greatest Ice Cream.

The same older woman he'd seen upon his arrival was scooping up what looked to be peach ice cream for a family of tourists who'd probably seen that sign on the road and come west.

The kids were jumping and yelling. The boy wanted Cove Chocolate and the girl wanted Basque Vanilla.

"You've only got the six flavors?" the woman asked.

"Yes, just six. We vary them according to the season. We don't mass-produce anything."

The boy whined that now he wanted blueberry ice cream. The chocolate looked too dark.

The older woman behind the counter smiled down at him and said, "You can't have it. Either pick another flavor or shut up."

The mother gasped and stared. "You can't act like that toward our son. Why, he's—"

The older woman smiled back, straightened her lacy white cap, and said, "He's what, ma'am?"

"He's a brat," the husband said. He turned to his son. "What do you want, Mickey? You see the six flavors. Pick one now or don't have any."

"I want Basque Vanilla," the girl said. "He can have worms."

"Now, Julie," the mother said, then licked the ice cream cone the woman handed her. "Oh, goodness, it's wonderful. Fresh peaches, Rick. Fresh peaches. It's great."

The woman behind the counter smiled. The boy took a chocolate triple-dip cone.

James watched the family finally leave.

"Yes, can I help you?"

"I'd like a peach cone, please, ma'am."

"You're new to town," she said as she pulled the scoop through the big tub of ice cream. "You traveling through?"

"No," James said, taking the cone. "I'll be here for a while. I'm trying to find Marge and Harve Jensen."

"Never heard of them."

James took a lick. He felt as though sweet peaches were sliding down his throat. The woman was a good liar. "The lady was right. This is delicious."

"Thank you. This Marge and Harve—"

James repeated the story he'd told to Thelma and Martha and the old men. When he finished, he stuck out his hand and said, "My name's James Quinlan. I'm a private investigator from Los Angeles."

"I'm Sherry Vorhees. My husband's the local preacher, Reverend Harold Vorhees. I have a four-hour shift here most days."

"A pleasure, ma'am. Can I treat you to an ice cream?"

"Oh, no, I have my iced tea," she said and sipped out of a large plastic tumbler. It was very pale iced tea.

"You know, I'd like some iced tea, if you don't mind," Quinlan said.

Sherry Vorhees winked at him. "Sorry, sir, but you don't want my kind of iced tea, and we don't have any of the other kind."

"Just ice cream, then. You've never heard of this Marge and Harve? You don't remember them coming through here some three years ago? In a Winnebago?"

Sherry thought he was handsome, just like that Englishman who'd played in two James Bond films, but this man was American and he was bigger, a lot taller. She really liked that dimple in his chin. She'd always wondered how men shaved in those tiny little holes. And now this lovely man wanted to know about these two old folk. He was standing right in front of her licking his peach ice cream cone.

"A lot of folk come to The Cove for the World's Greatest Ice Cream," she said, still smiling at him. "Too many to remember individuals. And three years ago—Why, at my age I can barely remember what I cooked Hal for dinner last Tuesday."

"Well, you think about it, please, Mrs. Vorhees. I'm staying at Thelma's Bed and Breakfast." He turned as the front doorbell jingled. A middle-aged woman came in. Unlike Martha, this one was dressed like a gypsy, a red scarf tied around her head, thick wool socks and Birkenstocks on her feet. She was wearing a long skirt that looked organic and a dark red wool jacket. Her eyes were dark and very beautiful. She had to be the youngest citizen in the town.

"Hello, Sherry," she said. "I'll relieve you now."

"Thanks, Amabel. Oh, this is James Quinlan. Mr. Quinlan, this is Amabel Perdy. He's a real private detective from Los Angeles, Amabel. He's here to try to find out what happened to an old couple who might have come through The Cove to buy ice cream. What was their name? Oh, yes, Harve and Marge."

Amabel raised her dark gypsy eyebrows at him. She was very still, didn't say anything, just looked at him, completely at ease.

So this was the aunt. How fortunate that she was here and not at home, where he hoped to find Sally Brainerd. Amabel Perdy, an artist, an old hippie, a former schoolteacher. He knew she was a widow, had been married to another artist she'd met in SoHo many decades ago. His art had never amounted to much. He'd died some seventeen years ago. James also knew now that she'd turned down Purn Davies. He noted she didn't look anything like her niece.

"I don't remember any old folk named Harve and Marge," Amabel said. "I'm going in the back to change now, Sherry. Ring out, okay?"

She was the best liar yet. He tamped down his dratted curiosity. It didn't matter. Sally Brainerd was the only thing that mattered.

"How's your little niece doing, Amabel?"

Amabel wished Sherry wouldn't drink so much iced tea. It made her run off at the mouth. But she said pleasantly, "She's doing better. She was so exhausted from her trip."

"Yes, of course." Sherry Vorhees continued to sip out of that big plastic tumbler and smile at James. That English actor's name was Timothy Dalton. Beautiful man. She liked James Quinlan even better. "There's not much to do here in The Cove. I don't know if you'll last out the week."

"Who knows?" James said, tossed his napkin into the white trash bin, and left the ice cream shop.

His next stop was Amabel Perdy's house, the small white one on the corner of Main Street and Conroy Street. Time to get it done.

When he knocked on the trim white door, he heard a crash from inside. It sounded as though a piece of furniture had been knocked down. He knocked louder. He heard a woman's cry of terror.

He turned the knob, found the door was locked. He put his shoulder against the door and pushed really hard. The door burst inward.

He saw Susan St. John Brainerd on her knees on the floor, the telephone lying beside her. He could hear the buzz of the dial tone. Her fist was stuffed in her mouth. She'd probably terrified herself when she screamed—that or she was afraid someone would hear her. Well, he had, and here he was.

She stared at him as he flew into Amabel's small living room, huddled herself against the wall like he was going to shoot her, jerked her fist out of her mouth, and screamed again.

Really loud.

FOUR

"Stop screaming," he yelled at her. "What's the matter? What happened?"

Sally knew this was it. She'd never seen him before. He wasn't old like everyone else in this town. He didn't belong here. He'd tracked her here. He was here to drag her back to Washington or force her to go back to that horrible place. Yes, he could work for Beadermeyer, he probably did. She couldn't go back there. She stared at the big man who was now standing over her, looking at her strangely, as if he was really concerned, but she knew he wasn't, he couldn't be, it was a ruse. He was here to hurt her.

"The phone," she said, because she was going to die and it didn't matter what she said. "It was someone who called and he scared me."

As she spoke, she slowly rose and began backing away from him.

He wondered if she had a gun. He wondered if she'd turn and run to get that gun. He didn't want this to turn nasty. He lunged for her, grabbed her left arm as she cried out, twisted about, and tried to jerk away from him.

"I'm not going to hurt you."

"Go away! I won't go with you, I won't. Go away."

She was sobbing and panting, fighting him hard now, and he was impressed with the way she jabbed him with her knuckles just below his ribs where it hurt really good, then raised her leg to knee him.

He jerked her back against him, then wrapped his arms around her, holding her until she quieted. She had no leverage now, no chance to hurt him. She was a lightweight, but the place where she'd gotten him below his ribs really hurt.

"I'm not going to hurt you," he said again, his voice calm and low. He was one of the best interviewers in the FBI because he could modulate his voice to make it gentle and soothing, mean and vicious, whatever was necessary to get what he needed.

He said now, in his easy and soft tone, "I heard you cry out and thought someone was in here with you, attacking you. I was just trying to be a hero."

She stilled, just stood there, her back pressed against his chest. The only sound breaking the silence was the dial tone from the telephone.

"A hero?"

"Yeah, a hero. You okay now?"

She nodded. "You're really not here to hurt me?"

"Nope. I was passing by when I heard you scream."

She sagged with relief. She believed him. What should she do now?

He let her go and took a quick step back. He leaned down and picked up the telephone, dropped the receiver into the cradle, and set it back on the table.

"I'm sorry," she said, her arms wrapped around herself. She looked as white as a cleric's collar. "Who are you? Did you come to see Amabel?"

"No. Who was that on the phone? Was it an obscene caller?"

"It was my father."

He tried not to stare at her, not to start laughing at what she'd said. Her father? *Lady, they buried him two days ago, and it was very well attended. If the FBI weren't investigating him, even the president would have been there.* He made a decision and acted on it. "I take it that he's not a nice guy, your father?"

"No, he's not, but that's not important. He's dead."

James Quinlan knew her file inside out. All he needed was to have her flip out on him. He'd found her, he had her now, but she was obviously close to the edge. He didn't want a fruitcake on his hands. He needed her to be sane. He said very gently, his voice, his body movements all calm, unhurried, "That's impossible, you know."

"Yes, I know, but it was still his voice." She was rubbing her hands over her arms. She was staring at that phone, waiting. Waiting for her dead father to call again? She looked terrified, but more than that she looked confused.

"What did he say? This man who sounded like your dead father?"

"It was my father. I'd know that voice anywhere." She was rubbing harder. "He said that he was coming, that he'd be here with me soon and then he'd take care of things."

"What things?"

"Me," she said. "He'll come here to take care of me."

"Do you have any brandy?"

Her head jerked up. "Brandy?" She grinned, then laughed, a small, rusty sound, but it was a laugh. "That's what my aunt's been sneaking into my tea since I got here yesterday. Sure, I've got brandy, but I promise you, even without the brandy I won't get my broomstick out of the closet and fly out of here."

He thrust out his hand. "That's good enough for me. My name's James Quinlan."

She looked at that hand, a strong hand, one with fine black hairs on the back of it, long fingers, well-cared-for nails, buffed and neat. Not an artist's hands, not like Amabel's, but capable hands. Not like Scott's hands either. Still, she didn't want to shake James Quinlan's hand, she didn't want him to see hers and know what a mess she was. But there was no choice.

She shook his hand and immediately withdrew hers. "My name's Sally St. John. I'm in The Cove to visit my aunt, Amabel Perdy."

St. John. She'd only gone back to her maiden name. "Yes, I met her in the World's Greatest Ice Cream Shop. I would have thought she lived in a caravan and sat by a campfire at night reading fortunes and dancing with veils."

She made a stab at a laugh again. "That's what I thought too when I first got here. I hadn't seen her since I was seven years old. I expected her to whip out some tarot cards, but I was very glad she didn't."

"Why? Maybe she's good at tarot cards. Uncertainty's a bitch."

But she was shaking her head. "I'd rather have uncertainty than certainty. I don't want to know what's going to happen. It can't be good."

No, he wasn't going to tell her who he was, he wasn't going to tell her that she was perfectly right, that what would happen to her would be bad. He wondered if she'd killed her father, if she hadn't run to this town that was on the backside of the Earth to protect her mother. Others in the Bureau believed it was a deal gone sour, that Amory St. John had finally screwed over the wrong people. But he didn't believe that for a minute, never had, which was why he was here and no other agents were. "You know, I'd sure like some brandy."

"Who are you?"

He said easily, "I'm a private investigator from Los Angeles. A man hired me to find his parents, who disappeared from around here some three years ago."

She was weighing his words, and he knew she was trying to determine if he was lying to her. His cover was excellent because it was true, but even that didn't matter. He was a good liar. He could tell his voice was working on her.

She was so thin, her face still had that bloodless look, the color leached out by the terror of that phone call. Her father? He was coming to take care of her? This was nuts. He could handle sane people. He didn't know what he'd do if she flipped out.

"All right," she said finally. "Come this way, into the kitchen."

He followed her to a kitchen that was straight out of the 1940s—the brownish linoleum floor with stains older than he was. It was clean but peeling up badly near the sink area. All the appliances were as old as the floor, and just as clean. He sat down at the table as she said, "Don't lean on it. One of the legs is uneven. See, Aunt Amabel has magazines under it to make it steady."

He wondered how long the table had been like that. What an easy thing to fix. He watched Susan St. John Brainerd pour him some brandy in a water glass. He watched her pause and frown. He realized she didn't know how much to pour.

"That's good," he said easily. "Thank you." He waited until she'd poured herself a bit, then gave her a salute. "I need this. You scared the evil out of me. Nice to meet you, Susan St. John."

"And you, Mr. Quinlan. Please call me Sally."

"All right—Sally. After all our screams and shouts, why not call me James?"

"I don't know you, even if I did scream at you."

"The way you gouged me in the ribs, I'd give up before I'd let you attack me like that again. Where'd you learn to do that?"

"A girl at boarding school taught me. She said her brother was the meanest guy in junior high and he didn't want a wuss for a sister so he taught her all sorts of self-defense tricks."

He found himself looking down at her hands. They were as thin and pale as the rest of her. She said, "I never tried it before—seriously, I mean. Well, I did, several times, but I didn't have a chance. There were too many of them."

What was she talking about? He said, "It worked. I wanted to die. In fact, I'll be hobbled over for the next couple of days. I'm glad you missed my groin."

He sipped his brandy, watching her. What to do? It had seemed so simple, so straightforward before, but now, sitting here, facing her, seeing her in the flesh as a person and not only as his key to the murder of Amory St.

John, things weren't so clear anymore. He hated it when things weren't clear. "Tell me about your father."

She didn't say anything, shook her head.

"Listen to me, Sally. He's dead. Your father is dead. That couldn't have been him on the phone. That means that it must have been either a recording of his voice or a person who could mimic him very well."

"Yes," she said, still staring into the brandy.

"Obviously someone knows you're here. Someone wants to frighten you."

She looked up at him then, and remarkably, she smiled. It was a lovely smile, free of fear, free of stress. He found himself smiling back at her. "That someone succeeded admirably," she said. "I'm scared out of my mind. I'm sorry I attacked you."

"I would have attacked me too if I had burst through the front door like that."

"I don't know if the call was long distance. If it was long distance, then I've got some time to decide what to do." She paused, then stiffened. She didn't move, but he got the feeling that she'd just backed a good fifteen feet away from him. "You know who I am, don't you? I didn't realize it before, but you know."

"Yes, I know."

"How?"

"I saw your photo on TV, also some footage of you with your father and your mother."

"Amabel assures me that no one in The Cove will realize who I am. She says no one besides her has a TV except for Thelma Nettro, who's older than dust."

"You don't have to worry that I'll shout it around. In fact, I promise to keep it to myself. I was in the World's Greatest Ice Cream Shop when I met your aunt. A Sherry Vorhees mentioned that you were visiting. Your aunt didn't say a word about who you were." Lying was an art, he thought, watching her assess his words. The trick was always to lean as much as possible toward the exact truth. It was a trick some of the town's citizens could benefit from.

She was frowning, her hands clasped around the glass. Her foot was tapping on the linoleum.

"Who is after you?"

Again she gave him a smile, but this one was mocking and underlaid with so much fear he fancied he could smell it. She fiddled with the napkin holder, saying while she straightened the napkins that had dumped onto the table, "You name someone and he'd probably be just one in a long line."

She was sitting across from one of those someones. He hated this. He'd thought it would be so easy. When would he learn that people were never what they seemed? That smile of hers was wonderful. He wanted to feed her.

She said suddenly, "The strangest thing happened last night. I woke up in the middle of the night at the sound of a person's cry. It was a person, I know it was. I went into the hall upstairs to make sure something wasn't happening to Amabel, but when the cry came again I knew it was from outside. Amabel said I'd imagined it. It's true that I'd had a horrible nightmare, a vivid memory in the form of a dream, actually, but the screams pulled me out of the dream. I know that. I'm sure of it. Anyway, I went back to bed, but I know I heard Amabel leave the house after that. You're a private detective. What do you make of that?"

"You want to be my client? It'll cost you big bucks."

"My father was rich, not me. I don't have a cent."

"What about your husband? He's a big tycoon lawyer, isn't he?"

She stood up like a shot. "I think you should leave now, Mr. Quinlan. Perhaps it's because you're a private detective and it's your job to ask questions, but you've crossed the line. I'm none of your business. Forget what you saw on TV. Very little of it was true. Please go."

"All right," he said. "I'll be in The Cove for another week. You might ask your aunt if she remembers two old folk named Harve and Marge Jensen. They were in a new red Winnebago, and they probably drove into town to buy some of the World's Greatest Ice Cream. Like I told you, the reason I'm here is because their son hired me to find them. It's been over three years since they disappeared." Although he'd already asked Amabel himself, he wanted Sally to ask her as well. He'd be interested to see if she thought her aunt was lying.

"I'll ask her. Good-bye, Mr. Quinlan."

She dogged him to the front door, which, thankfully, was still attached to its ancient hinges.

"I'll see you again, Sally," he said, gave her a small salute, and walked up the well-maintained sidewalk.

The temperature had dropped. A storm was blowing in. He had a lot to do before it hit. He quickened his step. So her husband was off-limits. Was she scared of him? She wasn't wearing a wedding band, but the evidence of one had been in that thick white line on her finger.

He'd really blundered—that wasn't like him. Usually he was very cautious, very careful, particularly with someone like her, someone fragile, someone who was teetering right on the brink.

Nothing seemed straightforward now that he'd met Susan St. John, that thin young woman who was terrified of a dead man who had called her on the phone.

He wondered how long it would be before Susan St. John discovered he'd lied through his teeth. It was possible she would never find out. Nearly everything he knew was in the file the FBI had assembled on her. If she found out he knew more than had ever been dished out to the public, would she take off? He hoped not. He was curious now about those human cries she'd heard in the middle of the night. Maybe her aunt had been right and she had dreamed it—being in a new place, she had every reason to be jumpy. And she had admitted to having a nightmare. Who knew?

He looked around at the beautiful small houses on either side of the street. There were flowers and low shrubs planted everywhere, all protected from the ocean winds with high-sided wooden slats on the western side. He imagined storms off the ocean could devastate any plant alive. The people were trying.

He still didn't like the town, but it didn't seem so much like a Hollywood set anymore. Actually it didn't look at all like Teresa's hometown in Ohio. There was an air of complacency about it that didn't put him off. He had a sense that everyone who lived here knew their town was neat and lovely and quaint. The townspeople had thought about what they wanted to do and they'd done it. The town had genuine charm and vitality, he'd admit that, even though he hadn't seen a single child or young person since he'd driven in some three hours before.

IT was late at night when the storm blew in. The wind howled, rattling the windows. Sally shivered beneath the mound of blankets, listening to the rain slam nearly straight down, pounding the shingled roof. She prayed there were no holes in the roof, even though Amabel had said earlier, "Oh, no, baby. It's a new roof. Had it put on just last year."

How long could she remain here with Amabel? Now that she was safe, now that she was hidden, she was free to think about the future, at least a future of more than one day's duration. She thought about next week, about next month.

What was she going to do? That phone call—it had yanked her right back to the present, and to the past. It had been her father's voice, no question about that. A tape, just like James Quinlan had said, a tape or a mimic.

Suddenly there was a scream, long and drawn out, starting low and ending on a crescendo. It was coming from outside the house.

She ran toward her aunt's bedroom, not feeling the cold wooden floor beneath her bare feet, no, just running until she forced herself to draw up and tap lightly on the door.

Amabel opened the door as if she'd been standing right there, waiting for her to knock. But that wasn't possible, surely.

She grabbed her aunt's arms and shook her. "Did you hear the scream, Amabel? Please, you heard it, didn't you?"

"Oh, baby, that was the wind. I heard it and knew you'd be frightened. I was coming to you. Did you have another nightmare?"

"It wasn't the wind, Amabel. It was a woman."

"No, no, come along now and let me help you back to bed. Look at your bare feet. You'll catch your death of something. Come on now, baby, back to bed with you."

There was another scream, this one short and high-pitched, then suddenly muffled. It was a woman's scream, like the first one.

Amabel dropped her arm.

"Now do you believe me, Amabel?"

"I suppose I'll have to call one of the men to come and check it out. The problem is, they're all so old that if they go out in this weather, they'll probably catch pneumonia. Maybe it was the wind. What woman would be screaming outside? Yes, it's this bloody wind. It's impossible, Sally. Let's forget it."

"No, I can't. It's a woman, Amabel, and someone is hurting her. I can't go back to bed and forget it."

"Why not?"

Sally stared at her.

"You mean when your papa hit your mama you tried to protect her?"

"Yes."

Amabel sighed. "I'm sorry, baby. You did hear the wind this time, not your mama being punched by your papa."

"Can I borrow your raincoat, Amabel?"

Amabel sighed, hugged Sally close, and said, "All right. I'll call Reverend Vorhees. He's not as rickety as the others, and he's strong. He'll check it out."

When Reverend Hal Vorhees arrived at Amabel's house, he had three other men with him. "This is Gus Eisner, Susan, a fellow who can fix anything with wheels and a motor."

"Mr. Eisner," Sally said. "I heard a woman scream, twice. It was an awful scream. Someone was hurting her."

Gus Eisner looked as if he would have spat if there'd been a cuspidor in the corner. "The wind, ma'am," he said, nodding, "it was the wind. I've heard it all my life, all seventy-four years, and it makes noises that sometimes have made my teeth ache. Just the wind."

"But we'll look around anyway," Hal Vorhees said. "This here is Purn Davies, who owns the general store, and Hunker Dawson, who's a World War Two vet and our flower expert." Sally nodded, and the reverend patted her shoulder, nodded to Amabel, and followed the other men out the front door. "You ladies stay safe inside now. Don't let anyone in unless it's us."

"The little females," Sally said. "I feel like I should be barefoot and pregnant, making coffee in the kitchen."

"They're old, baby, they're just old. That generation gave their wives an allowance. Gus's wife, Velma, wouldn't know a bank statement if it bit her ankle. But things balance out, you know. Old Gus is night-blind. Without Velma, he'd be helpless after dark. Don't mind their words. They care, and that's a good feeling, isn't it?"

Just as she opened her mouth to reply, there was a third scream, this one fast and loud, and then it ended, cut off abruptly. It was distant, hidden, and now it was over.

Sally knew deep down that there wouldn't be another scream. Ever again. She also knew it wasn't the damned wind.

She looked at her aunt, who was straightening a modern painting over the sofa, a small picture painted in patternless swirls of ochre, orange, and purple. It was an unsettling painting, dark and violent.

"The wind," Sally said slowly. "Yes, no more than the wind." She wanted to ask Amabel if Gus were night-blind, what good would he be out searching for a victim in the dark?

THE next morning dawned cool and clear, the sky as blue in March as it would be in August. Sally walked to Thelma's Bed and Breakfast. Mr. Quinlan, Martha told her, was having his breakfast.

He was seated in isolated splendor amid the heavy Victorian furnishings in Miss Thelma's front room. On the linen-covered table was a breakfast more suited to three kings than one man.

She walked straight to him, waited until he looked up from his newspaper, and said, "Who are you?"

FIVE

It had never occurred to him that she would confront him, not after he'd seen her huddled on the floor when he burst into her aunt's living room. But she had tried to knee him and she'd also punched him just below the ribs. She had fought back. And here she was today, looking ready to spit on him. For some obscure reason, that pleased him. Perhaps it was because he didn't want his prey to be stupid or cowardly. He wanted a chase that would challenge him.

How could she have found out so quickly? It didn't make sense.

"I'm James Quinlan," he said. "Most people call me Quinlan. You can call me whatever you want to. Won't you sit down, Sally? I assure you there's enough food, though when I finish one plate Martha brings in another one. Does she do the cooking?"

"I don't know. Who are you?"

"Sit down and we'll talk. Or would you like a section of the newspaper? It's the *Oregonian,* a very good paper. There's a long article in here about your father."

She sat down.

"Who are you, Mr. Quinlan?"

"That didn't last long. It was James yesterday."

"I have a feeling that nothing lasts very long with you."

She was right about that, he thought, as he had a fleeting image of Teresa laughing when he'd whispered to her as he'd come inside her that if she ever had another man she would find out what it meant to be half empty.

"What other feelings do you have, Sally?"

"That you love problems, that you get a problem in your hands and shape and mold and twist and do whatever you have to do to solve that problem. Then you lose interest. You look for another problem."

He stared at her and said aloud, though he didn't realize he was doing so, "How do you know that?"

"Mr. Quinlan, how did you know my husband is a lawyer? That wasn't on TV. There was no reason for it to be. Or if he had been shown, they certainly would have had no reason to discuss his profession or anything else about him."

"Ah, you remembered that, did you?"

"Delaying tactics don't become you. What if I told you I have a Colt forty-five revolver in my purse and I'll shoot you if you don't tell me the truth right now?"

"I'd probably believe you. Keep your gun in your purse. It was on TV— your good old husband escorting your mother to your dad's funeral. You just didn't see it." Thank God he'd heard Thelma and Martha discussing it yesterday. Thank God they hadn't really been interested. Washington, D.C., was lightyears from their world. "If you think there's anything private about you now, forget it. You're an open book."

She had seen it, she'd forgotten, just plain forgotten. She'd made a mistake, and she couldn't afford to make any more. She remembered eating that wonderful ham sandwich when she'd first arrived, sitting with Amabel, watching her black-and-white set, listening and watching and knowing that Scott was with her mother. She hadn't watched TV before or since. She prayed she wasn't an open book. She prayed no one in The Cove would ever realize who she was.

"I forgot," she said and picked up a slice of unbuttered toast. She bit into it, chewed slowly, then swallowed. "I shouldn't have, but I did."

"Tell me about him."

She took another bite of toast. "I can't afford you, remember, James?"

"I sometimes do *pro bono.*"

"I don't think so. Have you discovered anything about the old couple?"

"Yes, I have. Everyone I've spoken to is lying through their collective dentures. Marge and Harve were here, probably at the World's Greatest Ice Cream Shop. Why doesn't anyone want to admit it? What's to hide? So they had ice cream—who cares?"

He pulled up short, staring at the pale young woman sitting across from him. She took another bite of the dry toast. He lifted the dish of homemade strawberry jam and handed it to her. She shook her head. He'd never in his life told anyone about his business. Of course, old Marge and Harve weren't really his business, not really, but then again, why had everyone lied to him?

More to the point, why had he said anything about that case to her? She was a damned criminal, or at least she knew who had offed her father. If there was one thing he was sure of, it was that.

Whatever else she was—well, he'd find out. She had come to him. Confronted him. It saved him the trouble of seeking her out again.

"You're right. That doesn't make any sense. You're sure folk lied to you?"

"Positive. It's interesting, don't you think?"

She nodded, took another bite of toast, and chewed slowly. "Why don't I ask Amabel why no one admits to remembering them?"

"No, I don't think so. I'm the private investigator here. I'll do the asking. It's not your job."

She shrugged.

"It's too early for the World's Greatest Ice Cream," he said. "Maybe you'd like to go for a walk on the cliffs? You look pale. A walk would put some color in your cheeks."

She gave it a lot of thought. He said nothing more, watched her eat the rest of that dry toast that had to be cold as a stone. She stood, brushed the crumbs from the legs of her brown corduroy slacks, and said, "I need to put on my sneakers. I'll meet you in front of Amabel's house in ten minutes."

"Excellent," he said, and meant it. Now he was getting somewhere. He'd open her up soon enough, just like a clam. Soon she would tell him all about her husband, her mother, her dead father, who hadn't called her on the phone. No, that was impossible.

She also seemed perfectly normal, and that bothered him as well. When he'd found her hysterical and frightened yesterday, it had been what he'd expected. But this calm, this open smile that, to his critical eye, held no malice or guile, made him feel he'd missed the last train to Saginaw.

When he met her in front of her aunt's house, she smiled at him. Where the hell was her guile?

Fifteen minutes later she was talking as if there wasn't a single black cloud in her world. ". . . Amabel told me that The Cove was nothing until a developer from Portland bought up all the land and built vacation cottages. Everything went smoothly until the sixties; then everyone simply forgot about the town."

"Someone sure remembered, someone with lots of money. The place is a picture postcard." He remembered old Thelma Nettro had told him the same thing.

"Yes," she said, kicking a small pebble out of her path. "It's odd, isn't it? If the town died, then how was it resurrected? There's no local factory to employ everyone, no manufacturing of any kind. Amabel said the high school closed back in 1974."

"Maybe one of them has discovered how to tap into the Social Security computer system."

"That would only work in the short term. The fund only has money for, what is it? Fifteen months? It's scary. No one would want to count on that."

They stood on the edge of a narrow promontory and looked down at the fierce white spume, fanning upward when the waves hit the black rocks.

"It's beautiful," she said as she drew in a deep breath of the salt air.

"Yes, it is, but it makes me nervous. All that unleashed power. It has no conscience. It can kill you so easily."

"What a romantic thing to say, Mr. Quinlan."

"Not at all. But I'm right. It doesn't know the good guys from the bad guys. And it's James. You want to climb down? There's a path over there by that lone cypress tree that doesn't look too dangerous."

"I don't want you fainting on me, if you get too close to all that unleashed power."

"Threaten to knee me and I'll forget about fainting for the rest of my life."

She laughed and walked ahead of him. She quickly disappeared around a turn in the trail. It was a narrow path, strewn with good-sized rocks, snaggled low brush, and it was too steep. She slipped, gasped aloud, and grabbed at a root.

"Be careful!"

"Yes, I will be. No, don't say it. I don't want to go back. We'll both be very careful. Just another fifty feet."

The trail stopped. From the settled look of all the brush and rocks, there'd been an avalanche some years before. They could probably climb over the rocks, but Quinlan didn't want to take the chance. "This is far enough," he said, grabbing her hand when she took another step. "Nope, Sally, this is it. Let's sit here and commune with all that unleashed power."

There was no beach below, just pile upon pile of rocks, forming strange shapes as richly imagined as the cloud formations overhead. One even made a bridge from one pile to another, with water flowing beneath. It was breathtaking, and James was right, it was a bit frightening.

Seagulls whirled and dove overhead, squawking and calling to each other.

"It isn't particularly cold today."

"No," she said. "Not like last night."

"I'm in the west tower room at Thelma's Bed and Breakfast. The windows shuddered the whole night."

Suddenly she stood up, her eyes fixed on something off to the right. She shook her head, whispering, "No, no, it can't be."

He was on his feet in an instant, his hand on her shoulder. "What is it?"
She pointed.

"Oh, no," he said. "Stay here, Sally. Stay right here and I'll check it out."

"No, I won't stay put."

"Yes you will." He set her aside and made his way carefully through the rocks until he was standing five feet above the body of a woman, the waves washing her against the rocks, then tugging her back, back and forth. There was no blood in the water. "Oh, no," he said again.

She was at his side, staring down at the woman. "I knew it," she said. "I was right, but nobody would listen to me."

"We've got to get her out before there's nothing left of her," he said. He sat down, took off his running shoes and socks, and rolled up his jeans. "Stay here, Sally. I mean it. I don't want to have to worry about you falling into the water and washing out to sea."

Quinlan finally managed to haul her in. He wrapped the woman, what was left of her, in his jacket. His stomach was churning. He waved to Sally to start climbing back up the path. He didn't allow himself to think that what he was carrying had once been a living, laughing person. It made him sick. "We'll take her to Doc Spiver," Sally called over her shoulder. "He'll take care of her."

"Yeah," he said to himself, "I just bet he will." An old man in this one-horse town would probably say that she'd been killed accidentally by a hunter shooting curlews.

Doc Spiver's living room smelled musty. James wanted to open the windows and air the place out, but he figured the old man must want it this way. He pulled out his cell phone and called Sam North, a homicide detective with the Portland police department. Sam wasn't in, so James left Doc Spiver's number. "Tell him it's urgent," he said to Sam's partner, Martin Amick. "It's really urgent."

He watched Sally St. John Brainerd pace back and forth over a rich wine-red Bokhara carpet. It was fairly new, that beautiful carpet. "What did you mean when you said you knew it?"

"What? Oh, I heard her scream last night. There were three screams, and at the last one I knew someone had killed her. It was cut off so quickly, like someone hit her hard and that was it.

"Amabel thought it was the wind because it was howling—no doubt about that, but I knew it was a woman's scream, just like the one the first night I was here. I told you about that. Do you think it was the same woman?"

"I don't know."

"Amabel called Reverend Vorhees and he came with three other men and they went on a search. When they came back they said they hadn't found anything. It was the wind, they said. Reverend Vorhees patted me again, like I was a child, an idiot."

"Or worse, a hysterical woman."

"Exactly. Someone killed her, James. It couldn't have been an accident. I heard her scream the night I arrived and then last night. Last night, they killed her."

"What do you mean, 'they'?"

She shrugged, looking a bit confused. "I don't know. It just seems right."

James's cell phone played the first bar of "Fly Me to the Moon." He answered it. It was Sam North calling him back. Sally listened to his end of the conversation.

"Yes, a woman anywhere from young to middle-aged, I guess. The tide washed her in, and she'd been battered against the rocks for a good number of hours. I don't know how long. What do you want to do, Sam?"

He listened, then said, "A little town called The Cove about an hour or so southwest of you. You know it? Good. The local doctor is looking her over now, but they have no law enforcement, nothing like that. Yes? All right. Done. His name is Doc Spiver, on the end of Main Street. You've got my number. Right. Thanks, Sam."

He said as he punched off, "Sam's calling the county sheriff. He says they'll send someone over to handle things."

"Soon, I hope," Doc Spiver said, walking into the small living room, wiping his hands—an obscene thing to be doing, Sally thought, staring at those old liver-spotted hands, knowing what those hands had been touching. There was a knock on the front door and Doc Spiver called out, "Come along in!"

It was Reverend Hal Vorhees. On his heels were the four old men who spent most of their time sitting around the barrel playing cards.

"What's going on, Doc? Excuse me, ma'am, but we heard you'd found a body at the bottom of the cliffs."

"It's true, Gus," Doc Spiver said. "Do all of you know Mr. Quinlan and Sally, Amabel's niece?"

"Yes, we do, Doc," Purn Davies, the man who'd wanted to marry Amabel, said. "Now what's happening? Be quick telling us. I don't want the ladies to hear about it and be distressed."

"Sally and Mr. Quinlan found a woman's body."

"Who is she? Do you recognize her?" This from Hal Vorhees.

"No. She's not from around here, I don't think. I couldn't find anything on her clothes either. You find anything, Mr. Quinlan?"

"No. The county sheriff is sending someone over soon. A medical examiner as well."

"Good," Doc Spiver said. "Look, she could have been killed by anything. Me, I'd say it was an accident, but who knows? I can't run tests, and I haven't the tools or equipment to do an autopsy. As I said, I vote for accident."

"No," Sally said. "No accident. Someone killed her. I heard her screaming."

"Now, Sally," Doc Spiver said, holding out his hand to her, that hand he'd been wiping, "you're not thinking that the wind you heard was this poor woman screaming."

"Yes, I am."

"We never found anything," Reverend Vorhees said. "We all looked a good two hours."

"You just didn't look in the right place," Sally said.

"Would you like something to calm you?"

She stared at the old man who had been a doctor for many more years than her mother had been alive. She'd met him the previous day. He'd been kind, if a little vague. She knew he didn't want her here, that she didn't belong here, but as long as she was with Amabel, he would continue being kind. Come to think of it, all the folk she'd met had been kind, but she still felt they didn't want her here. It was because they'd found out she was a murdered man's daughter—that had to be it. She wondered if they would turn her in now that she and James had found the woman's body, the woman Sally had heard screaming.

"Something to calm me," she repeated slowly, "something to calm me." She laughed, a low, very ugly laugh that brought Quinlan's head up.

"I'd better get you something," Doc Spiver said, turned quickly, and ran into an end table. The beautiful Tiffany lamp crashed to the floor. It didn't break.

He didn't see it, James realized. The damned old man was going blind. He said easily, "No, Doc. Sally and I will be on our way now. The detective from the Portland police will tell the sheriff to come here. If you'd let them know we'll be at Amabel's house?"

"Yes, certainly," Doc Spiver said, not looking at them. He was on his knees, touching the precious Tiffany lamp, feeling all the lead seams to make certain it wasn't cracked.

They left him still on the floor. All the other men were silent as death in the small living room with its rich wine-red Bokhara carpet.

"Amabel told me he was blinder than a bat," Sally said as they stepped out into the bright afternoon sunlight. She stopped cold.

"What's wrong?"

"I forgot. I can't have the police knowing I'm here. They'll call the police in Washington, they'll send someone to get me, they'll force me to go back to that place or they'll kill me or they'll—"

"No, they won't. I already thought of that. Don't worry. Your name is Susan Brandon. They'll have no reason to question that. Just tell them your story and they'll leave you be."

"I have a black wig I wore here. I'll put it on."

"Couldn't hurt."

"How can you know they'll just want to hear my story? You don't know what's going on here any more than I do. Oh, I see. You don't think they'll believe I heard a woman screaming those two nights."

He said patiently, "Even if they don't believe you, it doesn't make a whole lot of sense that they'd then have a murdered woman on their hands, does it? You heard a woman's screams. Now she's dead. I don't think there's a whole lot of other possible conclusions. Get a grip, Sally, and don't fall apart on me now. You're going to be Susan Brandon. All right?"

She nodded slowly, but he didn't think he had ever seen such fear on a face in all his years.

He was glad she had a wig. No one could forget her face, and the good Lord knew it had been flashed on TV enough times recently.

SIX

David Mountebank had hated his name ever since he'd looked it up in the dictionary and read it meant boastful and unscrupulous. Whenever he met a big man, a big man who looked smart, and he had to introduce himself, he held himself stiff and wary, waiting to see if the guy would make a crack. He braced himself accordingly as he introduced himself to the man before him now.

"I'm Sheriff David Mountebank."

The man stuck out his hand. "I'm James Quinlan, Sheriff Mountebank. This is Susan Brandon. We were together when we found the woman's body two hours ago."

"Ms. Brandon."

"Won't you be seated, Sheriff?"

He nodded, took his hat off, and relaxed into the soft sofa cushions. "The Cove's changed," he said, looking around Amabel's living room as if he'd found himself in a shop filled with modern prints that gave him indigestion. "It seems every time I come here, it just keeps looking better and better. How about that?"

"I wouldn't know," Quinlan said. "I'm from L.A."

"You live here, Ms. Brandon? If you do, you've got to be the youngest sprout within the town limits, although there's something of a subdivision growing over near the highway. Don't know why folks would want to live near the highway. They don't come into The Cove except for ice cream, leastwises that's what I hear."

"No, Sheriff. I'm visiting my aunt. A short vacation. I'm from Missouri."

Sheriff Mountebank wrote that down in his book, then sat back, scratched his knees, and said, "The medical examiner's over at Doc Spiver's house checking out the dead woman. She'd been in the water a good while, at least eight hours, I'd say."

"I know when she died," Sally said.

The sheriff merely smiled at her and waited. It was a habit of his, just waiting, and sure enough, everything he ever wanted to hear would pop out of a person's mouth to fill in the silence.

He didn't have to wait long this time because Susan Brandon couldn't wait to tell him about the screams, about how her aunt had convinced her it was the wind that first night, but last night she'd known—just known—it was a woman screaming, a woman in pain, and then that last scream, well, someone had killed her.

"What time was that? Do you remember, Ms. Brandon?"

"It was around two-oh-five in the morning, Sheriff. That's when my aunt went along with me and called Reverend Vorhees."

"She called Hal Vorhees?"

"Yes. She said he was the youngest man and the most physically able. He brought over three elderly men with him. They searched but couldn't find anything."

"That was probably the same group over at Doc Spiver's. They were all sitting around looking at each other. This kind of thing hits a small town like The Cove real hard."

David Mountebank took down their names. He said without preamble, without softening, "Why are you wearing a black wig, Ms. Brandon?"

Without a pause she said, "I'm having chemotherapy, Sheriff. I'm nearly bald."

"I'm sorry."

"That's all right."

At that moment, Quinlan knew he would never again underestimate Sally Brainerd. He wasn't particularly surprised that the sheriff could tell it was a wig. She looked frankly ludicrous in that black-as-sin wig that made her look like Elvira, Mistress of the Dark. No, she was even paler than Elvira. He was impressed that the sheriff had asked her about the wig. Maybe there'd be a prayer of finding out who the woman was and who had killed her. He could see that David Mountebank wasn't stupid.

"Doc Spiver thinks this is all a tragic accident," the sheriff said, writing with his pencil on his pad even as he spoke.

James said, "The good doctor is nearly blind. He could have just as easily been examining the table leg and not the dead woman."

"Well, it appears the doctor admitted that readily enough. He said he couldn't imagine who could have killed her, not unless it was someone from the outside. That means beyond Highway 101A. The four other fellows there didn't know a blessed thing. I guess they were there for moral support. Now, Mr. Quinlan, you're here on business?"

Quinlan told him about the old couple he was looking for. He didn't say anything about the townspeople lying to him.

"Over three years ago," the sheriff said, looking at one of Amabel's paintings over Sally's head, this one all pale yellows and creams and nearly blueless blues, no shape or reason to any of it, but it was nice.

"Yeah, probably too long a time to turn anything up, but the son wanted to try again. I'm using The Cove as my headquarters, checking here first, then fanning out."

"Tell you what, Mr. Quinlan, when I get back to my office I'll do some checking. I've been sheriff only two years. I'll see what the former sheriff had to say about it."

"I'd appreciate that."

There was a knock at the front door. Then it opened and a small, slender man came into the living room. He was wearing wire-rim glasses and a fedora. He took off his hat, nodded to the sheriff, and bowed to Sally. "Sheriff, ma'am." He then looked at Quinlan, just looked at him, like a little dog ready to go after the mastodon if his master gave the command.

Quinlan stuck out his hand. "Quinlan."

"I'm the medical examiner. We're removing the body now, Sheriff. I just wanted to give you a preliminary report." He paused, a dramatic pause, Quinlan knew, and grinned. He'd seen it many times before. Medical examiners hardly ever had the limelight. It was their only chance to shine, and this man was trying his best to light up the room.

"Yes, Ponser? Get on with it."

That wasn't as good a name as Mountebank, but it was close. Quinlan looked over at Sally, but she was staring at her shoes. She was listening, though; he could see the tension in her body, practically see the air quiver around her.

"Someone strangled her," Ponser said cheerfully. "It's pretty obvious, but I can't say for sure until I've done the autopsy. Perhaps the killer believed it wouldn't be evident after she'd been in the water, but he was wrong. On the other hand, if the tide hadn't washed her in, then her body would never have been found and it would have been academic."

"That's what they wanted," Sally said. "They didn't want her found. Even with the tide washing her up, how many people ever go down there? They're all old. It's dangerous. James and I finding her, that was just plain bad luck for them."

"Yes, it certainly was," the sheriff said. He rose. "Ms. Brandon, could you try to pinpoint the direction and the distance of those screams you heard? Were they from the same direction and distance both nights?"

"That's an awfully good question," Sally said slowly. "It would help, yes, it would. Both nights the screams were close, that or she really screamed loudly. I think they came both times from across the way. It was close, so very close—at least I think it was."

"Ah, there's a nice long row of neat little cottages lining the street across from this house. Surely someone must have heard something. If you remember anything else, here's my card. Call me anytime."

He shook Quinlan's hand. "You know, what I can't figure out is why someone was holding the woman prisoner."

"Prisoner?" Sally said, just staring at the sheriff.

"Naturally, ma'am. If she wasn't being held against her will, then why would you have heard the screams two different nights? The killer was holding her for some reason, a reason so powerful he only killed her that second night when she got loose and screamed again. But I've gotta ask myself, why keep someone prisoner if you're not planning on doing away with her anyway? Or maybe he was thinking of ransom and that's why he kept her alive. Maybe he was planning on killing her all along. Maybe he's a real psycho. I don't know, but I'll find out. I haven't heard a thing about anyone missing.

"Questions, I'm filled with them. As soon as we can get a photograph of the woman, then my deputies will be crawling all over the subdivision like army ants. I hope she's local, I really do."

"It would make your job a whole lot easier," Quinlan said. "Give me a relative or a husband any day and I'll find you a dozen motives."

"Yes, Mr. Quinlan, that's surely the truth."

"Nothing like a good mystery to stir a man's blood."

"I prefer mine to yours, Mr. Quinlan. Finding two missing people after three years isn't likely. Well, I'll be on my way now. A pleasure to meet you, Ms. Brandon."

He said to Quinlan as they walked to the door, "Now, this murdered woman, I'll find out who was holding her and then we'll see what kind of motive we've got for a brutal murder. I wonder why they threw her body over the cliff?"

"Instead of burying her?"

"Yeah. You know what I think now? I think someone was furious that she got loose and made a racket. I think someone was so furious he killed her and just threw her away like so much trash. I want to catch him badly."

"I would too, Sheriff. I think you might just be right."

"You in town long, Mr. Quinlan?"

"Another week or so."

"And Ms. Brandon?"

"I don't know, Sheriff."

"A shame about the cancer."

"Yes, a real shame."

"She gonna be all right?"

"That's what her doctors believe."

Sheriff David Mountebank shook Quinlan's hand, nodded back at Sally—who'd heard everything they said, even though they'd been speaking low—and took his leave.

Sally wondered why her aunt had left before the sheriff came. Amabel had said only, "Why would a sheriff want to talk to me? I don't know anything."

"But you heard the screams, Amabel."

"No, baby, you did. I never did think they were screams. You don't want me calling you a liar in front of the law, do you?" And with that, she took off.

Sally said now to Quinlan, "The sheriff isn't dumb."

"No, he isn't. But you got him, Sally, with that chemo business. Where is your aunt?"

"I don't know. She left."

"But she knew the sheriff would be here."

"Yes, but she said she didn't know anything. She said she didn't hear any screams and didn't want to make me look bad if she had to tell him that."

"You mean like a hysterical girl or a liar?"

"That's about it. When she does talk to him, she'll probably lie. She loves me. She wouldn't want to hurt me."

But she hadn't loved her enough to lie for her this time, Quinlan thought. Strange family.

"Any more phone calls?"

Sally shook her head, her eyes going automatically to the telephone, sitting next to a lamp on an end table.

"Do you have a cell phone?"

She shook her head again.

"But someone knows you're here."

"Yes, someone."

He dropped it. He didn't want to push anymore, at least not right now. She'd been through quite enough for one day. But she hadn't lost it. She'd hung in there. "I'm proud of you," he said, without thinking.

She blinked as she looked up at him. He was still standing by the front door, leaning against the wall, his arms crossed over his chest. "You're proud of me? Why?"

He shrugged and walked over to her. "You're a civilian, but you didn't fall apart."

If only he knew, she thought, as she rubbed where that ring had been, so tight on her finger, paralyzing her.

"Sally, what's wrong?"

She jumped to her feet. "Nothing, James, nothing at all. It's lunchtime. You hungry?"

He wasn't, but she had to be, if that single piece of dry toast was all she'd eaten so far today. "Let's go back to Thelma's and see what's cooking," he said, and she agreed. She didn't want to be alone. She didn't want to be in this house alone.

The old lady was sitting in the dining room slurping minestrone soup, her diary open and facedown in her lap, the old-fashioned fountain pen beside her plate. What did she write in that diary? What could be so bloody interesting? When she saw them, she yelled, "Martha, bring me my teeth. I can't be a proper hostess without my teeth."

She shut her mouth, not saying another word until poor Martha hurried into the dining room and slipped the old lady her teeth. Thelma turned, then turned back, giving them a big porcelain smile.

"Now, what's all this I hear about you two finding a dead body?"

James said, "We're hungry. Any chance for some of your soup?"

Thelma yelled, "Martha, bring two more bowls of your minestrone!"

She waved them to two seats across from her. She stared at Sally, who was no longer wearing her wig. "So you're Amabel's niece, are you?"

Sally nodded. "Yes, ma'am. It's a pleasure to meet you."

The old lady snorted. "You wonder why I'm not dead yet. But I'm not, and I make sure I see Doc Spiver every day to tell him so. He pronounced me dead three years ago, did you know that?"

Quinlan imagined everybody did, many times over. He just smiled and shook his head. He reached beneath the table and squeezed Sally's hand. She went rigid, then slowly he felt her relax. Good, he thought, she was beginning to trust him, and that made him feel like a shit.

Martha set two places in front of them, then served two bowls of soup.

"Martha always had men hanging around her, but they were rotters, all of them. They only wanted her cooking. What did you do with young Ed, Martha? Did you cook for him or demand that he go to bed with you first?"

Martha shook her head. "Now, Thelma, you're embarrassing poor little Miss Sally here."

"And me, too," Quinlan said and spooned some of the soup into his mouth. "Martha," he said, "I'm not a rotter and I'd surely marry you. I'd do anything for you."

"Go along, Mr. Quinlan."

"A big man like you embarrassed, James Quinlan?" Thelma Nettro laughed. Sally was thankful she was wearing her teeth. "I think you've been around several blocks, boy. I bet I could take off my clothes and it wouldn't faze you."

"I wouldn't bet on it, ma'am," Quinlan said.

"I'll bring in the chicken parmigiana," Martha said. "With garlic toast," she said over her shoulder.

"She keeps me alive," Thelma said. "She should have been my daughter but wasn't. It's a pity. She's a good girl."

This was interesting, Quinlan thought, but not as interesting as the soup. They all gave single-minded concentration to the minestrone until

Martha reappeared with a huge tray covered with dishes. The smells nearly put Quinlan under the table. He wondered how long he'd have a hard stomach if Martha cooked all his meals.

Thelma took a big bite of chicken parmigiana, chewed like it was her last bite on earth, sighed, then said, "Did I tell you that my husband, Bobby, invented a new, improved gyropilot and sold it to a huge conglomerate in San Diego? They were hot for it, it being the war and all. Yep, that's what happened. I know it made airplanes fly even more evenly at the same height on a set course than before. With that money, Bobby and I moved here to The Cove. Our kids were grown and gone by then." She shook her head, smiled, and said, "I'll bet that body was a real mess when you found it."

"Yes," Sally managed to say, reeling a bit. "The poor woman had been thrown over the cliff. Evidently she was caught in the tide."

"So who is she?"

"No one knows yet," Quinlan said. "Sheriff Mountebank will find out. Did you hear a woman screaming, Ms. Nettro?"

"You can call me Thelma, boy. My sweet Bobby died in the winter of 1956, just after Eisenhower was elected—he called me Hell's Bells, but he always smiled when he said it, so I didn't ever get mad at him. A woman screaming? Not likely. I like my TV loud."

"It was in the middle of the night," Sally said. "You would have been in bed."

"My hair curlers are so tight, I can't hear a thing. Ask Martha. If she's not trying to find herself a man, she's lying in bed thinking about it. Maybe she heard something."

"All right," Quinlan said. He took a bite of garlic toast, shivered in ecstasy at the rich garlic and butter taste, and said, "The woman was screaming close by, perhaps across the way from Amabel's house. She was someone's prisoner. Then that someone killed her. What do you think?"

Thelma chewed another bite of chicken, a string of mozzarella cheese hanging off her chin. "I think, boy, that you and Sally here should go driving someplace and neck. I've never before seen a girl in such a twitter as poor Sally here. She's a mess. Amabel won't say anything except that you've had a rough time and you're trying to get over a bad marriage. She said none of us were to say a word to anybody, that you needed peace and quiet. You don't have to worry, Sally, no one from The Cove will call and tell on you."

"Thank you, ma'am."

"Call me Thelma, Sally. Now, how much does either of you know about that big-time murdered lawyer back in Washington?"

James thought Sally would faint and fall into her chicken parmigiana.

She looked whiter than death. He said easily, "No more than anybody else, I suspect. What do you know, Thelma?"

"Since I'm the only one with a real working TV, I know a world more than anybody else in this town. Did you know the missing daughter's husband was on TV, pleading for her to come home? He said he was worried she wasn't well and didn't know what she was doing. He said she wasn't responsible, that she was sick. He said he was real concerned about her, that he wanted her back so he could take care of her. Did you know that? Isn't that something?"

She wouldn't faint into the parmigiana now. Quinlan felt her turn into stone. "Where did you hear that, Thelma?" he asked mildly, even as he doubted he ever wanted another bite of chicken parmigiana in his life.

"It was on FOX. You can find out everything on FOX."

"Do you remember anything else he said?"

"That was about it. He pleads real well. Looked very sincere. A handsome man, but there's something too slick about him. From what I could tell he's got a weak chin. What do you two think about that?"

"Not a thing," Sally said, and James was pleased that her voice didn't sound scared, though he knew she had to be.

Thelma didn't seem to realize that her audience had stopped eating. She cackled, saying, "I like James. He's not all soft and smooth like that poor girl's husband. No, James doesn't put all that mousse in his hair. I bet that poor girl's husband wouldn't use that nice big gun James has under his coat. No, he'd have one of those prissy little derringers. He's too slick for my tastes.

"Now that James is here, Sally, I recommend that you use him. That's what my husband always said to me. 'Thelma,' he'd say, 'men love to be used. Use me.' I still miss Bobby. He caught pneumonia, you know, back in 1956. Killed him in four days. A pity." She sighed and took another bite of chicken parmigiana.

"I feel like I swallowed five cloves of garlic," Quinlan said after they managed to escape, Sally pleading a stomachache.

"Yes, but it was delicious until Thelma mentioned Scott."

"He wants to take care of you."

"Oh, I'm sure he does."

He wished she'd tell him about her husband and what he'd done to her. The fear in her voice wasn't as strong as the bitterness. When she'd gotten that phone call from someone pretending to be her father—now, that was fear. She turned to face him. She looked paler, if that were possible, and pinched, as if the life were being drained out of her. "You've been kind to me and I appreciate it, but I've got to be leaving now. I can't stay here any longer. Now that he's gotten on TV about me, someone will have seen it. Someone will call. I've got to leave. And you know what else? Thelma knows. She was playing with me."

"No one will call because no one saw him. If he'd offered a reward, then I'd bet on Thelma calling up in a flash, cackling all the while. Yes, Thelma knows, but she'll stop at taunting you. Look, Sally, no one else knows who you are. All you are is Amabel's niece. I'd even wager that if anyone did find out they wouldn't say a word. Loyalty—you know what I mean?"

"Actually," she said, "I don't."

Dear God, he thought as he stepped along with her, what had her life been like? He didn't remember a TV in his tower bedroom. He hoped there was one. He wanted to see Scott Brainerd pleading to his wife to return to him.

"Don't go," he said to her when they reached Amabel's cottage. "You know, it isn't all that hard to be loyal if it doesn't cost you anything. There's no need to. Let things spin out, just stay out of it. Besides, you don't have any money, do you?"

"I have credit cards, but I'm afraid to use them."

"They're very easy to trace. I'm glad you didn't use them. Look, Sally, I've got some friends back in Washington. Let me put in a couple of calls and see what's really happening, okay?"

"What friends?"

He smiled down at her. "I can't put a thing over on you, can I?"

"Not when it hits me in the nose," she said, and smiled back at him. "It doesn't matter, James. If you want to talk to some people, go ahead. Remember, though, I don't have any money to pay you."

"*Pro bono,*" he said. "I hear even government agencies do some work for free."

"Yeah, like they use our taxes to pay for midnight volleyball."

"Basketball. That was a while back."

"Your friends work for the feds?"

"Yep, and they're good people. I'll let you know what's cooking—if they know anything, of course."

"Thank you, James. But you know, there's still the person who called me pretending to be my father. That person knows where I am."

"Whoever comes, if he comes, has my big gun to contend with. Don't worry."

She nodded, wished he could touch her hand, squeeze it, pat her cheek, anything, to make her feel less threatened, less hunted. But he couldn't, she knew that, just as she knew she didn't know him at all.

So he was her protector now, Quinlan realized, shaking his head at himself. He would protect her from any guy who came here wanting to drag her back or hurt her.

That was a good joke on him, he thought, as he walked back to Thelma's Bed and Breakfast.

He was her main hunter.

SEVEN

When the phone rang, Sally was in the kitchen slicing a turkey breast Amabel had brought home from Safeway. Her aunt called out, "It's for you, Sally."

James, she thought, smiling, as she wiped her hands. She walked into the living room to see Martha with her aunt, the two of them smiling at her, saying nothing now, which was only polite since they'd probably been talking about her before she'd come into the room.

"Hello?"

"How's my little girl?"

She froze. Her heart pounded fast and painfully hard. It was him. She remembered his voice too well to believe now that it was someone pretending to be Amory St. John.

"You don't want to talk to me? You don't want to know when I'm going to come get you, Sally?"

She said clearly, "You're dead. Long dead. I don't know who killed you, but I wish I had. Go back to hell where you belong."

"Soon, Sally. I can't wait, can you? Very soon now I'll have you with me again."

"No, you won't," she screamed and slammed down the receiver.

"Sally, what is going on? Who was that?"

"It was my father," she said and laughed. She was still laughing as she walked up the stairs.

Amabel called after her, "But Sally, that couldn't have been someone trying to make you believe it was your father. That was a woman on the line. Martha said she sounded all fuzzy, but it was a woman. She even thought it sounded a bit like Thelma Nettro, but that couldn't be. I didn't know of any woman who knew you were here."

Sally stopped on the second step from the top. The steps were narrow, and too steep. She turned slowly and looked back downstairs. She couldn't see her aunt or Martha. She didn't want to see them. A woman? Maybe Thelma Nettro? No way.

She ran back down the stairs into the living room. Placid Martha was looking distressed, her hands clasping and unclasping her pearls, her glasses sliding down her nose.

"My dear," she began, only to stop at the ferocious look of anger on the girl's face. "Whatever is wrong? Amabel's right. It was a woman on the phone."

"When I answered it wasn't a woman on the phone. It was a man pretending to be my father." It had been her father. She knew it, knew it deep down. She was so scared she wondered if a person could die of just being scared, nothing else, just being scared.

"Baby," Amabel said, rising, "this is all very confusing. I think you and I should talk about this later."

Sally turned without another word and walked slowly upstairs. She was leaving now. She didn't care if she had to walk and hitchhike. She knew all the stories about the dangers of a woman alone, but they didn't come close to the danger she felt bearing down on her now. How many people knew she was here? The man pretending to be her father, and now a woman? She thought of that nurse. She'd hated that nurse so much. Sally couldn't even remember her name now. She didn't want to. Could it have been that nurse?

She stuffed her clothes in her duffel bag and then realized she had to wait. She didn't want to fight with Amabel. She heard Amabel lock up the cottage. She heard her walk up the stairs, her step brisk and solid. Sally got quickly into bed and pulled the covers up to her chin.

"Sally?"

"Yes, Amabel. Oh, goodness, I was nearly asleep. Good night."

"Yes, good night, baby. Sleep well."

"All right."

"Sally, about that phone call—"

She waited, not saying a word.

"Martha could have been mistaken. It's quite possible. Her hearing isn't all that good anymore. She's getting old. It could even have been a man disguising his voice like a woman's just in case you didn't answer the phone.

I can't imagine that it could have been Thelma. Baby, nobody knows who you are, nobody."

Amabel paused. Sally could see her silhouetted in the doorway from the dim light in the corridor. "You know, baby, you've been through a lot, too much. You're frightened. I would be too. Your mind can do funny things to you when you're frightened. You know that, don't you?"

"Yes, I understand that, Amabel." She wasn't about to tell Amabel that Thelma knew who she was.

"Good. You try to sleep, baby." She didn't come in to kiss her good night, for which Sally was grateful. She lay there, waiting, waiting.

Finally, she slipped out of bed, pulled on her sneakers, picked up her duffel bag, and tiptoed to the window. It slid up easily. She poked her head out and scanned the ground as she'd done earlier. This was the way out. It wasn't far to the ground, and she knew there was no way she could get down those stairs without Amabel hearing her.

No, she'd be just fine. She climbed out the window and sat on the narrow ledge. She dropped the duffel bag and watched it bounce off the squat, thick bushes below. She drew a deep breath and jumped.

She landed on James Quinlan.

They both went down, James rolling, holding her tight against him.

When they came to a stop, Sally reared up on her hands and stared down at him. There was a half-moon, more than enough light to see his face clearly.

"What are you doing here?"

"I knew you'd run after that telephone call."

She rolled off him and rose, only to collapse again. She'd sprained her ankle. She cursed.

He laughed. "That's not good enough for a girl who didn't go to finishing school in Switzerland. Don't you know some down and dirty street curses?"

"Go to hell. I sprained my damned ankle and it's all your fault. Why couldn't you mind your own damned business?"

"I didn't want you out on the road hitchhiking with some lowlife who could rape you and cut your throat."

"I thought of that. I'd rather take that risk than stay here. He knows I'm here, James, you know that. I can't stay here and wait for him to come and take me. That's what he said. He said soon he'd be here for me."

"I was reading a newspaper when Martha came in all worried and told

Thelma about a woman calling you, a woman you said wasn't a woman but your father. She said you were really distressed. She didn't understand why you'd be so upset to hear from your father. I knew you'd probably try to run; that's why I'm here, having you crush me into the ground."

She sat there on the ground next to him, rubbing her ankle, just shaking her head. "I'm not crazy."

"I know that," he said patiently. "There's an explanation. That's why you're not going to run away. Now *that's* crazy."

She came up on her knees, leaning toward him, her hands grasping his jacket lapels. "Listen to me, James. It was my father. No fake, no imitation. *It was my father.* Amabel said it could have been a man disguising his voice as a woman's if I wasn't the one to answer the phone. Then she turned around and told me how much strain I've been under. In other words, I'm crazy."

He took her hands in his, just held them, saying nothing. Then he spoke. "As I said, there's always an explanation. It probably was a man. We'll find out. If it wasn't, if it truly was a woman who asked for you, then we'll deal with that too. Trust me, Sally."

She sat back. Her ankle had stopped throbbing. Maybe it wasn't sprained after all.

"Tell me something."

"Yes?"

"Do you think someone could be trying to gaslight you?"

What did he know? She searched his face for the lie, for knowledge, but saw none of it.

"Is it possible? Could someone be trying to make you crazy? Make you doubt your sanity?"

She looked down at her clasped hands, at her fingernails. She realized that she hadn't chewed her nails since she'd been in The Cove. Not since she'd met him. They didn't look so ragged. She said finally, not looking at him, because it was awful, what she was, what she had been, perhaps what she still was today, right now, "Why?"

"I'd have to say that someone's afraid of you, afraid of what you might possibly know. This someone wants to eliminate you from the game, so to speak." He paused, looking toward the ocean, fancying he could hear the crashing waves, but he couldn't; Amabel's cottage was just a bit too far for that. "The question is why this someone would go this route. You're about the sanest person I know, Sally. Who could possibly think he could make you believe you were nuts?"

She loved him for that. Loved him without reservation, without any question. She gave him a big grin. It came from the deepest part of her, a place that had been empty for so long she'd forgotten that it was possible to feel this good, this confident in herself, and in someone else.

"I was nuts," she said, still grinning, feeling the incredible relief of telling someone the truth, of telling him. "At least that's what they wanted everyone to believe. They kept me drugged up for six months until I finally got it together enough to hide the medication under my tongue and not swallow it. The nurse always forced my mouth open and ran her fingers all inside to make sure I'd taken the pills. I don't know how I managed to keep the pill hidden, but I did. I did it for two days, until I was together enough. Then I escaped. And then I got the ring off my finger and threw it in a ditch."

He knew she'd been in a sanitarium, a very expensive, posh little resort sanitarium in Maryland. All very private. But this? She'd been a prisoner? Drugged to her gills?

He looked at her for a long time. Her smile faltered. He shook his head at her, cupped her face in his hand, and said, "How would you like to come back to Thelma's place and share my tower room with me? I'll take the sofa and you can have the bed. I won't make any moves on you, I swear. We can't sit here for the rest of the night. It's damp and I don't want either of us to get sick."

"And then what?"

"We'll think more about that tomorrow. If it was a woman who put the call through, then we need to figure out who it could have been. And I want to know why you were in that place for six months."

She was shaking her head even as he spoke. He knew she regretted spilling it to him now. After all, she didn't know him, didn't have a clue if she could trust him or not. She said, "You know, I have another question. Why did Martha answer Amabel's phone and not Amabel?"

"That's a good one, but the answer's probably as simple as that Martha happened to be standing next to the phone when it rang. Don't get paranoid, Sally."

He carried her duffel bag, his other hand under her arm. She was limping, but it wasn't bad, not a sprain, as she'd feared. He didn't want to haul her over to Doc Spiver's. Only the good Lord knew what that old man might do. Probably want to give her artificial respiration.

He had a key to the front door of Thelma's Bed and Breakfast. All the lights were out. They walked to his tower room without waking Thelma or Martha. James knew there was only one other guest, who had come in today, an older woman who'd been nice and smiling and had said that she was here to visit her daughter in the subdivision, but she'd always wanted to stay here, in one of the tower rooms. Thank God, she'd said, that there were two. Which meant she was on the other side of the huge house.

He switched the bedside lamp on low only after he had closed the venetian blinds. "There. It's charming, isn't it? There's no TV."

She wasn't looking at him or the window. She was moving as fast as a shot toward the door. She knew she didn't remotely love him anymore. She was afraid. She was in this man's room, a man she didn't know, a man who was sympathetic. She hadn't known sympathy in so long that she'd fallen for it without thought, without question. James Quinlan was quite wrong. She was as nuts as they came.

"Sally, what's wrong?"

She was tugging on the doorknob, trying to turn it, but the door didn't open. She realized the key was still in the lock. She felt like a fool.

He didn't make any movement of any kind. He didn't even stretch out his hand to her. He just said in his calm, deep voice, "It's all right. I know you're scared. Come now and sit over here. We'll talk. I won't hurt you. I'm on your side."

A lie, he thought, another damned lie. The chance of his ever being anywhere near her side was just about nil.

She walked slowly away from the door, stumbled against a small end table, and sat down heavily on the sofa. It was chintz with pale blue and cream flowers.

She was rubbing her hands together, just like Lady Macbeth, she thought. She raised her face. "I'm sorry."

"Don't be dumb. Now, would you like to try to sleep or talk awhile?"

She'd already told him too much. He was probably reconsidering his comment that she was the sanest person he knew. And he wanted to know why she'd been in that place? No, she couldn't bear that. Thinking about it was too much. She couldn't imagine talking about it. If she did, he'd know she was paranoid, delusional.

"I'm not crazy," she said, staring at him, knowing he was in the shadows and so was she, and neither of them could read the other's expression.

"Well, I just might be. I still haven't found out what happened to Harve and Marge Jensen, and you know what? I'm not all that interested anymore. Now, I called a friend at the FBI. No, don't look like you're going to dive for the door again. He's a very good friend, and I just got some information from him." Lies mixed with truth. It was his business, his lies having to be better than the bad guy's lies.

"What's his name?"

"Dillon Savich. He told me the FBI is looking high and low for you, but no sign as yet. He said they're convinced you saw something the night of your father's murder, that you probably saw the person who killed him, that it was probably your mother, and you ran to protect her. If it wasn't your mother, then it was someone else, or you.

"Your dad wasn't a nice man, Sally. Turns out he was being investigated by the FBI for selling weapons to terrorist countries like Iran and Syria. In any case, they're convinced you know something." He didn't ask her if it was true. He sat there on the other end of that chintz sofa with its feminine pale blue and cream flowers and waited.

"How do you know this Dillon Savich?"

He realized then that she might be scared half out of her mind, but she wasn't stupid. He'd managed to say everything that needed to be said without blowing his cover. But she hadn't responded. She still didn't trust him, and he admired her for that.

"We went to Princeton together in the nineties. He always wanted to be an agent, always, like his dad. We've kept in touch. He's good at his job. I trust him."

"It's difficult to believe he spilled all this out to you."

Quinlan shrugged. "He's frustrated. They all are. They want you, and you're gone without a trace. He was probably praying that I knew something and would tell him if he whetted my appetite."

"I didn't know about my father being a traitor. But on the other hand, I'm not surprised. I guess I've known for a very long time that he was capable of just about anything."

She was sitting very quietly, looking toward the door every couple of seconds silent now. She looked exhausted, her hair was ratty, there was a smudge of dirt on her cheek from her jump and a huge grass stain on the leg of her blue jeans. He wished she'd tell him what she was thinking. He wished she'd come clean and tell him everything.

Then, he thought, it might be a good idea to take her to dinner.

He laughed. He was the crazy one. He liked her. He hadn't wanted to. He'd only wanted to see her as the main piece to his puzzle, the linchpin that would bring it all together.

"Did you tell this Dillon Savich anything?"

"I told him I wouldn't go out with his sister-in-law again. She's always popping bubble gum in her mouth."

She blinked at him, then smiled—a small, tight smile, but it was a smile.

He rose and offered her his hand. "You're exhausted. Go to bed. We can deal with this in the morning. The bathroom's through there. It's a treat, all marble and a water-saver toilet in pale pink. Take a nice long shower; it'll help bring down the swelling in your ankle. Thelma even provides those fluffy white bathrobes."

He had let her off the hook, even though he guessed he could have gotten more out of her if he'd tried even a little bit. But she was near the edge, and not only because of that damned phone call.

Who was the dead woman they'd found being pulled in and out by the tide at the base of the cliff?

EIGHT

They were eating breakfast the next morning, alone in the large dining room. The woman who'd checked in the day before wasn't down yet, nor was Thelma Nettro.

Martha had said as she took their order, "Thelma sometimes likes to watch the early talk shows in bed. She also writes in that diary of hers. Goodness, she's kept a diary for as long as I can remember."

"What does she write in it?" Sally asked.

Martha shrugged. "I guess just the little things that happen every day. What else would she write?"

"Eat," Quinlan told Sally when Martha placed a plate stacked with blueberry pancakes in front of her. He watched her butter them, then pour Martha's homemade syrup over the top. She took one bite, chewed it slowly, then carefully laid her fork on the edge of the plate.

Her fork was still there when Sheriff David Mountebank walked in, Martha at his heels offering him food and coffee. He took one look at Sally's pancakes and Quinlan's English muffin with strawberry jam and said yes to everything.

They made room for him. He looked at them closely, not saying anything, just looking from one to the other. Finally he said, "You're a fast worker, Mr. Quinlan."

"I beg your pardon?"

"You and Ms. Brandon are already involved? Sleeping together?"

"It's a long story, Sheriff," Quinlan said, then laughed, hoping it would make Sally realize how silly it was.

"I think you're a pig, Sheriff," Sally said pleasantly. "I hope the pancakes give you stomach cramps."

"All right, so I'm a jerk. But what are you doing here? Amabel Perdy called my office real early and told me you'd disappeared. She was frantic. Incidentally, your hair sure grew back fast."

No black wig. Face him down, she thought, face him down. She said, "I was going to call her after breakfast. It's only seven in the morning. I didn't want to wake her. Actually, I'm surprised Martha didn't call her to tell her I was here."

"Martha must have assumed that Amabel already knew where you were. Now what's going on here?"

"What did her aunt tell you, Sheriff?"

David Mountebank recognized technique when he saw it. He didn't like to have it used on him, but for the moment, he knew he should play along. For a simple PI this man was very good.

"She said you'd gotten an obscene phone call last night and panicked. She thought you must have run away. She was worried because you don't have a car or any money."

"That's right, Sheriff. I'm sorry she worried you all for nothing."

Quinlan said, "I rescued the damsel, Sheriff, and slept on the sofa. She liked the tower room. She ignored me. Have you found out anything about the murdered woman?"

"Yes, her name was Laura Strather. She lived in the subdivision with her husband and three kids. They thought she was visiting her sister up in Portland. That's why no missing person report was filed on her. The question is, why was she being held a prisoner over here in The Cove and who killed her?"

"Have your people checked all the houses across from Amabel Perdy's cottage?"

The sheriff nodded. "Depressing, Quinlan, depressing. No one knows a thing. No one heard a thing—not a TV, not a telephone, not a car backfiring, not a woman screaming. Not on either night. Not a bloody thing." He looked over at Sally, but couldn't speak until Martha delivered his pancakes.

She looked at each of them, then smiled and said, "I'll never forget my mama showing me an article in the *Oregonian* written by this man called Qumquat Jagger way back in the early fifties. 'The Cove sunsets are a dramatic sight as long as one has a martini in the right hand.' I've long agreed with him on that." She added easily, "It's too early for a martini or a sunset—how about a bloody mary? All of you look on edge."

"I'd love one," Sheriff Mountebank said, "but I can't." Quinlan and Sally shook their heads. "Thank you, though, Martha," Quinlan said.

She checked to see that they had everything they could possibly want, then left the dining room.

After David Mountebank had eaten half the pancakes, he looked at Sally again and said, "If you had called me about hearing that woman screaming, I'm not certain I would have believed you. I would have searched, naturally, but I'd probably have thought you'd had a nightmare. But then you and Quinlan found a woman's body. Was she the woman you heard screaming? Probably so. You were telling the truth then, and all the old folk in this town are deaf. Either of you have any ideas?"

"I didn't even think about calling a sheriff," Sally said. "But I probably wouldn't have. My aunt wouldn't have wanted that."

"No, probably not. The folk in The Cove like to keep things to themselves." The sheriff grinned at her then. "I don't know if you're my best witness in any case, Ms. Brandon, since I find you've slept in Quinlan's tower room. And you lied to me about your hair."

"I have several wigs, Sheriff. I like wigs. I thought you were impertinent to ask me, so I said I had cancer to guilt you."

David Mountebank sighed. Why did everybody have to lie? It was exhausting. He looked at her again. This time he frowned. "You look familiar," he said slowly.

"James tells me I look like his former sister-in-law. Amabel thinks I look like Mary Lou Retton, although I'm nearly a foot taller. My mom said I was the image of her Venezuelan nanny. Don't tell me, Sheriff, that I remind you of your Pekingese."

"No, Ms. Brandon, be thankful you don't look like my dog. His name is Hugo and he's a rottweiler."

Sally waited, trying not to clench her hands, trying to look amused, trying to look like she was all together and not ready to fall apart if he poked his finger at her and said he was taking her in. She watched his frown smooth away as he turned to James.

"I checked the files from the previous sheriff. Her name was Dorothy Willis, and she was very good. Her notes on those missing old folks were very thorough. I made copies and brought them to you." He reached in his pocket and pulled out a thick envelope.

"Thank you, Sheriff," Quinlan said, not knowing for several moments who David Mountebank was talking about. Then he remembered Harve and Marge Jensen.

"I read over them last night. Everybody believed there was foul play, what with their Winnebago being found in a used car lot in Spokane. It's just that nobody knew anything. She wrote that she spoke to nearly everybody in The Cove but came up with nothing. Nobody knew a thing. Nobody remembered the Jensens. She even sent off the particulars to the FBI just in case something like this had happened elsewhere in the country. That's it, Quinlan. Sorry, but there's no more. No leads of any kind." He ate another helping of pancakes, drank his black coffee down, then shoved back his chair. "Well, you're all right, Ms. Brandon, so at least I don't have to worry about you. It's strange, you know? Nobody else heard that woman scream. Real strange."

He shook his head and walked out of the dining room, saying over his shoulder, "You look best with your own hair, Ms. Brandon. Lose the wigs. Trust me. My wife says I've got real good taste."

"Sheriff, what happened to Dorothy Willis?"

David Mountebank stopped then. "A bad thing, a very bad thing. She was shot by a teenage boy who was robbing a local 7-Eleven. She died."

When Thelma Nettro made her appearance some ten minutes later, looking for all the world like a relic from Victorian days, her teeth in her mouth, white lace at her parchment throat, the first words out of her mouth were, "Well, girl, is James here a decent lover?"

"I don't know, ma'am. He wouldn't even kiss me. He said he was too tired. He even hinted at a headache. What could I do?"

Old Thelma threw her head back, and that scrawny neck of hers worked ferociously to bring out fat, full laughs. "Here I thought you were a wimp, Sally. That's good. Now, what's this Martha tells me about how a woman who was really your dead daddy called you at Amabel's last night?"

"There was no woman when I got on the line."

"This is very strange, Sally. Why would anyone do this? Now, if it had been James on the phone, well, that would have been another matter. But if he gets all that tired, well, then maybe you'd best forget him."

"How many husbands did you have, Thelma?" Quinlan asked, knowing that Sally was reeling, giving her time to get herself together.

"Just Bobby, James. Did I tell you Bobby invented a new improved gyropilot? Yes, well, that's why I've got more money than any of the other poor sods in this place. All because of Bobby's invention."

"It looks to me like everyone has money," Sally said. "The town is charming. Everything looks new, planned, like everyone put money in a pot and decided together what they wanted to do with it."

"It was something like that," Thelma said. "It's all barren by the cliffs now. I remember back in the fifties there were still some pines and firs, even a few poplars close to the cliffs, all bowed down, of course, from the violent storms. They're all gone now, like there'd never been anything there at all. At least we've managed to save a few here in town."

She then turned in her chair and yelled, "Martha, where's my peppermint tea? You back there with young Ed? Leave him alone and bring me my breakfast!"

James waited two beats, then said easily, "I sure wish you'd tell me about Harve and Marge Jensen, Thelma. It was only three years ago, and you've got the sharpest mind in town. Hey, maybe there was something interesting about them and you wrote about it in your diary. Do you think so?"

"That's true enough, boy. I'm sure smarter than poor Martha, who doesn't know her elbow from the teakettle. And she just never leaves those pearls of hers alone. I've replaced them at least three times now. I even let her think for a while that I was the one who called Sally. I like to tease her; it makes life a bit more lively when she's twisting around like a sheet in a stiff wind. I'm sorry, but I don't remember any Harve or Marge."

"You know," Sally said, "that phone call could have been local. The voice was so clear."

"You think maybe I called you, girl, then pretended to be your daddy? I like it, but there's no way I could have gotten a tape of your daddy's voice. Who cares, anyway?"

"So you admit you know who I am?"

"Sure I do. It took you long enough to catch on. No need to worry, Sally, I won't tell a soul. No telling what some of these young nitwits around town would do if they found out you were that murdered big-shot lawyer's daughter. No, I won't tell anybody, not even Martha."

Martha brought in the peppermint tea and a plate filled with fat browned sausages, at least half a dozen of them. They were rolling on the plate in puddles of grease. Sally and Quinlan both stared at that plate.

Thelma cackled. "I want the highest cholesterol in history when I croak. I made Doc Spiver promise that when I finally shuck off this mortal snakeskin, he'll check. I want to be in the book of records."

"You must be well on your way," Quinlan said.

"I don't think so," Martha said, hovering by Thelma's left hand. "She's been eating this for years now. Sherry Vorhees says she'll outlive us all. She says her husband, Reverend Hal, doesn't have a chance against Thelma. He's already wheezing around and he's only sixty-eight, and he isn't fat. Strange, isn't it? Thelma wonders who's going to do her service if Reverend Hal isn't around."

"What does Sherry know?" Thelma demanded, talking while she

chewed on one of those fat sausages. "I think she'd be happier if Reverend Hal would pass on to his just reward, although I don't know how just he'd find it. He might find himself plunked down in hell and wonder how it could happen to him since he's so holy. He's reasonable most of the time, is Hal. It's when he's near a woman alone that he goes off the deep end and starts mumbling about sin and hell and temptations of the flesh. It appears he believes sex is a sin and rarely touches his wife. No wonder they don't have any kids. Not a one, ever. Fancy that. It's hard to believe, since he is a man, after all. But still, all poor Sherry does is drink her iced tea, fiddle with her chignon, and sell ice cream."

"What's wrong with that?" Sally asked, thinking that the Mad Hatter's tea party couldn't have been weirder than Thelma Nettro at breakfast. "If she were unhappy, wouldn't she leave?" *Yeah, like you did, but not in time.* Some of the grease around the sausages was beginning to congeal.

"Her iced tea is that cheap white wine. I don't know how her liver is still holding up after all these years."

Sally swallowed, looking away from those sausages. "Amabel told me that when you first opened the World's Greatest Ice Cream Shop, you stored the ice cream in Ralph Keaton's caskets."

"That's right. It was Helen's idea. She's Ralph's wife and the one who had the recipe. It was her idea that we start the ice cream shop. She used to be a shy little thing, looked scared whenever she had to say anything. If Ralph said boo she'd fade behind a piece of furniture. She's changed now, speaks right up, tells Ralph to put a sock in it whenever she doesn't like something he does. All because of that recipe. She's really blossomed with her ice cream success."

"Poor old Ralph. He needs business, but none of us will die for him. I think he's hoping the husband of that dead woman will ask him to lay her out."

Sally couldn't stand it anymore. She rose, tried to smile, and said, "Thank you for breakfast, Thelma. I've got to go home now. Amabel must be worried about me."

"Martha called her and told her you were here with James. She didn't have a word to say to that."

"I'll thank Martha," Sally said politely. She waited for James to join her. It was raining outside, a dark, miserably gray day.

"Well, damn," James said. He walked back into the foyer and fetched an umbrella from the stand. He said as they walked down the street, "I'll bet you the old men are playing cards in Purn Davies's store. I can't imagine them missing the ritual."

"Sheriff Mountebank will realize who I am, James. It's just a matter of time."

"I don't think so. He probably saw your picture on TV, but that would have been last week at the latest. He won't make the connection."

"I'm sure the authorities would have sent photos out to everyone."

"This is a backwater, Sally. It costs too much to fax photos to every police and sheriff office in the country. Don't worry about it. The sheriff doesn't have a clue. The way you answered him polished it off."

His eyes were as gray as the rain that was pouring down. He wasn't looking at her, but straight ahead, his hand cupping her elbow. "Watch the puddle."

She took a quick step sideways. "The town doesn't look quite so charming in this rain, does it? Main Street looks like an old abandoned Hollywood set, all gray and forlorn, like no one's lived here forever."

"Don't worry, Sally."

"Maybe you're right. Are you married, James?"

"No. Watch your step here."

"Okay. Have you ever been married?"

"Once. It didn't work out."

"I wonder if any marriages ever work out."

"You an expert?"

She was surprised at the sarcasm but nodded, saying, "A bit. My parents didn't do well. Actually . . . no, never mind that. I didn't do well, either. That's just about one hundred percent of my world, and it's all bad."

They were walking past Purn Davies's general store. Quinlan grinned and took her hand. "Let's go see what the old guys are up to. I'd like to ask them firsthand if it's true that nobody heard anything the night that poor woman was murdered."

Purn Davies, Hunker Dawson, Gus Eisner, and Ralph Keaton were seated around the barrel, a game of gin rummy under way. There was a fire in a wood-burning stove that looked to be more for show than for utility, a handsome antique piece. A bell over the door rang when Quinlan and Sally came through.

"Wet out there," Quinlan said, shaking the umbrella. "How you all doing?"

There were two grunts, one okay, and Purn Davies actually folded his cards facedown and got up to greet them. "What can I do for you folks?"

"You meet Amabel Perdy's niece, Sally St. John?"

"Yep, but it weren't much of a meeting. How you doin', Miz Sally? Amabel all right?"

She nodded. She hoped she could keep her fake names straight. Brandon for Sheriff Mountebank and St. John for everyone else.

There was more than polite interest in his question about Amabel, and it made Sally smile. "Amabel's fine, Mr. Davies. We didn't have any leaks during the storm. The new roof's holding up really well."

Hunker Dawson, who was sitting there pulling on his suspenders, said, "You had us all out looking for that poor woman who went and fell off that cliff. It was cold and windy that night. None of us liked going out. There weren't nothing to find anyway."

NINE

Sally's chin went up. "Yes, sir. I heard her scream and of course I would alert you. I'm sorry you didn't find her before she was murdered."

"Murdered?" The front legs of Ralph Keaton's chair hit hard against the pine floor. "What the dickens do you mean, murdered? Doc said she must have fallen, said it was a tragic accident."

Quinlan said mildly, "The medical examiner said she'd been strangled. Evidently whoever killed her didn't count on her body washing back up to land. More than that, whoever killed her didn't even consider that if she did wash up there would be anyone around down there to find her. The walk down that path is rather perilous."

"You saying that we're too rickety to walk down that path, Mr. Quinlan?"

"Well, it's a possibility, isn't it? You're certain none of you heard her scream during the night? Cry out? Call for help? Anything that wasn't a regular night sound?"

"It was around two o'clock in the morning," Sally said.

"Look, Miz Sally," Ralph Keaton said, rising now, "we all know you're upset about leaving your husband, but that don't matter. We all know you came here to rest, to get your bearings again. But you know, that kind of thing can have some pretty big effects on a young lady like yourself, like screwing up how you see things, how you hear things."

"I didn't imagine it, Mr. Keaton. I would think that I had if Mr. Quinlan and I hadn't found the woman's body the very next day."

"There is that," Purn Davies said. "Could be a coincidence. You havin' a dream because of you leaving your husband—that's what Amabel told us—or hearing the wind howling, and the woman jumping off that cliff. Yeah, all a coincidence."

Quinlan knew there was nothing more to be gained. They'd all dug in their heels. Both he and Sally were outsiders. They weren't welcome, only tolerated, barely. He thought it was interesting that Amabel Perdy seemed to have enough control over the townspeople so none of them had revealed to the cops that Sally was here, no matter how much she was obviously upsetting them. He prayed that Amabel's hold on them would last. Maybe he should tone things down, to be on the safe side. "Mr. Davies is right, Sally," Quinlan said easily. "Who knows? We sure don't. But, you know, I wish you'd remember something about Harve and Marge Jensen."

Hunker Dawson turned so fast he fell off his chair. There was pandemonium for a minute. Quinlan was beside him in an instant, making sure that he hadn't hurt himself. "I'm a clumsy old geek," Hunker said, as Quinlan carefully helped him to his feet.

"What happened to you?" Ralph Keaton shouted at him, all red in the face.

"I'm a clumsy old geek," Hunker said again. "I wish Arlene were still alive. She'd massage me and make me some chicken soup. My shoulder hurts."

Quinlan patted his arm. "Sally and I will drop by Doc Spiver's house and tell him to come over here, all right? Take two aspirin. He shouldn't be long."

"Naw, don't do that," Ralph Keaton said. "No problem. Hunker here is just whining."

"It's no problem," Sally said. "We were going to walk by his house anyway."

"Well, all right, then," Hunker said and let his friends lower him back into his chair. He was rubbing his shoulder.

"Yes, we'll get Doc Spiver," Quinlan said. He shook open the umbrella and escorted Sally out of the general store. He paused when he heard the old men talking quietly. He heard Purn Davies say, "Why shouldn't they go to Doc's house? You got a problem with that, Ralph? Hunker doesn't, and he's right. Listen to me, it don't matter."

"Yeah," Gus Eisner said. "I don't think Hunker could make it over there, now could he?"

"Probably wouldn't be smart," Purn Davies said slowly. "No, let Quinlan and Sally go. Yeah, that's best."

The rain had become a miserable drizzle, chilling them to the bone. He said, "None of them is a very good liar. I wonder what all that talk of theirs meant."

All that he was implying blossomed in her mind, and she felt more than the chill, damp air engulfing her. "I can't believe what you're suggesting, James."

He shrugged. "I guess I shouldn't have said anything. Forget it, Sally."

She couldn't, of course. "They're old. If they do remember the Jensens, they're afraid to admit it. As for the other, it was harmless."

"Could be," James said.

They walked in silence to Doc Spiver's house, and Quinlan knocked on the freshly painted white door. Even in the dull morning light, the house looked well cared for. Like all the other houses in this bloody little town.

No answer.

Quinlan knocked again, calling out, "Doc Spiver? It's Quinlan. It's about Hunker Dawson. He fell and hurt his shoulder."

No answer.

Sally felt something hard and dark creep over her. "He must be out with someone else," she said, but she was shivering.

Quinlan turned the doorknob. To his surprise it wasn't locked. "Let's see," he said and pushed the door open. The house was warm, the furnace going full blast.

There were no lights on, and there should have been, what with all the dull gray outside. It was as gray inside the house, the corners as shadowy, as it was outdoors.

"Doc Spiver?"

Suddenly James turned, took her by the shoulders, and said, "I want you to stay here in the hallway, Sally. Don't budge."

She smiled up at him. "I'll look in the living room and dining room. Why don't you check upstairs? He's not here, James."

"Probably not." He turned and headed up the stairs. Sally felt the impact of the heat. It was hotter now, almost burning, making her mouth dry. She quickly switched on the hallway light. Odd, but it didn't help. It was still too dark in here. Everything was so still, so motionless. There didn't seem to be any air. She tried to draw in a deep breath but couldn't. She looked at the arch that led into the living room.

Suddenly she didn't want to go in there. But she forced herself to take one step at a time. She wished James were right beside her, talking to her, dispelling the horrible stillness. For God's sake, the old man simply wasn't here, that was all.

She tried to take another deep breath. She took another step. She stood in the open archway. The living room was just as dim and gray as the hallway. She quickly switched on the overhead lights. She saw the rich Bokhara carpet, the Tiffany lamp that Doc Spiver had knocked over because he hadn't seen it. It wasn't broken or cracked, as far as she could tell. She took a step into the living room.

"Doc Spiver? Are you here?"

There was no answer.

She looked around, not wanting to go farther, to take one more step into that room. She saw a blur, something moving quickly. She heard a loud thump on the hardwood floor, then the raucous sound of a rocking chair. There was a loud, indignant meow, and a huge gray cat leaped off the back of the sofa to land at her feet. Sally shrieked. Then she laughed, a horrible laugh that made her sound crazy. "Good kitty," she said, her voice so thin she was surprised she could breathe. The cat skittered away.

She heard the rocking chair moving, back and forth, back and forth, creaking softly now. She stifled the scream in her throat. The cat had hit the rocking chair and made it move, nothing more. She drew a deep breath and walked quickly to the far side of the living room. The rocker was moving slowly, as if someone were putting pressure on it, somehow making it move. She walked around to the front of the chair.

The air was as still and dead as the old man slumped low in the old bentwood rocker, one arm hanging to the floor, his head bowed to his chest. His fingernails scraped gently against the hardwood floor. The sound was like a gun blast. She stifled a scream behind the fist pressed against her mouth. Then she took several fast breaths. She stared in fascination at the drops of blood that dripped slowly, inexorably, off the end of his middle finger. She turned on her heel and ran back into the hallway.

She yelled, her voice hoarse with terror and the urge to vomit. "James! Doc Spiver is here! James!"

"ONE wonders—if you weren't here, Ms. Brandon, would there have been two deaths?"

Sally sat on the edge of Amabel's sofa, her hands clasped in her lap, rocking gently back and forth, just like old Doc Spiver had in that rocking chair. James was sitting on the arm of the sofa, as still as a man waiting in the shadows for his prey to pass by. Now where, David Mountebank wondered, had that thought come from? James Quinlan was a professional, he knew that for sure now, knew it from the way Quinlan had handled the scene at Doc Spiver's house more professionally than David would have, the way he had kept calm, detached. All of it screamed training that had been extensive, had been received by someone who already had all the necessary skills—and that easy, calm temperament.

Quinlan was worried about Sally Brandon, David could see that, but there was something else, something more that was hidden, and David hated that, hated the not knowing.

"Don't you agree, Ms. Brandon?" he asked again, pressing now, gently, because he didn't want her to collapse. She was too pale, too drawn, but he had to find out what was going on here.

She said finally, with great simplicity, "Yes."

"All right." He turned to Quinlan and gave him a slow smile. "Actually, you and Sally arrived at nearly the same time. That's rather an odd coincidence, isn't it?"

He was too close, James thought, but he knew David Mountebank couldn't possibly know anything. All he could do was guess.

"Yes," he said. "It's also one that I would have willingly forgone. Amabel should be back soon. Sally, would you like some tea?"

"His fingernails scraped against the hardwood floor. It scared me silly."

"It would scare me silly, too," David said. "So, both of you were there because Hunker Dawson fell off his chair and hurt his shoulder."

"Yes," James said. "That's it. Nothing sinister, just being good neighbors. Nothing more except what a couple of the old men said when we were leaving. Something about it didn't matter. That Hunker shouldn't go. To let us go, that it was time."

"You aren't saying that they knew he was dead and wanted you and Sally to be the ones to find him?"

"I have no idea. It doesn't make any sense, really. I just thought I'd pour out everything."

"Do you think he killed himself?"

Quinlan said, "If you look at the angle of the shot, at how the gun fell, at how his body crumpled in, I think it could go either way. Your medical examiner will find out, don't you think?"

"Ponser is good, but he isn't that good. He didn't have the greatest training. I'll let him have a go at it, and if it turns out equivocal, then I'll call Portland."

Sally looked up then. "You really think he could have killed himself, James?"

He nodded. He wanted to say more, but he knew he couldn't, even if the sheriff weren't here. He had to rein in all the words that wanted to speak themselves to her. It was too much.

"Why would he do that?"

Quinlan shrugged. "Perhaps he had a terminal illness, Sally. Perhaps he was in great pain."

"Or maybe he knew something and couldn't stand it. He killed himself to protect someone."

"Where did that come from, Ms. Brandon?"

"I don't know, Sheriff. It's all just hideous. Amabel told me after we found that poor woman that nothing ever happened here, at least nothing more than Doc Spiver's cat, Forceps, getting stuck in that old elm tree in his backyard. What will happen to the cat?"

"I'll make sure Forceps has a new home. I'll bet one of my kids will beg me to bring the damned cat home."

"David," Quinlan said, "why don't you just break down and call her Sally?"

"All right, if you don't mind. Sally." When she nodded, he was struck again at how familiar she looked to him. But he couldn't nail it down. More likely, she just looked like someone he'd known years ago, perhaps.

"Maybe James and I should leave so nothing else will happen."

"Well, actually, ma'am, you can't leave The Cove. You found the second body. There are so many questions and not enough answers. Quinlan, why don't you and I make Sally some tea?"

Sally watched them walk out of the small living room. The sheriff stopped by one of Amabel's paintings, this one of oranges rotting in a bowl. Amabel had used globs of paint on those parts of the oranges that were rotting. It was a disturbing painting. She shivered. What did the sheriff want to talk to James about?

DAVID Mountebank watched Quinlan pour water into the old kettle and turn on the heat beneath it. "Who are you?" he asked.

James stilled. Then he took down three cups and saucers from the cabinet. "You like sugar or milk, Sheriff?"

"No."

"How about brandy? That's what I'm putting in Sally's tea."

"No, thank you. Answer me, Quinlan. There's no way you're a PI, no way in hell. You're too good. You've had the best training. You're experienced. You know how to do things that normal folk just wouldn't know."

"Well, shit," James said. He pulled out his wallet and flipped it open. "Special Agent James Quinlan, Sheriff. FBI. A pleasure to meet you."

"Hot damn," David said. "You're here undercover. What's going on?"

TEN

James poured a finger of brandy into the cup of tea. He grinned when the sheriff held out his hand. "No, hold on a second, I want to give this to Sally. I want to make sure she's hanging in there. She's a civilian. This has been incredibly tough on her. Surely you can understand that."

"Yes. I'll wait for you here, Quinlan."

James returned after just a moment to see the sheriff staring out the kitchen window over the sink, his hands on the counter. He was a tall man, a runner, rangy and lean. He was probably only a few years older than James. He had a quality of utter concentration about him, something that made people want to talk to him. James admired that, but he wasn't about to talk. He was beginning to like David Mountebank, but he wasn't about to let that sway him either.

Quinlan said quietly, not wanting to startle him, "She's asleep. I covered her with one of Amabel's afghans. But let's keep it down, all right, Sheriff?"

He turned slowly and gave Quinlan a glimpse of a smile. "Call me David. What's going on? Why are you here?"

Quinlan said calmly, "I'm not really here to find out about Marge and Harve Jensen. They're my cover. But their disappearance remains a mystery. And it's not only them. You were right. The former sheriff sent everything off to the FBI, including reports on two more missing persons—a biker and his girlfriend. Other towns up and down the coast have done the same thing. There's a nice fat file now on folks who have simply disappeared around here. The Jensens were the first, evidently, so I'm sticking to them. I've told everyone I'm a PI because I don't want to scare these old folks. They'd freak if they knew an FBI agent was in their midst doing God knows what."

"It's a good cover, since it's real. I don't suppose you'll tell me what's really going on?"

"I can't, at least not right now. Can you be satisfied with that?"

"I guess I'll have to be. You discover anything yet about the Jensens?"

"Yeah—all these respectable old folk are lying to me. Can you beat that? Your parents or grandparents lying through their teeth over something as innocuous as a pair of old people in a Winnebago probably coming into town to buy the World's Greatest Ice Cream?"

"Okay, then. They do remember Harve and Marge, but they're afraid to talk, afraid to get involved. Why didn't you come talk to me right away? Tell me who you were and that you were undercover?"

"I wanted to keep things under wraps for as long as possible. It makes it easier." Quinlan shrugged. "Hey, then if I didn't find anything, well, no harm done and who knows? I might discover something about all these old folks who have disappeared."

"You would have succeeded in keeping your cover from me if two people weren't dead. You're too good, too well trained." David Mountebank sighed, took a deep drink of the brandied tea James handed him, shuddered a bit, then grinned as he patted his belly. "That'll put optimism back in your pecker."

"Yeah," Quinlan said.

"What are you doing with Sally Brandon?"

"I sort of hooked up with her the first day I was here. I like her. She doesn't deserve all this misery."

"More than misery. Seeing that poor woman's body banging up against the rocks at the base of those cliffs was enough to give a person nightmares for the rest of her life. But finding Doc Spiver with half his head blown off was even worse."

David took another drink of his tea. "I sure won't forget this remedy. You think that by any wild chance these two deaths are related in any way to the FBI missing persons files, to this Harve and Marge Jensen and all the others?"

"That's far-fetched for even my devious brain, but it makes you wonder, doesn't it?"

He was doing it to him again, David thought, without rancor. He was smooth, he was polite, he wasn't about to spill anything he didn't want to spill. It would be impossible to rattle him. He wondered why the devil he was really here. Well, Quinlan would tell him when he was good and ready.

David said slowly, "I know you won't tell me why you're really here, but I've got enough on my plate right now, so I don't plan to stew about it. You keep doing what you're doing, and if you can help me at all, or I can help you, I'll be here."

"Thanks, David. I appreciate it. The Cove is an interesting little town, don't you think?"

"It is now. You should have seen it three or four years ago. It was as ramshackle as you could imagine, everything run-down, only old folks here. All the young ones hightailed it out of town as soon as they could get. Then prosperity. Whatever they did, they did it well and with admirable planning.

"Maybe some relative of one of them died and left a pile of money, and that person gave it to the town. Whatever, the place is a treat now. Yep, it shows that folk can pull themselves out of a ditch if they put their minds to it. You've got to respect them."

David set his empty cup in the sink. "Well, I'm back to Doc Spiver's house. I've got exactly nothing, Quinlan."

"If I uncover something, I'll call."

"I won't hold the lines open. I just realized that these two deaths have got to be real hard on the townsfolk. Here I am, nearly accusing one of them of holding the woman prisoner before killing her. Hey, I was even thinking those four old men already knew that Doc Spiver was dead when you volunteered to go fetch him for Hunker Dawson, that maybe they'd had something to do with it. That's crazy. They're good people. I want to get this cleared up as soon as possible."

"As I said, I'll tell you if I find something."

David didn't know if that was the truth, but Quinlan sounded sincere enough. Well, he should. He'd been trained by the best of the best. David had a cousin, Tom Neibber, who had washed out of Quantico back in the early nineties, only gotten through the fourth week out of sixteen. He'd thought his cousin had what it took, but he hadn't made it.

David turned in the kitchen doorway. "It's funny, but inescapable. Sally wasn't expected here. Whoever killed Laura Strather was already holding her prisoner. If Sally hadn't heard the woman scream that first night she was here, you can bet no one else would have—but that's exactly what happened. If you and Sally hadn't been out there on the cliffs, that woman's body would never have been found. There would never have been a crime. Nothing, just another missing persons report put out by the husband.

"Now, Doc Spiver, that's different. The killer didn't care if Doc was found, just didn't care."

"Don't forget, it could be suicide."

"I know, but it doesn't smell right, you know?"

"No, I don't know, but you keep smelling, David. I do wonder that no-body heard a blessed thing. Hardly seems possible, does it? People are too contrary to all agree with each other. Now, that must smell big time to you."

"Yeah, it does, but I still think the old folk are just afraid. I'll be around, Quinlan. Take care of Sally. There's something about her that makes you want to put her under your coat and see that nothing happens to her."

"Maybe right now, but I imagine that usually if you tried that she'd punch your lights out."

"I get the same feeling—probably she would have some time ago, but not now. No, there's something wrong there, but I fancy you're not going to tell me what."

"I'll be talking to you, David. Good luck with that autopsy."

"Oh, yeah, I got to call my wife. I think she can forget me being home for dinner."

"You married?"

"You saw my wedding ring first thing, Quinlan. Don't be cute. I even mentioned one of my kids. I've got three little ones, all girls. When I come through the front door, two of them climb up my legs and the third one drags a chair over to jump into my arms. It's a race to see who gets her arms around my neck first."

David gave him a lopsided grin, a small salute, and left.

NO one could talk about anything else. Just Doc Spiver and how two out-siders had found him lying in his rocking chair, blood dropping off his fin-gertips, half his head blown off.

He'd killed himself—everyone agreed to that—but why?

Terminal cancer, Thelma Nettro said. Her own grandpa had had can-cer, and he would have killed himself if he hadn't died first.

He was nearly blind, Ralph Keaton said. Everybody knew he was pleased because when they got the body back, Ralph would lay him out. Yeah, Ralph said, Doc couldn't stand it that he wasn't really an honest-to-goodness doctor anymore.

He was hurt because some woman rejected him, Purn Davies said. Everyone knew that Amabel had turned Purn down some years before and he was still burning with resentment.

He just got tired of life, Helen Keaton said, as she scooped out a triple-dip chocolate pecan cone for Sherry Vorhees. Lots of old people got tired of living. He did something about it and didn't sit around whining for ten years until the devil finally took him.

Maybe, Hunker Dawson said, just maybe Doc Spiver had something to do with that poor woman's death. It made sense he'd kill himself then, wouldn't it? The guilt would drive a fine man like Doc Spiver to shoot himself.

There were no lawyers in town, but the sheriff found Doc Spiver's will soon enough. He had some $22,000 in a bank in South Bend. He left it all to what he called the Town Fund, headed by Reverend Hal Vorhees.

Sheriff David Mountebank was surprised when he was told about the Town Fund. He'd never heard about such a thing. What effect would this Town Fund have had on people's motives? Of course, he didn't know yet if someone had put the .38-caliber pistol in Doc's mouth and pulled the trigger, then pressed the butt into Doc's hand.

Premeditated murder, that was. Or Doc Spiver had put the gun in his own mouth. Ponser called David at eight o'clock that evening. He'd finished the autopsy and now he was equivocating, the putz. David pushed him, and he ended up saying it was suicide. No, Doc Spiver didn't have any terminal illness—at least Ponser hadn't seen anything.

Amabel said to Sally that same evening, "I'm thinking you and I should go to Mexico and lie on a beach."

Sally smiled. She was still wearing Amabel's bathrobe because she couldn't seem to get warm. James hadn't wanted to leave her, but then it seemed he remembered something that had made him go back to Thelma's. She'd wanted to ask him what it was, but she hadn't. "I can't go to Mexico, Amabel. I don't have my passport."

"Alaska, then. We could lie around on the snowbanks. I could paint and you could do—what, Sally? What did you do before your daddy got killed?"

Sally got colder. She pulled the bathrobe tighter around her and moved closer to the heat register. "I was Senator Bainbridge's senior aide."

"Didn't he retire?"

"Yes, last year. I didn't do anything after that."

"Why not?"

Vivid, frenzied pictures went careening through her mind, shrieking as loudly as the wind outside. She clutched the edge of the kitchen table.

"It's all right, baby, you don't have to tell me. It really doesn't matter. Goodness, what a day it's been. I'm going to miss Doc. He's been here forever. Everyone will miss him."

"No, Amabel, not everyone."

"So you don't think it was suicide, Sally?"

"No," Sally said, drawing a deep breath. "I think there's a madness in this town."

"What a thing to say! I've lived here for nearly thirty years. I'm not mad. None of my friends is mad. They're all down-to-earth folk who are friendly and care about each other and this town. Besides, if you were right, then the madness didn't begin until after you arrived. How do you explain that, Sally?"

"That's what the sheriff said. Amabel, do you really believe that Laura Strather, the woman James and I found, was brought into town by a stranger and held somewhere before he murdered her?"

"What I think, Sally, is that your brain is squirreling around, and it's not healthy for you, not with everything else upside down in your life. Just don't think about it. Everything will be back to normal soon. It's got to be."

That night, at exactly three o'clock in the morning, a blustery night with high winds but no rain, something brought Sally awake. She lay there a moment. Then she heard a soft tap on the window. At least it wasn't a woman screaming.

A branch from a tree, she thought, turning over and pulling the blanket up to her nose. Just a tree branch.

Tap.

She gave up and slid out of bed.

Tap.

She didn't remember that there wasn't a tree high enough until she'd pulled back the curtain and stared into her father's ghastly white, grinning face.

Amabel found her on her knees in the middle of the floor, her arms wrapped around herself, the window open, the curtains billowing outward, pulled by the wind, screaming and screaming until her throat closed and no sound came from her mouth.

QUINLAN made a decision then and there. "I'm taking her back to Thelma's. She'll stay with me. If something else happens, I'll be there to deal with it."

She'd called him thirty minutes before, gasping out her words, begging him to come and make her father leave her alone. He'd heard Amabel in the background telling her she was in no shape to be on the phone to anybody, much less to that man she didn't even know, to put down the phone, she was just excited, there hadn't been anyone there, it had been her imagination. Just look at all she'd been through.

And she was still saying it, ignoring Quinlan. "Baby, think. You were sound asleep when you heard the wind making strange noises against the window. You were dreaming, like those other times. I'll bet you weren't even awake when you pulled the curtains back."

"I wasn't asleep," Sally said. "The wind had awakened me. I was lying there. And then came the tapping."

"Baby—"

"It doesn't matter," Quinlan said, impatient now, knowing that Sally would soon think that she was crazy, that she'd imagined it all. He prayed to God that she hadn't. But she had been in that sanitarium for six months. She'd been paranoid, that's what was in the file. She'd also been depressed and suicidal. They'd been worried that she would harm herself. Her doctor hadn't wanted her released. Her husband had agreed. They wanted her back. Her husband was first in line. He wondered about the legalities of getting a person committed if that person didn't volunteer.

Why hadn't Sally's parents done anything about it? Had they believed her to be nuts too? But she was a person with legal rights. He had to check on how they'd gotten around it.

He said now, "Amabel, could you please pack Sally's things? I'd like all of us to get some sleep before morning."

Amabel pursed her lips. "She's a married woman. She shouldn't be going off with you."

Sally started laughing, a low, hoarse, very ugly laugh.

Amabel was so startled that she didn't say anything more. She went upstairs to pack the duffel bag.

Thirty minutes later, after four o'clock in the morning, Quinlan let Sally into his tower room.

"Thank you, James," she said. "I'm so tired. Thank you for coming for me."

He'd come for her, all right. He'd been off like a shot to get her. Damnation, why couldn't anything turn out the way it was supposed to, the way he'd planned? He was in the middle of a puzzle, and all he had was scattered pieces that didn't look like they would ever fit together. He put her to bed, tucked the covers around her, and without thinking about it, kissed her lightly on the mouth.

She didn't respond, just looked up at him.

"Go to sleep," he said, gently pushing her hair back from her face. He pulled the string on the bedside lamp. "We'll work it all out. Don't worry anymore."

That was a promise and a half. It scared the hell out of him.

"That's what he said on the phone, that he was coming for me. Soon, he said, very soon. He didn't lie, did he? He's here, James."

"Someone's here. We'll deal with it tomorrow. Go to sleep. I'm here, and I won't leave you alone, not anymore."

SHE was usually alone. At the beginning some of the patients had tried to talk to her, in their way, but she'd turned away from them. It didn't matter really because most of the time her brain was fuzzy, so completely disconnected from anything she could identify either outside herself or inside that she was as good as lost in a deep cave. Or she was floating up in the ether. There was no reality here, no getting up at six in the morning to run up Exeter Street over to Concord Avenue, covering a good two miles, then run home, jump in the shower, and think about all she had to do that day while she washed her hair.

Senator Bainbridge went to the White House at least twice a week. Many times she was with him, keeping together all his notes for the topics to be discussed. It was easy for her to do that since she'd written most of the notes and knew more than he did about his stands on his committee projects. She'd done so much, been involved in so many things—press releases, huddling with staff and the senator when a hot story broke and they tried to determine the best position for the senator to take.

There were always fund-raisers, press parties, embassy parties, political parties. So much, and she'd loved it, even when she would fall exhausted into bed.

At first Scott had told her how proud he was of her. He'd seemed excited to be invited to all the parties, to meet all the important players. At first.

Now she did nothing. Someone washed her hair twice a week. She scarcely noticed unless they let water run down her neck. She didn't have any muscles anymore, even though someone took her for long walks every day, just like a dog. She'd wanted to run once, just run and feel the wind against her face, feel her face chapping, but they didn't let her. After that they gave her more drugs so she wouldn't want to run again.

And he came, at least twice a week, sometimes more. The nurses adored him, saying behind their hands how devoted he was. He would sit with her in the common room a few minutes, then take her hand and lead her back to her room. It was a stark white room with nothing in it to use in attempting suicide—nothing sharp, no belts.

He had furnished it for her, she'd heard once, with the advice of Dr. Beadermeyer. It was a metal bed covered with fake wood, fake so that it wouldn't splinter so she could stick a fragment through her own heart. Not that such a thing would ever occur to her, but he talked about it and laughed, saying as he cupped her face in his hand that he would take care of her for a very long time.

Then he'd strip off her clothes and make her lie on her back on the bed. He would walk around the bed, looking at her, talking to her about his day, his work, about the woman he was currently sleeping with. Then he'd unzip his trousers and show her himself, tell her how lucky she was to get to see him, that he would let her touch him but he didn't quite trust her yet.

He'd touch her all over. He'd rub himself. Before he came, he'd hit her at least once, usually in the ribs.

Once when his head was thrown back in his orgasm, she saw through the fog in her eyes that there were two people at the window opening in the door, staring at them, talking even as they looked. She'd tried to push him away, but it hadn't worked. She had so little strength. He'd finished, then leaned down, seen the hatred in her eyes, and struck her face. It was the only time he had ever hit her in the face.

She remembered once how he'd turned her onto her belly, pulling her back toward him, and how he'd said that maybe one day he'd let her have him, let her feel him going into her, deep, and it would hurt because he was big, didn't she agree? But no, she didn't deserve him yet. And who cared? They had years ahead of them, years to do all sorts of things. And he'd told her about when he finally allowed his mistresses to have him and what they did to please him.

She hadn't said anything. He'd struck her for that, with his belt. He hadn't stopped for a very long time. She remembered screaming, begging, screaming some more, trying to wriggle away from him, but he'd held her down. He hadn't stopped.

IT was five A.M. when Quinlan was jerked out of a deep sleep by her scream, loud, piercing, so filled with pain and helplessness that he couldn't bear it. He was at her side in an instant, pulling her against him, trying to soothe her, saying anything that came to mind, just talking and talking to bring her out of the dreadful nightmare.

"It hurt so much, but he didn't care, he kept hitting and hitting, holding me down so I couldn't move, couldn't escape. I screamed and screamed, but nobody cared, nobody came, but I know those faces were looking in the window and they loved it. Oh, God, no, make it stop. STOP IT!"

So it was a nightmare about her time in that sanitarium—at least that's what it sounded like. It sounded sadistic and sexual. What was going on here?

His hand was busy in her hair, stroking up and down her back, talking to her, talking, talking.

Her horrible gasping breaths slowed. She hiccuped. She leaned back, wiping her hand across her nose. She closed her eyes a moment, then began to tremble.

"No, Sally, I'm here, it's all right. Relax against me, that's it. Breathe real slow. Good, that's fine." He stroked her back, felt the shivering slowly ease. What had she dreamed? A memory distorted by the unconscious could be hideous.

"What did he do to you?" He spoke slowly, softly against her temple. "You can tell me. It'll make it go away faster if you talk about it."

She whispered against his neck, "He came, at least twice a week, and every time he took off my clothes and looked at me and touched me and told me things he'd done that day, the women he'd taken.

"People watched through that window in the door, the same people, as if they had season tickets or something. It was horrible, but most of the time I lay there because my brain wasn't working. But that one time, it hurt so badly, I remember having my thoughts and feelings come together enough to feel the humiliation, so I tried to get away from him, to fight him, but he kept hitting me and hitting me, first with his hand, then with his belt. It pleased him that he'd made me bleed. He told me maybe sometime in the future, when I'd earned the honor, he'd come into me. I wouldn't have to worry because he wasn't HIV-positive, not that I would anyway because I was crazy. That's what he said, 'You won't remember a thing, will you, Sally, because you're crazy?' "

Even though Quinlan was so tense he imagined that if someone hit him he would just shatter into myriad pieces, Sally was now leaning limp against him, her breathing low, calmer. He'd been right. Talking about it out loud had eased her, but not him, good Lord, not him.

Could she have imagined it all? For the longest time he couldn't speak. Finally he said, "Was it your husband who did this to you, Sally?"

She was asleep, her breath even and slow against his chest. He realized then that he was wearing only his boxers. Who cared? He eased her back and tried to pull away from her. To his pleasure and consternation, she clutched her arms around his back. "No, please, no," she said. She sounded asleep.

He eased down beside her, lying on his back, pressing her face against his shoulder. He hadn't planned on this, he thought, staring up at the dark ceiling. She was breathing deeply, her leg across his belly now, her palm flat on his chest. Any lower with that hand or any lower with her thigh and he would be in big trouble.

He was already in big trouble. He kissed her forehead, squeezed her more closely against him, and closed his eyes. At least the bastard hadn't raped her. But he'd beat her.

Surprisingly, he fell asleep.

ELEVEN

"Yeah, right," Quinlan said to himself as he got to his feet. There were two nice male footprints below Sally's bedroom window at Amabel's house and, more important, deep impressions where the feet of the ladder had dug into the earth.

There were small torn branches on the ground, ripped away by some-one who had moved quickly, dragging that long ladder with him. He dropped to his haunches again and measured the footprints with his right hand. Size eleven shoe, about his own size. He took off his loafer and set it gently into the indentation. Nearly a perfect fit. All right, then, an eleven and a half.

The heels were pretty deep, which meant he wasn't a small man, per-haps about six feet and one hundred eighty pounds or so. Close enough. He looked more carefully, measuring the depth of the indentations with his fin-gers. One went deeper than the other, which was odd. A limp? He didn't know. Maybe it was just an aberration.

"What have you got, Quinlan?" It was David Mountebank. He was in his uniform, looking pressed and well shaved, and surprisingly well rested. It was only six-thirty in the morning. "You thinking about eloping with Sally Brandon?"

Quinlan rose slowly, as he said in an easy voice, "Actually someone tried to get into the house last night and really scared Sally. And yes, if you're interested, she should still be sleeping in Thelma's tower room, my room."

"Someone tried to break in?"

"Yeah, that's about it. Sally woke up and saw the man's face in the window. It scared the bejesus out of her. When she screamed, it must have scared the bejesus out of the guy as well, because he was out of here."

David Mountebank leaned against the side of Amabel's cottage. It looked like it had been freshly painted not six months ago. The dark green trim around the windows was very crisp. "What's really going on, Quinlan?"

He sighed. "I can't tell you. Call it national security, David."

"I'd like to call that bullshit."

"I can't tell you," Quinlan repeated. He met David's eye. He never flinched. David could have drawn a gun on him and he wouldn't have flinched.

"All right," David said finally. "Have it your way, at least for now. You promise me it doesn't have anything to do with the two murders?"

"It doesn't. The more I mull it over, the more I think the woman's murder is somehow connected to Harve and Marge Jensen's disappearance three years ago, even though just yesterday I told you I couldn't imagine it. I don't know how or why, but you've got things that don't smell right. Well, I have things that twist and turn in my gut. That's my intuition. I've learned over the years never to ignore it. Things are somehow connected. I just have no idea how or why or if I'm just plain not thinking straight.

"As for Sally, let it go, David. I'd consider that I owed you good if you'd let it go."

"It was *two* murders, Quinlan."

"Doc Spiver?"

"Yeah. I got a call from the M.E. in Portland, a woman who was trained down in San Francisco and really knows her stuff. Would that there were M.E.s everywhere who knew what they were doing. I got his body to her late last night, and she agreed to do the autopsy immediately, bless her. She determined there was no way he would have sat himself down in the rocking chair, put the gun in his mouth, and pulled the trigger."

"That takes care of the theory that Doc Spiver murdered the woman and then felt so guilty that he killed himself."

"Blows it straight into the ground."

"You know what it sounds like to me? Maybe the person really believed everyone would think Doc Spiver killed himself. Maybe an older person who doesn't know all about things a good M.E. can determine. Your man Ponser didn't know, after all. You could say you lucked out because of how good the M.E. is in Portland."

"That sounds right to me." He sighed. "What we've got is a killer loose, Quinlan, and I'm so stuck I don't know what to do.

"My men and I have been questioning every person in this beautiful little town, and like with Laura Strather, no one knows a thing. I still can't buy it that one of the local folk is involved in this."

"One of them is, David, no way around it."

"You want me to take plaster casts of those footprints?"

"No, don't bother. But take a look, one impression goes deeper than the other. You ever see anything like that?"

David was down on his hands and knees, studying the footprints. He measured the depth with his pinkie finger, as Quinlan had done. "Strange," he said. "I don't have a clue."

"I was thinking the guy had a limp, but it wouldn't look like that if he did. There'd be more of a rolling to one side, but there's not."

"You got me, Quinlan." David stood up and looked toward the ocean. "It's going to be a beautiful day. I used to bring my kids here at least twice a week for the World's Greatest Ice Cream. I haven't wanted them to get near The Cove since that first murder."

And, Quinlan knew, besides that killer, there was another man here who was out to make Sally believe she was crazy. It had to be her husband, Scott Brainerd.

He dusted his hands off on his dark brown corduroy pants. "Oh, David, which one got to you first?"

"What?"

"Which of your daughters got her arms around your neck first?"

David laughed. "The littlest one. She climbed right up my leg like a monkey. Her name's Deirdre."

James left David Mountebank and returned to Thelma's Bed and Breakfast.

When he opened the door to his tower room, Sally was standing in the doorway of the bathroom. Her hair was wet and plastered to her head, strands falling to her shoulders. She had a towel in her left hand. She stared at him.

She was stark naked.

She was so damned thin and so damned perfect, and he realized it in the split second before she pulled the towel in front of herself.

"Where did you go?" she asked, still not moving, just standing there, wet and thin and perfect, and covered with a white towel.

"He wears an eleven-and-a-half shoe."

She tightened the towel, rolling it over above her breasts. She continued to stare at him.

"The man pretending to be your father," he said, watching her closely.

"You found him?"

"Not yet, but I found his footprints beneath your bedroom window and the indentations of the ladder feet. Yeah, our man was there. What size shoe does your husband wear, Sally?"

She was very pale. Now she was so colorless that he imagined even her hair was fading as he looked at her. "I don't know what size. I never asked, I never bought him shoes. My father wears an eleven and a half."

"Sally, your father is dead. He was murdered more than two weeks ago. He was buried. The cops saw the body. It was your father. The man last night, it wasn't your father. If you can't think of any other man who's trying to drive you nuts, then it has to be your husband. Did you see him the night your father was murdered?"

"No," she whispered, backing away from him, retreating into the bathroom, shaking her head, wet strands of hair slapping her cheeks. "No, no."

She didn't slam the door, just quietly pushed it closed. He heard the lock click on the other side.

He knew he would never look at her in quite the same way again. She could be wearing a bear coat and he knew he would still see her standing naked in the bathroom doorway, so pale and beautiful that he'd wanted to pick her up and very gently lay her on his bed. But that would never happen. He had to get a grip.

"Hi," he said when she came out a while later, wrapped in one of the white robes, her hair dry, her eyes not meeting his.

She nodded, her eyes still on her bare feet, and began to collect her clothing.

"Sally, we're both adults."

"What's that supposed to mean?"

At least she was looking at him now, and there wasn't an ounce of fear in her voice or in her eyes. He was pleased. She trusted him not to hurt her.

"I didn't mean as in consenting adults. I only meant that you're no more a kid than I am. There's no reason for you to be embarrassed."

"I suppose you'd be the one to be embarrassed since I'm so skinny and ugly."

"Yeah, right."

"What does that mean?"

"It means I think you're very—no, never mind that. Now, smile."

She gave him a ghastly smile, but again, there was no fear in it. She did trust him not to rape her. He heard himself say, completely unplanned, "Was it your husband who humiliated you and beat you in that sanitarium?"

She didn't move, didn't change expressions, but she withdrew from him. She shut down.

"Answer me, Sally. Was it your damned husband?"

She looked at him straight on and said, "I don't know you. You could be the man calling me, mimicking my father, you could be the man last night at my window. He could have sent you. I want to leave now, James, and never come back here. I want to disappear. Will you help me do that?"

He wanted to help her. He wanted to disappear with her. He wanted— He shook his head. "That's no answer to anything. You can't run forever, Sally."

"I wouldn't bet on it." She turned, clutching her clothes to her chest, and went back into the bathroom.

He started to shout through the bathroom door that he liked the small black mole on the right side of her belly. But he didn't. He sat down on the chintz sofa and tried to figure things out.

"THELMA," he said after he'd swallowed a spoonful of the lightest, most beautifully seasoned scrambled eggs he'd ever tasted in his life, "if you were a stranger and you wanted to hide here in The Cove, where would you go?"

Thelma ate one of her fat sausages, wiped the grease off her chin, and said, "Well, let me see. There's that dilapidated little shack up on that hillock behind Doc Spiver's house. But I tell you, boy, I'd have to be real desperate to hole up in that place. All filled with dirt and spiders and probably rats. Nasty place that probably leaks real bad when it rains." She ate another sausage—forked the whole thing up and stuffed it into her mouth.

Martha came up beside her and handed her a fresh napkin. Thelma gave her a nasty look. "You think I'm one of those old ladies who will dribble on themselves if a handmaiden isn't right on the spot to keep her clean?"

"Now, Thelma, you've been twisting the other napkin around until it's a crumpled ball. Here, take this one. Oh, look, you got some sausage grease on your diary. You've got to be more careful."

"I need more ink. Go buy me some, Martha. Hey, you got young Ed back there in the kitchen? You're feeding him, aren't you, Martha? You're buying my food with my money and you're feeding him so he'll go to bed with you."

Martha rolled her eyes and looked at Sally's plate. "You don't like the toast? It's a little on the pale side. You want it better toasted?"

"No, no, it's fine, truly. I'm just not hungry this morning."

"No man wants a skinny post, Sally," Thelma said, taking a noisy bite of toast. "A man's got to have something he can hang on to. Look at Martha, bosom so big young Ed can't even walk past without seeing her poking out at him."

"Young Ed has prostate trouble," Martha said, raising a thick black eyebrow, and she left the dining room, saying over her shoulder, "I'll buy you some black ink, Thelma."

"I'M coming with you."

"But—"

Sally shook her head and walked across the street toward the World's Greatest Ice Cream Shop. She was limping only slightly today. A bell tinkled when she opened the door.

Amabel, dressed like a gypsy with a cute white apron, stood behind the counter, scooping up a peach double-dip cone for a young woman who was talking a mile a minute.

". . . I heard that two people have been murdered here in the last several days. That's incredible! My mama said The Cove was the quietest little place she knew about, she said nothing ever happened here, that it had to be one of those gangs from down south come up here to stir up misery."

"Hello, Sally, James. How are you this morning, baby?"

As she spoke, she handed the cone to the young woman, who immediately began licking and moaning in ecstasy.

"I'm fine," Sally said.

"That will be two dollars and sixty cents," Amabel said.

"Oh, it's wonderful," the young woman said. She alternately dug in her wallet and ate the ice cream.

Quinlan smiled at her. "It is excellent ice cream. Why don't you keep eating and I'll treat you?"

"Taking ice cream from a stranger is okay," Sally said. "Besides, I know him. He's harmless."

Quinlan paid Amabel. Nothing else was said until the young woman left the shop.

"There hasn't been another call," Amabel said. "Either from Thelma or from your father."

"He knows that I've left your house," Sally said thoughtfully. "That's good. I don't want you in any danger."

"Don't be ridiculous, Sally. There's no danger for me."

"There was for Laura Strather and Doc Spiver," Quinlan said. "You be careful, Amabel. Sally and I are going exploring. Thelma told us about this shack up the hill behind Doc Spiver's house. We're going to check it out."

"Watch out for snakes," Amabel called after them.

Which kind? Quinlan wondered.

Once they were rounding the corner to Doc Spiver's house, Sally said, "Why did you tell Amabel where we were going?"

"Seeding," he said. "Watch your step, Sally. You're not all that steady on your ankle yet." He held back the stiff, gnarly branch of a yew tree. There was a barren hill behind the house, and tucked into a shallow recess was a small shack.

"What do you mean, seeding?"

"I don't like the fact that your dear auntie has treated you like you're so high-strung no one should trust what you say. I told her that to see if perhaps something might happen. Then if it does—"

"Amabel would never hurt me, never."

He looked down at her and then at the shack. "Is that what you believed about your husband when you married him?"

He didn't wait for her to answer him, just pushed open the door. It was surprisingly solid. "Watch your head," he said over his shoulder as he stooped down and walked into the dim single room.

"Yuck," Sally said. "This is pretty bad, James."

"Yeah, I'd say so." He didn't say anything else, just began to look around as he imagined the sheriff had done only days before. He found nothing. The small space was empty. There were no windows. It would be pitch black when the door was closed. Just plain nothing. A modicum of hope, that was all he'd had, but still, he was more than a modicum disappointed. "I'd say that if Laura Strather was kept prisoner here, the guy holding her was very thorough cleaning up. There's nothing, Sally, not a trace of anything."

"He's not hiding in here, either," she said. "And that's what we're really doing here, isn't it?"

"Both, really. I have a feeling that your *father* wouldn't lower himself to stay in this place. There aren't even any free bathrobes."

THAT afternoon they ate lunch at the Hinterlands. This week Zeke was serving Spam burgers and variations on meat loaf.

They both ordered Zeke's original-recipe meat loaf.

"The smells make me salivate," Quinlan said, inhaling. "Zeke puts garlic in his mashed potatoes. Breathe deeply enough and no vampire will come near you."

Sally was toying with the curved slice of carrot in her salad. "I like garlic."

"Tell me about that night, Sally."

She'd picked up the carrot and was chewing on it. She dropped it. Then she picked it up again and slowly began eating it. "All right," she said finally. She smiled at him. "I might as well trust you. If you're going to betray me, then I might as well hang it up. The cops are right. I was there that night. But they're wrong about everything else. I don't remember a thing, James, not a blessed thing."

Well, hell, he thought, but he knew she was telling him the truth. "Do you think someone struck you?"

"No, I don't think so. I've thought and thought about it and all I can figure out is that I just don't want to remember, can't bear to, I guess, so my brain just closed it down."

"I've heard about hysterical amnesia and even seen it a couple of times. What usually happens is that you will remember, if not tomorrow, then next week. Your father wasn't killed in a horrific way. He was shot neatly through the heart, no muss, no fuss. So, it would seem to me that the people involved in his death shook you so much that's the reason you've blocked it all out."

"Yes," she said slowly, then turned around and saw the waitress bringing their plates. The smell of garlic, butter, roasted squash, and the rich aroma of the meat loaf filled the air around them.

"I couldn't live here and stay trim," James said. "It smells delicious, Nelda."

"Catsup for the meat loaf?"

"Does a shark have a fin?"

Nelda, the waitress, laughed and set a Heinz bottle between them. "Enjoy," she said.

"Nelda, how often do young Ed and Martha eat here?"

"Oh, maybe twice a week," she said, looking a bit startled. "Martha says she gets tired of her own cooking. Young Ed is my older brother. Poor man. Every time he wants to see Martha, he has to endure Thelma's jokes. Can you believe that old woman is still alive, writing in that diary of hers every day and eating that sausage?"

"That's interesting," James said when Nelda left them. "Eat, Sally. That's right. You're perfect, but I'd be worried for you in a strong wind."

"I used to run every day," she said. "I used to be strong."

"You will be again. Just stick with me."

"I can't imagine running in Los Angeles. All I ever see is pictures of horrible fog and cars stacked up on the freeways."

"I live in a canyon. It's got healthy air and I run there as well."

"Somehow I can't imagine you living in Southern California. You just don't seem the type. Does your ex-wife still live there?"

"No, Teresa is back east. She married a crook, interestingly enough. I hope she doesn't have kids with the guy. Their genetic potential is hair-raising."

She laughed, actually laughed. It felt as wonderful to her as it felt to James hearing it.

"You have any idea how beautiful you are, Sally?"

Her fork stilled over the meat loaf. "You're into crazy freaks?"

"If you ever say anything like that again, you'll piss me off. When I get pissed off I do strange things, like take off all my clothes and chase ducks in the park." The tension fell away from her. He had no idea why he'd told her she was beautiful; it had just slipped out. Actually, she was more than beautiful—she was warm and caring, even while she was living this nightmare. He wished he knew what to do.

"You said you don't remember about that night your father was killed. Do you have other gaps in your memory?"

"Yes. Sometimes when I think about that place, very sharp memories will come to me, but I couldn't swear if they are truly memories or just weird images stewed up by my brain. I remember everything very clearly until about six months ago."

"What happened six months ago?"

"That's when everything went dim."

"What happened six months ago?"

"Senator Bainbridge retired suddenly, and I was out of a job. I remember that I was going to interview with Senator Irwin, but I never got to his office."

"Why not?"

"I don't know. I remember it was a sunny day. I was singing. The top was down on my Mustang. The air was sharp and warm." She paused, frowning, then shrugged. "I always sang when the top was down. I don't remember anything else, but I know I never saw Senator Irwin."

She said nothing more. She was eating her meat loaf. She probably didn't realize she was eating, but he wanted her to keep at it. He guessed he wanted her to eat more than he wanted her to talk. At least for now. What had happened?

James paid their bill and walked outside while Sally went to the women's room. He wondered how he was going to keep his hands off her when they got back to his tower bedroom.

TWELVE

He heard a whisper of sound that didn't belong in that small narrow space beside the Hinterlands. He turned around, wondering if Sally had come out of the cafe without his seeing her. That was when he heard it again. There it was, a whisper of sound. He pivoted quickly on his heel, his hand inside his jacket on the butt of his SIG-Sauer, a 9mm semiautomatic pistol that fit his hand and his personality perfectly. He was at one with that pistol, as he'd never been with any other before in his professional life. He was pulling it out, smooth and quick, but still, he was too late. The blow struck him just over his left ear. He went down without a sound.

"James?" Sally stuck her head out the door of the cafe. There was no one around. She waved to Nelda, then turned back. Where was James? She frowned and stepped down. She heard a scraping sound, then she knew she heard a whisper—a man's whisper? James? She wheeled about to look in that sliver of space beside the building.

What she saw was James lying on his side on the ground, a trickle of blood trailing down his cheek toward his chin. She yelled his name and skidded onto her knees beside him, shaking him, then drawing back. She sucked in her breath. Gently she laid her fingers on the pulse in his throat. It was strong and slow. Thank God, he was all right. What was going on here? But then she knew.

It was her father, he'd finally come to get her, just as he'd promised he would. He'd hurt James, probably because he'd been protecting her.

She looked up for help, praying to see anyone, it didn't matter how old he was, just anyone. There was no one around, not a single soul.

Oh, God, what should she do? She was leaning down to look at the wound when the blow crashed directly down on the back of her head and she crumpled over James.

* * *

SHE heard the sound. It came at short intervals. It was water, one drop after another, hitting metal.

Plop.

She opened her eyes but couldn't seem to focus. Her brain felt loose, as if it were floating inside her head. She couldn't seem to think; she could only hear that plop. She knew something wasn't right. She tried to remember but couldn't quite make her brain fasten onto something that would trigger a thought, any thought, anything that had happened to her before she was here, wherever here was.

"You're awake. Good."

A voice, a man's voice, *his* voice. She managed to follow the sound of his voice. It was Dr. Beadermeyer, the man who had tormented her for six long months.

Yes, she remembered that, not all of it, but enough to have it burn through her sleep and terrify her over and over in nightmares that still brought vivid pain.

Suddenly she remembered. She'd been with James. Yes, James Quinlan. He'd been struck on the head. He was lying unconscious on the ground in that small slice of land next to the Hinterlands.

"Nothing to say, Sally? I cut back on the dosage so you could talk to me." She felt a sharp slap on her cheek.

"Look at me, Sally. Don't pretend you're off in outer space. I know this time you can't be." He slapped her again.

He grabbed her shoulders and shook her hard.

"Is James all right?"

He stopped shaking her. "James?" He sounded surprised. "Oh, that man you were with in The Cove. Yes, he's fine. No one wanted to take the risk of killing him. Was he your lover, Sally? You had him less than a week. That's moving fast. He must have been desperate.

"Just look at you, all skinny and pathetic, your hair in strings, your clothes bagging around you. Come on, Sally, tell me about James. Tell me what you told him."

"I told him about you," she said. "I had a nightmare and he helped me through it. I told him what a piece of slime you are."

He slapped her again, not too hard, but hard enough to make her shrink away from him.

"You're rude, Sally. And you're lying. You've never lied well and I can always tell. You might have dreamed, but you didn't tell him about me. You want to know why? It's because you're crazy and I'm so deep a part of you that if you were to tell anyone about me, why, you'd collapse in on yourself and die. You can't exist without me, Sally.

"You were away from me for two weeks, and look what happened. You're a mess. You tried to pretend you were normal. You lost all your manners. Your mother would be appalled. Your husband would back away from you in disgust. As for your father, well—well, I suppose it's not worth speculating now that he's shuffled off his mortal coil."

"Where am I?"

"Ah, that's supposed to be the first thing out of your mouth, if books and TV stories are to be believed. You're back where you belong, Sally. Look around you. You're back in your room, the very same one decorated especially for you by your dear father. I've kept you under for nearly a day and a half. I let up on the dosage about four hours ago. You took your time coming to the surface."

"What do you want?"

"I have what I want; at least I have the first installment of what I want. And that's you, my dear."

"I'm thirsty."

"I'll bet you are. Holland, where are you? Bring some water to our patient."

She remembered Holland, a skinny, furtive little man who'd been one of the two men to stare through the small square window while he was hitting her and caressing her, humiliating her. Holland had thinning brown hair and the deadest eyes she'd ever seen. He rarely said anything, at least to her.

She said nothing more until he appeared at her side, a glass of water in his hand.

"Here you are, Doctor," he said in that low, hoarse voice of his that lay like a covering of loose gravel in all those nightmares, making her want to be drugged so she wouldn't realize he was around her.

He was standing behind Beadermeyer, looking down at her, his eyes dead and hungry. She wanted to vomit.

Dr. Beadermeyer raised her and let her drink her fill.

"Soon you'll want to go to the bathroom. Holland will help you with that, won't you, Holland?"

Holland nodded, and she wanted to die. She fell back against the pillow, a hard, institutional pillow, and closed her eyes. She knew deep down she couldn't keep herself intact in this place again. She also realized that she would never escape again. This time it was over for her.

She kept her eyes closed, didn't turn toward him. "I'm not crazy.

I was never crazy. Why are you doing this? He's dead. What does it matter?"

"You still don't know, do you? You still have no memory of any of it. I realized that almost immediately. Well, it isn't my place to tell you, my dear." She felt him pat her cheek. She flinched.

"Now, now, Sally, I'm not the one who tormented you, though I must admit that I enjoyed the one tape I saw. Except you weren't even there, you were flopping back, your eyes closed, letting him do whatever he wanted.

"You didn't have any fight in you. Why, you were so out of it, you barely flinched when he hit you. But even then you weren't afraid. I could tell. The contrast, at least, made for fascinating viewing."

She felt gooseflesh rise on her arms as remnants of memories flooded her—the movement of his hands over her, the pushing and slapping, the caressing that turned to pain.

She heard the bed ease up and knew that Dr. Beadermeyer was standing beside her, looking down at her. She heard him say softly, "Holland, if she gets away again, I'll have to hurt you badly. Do you understand?"

"Yes, Dr. Beadermeyer."

"It won't be like last time, Holland. I made a mistake on your punishment last time. You rather liked that little shock therapy, didn't you?"

"It won't happen again, Dr. Beadermeyer." Was there disappointment in that frightening little man's voice?

"Good. You know what happened to Nurse Krider when she let her hide those pills under her tongue. Yes, of course you do. Be mindful, Holland.

"I must go now, Sally, but I'll be with you again this evening. We'll have to get you away from the sanitarium, probably tomorrow morning. The decision what to do with you hasn't been made yet. But you can't stay here. The FBI, this Quinlan fellow, he's got to know all about this place. I'm sure you did tell him some things about your past. And they'll come. But that isn't your problem.

"Now, let me give you a little shot of something that will make you drift and really feel quite good about things. Yes, Holland, hold her arm for me."

Sally felt the chill of the needle, felt the brief sting. Within moments, she felt herself begin to drift out of her brain, to float in nothingness. She felt the part of her that was real, the part of her that wanted life—such a small flicker, really—struggling briefly before it succumbed. She sighed deeply and was gone from herself.

She felt hands on her, taking off her clothes. She knew it was Holland. Probably Dr. Beadermeyer was watching.

She didn't struggle. There was nothing more to care about.

QUINLAN woke up with a roaring headache that beat any hangover he'd ever had in college. He cursed, held his head in his hands, and cursed some more.

"You've got the mother of all headaches, right?"

"David," he said, and even that one word hurt. "What the devil happened?"

"Someone hit you good just above your left ear. Our doctor put three stitches in your head. Hold still and I'll get you a pill."

Quinlan focused on that pill. It had to help. If it didn't, his brain would break out of his skull.

"Here, Quinlan. It's strong stuff; you're supposed to have one every four hours."

Quinlan took it and downed the entire glass of water. He lay back, his eyes closed, and waited.

"Dr. Grafft said it would kick in quickly."

"I sure hope so. Talk to me, David. Where's Sally?"

"I'll tell you everything. Lie still. I found you unconscious in that narrow little strip of alley beside the Hinterlands. Thelma Nettro had reported you and Sally missing, so I started looking.

"When I found you lying there, I thought you were dead. I slung you over my shoulder and brought you to my house. Dr. Grafft met me here and stitched you up. I don't know about Sally. She's gone, Quinlan. No trace, nothing. It's like she was never even here."

If he didn't hurt so badly, Quinlan would have yelled. Instead, he lay there, trying to figure things out, trying to think. For the moment, it was beyond him.

Sally was gone. That was all that was real to him. Gone, not found dead. Gone. But where?

He heard children's voices. Surely that couldn't be right. He heard David say, "Deirdre, come here and sit on my lap. You've got to keep very quiet, okay? Mr. Quinlan isn't feeling well, and we don't want to make him feel worse."

He heard a little girl whisper, but he couldn't make it out. He remembered that Deirdre meant sorrow. He slept.

He awoke to see a young woman with a pale complexion and very dark red hair looking at him. She had the sweetest face he'd ever seen. "Who are you?"

"I'm Jane, David's wife. You lie still, Mr. Quinlan." He felt her cool palm on his forehead. "I've got some nice hot chicken soup for you. Dr. Grafft said to keep it light until tomorrow. You open your mouth and I'll feed you. That's right."

He ate the entire bowl and began to feel human. "Thank you," he said, and slowly, her hand under his elbow, he sat up.

"Your head ache?"

"It's just a dull thud now. What time is it? Rather, what day is it?"

"You were hurt early this afternoon. It's eight o'clock in the evening now. I hope the girls didn't disturb you."

"No, not at all. Thank you for taking me in."

"Let me get David. He's tucking the girls into bed. He should be about through with the bedtime story."

Quinlan sat there, his head back against the cushions of the sofa, a nice comfortable sofa. The headache was gone now. He could get out of here soon. He could find Sally. He realized he was scared to his socks. What had happened to her?

Her father had come for her just as he'd promised he would. No, that was ridiculous. Amory St. John was long dead.

"You want some brandy in hot tea?"

"Nah, my pecker doesn't need optimism." Quinlan opened his eyes and smiled at David Mountebank. "Your wife fed me. Great soup. I appreciate you taking me in, David."

"I couldn't leave you with Thelma Nettro, now, could I? I wouldn't leave my worst enemy there. That old lady gives me the willies. It's the weirdest thing. She always has that diary of hers with her and that fountain pen in her hand. The tip of her tongue is practically tattooed from the pen tip."

"Tell me about Sally."

"Every man I could round up is talking to everybody in The Cove and looking for her. I've got an APB out on her—"

"No APB," James said, sitting up straight now, his face paling. "No, David, cancel it now. It's critical."

"I won't buy any more of this national security crap, Quinlan. Tell me why or I won't do it."

"You're not being cooperative, David."

"Tell me and let me help you."

"She's Sally St. John Brainerd."

David stared at him. "She's Amory St. John's daughter? The daughter who's nuts and who ran away from that sanitarium? The woman whose husband is frantic about her safety? I knew she looked familiar. Damn, I'm slipping fast. I should have made the connection. Ah, that's the reason for the black wig. Then she forgot to put it on, didn't she?"

"Yeah, that and I told her to relax, that you would never connect her to Susan Brainerd, at least I prayed you wouldn't."

"I wish I could say I would have, but I probably never would have unless I saw her in person and then saw her again on TV. What were you doing with her, Quinlan?"

Quinlan sighed. "She doesn't know I'm FBI. She bought that story about me being a PI and looking for those old folks who disappeared around here three years ago. I came here because I had this feeling she would run here, to her aunt. I was just going to take her back."

"But why is the FBI involved in a homicide?"

"The homocide's only part of it. We're in it for other reasons."

"I know. You're not going to tell me the rest of it."

"I'd prefer not to yet. As I was saying, I was going to take her back, but then—"

"Then what?"

"Her father phoned her twice. Then she saw his face at her window in the middle of the night."

"And you found her father's footprints on the ground the next morning. Her father's dead, murdered. Quinlan, what's going on here?"

"I don't know. But I've got to find her. Someone was trying to make her believe she's crazy. And that aunt of hers didn't help a bit, kept telling her in an understanding, tender voice that she'd be hearing things and seeing things too if she'd been through all that Sally had, and she had been in that sanitarium for so long, and that would make her think differently, wouldn't it?

"Then the two murders. I've got to find her. Everything else is nuts, but not Sally."

"When you feel well enough, you and I will go see her aunt. I already spoke to her, but she said that she hadn't seen Sally, that she was staying with you at Thelma's Bed and Breakfast. We searched your tower bedroom. Her duffel bag was gone and all her clothes, her blow dryer, everything. It's like she was never there. Look, Quinlan, maybe when she saw you unconscious, she got really scared and ran."

"No," James said, looking David straight in the eye. "I know she wouldn't leave me, not if I were lying there unconscious. She wouldn't."

"It's like that, is it?"

"God only knows, but she has a thick streak of honor and she cares about me. She wouldn't have left."

"Then we've got to find her. Another thing—I'm an officer of the law. Now that I know who she is, it's my duty to report her."

"I'd appreciate it if you'd wait, David. There's more at stake here than Amory St. John's murder, lots more. Trust me on this."

David looked at him for a long time. Finally, he said, "All right. Tell me what I can do to help."

"Let's go see Aunt Amabel Perdy."

DR. Alfred Beadermeyer was enjoying himself. Sally didn't know the small new mirror in her room was two-way. No one knew, at least he didn't think so. He watched her sit up slowly, obviously trying to coordinate her arms and legs. Since her brain was fuzzy, it was difficult for her, but she kept trying. He admired that in her, and at the same time he wanted to destroy it. It seemed to take her several moments to realize she was naked.

Then, very slowly, as if she were an old woman, she rose and walked to the small closet. She pulled out a nightgown she'd left there before she escaped. She didn't know it, but he had bought it for her. She slipped it over her head, teetering a bit but managing finally. Then she walked back to sit on the edge of the bed. She held her head in her hands.

He was getting bored. Wouldn't she do anything? Wouldn't she start yelling? Something? He had nearly turned to go when at last she raised her head and he saw tears streaming down her cheeks.

This was better. Soon she would be ready to listen to him. Soon now. He would hold off on another shot for an hour or so. He turned away and unlocked the door of the tiny room.

Sally knew she was crying. She could feel the wet on her face, taste the salt when it trickled into her mouth. Why was she crying? James. She remembered James, how he lay there, blood streaming from the wound over his left ear. He'd been so still, so very still. Beadermeyer had promised he wasn't dead. How could she believe that monster?

He had to be all right. She looked at the soft silk gown that slithered against her skin. It was a lovely peach color with wide silk straps over her shoulders. Unfortunately it bagged on her now. She looked at the needle marks in her arm. There were five pinpricks. He'd drugged her five times.

She felt her head begin to clear, slowly, so very slowly. More things, memories, began to filter through, take shape and substance.

She had to get out of here before he either killed her or took her someplace else, someplace where nobody could find her. She thought of James. He could find her if anyone could.

She forced herself to her feet. She took one step, then another. Soon she was walking slowly, carefully, but naturally. She stood in front of the narrow window and stared out onto the sanitarium grounds.

The mowed lawn stretched a good hundred yards before it butted against a heavily wooded area. Surely she could walk that far; she had before. She had to get to those woods. She could get lost in those woods, as she had before. Eventually she'd found her way out. She would again.

She walked back to the closet. There was a bathrobe and two more nightgowns, a pair of slippers. Nothing else. No pants, no dresses, no underwear.

She didn't care. She would walk in her bathrobe, to the ends of the earth if necessary. Then another veil lifted in her brain, and she remembered that she'd stolen one of the nurse's pantsuits that first time, and her shoes. Would it be possible to do that again?

Who had done this to her? She knew it wasn't her father. He was long dead. It had to be the man pretending to be her father, the man who'd called her, who'd appeared at her bedroom window. It could have been Scott, it could have been Dr. Beadermeyer, it could have been some man either of them had hired.

But not her father, thank God. That miserable bastard was finally dead. She prayed there was a hell. If there was, she knew he was there, in the deepest pit.

She had to get to her mother. Noelle would help her. Noelle would protect her, once she knew the truth. But why hadn't Noelle ever come to see her during the six months here? Why hadn't she demanded to know why her daughter was here? As far as Sally knew, Noelle hadn't done anything to help her. Did she believe her daughter was crazy? Had she believed her husband? Had she believed Sally's husband?

How to get out of here?

AMABEL said, "Would either of you gentlemen care for a cup of coffee?"

"No," Quinlan said curtly. "Tell us where Sally is."

Amabel sighed and motioned the two men to sit down. "Listen, James, I already told the sheriff here that Sally must have gotten scared when she saw you were hurt, and she ran. That's the only explanation. Sally's not a strong girl. She's been through a lot. She was even in an asylum. You don't look shocked. I'm a bit surprised that she told you about it. Something like that shouldn't be talked about.

"But listen, she was very ill. She still is. It makes sense that she would run again, like she ran away from what happened in Washington. If you doubt me, go to Thelma's. Martha told me that all of Sally's things were gone from your room. Isn't that odd? She left not even a memory of herself in that room.

"It was like she wanted to erase her very self." She paused a moment, then added in a faraway gypsy's voice, "It's almost as if she was never really there at all, as if we all just imagined she was here."

Quinlan jumped to his feet and stood over her. He looked menacing but David didn't say a word, just waited. Quinlan stuck his face near hers and said slowly and very distinctly, "That's bullshit, Amabel. Sally wasn't an apparition, nor was she nuts, as you implied to her, like you're implying to us now. She didn't imagine hearing a woman scream those two nights. She didn't imagine seeing her father's face at her bedroom window in the middle of the night. You tried to make her doubt herself, didn't you, Amabel? You tried to make her think she was crazy."

"That is ridiculous."

Quinlan moved even closer, leaning over her now, forcing her to press her back against the chair. "Why did you do that, Amabel? You said you knew she was in a sanitarium. You knew, didn't you, that someone put her there and kept her for six months drugged to her eyebrows? You didn't try to assure her that she was as sane as anyone—no, you kept on with the innuendos.

"Don't deny it, I heard you do it. You tried to make Sally doubt herself, her reason. Why?"

But Amabel smiled sadly at him. She said to David, "Sheriff, I've been very patient. This man only knew Sally for a matter of days. I'm her aunt. I love her. There's no reason I would ever want to hurt her. I would always seek to protect her. I'm sorry, James, but she ran away. It's as simple as that. I pray the sheriff will find her. She's not strong. She needs to be taken care of."

Quinlan was so angry he was afraid he'd pull her out of the chair and shake her like a rat. He backed off and began pacing around the small living room. David watched him for a moment, then said, "Mrs. Perdy, if Sally ran, can you guess where she would go?"

"To Alaska. She said she wanted to go to Alaska. She said she preferred Mexico, but she didn't have her passport. That's all I can tell you, Sheriff.

Of course, if I hear from her, I'll call you right away." Amabel rose. "I'm sorry, James. You know who Sally is. It's likely you've told Sheriff Mountebank her real name. There's a lot for her to face, and she'll have to face it eventually. As to her mental status, who's to say? All we can do is pray."

James wanted to wrap his fingers around her gypsy neck and squeeze. She was lying, damn her, but she was doing it very well. Sally wouldn't have run away, not with him lying unconscious at her feet. She wouldn't.

That meant that someone had her.

And that someone was the person who had pretended to be her father. James would bet on it. Now he knew what to do. He even had a good idea where she was, and it curdled his blood to think about it.

THIRTEEN

It was a black midnight, not even a sliver of moon or a single star to cast a dim light through that cauldron sky. Roiling black clouds moved and shifted, but never revealed anything except more blackness.

Sally stared out the window, drawing one deep breath after another. They would be here soon to give her another shot. No more pills, she'd heard Beadermeyer say; she just might be able to hide them again in her mouth. He announced that he didn't want her hurt again, the bastard.

There was a new nurse—her name tag said Rosalee—and she was as blank-faced as Holland. She didn't speak to Sally except to tell her tersely what to do and when and how to do it. She watched Sally go to the bathroom, which, Sally supposed, was better than having Holland standing there.

Dr. Beadermeyer didn't want her hurt? That could only be because he himself wanted to be the one to hurt her. She'd seen no one except Beadermeyer and Holland and Nurse Rosalee. They'd forced her to keep to her room. She had nothing to read, no TV to watch. She didn't know anything about her mother or about Scott. Most of the time she was so drugged she didn't care, didn't even know who she was, but now she knew, now she could reason, and she was getting stronger by the minute.

If only Beadermeyer would wait just a few more minutes, maybe fifteen minutes, then she'd be ready.

But he didn't give her even two more minutes. She jumped when she heard him unlock the door. No time to get into position. She stood stiffly by the window in her peach silk nightgown.

"Good evening, my dear Sally. You're looking chipper and really quite lovely in that nightgown. Would you like to take it off for me now?"

"No."

"Ah, so you've got your wits together, have you? Just as well. I'd like to have a conversation with you before I send you back into the ether. Do sit down, Sally."

"No, I want to stay as far away from you as possible."

"As you wish." He was wearing a dark blue crew sweater and black slacks. His black hair was slicked back as if he'd just had a shower. His teeth were white, the front two top teeth overlapping.

"Your teeth are ugly," she said now. "Why didn't you wear braces as a kid?"

She'd spoken without thinking, another indication that her mind wasn't completely clear yet.

He looked as if he wanted to kill her. Without conscious thought, he raised his fingers to touch his teeth, then dropped his arm. There was only a thin veil of shadow separating them now, but she recognized the anger in him, knew he wanted to hurt her.

He got control of himself. "Well, you're a little bitch tonight, aren't you?"

"No," she said, still watching him, her body tensed, knowing he wanted to attack her, hurt her badly. She didn't know she could hate a person as much as she hated him. Other than her father. Other than her husband.

Finally, he sat down in the single chair and crossed his legs. He removed his glasses and put them on the small circular table beside the chair. There was a carafe of water and a single glass on the table, nothing more.

"What do you want?" The carafe was plastic—even if she struck him squarely on the head, it wouldn't hurt him. But the table was sturdy. If only she were fast enough, she could grab it and smash him with it. But she knew she would have to be free of the drugs for at least another hour to be fast enough, strong enough, to bring him down. Could she keep him talking that long? She doubted it, but it was worth a try.

"What do you want?" she said again. She couldn't bring herself to take a step closer to him.

"I'm bored," he said. "I'm making so much money, but I'm never free to leave this place. I want to enjoy my money. What do you suggest?"

"Let me go, and I'll see that you get even more money."

"That would defeat the purpose, wouldn't it?"

"Do you mean that you have other people in here who are perfectly sane? Other people you're holding prisoner? Other people you're being paid to keep here?"

"This is a very small, very private place, Sally. Not many people know about it. I gain all my patients through referrals, carefully screened referrals.

"Just listen to me. This is the first time I've ever talked to you as an adult. Six months I had you with me, six whole months, and you were always as interesting as a jointless doll, except for that time you jumped through the window in my office. If anything proved to your dear mother that you were nuts, that story did. That made me sit up and take notice of you, but not for long. This is much better. If only I could trust you not to try to escape me again, I would keep you just as you are now."

"How do you imagine that I can escape?"

"Unfortunately Holland is quite stupid, and he's the one who tends you most often. I do believe Nurse Rosalee is a bit afraid of you. Isn't that odd? As for Holland, he begged me to let him take care of you, the pathetic creature. Yes, I can imagine you waiting behind that door for him to come in.

"What would you do, Sally? Hit him on the head with this table? That would stun him. Then you could strip off his clothes, though I doubt you'd enjoy stripping him as much as he enjoys stripping you. No, you see, I'm in a bind. And please don't move. Remember, I'm not Holland. Stay where you are or you get a nice big shot right now."

"I haven't moved an inch. Why am I here? How did you find me? Amabel had to call to tell you where I was. But why? And who wanted me back here? My husband? Were you the one who pretended to be my father or was it Scott?"

"You speak of your poor husband as if he's a stranger to you. It's that James Quinlan, isn't it? You slept with him, you enjoyed him, and now you want to dump poor Scott. I would never have taken you for such a fickle woman, Sally. Wait until I tell Scott what you've done."

"When you speak to Scott Brainerd, tell him I fully intend to kill him when I'm free of this place. And I will be free soon, Dr. Beadermeyer."

"Ah, Sally, I'm sure that Scott wants me to make you more malleable. He doesn't like women who are aggressive, all tied up in their careers. Trust me to see to it, Sally."

"Either you or Scott called me up in The Cove pretending to be my father. Either you or Scott came to The Cove and climbed that silly ladder to scare me silly, to make me think I was crazy. There's no one else. My father is dead."

"Yes, Amory is dead. I think personally that you killed him, Sally. Did you?"

"I don't know if you really want the truth. I have no memory of that night. It will come back, though. It has to."

"Don't count on it. One of the drugs I'm giving you is excellent at suppressing memory. No one really knows yet what the long-term side effects will be. And you will be taking it forever, Sally."

He rose and walked to her. "Now," he said. He was smiling. She couldn't help herself. When he reached for her, she cracked a fist as hard as she could against his jaw. His head flew back. She hit him again, kicked him in the groin with all her strength, and ran to grab that table.

But she stumbled, her head spinning, nausea flooding through her. Her legs collapsed beneath her. She fell to the floor.

She heard him panting behind her. She had to get to that table. She struggled to her feet, forced one foot in front of the other. He was close behind her now, panting, panting, he was in pain, she'd hurt him. If she didn't knock him out, he would take great pleasure in hurting her. Please, God, please, please.

She clutched the table, lifted it, turned to face him. He was so close, his arms stretched out toward her, his fingers curved, coming toward her throat.

"Holland!"

"No," she said and swung the table at him. But it was a puny effort, and he blocked it with his shoulder.

"Holland!"

The door flew open and Holland ran into the room.

"Hold the little bitch, hold her!"

"No, no." She backed away from the men, but there was no room, only the narrow bed and the table she held as a shield in front of her.

Dr. Beadermeyer was holding his crotch, his face still drawn in pain. Good, she'd hurt him. Anything he did to her would be worth it. She'd hurt him.

"That's enough, Sally." Holland's voice, soft and hoarse, terrifying.

"I'll kill you, Holland. Stay away from me." But it was an empty threat. Her arms were trembling, her stomach roiling now. She tasted bile. She dropped the table, fell to her knees, and vomited on Dr. Beadermeyer's Italian loafers.

* * *

"YOU either help me or you don't, Savich, but you don't tell a soul about this."

"Quinlan, do you know what you're asking?" Dillon Savich leaned back in his chair, nearly tipping it over, but not quite because he knew exactly how far to go. His computer screen was bright with the photo of a man's face, a youngish man who looked like a yuppie broker, well dressed, easy smile, well-groomed hair and clothes.

"Yes. You're going with me to that sanitarium and we're going to rescue Sally. Then we're going to clean up this mess. We'll be heroes. You won't be gone from your computer for more than a couple of hours. Maybe three hours if you want to be a hero. Take your laptop and the modem. You can still hook into any system you want."

"Marvin will cut our balls off. You know he hates it when you try to go off on your own without talking to him."

James said, "We'll give Marvin all the credit. The FBI will shine. Marvin will be grinning from ear to ear. He'll give the credit to his boss, Mr. Maitland, so he won't cut Marvin's balls off. Mr. Maitland will be happy as a loon.

"And on and on it goes. Sally will be safe and we'll get this damned murder solved."

Savich said, "You still ignore the fact that she might have killed her father herself. It's a possibility. What's wrong with you? How can you ignore it?"

"Yes, I do ignore it. I have to. But we'll find out, won't we?"

"You're involved with her, aren't you? It was only one week you were with her. What is she, some sort of siren?"

"No, she's a skinny little blonde who's got more grit than you can begin to imagine."

"I don't believe this. No, shut up, Quinlan, I've got to think." Savich leaned forward and stared fixedly at the man's photo on the computer screen. He said absently, "This creep is probably the one who's killing the homeless people in Minneapolis."

"Leave the creep for the moment. Think, brood, whatever. You're going to try to figure all the odds. You're going to weigh every possible outcome with that computer brain of yours. Have you developed a program for that yet?"

"Not yet, but I'm close. Come on, Quinlan, my brain is why you love me. I've saved your butt at least three times. You wouldn't trade me for any other agent. Shut up. I've got to make an important decision here."

"You've got ten minutes. Not a second more. I've got to get to her. God knows what they're doing to her, what they're giving her. She could be dead. Or they could have already moved her. If the guy who hit me bothered to check my ID, then they know I'm FBI. We haven't got much time even if they didn't check. I know they'll move her; it only makes sense."

"Why are you so sure she's at the sanitarium?"

"They wouldn't take the chance of taking her anywhere else."

" 'They' who? No, you don't know. Ten minutes, then. No, shut up, Quinlan."

"Thank God, you've already been to the gym this morning or I'd have to wait for you to lift your bloody weights. I'm getting some coffee."

Quinlan walked down to the small lounge at the end of the hall. It wasn't that the fifth floor was ugly and inhospitable. It couldn't be, since they let tourists get within a floor of them. It didn't look all that institutional, only a bit tired. The linoleum was still pale brown with years of grit walked deep into it.

He poured a cup of coffee, sniffed it first, then took a cautious sip. Yep, it still made his Adam's apple shudder, but it kept the nerves finely tuned. Without it an agent would probably fold up and die.

He needed Savich. He knew that Savich would set up an appropriate backup in case it turned out they couldn't handle the job. He'd been tempted to go directly from Dulles to Maryland to that sanitarium, but he'd given the matter a good deal of thought. He was in this up to his neck, and he wanted to save Sally's neck as well.

He had no idea about the security at Beadermeyer's sanitarium, but Savich would find out and then they'd get over there. He couldn't take the chance of alerting his boss, Brammer. He couldn't take the chance that Sally could be plowed under in the fallout.

He drank more coffee, felt the caffeine jolt hit his brain and stomach at about the same time.

He wandered back into Savich's office. "It's been ten minutes."

"I've been waiting for you, Quinlan. Let's go."

"Just like that? No more arguments? No more telling me there's a thirteen percent chance that one of us will end up in a ditch with a knife in his throat?"

"Nope," Savich said cheerfully. He pulled several sheets out of his printer and rose.

"Here's the layout for the sanitarium. I think I've found exactly where it's safest for us to go in."

"You made up your mind before you even kicked me out."

"Sure. I wanted to get a look at the plans, didn't really know if I could get my paws on them, but I did. Come here and let me show you the best way into this place. Tell me what you think."

"DID you make her brush her teeth and wash her mouth out?"

"Yes, Dr. Beadermeyer. She spit the mouthwash on me, but she did get a bit of it in her mouth."

"I hate the smell of vomit," Beadermeyer said as he looked down at his shoes. He'd cleaned them as best he could. Just thinking about what she'd done made him want to hit her again, but it wouldn't gain him any pleasure. She was unconscious.

"She'll be out of it for a good four hours. Then I'll lighten the dose to keep her pleasantly sedated."

"I hope the dose isn't too high."

"Don't be a fool. I have no intention of killing her, at least not yet. I don't know yet what will happen. I'm taking her out of here tomorrow morning."

"Yes, before he comes to get her."

"Why do you say that, Holland? You don't know anything."

"I was sitting beside her after you gave her the shot, and she was whispering that she knew he'd come here, she knew it."

"She's crazy. You know that, Holland."

"Yes, Doctor."

He knew. Quinlan could find out everything he wanted to know about the sanitarium within computer minutes. He felt the wet of his own sweat in his armpits. This shouldn't have happened. He wondered if he should get her out of there tonight, right now.

They should have killed that agent while they'd had him, and because they'd been afraid to, now he would have to deal with it.

If he was smart, if he wanted to make sure he was safe, he'd get Sally out of there now.

Where to take her? He was tired. He rubbed the back of his neck as he walked back to his office.

Mrs. Willard hadn't left any coffee for him. He sat down behind the mahogany desk that kept patients a good three and a half feet from him and leaned back in his chair.

When would Quinlan and his FBI buddies show up? He would show up, Beadermeyer knew it. He'd followed her to The Cove. He would come here for sure. But how soon? How much time did he have? He picked up the telephone and dialed. They would have to make a decision now. There was no more time for playing games.

THE night was black as pitch. Quinlan and Savich left the Oldsmobile sedan about twenty yards down the road from the wide gates of the Beadermeyer Sanitarium. The words were scrolled in fancy script letters on top of the black iron gates.

"Pretentious bastard."

"Yeah," Savich said. "Let me think if there's anything more to tell you about our doctor. First of all, I don't think many people have this information.

"He's brilliant and unscrupulous. Word has it that if you're rich enough and discreet enough and you want someone under wraps badly enough, then Beadermeyer will take that person off your hands. It's rumors, of course, but who knows? Who did Sally anger enough to get her sent here? Look, Quinlan, maybe she's really sick."

"She isn't sick. Who sent her here? I don't know. She never would tell me. She never even mentioned Beadermeyer by name. But it has to be him. Keep that flashlight down, Savich. Yeah, better. Who knows what kind of security he has?"

"That I couldn't find out, but hey, the fence isn't electrified."

They were both wearing black, including heavily lined black gloves. The twelve-foot-high fence was no problem. They dropped lightly to the spongy grass on the other side.

"So far, so good," Quinlan said, keeping the flashlight low and moving it in a wide arc.

"Let's stay close to the tree line."

The two men moved quickly, hunkered down, the flashlight sending out a low beam just in front of them.

"Not good," Savich said.

"What? Oh, yeah." Two German shepherds came galloping toward them.

"I don't want to kill them."

"You won't have to. Stand still, Savich."

"What are you going—"

Savich watched Quinlan pull a plastic-wrapped package from inside his black jacket. He peeled it open to show three huge pieces of raw steak.

The dogs were within twelve feet of them. Still Quinlan held perfectly still, waiting, waiting.

"Another second," he said, then threw one piece of raw steak in one direction and a second piece in the other direction. The dogs were on the meat in an instant.

"Let's get moving. I'm going to save this last piece as getaway meat."

"Not a bad security system," Savich said.

They were running now, keeping low, the flashlight off because there were a few lights on in the long, sprawling building in front of them, enough to light their way.

"You said the patient rooms are all in the left wing."

"Right. Beadermeyer's office is in the far end of the right wing. If he's still here, he's a good distance away."

"There should only be a small night shift complement."

"I hope. I didn't take the time to access their personnel and administration files. I don't know how many employees work the night shift."

"Useless machine."

Savich laughed. "Don't accuse me of being married to my computer when you're at your club most weekends wailing away on your sax. Whoa, Quinlan, stop."

They froze in an instant, pressed against the brick building, behind two tall bushes. Someone was coming, walking briskly, a flashlight in his hand.

He was whistling the theme from *Gone With the Wind*.

"A romantic security guard," Quinlan whispered.

The man waved the flashlight to both sides and back again to the front. He never stopped whistling. The light flowed right over their bent heads, showing the guard only black shadows.

"I hope she's here," Quinlan said. "Beadermeyer has to know I'll come here. If he's the one who hit me, then he would have checked my ID. What if they've already taken her away?"

"She's here. Stop worrying. If she isn't, well, then, we'll find her soon enough. Did I tell you I had a date tonight? I had a date and look what I'm doing. Playing Rescue Squad with you. Stop worrying. You're smarter than Beadermeyer. She's still here, I'll bet you on it. I get the feeling there's more arrogance in this Beadermeyer than in most folk. I think he believes he's invincible."

They were moving again, bent nearly double, no flashlight, just two black shadows skimming over the well-manicured lawn.

"We've got to get inside."

"Soon," Savich said. "Up ahead. Then it's going to be tricky. Imagine seeing the two of us dressed like cat burglars roaming down the halls."

"We'll find a nurse soon enough. She'll tell us."

"We're nearly to the back emergency entrance. Yeah, here we are. Help me pull up the doors, Quinlan."

They gently eased the doors back down. He turned on the flashlight. They were in an enclosed space that could hold at least six cars. There were four cars there. They made their way around them, then Quinlan turned and trained his flashlight on the license plates.

"Look, Savich. Good guess, huh? The moron would have a luxury plate—BEADRMYR. So he's still here. I wouldn't mind running into him."

"Marvin would not be a happy camper."

Quinlan laughed.

Savich used one of his lock picks to get into the door. It only took a moment.

"You're getting good at this."

"I practiced for at least six hours at Quantico. They have about three dozen kinds of locks. They use a stopwatch on you. I came in sixth."

"How many agents were entered?"

"Seven. Me and six women."

"I want to hear more about this later."

They were in a long hallway, low lights giving off a dim, mellow glow. There were no names on the doors, only numbers.

"We've got to get us a nurse," Savich said.

They turned a corner to see a nurses' station just ahead. There was only one woman there, reading a novel. She looked up every once in a while at the TV screen in front of her. They were nearly upon her when she saw them. She gasped, her novel dropping to the linoleum floor as she tried to scoot off her chair and run.

Quinlan grabbed her arm and gently pressed his hand over her mouth. "We won't hurt you. Hold still. You got her chart, Savich?"

"Yep, here it is. Room two twenty-two."

"Sorry," Quinlan said quietly as he struck her in the jaw. She collapsed against him and he lowered her to the floor, pushing her under the desk.

"We passed two twenty-two. Quick, Savich, I've got a feeling that our charmed existence is about to be shot down in flames."

They ran swiftly down the hallway, back the way they had come. "Here it is. No light. Good."

Quinlan slowly pushed at the door. It was locked, as he'd known it would be. He motioned Savich forward. Savich examined the lock, then pulled out a pick. He didn't say a word, just changed to another pick. After a good three minutes, the lock slid open.

Quinlan pushed the door open. The soft light from the hallway beamed into the room, right on the face of a man who was seated on a narrow bed, leaning over a woman.

He whipped around on the bed, half rising, his mouth open to yell.

FOURTEEN

"I didn't know you could move that fast," Savich said in admiration after Quinlan had leaped across to the bed and slammed his fist into the man's mouth before he could let out a single sound. He dumped him off the bed to the floor.

"Is this Sally Brainerd?"

Quinlan looked briefly at the small man whose nose was flooding blood, then up at the woman on the bed. "It's Sally," he said, such rage in his voice that Savich stared at him for a moment. "Let me get that door closed and then we'll use our flashlights. Take the little guy and tie him up with something."

Quinlan shone the flashlight in her face. He was shocked at her pallor and the slackness of her flesh. "Sally," he said, gently slapping her face.

She didn't respond.

"Sally," he said, shaking her this time. The covers slid down and he saw that she was naked. He looked over at the slight man who was now tied up as well as unconscious. Had he been planning to rape her?

She was deeply unconscious. He shone the light on her bare arms. There were six needle marks.

"Look, Savich. Look what they've done to her."

Savich ran his fingers lightly over the needle marks. "It looks like they gave her a real heavy dose this time," he said as he leaned down and pulled up her eyelids. "Real heavy dose."

"They'll pay. See what kind of clothes are in the closet."

Quinlan noticed that her hair was neatly brushed and smoothed back from her forehead. That little man who'd been leaning over her, he'd done that. Quinlan knew it. He felt himself shiver. What went on in this place?

"Here's a nightgown and a robe and a pair of slippers. Nothing more."

Quinlan got her into the gown and robe within minutes. It was difficult dressing an unconscious person, even a small one. Finally, he lifted her over his shoulder. "Let's get the hell out of Dodge."

They were through the back emergency door and nearly out of the garage when the sirens went off.

"The nurse," Quinlan said. "We should have tied her up."

"We've got time. We'll make it."

When Quinlan tired, Savich took Sally. They were almost to the fence when the German shepherds, barking louder than the hounds of Baskerville, came racing smoothly toward them.

Quinlan tossed out the other piece of meat. They didn't stop to see what the dogs did with it.

When they got to the fence, Quinlan climbed it faster than he'd ever climbed anything in his life. At the top, he straddled the fence on his belly and leaned back toward Savich as far as he could. "Hand her up to me."

"She's boneless," Savich said, trying to get a firm grip on her. On the third try, Quinlan got hold of her wrists. He slowly pulled her up. He held her around the waist until Savich was on top of the fence beside him. His arms were cramping by the time Savich swiveled around and leaped to the ground. He brought her around and began to lower her. "Hurry, Quinlan, hurry. Okay, another couple of inches. There, I've got her. Get down here!"

The dogs were barking louder. The meat had stopped them for all of forty-five seconds.

They heard several men yelling.

Guns fired, one bullet sparked off the iron fence, so close to Quinlan's head that he felt the searing heat from it.

A woman's sharp yell sounded behind the men.

"Let's go," Quinlan said as he hefted Sally over his shoulder and ran as fast as he could toward the Oldsmobile.

The guns didn't stop until they'd raced around the bend and were out of sight.

"If they let the dogs out on us, we're in trouble," Savich said.

Quinlan hoped they didn't. He didn't want to shoot those beautiful dogs.

He was relieved when they slammed the car doors some two minutes later. "Thank God for good-sized favors."

"You've got that right. Hey, that was fun. Now, your apartment, Quinlan?"

"Oh, no, we're going to Maryland, only another hour up the road, Savich. I'll give you directions. What surprises me is that they took her back to this place at all. They must have figured I'd come here first thing. I'll bet you she would have been gone tomorrow morning. So, I'm not going to be as stupid. No way we're going back to my place."

"You're right. When someone hit you over the head in The Cove, he would have searched your pockets. They know you're FBI. That's why they didn't kill you; I'd bet my StairMaster on it. It would have been too big a risk for them."

"Yeah. We're going to my parents' lake cottage. It's safe. No one knows about it except you. You haven't told anyone, have you?"

Savich shook his head. "What are you going to do with her, Quinlan? This is highly irregular."

Quinlan was holding her in his lap, her head cradled on his arm. He'd covered her with his black jacket. It was warm in the car. "We're going to wait until she comes out from under this drug, then see what she knows. Then we're going to clean everything up. How's that sound to you?"

"Like we'll be a couple of heroes." Savich sighed. "Marvin will probably try to transfer us to Alaska for not being team players. But, hey, don't sell a hero short."

SHE woke up to see a strange man looking down at her, his nose not more than six inches from hers. It took her a moment to realize that he was indeed flesh and blood and not some specter dredged up from a drugged vision. Her lips felt cracked. It was hard to make herself talk, but she did.

"If Dr. Beadermeyer sent you, it won't matter." She spit on him.

Savich jerked back, wiped the back of his hand across his nose and cheek. "I'm a hero, not a bad guy. Beadermeyer didn't send me."

Sally tried to sift through his words, make some sense of them. Her brain still felt like it wanted to sleep, like parts of it were numb, like an arm or leg that had been in a single position for too long. "You're a hero?"

"Yeah, a real live hero."

"Then James must be here."

"You mean Quinlan?"

"Yes. He's a hero too. He was the first hero I ever met. I'm sorry I spit on you, but I thought you were another one of those horrible men."

"It's okay. You lie still and I'll get Quinlan."

What did he think she would do? Jump up and race out of here, wherever here was?

"Good morning, Sally. Don't spit on me, okay?"

She stared up at him, so thirsty she could barely squeak out another word. Her brain was at last knitting itself back together, and all she could do was throw up her arms and pull him down to her. She said against his throat, "I knew you'd come. I just knew it. I'm so thirsty, James. Can I have some water?"

"You all right? Really? Let me up just a little, okay?"

"Yes. I'm so glad you're not dead. Someone hit you and I was bending over you." She pulled back from him, her fingers lightly tracing over the stitched wound over his left ear.

"I'm okay—don't worry about it."

"I didn't know who'd done it to you. Then someone hit me over the head. I woke up with Beadermeyer leaning over me. I was back in that place."

"I know, but you're with me now and no one can possibly find you." He said over his shoulder, "Savich, how about some water for the lady?"

"It's the drugs he gives me. They make my throat feel like a desert."

She felt the tightening in him at her words.

"Here, I'll hold the glass for you."

She drank her fill, then lay back and sighed. "I'll be back to normal in about ten more minutes—at least that's my best guess. James, who is that man I spit on?"

"He's a good friend of mine, name of Dillon Savich. He and I got you out of the sanitarium last night. Savich, come and say hello to Sally."

"Ma'am."

"He said he was a hero, just like you, James."

"It's possible. You can trust him, Sally."

She nodded, such a slight movement really, and he watched her eyes close again. "You're not ready to eat something?"

"No, not yet. You won't leave, will you?"

"Hello, Sally."

He would have sworn that the corners of her mouth turned up a bit into a very slight smile. Without thinking, he leaned down and kissed her closed mouth. "I'm glad I've got you again. When I woke up in David Mountebank's house, my head pounding like a watermelon with a stake in it, he told me you were gone. I've never been so scared in my life. You're not going to be out of my sight again, Sally."

"That sounds good to me," she said. In the next moment, she was asleep. Not unconscious but asleep, real sleep.

Quinlan rose and looked down at her. He straightened the light blanket over her chest. He smoothed her hair back on the pillow. He thought of that little man they'd found in her room and knew that if he ever saw him again, he'd kill him.

And Beadermeyer. He couldn't wait to get his hands on Dr. Beadermeyer.

"How does it feel to be the most important person in the whole universe, Quinlan?"

Quinlan kept smoothing down the blanket, his movements slow and calm. Finally he said, "It scares the sin out of me. You want to know something else? It doesn't feel bad at all. How much credit am I going to have to give you?"

THAT evening, the three of them were sitting on the front veranda of Quinlan's cottage, looking out over Louise Lynn Lake. For an evening in March, it was balmy. The cottage faced west. The sun was low on the horizon, making the water ripple with golds and startling pinks.

Quinlan said to Sally, "It's narrow, not all that much fun for boaters unless you're a teenager and like to play chicken. And you can see at least four different curves from here. Well, the sucker has so many curves that—"

"So many curves that what?" Savich asked, looking up from the smooth block of maple he was carving.

"We are not a comedy routine," Quinlan said, grinning to Sally. "Come on now, the lake has so many curves that it very nearly winds back onto itself."

Savich said, as he watched a curling sliver of maple drift to the wooden floor, "You sometimes don't know if you're coming or going."

"You're very good friends," Sally said. "You know each other quite well, don't you?"

"Yeah, but we're not going to get married. Quinlan snores like a pig."

She smiled. It was a good smile, Dillon thought, not a forced smile. Now, that showed she knew she was safe here.

"You want some more iced tea, Sally?"

"No, I like sucking on the ice. There's plenty."

Quinlan lifted his legs and put his feet on the wooden railing that circled the front veranda. He was wearing short, scuffed black boots, old faded blue jeans that looked quite lovely on him—it was surely a shock that she could even think of something like that—and a white shirt with the sleeves rolled up to the elbows.

He was also wearing a shoulder holster, and there was a gun in it. She hadn't realized that private investigators wore guns all the time. He was comfortable with it, like it was simply another item of clothing. It looked part of him. He was long and solid and looked hard as nails. She remembered how she'd hauled his face down to hers when she'd come out of the drugged sleep. How he'd let her. How he'd kissed her when he thought she was asleep again. She'd never met a man like him before in her life—a man to trust, a man to believe, a man who cared what happened to her.

"Has your head cleared?" Savich asked. She turned to see him gently rubbing his thumbs over the maple, over and over and over.

"Why are you doing that?"

"What? Oh, it warms the wood and makes it shine."

"What are you carving?"

"You, if you don't mind."

She blinked at him, swallowed a piece of ice she was sucking, and promptly fell to coughing. James leaned over and lightly slapped her between the shoulder blades.

When she got her breath, she said, "Why ever would you want to immortalize me in any way? I'm nothing at all, nothing—"

"Shut up, Sally."

"Why, James? Someone wants me out of the way, but that doesn't make me important. It only makes what I appear to know of interest to someone."

"I guess maybe it's time we got to that," Savich said. He set down the piece of maple and turned to face Sally.

"If we're to help you, you must tell us everything."

She looked from Dillon Savich to James. She frowned down at her hands. She carefully set the glass down on the rattan table beside her.

She looked at James again, nodding at his shoulder holster. "I was thinking that I never realized that private investigators wore guns all the time. But you do, don't you? Another thing—it looks natural on you, like you were born wearing it. You're not a private investigator, are you, James?"

"No."

"Who are you?"

He was very still, then he looked at her straight in the face and said, "My name is James Quinlan, just as I told you. What I didn't tell you was that I'm Special Agent James Quinlan, FBI. Savich and I have worked together for five years. We're not really partners, since the FBI doesn't operate that way, but we're on a lot of cases together.

"I came to The Cove to find you."

"You're with the FBI?" Saying the words made gooseflesh ripple over her arms, made her feel numb and cold.

"Yes. I didn't tell you immediately because I knew it would spook you.

I wanted to get your confidence and then bring you back to Washington and clear up all the mess."

"You certainly succeeded in gaining my confidence, Mr. Quinlan."

He winced at her use of his surname. He saw that Savich wanted to say something, and held up his hand. "No, let me finish it. Look, Sally, I was doing my job. Things got complicated when I got to know you. And then there were the two murders in The Cove, your father calling you on the phone and then appearing at your bedroom window.

"I decided not to tell you because I didn't know what you'd do. I knew you were in possible danger and I didn't want you running away. I knew I could protect you—"

"You failed at that, didn't you?"

"Yes." She was angry; it was sharp and clear in her voice. He wished he could change things, but he couldn't. He had to try to make her understand. If he didn't get her to come around, then what would happen?

She rose slowly to her feet. She was wearing blue jeans that looked like a second skin. Savich had misjudged and bought her a pair of girl's jeans at the Kmart in the closest town, Glenberg. Even the blouse was tight, the buttons pulling apart.

The look on her face was remote, distant, as if she really weren't standing on the old veranda any longer, between the two of them. She said nothing for a very long time, and stared at the lake. Finally she said, "Thank you for getting me out of that place last night. He wouldn't leave my head clear enough so I could figure out how to escape again. I don't think I would ever have gotten free. I owe you both a lot for that. But now I'm leaving. I have a good number of things to resolve. Good-bye, James."

FIFTEEN

"You're not leaving, Sally. I can't let you leave."

She gave him a look that was so immensely damning of what he was and what he'd done, he couldn't stand it.

"Listen, Sally, please. I'm sorry. I did what I believed was right. I couldn't tell you, please understand that. You were coming to trust me. I couldn't take a chance that you'd react the way you're reacting now."

She laughed. Just laughed. She said nothing at all.

Savich rose, saying, "I'm going for a walk. I'll be back to make dinner in an hour."

Sally watched him stride down the narrow trail toward the water. She supposed he was a fine-looking man, not as fine-looking as James, of course. She didn't like all his big muscles, but she supposed some people did.

"Sally."

She didn't want to turn back to him. She didn't want to speak to him anymore, give him any of her attention, listen to his damning words that made so much sense to him and had utterly destroyed her.

No, she'd rather watch Dillon Savich, or the two boats that were rocking lazily in the smooth evening waters. It would be sunset soon. The water was beginning to turn the color of cherries.

"Sally, I can't let you leave. Besides, where would you go? I don't know where you'd be safe. You thought you'd have a refuge in The Cove. You didn't. Your dear auntie Amabel was in on it."

"No, that's impossible."

"Believe it. I have no reason to lie to you. David and I both visited her after I got on my feet again. She claimed you'd seen me unconscious and decided to run away. She said that you had probably run to Alaska, that you couldn't go to Mexico because you didn't have a passport. She said that you'd been ill—in an institution, as a matter of fact—and that you were still unstable, still very weak in the head. My gut tells me that your auntie is in this mess up to her eyeballs."

"She welcomed me. She was sincere. You're wrong, James, or you're just plain lying."

"Maybe she was sincere at first. But then someone got to her. What about the two murders in The Cove, Sally? The woman's screams you heard that Amabel claimed were a result of the wind, that or the result of you being so bloody nuts."

"So you used those old people—Marge and Harve, who drove to The Cove in their Winnebago and then disappeared—as your, what do you call it? Oh, yes, your cover. The sheriff believed you completely, didn't he?"

"Yes, he did. And what's more, the investigation will open again, since a whole bunch of other folk have disappeared in that area as well. Being a PI hired by their son from L.A. was my cover. It worked. After the murders happened, I didn't know what to think. I knew it couldn't have anything to do with you directly."

He stopped, plowing his fingers through his hair. "Damn, we're getting off the subject, Sally. Forget about The Cove. Forget Amabel. She and her town are three thousand miles away. I want you to try to understand why I did what I did. I want you to understand why I had to keep silent about who I really am and why I was at The Cove."

"You want me to agree that it was fine for you to lie to me, to manipulate me?"

"Yes. You lied to me as well, if you'll recall. All you had to do was scream your head off when your so-called father called you, and I was manipulated up to my ears. A beautiful woman appealing to my macho side. Yeah, I was hooked from that moment."

She was staring at him as if he'd lost his mind.

"Sally, I came flying into the room like a madman to see you on the floor, staring at that phone like it was a snake ready to bite you, and I was a goner."

She waved away his words. "Someone was after me, James. Nobody was after you."

"It didn't matter."

She began to laugh. "Actually there were two someones after me, and you were the second, only I was too stupid, too pathetically grateful to you, to realize it. I'm leaving, James. I don't want to see you again. I can't believe I thought you were a hero. When will I stop being such a credulous fool?"

"Where will you go?"

"That's none of your business, Mr. Quinlan. None of what I do is any of your business anymore."

"The hell it isn't. Listen, Sally. Tell me the truth about something. When Savich and I got into your room at the sanitarium, there was this pathetic little guy who looked crazy as a loon sitting on the bed beside you, looking down at you. Did he ever hurt you? Beat you? Rape you?"

"Holland was there in my room?"

"Yeah, you were naked and he was leaning down over you. I think he'd combed and straightened your hair. Did he rape you?"

"No," she said in a remote voice. "No one raped me. As for Holland, he did other things, things Dr. Beadermeyer told him to do. He never hurt me— well, that's not important."

"Then who did hurt you? Beadermeyer? Your husband? Who was that man you told me about in your nightmare?"

She gave him a long look, and again that look was filled with quiet rage.

"You are nothing more to me. None of this is any of your business. I'm leaving now, James."

She turned away from him and walked down the wooden steps. It was chilly now. She wasn't wearing anything but that too-small shirt and jeans.

"Come back, Sally. I can't let you go. I won't let you go. I won't see you hurt again."

She didn't even slow down, just kept walking, in sneakers that were probably too small for her as well. He didn't want her to get blisters. He'd planned to go shopping for her tomorrow, to buy her some clothes that fit her, to—he was losing it.

He saw Savich standing near the water line, unaware that she was walking away.

"Sally, you don't know where you are. You don't have any money."

Then she did stop. She was smiling as she turned to face him. "You're right, but it shouldn't be a problem for long. I really don't think I'm afraid of any man anymore. Don't worry. I'll get enough money to get back to Washington."

It sent him right over the edge. He slammed his hand down on the railing and vaulted over to land lightly only three feet away from her. "No one will ever hurt you again. You will not take the chance of some asshole raping you. You will stay with me until this is over. Then I'll let you go if you don't want to stay."

She began to laugh. Her body shook with her laughter. She sank slowly to her knees, hugging herself, laughing and laughing.

"Sally!"

She stared up at him, her palms on her thighs. She laughed, then said, "Let me go? You'd keep me if I didn't want to leave? Like some sort of pathetic stray? That's good, James. I haven't known a single person for a very long time who cared one whit about anyone, including me, not that it mattered. Please, no more lies.

"I'm a case for you, nothing more. If you solve it, think of your reputation. The FBI will probably make you director. They'll kiss your feet. The president will give you a medal."

She gasped, out of breath now, hiccuping through the laughter that welled up from her throat. "You should have believed my file, James. Yes, I'm sure the FBI has a very thick file on me, particularly my stint in the loony bin. I'm crazy, James. No one should believe I'm a credible witness, despite the fact that you want very badly to have someone to lock up, anyone.

"I won't tell you anything. I don't trust you, but I do owe you for rescuing me from that place. Now let me go before something horrible happens."

He came down on his knees in front of her. Very slowly, he pulled her arms to her sides. He brought her forward until her face was resting against his shoulder. He rubbed his hands up and down her back. "It's going to be all right, I swear it to you. I swear I won't screw up again."

She didn't move, didn't settle against him, didn't release the terrible rage that had been deep inside her for so long she didn't know if she could ever confront it, or speak about it, because it could very well destroy her, and the sheer magnitude of it would destroy others as well.

It bubbled deep, that rage, and now with it was a shattering sense of betrayal. She'd trusted him and he'd betrayed her. She felt stupid for having believed him so quickly, so completely.

Sally marveled that she felt such passion, such a hideous need to hurt as she'd been hurt. She'd thought he'd drained such savage feelings out of her long ago. It felt incredible to feel rage again, to feel sweat rise on her flesh, to want to do something, to want vengeance. Yes, she wanted vengeance.

She lay against him, thinking, wondering, calming herself, and in the end of it all, she still didn't know what to do.

"You've got to help me now, Sally."

"If I don't, then you'll take me to the FBI dungeon and they'll give me more drugs to make me tell the truth?"

"No, but the FBI will get all the truth sooner or later. We usually do. Your father's murder is a very big deal, not only his murder but lots of other things that are connected to it. Lots of folk want to be in on catching his murderer. It's important for a lot of reasons. No more crap about not being credible. If you'll help me now, you'll be free of all this evil."

"Funny that you call it evil."

"I don't know why I did. That sounds a bit melodramatic, but somehow it came out. Is it evil, Sally?"

She said nothing, just stared ahead, her thoughts far away from him, and he hated it. He wanted to know what was going through her mind. He imagined it wasn't pleasant.

"If you help me, I'll get your passport and take you to Mexico."

That brought her back for a moment. She said with a quirky smile that she probably hadn't worn on her face in a very long time, "I don't want to go to Mexico. I've been there three times and got vilely sick every time."

"There's this drug you can take before going. It's supposed to keep your innards safe from the foreign bugs. I used it once when I went down to

La Paz on a fishing trip with my buddies and I never got sick and we were on the water most of the time."

"I can't imagine you ever getting sick from anything. No bug would want to take up residence inside you. Too little to show for it."

"You're talking to me."

"Oh, yes. Talking calms me. It makes all that bile settle down a bit. And listen to you, talking to the little victim, trying to soothe and calm her, gain her trust. You're really very good, the way you use your voice, your tone, your choice of words.

"Forget it, James. I've got even more to say. In fact, I think I've got it all together now.

"If you'll notice, Mr. Quinlan, I've got your gun pointed at your belly. Try to squeeze me or hurt me or jerk it away from me with one of your fancy moves, and I'll pull the trigger."

He felt then the nose of his SIG-Sauer pressing against his gut. He hadn't felt it even a second before. How had she gotten it out of his shoulder holster? The fact that she'd gotten it without his realizing it scared him more than knowing the pistol had a hair trigger and her finger was on it.

He said against her hair, "I guess this means you're still pissed at me, huh?"

"Yes."

"I guess this means you don't want to talk about Mexico anymore? You don't like deep-sea fishing?"

"I've never done it. But no, the time for talking is over."

He said very quietly and slowly, "That gun is perfectly balanced and will respond practically to your thoughts. Please be careful. Sally, don't think any violent thoughts, okay?"

"I'll try not to, but don't push me. Now, James, fall over onto your back and don't even think about kicking out with your feet. No, don't stiffen up like that or I'll shoot you. I've got nothing to lose. Don't ever forget that."

"It's not a good idea, Sally. Let's talk some more."

"FALL ON YOUR BACK!"

"Well, hell." He dropped his arms to his sides as he keeled over backward. He could have tried kicking up, but he couldn't be sure that he wouldn't hurt her badly. He lay on his back watching her rise to stand over him, the pistol in her hand. She looked very proficient with that gun. She never looked away from him, not even for an instant.

"Have you ever fired a gun before?"

"Oh, yes. You needn't worry that I'll shoot myself in the foot. Now,

James, don't even twitch." She backed away from him, up the steps to the veranda. She got his jacket, felt inside the breast pocket, and found his wallet. "I hope you've got enough money," she said.

"I went to the cash machine just before coming to rescue you, dammit."

"That was nice of you. Don't worry, James." She gave him a small salute with his gun, then threw his jacket over her arm. "Your good buddy will be back soon to make your dinner. I think I heard him talking about some trout. The lake doesn't look polluted, so maybe it won't poison you. Did I ever tell you that my father headed up this citizens' committee that was always haranguing against pollution?

"But who cares, when it comes right down to it? No, don't say it. I'm talking. It feels rather good actually. So you see, no matter what else the bastard did, he did accomplish some good.

"Oh, yeah, Mr. Quinlan, you wanted to know all the juicy details about who did what to me in the sanitarium. You're dying to know who did it, who put me there. Well, it wasn't Dr. Beadermeyer or my husband. It was my father."

And how, she wondered, could she ever get vengeance on a dead man? She was off in a flash, running faster than he'd thought she could, dust kicking up behind her sneakers.

She was at the car when he jumped to his feet. He didn't think, just sprinted as fast as he could toward the Oldsmobile. He saw her stop by the driver's door and aim quickly, then he felt the dirt spray his jeans leg as a bullet kicked up not a foot from his right boot. Then she was inside. The car engine revved. She was fast.

He watched her throw the car in reverse, watched her back it out of the narrow driveway onto the small country road. She did it well, coming close to that elm tree but not touching the paint job on the car, which was nice of her because the government was never pleased when it had to repaint bureau cars.

He was running after her again, knowing he had to do something, but not knowing what, just accepting that he was a fool and an incompetent ass and running, running.

Her father had beat her and fondled her and humiliated her in the sanitarium? He'd been the one to put her there in the first place?

Why?

It was nuts, the whole thing. And that's why she hadn't told him. Her father was dead, couldn't be grilled, and the whole thing did sound crazy.

"Rein in, Quinlan," Savich shouted from behind him. "Come on back. She's well and truly gone."

He turned to see Savich run up behind him. "Last time I checked your speed on the track you couldn't beat an accelerating Olds."

"Yeah, yeah. Okay, it's all my fault. You don't have to say it."

"There's hardly any need to say it. How did she get your gun?"

Quinlan looked at his longtime friend, shoved his hands in the pockets of his jeans, and said in the most bewildered voice Savich had ever heard from him, "I was holding her against me, trying to make her understand that I did what I had to do and I wasn't betraying her, really I wasn't, and I thought perhaps she was coming around.

"Looks like I really screwed up on this one. I never felt a thing. Nothing. Then she told me she was pointing the gun in my gut. She was."

"I don't think I like having a partner who's so besotted that he can't even keep his own gun in his holster."

"Is that some sort of weird sexual innuendo?"

"Not at all. Our cell phones are inside. I hope she didn't take them."

"She never went inside the cottage."

"Thank God for small favors. It's about time we got one."

Quinlan said, "Are your connections good enough to get us another one?"

"If not, I'll call my aunt Paulie. Between her and Uncle Abe, they've got more connections than the pope."

SIXTEEN

She knew James would come here, maybe not immediately, but soon enough. She also knew she had time. Too bad she hadn't thought to take their cell phones. That would have really slowed him up. But she had enough of a head start.

She pulled the Oldsmobile into an empty parking spot off Cooperton Street. She locked the door and walked slowly, wearing James's jacket, which should make her look very hip, toward number 337, the gracious Georgian red-brick home on Lark Street. Lights were on downstairs. She prayed Noelle was there and not the police or the FBI.

She huddled low and ran along the tap line of shrubbery toward the downstairs library. Her father's office. The room where she'd first seen her father strike her mother. That had been ten years ago. Ten years. What had happened to those years? College, with nightly phone calls and more visits than she cared to make, even unexpected visits during the week to make sure her father wasn't beating her mother.

She'd sensed the festering anger in her father at her interference, but his position, more highly visible by the year, his absolute horror of anyone finding out that he was a wife beater, kept him in line, at least most of the time. As it turned out, she found out that if he was pissed off, he would beat her mother as soon as Sally left to go back to college. Not that her mother would ever have told her.

On one visit she'd forgotten a sweater and had gone quickly back home to get it. She'd opened the front door with her key and walked into the library, in on a screaming match with her mother cowering on the floor and her father kicking her.

"I'm calling the police," she said calmly from the doorway. "I don't care what happens. This will stop and it will stop now."

Her father froze, his leg in mid-kick, and stared at her in the doorway. "You damned little bitch. What the hell are you doing here?"

"I'm calling the police now. It's over." She walked back into the foyer to the phone that sat on the small Louis XVI table, beneath a beautiful gilt mirror.

She'd dialed 9-1- when her hand was grabbed. It was her mother. It was Noelle, and she was crying, begging her not to call the police, begging, on her knees, begging and begging, tears streaming down her face.

Sally stared down at the woman who was clutching at her knees, tears of pain grooving down her cheeks. Then she looked at her father, who was standing in the doorway to the library, his arms crossed over his chest, his ankles crossed, tall and slender, beautifully dressed in cashmere and wool, his hair thick and dark, with brilliant gray threading through it, looking like a romantic lead in the movies. He was watching her.

"Go ahead, do it," he said. "Do it and just see what your mother will do when the cops get here. She'll say you're a liar, Sally, that you're a jealous little bitch, that you don't want her to have my affection, that you've always resented her, resented your own mother.

"Isn't that why you're coming home all the time from college? Go ahead, Sally. Do it. You'll see." He never moved, just spoke in that intoxicating, mesmerizing voice of his, one that had swayed his colleagues and clients for the past thirty years. He kept a hint of a Southern drawl, knowing it added just the right touch when he deftly slurred the word he wanted to emphasize.

"Please, Sally, don't. Don't. I'm begging you. You can't. It would ruin everything. I can't allow you to. It's dangerous. It's all right, Sally. Just don't call, please, don't call."

She gave her mother and her father one last look and left. She did not return until after her graduation seven months later.

Maybe her father was beating her mother less simply because Sally wasn't coming home anymore.

Funny that she hadn't been able to remember that episode until now. Not until—not until she'd gone to The Cove and met James and her life had begun to seem like a life again, despite the murders, despite her father's phone calls, despite everything.

She must really be nuts. The man had betrayed her. There was no way around that. He'd saved her too, but that didn't count, it was more of the job. She still marveled at her own simplicity. He was FBI. He'd tracked her down and lied to her.

She huddled down even more as she neared the library windows. She looked inside. Her mother was reading a book. She was sitting in her husband's favorite wing chair, reading a book. She looked exquisite. Well, she should. The bastard had been dead for a good three weeks. No more bruises. No more chance of bruises.

Still, Sally waited. No one else was in the house.

"YOU'RE sure she's going home, Quinlan?"

"Not home. She's going to her mother's house. Not her husband's house. You know my intuition, my gut. But to be honest about it, I know her. She feels something for her mother. That's the first place she'll go. I'll bet you both her father and her husband put her in that sanitarium in the first place. Why? I haven't the foggiest idea. I do know, though, that her father was a very evil man."

"I assume you'll tell me what you mean by that later?"

"Drive faster, Savich. The house is number three thirty-seven on Lark. Yeah, I'll tell you, but not now. Let's get going."

"HELLO, Noelle."

Noelle St. John slowly lowered her novel to her lap. Just as slowly, she looked up at the doorway to see her daughter standing there, wearing a man's jacket that came nearly to her knees.

Her mother didn't move, stared at her. When she was younger, her mother was always holding her, hugging her, kissing her. She wasn't moving now. Well, if she believed Sally was crazy, then it made sense. Did

Noelle think her daughter was here to shoot her? She said in a soft, frightened voice, "Is it really you, Sally?"

"Yes. I got away from the sanitarium again. I got away from Dr. Beadermeyer."

"But why, darling? He takes such good care of you. Doesn't he? Why are you looking at me like that, Sally? What's wrong?"

Then nothing mattered, because her mother was smiling at her. Her mother jumped to her feet and ran to her, enfolding her in her arms. Years were instantly stripped away. She was small again. She was safe. Her mother was holding her. Sally felt immense gratitude. Her mother was here for her, as she'd prayed she would be.

"Mama, you've got to help me. Everyone is after me."

Noelle stood back, smoothing Sally's hair, running her hands over her pale face. She hugged her again, whispering against her cheek. "It's all right, sweetheart. I'll take care of everything. It's all right." Noelle was shorter than her daughter, but she was the mother and Sally was the child, and to Sally she felt like a goddess.

She let herself be held, breathed in her mother's fragrance, a scent she'd worn from Sally's earliest memories. "I'm sorry, Noelle. Are you all right?"

Her mother released her, stepping back. "It's been difficult, what with the police and not knowing where you were and worrying incessantly. You should have called me, Sally. I worried so much about you."

"I couldn't. I imagined that the police had your phone bugged. They could have traced me."

"I don't think there's anything wrong with the phones. Surely they wouldn't dare plant devices like that in your father's home?"

"He's dead, Noelle. They'd do anything. Now, listen. I need you to tell me the truth. I do know that I was here the night that he was murdered. But I don't remember anything about it. Only violent images, but no faces. Only loud voices, but no person to go with the voices."

"It's all right, love. I didn't murder your father. I know that's why you ran away. You ran away to protect me, as you tried to protect me for all those years.

"Do you believe me? Why would you think I'd know anything about it? I wasn't here myself. I was with Scott, your husband. He's so worried about you. All he can talk about is you and how he prays you'll come home. Please tell me you believe me. I wouldn't kill your father."

"Yes, Noelle, I believe you—although if you had shot him I would have applauded you. But no, I never really believed you did. But I can't remember. I plain can't remember, and the police and the FBI, they all believe I know everything that happened that night. Won't you tell me what happened, Noelle?"

"Are you well again, Sally?"

She stared at her mother. She sounded vaguely frightened. Of her? Of her own daughter? Did she think she would murder her because she was insane? Sally shook her head. Noelle might look a bit frightened, but she also looked exquisite in vivid emerald lounging pajamas. Her light hair was pinned up with a gold clip. She wore three thin gold chains. She looked young and beautiful and vital. Perhaps there was some justice after all.

"Listen to me, Noelle," Sally said, willing her mother to believe her. "I wasn't ever sick. Father put me in that place. It was all a plot. He wanted me out of the way. Why? I don't know. Maybe just plain revenge for the way I'd thwarted him for the past ten years. Surely you must have guessed something. Doubted him when he told you. You never came to see me, Mama, never."

"Your father told me, and you're right, I was suspicious, but then Scott broke down—he was in tears—and he told me about all the things you'd done, how you simply weren't yourself anymore and there hadn't been any choice but to put you in the sanitarium. I met Dr. Beadermeyer. He assured me you would be well cared for.

"Oh, Sally, Dr. Beadermeyer told me it would be better if I didn't see you yet, that you were blaming me for so many things, that you hated me, that you didn't want to see me, that seeing me would make you worse and he feared you'd try to commit suicide again."

But Sally wasn't listening to her. She felt something prickle on her skin, and she knew, she *knew* he was close. She also knew that her mother wasn't telling her the truth about the night her father was murdered. Why? What had really happened that night? There was no time now.

Yes, James was close. There was no unnatural sound, no real warning, yet she knew.

"Do you have any money, Noelle?"

"A few dollars, Sally, but why? Why? Let me call Dr. Beadermeyer. He's already called several times. I've got to protect you, Sally."

"Good-bye, Noelle. If you love me—if you've ever loved me—please keep the FBI agent talking as long as you can. His name is James Quinlan. Please, don't tell him I was here."

"How do you know the name of an FBI agent?"

"It's not important. Please don't tell him anything, Noelle."

* * *

"MRS. St. John, we saw the car parked on Cooperton. Sally was here. Is she still here? Are you hiding her?"

Noelle St. John stared at his ID, then at Savich's. Finally, after an eternity, she looked up and said, "I haven't seen my daughter for nearly seven months, Agent Quinlan. What car are you talking about?"

"A car we know she was driving, Mrs. St. John," Savich said.

"Why are you calling my daughter by her first name? Indeed, Sally is her nickname. Her real name is Susan. Where did you get her nickname?"

"It doesn't matter," Quinlan said. "Please, Mrs. St. John, you must help us. Would you mind if we looked through your house? Her car is parked down the street. She's probably hiding here in the house waiting for us to leave before she comes out."

"That's ridiculous, gentlemen, but look to your hearts' content. None of the help sleep here, so the house is empty. Don't worry about frightening anyone." She smiled at them and walked with her elegant stride back into the library.

"Upstairs first," Quinlan said.

They went methodically from room to room, Savich waiting in the corridor as Quinlan searched, to ensure that Sally couldn't slip between adjoining rooms and elude them. When Quinlan opened the door to a bedroom at the far end of the hall, he knew immediately that it had been hers. He switched on the light. It wasn't a frilly room with a pink or white canopied bed and posters of rock stars plastering the walls. No, three of the walls were filled with bookshelves, all of them stuffed with books. On the fourth wall were framed awards, writing awards beginning with ones for papers she'd written in junior high school on the U.S. dependence on foreign oil and the gasoline crisis, on Saddam's quasi victory in Desert Storm. There was a paper that had won the Idleberg Award and appeared in the *New York Times.* The high school awards were for papers that ran more toward literary themes.

Then they stopped, somewhere around the end of high school—no more awards, no more recognition for excellent short stories or essays, at least no more here in this bedroom. She'd gone to Georgetown University, majored in English. Again, no more sign that she'd ever written another word or won another prize.

"Quinlan, what are you doing? Is she in there or not?"

He was shaking his head when he rejoined Savich. He said, "Sally isn't here. Sure, she was here, but she's long gone. Somehow she knew we were close. How, I don't know, but she knew. Let's go, Savich."

"You don't think her mother would have any idea, do you?"

"Get real." But they asked Mrs. St. John anyway. She gave them a blank smile and sent them on their way.

"What now, Quinlan?"

"Let me think." Quinlan hunched over the steering wheel, wishing he had a cup of coffee, not good coffee, but the rotgut stuff at the Bureau. He drove to FBI headquarters at Tenth and Pennsylvania, the ugliest building ever constructed in the nation's capital.

Ten minutes later, he was sipping on the stuff that could be used to plug a hole in a dike. He made Savich a cup of tea and set it near the mouse pad at his right hand.

"Okay, she's got the Oldsmobile."

"No APB, Savich."

Savich swiveled around in his chair, the computer screen glowing behind his head. "You can't keep this a two-man hunt, Quinlan. We lost her. You and I, my friend, lost a rank amateur. Don't you think it's time to spread the net?"

"Not yet. She's also got my wallet. See what you can do with that."

"If she keeps purchases below fifty dollars, chances are no one will check. Still, if someone does check, we'll have her almost instantly. Hold on a minute and let me set that up."

Savich had big hands, long, blunt fingers. Quinlan watched those unlikely fingers race over the computer keys. Savich hit a final key and nodded in satisfaction. "There's just something about computers," he said over his shoulder to Quinlan. "They never give you trouble. They never contradict you. You tell 'em what to do in simple language and they do it."

"They don't love you, either."

"In their way they do. They're so clean, Quinlan. Now, if she uses one of your credit cards and there's no check, then I've got her within eighteen hours. It's not the best, but it'll have to do."

"She might have to use a credit card, but she'll keep it below fifty dollars. She's not stupid. Did you know she won a statewide contest for a paper she wrote about how much credit card crooks cost the American public? You'd better believe she knows she's bought eighteen hours, and she might figure that's just enough, thank you."

"How do you know that? Surely you had other things to talk about with her? You had two murders in that little picturesque town, and the two of you found both bodies. Surely that's enough fodder for conversation for at least three hours."

"When I was in her bedroom I saw that the walls are loaded with awards for papers, short stories, essays, all sorts of stuff that she wrote. That credit card essay was one of them. She must have been all of sixteen when she wrote it."

"So she's a good writer, even a talented writer. She's still a rank amateur. She's scared. She doesn't know what to do. Everyone is after her, and we're probably the best-meaning of the lot, but it didn't matter to her. She still poked your own gun in your belly."

"Don't whine. She has around three hundred dollars in cash. That's not going to take her far. On the other hand, she got all the way across the country on next to no money at all riding a Greyhound bus."

"You don't keep your PIN number in your wallet, do you?"

"No."

"Good. Then she can't get out any more cash in your name."

Quinlan sat down in a swivel chair beside Savich's. He steepled his fingers and tapped the fingertips together rhythmically. "There's something she said, Savich, something that nearly tore my guts apart, something about no one she'd been around cared about anybody but himself. I think she trusted me so quickly because something inside her desperately needs to be reaffirmed."

"You're sounding like a shrink."

"No, listen. She's scared just like you said, but she needs someone to believe her and care about what happens to her, someone to accept that she isn't crazy, someone simply to believe her, without reservation, without hesitation.

"She thought I did, and she was right, only, you know the answer to that. She was locked up in that place for six months. Everyone told her she was nuts. She needs trust, complete unquestioning trust."

"So who would give her unconditional trust? Her mother? I can't believe that, even though Sally went to see her first. There's something weird going on with Mrs. St. John. It's sure not her husband, Scott Brainerd, although I'd like to meet the guy, maybe rearrange his face a bit."

Quinlan got out her file. "Let's see about friends."

He read quietly for a very long time while Savich put all systems in place to kick in whenever Sally used one of the credit cards.

"Interesting," Quinlan said, leaning back and rubbing his eyes. "She had several very good women friends, most of them associated with Congress. Then after she married Scott Brainerd, the friends seemed to fade away over the period before Daddy committed her to Beadermeyer's charming resort."

"That cuts things down, but it doesn't help us. You don't think she'd go to her husband, do you? I can't imagine it, but—"

"No way."

There was a flash and a beep on the computer screen. "Well, I'll be swiggered," Savich said, rubbing his hands together. He punched in several numbers and added two more commands.

"She used a credit card for gas. The amount is twenty-two fifty, but it's their policy to check all credit cards, regardless of the amount. She's in Delaware, Quinlan, outside of Wilmington. A bit of luck for the good guys."

"Wilmington isn't that far from Philadelphia."

"It isn't that far from anywhere, except maybe Cleveland."

"No, that's not what I meant. Her grandparents live on the Main Line just outside of Philadelphia. Real ritzy section. Street name's Fisher Road."

"Fisher Road? Doesn't sound ritzy."

"Don't let the name fool you. I have a feeling Fisher Road will wind up being one of those streets with big stone mansions set back a good hundred feet from the road. Gates too, I'll bet."

"We'll see soon enough. It's her mother's parents who live there. Their name is Harrison. Mr. and Mrs. Franklin Ogilvee Harrison."

"I don't suppose Mrs. Harrison has a name?"

"Nah, if the guy is rich and old, that's the way they do it. I've wondered if sometimes they just make up that highbrow middle name for effect."

SEVENTEEN

"I meant to tell you why Sally used a credit card and not some of your three hundred bucks."

Savich was driving, handling his Porsche with the same ease and skill he used with computers.

Quinlan was reading everything he had on the grandparents with a small penlight. He had to look up every few minutes so he wouldn't throw up. "I hate reading in a car. My sister used to read novels all the time—in the back seat—never bothered her for an instant. I'd look at a picture and want to throw up. What did you say, Savich? Oh, yeah, why Sally used the credit card. While you were getting your coat, I checked the rest of the information they gave on the credit card check. The license plate number was different. She bought a clunker, probably used about every cent of that three hundred bucks."

Savich grunted. "Hand me the thermos. Another hour and we'll be there."

"It took time for her to sell the Olds and buy the clunker. It cut down on her lead. Let's say she's got two hours on us. That's not too bad."

"Let's hope she doesn't realize you're anywhere in the vicinity, like you seem to believe she did last time at her mother's."

"She did know. Listen to this. Mr. Franklin Ogilvee Harrison is the president and CEO of the First Philadelphia Union Bank. He owns three clothing stores called the Gentleman's Purveyor. His father owned the two largest steel mills in Pennsylvania, got out before the bottom fell out, and left his family millions. As for Mrs. Harrison, she comes from the Boston Thurmonds, who are all in public office, lots of old money from shipping. Two daughters, Amabel and Noelle, and a son, Geoffrey, who's got Down's syndrome and is kept at a very nice private place near Boston."

"You want to stop at that gas station in Wilmington? We'll be there in half an hour."

"Let's do it. Someone will remember the kind of car she was driving."

"If she got something for three hundred bucks, it would really stand out."

But the guy who'd sold her the gas had gone home. They drove straight on to Philadelphia.

SALLY looked from her grandfather Franklin to her grandmother Olivia. She'd seen them two or three times a year every year of her life, except this past year.

Their downstairs maid, Cecilia, had let her in, not blinked an eye at her huge men's coat over the too tight blouse and jeans, and calmly led her to the informal study at the back of the house. Her grandparents were watching reruns of *Friends* on TV.

Cecilia didn't announce her, just left her there and quietly closed the door. Sally didn't say anything for a long time. She stood there, listening to her grandfather give an occasional chuckle. Her grandmother had a book on her lap, but she wasn't reading; she was watching TV as well. They were both seventy-six, in excellent health, and enjoyed the Jumby Bay private resort island off Antigua twice a year.

Sally waited for a commercial, then said, "Hello, Grandfather, Grandmother."

Her grandmother's head jerked around, and she cried out, "Susan!"

Her grandfather said, "Is that really you, Susan? By all that's holy, my poor child, whatever are you doing here?"

Neither of them moved from the sofa. They seemed nailed to their seats. Her grandmother's book slid from her lap to the beautiful Tabriz carpet.

Sally took a step toward them. "I hoped you could give me some money. There are a lot of people looking for me, and I need to hide someplace. I only have about seventeen dollars."

Franklin Harrison rose slowly. He was wearing a smoking jacket and an ascot—she hadn't known those things were still even made. She suddenly had an image of him wearing the same thing when she'd been a very young girl. She remembered how he'd held her and let her stroke the soft silk of the ascot. His white hair was thick and wavy, his eyes a dark blue, his cheekbones high, but his mouth was small and tight. It seemed smaller and tighter now.

Olivia Harrison rose as well, straightening the silk dress she was wearing. She held out her hand. "Susan, dear, why aren't you with that lovely Dr. Beadermeyer? You didn't escape again, did you? That's not a good thing for you, dear, not good for you at all, particularly with all the scandal that your father's death has produced."

"He didn't just die, Grandmother, he was murdered."

"Yes, we know. All of us have suffered. But now we're concerned about you, Susan. Your mother has told us how much Dr. Beadermeyer has done for you, how much better you've gotten. We met him once and were very impressed with him. Wasn't that nice of him to come to Philadelphia to meet us? You are better, aren't you, Susan? You aren't still seeing things that aren't there, are you? You're not still blaming people for things they didn't do?"

"No, Grandmother. I never did any of those things." Strange how neither of them wanted to come close to her.

"You know, dear," her grandmother continued in that gentle voice of hers that masked pure iron, "your grandfather and I have discussed this, and we hate to say it, but it's possible that you're like your uncle Geoffrey. Your illness is probably hereditary, and so it isn't really your fault. Let me call Dr. Beadermeyer, dear."

Sally could only stare at her grandmother. "Uncle Geoffrey was born with Down's syndrome. It has nothing to do with mental illness."

"Yes, but it perhaps shows that instability can be somewhat genetic, passed down from a mother or a father to the daughter. But that's not important. What's important is getting you back to that nice sanitarium so Dr. Beadermeyer can treat you. Before your father died, he called us every week to tell us how much better you were getting. Well, there were weeks with setbacks, but he said that in the main, you were improving with the new drug therapies."

What could she say to that? Tell them all the truth as she remembered it and watch their faces go from disbelief to fury on her account? Not likely.

She saw the years upon years of inflexibility, the utter rigidity, in her grandmother. She remembered what Aunt Amabel had told her about when Noelle had come home, beaten by her husband, when Sally was just a baby. How they hadn't believed Noelle.

It had always been there, of course, this rigidity, but since Sally had seen her grandmother so infrequently, she'd never had it turned on her. More clearly than ever, Sally could see now how her grandmother had treated her daughter Noelle when she'd come here begging for help. She shuddered.

"Well," her grandfather said, all hale and hearty, so good-natured, so weak, "it's good to see you, dear. I know you don't have time to stay, do you? Why not let us send you back to Washington? Like you grandmother said, this Beadermeyer fellow seemed to be doing you a great deal of good."

She looked from one to the other. Her grandfather, as tall as James, or at least he used to be, a man who had lived his life by a set of rules of his wife's making—or perhaps his father's—a man who didn't mind if someone strayed from the proper course but who wouldn't defend that person if his wife was anywhere near.

She'd always believed him so dear, so kind, but he wasn't coming anywhere near her, either—she wondered what he really thought of her. She wondered why he had that tight, mean mouth. She said, "I was in The Cove. I stayed for a while with Aunt Amabel."

"We don't speak of her," her grandmother said, taller now because her back had gotten stiffer. "She made her bed and now she must—"

"She's very happy."

"She can't be. She disgraced herself and her family, marrying that absurd man who painted for a living, *painted pictures!*"

"Aunt Amabel is an excellent artist."

"Your aunt dabbled at many things, nothing more. If she were a good painter, then why haven't we heard of her? You see, no one has. She lives in this backwater town and exists on a shoestring. Forget about Amabel.

Your grandfather and I are sorry you saw her. We can't give you money, Susan. I'm sure your grandfather would agree. Surely you understand why."

She looked her grandmother right in the eye. "No, I don't understand. Tell me why you won't give me money."

"Susan, dear," her grandmother said, her voice all low and soothing, "you're not well. We're sorry for it and a bit stunned, since this sort of thing has never before been in the family except, of course, for your uncle Geoffrey.

"We can't give you money because you could use it to hurt yourself even more. If you would sit down, even stay the night, we will call Dr. Beadermeyer and he can come and get you. Trust us, dear."

"Yes, Susan, trust us. We've always loved you, always wanted the best for you."

"You mean the way you sent your daughter, my mother, back to a man who beat her?"

"Susan!"

"It's true, and both of you know it. He beat the living shit out of her whenever he felt like it."

"Don't use that kind of word in front of your grandmother, Susan," her grandfather said, and she saw that mouth of his go stern and tight.

She looked at him, wondering why she'd even come here, but still, she had to try. She had to have money.

"I tried to protect Noelle for years, but I couldn't save her because she let him do it—do you hear me?—Noelle let him beat her. She was like all those pathetic women you hear about."

"Don't be stupid, Susan," her grandmother said in a voice that could have crushed gravel. "Your grandfather and I have discussed this, and we know that battered wives are weak and stupid women. They're dependent. They have no motivation. They have no desire to better themselves. They aren't able to leave their situations because they've bred like rabbits and the men they're married to drink and don't have any money."

"Your grandmother is perfectly correct, Susan. They aren't our kind at all. They are to be pitied, certainly, but don't ever put your dear mother in that class."

"Amabel told me how Noelle came here once—it was early on in her marriage—and told you both what my father was doing. You didn't want to hear about it. You insisted she go back. You turned her away. You were horrified. Did you even think she was making it up?"

Sally thought for a wild moment that this was surely the wrong way to go about getting money from them. She hadn't realized all this resentment toward them was bottled up inside her.

"We will not speak of your mother to you, Susan," her grandmother said. She nodded slightly to her husband, but Susan saw it. He took a step toward her. She wondered if he would try to hold her down and tie her up and call Dr. Beadermeyer. In that moment, she truly wanted him to try. She wouldn't mind hitting that tight, mean mouth of his that masked weakness and preached platitudes.

She took a step back, her hands in front of her. "Listen, I need some money. Please, if you have any feeling for me at all, give me some money."

"What are you wearing, Susan? That's a man's jacket. What have you done? You haven't harmed some innocent person, have you? Please, what have you done?"

She'd been a fool to come here. What had she expected? They were so set in their ways that a bulldozer couldn't budge them. They saw things one way, only one—her grandmother's way.

"You're not well, are you, Susan? If you were, you wouldn't be wearing those clothes that are so distasteful. Would you like to lie down for a while and we can call Dr. Beadermeyer?"

Her grandfather was moving toward her again, and she knew then that he would try to hold her here.

She had a trump card, and she played it. She even smiled at the two old people who perhaps had loved her once, in their way. "The FBI is after me. They'll be here soon. You don't want the FBI to get me, do you, Grandfather?"

He stopped cold and looked at his wife, whose face had paled.

She said, "How could they possibly know you were coming here?"

"I know one of the agents. He's smarter than anyone has a right to be. He also has this gut instinct about things. I've seen him in action. Count on it. He'll be here soon now with his partner. If they find me here, they'll take me back. Then everything will come out. I'll tell the world how my father—that larger-than-life, very rich lawyer—beat my mother and how you didn't care, how you ignored it, how you pretended everything was fine, happy to bask in the additional glory that such a successful son-in-law brought you."

"You're not a very nice girl, Susan," her grandmother said, two spots of bright red appearing on her very white cheeks. Anger, probably. "It's because you're ill, you know. You didn't used to be this way."

"Give me money and I'll be out of here in a flash. Keep talking, and the FBI will be here and haul me off."

Her grandfather didn't look at his wife this time. He pulled out his wallet. He didn't count the money, just took out all the bills, folded them, and thrust them toward her. He didn't want to touch her. She wondered about that again. Was he afraid he'd go nuts if he did?

"You should immediately drive back to Dr. Beadermeyer," he said to her, speaking slowly, as if she were an idiot. "He'll protect you. He'll keep you safe from the police and the FBI."

She stuffed the bills into her jeans pocket. It was a tight fit. "Good-bye, and thank you for the money." She paused a moment, her hand on the doorknob. "What does either of you know about Dr. Beadermeyer?"

"He came highly recommended, dear. Go back to him. Do as your grandfather says. Go back."

"He's a horrible man. He held me prisoner there. He did terrible things to me. But then again, so did my father. Of course, you wouldn't believe that, would you? He's so wonderful—rather, he was so wonderful. Doesn't it bother you that your son-in-law was murdered? That's rather low on the social ladder, isn't it?"

They stared at her.

"Good-bye." But before she could leave the room, her grandmother called out. "Why are you saying things like this, Susan? I can't believe that you're doing this. Not only to us but to your poor mother as well. And what about your dear husband? You're not telling lies about him, are you?"

"Not a one," Sally said and slipped out of the room, closing the door behind her. She grinned briefly.

Cecilia was standing in the hall. She said, "I didn't call the cops. No one else is here. You don't have to worry. But hurry, Miss Susan, hurry."

"Do I know you?"

"No, but my mama always took care of you when your parents brought you here every year. She said you were the brightest little bean and so sweet. She told me how you could write the greatest poems for birthday cards. I still have several cards she made me that have your poems on them. Good luck, Miss Susan."

"Thank you, Cecilia."

"I'M Agent Quinlan and this is Agent Savich. Are Mr. and Mrs. Harrison here?"

"Yes, sir. Come with me, please." Cecilia led them to the study, just as she'd led Sally Brainerd there thirty minutes before. She closed the door after they'd gone in. She thought the Harrisons were now watching the Home Shopping Network. Mr. Harrison liked to see how the clothes hawked there compared with his.

She smiled. She wasn't about to tell them that Sally Brainerd now had money, although she didn't know how much she'd gotten from that niggardly old man. Only as much as Mrs. Harrison allowed him to give her. She wished Sally good luck.

SALLY stopped at an all-night convenience store and bought herself a ham sandwich and a Coke. She ate outside, well under the lights in front of the store. She waited until the last car had pulled out, then counted her money.

She laughed and laughed.

She had exactly three hundred dollars.

She was so tired she was weaving around like a drunk. The laughter was still bubbling out. She was getting hysterical.

A motel, that was what she needed, a nice, cheap motel. She needed to sleep a good eight hours, then she could go on.

She found one outside Philadelphia—the Last Stop Motel. She paid cash and endured the look of the old man who really didn't want to let her stay but couldn't bring himself to turn away the money she was holding in her hand.

Tomorrow, she thought, she would have to buy some clothes. She'd do it on a credit card and only spend $49.99. Fifty dollars was the cutoff, wasn't it?

She wondered, as she finally fell asleep on a bed that was wonderfully firm, where James was.

"WHERE to now, Quinlan?"

"Let me stop thinking violent thoughts. Damn them. Sally was there. Why wouldn't they help us?"

"They love her and want to protect her?"

"I don't think so. I got cold when I got within three feet of them."

"It was interesting what Mrs. Harrison said," Savich said as he turned on the ignition in the Porsche. "About Sally being ill and she hoped soon she would be back with that nice Dr. Beadermeyer."

"I'll bet you a week's salary that they called the good doctor the minute Sally was out of there. Wasn't it strange the way Mrs. Harrison tried to make Mr. Harrison look like the strong, firm one? I'd hate to go toe-to-toe with that old battle-ax. She's the scary one in that family. I wonder if they gave her any money."

"I hope so," James said. "It makes my belly knot up to think of her driving a clunker around without a dime to her name."

"She's got your credit cards. If they didn't give her any money, she'll have to use them."

"I'll bet you Sally is dead on her rear. Let's find a motel, and then we can take turns calling all the motels in the area."

They stayed at a Quality Inn, an approved lodging for FBI agents. Thirty minutes later, Quinlan was staring at the phone, just staring, so surprised he couldn't move.

"You found her? This fast?"

"She's not five miles from here, at a motel called the Last Stop. She didn't use her real name, but the old man thought she looked strange, what with that man's coat she was wearing and those tight clothes he said made her look like a hooker except he knew she wasn't, and that's why he let her stay. He said she looked scared and lost."

"Glory be," Savich said. "I'm not all that tired anymore, Quinlan."

"Let's go."

EIGHTEEN

Sally took off her clothes—peeled the jeans off, truth be told, because they were so tight—and lay on the bed in the full-cut girls' cotton panties that Dillon Savich had bought for her. She didn't have a bra, which was why she had to keep James's coat on. The bra Savich had bought—a training bra— she could have used when she was eleven years old.

The bed was wonderful, firm—well, all right, hard as a rock, but that was better than falling into a trough. She closed her eyes.

She opened her eyes and stared at the ceiling. Through the cheap drapes she could see an all-night flashing neon sign: HOT HARVEY'S TOPLESS GIRLS.

Great part of town she'd chosen.

She closed her eyes again, turned on her side, and wondered where James was. In Washington? She wondered what Noelle had said to him. Why hadn't Noelle told her the truth about that night? Maybe she would have if there'd been more time. Maybe. Had Noelle told her the truth, that both her father and her husband had conspired to put her in Beadermeyer's sanitarium? Both of them? And Noelle had bought it?

She wondered if her grandparents had called Dr. Beadermeyer, and if the Nazi was on his way to Philadelphia. No, he'd wait. He wouldn't want to chase shadows, and that's exactly what she was and planned to be. No one could catch her now. The three hundred dollars would get her to Maine. She'd go to Bar Harbor, get a job, and survive. The tourists would flow in in only three months; then she would have more cover than she'd ever need. No one would find her there. She knew she was seeing Bar Harbor through a seven-year-old's eyes, but it had been so magical; surely it couldn't be all that different now.

Where was James? He was close, she knew it. She hadn't exactly felt him close, but as she'd told her grandparents, he was smarter than he had a right to be.

She devoutly hoped he was at home in Washington, in bed fast asleep, the way she should be right now but wasn't. How close was he?

She thought about it a few more minutes, then got out of bed. She would get to Bar Harbor sooner than expected. Still, she'd spent $27.52 on this room. To waste that money was appalling, but she couldn't sleep.

She was out of the room within five minutes. She revved up her motorcycle and swung back onto the road, the garish lights from Hot Harvey's Topless Girls haloing around her helmeted head. It was odd, she thought, as she passed a Chevrolet—she would swear that James was nearby. But that wasn't possible.

JAMES was the navigator and on the lookout for the Last Stop Motel. When she pulled out not fifty feet ahead of them, at first he couldn't believe it. He shouted, "Wait, Savich, wait. Stop."

"Why, what's wrong?"

"It's Sally."

"What Sally? Where?"

"On the motorcycle. I'd recognize my coat anywhere. She didn't buy a clunker, she bought a motorcycle. Let's go. What if we'd been thirty seconds later?"

"You're sure? That's Sally on that motorcycle? Yeah, you're right, that is your coat. It looks moth-eaten even from here. How do you want me to curb her in? It could be dangerous, what with her on that bike."

"Hang back for a while and let's think about this."

Savich kept the Porsche a good fifty feet behind Sally.

"That was a smart thing she did," Savich said. "Buying a motorcycle."

"They're dangerous. She could break her neck riding that thing."

"Stop sounding like you're her husband, Quinlan."

"You want me to break your upper lip? Hey, what's going on here?"

Four motorcycles passed the Porsche and accelerated toward the single motorcycle ahead.

"This is all we need. A gang, you think?"

"Why not? Our luck has sucked so far. How many rounds of ammunition do you have?"

"Enough," Savich said briefly, his hands still loose and relaxed on the steering wheel, his eyes never leaving the road ahead. Traffic was very light going out of Philadelphia at this time of night.

"You feeling like the Lone Ranger again?"

"Why not?"

THE four motorcycles formed a phalanx around Sally.

Don't panic, Sally, Quinlan said over and over to himself. Just don't panic.

She'd never been so scared in her life. She had to laugh at that. Well, to tell the truth, at least she hadn't been this scared in the last five hours. Four of them, all guys, all riding gigantic Harleys, all of them in dark leather jackets. None of them was wearing a helmet. She should tell them they were stupid not to wear helmets. Maybe they didn't realize she was female. She felt her hair slapping against her shoulders. So much for that prayer.

What to do? More to the point, what would James do?

He'd say she was outnumbered and to get out of there. She twisted the accelerator grip hard, but the four of them did the same, seemingly content for the moment to keep their positions, hemming her in and scaring the hell out of her.

She thought of her precious two hundred and seventy-something dollars, all the money she had in the world. No, she wouldn't let them take that money. It was all she had.

She shouted to the guy next to her, "What do you want? Go away!"

The guy laughed and called out, "Come with us. We've got a place up ahead you'll like."

She yelled, "No, go away!" Was the idiot serious? He wasn't a fat, revolting biker, like the stereotype was usually painted. He was lean, his hair was cut short, and he was wearing glasses.

He swerved his bike in closer, not a foot from her now. He called out,

"Don't be afraid. Come with us. We're turning off at the next right. Al—the guy on your right—he's got a nice cozy little place not five miles from here. You could spend some time with us, maybe sack out. We figure you must have rolled some guy for that coat—whatever, it doesn't matter. Hey, we're good solid citizens. We promise."

"Yeah, right," she shouted, "like the pope. You want me to come with you so you can rob me and rape me and probably kill me. Go to hell, buster!"

She sped up. The bike shot forward. She could have sworn she heard laughter behind her. She felt the gun in James's coat pocket. She leaned down close to the handlebars and prayed.

"LET'S go, Savich."

Savich accelerated the Porsche and honked at the bikers, who swerved to the side of the highway. They heard curses and shouts behind them. Quinlan grinned.

"Let's keep us between her and the bikers," Quinlan said. "What do you think? Are we going to have to follow her until she runs out of gas?"

"I can get ahead of her, brake hard, and swing the car across the road in front of her."

"Not with the bikers still back there, we can't. Stay close."

"In exactly one more minute she's going to look back," Savich said.

"She's never seen the Porsche."

"Great. So she'll think not only some insane bikers are after her but also a guy in a sexy red Porsche."

"If I were her, I'd opt for you."

WHY didn't the car pass her?

She pulled even farther over toward the shoulder. Still the car didn't pull around. There were two bloody lanes. There were no other cars around. Did the idiot want three lanes?

Then something slammed into her belly. The guy in that Porsche was after her. Who was he? He had to be connected with Quinlan—she'd bet her last dime on it.

Why hadn't she stayed in her motel room, quiet on that nice hard bed, and counted sheep? That's probably what James would have done, but no, she had to come out on a motorcycle after midnight.

Then she saw a small, gaping hole in the guardrail that separated the eastbound lanes from the westbound. She didn't think, just swerved over in a tight arc and flew through that opening. There was a honk behind her from a motorist who barely missed her. He cursed at her out his window as he flew by.

There was lots of traffic going back into Philadelphia. She was safer now.

"I can't believe she did that," Quinlan said, his heart pounding so loud his chest hurt. "Did you see that opening? It couldn't have been more than a foot. I'm going to have to yell at her when we catch her."

"Well, she made it. Looked like a pro. You told me she had grit. I'd say more likely she's got nerves of steel or the luck of the Irish. And yeah, you're sounding like you're her husband again. Stop it, Quinlan. It scares me."

"Nothing short of a howitzer firing would scare you. Pay attention now and stop analyzing everything I say. We'll get her, Savich. There's a cut-through up ahead."

It took them some time to get her back in view. She was weaving in and out of the thicker traffic going back toward the city.

"Hang on," Quinlan said over and over, knowing that at any instant someone would cut her off, someone else wouldn't see her and would change lanes and crush her between two cars.

"At least she thinks she's lost us," Savich said. "I wonder who she thought we were."

"I wouldn't be surprised if she guessed it was me."

"Nah, how could that be possible?"

"It's my gut talking to me again. Yeah, she probably knows, and that's why she's driving like a bat out of hell. Look out, Savich. Hey, watch out, bubba!" Quinlan rolled down the window and yelled at the man again. He turned back to Savich. "Damned Pennsylvania drivers. Now, how are we going to get her?"

"Let's tail her until we get an opportunity."

"I don't like it. The bikers are back, all four of them."

The four bikers fanned through the traffic, coming back together when there was a break, then fanning out again.

Sally was feeling good. She was feeling smart. She'd gotten them, that jerk driving that Porsche and the four bikers. She'd gone through that opening without hesitation, and she'd done it without any problem. It was a good thing she hadn't had time to think about it, otherwise she would have wet her pants. She was grinning, the wind hitting hard against her teeth, making them tingle. However, she was going in the wrong direction.

She looked at the upcoming road sign. There was a turn onto Rancor Road half a mile ahead. She didn't know where Rancor Road went, but from what she could see, it wove back underneath the highway. That meant a way back east.

She guided her bike over to the far right lane. A car honked, and she could have sworn she felt the heat of it as it roared past her. Never again, she thought, never again would she get on a motorcycle.

Although why not? She was a pro.

She'd driven a Honda 350, exactly like this one, for two years, beginning when she was sixteen. When she told her father she was moving back home, he refused to buy her the car he'd promised. The motorcycle was for the interim. She saved her money and got the red Honda, a wonderful bike. She remembered how infuriated her father had been. He'd even forbidden her to get near a motorcycle.

She'd ignored him.

He'd grounded her.

She hadn't cared. She didn't want to leave her mother in any case. Then he'd shut up about it. She had the sneaking suspicion that he wouldn't have cared if she'd killed herself on the thing.

Not that it mattered. He'd gotten his revenge.

She didn't want to think about that.

She took the turn onto Rancor Road. Soon now, she'd be going back in the other direction, and no one would be after her this time. The road was dark, no lights at all. It was windy. There were thick, tall bushes on both sides. There was no one on the road. What had she done? She smelled the fear on herself. Why had she turned off? James wouldn't have turned off.

She was a fool, an idiot, and she'd pay for it.

It happened so fast she didn't even have time to yell or feel scared. She saw the lead biker on her left, waving to her, calling to her, but she couldn't understand his words. She jerked her bike to the right, hit a gravel patch, slid into a skid, and lost control. She went flying over the top of the bike and landed on the side of the two-lane road, not on the road but in the bushes that lined the road.

She felt like a meteor had hit her—a circle of blinding lights and a whoosh of pain—then darkness blacker than her father's soul.

Quinlan didn't want to believe what he'd just seen. "Savich, she's hurt. Hurry, dammit, hurry."

The Porsche screeched to a halt not six feet from where the four bikers were standing over Sally. One of them, tall, lanky, short hair, was bending over her.

"Okay, guys," Quinlan said, "back off now."

Three of them twisted around to see two guns pointed at them. "We're FBI and we want you out of here in three seconds."

"Not yet." It was the lead biker, who was now on his knees beside her.

"What are you doing to her?"

"I'm a doctor—well, not fully trained, but I am an intern. Simpson's the name. I'm trying to see how badly hurt she is."

"Since you're the one that knocked her off the road, that sounds weird."

"We didn't force her off the road. She went into a skid. Actually, we followed because we saw you go back after her. Hey, man, we want to help her."

"As I said, we're FBI," Quinlan repeated, looking at the man. "Listen, she's a criminal. A big-time counterfeiter. Is she going to be all right? Can you tell if she broke anything? Savich, keep an eye on these bozos."

Quinlan dropped to his knees. "Can I take off her helmet?"

"No, let me. I guess maybe we should wear helmets. If she hadn't had one on, she might have scrambled her brains, and not necessarily left them inside her head. You're really FBI? She's really a criminal?"

"Of course she is. What are you doing? Okay, you're seeing if her arms are broken. She'd better be all right or I'll have to flatten you. You scared her to death. Yeah, she's your typical criminal type. Why isn't she conscious yet?"

At that moment Sally moaned and opened her eyes. It was dark. She heard men's voices, lots of them. Then she heard James.

"No," she said. "No, it's not possible you caught me. I didn't think it could be you. I was wrong again."

He leaned down over her and said one inch from her nose, "I caught you, all right. And this is the last time I'm going to do it. Now be quiet and lie still."

"I wouldn't have guessed she was a criminal," Simpson said. "She looks as innocent and sweet as my kid sister."

"Yeah, well, you never know. It's taken us a long time to catch up with her. We didn't know she'd gotten ahold of a bike. She was in a car six hours ago.

"All right, Sally, are you all right? Anything hurt? Nothing's broken, right? Can't you take off her helmet now?"

"Okay, but let's do it real carefully."

Once the helmet was off, she breathed a sigh of relief. "My head hurts," she said. "Nothing else does except my shoulder. Is it broken?"

The biker felt it very gently. "No, not even dislocated. You probably landed on it. It'll be sore for a while. I think you should go to the hospital and make sure there are no internal injuries."

"No," she said. "I want to get on my bike and get out of here. I've got to get away from this man. He betrayed me."

"What do you mean, he betrayed you?"

"He drew me in and made me trust him. I even slept with him one night, but that was in Oregon. Then he had the gall to tell me he'd lied to me, he was an FBI agent. He told me that here, not in Oregon."

"You're sure her brains aren't scrambled?" Savich asked, pressing a bit closer.

"She made perfectly good sense," Quinlan said. "If you can't add anything sensible, Savich, keep quiet."

Quinlan touched the biker's arm. "Thanks for your help. The four of you can go now."

"Can I see identification?"

Quinlan smiled through his teeth. "Sure thing. Savich, show the man our ID again. He didn't get a good enough look the first time."

The biker studied it closely, then nodded. He looked back down at Sally, who'd propped herself up on her elbows. "I still can't believe she's a crook."

"You should see her grandmother. A glacier, that old lady. She's the head of the counterfeiting ring. Leads her husband around by the ear. She's a terror, and this one is going to be her spitting image."

Once the bikers had roared off, Quinlan said to Sally, "We're going to take you to the hospital now."

"No."

"Don't be an idiot. You could have hurt your innards."

"If you force me to a hospital, I'll announce to the world who I am and who you are."

"No, you won't."

"Try me."

He realized he was being blackmailed, but not for anything he had done. She would be the only one to be hurt if she did as she promised. He believed her.

"How are you, Sally?"

"Agent Savich? You were the jerk driving the Porsche? And James was sitting right beside you telling you what to do. I should have known. Well, I did know, deep down."

"Yeah," Savich said, wondering why it didn't occur to her to give him any of the credit. "Let me help you up. You don't look half bad in Quinlan's coat. A little long, but other than that, it's a perfect fit. Anyone who can ride a motorcycle like you do has to have the broadest shoulders in the land."

"How did you find me? Oh, dear, my head." She shook her head, then blinked her eyes. "It's only a bit of a headache. My shoulder hurts a little, but that's all. No hospital."

Quinlan couldn't stand to see her weaving around, his coat torn at the left shoulder, two buttons popped on her blouse. "You're not wearing a bra."

Sally looked down at the gaping blouse. There was no way she could pull it together. She buttoned James's coat. "This blind man here got me a training bra when he went out, and bought all these charming duds that are three sizes too small. I couldn't even get the thing fastened."

"Well, I didn't know what size. Sorry it didn't get the job done."

She kicked him in the shin.

"I didn't mean it like that," Savich said, rubbing his leg. "I'll think of something and tell you later."

"You'd better not."

Quinlan took her arm and gently pulled her toward him. "It's all right now, Sally. It's all right."

He pulled her against him. "Are you sure you don't want to have a doctor check you out?"

"No doctor. I hate doctors."

That made sense to him. He didn't point out that a doctor wasn't the same as a shrink. He wondered in that moment if Beadermeyer even was a doctor. He said to Savich, "When you get a minute, do some checking on Beadermeyer. I'm beginning to wonder if he's just a ruthless crook." To Sally he said, "All right. But you need to rest. Let's find a place to stay the night."

"How did you find me?"

"We just missed you at your grandparents' house, just as we did at your mother's. We figured you had to be as tired as we were, so we called all the motels in this area. It was easy. You've got a lot to learn about running, Sally."

She realized then that she'd lost, she'd really lost. And it had been so easy for them. If they hadn't tracked her down on the highway, then James would have come into her motel room. Easy, too easy. She was a turkey. She looked down at her dead Honda 350, at its twisted frame and blown back tire.

"My bike is ruined. I just bought it. I was getting it broken in."

"It's all right. It doesn't matter."

"That bike cost me nearly all my money."

"Since it was my three hundred dollars, I'm willing to write it off."

Everything had turned upside down. Nothing was as it should be. She eased her hand into the coat and pulled out his gun. She pressed it against his lower ribs.

NINETEEN

"Not again, Sally," he said, but still he was careful not to move.

"She's got your gun on you again, Quinlan?"

"Yes, but it's okay. I think she's learned a bit more since the last time she did it.

"Sally, it's over now. Come on, sweetheart, pull that sucker back. Whatever you do, don't forget that hair trigger. I think I'll have it modified a bit next time I'm at Quantico. Actually, if you could slip it back into my shoulder holster once we're in the car, I'd appreciate it. My shoulder holster's been empty since you stole my gun. I feel half-dressed."

"I don't want to shoot you, James, but I do want to get away from you. You did betray me. You know I can't trust you. Let me go, please."

"Nope, not ever again. You know you can trust me. It pisses me off that you're even questioning that. Listen up, Sally. You're with me now until all this is over. Would you rather trust your mother or your grandparents? Oh, yeah, your sweet little granny is a piece of work."

"No, I don't trust any of them. Well, I do trust Noelle, but she's all confused and doesn't know what to believe—whether I'm a lunatic or not. I'd bet that all of them have called Beadermeyer, even Noelle. If she called him it wasn't to turn me in, it was to get some answers. Oh, no, do you think Beadermeyer would hurt her?"

Quinlan didn't think he would hurt her unless her own skin was in really deep trouble, which it would be shortly, but not yet. But he said, "I don't know. Beadermeyer could do anything if he felt threatened, which he probably does, since we busted you out of his sanitarium. Hey, did you know I even threw meat to those dogs to save you?"

She looked up at him in the darkness. "What dogs?"

Savich said, "There were guard dogs at the sanitarium, Sally. James tossed meat to them so they wouldn't tear our throats out. One of the dogs was leaping up trying to get James's ankle when he was carrying you up that fence."

She could see the shadows and blurred lines of his face. "Well," she said at last, aware that she couldn't hold that gun up for much longer because her shoulder hurt like the very devil, "damnation."

"That's what we've been thinking for the past six hours," Savich said. "Come on, Sally, give it up. Quinlan's determined to help you. He's determined to protect you. Let him be possessive. I've never before seen him like this. It's a real treat.

"Come on, you guys. Let's get out of here before some motorists come by and stop or worse, someone calls the local cops."

Quinlan didn't even think about it: he scooped her up in his arms and carried her to the Porsche.

"You're no he-man," she said in the bitterest voice he'd ever heard. "It was only a six-foot walk. A nerd could have carried me that far."

"It's my gun," he said, leaning down and lightly kissing her ear. "It's heavy." When he settled her on his lap in the passenger side of the Porsche, he held out his hand for the gun.

She looked at him for a very long time. "You're really feeling possessive about me?"

"You stole my money, my credit cards, my car, and the photos of my nieces and nephews. I had to catch you so I could get that stuff back."

"Jerk." She gave him the gun.

"Yeah, that's me," he said. "Thanks, Sally. No more trying to run away from me?" he asked as he tossed the gun into the back seat.

"I don't know."

"Tell you what, I won't strain your options. I'll handcuff you to me, how's that?"

She didn't answer, her head pressed against his shoulder. She hurt, he realized, and here he'd been teasing her. "Rest," he said. He looked at Savich. "How about finding us a nice motel?"

"Contradiction in terms. Are you paying or is the FBI?"

"Hey, I'm rich now that I've got my credit cards back. It's on me, all except your room."

"TOMORROW we'll buy you some clothes that fit."

She was standing there, staring at the large motel room. There was a sitting area and a TV and a king-size bed.

She turned to look at him. "It's payback time?"

He cocked his head to one side. "What do you mean?"

She nodded toward the bed. "I gather I'm to sleep with you in that bed."

"I was going to ask that you take the sofa. It's too short for me."

She gave him a baffled look, then walked to the bathroom, saying over her shoulder, "I don't understand you. Why aren't you furious with me? Why aren't you yelling? I'm not used to reasonable people, particularly reasonable men. Look at you, the very image of long-suffering Job."

A bruise was coming up along her jaw. He wondered how badly her shoulder was hurt. "I would be pissed at you if I hadn't seen you go flying off that motorcycle. You gave me a gray hair with that stunt."

"I hit gravel. There was nothing I could do."

"Take a nice long shower. It should help your aches and bruises."

Five minutes later there was a knock on the adjoining door.

Quinlan opened it up. "She's in the shower. Come on in."

Savich was carrying a big bag from Burger King and a container holding three big soft drinks. He set them down on the table and sat down on the sofa.

"What a mess. At least it seems like she's not going to try to run again. I didn't know you had such charm."

"Hang around and maybe you'll get a few pointers."

"What are we going to do, Quinlan? We've got to call Brammer. We don't even know what's going on with the rest of the investigation."

"It occurred to me that it's the weekend. This is Friday night—well, actually Saturday morning. We're sort of off duty. We've got until Monday before we have to be the good guys again, right?"

Savich was leaning back against the sofa, his eyes closed. "Brammer will have our balls for breakfast."

"Nah. He would have had our balls if we'd lost Sally. But we didn't. Everything will be fine now."

"I can't believe your wild-eyed optimism," Savich said, opening his eyes and sitting up when he heard the shower turn off. "They have all sorts of those little shampoos and conditioners and stuff in the bathrooms."

"Your point?"

The blow dryer went on.

"No point, really. Let's eat," Savich said. He took the beef patty out of his hamburger bun, took a big bite, and said, with his mouth full, "I'm stressed. I need to work out. Thank God tomorrow's Saturday. But the gym will be crowded."

* * *

IT was nearly three o'clock in the morning. It was quiet and dark in the room. He knew she was still awake. It was driving him nuts.

"Sally?" he said finally. "What's wrong?"

"What's wrong?" She started to laugh. "You have the feelings of a rhino. You ask me *what's wrong?*"

"Okay, you have a point, but you need to sleep and so do I. I can't go to sleep until you do."

"That's nonsense. I haven't made a sound."

"I know, that's what's so crazy about it. I know you're scared to death, but if you'll remember, I promised you I'd protect you. I promised that we'd get this mess all cleared up. You know I can't do it without you."

"I told you, James, I don't remember that night. Not a single thing. There are images and sounds, but nothing solid. I don't know who killed my father. He may not even have been killed when I was there. On the other hand, I could have shot him. I hated him more than you can begin to imagine. Noelle swore to me she didn't kill him. There was more, but she didn't have time to tell me—if, that is, she would have told me in any case."

"You know you were there when he was shot. You know very well you didn't shoot him. But we'll get back to that later."

"I think my mother didn't tell me the truth because she knows I did shoot him. She's trying to protect me, not the other way around."

"No, you didn't shoot him. Maybe it was because she didn't have time since we showed up. Or maybe it was because she's protecting somebody else. We'll find out everything. Trust me. She told the cops and us that she'd been out all evening, alone, at a movie."

"Well, she told me she'd been with Scott. Which means she had a witness to prove she didn't kill my father."

"Scott? Your husband?"

"Don't be cute. You know he's my husband, but for only a very short time longer."

"All right. We'll take care of things. Now, it's late. We've got to get some sleep.

"I just wanted to tell you that you ran a good race, Sally, real good. When I happened to spot you leaving the motel on that motorcycle, I nearly dropped my teeth. That was real smart of you to ditch the car and buy a bike. It took us totally by surprise."

"Yes, but it didn't matter when it came right down to it, did it?"

"No, thank God. Savich and I are good. That and lucky as dogs on the loose in an Alpo factory. Where were you going?"

"To Bar Harbor. My grandfather gave me three hundred dollars. It was all he had in his wallet. When I counted it, I became aware of a certain irony."

"You're kidding. Three hundred exactly?"

"Right on the button."

"I didn't particularly care for your grandparents. The maid showed us into this back study. They were watching some Home Shopping show. I've got to say that was a surprise. Mr. Franklin Ogilvee Harrison and wife watching that plebian show."

"That would have surprised me too."

"Sally, would you like to come here to the big bed? No, don't freeze up on me. I can see you freezing from here. I'll bet your shoulder aches too, doesn't it?"

"Only a little bit. More sore than aches. I was very lucky."

"You're right about that. Come on now, I promise not to attack you. Remember how well we both slept in The Cove in my tower bedroom? It can't have bothered you all that much since you were willing to tell the bikers about it quick enough."

The silence lasted for a full minute. She said, "Yes, I remember. I don't know why I opened my mouth and blabbed it to total strangers. I had that horrible nightmare."

"No, you remembered what had happened to you. It was a nightmare, but it was real. It was your father. At least you finally told me that.

"Come here, Sally. I'm exhausted and even you—super female—have got to be teetering on the edge a bit."

To his relief and pleased surprise, she was standing beside the bed in the next moment, looking down at him. She was wearing his white undershirt. He pulled the cover back.

She slipped in and lay on her back.

He lay on his back four inches away from her.

"Give me your hand."

She did. He squeezed her fingers. "Let's get some sleep."

Surprisingly, they did.

When Quinlan awoke the following morning, she was sprawled on top of him, her arms wrapped around his neck, her legs parted, lying directly on top of his. The undershirt had ridden up to her waist.

Oh, damn, he thought, trying not to move, trying to tell himself that this was just something else a professionally trained FBI agent had to learn how to deal with. So it hadn't been covered in the sixteen-week training course at Quantico. No big deal. He had experience. He wasn't sixteen. He breathed through his teeth.

Yes, he would handle this situation with poise and composure. He felt the heat of her through his boxer shorts. He was just a smidgen of material away from her, that was all, and he knew that composure was a big thing at this point.

"Sally?"

"Hmm?"

He was harder than his uncle Alex's divining rod. No way he was going to scare her. As gently as he could, he pushed her off him onto her back. The only thing was that she didn't let go of him. He had no choice but to come down over her. Now Uncle Alex's divining rod was between her legs, where it belonged.

What was poise anyway? It didn't seem too important right at that moment.

"Sally, I'm in a bad way. Let me go, okay?"

Her arms eased around his neck but she kept her fingers laced.

He could have easily pulled away from her, but he couldn't bring himself to do it. She was slight and warm and he thought where he was and where she was a very nice thing. He loved the feel of her arms tight about his neck. He liked her warm breath against his neck.

He thought having her here beneath him until he croaked would be a very nice thing.

He was staring down at her. He opened his mouth and said, "Sally, would you marry me?"

Her eyes came open in a flash. "What did you say?"

"I asked you to marry me."

"I don't know, James. I'm already married."

"I forgot that. Sally, please don't move. Do you want to take your arms off my neck?"

"No, not really. You're warm, James, and I like your weight on me. I feel safe and like everything might be all right. Somebody would have to go through you to get to me. They'd never make it; you're too solid, too strong. Please don't roll off me."

Solid and strong was he? "You're sure you're not afraid? After what happened to you at the sanitarium, I don't want to scare you."

She frowned even as she tightened her arms around his neck. "It's odd, but you never scared me except when you came roaring through Amabel's door like a bull that day when my father called me for the first time. But after that, not at all, not even when you walked in on me when I'd come out of the shower."

"You were so beautiful, I thought I'd lose it for sure."

"Me? Beautiful?" She snorted, and he was charmed. "I'm a stick, but you're nice to say it."

"It's true. I looked at you and thought, She's perfect. I really like that little black mole on the side of your belly, beside your left pelvic bone."

"Oh, dear, you saw that much of me?"

"Oh, yes. A man's eyes can move real fast when the motivation is there. Why don't you dump Scott Brainerd and then you can marry me?"

"I don't think he'll mind at all," she said after a moment. "Actually he's already dumped me, despite those pleas he made on TV." She was rubbing her hands over his shoulders and upper back. His skin was warm and smooth. "Shortly after we were married, I knew it had been a mistake. I was as busy as he was, always on the go, always going out t. meetings and parties and functions in the evenings, always talking to people on the phone, always having people over. I loved it, and he seemed to at first.

"Then he told me he'd thought I would give all that up when we got married. Evidently he expected me to sit around until he got home and then feed him and probably rub his back and listen to him talk about his day, and then strip if he wanted sex. At least that's what he'd expected. Where he got that idea I'll never know.

"I tried to talk to him about it, but he would shake his head and tell me over and over that I was a crummy wife, that I was unreasonable. He said I'd lied to him. That wasn't true. It came as a total shock to me after we were married when he started pitching fits over my schedule. While we were dating it had been the same and he never said a word. Once he even told me how proud he was of me.

"When I finally told him that I knew he was having an affair and that I wanted out, he said I was imagining things. He said I was being silly, at least at first he said that. Then just days later he said I was losing it, that I was paranoid but that he wouldn't divorce me because I was going crazy. It wouldn't be right. No, he wouldn't do that to me. I didn't understand what he was talking about until about four days later.

"He was sleeping with another woman, James, I would bet my life on it. After I was locked away in Beadermeyer's sanitarium, I don't know what he did. I was kind of hoping that I'd never have to see him again. And I didn't. Just my father came out. But Scott had to be in on it with my father. He was and is my husband, after all. And he had told me I was nuts."

Interesting, he thought. "Yes," he said. "He was in on it, up to his little shyster's ears. Who was he having an affair with?"

"I don't know. Probably someone at work, at TransCon. Scott's big into power."

"I'm sorry," he said, and dipped down and kissed her ear, "but you're going to have to see him again, at least one more time. Good thing is, I'm your hero and I'm even official, so you don't have to worry.

"Sally, maybe Scott killed your father. Maybe your mother is protecting him."

"No, Scott's a worm. He's a stingy, cowardly little worm. He wouldn't have the guts to kill my father."

"All right." So much pain, he thought, too much. It would all work out, it had to.

He leaned down and kissed her mouth this time. Her lips parted, and he wanted more than anything to go deep into her mouth—he pulled back. He realized her world was spinning out of control right now. He didn't want to add any more confusion to her life. Good Lord, he'd asked her to marry him.

"Perhaps that would be good," she said and pulled him down so she could kiss him.

"What would be good?" he said in her mouth.

"To get married. To you. You're so normal, so big and normal. You didn't have a screwed-up childhood, did you?"

"No. I've got two older sisters and an older brother. I was the baby of the family. Everyone spoiled me rotten. My family wasn't particularly dysfunctional. No one hit anyone. We kids beat the crap out of each other, but that's normal enough. I was big into sports, any and every sport, but my passion was and still is football. Sundays were created for football. I always go into withdrawal after the Super Bowl. Do you like football?"

"Yes. I had a woman gym teacher at my school who was from San Francisco. She was nuts about football and taught us the game. We got very good. The only problem was that there wasn't another girls' team around for us to play. I don't like basketball or baseball."

"I can live with that. I'll even play touch football with you."

She kissed his neck. He shuddered as he felt her opening even more beneath him. He said quickly, "My big screw-up was marrying Teresa Raglan when I was twenty-six. She was from Ohio, seemed perfect for me.

"She's a lawyer, just like your husband and dear old dad. It turned out she fell in love with a guy in the Navy who was selling secrets to whoever was interested. I was the one who caught him. She defended him. She got him off, then left me and married him."

"That's pretty amazing, James. What happened to her?"

"They live in Annandale, Virginia. The guy's some sort of lobbyist, gets paid really well, and they seem to be doing great. I see them every once in a while. No, don't romanticize it and pretend that I was a brokenhearted wreck. I wasn't. I was shocked and furious for a while, before Savich pointed out the absurdity of it all.

"The good guy catches the bad guy. The good guy's wife defends the bad guy and gets him off and then marries him. Pretty deep stuff to walk in. He was right. The whole thing was like a bad melodrama or a TV soap."

"James, you're wonderful. Even in all this mess, you can laugh and make me laugh, and you weren't angry that I poked a gun in your stomach and stole your car. I had to ditch the car, James. Then I bought the motorcycle. I had to get away. I think if you could forget who you are and come to Bar Harbor with me, everything would be better than what it's going to be soon. I used to love life, James, before—well, that's not important right now."

"It is important. You want to know something else? Something else that will prove how great I am?"

"What's that?"

"I didn't even get pissed when you pulled my gun on me the second time."

"Well, that settles it then, doesn't it?" She moved beneath him, and he thought he'd lose it for sure. He was hard against her, and his heart was pounding deep and fast against her chest.

He hadn't intended to let things get this out of hand, at least he hadn't before she shifted beneath him, her legs wide now, his legs between hers.

He kissed her, then said into her mouth, "You're beautiful, and you can feel how much I want you. But we can't let this happen. I don't have any condoms. The last thing you need is to get pregnant."

He heard Savich moving about in the adjoining room. "Besides, Savich is awake and up. It's nearly seven o'clock. We need to get back home."

She turned her face away from him. Her eyes were closed. He thought she must be in pain, from either her head or her shoulder. Without thinking, he reared back and pulled his undershirt over her head. She blinked up at him and made a move to cover herself.

No, he thought, she wasn't ready for this. "It's all right. I want to see how badly your shoulder is hurt. Hold still."

He was on his knees between her legs, bending over her, his hands gentle as they lightly touched her left shoulder. She winced. "There. Okay, hold still, let me feel around a bit more." She looked like the Italian flag, the bruises raw and bright, slashing downward to her breasts and over her shoulder cap to her upper arm. Some of the colors were smearing into each other, green the predominant one.

He leaned down and kissed her shoulder.

He felt her hands clenching his arms. "I'm sorry you got hurt." He kissed her again, on her left breast this time. He laid his cheek against her breast and listened to her heartbeat, so clear and strong, and now it was speeding up. Why not? he thought. He raised his head and smiled at her.

"A woman who's lived with as much stress as you must have release. It's the best medicine." He kissed her again, and eased off her onto his side. He slid his palm down her body, lightly caressing her belly, then his fingers found her. He felt the excitement of what he was doing to her break through her embarrassment.

He lifted his head and smiled at her dazed face. "It's all right, sweetheart. You need this. God knows I do, too."

He began kissing her again, talking into her mouth, sex words that were crude and raw and exciting. When she came, he took her cries in his mouth, held her tightly against him, and wished like mad that he could come inside her.

But he couldn't.

Savich knocked lightly on the adjoining door.

"Quinlan, Sally, you guys awake?"

He looked down at the bluest eyes he'd ever seen. She was staring at him as if she couldn't believe what had happened.

"You okay?"

She stared up at him, mute.

"Hey, Quinlan, you up? Come on, you guys, we've got miles to go."

"That's the guy who owns the Porsche," Quinlan said. "We've got to hang on to him." He kissed the tip of her nose and forced himself to leave her.

TWENTY

"I like your apartment."

He grinned at the back of her head. "Easy for you to say since it's got more character than that motel room—"

She turned to face him, no longer dressed in the too-tight jeans, his coat that had hung halfway down her legs, and the blouse that had gaped open over her breasts.

They'd stopped at the Macy's in Montgomery Plaza on the way back to Washington. Savich had bowed out, heading for the computer software store in the mall. James and Sally had enjoyed themselves immensely, arguing over everything from the color of her nightgown to the style of her shoes. She left wearing dark brown corduroy slacks that fit her very nicely, a cream pullover wool sweater over a brown turtleneck, and neat brown leather half boots.

He was carrying his own coat—the one she'd taken—over his arm. He doubted the dry cleaners would be able to get out the grease stains from her motorcycle accident.

"I've heard that men living alone usually live in a dump—you know, empty pizza cartons all over everywhere, including the bathroom, dead plants, and horrible furniture they got from their mother's attic."

"I like to live well," he said, and realized it was true. He didn't like mess or secondhand furniture, and he loved plants and impressionist paintings. He was lucky to have Mrs. Mulgravy live next to him. She saw to everything when he was gone, particularly his precious African violets.

"You do very well with plants."

"I think the secret is that I play my sax to them. Most of them prefer blues."

"I don't think I like the blues," she said, still looking at him intently.

"Have you ever listened to Dexter Gordon? John Coltrane? Gordon's album *Blue Notes* makes your heart weep."

"I've heard of Gato Barbieri."

"He's great too. I learned a lot from him and Phil Woods. There's hope for you yet, Sally. You've got to give the wailing and the rhythm a chance."

"That's your hobby, James?"

He looked a bit embarrassed. "Yeah, I play the saxophone at the *Bonhomie Club* on Friday and Saturday nights. Except when I'm not in town, like last night."

"Are you playing tonight?"

"Yes, but no, not now. You're here."

"I'd love to hear you. Why can't we go?"

He gave her a slow smile. "You'd really like to go?"

"I'd really like to go."

"Okay. The chances are nobody would even begin to recognize you, but let's get you a wig anyway, and big dark glasses." He knew that tomorrow he, Sally, and Savich would leap into this mess feetfirst. He couldn't wait to meet Scott Brainerd. He couldn't wait to meet Dr. Beadermeyer. He hadn't told Sally yet. He wanted to give her today with no hassles from him, from anybody. He wanted to see her smile.

"James, do you think I could call a couple of my friends?"

"Who are they?"

"Women who work on the Hill. I haven't spoken to them since more than six months ago. Well, I did call one of them before I left Washington to go to The Cove. Her name is Jill Hughes. I asked her for a loan. She agreed, very quickly, and wanted to meet me. There was something about how she acted—I didn't go. I'd like to call Monica Freeman. She was my very best friend. She was out of town before. I want to see how she acts, what she has to say to me. Perhaps I'm paranoid, but I want to know who's there for me."

She didn't sound the least bit sorry for herself. Still, he felt a knife twist in his gut.

"Yeah," he said easily, "let's give Monica a call and see if someone's gotten to her as well." He handed her his cell phone.

She called Monica Freeman, a powerhouse administrator in HUD. She was embarrassed because she had to call Information for the number. She'd known it as well as her own before Scott.

The phone rang twice, three times, then, "Hello."

"Monica? It's Sally."

James was bent over, writing something.

There was a long pause. "Sally? Sally Brainerd?"

"Yes. How are you, Monica?"

"Sally, where are you? What's going on?"

James slid a sheet of paper under her hand. Sally read it, nodded slowly, then said, "I'm in trouble, Monica. Can you help me? Can you loan me some money?"

There was another long pause. "Sally, listen. Tell me where you are."

"No, Monica, I can't do that."

"Let me call Scott. He can come and get you. Where are you, Sally?"

"You never called him Scott before, Monica. You didn't like him, remember? You used to call him a jerk when you knew I was listening. You wanted to protect me from him. You used to tell me he was into power and that he was trying to separate me from all my friends. Don't you remember how you'd call after Scott and I were first married and ask me first thing if Scott was gone so we could really talk? You didn't like him, Monica. Once you told me I should kick him in the balls."

There was utter silence, then, "I was wrong about him. He's been very concerned about you, Sally. He came to me hoping you would call and that I would help him.

"Scott's a good man, Sally. Let me call him for you. He and I can meet you someplace, we—"

Sally very gently punched the off button on the cell phone.

To her surprise James was grinning. "Hey, maybe we've got your husband's lover. Am I jumping too fast here? Yeah, probably, but what do you think? Maybe he's a real stud, may he's got both Jill and Monica. Could he do it, do you think?"

She'd been thinking that hell couldn't feel worse than she felt right now, but he'd put a ridiculous twist on it, like the best of the spin doctors. "I don't know. She's certainly changed her tune, just like Jill. Two? I doubt it, James. He was always so busy. I think his deals were more exhilarating to him than mere sex."

"What kind of deals?"

"He was in my dad's law firm, something I didn't know until after we were married. That sounds weird but it's true. He didn't want me to know, obviously, until after we were married. He was in international finance, working primarily with the oil cartel. He would come home rubbing his hands together, telling me how this deal or that deal would impress everybody, how he'd gotten the better of such and such a sheikh and had just brought in a cool half million. Deals like that."

"How long were you married to him?"

"Eight months." She blinked and fiddled with the leaves of a healthy philodendron. "Isn't it odd? I don't count the six months in the sanitarium."

"That's not a very long time for a marriage, Sally. Even mine—a semi-unmitigated disaster—lasted two years."

"I realized right after we were married that my father was as much a part of the marriage as we were. I'm willing to bet he offered me up to Scott as part of a deal between the two of them."

She drew a deep breath. "I think my father put me in the sanitarium as revenge for all those years I protected Noelle. I'm willing to bet that another part of the revenge was to get Scott to marry me. He got to Scott, and Scott did what he was told. All revenge.

"When I told Scott I wanted a divorce, he told me I was crazy. I told him he could marry my father if he wanted a St. John so badly. Maybe two days after that, I was in that sanitarium—at least I think it was two days. The time still gets all scrambled up."

"But he had a lover. Perhaps Monica, perhaps Jill. Perhaps someone we don't know at all. How quickly were you sure about this affair?"

"About three months after we were married. I'd decided to try to make a go of it, but when I found a couple of love notes, unsigned, and two motel receipts, I didn't care enough to try. Between that and my father, always in the background, I just wanted to get out."

"But your father didn't let you get out."

"No."

"Obviously your father knew everything about your marriage. Scott must have told him immediately when you asked for a divorce for your father to have taken action so quickly. Who knows? Maybe it was Scott's idea. Do you want to call anyone else?"

"No, that leaves just Rita. I don't think I could take it if Rita started on me about calling Scott. This was enough—much too much, as a matter of fact."

"Okay, no more work today, all right?"

"That was work?"

"Certainly. We filled in another piece of the puzzle."

"James, who knocked both of us out in The Cove and brought me back to Dr. Beadermeyer's?"

"Beadermeyer or a henchman. Probably not Scott. It was probably the guy who played the role of your father that night in your bedroom window. But now that you've got me, you don't have to be depressed at the number of bad people in the world."

"They all seem to have congregated around me. Except Noelle."

He wanted to ask her to go over everything with him, from the day she met Scott Brainerd to now, but he didn't. Give her the day off, make her smile. Maybe they could make love in front of the fireplace. He wanted to make love to her very much. His fingers itched remembering the feel of her, the way she moved against his fingers, the softness of her. He tried to focus on his African violets.

THAT evening she pulled her hair back tight, securing it with a clip at the nape of her neck. She put on a big pair of dark sunglasses. "No one would recognize you," Quinlan said, coming up behind her and putting his hands lightly on her shoulders.

"But let's get you a wig anyway. You know something? Your father was killed, what, three weeks ago or so? It was splashed all over TV, all over every tabloid, every newspaper. You, the missing daughter, got the same treatment. Why take the chance on someone recognizing you? I have to tell you, I like you in those sunglasses. You look mysterious. Are you really the same woman who's agreed to marry me? The same woman who woke me up this morning lying on top of me?"

"I'm the same woman. James, really, the other—I thought that was maybe a glitch on your part. You really mean it?"

"Nah, I just wanted to get you in bed and make you come."

She poked him in the stomach.

"Yeah, Sally, I really meant it."

THE *Bonhomie Club* on Houtton Street was in an old brick building set in the middle of what they called a "border" neighborhood. It was accepted wisdom to take a cab to and from the club or else take a huge risk of losing your entire car, not just the hubcaps.

James had never really thought about the possible dangers in this area until he handed Sally out of the cab. He looked around at the streetlights, many of them shot out.

There was litter on the sidewalks, none in front of the club because Ms. Lilly didn't like trash—real trash, white trash, any kind of trash.

"Like I told you, boy," she'd said when she hired him some four years before, "I like the look of you. No earrings, no tattoos, no bad teeth, and no paunch.

"You'll have to watch the gals, now, they're a horny bunch and one look at you and they're gonna have visions of sugar cocks dancing in their heads." And she howled at her own humor while James, an experienced agent, a man who'd heard just about every possible combination of crude words, stood there, embarrassed to his toes. She tweaked his earlobe between two fingers with inch-long bright pink fingernails and laughed some more. "You're gonna do fine, boy, just fine."

And he had. At first the customers, a loyal bunch, the large majority of them black, had looked at him like he was something escaped from the zoo, but Lilly had introduced him, made three off-color jokes about his sax playing, his sex playing, and his red sox playing.

She was one of his best friends. She'd even given him a raise in January.

"You'll like Ms. Lilly," Quinlan said to Sally as he shoved open the heavy oak door of the club. "I'm her token white." Marvin the Bouncer was inside, a heavy scowl on his ugly face until he saw it was Quinlan.

"Hullo, Quinlan," he said. "Who's the chicky?"

"The chicky is Sally. You can call her Sally, Marvin."

"Hello, Marvin."

But Marvin wasn't up for names. He nodded. "Ms. Lilly is back in her office playing poker with the mayor and some of his lame-assed cronies. No, James, there ain't no drugs. You know Ms. Lilly, she'd shoot anybody before she'd let 'em take a snort.

"She'll be out before it's time for you to play. As for you, Chicky, you stay in my eyesight once James is up there wailing his heart out on the stage, all right?"

"She's a cute little chicky, Quinlan. I'll take care of her."

"I appreciate it, Marvin. She is cute, and a lot of bad people are chasing her. If you could keep an eye on her, I can wail on my sax without worry."

"Ms. Lilly is going to try to feed her, Quinlan. She doesn't look like she's had a good meal in a month. You hungry, Chicky?"

"Not yet, but thank you, Marvin."

"A chicky with real good manners. It warms a man's heart, Quinlan."

"Amazing," Sally said and nothing more. But she was smiling. She gave Marvin a small wave.

"He'll watch over you, not to worry."

"Actually I hadn't even thought about it. I can't believe you just spit out the truth to him."

"Ah, Marvin didn't believe me. He thought I was worried some guy would hit on you, that's all."

Sally looked around the dark, smoky interior of the *Bonhomie Club*. "It's got lots of character, James."

"It gains more by the year. I think it's because of the aging wood. That bar is over a hundred years old. It's Ms. Lilly's pride. She won it in a poker game from a guy up in Boston. She always calls him Mr. Cheers."

"Lots of character."

He grinned down at her. "Tonight's for fun, all right? You look gorgeous, you know that? I like that sexy little top."

"You're into jet beads, are you?" But she was pleased. He'd insisted on buying it for her at Macy's. She actually smiled. She felt good, light and easy. Tonight, she thought, tonight was for fun. It had been so long. Fun. She'd simply forgotten.

Nightmares could wait for tomorrow. Maybe when James took her home he'd want to kiss her some more, maybe even make love to her. She could still feel the warmth of his fingers on her.

"You want a drink?"

"I'd love a white wine. It's been so long."

He raised an eyebrow. "I don't know if Fuzz the Bartender has ever heard of such a thing. You sit down and let the atmosphere soak into your bones. I'll go see what Fuzz has got back there."

Fuzz the Bartender, she thought. This was a world she'd never imagined. She'd cheated herself.

She looked up to see James gesturing back at her and an immense black man with a bald head shiny as a cue ball grinning at her, waving a dusty wine bottle. She waved back and gave a thumbs-up.

Where did the name Fuzz come from?

There were only about half a dozen whites in the club, four men and two women. But no one seemed to care what color anyone was.

An Asian woman with long, board-straight black hair to her waist was playing the flute on the small wooden stage. The song was haunting and soft.

The conversation was a steady hum, never seeming to rise or fall. James put a glass of white wine in front of her.

"Fuzz said he got the wine a couple of years ago from this guy who wanted whiskey but was broke. Fuzz got this bottle of wine in trade."

She sipped it and gulped. It was awful and she wouldn't have traded it for a glass of Balen-Craig. "It's wonderful," she called out to Fuzz the Bartender.

James sat beside her, a beer in his hand. "The wig's not bad, either. A little too red for my taste, a little too curly, but it'll do for tonight."

"It's hot," she said.

"If you can hold on, I'll try to think of something indecent to do with that thing when we get home."

At nearly nine o'clock, he kissed her mouth, tasted the white wine, and grimaced.

"That's rotgut."

"It's wonderful rotgut. Don't say anything to Mr. Fuzz."

James laughed, swung his saxophone case off the other chair, and wove his way through the tables to the stage.

She couldn't take her eyes off him. He hugged the flutist, then pulled a lower stool forward to the microphone. He took his saxophone out of the case, polished it a bit with a soft cloth, checked the reed. Then he began to warm up.

She didn't know what she'd expected, but the sound coming out of that sax would make the devil weep. He played scales, bits and pieces of old songs, skipped from high notes to low ones, testing, soft, then loud.

"So you're the little white girl who's hooked my Quinlan, are you?"

TWENTY-ONE

"I won't be so little in another six months."

"Why's that?"

"I'm not usually so skinny. I'll fatten up."

"Maybe my Quinlan will even get you pregnant. You watch out, Sally, all the ladies salivate while he's playing. Poor boy, he tells himself it's because of his beautiful music. And he does look so soulful while he's playing."

She shook her head, her voice mournful. "I don't have the heart to tell him it's his sexy body and gorgeous eyes. Ah, now he's playing Sonny Rollins, my favorite. Well, aren't I forgetful? I'm Ms. Lilly," the huge black woman said, grinned wide, and pumped Sally's hand.

"I'm Sally."

"I know. Fuzz told me. Then Marvin told me. They said it looks like my Quinlan has got it real bad. He's never had it even mild before. This should be interesting. Hey, you aren't planning on having your way with him and then kissing him off, are you?"

"Kiss him off? Kiss off James?"

"What I mean is, you aren't married, are you? You're not using my Quinlan just to take care of your needs? I hear he's a treat in bed, so that would make sense, even though I don't like it."

"Actually, no, I'm not going to kiss him off," Sally said. She sipped at Mr. Fuzz's white wine. "I like your dress. It's magnificent."

Ms. Lilly preened and pressed her arms against her impressive breasts. The resulting cleavage made Sally stare. She'd never seen so much outside of a *Playboy* magazine.

"You like the white satin? So do I. I hear tell that a woman built along statuesque lines like I am isn't supposed to wear white, but hey, I like it. It makes me feel young and virginal. It makes me feel ready to go out and try a man for the first time.

"Now, you sit here and listen to my Quinlan. That's Stan Getz he's playing now. He makes old Stan sound like a sinful angel. Quinlan's good. You really listen now."

"I'll listen good."

Ms. Lilly patted her on the back, nearly sending her face into the glass of wine, and moved away like a ship under sail to a booth that was very near the stage.

Quinlan began to play a sexy, weeping, slow blues song. It sounded like John Coltrane, but she couldn't be completely sure. It was still so new to her.

She noticed for the first time that no one was talking. There was total quiet in the club. Everyone was focused on James.

She watched at least four women get up and move closer to the stage. He played beautifully. His range was excellent, each note full and sweet, enough to break your heart. She felt a lump in her throat and swallowed. The song he was playing cried torrents, the notes sweeping lazily from a high register to low, deep notes that tore at the soul. His eyes were closed. His body was swaying slightly.

She knew she loved him, but she wasn't about to admit it here and now, knowing that it was his damned music making her feel as mushy as the grits Noelle had tried to make for her once. Men in uniforms and men playing soul music—a potent combination.

James spoke into the microphone. "This one's for Sally. It's from John Coltrane's *A Love Supreme*."

If she'd ever doubted what he felt about her, that song put an end to it. She gulped down Mr. Fuzz's white wine and her tears.

Two more women moved closer to the stage, and Sally smiled.

When James finished, he waved to her. Then he cleared his throat and called out, "I got a request for Charlie Parker."

She listened, took a last sip of Mr. Fuzz's wine, and realized she had to go to the bathroom.

She slipped out of her chair, looked at Fuzz the Bartender, who was pointing to an open door beside the bar. She smiled and walked past him, saying, "Can I have another glass when I come out, Mr. Fuzz?"

"You sure can, Sally. I'll have it waiting." When she came out of the women's bathroom, she was smiling. She could hear James getting into his next song, one she recognized, a soft, searching song she hadn't realized was blues.

Suddenly she knew she wasn't alone. She felt someone very close to her, just behind her. She heard breathing, a lot of soft breathing.

The corridor was narrow. There hadn't been any other women in the bathroom. But that was silly. It had to be another woman.

But it wasn't a woman.

It was Dr. Beadermeyer. There were two men standing behind him. One of them was holding a needle in his hand.

He took her arm with a lover's light grasp. It changed quickly enough. She felt her skin pulling and sinking in at the increasing pressure of his fingers.

With his other hand, he grabbed her jaw to hold her still. He leaned over and lightly kissed her.

"Hello, Sally. How lovely you look, my dear. You shouldn't be drinking, you know, it doesn't go well with the kind of drugs your body is used to. I watched you drinking that dreadful stuff. Why are you here? I assume that man up there making a fool of himself in this backwater hole-in-the-wall is James Quinlan, that FBI agent you were with in The Cove? He's not bad looking, Sally. Now I know he's your lover. A man like that wouldn't stay with a woman unless she delivered.

"How desolate poor Scott will be when he finds out. Let's go now, my dear girl. It's time you came back to your little nest. A different nest. This time that bastard won't come to get you." It couldn't be him, but it was. Her father was dead. Why did he still want her so badly?

"I'll hold her. Bring the needle. Let's get out of this godforsaken place."

"I wouldn't go to heaven with you."

"Of course you will, my dear girl."

He was gripping her arm hard now, pulling her back against him, one hand over her mouth. She shoved her right elbow hard into his stomach.

He sucked in his breath, and she jerked free. "James! Marvin!" Then she screamed once, right before a hand smashed down over her mouth.

"Damn it, grab her! Gag her. Give her the shot!"

She grabbed the edge of a small table below the public telephone and gave it a shove, sending it crashing over, knocking against one of the men with Beadermeyer. She screamed once more, just a whisper of sound this time because the man's hand was hard over her mouth, covering her nose as well and she couldn't breathe. She was jerking, kicking back with her heels, feeling flesh, but still the man held her.

She felt fingers fumbling around her arm.

A needle.

He was going to shove a needle into her arm. He was going to make her into a zombie again. She kicked back as hard as she could. For an instant the man's hand loosened over her nose and mouth.

She leaned down and bit the man's hand, the hand that held that needle, and yelled again. "James!"

The hand went back over her mouth. A man was cursing, another man was jerking at her other arm, but she managed to send her left arm back hard, hitting him in the belly. The touch of the needle fell away. She heard a thunk on the wooden floor. He'd dropped the needle.

"I should have known you two goons would muck it up. Pick up the damned needle, you idiot. It's dark in here, but not dark enough. I knew I should have knocked her out. Or shot the little bitch. Damn, let's get out of here. Forget the needle, forget her."

It was Dr. Beadermeyer and he was furious.

Then she heard Fuzz the Bartender yelling the ripest obscenities she'd ever heard. The man released her. She staggered, then screamed, "You've lost, you damned bastard. Run and take your two dogs with you or James will kill you!"

He was panting hard, enraged. "I thought it would be easy, just slip a needle into your arm. You've changed, Sally, but this isn't the end of it."

"Oh, yes, it is. I'm going to put you out of business, you Nazi worm. I'm going to put you in jail, and I hope every one of those big inmates takes a fancy to you."

He raised his arm to hit her, but his two men crashed into him as they tried to get down the narrow hallway to the exit.

"Stop it, you fools," he screamed at them. Then they were all racing toward the back emergency exit. The door pounded open, then slammed shut.

She looked up to see Marvin the Bouncer bolting toward her like a runaway train. She heard Fuzz the Bartender crashing through the tables, yelling even riper obscenities.

She realized the whole incident had taken only seconds. It had seemed longer than a winter blizzard.

She took two steps forward. She saw James leaping off the stage. She saw him pull out his gun.

She saw Ms. Lilly pick up a baseball bat and stride toward her like an amazon angel.

It had all happened so quickly. Yet she'd felt the fear of a lifetime. To have a needle shoved into her arm again. No, she couldn't have borne that, not again.

Then she realized the fear was dimming, falling away.

She'd won. She'd beaten him. She wished she could have shot him. Or stuck a knife in his guts.

Marvin the Bouncer took one quick look at her, then slammed open the emergency exit door and ran outside.

Fuzz the Bartender streaked past her and out the door behind Marvin. She heard pounding footsteps. Lots of them. She prayed they'd catch Beadermeyer.

She suddenly felt so weak she couldn't hold herself up. She sank to her knees and leaned against the wall. She wrapped her arms around her bent knees and leaned her face against her legs.

"Sally, hang on, I'll be right back." It was James running after Marvin and Fuzz.

"Well, my girl, Marvin told me that James said you had bad guys after you. I don't mind this—even though it did interrupt one of my favorite songs. What fools those guys were to try to get you here. They must have really been desperate. Either that or stupid. I'll bet stupid."

Ms. Lilly shook her head, the thick black coils of hair never budging. "You ready to get up now, Sally?"

"Is the little chicky all right?"

"Yes, Marvin, she's just catching her breath. I think she did a good job on those guys. I don't suppose you nabbed the jerks?"

"No, Ms. Lilly. We got close, but they pulled away in this big car. Quinlan put a bullet through the back window, but then he stopped. He said he knew who it was and he was going to get the bastard tomorrow. Then he laughed and rubbed his hands together. It was hard because he was still holding that cannon of his."

Marvin the Bouncer turned. "Ain't that right, Quinlan?"

"It was Beadermeyer, wasn't it, Sally?"

She raised her head. She wasn't hyperventilating anymore. She was feeling just fine, thank you.

Ms. Lilly grabbed her arm and pulled her to her feet. "There you go.

Fuzz, get Sally some more of that wonderful white wine you've got stashed."

"Yes, it was Beadermeyer with two goons and a needle. I think the needle's still over there on the floor. I managed to knock it away."

Marvin gave her an approving nod. "I knew you were skinny but not helpless. That was good, Chicky."

"Thank you, Marvin. Thank all of you."

"You're welcome," Ms. Lilly said. She turned and shouted, "Okay, everyone back to their tables. Everything's okay now. This will teach any of you who want to screw around with Marvin that it isn't smart. They smashed the guys who were trying to mug Sally. It's all over now.

"Quinlan, get your very nice butt back up there on the stage and play me my Dexter Gordon. What do you think I pay you for anyway?"

"My music," James said. "Sally, I want you right next to the stage, all right?" But before he left, he picked up the needle, wrapped it in a napkin, and put it in his shirt pocket.

"I want to know what that yahoo was going to give you. We'll take this to the FBI lab tomorrow. Come on, Sally."

"I'll bring the wine," Fuzz said.

HE paced from one end of the living room to the other, back and forth. Savich was sitting comfortably in a big overstuffed chair, hunched over the keyboard of his laptop, MAX.

Sally wasn't doing anything except watching James. "I guess I've had enough," she said finally.

Both men looked at her.

She smiled. "I don't want to wait until tomorrow. I want to get it over with tonight. Let's go see my mother. She knows what happened that night my father was murdered. At least she knows a lot more than she's told you or the police or me. I'd like to know the truth."

"Better yet," Savich said, looking back down at his computer screen, "let's get all three of them together—your mother, your husband, and Dr. Beadermeyer. You think the time is right, Quinlan?"

"I don't know," Quinlan said. "Maybe it's too soon." He gave Sally a worried look. "You really sure about this, Sally?"

She looked strong, her thin shoulders back, those soft blue eyes of hers hard and steady. She looked ready to take on a grizzly. "I'm sure."

It was all he needed. Yeah, it was time to find out the truth. He nodded.

"Maybe they'll be tired," Savich said. "Well, here we go. Finally I've found it." He gave them a big grin. "I'm good," he said, rubbing his hands together. "Real good."

"What are you talking about?" Quinlan said, striding over to Savich. He leaned down to look at the screen.

"Everything we ever wanted to know about Dr. Alfred Beadermeyer. His real name is Norman Lipsy and he's Canadian. He did go to medical school—McGill, in Montreal.

"My, my, he has a specialty in plastic surgery. And there's lots more. Sorry it took me so long. I never considered he'd be Canadian, not with a name like Beadermeyer. I wasn't getting into the right databases." He rubbed his hands together. "I found him on a cosmetic surgeons roster, along with a photo. Said he graduated from McGill."

"This is incredible," Quinlan said. "Excellent, Savich."

"Now, before we're off, let me try a couple more things on Scott Brainerd. Where'd he get his law degree, Sally?"

"Harvard."

"Yeah, it does show him graduating Harvard with honors. Too bad. I was hoping maybe he'd lied about that."

Quinlan said, "You're still sure, Sally? You ready to see Scott? Beadermeyer? After what he tried tonight? You're sure?"

"Yes, I'm sure. No more. It's crazy. It's got to end. If I killed my father, I want to know. If Noelle or someone else did, then let's find out. I won't fall apart, James. I can't stand this fuzziness anymore, this constant mess of blurred images, the voices that are all melting together."

Quinlan said very slowly, in that wonderful soothing voice of his, "Before we leave I want to go over some more things with you. You up to it?"

"Oh, yes," she said. "I'm ready. We already talked about Scott and my father." She stopped, her fingers rubbing the pleats in her corduroy slacks.

"What is it?"

"It's about my father. And my mother." She looked down at her hands. Thin hands, skinny fingers, short fingernails. At least she hadn't bitten them since she'd met James.

"What is it, Sally? Come now, no more secrets."

"He beat my mother, viciously. I caught him doing it when I was sixteen. That was when I moved back from the girls' school in Virginia. I tried to protect her—"

Savich's head came up. "You're saying your father, the senior legal counsel of TransCon International, was a wife beater?"

"Why am I not surprised?" Quinlan said. He sat beside her and took one of her hands and waited, saying nothing more. She'd lived through that?

"My mother—Noelle—she wouldn't do anything about it. She just took it. I guess since he was so well known and respected and rich, and she was part of it, she couldn't bear the humiliation or losing all she had.

"I remember I always looked forward to parties, diplomatic gatherings—he was invited to all of them—those lavish lobbyist banquets, intimate little power lunches where wives were trotted out to show off, magazine interviews, things like that, because I knew he wouldn't dare hit Noelle then—there'd be photos taken of the two of them together. He knew that I knew, and that made him hate me even more.

"When I didn't leave the District to go to college, I thought he would kill me. He'd really counted on my leaving. He hadn't dreamed that I'd still be at home, watching him.

"I'll never forget the hatred in his eyes. He was very handsome, you know, thick, dark hair with white threaded through, dark blue eyes, tall and slender. High cheekbones, sculpted elegantly to make him look like an aristocrat.

"Actually, he's an older version of Scott. Isn't that strange that I thought I fell in love with a man who looked like my father?"

"Yeah," Savich said. "I'd say that's plain not good. It's a good thing that Quinlan here doesn't look like anybody except himself."

"Tell us the rest of it, Sally," Quinlan said.

"I came home at random times. He knew I would. Once when I'd been visiting Noelle, after I left, I realized I'd forgotten my sweater. I went back into the house and there he was, kicking my mother. I went to the phone to dial nine-one-one. As far as I was concerned, it was the last straw. You won't believe it, but my mother crawled to me, grabbed my leg, and begged me not to call the cops. My father stood there in the library doorway and dared me to do it. He dared me, all the while watching my mother sobbing and pleading, on her knees, her nails digging into my jeans. It was horrible. I put down the phone and left. I never went back."

"But he didn't take his revenge until six months ago," Savich said. "He waited—what?—some five years before he went after you."

"That's not quite true. He started his revenge with Scott. I'm convinced of that now. Yes, he was behind my marriage to Scott. There weren't any men in my life before that. I worked for Senator Bainbridge right out of college. I was happy. I never saw my parents. I had friends. I'd see my father every once in a while, by accident, and I could tell that he still hated my guts.

"I remember once at a party, I ran into my mother in the women's room. She was combing her hair and her long sleeve had fallen away. There was a horrible purple bruise on her arm. I remember looking at it and saying, 'What kind of monster in you allows you to let that bastard beat you?'

"She slapped me. I guess I deserved it."

"You do remember actually going to your parents' house the night your father was killed?"

"Yes, but nothing else is clear. How was I sure my father was dead? I don't know. But I did know, and I guess I must have believed that Noelle finally couldn't stand the beatings anymore. Yes, that's what I must have thought, although all that isn't particularly clear."

She began to rub her temples with the palms of her hands. "No, I don't know, James. I think I remember screams, I think I can see a gun, but nothing else, just these images. And maybe blood. I remember blood. But my father? Dead? Was Noelle there? I can't swear to anything. I'm sorry. I'm no help at all."

But Quinlan wasn't worried. He looked over at Savich whose fingers were tap-dancing on his laptop, nary a furrow of worry on his brow. He knew that Savich was hearing everything they said. He also knew Savich wasn't worried either.

Quinlan had pulled this off before. They had lots to work with. Sally was ready.

He said slowly, more to himself really, so she would get calm again, "So your father bided his time."

"Yes. It wasn't until after we were married that I found out my father was Scott's boss. He'd never told me what firm he was with. He was vague and I didn't really pay attention. It was all downhill from there, once I found out."

Quinlan paced his living room, not nervous pacing, just rhythmic strides. Savich worked MAX's keyboard. Sally rubbed the dust off the small rubber tree that sat in a beautiful oriental pot next to the sofa.

Quinlan stopped. He smiled at Sally. "I think it's time you made some phone calls, Sally. I think it's time we get the gang together and do some rattling. We'll see what falls out." He handed her the phone.

"Mom, then Scott, then Beadermeyer."

TWENTY-TWO

"You want to know what's driving me crazy?" Savich said, looking up from the keyboard and stretching. "I want to know why Beadermeyer is still after you. It was your father who had you put away there. He's dead. Why would Beadermeyer care anymore? Who's following in your old man's footsteps? You said Scott had to be in on it? But why would he care now? Wouldn't he just want that divorce so he could get on with his life? You sure you're up for this, Sally?"

"Yes, I'm up for it. In fact, I can't wait. I want to spit in Beadermeyer's face. As for why they took me again, I've thought and thought, but I can't think of a decent reason. Now let me make those calls."

She took the phone and dialed. There wasn't any wait at all. "Mom? It's me, Sally. I wondered if I could come over. I need to talk to you, Mom. Yes, right now. Is that all right?"

Slowly, she pressed the off button. She started to dial Scott's number. Quinlan lightly touched his hand to hers and shook his head. "No, I think your mom will get the other players there."

"He's right," Savich said. "If she doesn't, then we'll talk to her alone. We need to anyway. We need to know exactly where she stands in all of this mess."

"James is right," Sally said and swallowed hard. "The others will be there. But know this—she was protecting me. I'd bet my life on it."

He wanted to hug her, but he didn't. He watched her blink back the tears and swallow until she had control again. Sally had guts. She also had him.

He said, "Okay. Let me make some phone calls, then we'll get this show on the road."

THIRTY minutes later James rapped the griffin-head knocker of the St. John home.

Noelle St. John answered the door herself. She was wearing a pale blue silk dress. Her hair, blonder than Sally's, was twisted up in a neat chignon. She looked elegant, tense, and very pale. She hesitated a moment, then held out her arms to her daughter. Sally didn't move. Noelle St. John looked as if she was ready to burst into tears. She lowered her arms to her sides.

She said quickly, her words running together as if she couldn't get them out fast enough, "Oh, Sally, you've come. I've been so worried. When your grandparents called me I didn't know what to do. Come in, love, come in. We'll get this all straightened out." Then she saw Quinlan in the shadows.

"You."

"Yes, ma'am. May I come in as well?"

"No, you may not. Sally, what's going on here?"

"Sorry—no me, then no Sally."

She looked from Sally to Quinlan, shaking her head. She looked confused.

"Noelle, it's all right. Let us in."

She was shaking her head, back and forth. "But he's FBI, Sally. I don't want him here. He was here before with another man, and they searched the house for you. Why would you want him with you? It doesn't make sense. The last person you want around you is a cop. He's lied to you. He's manipulating you. He's making you more confused."

"No, Noelle, I'm not confused at all about this."

"But Sally, when your grandparents called me, they told me he was right behind you and you claimed you knew he would be. You said he was smart. But they said you wanted to escape and go into hiding. You said the same thing to me. Why are you with him? Why do you want to be with him?"

"He caught me. I'm an amateur and he's not. And trust me, you want him with me, too." Sally took a small step forward and lightly laid her fingertips on her mother's arm.

"That's me, ma'am, real smart. Special Agent James Quinlan. I'm pleased you remember me."

"I wish I didn't remember, sir," Noelle said. She looked back over her shoulder. James smiled, knowing now that there was someone else in the living room. Scott Brainerd? Dr. Beadermeyer? Or both of them? He sure hoped both of them were. "Both of us or neither of us," he said. "It's chilly out here. Make up your mind, ma'am."

"All right, but I don't know why you're with her. You've no right, none at all. Sally's my daughter, she's ill, the FBI can't hold her since she's mentally unstable, nor can the police. She's my responsibility, I'm her guardian, and I say she's going back to the sanitarium. It's the only way she can be protected."

"All that?" James said, looking amazed. Noelle looked at him as if she'd like to smack his face. "She doesn't look unstable to me. I'll bet she could withstand being beaten with rubber hoses, even having her fingernails yanked out. There's not an unstable cell in Sally's brain."

"She's been very ill for the past six months," Noelle said, as she stood back.

They walked past her into the foyer. There were fresh flowers on the beautiful antique table with the large gilded mirror hanging over it. There had always been fresh flowers in that hideous oriental vase, Sally thought, usually white and yellow chrysanthemums.

"Come along into your father's study, Sally. Let's get this over with. Then I'll make certain you're safe again."

"Safe again?" Sally whispered. "Is she nuts?"

Quinlan hugged her quickly against him, and when she looked up at him, he winked at her. "Don't worry."

"Well, well, what a surprise," he said when he saw Dr. Beadermeyer standing by the fireplace. He'd studied the man's photo so many times he felt as if he'd interviewed him, even though they'd never met in the flesh before. Was he the bastard who'd struck him on the head at The Cove? He'd find out soon enough.

He turned to the other man. "And this, I take it, is your husband, Sally? That famous deal-maker Scott Brainerd? Who worked for your father? Who probably married you because your father ordered him to?"

"Her name's Susan," the man said. "Sally is a little girl's name. I never liked it. I call her Susan." He took a step forward, then stopped. "You're looking a bit on edge, Susan, and no wonder. What are you doing with him? Noelle told me he's an FBI agent—"

"Special agent," Quinlan said, wanting to goad this little weasel until he gnashed his teeth. "I've always been a special agent."

"He caught up with her," Noelle said, "and he brought her back. I don't know why he's here, but we must convince him that since Sally isn't well, she wasn't responsible for killing her father. We can protect her. Dr. Beadermeyer can take her back to the sanitarium and keep her safe."

"Since Father's dead," Sally said, staring her mother right in the eye, "that raises a whole lot of questions. For example, since he's no longer with us, then who will come and beat me and fondle me and humiliate me every week?"

Her mother stared at her, her mouth working, but no sound came out. Her face was leached of color. She looked sick now, and uncertain. "Oh, God, no, Sally, that's not possible. Your father and Scott and Dr. Beadermeyer, they all told me every week how well you were doing, what fine care you were getting. No, this can't be true."

"She shouldn't speak of her dead father like that," Dr. Beadermeyer said.

"He's right. This just proves how ill she is," Scott said. "She's making this up. Amory beat his own daughter? Fondled her? That's crazy, she's crazy, she just proved it."

"It's classic," Dr. Beadermeyer said from his staged pose by the fireplace. "Some patients fantasize so strongly that they begin to believe what their minds dredge up. It's usually things that they've always wanted, deep down.

"Your father was a handsome man, Sally. Girls have sexual feelings about their fathers. It's nothing to be ashamed of. The only reason you fantasize that he's come to you is because you wanted it so badly. The beating part, the humiliating part, is so you can forgive yourself for these feelings by making yourself helpless so that you couldn't prevent it."

"That's really good," Quinlan said. "You're Dr. Beadermeyer, I take it. Such a pleasure to finally meet you."

"Sorry I can't say the same about you. I'm here to take Sally back with me, and even though you're FBI there's nothing you can do about it."

"Why did you try to kidnap her from the *Bonhomie Club* three hours ago?"

"Alfred? What's he talking about?"

"A mere misunderstanding, my dear Noelle. I found out where Sally was. I thought I could simply take her with no fuss no bother but it didn't work out."

"It didn't work out?" Sally repeated. "You tried to kidnap me and shove a needle in my arm, and all you can say is it didn't work out?"

He merely smiled at her and shrugged again.

"He brought two goons with him, Noelle," Quinlan said. "All three of them grabbed Sally when she came out of the bathroom and tried to give her a shot." He turned back to Beadermeyer. He wanted very badly to wring the bastard's neck. "We nearly got you, you miserable excuse for a human. At least you have to have your rear window replaced."

"No problem," Beadermeyer said. "It wasn't my car."

"What is going on here?" Scott said. "Noelle told me Sally escaped. Now she's with an FBI agent. Dr. Beadermeyer told me Sally met this man in this hick town in Oregon and they're lovers. That's not possible. Sally, you're still my wife. What's going on here?"

Quinlan smiled benignly at all of them. "Why don't you consider me a sort of lawyer for her? I'm here to see that you don't run all over her or that the good doctor here doesn't try to shove another needle into her."

He eyed Scott Brainerd. Tall, slim, beautifully dressed, but that handsome face of his looked haggard. There were dark circles beneath his eyes. He didn't look happy about any of this, and more, he looked scared. He should. Quinlan could tell that he wasn't carrying a gun. He was nervous, part of him always moving, his hands fidgeting. He pulled a pipe out of the pocket of his lovely English jacket. A shoulder holster would ruin the line of that jacket. The bastard.

Quinlan said nothing more, watched him light his pipe. He imagined he used the delay to good advantage when he was in negotiations. It also gave his hands something to do when he was nervous or scared, like now.

"You're the man who took Sally away from me, aren't you? You're the one who broke into the sanitarium?"

James smiled at Beadermeyer. "Yeah, right on both counts. How are the German shepherds? They're fine dogs, both with a taste for good raw steak."

"You had no right to break into my facility. I'll sue your butt off."

"Just be quiet, Alfred," Noelle said, "and you too, Mr. Quinlan. Sally, why don't you sit down? Would you like a cup of tea? You look exhausted. You need to rest. You're so thin."

Sally looked at her mother and slowly shook her head. "I'm sorry, Noelle, but I'm afraid you'd let Dr. Beadermeyer drug the tea."

The woman looked as if she'd been hit. She looked frantic. She took a step toward Sally, her hand out. "Sally, no, I'm your mother. I wouldn't hurt you. Please, don't do this. All I want is what's best for you."

Sally was shaking. James took her arm in a firm grip and led her to a small settee. He stayed close to her, knowing it was important for her to feel him beside her, feel the warmth of him, the solidness of him. He put his hands behind his head and eyed them all from beneath his lowered lashes.

He said to Scott Brainerd, who was now puffing furiously on his pipe, "Tell me about how you first met Sally."

"Yes, Scott, do tell him," Sally said.

"If I do, will you tell him to get out of our lives?"

"It's a possibility," Quinlan said. "Tell you what I can promise for sure. I won't throw Sally in the slammer."

"Good," Noelle said. "She needs to be kept safe. Dr. Beadermeyer will see to it. He's promised me he would."

Their litany, James thought, their damned litany. Was Noelle a part of this? Or could she be this gullible? Couldn't she really see Sally? See that she was perfectly all right?

Scott began to pace, looking at Noelle, who was staring intently at her daughter, as if to read her thoughts, then at Beadermeyer, who was lounging in his large wing chair, trying to copy the damned agent.

"I met her at the Whistler exhibition at the National Gallery of Art. It was an exciting evening. They were displaying sixteen of Whistler's Japanese paintings. Anyway, Sally was there partying with her friends, like she always did. One of the Smithsonian lawyers introduced us. We talked, then had coffee. I took her to dinner.

"That's how it began, nothing more, nothing less. We discovered we had a lot in common. We fell in love. We married."

Beadermeyer rose and stretched. "Vastly romantic, Scott. Now, it's late and Sally needs her rest. It's time for us to leave, Sally."

"I don't think so," Sally said, her voice as calm as could be. James felt the shaking in her arm. "I'm twenty-six years old. I'm perfectly sane. You can't make me go back with you. Incidentally, Scott, you didn't tell James why you neglected to mention that you worked for my father until after we were married."

"You never asked, did you, Sally? You were caught up with your own career, all your fancy parties and wild friends. You didn't really care what I did. You never asked."

"I asked, but you never came right out with it. You told me it was a law firm and left it at that. I remember asking you, but you wouldn't give much out, ever."

Quinlan felt the ripple beneath the flesh of her hand. He squeezed slightly but kept quiet. She was doing fine. He was pleased and optimistic. He was fast getting the measure of all three people. Soon, he thought, soon now.

Sally paused a moment, then said calmly, "I certainly didn't care after I found out you were having an affair."

"That's a lie! I wasn't having an affair. I was faithful to you. I've always been faithful to you, even during these past six months."

Noelle cleared her voice. "This is leading nowhere. Sally, you're saying that you're sane, that indeed your father abused you in the sanitarium—"

"So did Dr. Beadermeyer. He had this creepy little attendant called Holland who liked to bathe me, strip me, fix my hair, and sit on the side of my bed staring at me."

Noelle turned to Beadermeyer. "Is this true?"

He shrugged. "A bit of it. She did have an attendant named Holland.

He's gone now. Perhaps once he might have been out of line. These things happen, Noelle, particularly when a patient is as sick as Sally is. As for the rest of it, it's part of her illness—the delusions, the dark fantasies. Believe me, just as you believed your husband and Scott. Scott lived with her. He saw the disintegration. Isn't that right, Scott?"

Scott nodded. "It was frightening. We're not lying, Noelle."

Noelle St. John believed them. Quinlan saw it on her face, the look of new resolve, the new certainty, the profound pain she felt.

She said to her daughter, "Listen, Sally, I love you. I've loved you forever. You will get better. I don't care what it costs. You'll have the best care. If you don't like Dr. Beadermeyer, we'll find you another doctor. But for now, please, go back with him to the sanitarium so you can be protected.

"You were judged mentally incompetent by Judge Harkin. You don't even remember the hearing, do you? Well, no wonder. You were so ill, you sat through the whole thing, didn't say a thing, stared straight ahead. I spoke to you, but you looked through me. You didn't even recognize me. It was horrible.

"I'm your guardian now that your father is dead. Both Scott and I are, as a matter of fact. Please trust me, Sally. I only want what's best for you. I love you."

Scott said, "Agent Quinlan, you could hold her for a day, maybe, but that's all. The judge has already ruled that she isn't responsible for her actions. You can't do anything to her. No one would consider having her stand trial for the murder of her father."

She kept her head, though Quinlan knew that shook her. This was some group. He still couldn't make up his mind about her mother. She seemed so sincere, so caring, but . . . Now they seemed certain she'd murdered her father? It was almost time for him to intervene, but not yet.

Sally said, raising her hand to stem her mother's words, "Noelle, did you know that Dr. Beadermeyer kept me drugged all the time? I told you that my father came and beat me twice a week, but did you know that Dr. Beadermeyer watched? Oh, yes, Doctor, I know about that two-way mirror. I also know you let others look through the door window when my father was fondling himself while I was lying naked on the bed."

She jumped to her feet, and Quinlan was sure she was going to attack Beadermeyer. He lightly touched her arm. Her muscles were frozen. She yelled, "Did you enjoy it, you filthy slug?"

She whirled around to face her mother. "I don't remember the hearing because he kept me drugged up so I wouldn't fight him or any of his keepers. Don't you understand? There was no way they could let up on the drugs. I would have blown them out of the water. Did you also know that sometimes my father would have him lighten the dosage so I'd be more alert when he came to abuse me? That's right, Noelle, believe it. My father, your husband. I'm not lying to you. I'm not making this up to defend my shattered ego. My father was a monster, Noelle. But you know that, don't you?"

Her mother screamed at her, "No more of that, Sally! No more of your crazy lies. I can't stand it, I just can't."

Scott Brainerd shouted, "That's right, Sally. That's more than enough. Apologize to your mother for those horrible things you're saying about her husband."

"But they're all true, and you know they are, Scott. Father couldn't have had me committed without your being in on it. Why did you want me put away, Scott?"

"It nearly killed me to have you committed," Scott said. "Nearly killed me. But we had to. You were going to harm yourself."

To Quinlan's relief, Sally actually managed to laugh. "Oh, that's really good, Scott. You're a wretched liar. Now, Noelle, when my father was beating me, or just holding me down while he stood over me, he'd laugh, tell me how he finally had me right where he wanted me, where I deserved to be.

"Goodness, I remember it all now. He said it was his revenge for all the years I tried to protect you, Noelle. He said being in this nice place would keep my mouth shut about the other, but I don't know what he meant by that."

"I do," Quinlan said. "We'll get to that later."

She smiled at him and nodded, then turned back to her mother. "Did he tell you how much he hated me? But I guess locking me away wasn't enough for him. I guess he wasn't beating you enough, Noelle, since he had to come and beat me as well. Twice a week. Like clockwork. He was a man of disciplined habits. I was so drugged I sometimes didn't even know, but Holland, that pathetic little creep, he would say, 'Yep, every Tuesday and Friday, the old guy's here to knock you around and beat off.'

"Of course, I do remember many of the times, particularly when they lightened the drugs. It pleased him that I knew it was him and I was helpless to stop him doing anything he wanted to do."

Noelle St. John turned on Dr. Beadermeyer. "She is sick, isn't she, Alfred? This can't be true, can it? And not just Amory but Scott too. Why, he's sworn to me that she's very ill. Just as you have."

Beadermeyer shrugged. It was the man's favorite response, Quinlan thought. "I think she believes what she's saying is true. She really is very ill. Because she believed he did this to her, she had to murder him to assuage her own guilt. I told you how she managed to hide the sedatives beneath her tongue and escape the sanitarium. She came straight here, like a homing pigeon, took her father's gun from his desk, and when he came in, she shot him. You heard the shot, Noelle. So did you, Scott. By the time I got here she was standing over him, watching the blood leak out of his chest, and all of you were staring at her. I tried to help her, but she turned that gun on me and escaped again."

Quinlan sat forward on the sofa. Ah, now it would come out. It was time. None of this surprised him. In a few minutes it wouldn't surprise Sally either.

Beadermeyer turned to Sally, and his voice was gentle as a soft rain on the windowpanes. "Come, my dear, I'll protect you from the police. I'll protect you from the FBI, from the press, from everyone. You must leave this man. You don't even know who he is."

"Susan," Scott said, "I'm sorry for all this, but I know you couldn't help yourself. All those delusions, those dreams, those fantasies, Dr. Beadermeyer told us you had. You did shoot Amory; you had the gun in your hand. Noelle and I saw you holding that gun, leaning down over him. We only want to help you, protect you. We didn't tell the police a thing. Dr. Beadermeyer left before they even came. No one accused you. We've been protecting you all along."

"I didn't kill my father."

"But you told me you didn't remember anything," Noelle said. "You told me you were afraid I'd done it and that was why you ran away. To protect you, I made the police suspect me, acted as guilty as I could, even though I hadn't killed him. What saved me was that they couldn't ever find the gun. Neither Scott nor I ever told the police that we were practically witnesses to the shooting. In fact, Scott didn't even tell them he was here. That made me a better suspect. They couldn't find you. The police are certain that you know I did it and that's why you ran. But I didn't, Sally, I didn't. You did."

"And I know she didn't, Susan," Scott Brainerd said, his pipe dangling loose in his right hand, cold now. "I met her in the hallway, and we came into the living room together. You were there, leaning over him, the gun in your hand. You have to go with Dr. Beadermeyer or else you'll wind up behind bars."

"Ah, yes," said Quinlan. "The good Dr. Beadermeyer, or should I call you Norman Lipsy, from the fair nation of Canada to our north?"

"I prefer Dr. Beadermeyer," the man said, with exquisite calm. He lounged more comfortably in his chair, a man without a care, relaxed, at ease.

"What's he talking about?" Scott said.

"Your good doctor here is a fake," Quinlan said. "That little hideaway of his is nothing more than a prison where he keeps folks that family or others want out of the way. I wonder how much money Sally's father paid him to keep her? Maybe you know, Scott? Maybe some of it was your money. I'll bet it was."

"I am a doctor, sir. You are insulting. I will sue you for libel."

"I have been to the sanitarium," Noelle said. "It's a clean, modern facility. The people there couldn't have been nicer. I didn't get to see Sally simply because she was so ill. What do you mean, people pay for Dr. Beadermeyer to hold their enemies prisoner?"

"It's true, Mrs. St. John, the simple truth. Your husband wanted Sally out of the way. Was it his final revenge against her for trying to protect you? I'll bet that's sure one part of it."

Quinlan turned to Sally. "I think you might have wasted your time protecting your mom, Sally. It seems to me that she would as soon throw you right back to the hounds."

"That's not true," Noelle said, twisting her hands now. "Don't believe him, Sally."

Quinlan just smiled at her. "In any case, your husband, Mrs. St. John, paid Norman Lipsy here a ton of money every month to keep his daughter drugged to her ears, to let him come visit his little girl and abuse her. Oh, yes, he did abuse her, humiliate her, treat her like a little sex slave. We have a witness."

TWENTY-THREE

Dr. Beadermeyer didn't change position or expression.

Scott actually jumped. As for Noelle, she turned as white as the walls.

"No," she whispered. "A witness?"

"Yes, ma'am. FBI agents picked up Holland. Before we came here, they called. He's singing, Norman. His little lungs are near to bursting with all the songs pouring out of his mouth.

"It's not only Sally who was kept there. There's a senator's daughter. Her name is Patricia. Dr. Beadermeyer gave her a lobotomy—and botched it, by the way."

"That isn't true, none of it."

"Now, Norman, the FBI will be at the sanitarium shortly with a search warrant, and they'll go through that office of yours like ants at a picnic lunch. All your dirty little secrets will be out. I have a friend at the *Washington Post*. All the world will soon know your secrets. All those poor people you've kept at your prison will be free again.

"Now, given all this, Noelle, do you still want to put any stock in this guy's word?"

Noelle looked from Quinlan to Dr. Beadermeyer. "How much did my husband pay you?" It was suddenly a new Noelle—straight shoulders, no longer pale and fragile-looking, but a strong woman whose eyes were narrowed now, whose jaw was locked and hard. He saw rage in those soft blue eyes of hers.

"It was only for her care, Noelle, nothing more. Her case is complex. She's paranoid schizophrenic. She's been mentally ill for some time. We tried a number of drugs to relieve her symptoms. But we were never fully successful. This thing she dreamed up about her father—it gave her enough to focus to escape and come to kill him. It's that simple and that complex. I did nothing wrong.

"This Holland—poor fellow—I took him in. He's very simple in the head. It's true he attended Sally. He was very fond of her in his moronic way. Only a fool would believe anything he said. He'd say whatever anyone wanted him to say. They'll realize quickly enough that he'll say anything, just to please them."

"For someone who's not a shrink, you're not bad, Norman," James said.

"What do you mean he's not a shrink?" Scott said.

"He's a cosmetic surgeon. He deals with the outside of the head, not the inside. He's a fake. He's a criminal. And he watched your husband hurt his own daughter. I have no reason to lie to you, Mrs. St. John."

Dr. Beadermeyer said, "All right, Noelle, if you no longer believe me, no longer trust my word, then I won't take Sally back with me. I'll leave. I've got nothing more to say. The only reason I came here was to help Sally."

He took a step forward, but James was up in an instant. Three steps and he had Dr. Beadermeyer's tie in his fist. He said very softly, right in his face, "Who is paying you to hold Sally now that her father's dead? Scott here? If so, why? Why was she put away? It wasn't just revenge, was it?" Quinlan knew, but he wanted to hear it out of Beadermeyer's mouth.

"Noelle is paying me only for her regular treatment, the same as I've always received."

"You still want to lie, do you? Well, I'll be able to tell you, Mrs. St. John, exactly the amount your dear husband was paying this little bastard as soon as the FBI finishes going through all his crooked little books."

"I'm calling my lawyer. You can't do this. I'll sue you, all of you."

"If Mrs. St. John was paying you only for Sally's care, then why did you come to The Cove, knock both Sally and me on the head, and haul her back to your sanitarium? Did you bill Noelle for the airfare? And your little excursion to the *Bonhomie Club* with those two goombas—will you send Noelle a bill for their services? How about that rear window I shot out? Don't you bill for overtime, Norman? No comment this time? Don't you even want to insist that you're such a dedicated doctor that you'll do anything to help your poor patients?" Quinlan turned to Noelle, who looked as if she'd love to have a knife. She was looking at Dr. Beadermeyer with very new eyes. "When I got to Sally in the sanitarium she was so drugged it took more than a day to clear her out. That sounds like great treatment, doesn't it, Noelle?"

"Oh, I believe you, Mr. Quinlan. I believe you now."

Dr. Beadermeyer shrugged and looked down at his fingernails.

"Maybe," James said, "it's Scott here who wants his wife kept under wraps?"

"That's ridiculous," Scott Brainerd yelled. "I never did anything. All I did was tell her father how worried I was about her."

Noelle said very calmly, "No, Scott, that isn't true. You're lying as well. All of you lied to me. If it had been just Amory, I wouldn't have bought it for a minute, but no, all of you were like a Greek chorus, telling me the same thing over and over until I believed you. I allowed you to put my little girl in that damn institution!"

Quinlan quickly stepped out of the way when he saw her coming. She dashed to Beadermeyer and slammed her fist into his jaw before he even had a chance to twitch. He reeled back against the mantelpiece. Noelle stepped back, panting. "You bastard." She whirled around to face Scott. "You vicious little worm, why did you do this to my daughter? How much did my husband pay you?"

Sally rose from the sofa. She walked to her mother. She put her arms around her. "Thank you," she said against her mother's hair. "Thank you. I hope I can hit Beadermeyer myself before this is all over."

Sally wiped her damp hands on her pants legs. She felt such a surge of relief that it made her mouth dry. She actually smiled as she said to Scott, "I'm divorcing you. It shouldn't take long, since I don't even want my poor ivy plant that's probably already dead anyway. My lawyer will serve the papers on you as soon as I can arrange it."

"You're crazy. No lawyer is going to do a thing you say."

"If you take another step toward her, Brainerd, I'll have to kill you. That or I'll let Noelle at you. Look at poor Norman, his lip is bleeding. You know, I like the thought of Sally as a widow."

James walked calmly up to Scott Brainerd, pulled back his fist, and rammed it into his stomach. "That's for Sally, Noelle, and me."

Scott yelped, bent over, breathing like he'd been shot, his arms clutching his middle.

"Sally," James said, rubbing his knuckles, wanting to hit Scott Brainerd again but knowing it wouldn't be smart, "one of my sisters-in-law is a lawyer. She'll handle the paperwork on the divorce. Severing ties with this slug shouldn't be difficult. It takes six months. Maybe I should kill him. You want to try running away, Scott?

"Oh, yes, I forgot to tell you guys, the FBI is also all over the private books in Amory St. John's firm. They've been doing that for a while now. That's the real reason the FBI got involved in the first place. It's all delicate stuff, so that's why we've kept it under wraps, but there's no reason for you not to know.

"Selling arms to places like Algeria, Iran, and Syria—well, we do tend to frown on stunts like that. And that's got to be the other reason, Sally, that your father and your husband locked you away. They must have believed that you would say something incriminating, something to prove that they were traitors."

"But I never saw a thing, never," Sally said. "Is that it, Scott?"

"No, damn you. I didn't have a thing to do with that."

"And her father manipulated you into coming on to Sally, into marrying her?"

"No, that's not true. All right, so I did agree to have her put away. That's because I believed she was sick."

"Why did you believe I was sick, Scott?"

He didn't say anything, waved his pipe at her. "You weren't a good wife. Your dad swore to me your career was something for you to do until you got married. He said you were like your mother, a woman who really wanted a husband to take care of and children to look after. I wanted a wife to stay home and take care of me, but you wouldn't do it. I needed you there, to help me, to understand me, but no, you never stayed there for me."

"That doesn't make her sick, Scott," Quinlan said.

"I refuse to say anything more about it," Scott said.

"Why am I not surprised that Amory was a traitor?" said Noelle. "But I'm not. Then maybe one of his clients murdered him. Maybe it wasn't Sally after all. Such a pity it wasn't Scott who murdered him. That's what you were, isn't it, Scott, you pathetic jerk?"

Good, Quinlan thought, she was trying to explain her husband's murder another way. He was pleased. He said, "That's what he was, Mrs. St. John. Now, you said you walked in here with Scott and found Sally literally standing over him with the smoking gun."

Noelle was frowning, her mouth working. She was thinking real hard. "Well, yes, but she said that she'd heard the shot and come running. She said she had picked the gun up. She said she was here to get money from me and leave."

Quinlan pulled a folded piece of paper out of his breast pocket. He unfolded it and scanned it. "This is your statement to the cops, Noelle. No mention of Sally. Too bad a neighbor reported seeing her running from the house. But you tried, Noelle, you tried.

"Were you really with Scott that night? Did you really run in here with him to see Sally over your husband's body?"

Scott threw his pipe at the fireplace. It fell with a loud crack against the marble hearth. "Of course I was with her! I was with her all evening."

Scott was still rubbing his belly, and that made Quinlan feel good. That bloody little worm. He turned back to Noelle.

"I'm pleased you tried to protect Sally. But I did wonder if you weren't in it along with these other sterling characters."

"I don't blame you," Noelle said. "I'd think I was a jerk too. But I'm not. I'm just plain stupid."

Sally smiled at her mother. "I'm stupid too. I married Scott, didn't I? Just take a good look at him."

Quinlan said, "Listen, Noelle. Only a real bad person would turn on her daughter after what she tried to do for you since she was sixteen. She was just a girl, and yet she tried to protect you. I want you to tell me this isn't true. Tell me you didn't kill your husband. Tell me you didn't kill that monster who'd been abusing you."

"I didn't kill him, I didn't. You believe me, don't you, Sally? You don't believe I killed your father, do you?"

There was no hesitation. Sally took her mother in her arms. "I believe you."

"But there's so much more, Sally," Quinlan said, his voice soft and smooth, the promise of truth in that voice. "It's time now to get it all out. I want you to think back now. Look at Noelle and think back to that night."

Sally drew back, her eyes on her mother. Then, slowly, she turned to Quinlan. "I now have a clear picture of my father, lying right over there, blood all over his chest. I'm sorry, James, but I don't remember anything else."

"Your mother said you had a gun. You don't remember taking the gun with you, Sally?"

She started to shake her head, then she stared down at her brown boots.

Quinlan said, "It was an antique Roth-Steyr pistol your father probably bought off an old English soldier from World War One. It has a ten-round clip, ugly devil, about nine inches long."

"Yes," Sally said slowly, moving away from him, walking toward the spot on the floor where she'd found her father's body, right in front of his huge mahogany desk. "Yes, I remember that pistol. He was very proud of it. The English ambassador gave it to him back in the 1970s. He'd done him a big favor.

"Yes, now I can see it clearly. I remember picking it up now, holding it. I remember thinking it was heavy, that it weighed my hand down. I remember it felt hot, like it had just been used."

"It is heavy. The sucker weighs a bit more than three pounds. Are you looking at it, Sally?"

She was standing there, apart from him, apart from all of them, and he knew she was remembering now, fitting those jagged memory pieces together, slowly, but he'd known she could do it.

"It's hot, Sally," he said. "It's burning your hand. What are you going to do with it?"

"I remember I was glad he was dead. He was wicked. He'd hurt Noelle all those years and he'd never paid for it. He'd always done exactly what he'd wanted to do. He'd gotten me. There'd never been any justice, until now.

"Yes, I can remember that's what I was thinking. 'You're dead, you miserable bastard, and I'm glad. Everyone is free from you now. You're dead.'"

"Do you remember Noelle coming in? Do you remember her screaming?"

She was looking down at her hands, flexing her fingers. "The gun is so hot. I don't know what to do with it. I can see you now, Noelle, and yes, there's Scott behind you. But you have your coats on. You weren't here at the house, you'd been out. Just Father is here, no one else.

"You started screaming, Noelle. Scott, you didn't do a blessed thing. You looked at me like I was some sort of wild dog, like you wanted to put me down."

"We thought you'd killed him," Scott said. "He wasn't even supposed to be at home that night. He was supposed to be in New York, but he came back unexpectedly. You grabbed that gun and you shot him."

But Sally was shaking her head, looking not frightened but thoughtful, her forehead furrowed. "No, I remember when I got here I tried the front door. I didn't expect it to be unlocked, but it was. Just as I turned the knob, I heard a shot. I ran into this room and there he was, on the floor, his chest covered with blood.

"I remember—" She paused, frowning ferociously. Then she pressed her knuckles against her forehead. "It's so vague, so fuzzy. Those damned drugs you gave me—I could kill you for that."

Quinlan said, "He's in so much trouble now, Sally, that killing him would be letting him off lightly. I want to see him spend all his money on lawyers. Then I want to see him rot in prison for the rest of his miserable life. Don't worry about him. You can do this. It's all vague, but it's there. What do you see?"

She was staring down at where his body had sprawled, arms flung out, his right palm up. So much blood. There had been so much blood. Noelle had laid a new carpet. But there'd been something strange, something she couldn't quite put her finger on, something . . .

"There was someone else there," she said. "Yes, there was someone else in the room."

"How did you get the gun?"

She said without hesitation, "It was on the floor. He was bending down to pick it up when I came into the room. He straightened up real fast and ran to the French doors."

She turned slowly and looked at the floor-to-ceiling windows that gave onto a patio and yard. There were high bushes and a fence between this house and the one next door.

"You're sure it was a man?"

"Yes, I'm sure. I can see his hand opening the handle on the French doors. He's wearing gloves, black leather gloves."

"Did you see his face?"

"No, he—" Her voice froze. She began to shake her head back and forth, back and forth. "No," she whispered, looking toward those French doors. "It's not possible. It's just not possible."

"You see him now, Sally?" Quinlan's voice was steady and unhurried.

She looked at James, then at her mother, at Scott, and finally at Dr. Beadermeyer. She said, "Maybe they're right, James. Maybe I am crazy."

"Who was he, Sally?"

"No, no, I'm crazy. I'm delusional."

"*Who was he?*"

She looked defeated, her shoulders bowed, her head lowered. She whispered, "He was my father."

"Ah," Quinlan said. Everything was falling neatly into place, though not yet for the others.

Noelle whispered, "Your father? Oh, Sally, that's impossible. Your father was lying dead on the floor. I saw him, I went down on my knees beside him. I even shook him. It was your father. I couldn't be wrong about that."

Scott waved his pipe at her, shaking his head, saying, "She's bloody crazy, crazier than we thought. Your father's dead, Sally, just like Noelle said. I saw him dead too. Don't forget there were the two of us."

Dr. Beadermeyer said, "It's all right, Sally. It's another symptom of your illness. Will you come with me now? I'll call your father's lawyer, and he can come and make sure this man doesn't take you to jail."

Quinlan let all their voices float over him for a moment. He stood up and walked to Sally. He took her hands in his. "Well done," he said, leaned down, and kissed her.

"You bastard, that's my wife! I don't want her, but she still is my wife."

He kissed her again. "Everything makes sense now." He turned to Dr. Beadermeyer. "Now it all fits. You're a cosmetic surgeon, Norman. You must be very good at it. Where did you find the man whose face you reworked into Amory St. John's?"

"You don't know what you're talking about. The murdered man was Amory St. John. No one doubted it. Why should they? There were no questions."

"That's because there was no reason to doubt it. Why would anyone check dental records, for example, if the wife of the deceased identified the body, if the face on the body looked like all the faces on all the photographs on the desk? It does bother me though that the medical examiner didn't see the scars from the surgery. You must be very good, Norman."

"Did you really do that, Dr. Beadermeyer?" Scott asked. "Did you really plan with Armory St. John to kill another man and have him take Amory's place? Was he planning to leave me to take the fall? It's the truth, isn't it? I'd be the one blamed because he was supposedly dead. And I didn't do all that much, I swear. There was Sally, but that was necessary because we knew she'd read several short messages I'd forgotten were in my briefcase. There wasn't any choice. I went along with him because I had to."

Quinlan hit him again, this time in the jaw. He rather hoped he'd broken it.

Beadermeyer looked down at Scott, who was now lying on his side, unconscious. "What a piece of nothing he is, but that's not my problem. Now, Agent, all this is nuts. Armory St. John was the one who died. I've had enough of this. I'm sorry, Sally. I've tried to help you, but now I don't care. I'm leaving."

"When the devil leaves hell, you sadistic monster," she said "is when I'd go with you."

"Best you find another comparison, Sally," Quinlan said. "I know for a fact that the devil roams the world. We've got two of his minions right here. So Sally's father is still paying you. That surely answers the rest of my questions."

"I'm leaving," Dr. Beadermeyer said and walked toward the door.

"I don't think you want to leave just yet," Savich said, stepping into the room.

"When that worm wakes up I want to hit him," Noelle St. John said. "Well, maybe I won't wait." She walked over to Scott and kicked him in the ribs. "As for you," she said to Dr. Beadermeyer, "if only Agent Quinlan will give me a rubber hose, I'll work you over but good. What all of you did to my daughter . . . I'd like to kill you."

"I'll make sure you get that rubber hose, Noelle," Quinlan said.

"I'm going to sue all of you. Police brutality, that's it, and libel. Look at poor Scott."

Sally went over and kicked Scott in the ribs. Then she walked into her mother's arms.

TWENTY-FOUR

Savich nodded to Quinlan and smiled at Sally. "That was well done. Quinlan's good at helping people remember."

He turned to Dr. Beadermeyer. "I don't think you want to leave yet. I've got lots more buddies coming any minute now. And they're all special agents, which means they can shoot off the end of your pinkie finger at fifty yards and make you sing out every secret you've had since you were two years old. They're really very good, so it's best that you stay put, Dr. Beadermeyer."

Noelle was staring at Dr. Beadermeyer. "I hope you rot in the deepest pit they can find to throw you in. Now, you miserable bastard, where is my husband? Who was the poor man both of you murdered?"

"That's an excellent question," Quinlan said. "Tell us, Norman."

It happened quickly. Dr. Beadermeyer pulled a small revolver out of his coat pocket. "I don't have to tell you anything, you son of a bitch. You've ruined my life, Quinlan. I have no home, no money, damn you, nothing. I'd love to kill you, but then I'd never know peace, would I?"

They heard several car doors slam.

"It's too late to whine, Norman," Quinlan said. "Now you're going to the slammer. You might consider cutting a deal. Tell us where Amory St. John is hiding. Tell us the name of that guy whose face you rearranged. Tell us the whole sordid story."

"Go to hell, Quinlan."

"Not for many years yet, I hope," Quinlan said. "So it was Amory St. John who was continuing to pay you to keep Sally a prisoner. Was it indeed her father who followed her to The Cove and peered at her through her bedroom window that night? Were you with him? Did the two of you knock us out and take Sally back to your wonderful sanitarium? Yeah, that sounds right. It was Amory St. John on the phone to his daughter, his own face staring in at her through the bedroom window."

"It's all a lie, all of it. I'm leaving now. Come here, Noelle. I don't think anyone will shoot if you're with me."

Sally said, "My father must have been furious when I saw him run out of this room. He would have thought I'd shout it to the world. That's why he wanted you to keep me in the sanitarium."

"Don't be ridiculous, Sally," Dr. Beadermeyer said. "You're crazy. You escaped from a mental institution. Even if you'd spouted all this out as soon as the cops got here, no one would have believed you, not a single soul."

"But it would have raised questions," Quinlan said. "I would have wondered and chewed on it. I'm a real FBI nerd when it comes to things like that. I wouldn't have let it go. Sally's right. That's why you and her father wanted to keep her locked up. She was out of the way permanently. And her father still believed she knew he was a traitor, or at least suspected he wasn't a solid citizen."

"Shut up. Come here, Noelle, or I'll shoot your bloody daughter."

"How much money are we talking here, Norman? A couple million? More? It just occurred to me why you wanted Sally so badly. She was your insurance policy, wasn't she? With her, you didn't have to worry that Amory St. John would kill you. Of course, he could have killed Sally too, but that would have raised questions inevitably.

"No, better for him to keep paying you off until he came up with a bright idea to rid himself of you. Have I gotten anything wrong, Norman? I love real-life wicked plots. Novels can't even come close."

Dr. Beadermeyer waved the gun. "Come here, Noelle."

Scott stirred on the floor, shook his head, and slowly sat up. He moaned and rubbed his jaw. "What's going on here? What are you doing, Dr. Beadermeyer?"

"I'm leaving, Scott. If you want to come along, you can. We've got Noelle. The cops won't take a chance of shooting because they might hit her. Come here, Noelle." He pointed the revolver at Sally. "Now."

Noelle walked slowly to where he stood. He grabbed her left arm and pulled her tightly against him. "We'll go out through the French doors. Nice and slow, Noelle, nice and slow. Ah, Scott, why don't you stay put? I never really liked you, always thought you were a no-account loser. Yes, you just stay here."

"What you're doing isn't smart, Norman," Quinlan said. "Believe me, it isn't smart at all."

"Shut up, you bastard." He kicked open the French doors and pulled Noelle through them. Quinlan didn't move, only shook his head. Savich said, "You did warn him, Quinlan."

There were voices, two shots. Then dead silence. Savich ran outside.

"Noelle!" Sally ran through the open French doors onto the patio, yelling her name over and over.

They turned to see Noelle stumble toward her daughter. The women embraced.

Quinlan said, "Now, Scott, why don't you tell us which woman is your lover—Jill or Monica?"

"Neither, damn you. I'm gay!"

"Now that's a kicker," Quinlan said.

Savich came back in. There was a huge grin on his face. "Poor old Norman Lipsy's got a nice big nick in his arm. Unfortunately, he'll be fine."

"I'm glad about that," Quinlan said. "I want to see him rot in jail with Bubba, his future boyfriend."

"Scott is gay, James?" Sally stared at her husband. "You're gay and you married me?"

"I had to," Scott said. "Your father's ruthless. I'd only done a little fiddling with some clients' accounts, but he discovered it. That's when he got me into the arms deals and told me I had to marry you. He also paid me, but believe me, it wasn't enough to bear you for those six months."

Quinlan laughed and pulled Sally against him. "I hope this doesn't depress you too much."

"I think I'll kick up my heels."

They heard Dr. Beadermeyer cursing outside, then moaning, complaining loudly that his arm was bleeding too much, that he'd die from blood loss, that the bastards wanted him to die.

They heard Savich laugh and say loudly, "Justice. I do like to see justice done."

Sally said, "There's no justice yet. James, where is my father?"

He kissed her on the mouth and hugged her. "We'll check first to see if his passport is gone. If it isn't, we'll have him soon enough."

"Another thing," Savich said, "where is that bloody Roth-Steyr pistol?"

"I remember running after my father out the French doors. I threw it in the bushes."

"The cops would have found it. They didn't."

"Then that means her father saw her throw it away and doubled back to get it," Quinlan said. And he smiled. "That pistol IDs him better than fingerprints."

"That poor man Dr. Beadermeyer operated on. I wonder who he was?"

"I don't think we'll ever know, Sally, unless Beadermeyer talks. He was cremated. Damnation, all the clues were there, staring me right in the face.

Your father had made out a new will about eight months ago, specifying that he wanted to be cremated immediately. Norman Lipsy was a cosmetic surgeon. You were certain it was your father on the phone. I should have believed you, but I truly thought you'd heard some sort of spliced tape recording of his voice. We'll get him, Sally. I promise."

Quinlan took her home and made her promise to stay there. He had to go to the office and see how the investigation was going.

"But it's after midnight."

"This is a big deal. The FBI building will be lit up from top to bottom, well, at least part of the fifth floor."

"Can I come with you?"

He pictured thirty men and women all talking at the same time, going over reams of paper, one group reviewing what they'd recovered from Amory St. John's office, another group delving into Dr. Beadermeyer's papers.

Then there was Dr. Beadermeyer to interview—ah, he wanted to get Norman in a room alone, just the two of them and a tape recorder and go at it. He nearly rubbed his hands together.

"Yes," he said, "you can come, but agents will latch on to you and question you until you want to curl up in the fetal position and sleep."

"I'm ready to talk," she said and grinned up at him.

"Oh, James, I'm so relieved. Scott is gay and my mother wasn't in on anything. There *is* someone here for me besides you."

MARVIN Brammer, head of the Criminal Investigative Division, wanted her examined by FBI doctors and shrinks.

Quinlan talked him out of it. Sally didn't get to see him do it, but she bet he was very good.

She ended up talking at length to Marvin Brammer. He, without realizing it, was positively courtly with her.

By the end of the hour-long interview, he'd gotten even more details of that night from her. Brammer was one of the best interviewers in the FBI, an organization known for its excellent interview skills. Maybe he was even better than Quinlan, but she doubted if James would admit that.

When she came out of Marvin Brammer's office, Brammer behind her with his hand lightly holding her elbow, there was Noelle sitting in the small waiting area, asleep. She looked young and very pretty. She looked, Sally thought, just like she should look. But she was worried about her father. What if he got to Noelle again? What if he got to her? She'd said all that to Mr. Brammer, but he'd reassured her again and again that they would have guards on the two of them. There was no chance Amory St.

John would get near either of them. Besides, he couldn't imagine the man being that stupid. No, everything would be all right.

"That's my mother," Sally said. "Isn't she beautiful? She's always loved me." She gave Brammer a smile that would have disarmed a rabid cynic.

Brammer cleared his throat. He ran his fingers lightly through his thick white hair. The word was that his interview skills had increased exponentially when his hair had turned white overnight after a shoot-out five years before in which he'd nearly been killed. You looked at him and you trusted him.

"From what Quinlan told me—he insisted on talking to Scott Brainerd—it seems that Scott did indeed embezzle client funds on a very small scale. But your father caught him, and that was it. He did some of your father's dirty work, so your father really had him. Ah, you were right, he did have a lover, a guy named Allen Falkes, in the British embassy. I'm sorry."

"Actually, all of this comes as quite a relief. I'm not hurt, Mr. Brammer," she said, and it was true. "I'm just surprised by all of it. I've really been used, haven't I?"

"Yes, but a lot of people are used every day. Not as grossly as you've been, but manipulated by those who are more powerful, those who are smarter, those who have more money. But as I said, that won't be a problem anymore, Mrs. Brainerd."

"Call me Sally. After all this, I don't think I ever want to have the Brainerd name attached to me again."

"Sally. A nice name. Warm and funny and cozy. Quinlan likes your name. He said it was a name that made him feel good, made him feel like he'd always get a ready smile, and probably a good deal more, but he didn't add that. Sometimes Quinlan has discretion, at least when he's on the job—or rather, when he's talking to me, his boss."

She said nothing to that.

Brammer really didn't know why he was doing it, but this thin young woman who'd been through more than her fair share for a lifetime, who didn't know the first thing about getting information out of people, had made him spill his guts—and she hadn't said a thing.

Actually, he wanted to take her home with him and feed her and tell her jokes until she was smiling and laughing all the time.

He said, impelled by all the protective instincts she fostered in him, "I've known Quinlan for six years. He's an excellent agent. He's smart and he's intuitive. He's got this sort of extra sense that many times puts him nearly in another person's head—or heart. Sometimes I'm not sure which. Sometimes I have to rein him in, yell at him because he plays a lone hand, which we don't like to have happen. Bureau agents are trained to be team players, except for those in New York City, of course, and Quinlan down here at headquarters. But I always know when he's doing it, even though he thinks he's fooling me.

"He also has this knack for making people remember things buried deep in their brains. He did that with you tonight, didn't he?"

"Yes. But, on the other hand, Mr. Brammer, you got even more out of me."

"Ah, but that's because Quinlan opened the spigot, so to speak. Now, in addition to being one of the best agents in this office, he's a very talented man. He plays the saxophone. He's from a huge family sprawled out all over the East Coast. His father retired two years ago, a big-time investment banker. His first wife, Teresa, was a big mistake, but that's over with. He hunkered down for a while, rethought lots of things, and then he came out of hibernation, and he got well. Now he's met you, and all he can do is smile and rub his hands together and talk about the future. Treat him well, Sally."

"As in be gentle with him?"

Marvin Brammer laughed. "Nah, beat on him, give him a run for his money, don't let him pull any of his smart-ass pranks on you."

"Pranks?"

He gave her a surprised grin, then shook his head. "You haven't known him all that long. You'll see, once you're married, Sally. Maybe even before you're married. I've heard that Quinlan's daddy is just the same. But Quinlan has something his daddy doesn't have."

"What's that?"

"You," Marvin Brammer said. He touched his palm lightly to her cheek. "Don't worry, Sally. We'll get your father, and he'll pay for what he's done. Quinlan was talking a mile a minute to bring me up to date. He told me about your father calling you twice and his face appearing in your bedroom window when you were staying at your aunt's house in this small town called The Cove. Of course, he thought it was someone mimicking your father. He said you knew it was your father. And that scared you. He told me he'd never doubt you about anything again. Now, Sally, let's get honest here. It's not only the murder of that unknown man, it's not just what he did to you, although that turns my stomach—it's the dirty dealings he's been pulling for several years now, the arms sales to very bad people. The feds will chew him up for that, and that, naturally, is why we got involved in the first place after his murder. I'm sorry he had to be your father. We believe that's another reason he locked you away in Beadermeyer's sanitarium. He did believe, according to Scott Brainerd, that you had seen some compromising papers. You don't remember seeing any papers that could have implicated your father in the arms dealing?"

She shook her head. "No, really, Mr. Brammer. But you do believe this was one of the reasons my father had me admitted to Dr. Beadermeyer's sanitarium?"

"It sounds probable. The other thing—the revenge angle—it seems reasonable, but frankly I don't think it's enough of a motive in itself. No, I think it was a bunch of things, but primarily that he knew Scott was losing you, and thus he, Amory St. John, was losing control. And he believed you'd seen some incriminating papers about the arms deals. There's more than enough there, Sally. What was uppermost in your father's mind? I don't know. We'll never know."

"You don't know how much he hated me. I'll bet even my mother believes it's enough of a motive."

"We'll find out when we catch him," Marvin Brammer said. "Then we'll make him pay. I'm sure sorry about all this, Sally. Not much of a decent childhood for you, but there's rottenness in some people, and that's just the way it is."

"What will happen to Dr. Beadermeyer?"

"Ah, Norman Lipsy. If only we'd thought to put Savich on him earlier. That man can make a computer tap-dance. We all laugh that he's not a loner like Quinlan because he's always got his computer tucked under his arm, a modem wrapped around his neck like a stethoscope. He can get into any system on the planet. He's amazing. We kid him that he sleeps with the bloody thing. I think that even if someone gave him a turn-of-the-century telephone, he could invent a modem that would work. Agents in the bureau don't have partners like cops do, but Quinlan and Savich, well, they always do well together.

"Good Lord, why'd I get off on that? You wanted to know about Norman Lipsy. He'll go to jail for a very long time. Don't spend any time worrying about him. He refused to say a thing. Said that Holland was a moron and a liar. But it doesn't matter. We've got the goods on him."

She shivered, her arms wrapped around herself. He wanted to comfort her somehow, but he didn't know what to do.

He said, "Believe me, Lipsy is going down hard. We don't as yet know all the people he's holding there against their will. Our people will interview each one, look at each one's file, speak to all the relatives. It'll shake out soon enough. I think when it's all over, lots of very rich, very famous folk aren't going to be happy.

"Also, Lipsy's an accessory to murder. He's gone for good, Sally. No need for you to worry about him."

What had that man done to her? He couldn't imagine. He really didn't want to be able to.

When Quinlan walked up, his eyes alight with pleasure at the sight of Sally, all skinny and pale, her hair mussed, her eyes bright at the sight of him, Marvin Brammer wandered back into his office thinking he couldn't remember the last time he'd talked so much.

She would pry every secret out of Quinlan and he wouldn't even know what she was doing. Better yet, she didn't even realize the effect she had on people.

Good thing she wasn't a spy; they'd all be in deep shit. He was also mighty relieved her mama hadn't been in on the nastiness.

TWENTY-FIVE

Quinlan brought her home to his apartment, to his bedroom, to his bed, and now he was holding her, lightly stroking his hand up and down her back.

She was so very thin. He could feel her pelvic bones, the thinness of her arms through her nightgown. He had the urge to phone out for Chinese food—lots of sugar in Szechwan beef and pot stickers—but he decided he'd rather be doing what he was doing. Besides, he'd already stuffed her to the gills with spaghetti, lots of Parmesan on top, and hot garlic bread that wasn't nearly as good as Martha's.

"James?"

"You're supposed to be asleep."

"Mr. Brammer was very nice to me. He told me a thing or two about you, too."

Quinlan stared at her. "You're kidding. Brammer is the biggest closed-mouth in the FBI. If they gave awards for it, he'd win hands down."

"Not tonight. Maybe he was tired or excited, like you were. Yep, he told me lots of things."

This was interesting. Quinlan cleared his throat against her hair. "Um, was all he talked about—it was all the case and the players?"

"Most of it, but not all." He felt her fingers playing over his bicep. He instantly flexed the muscle. A man, he thought, he was just a man who wanted his woman to know he was strong. He nearly laughed aloud at himself.

"What was the 'not all'?"

"You. He told me about you and your father and Savich."

"You'll like my old man. He's a kick. He had a heart attack last year but he seems okay now, thank God. He makes you so mad you want to punch his lights out, and then in the next second you're clutching your stomach, you're laughing so hard."

"A lot like you. That's what Mr. Brammer said."

She was caressing his bicep again. He flexed again. A man was a man. He guessed there was no getting away from it.

"He also said that you liked to play a lone hand but that he always knew what you were doing even if you would swear he didn't know a thing."

"I wouldn't doubt it, that old con man. He's got moles everywhere."

"Maybe now he's got a mole who's living with you."

"That's okay," Quinlan said and kissed her.

She was soft and giving, but she wasn't with him, not yet, and he couldn't blame her at all for that. He said against her warm mouth, "There's only your father left, Sally. We'll get him. He won't get away. There'll be a huge scandal, a big trial. Can you deal with that?"

"Yes," she said, her voice suddenly very cold and hard. "I can't wait, actually. I want to face him down. I want to tell the world how he beat his wife. I want to tell the world what he did to me. James?"

"Yeah?"

"Was there another woman in my father's life? Someone he was going to leave the country with?"

"Not that we know of, but that's a good thought. We'll have to keep an eye on it. It's early, very early. As I said, we have people going through every scrap of paper in your father's house and at his office. Everything will be scrutinized.

"You ain't seen scrutiny until you've seen the FBI do it. As for our Norman Lipsy, the cosmetic surgeon, he won't be going anywhere even with the best lawyers he can buy. He'll be questioned by agents until at least next Wednesday. It doesn't mean a thing that he hasn't talked yet. He will. Already they've found more than enough evidence to convict him on innumerable counts—kidnapping, collusion, conspiracy, that's the beginning. Now, Sally, you're still withdrawn from me. What is it? What's going on?"

"James, what if I was wrong? What if I was still drugged up so that I saw things that weren't really there? What if it wasn't my father running out those French doors? What if it was someone else? What if I didn't see anybody? What if I did shoot him and all the rest—well, it's games being played in my mind."

"Nah," he said and kissed her again. "Not in a million years. If there's one thing I know, it's crazy. You aren't crazy. I'll bet you don't even get PMS."

She hit his arm—he flexed the muscle—and she giggled.

"Now that's a wonderful sound. Forget all that crazy stuff, Sally. You saw your father. There's not one single doubt in my mind or in Brammer's mind or in Savich's or, I'll bet, in Ms. Lilly's, when we tell her.

"Your father must have stopped, seen you throw that prized pistol of his away and gone back to get it. That in itself is convincing, don't you see? If he didn't go back for the gun, then where is it? When we find him I'll bet you a Mexican meal at Taco Charlie's that he's got that Roth-Steyr."

She leaned up and kissed his mouth. "Goodness, I hope so. You were so sure I'd remember."

"I prayed harder than I did when I was seventeen and afraid Melinda Herndon might be pregnant."

"I'm so glad I didn't shoot him, regardless of the fact that I would have liked to. I wonder where he is."

"We'll find him. His passport's still here. The agents had Noelle go through his safe at home and his safety-deposit boxes. He could have had another passport made, that's always possible. They found some bankbooks from the Caymans and Switzerland. We'll get him. It won't take long."

She was quiet, utterly still against him. He liked to feel her push against him, he liked her touching him. He was still on an adrenaline high, but she had to be exhausted. She'd been through quite an experience. He sighed. He settled for a light kiss on her mouth. "You ready to sleep now?"

"I have this feeling, James," she said slowly, her breath warm against his neck. "It's weird and I can't explain it, but I don't think he's gone anywhere. That is, I don't think he's left the country. He's here, somewhere. I just don't know where. We don't have a beach house or a mountain cabin that I know of."

"That's interesting. We'll ask Noelle tomorrow. Now come on, Sally, I'm supposed to be the one with the famous intuition, the hyper gut instinct. You trying to show me up?"

Quinlan shifted his weight. He was still wearing his pants and shirt. He wished he wasn't wearing anything. Sally was in one of her new nightgowns, a cotton thing that came nearly up to her chin and went down to her ankles. He wished she wasn't wearing anything either. He sighed and kissed her right ear.

He wished all the adrenaline in his body would clear out. He was high and horny. To distract himself, he said, "I forgot to tell you. I got a call from David Mountebank—you remember the sheriff, don't you?"

"He's very nice. He took care of you." He felt her fingertips lightly touch where the stitches had been in his head. "Hardly even a ridge now."

"Yes, well, he still hasn't got a clue about the two murders, and yes, Doc Spiver was murdered, no doubt about it. He wants FBI help, officially, and he'll get it since we're talking about interstate shenanigans. He's convinced everybody that the older couple—Harve and Marge Jensen—were killed around there and that all the other missing folks are linked together as well. There'll be agents from the Portland office, and I'll be there from the Washington office. They'll crawl all over that damned town."

She was kissing his neck, her fingers lightly tugging on his chest hair. He said slowly, "I'm going, Sally. And yes, Brammer knows I'm going. He thinks it's a good idea. He wants me to talk to Amabel. We all want to know how she fits into all this. And, believe me, she's got to fit in somewhere. I think you should consider coming with me, Sally."

He had weighed the danger of her being in that small little town on the Oregon coast against the danger of her remaining here, without him, her father still at large. No, he wanted her with him. It was the only way he could protect her. There'd be enough agents hanging around The Cove, no one would have a chance of hurting her.

"How could she be involved, James? She loves me, doesn't she? She took me in. She—"

"Don't turn blind on me now. She's involved. When she told David and me how you would probably run because you were scared, well, then I was as sure as I could be that she was involved. How deeply, we'll find out."

"I've got my mother back now. I'd sure like to have Aunt Amabel, too. I'm praying really hard that she isn't involved."

"Not only do you have your mama back, you've got me, and you'll never lose me, I swear it. And you'll have all my family. They're obnoxious, loving pains in the butt, all in all a great family. Now, if Amabel is somehow involved with all this, we'll deal with it, you and I together."

He felt her palm slide down his chest, felt her fingers slip inside his shirt to caress him. He nearly bowed off the bed. No, she was exhausted, he couldn't let her do this, not now, not tonight.

He'd made up his mind. No way was he going to rush her on this. He shook his head and said, "Sally, are you certain?"

"Oh, yes," she said and kissed his chest. "Let me get this shirt off you, James."

He laughed. He was still laughing when her mouth was on his belly. Then he moaned and jerked with the power of it. He didn't think he'd ever stop moaning, stop wanting, until he was deep inside her. That was what he wanted more than anything, for her to accept him completely, to love him, to shout it to him, and to the world.

And when he was deep inside of her, he knew it was right, better than right. She was his lifeblood, his future. It was about the best thing he'd ever managed in his life.

She whispered against his chest, "I love you, James." He was shaking, heaving over her like a wild man, but she was just as wild, and that made him even wilder.

A man, he thought just before he shattered, a man needed to belong as much as a woman. A man needed to be desired, to be cherished, as much as a woman.

When she bit his neck, then cried out, he knew everything would be fine. "I love you, too," he said, his breath warm in her open mouth.

Life, he thought, on the edge of sleep, was weird. He'd gone to The Cove to find a crazy woman who could have murdered her father.

Instead he'd found Sally.

Actually, life was dandy.

TWENTY-SIX

The day was warm, the air salty with the ocean spray, the sun high overhead. The Cove had never looked more beautiful, Quinlan thought, as he helped Sally out of their rental car.

"It's a picture postcard," she said, looking around. "There are the four old men playing cards around the barrel. Look, there are at least six cars parked in front of the World's Greatest Ice Cream Shop. There's Martha coming out of the Safeway with two sacks of groceries. There's Reverend Vorhees walking with his head down like he's got to tell someone that he's sinned badly. How could anything bad happen here? It looks perfect. All calm, nobody running around waving an ax, yelling, no kids ruining buildings with graffiti."

"Yeah," Quinlan said. He was frowning.

"What's wrong?"

He shook his head. His intuition. She poked him in the ribs. He grabbed her hand and said only, "It's too perfect. Why is that, I wonder? How did it get to be so perfect? Look at all that paint, Sally. It's fresh. Nothing's run-down. Nothing's old. Everything is in tip-top shape.

"But enough of this postcard place. We're meeting David and two FBI agents from the Portland office over at Thelma's at two o'clock. It's about two now."

"I'll meet them and then go to Amabel's house, all right?"

He looked worried, and she punched him again on his arm. "Do you think she's going to lock me in a root cellar? Don't be silly, James. She's my aunt."

"Okay. I'll be along as soon as I can. Make sure Amabel knows that."

David Mountebank looked tired. He looked harassed. When he introduced Quinlan to the man and woman agents, he didn't sound like a happy camper. He sounded like he was being bossed around, which occasionally did happen when the feds came in and treated the local law as yokels. It had happened a lot in the past, but not as much now. He sure hoped that wasn't the case here. In the sixteen-week training program at Quantico, agents were told never to usurp local prerogatives.

Maybe he was wrong. Maybe David was depressed about these killings. He knew he'd be as depressed as hell himself.

Corey Harper and Thomas Shredder didn't look too happy either. They all shook hands and sat down in Thelma Nettro's parlor. Martha came in and beamed at them. "Sally. Mr. Quinlan. How nice to see you again. Now, would everyone like some coffee? And some of my special New Jersey cheesecake?"

"New Jersey cheesecake, Martha?" Quinlan asked as he kissed her cheek.

"It's better than any cheesecake from New York," she said and gave Sally a brief hug. "You folks get on with your business. I'll be right back."

"How's Thelma doing, Martha?" Sally asked.

"She's primping right now. Not for you, Sally, but for Mr. Quinlan. She even had me go out and buy her some pumpkin peach lipstick, if you can imagine." Martha tsked and left the large parlor.

"I'd like to get to work here," Thomas Shredder said with enough impatience in his voice to make Quinlan want to loll back, lock his arms behind his head, and take a snooze, just to aggravate him.

Shredder was about thirty, tall and lanky, and very intense, one of those men Quinlan tried to avoid like the plague. They made him nervous simply because they never laughed, wouldn't know a joke if it bit them, usually saw the forest but never the individual trees.

As for the woman, Special Agent Corey Harper, she hadn't said anything yet. She was tall, with light hair and very pretty blue-gray eyes. She also looked eager, sitting on the edge of the sofa, her notebook on her knee, her ballpoint pen poised above an open page. She looked as if she hadn't been out of Quantico for very long. He'd bet the Portland office was her first assignment.

"Corey told me all the excitement you had back in Washington," David Mountebank said, ignoring Thomas Shredder. "That was something. You okay, Sally?"

"Yes, fine now. They still haven't caught my father, but James promises me they will. It's just a matter of time."

Quinlan thought that Thomas Shredder was going to explode. He smiled at the man and said, "I came here looking for Sally. I was a private investigator—that was my cover—hired to locate two old people who disappeared over three years ago in this area. And that was true. These folk did disappear in this area. Funny thing was that when I started asking questions, bad things started happening. Sally, tell them about the woman's screams."

She did, leaving out the fact that Amabel hadn't believed it was really a woman screaming.

"We came across a woman's body the following morning when we were walking down the cliffs," Quinlan said. "She'd been murdered and thrown off the cliffs. Not a very nice thing to do. It's difficult not to believe that this was the same woman Sally heard screaming on two different nights. She must have been held prisoner somewhere close to Sally's aunt's cottage. Why was she being held prisoner? We have no idea. Now, I'm willing to wager the farm that the murders are tied directly to these missing folks."

"Yes, yes, we know all this," Shredder said, and he actually swatted at Quinlan as if he were a fly to be removed from the bread.

"We also know your opinion about this so-called tie-in. However, as yet we don't have any real proof that there is a tie-in. What we've got is two murders, one a longtime local in Doc Spiver and the other a woman from the subdivision, not at all local in the same sense. What we need is a tie-in between the two of them, not between them and the disappearance of these old folk over three years ago."

"Well, then," Quinlan said, "David, why don't you bring me up to date. What have you done since I flew home last week?"

Shredder interrupted, his voice fast and sharp, "Sheriff Mountebank didn't do much of anything. Ms. Harper and I have been here since Monday, not long enough to solve the crimes yet, but we're getting close, very close."

Corey Harper cleared her throat. "Actually, David had collected interviews from just about everyone in town. They're very thorough, but no one could tell him much of anything. Everyone is shocked and very depressed about the deaths, particularly Doc Spiver's."

"We've already started to repeat the interviews," Thomas Shredder said. "Someone must have seen something. We'll get it out of them. Old people have difficulty remembering unless they're prodded just right. It takes special training to learn how to do it."

"Nah," Quinlan said. "I did it perfectly even before my training. Another thing, David knows all these people. He'd know when they were lying and what about."

"That remains to be seen," Shredder said. Corey Harper looked embarrassed.

Martha appeared in the doorway, a huge tray resting on her arms.

Quinlan got up and took it from her. "He's such a nice boy," she said to Sally.

"Right there, Mr. Quinlan. Yes, that's right. Now, I know you don't want me listening to all this important talk, so I'll leave you with everything. You'll manage?"

"Yes, thank you, Martha," Quinlan said. "How's Ed?"

"Oh, that poor man. Thelma won't leave him alone. Now she's accusing him of compromising me and she's going to buy a shotgun. He's in the hospital right now having tests for that prostate of his. Poor man."

Thomas Shredder looked at Corey Harper, then at the tray. She bit her lip and began to place cups on saucers. Quinlan grinned at her and began to do the same. Sally poured a cup and said, "Cream, David?"

Thomas Shredder sat there while everyone served each other. Quinlan gave him a big grin and pointed to the last cup on the tray. "Help yourself, Thomas. Ah, best hurry—I bet these New Jersey cheesecakes are going to be inhaled."

"My, this is beyond delicious," Corey Harper said and took the last bite of her slice of cheesecake.

"James and I want to ask Martha to come back to Washington with us," said Sally. "She's the best cook I know. Her pasta makes you weep."

Quinlan knew that Shredder was going to blow up any minute. Well, he'd pushed the ass far enough. He said easily, "Forget the interviews, Thomas. We need to come at this from another angle. I know it sounds weird that the missing persons would have anything to do with the two murders, but the thing is that up until about the time Marge and Harve Jensen disappeared, The Cove was a run-down old shanty of a town. No paint on anything, potholes in the road, fences falling over, even the trees sagging, all the kids gone, just old people left, living on Social Security. My question is, why is The Cove so different now from what it was three, four years ago? Why did everything here begin to wake up about the same time that Harve and Marge disappeared?"

Corey said, "I didn't realize the timing."

"I did," David said, "but I never questioned it, Quinlan, for the simple reason that it was common knowledge that Doc Spiver had come into a lot of money right around then. Since he didn't have any heirs, he invested the money and used all the proceeds to improve the town. But you don't think so, Quinlan?"

"I think it's worth checking into, closely. I remember you telling me that in Doc Spiver's will he left his estate to the town and it amounted to about twenty thousand dollars. If he was that low, then the town would start sliding again, really soon, don't you think? Makes you wonder, doesn't it?

"I'll call Savich—he's a computer nerd at the Bureau—and get him going on it. Tell me which bank and the account number, David. Sally and I will be staying here. Give me a call, and I'll get to Savich."

"Is that Dillon Savich?" Corey Harper asked, looking up.

"Yeah, he's a genius with a computer, but don't tell him that because he'll think you're sucking up."

"I know. I did tell him that when I was in training at Quantico. He gave a couple of great lectures, and yeah, he probably did think I was sucking up."

"I've never heard of this Savich guy, at least not more than three times," Thomas Shredder said. "Who cares about a computer nerd? They're fine in their place, but this is the real world. What we do here is what really counts. Let's get back to why we're here in this godforsaken place."

David said slowly, "Regardless of whether or not the missing persons are somehow involved in these murders, what you're implying in a very subtle way is a tough pill to swallow, Quinlan. I've known these people most all my life. They're a bunch of tough old birds; they've had to be to survive all the economic disasters we've had. That one of them is a murderer curdles my breakfast. More than one of them murderers? No way."

"It's more than a tough pill," Thomas Shredder said with a goodly dose of sarcasm. "You're paranoid, Quinlan. That's nuts."

Quinlan shrugged. "This town looks like a Hollywood set. I remember that was my first thought when I came here. I want to know why and how that happened."

"All right, we've got a lead," David said, leaning forward. "I'm going to check more closely into Doc Spiver's bank account. Now, I've gotten together all the accounts for all the missing persons reported in this area for the past four years." David drew a deep breath. "There's about sixty."

"Whoa," Corey Harper said.

"James is wrong about this," Sally said. "My aunt has lived here for more than twenty years. She couldn't be part of a murder conspiracy of this magnitude. She couldn't."

"I hope I am wrong, Sally," he said as he took her hand. It was cold. He poured her some coffee and put the fragile china cup between her hands to warm them. "But there's lots of questions here. I can't think of another way to go on this."

"I can't either," David said.

"Well, I can," said Thomas Shredder, rising to stand in front of the fireplace. He struck a pose, looking like Hercule Poirot ready to deliver his solution. All he needed was a mustache to twirl.

"I hope this is good, Thomas," Quinlan said. "We've paid our admission. Now on with the show."

"Pinning these murders on several of the townspeople just doesn't make sense. As to tying it all to David's missing persons, let's just forget about that."

"But, Thomas," Corey began, but he raised a hand to silence her.

"It's a theory, nothing more. What we've got is solid fact. Let's get specific. I looked into Reverend Hal and Sherry Vorhees. They've lived here for twenty-seven years, true, but before that, they were in Tempe, Arizona. They had two little adopted boys. The two little boys ended up dead within a year after they came to the Vorheeses. One fell out of a tree and broke his neck. The other one got himself burned to death when he turned on the gas stove. Both were accidents, at least that's what was reported and accepted. Everyone felt real bad about it, said the Vorheeses were the nicest people, and he was a reverend, and why would God take both their children?

"But there were questions. It seems a couple of other children had accidents during the time the Vorheeses lived there. Then the Vorheeses left and came here. There weren't any more children."

He waited for applause and he got it.

"That's something," David Mountebank said. "Good going, Thomas. You got any more?"

"There's also some history on Gus Eisner, the old guy who fixes everything on wheels in this town. Turns out his wife, Velma, isn't his first wife. His first wife was murdered. He was accused of the crime, but the DA never had enough evidence to bring him to trial. One month later Gus marries Velma and they move here. From Detroit. We've got to check on every single soul in this town. Corey's checking on the Keatons."

"Yeah, you're right. We've got to check on all of them," Quinlan said, at which the other man stared at him, utterly surprised, a flicker of pleasure in those dark eyes of his. "I hope it's one or the other. But it still doesn't feel right."

"Look, Quinlan," Thomas Shredder said. "Since the doctor was murdered, we looked all through his background."

"Well, Thomas," Corey Harper said, interrupting him, "actually David ran all the checks on him."

"Yes," David said, sitting forward. "He came here in the late forties with his wife. She died in the mid-sixties of breast cancer. They had two boys, both dead now, one in Vietnam, the other in a motorcycle accident in Europe. There was a rich uncle who died. That's all I could find out, Quinlan."

"Okay. If the money didn't come from Doc Spiver, then it had to come from someplace else."

An ancient throat cleared in the doorway, grabbing their attention.

"Well, now, you're back, Sally, and you, Mr. Quinlan. I hear from Amabel that the FBI has nearly everything cleared up back in that capital of ours, that foul den of iniquity." She paused a moment, shaking her head. "Goodness, I'd sure like to visit there."

Thelma Nettro had opened the door and was standing there, leaning on her cane, beaming at all of them, the pumpkin peach lipstick smeared, some of it on her false front teeth.

"Hello, Thelma," Quinlan said and rose to go to her. He leaned down and kissed her cheek. "You're looking like a French model. How's tricks?"

TWENTY-SEVEN

"You've got a smart mouth on you, boy," Thelma said in high good humor. She patted Quinlan's cheek. "Help me to my chair and I'll tell you all about my tricks."

Once Quinlan had her settled, she said, "Now, what's this I hear on FOX—that Sally's father killed a man he'd paid some cosmetic surgeon to make look like him? He locked you up, Sally? Then he skipped out?"

"That's about it, Thelma," Sally said. "My father is still free, more's the pity, but they'll catch him. His face has been all over the TV. Someone will spot him. He didn't leave the country, his passport isn't missing."

"He could have gotten another passport," Thomas Shredder said. "Even today it can be done."

"So, you got some more FBI agents here. You want to solve those murders, huh?"

"Yes, ma'am," Corey Harper said.

"We all thought Doc had killed himself, but that woman from Portland said it wasn't so."

"The medical examiner," David said. "I was lucky she's so well trained and was available. Otherwise it might have passed as a suicide."

"Poor Doc," Thelma said. "Who'd want to stick a gun in his mouth? It isn't civilized—you know?"

"No, it isn't."

"As for that young woman with the three children, well, that was a pity too, but after all, she wasn't one of us. She was from that wretched subdivision."

"Yeah, Thelma, she lived all of five miles away," Quinlan said, seeing his irony floating gently over Thelma's head. "Fact is, though, she did die right here."

Quinlan sat himself back down beside Sally on the brocade sofa. When he spoke again, Sally immediately recognized that voice of his, low and soothing, intimate. That voice would get information out of a turnip. "Now, did you ever meet that rich uncle of Doc Spiver's, Thelma?"

"Nope, never did. I don't even remember where he lived, if I ever did know. But everyone knew about him and how he was older than God and how if we could hang on a bit longer then he'd croak and Doc would get the money.

"Of course, I have money, but not as much as that rich uncle had. We were all afraid that the old codger would use it all up on nursing homes, but he up and died in his sleep, Doc said, and then Doc got that big fat check. More zeros than anybody in this town had ever seen before, I'll tell you."

"Thelma," David said, "do you know of anyone in town who could have met his uncle?"

"Don't know, but I'll find out. Martha!"

The screech hurt Sally's ears. She winced even as she smiled because Corey had jumped and dropped her pen and notebook.

"Healthy set of lungs," Quinlan said.

Martha appeared in the doorway, wiping her hands on her apron.

"What are you making for dinner, Martha? It's getting on toward four o'clock."

"Your favorite eggplant parmigiana, Thelma, with lots of Parmesan cheese on top and garlic bread so snappy it will make your teeth dance, and a big Greek salad with goat cheese."

"The uncle, Thelma," Quinlan said easily.

"Oh, yes. Martha, did you ever meet Doc Spiver's rich uncle?"

Martha frowned deeply, then slowly shook her head. "No, just heard about him for years. Whenever things were looking real bad, we'd talk about him, discuss how old he was, what kind of ailments he had, try to figure out when he'd pass on. Don't you remember, Thelma? Hal Vorhees was always telling us we were ghouls, that it surely had to be a sin to discuss that poor old man, like we were holding prayer meetings for him to die."

"We were," Thelma said. "I'll bet Hal did a little praying when none of us were around. Well, I wasn't praying for myself because I wasn't poor like the rest of the town, but when Doc got that check, I was shouting along with everyone else."

"You've lived here since the forties, haven't you, Thelma?" David asked.

"Yes. I came here with my husband, Bobby Nettro, back in 1949. We already had grown kids, and we were rattling around in that big old house in Detroit. Came out here and decided this was the place for us." She gave a lusty sigh that sent a whistling sound through her false teeth. "Poor Bobby, he passed on in 1956, right after Eisenhower was reelected. He died of pneumonia, you know.

"But he left me well off, real well off. I got Martha to come live with me in the early seventies, and we did just fine. She was teaching school over in Portland, and she didn't like it, all those gangs and drugs and that young lust. Since I knew her mama before she passed on, I also knew Martha. We all kept in touch. But you know, Quinlan, I did fail her mama. I still can't find Martha a husband, and I promised her I would. Lord knows, I've been looking for more years now than I've got teeth."

"You don't have any teeth, Thelma," Martha said. "Why don't you chew on that nice pumpkin peach lipstick and think about that eggplant parmigiana?"

"Well, I used to have a healthy set of choppers. I'll tell you, Quinlan, it don't seem to matter how revved up she gets and how much she sticks her bosom out there for the old codgers to ogle. Now, take poor Ed—"

Martha rolled her eyes and left the room.

"Well, actually, could you tell us about your kids, Thelma?" Quinlan asked.

"Two boys, one died in the war—the Big War, not Korea or Vietnam. The other one, well, he lives back in Massachusetts. He's retired now, has grown-up grandkids, and they got kids, and that makes me so old I can't bear to think about it."

Sally smiled as she stood up and walked over to kiss Thelma's soft, wrinkled cheek. "I'm going to see Amabel now, Thelma, but James and I will be staying here in the tower room."

"You still taking advantage of him, huh, Sally? Poor little boy, he doesn't have a chance. The first time I saw the two of you together I knew you'd have his pants off him in no time at all."

"Thelma, have a piece of my New Jersey cheesecake."

Thelma turned to frown at Martha, who had just come back into the room with another tray of her cheesecakes.

"You're such a prude, Martha, such a prude. I'll just bet Ed has to beg for every little favor."

"I'll see you later," Sally said, grinning back at the two dumbstruck special agents from Portland, James, and David Mountebank.

"I'll be along shortly, Sally," Quinlan said. He was already asking

Thelma more questions when Sally went out the front door of Thelma's Bed and Breakfast.

The day was beautiful, warm, just a slight nip in the air, the salty tang swept in from the ocean soft as a bird's wing on her face.

Sally breathed in deeply. Sherry Vorhees was standing in front of the World's Greatest Ice Cream Shop. Sally waved, and Sherry waved back. Helen Keaton, whose grandmother had invented the ice cream recipe, came out of the shop behind her, looked over at Sally, and waved herself. Such nice women. Surely they couldn't know anything about the murders or those missing people.

"Our flavor this week is banana walnut cream," Helen called out. "Do come and try it with your Mr. Quinlan. My granny didn't exactly make it, but I like to try new flavors. Ralph loves the banana walnut, says it's so good it's got to be real bad for you."

Sally remembered that Ralph Keaton was the undertaker. She saw old Hunker Dawson, the World War Two veteran, who always wore his two medals across the pocket of his flannel shirts. He hiked up his baggy pants and yelled, "You're famous, Sally Brainerd. We didn't find out until after you'd left that you were crazy. But now you're not even crazy, are you? I think the news media were pissed about you not being crazy. They like crazy and evil better than innocence and victims."

"Yeah," Purn Davies called out, "the media all wanted you to be crazier than a loon and out offing folk. They sure didn't want to report that you weren't crazy. Then, though, they got your daddy."

"I'm glad they finally did," Sally called.

"Don't you worry none about your daddy, Sally," Gus Eisner yelled. "His face has been shown more times than the president's. They'll get him."

"Yeah," Hunker Dawson yelled. "Once the media get their hooks in him all right and proper, they'll forget everything else. They always do. It's always the grossest story of the day for them."

"I sure hope so," she yelled back.

"My wife, Arlene, was wavering on her rocker," Hunker shouted matter-of-factly, tugging on his old suspenders. "Wavering for years before she passed over."

Purn Davies yelled, "Hunker means she was a mite off in her upper works."

"These things happen," she said, but probably not loud enough for them to hear.

The four old men had suspended their card game and were all looking at Sally. Even when she turned away, she knew they were watching her as she walked down that beautiful wooden sidewalk, the railing all fresh white paint, toward Amabel's cottage. She saw Velma Eisner, Gus's wife, and waved to her. Velma didn't see her, just kept walking, her head down, headed for Purn Davies's general store.

Amabel's cottage looked fresh as spring, with newly planted beds of purple iris, white peonies, yellow crocus, and orange poppies, all perfectly arranged and tended. She looked around and saw flower boxes and small gardens filled with fresh flowers. Lots and lots of orange poppies and yellow daffodils. What a beautiful town. All the citizens took pride in how their houses looked, how their gardens looked. Every short sidewalk was well swept.

She wondered if The Cove now had a sister Victorian city in England.

She thought about what James had said about all those missing people. She knew the direction of his thoughts, but she wouldn't accept it.

She just couldn't. It was outrageous. She stepped onto Amabel's small porch and knocked on the door.

No answer.

She knocked again and called out.

Her aunt wasn't home. Well, she'd doubtless be back soon.

Sally knew where she wanted to go, had to go.

SHE stood in the center of the cemetery. It was laid out like a wheel, with the very oldest graves in the very center. It was as well tended as the town. The grass was freshly mowed, giving off that wonderful grass scent. She laid her hand lightly on top of a marble headstone that read:

ELIJAH BATTERY
BEST BARTENDER IN OREGON
DIED JULY 2, 1897
81 RIPE YEARS

The lettering grooves had been carefully dug out and smoothed again. She looked at other headstones, some incredibly ornate, others that had begun as wooden crosses and had obviously been replaced many times. Those that hadn't weathered well had been replaced.

Was nothing in this town overlooked? Was everything to be perfect, including every headstone?

She walked out from the center of the cemetery. Naturally, the headstones became newer. She finished with the 1920s, the 1930s, the 1940s, all the way to the present. The planners of the cemetery had been very precise indeed, working outward from the middle so that if you wanted to be buried here now, you'd be nearly to the boundaries.

She found Bobby Nettro's grave, on the fourth circle out from the center. It was perfectly tended.

As far as she could tell, they'd kept to this wheel plan since the beginning. There were so many graves now. She imagined that when the first townspeople decided to put the cemetery here they'd considered the plot of ground they were setting aside to be immense. Well, it wasn't. There was little space left, since the west side of the cemetery was bounded by the cliffs, and the east and north were bounded by the church and someone's cottage. The south nearly ran into the single path that led along the cliff.

She walked to the western edge of the cemetery. The graves here were new, as well tended as the others. She leaned down to look at the headstones. There were names, dates of birth and death, but nothing else. Nothing clever, nothing personal, nothing about being a super husband, father, wife, mother. Just the bare information.

Sally pulled a small notebook out of her purse and began to write down the names on the headstones. She walked around the periphery of the cemetery, ending up with a good thirty names. All the people had died in the early two-thousands to this year, two months before.

It didn't seem right. Thing was, this was a very small town, grown smaller with each decade. Thirty people had died in a period of only five years? Well, it was possible, she supposed. Some kind of flu epidemic that killed off old folk.

Then she noticed something else and felt the hair rise on her arms.

Every one of the headstones bore a man's name. Not a single woman's name. Not one. Not a single child's name. Not one. Only men's names. On one of the graves, it said BILLY with a date of death. Nothing more. What was going on here? No women died during this period of time, just men? It made no sense.

She closed her eyes a moment, wondering what the devil she'd discovered. She knew she had to get this list to David Mountebank and to James. She had to be sure that these people had lived here and died here. She had to be sure that these people had nothing to do with all the reported missing folk. The thought that there might be a connection made her want to grab James and run out of the town as fast as she could.

She shook her head even as she stared down at one headstone in particular. The name was strange—Lucien Gray. So it was an odd name; it didn't matter. All these names were legitimate, they had to be. These were all local people who'd just happened to die during this four-year stretch. Yeah, and only men died. She found herself looking for Harve Jensen's grave. Of course there wasn't one. But there was that one headstone with Lucien Gray scripted on it. It looked very new, very new indeed.

She was beginning to sweat even as her brain raced ahead.

No, no. This town was for real.

This town was filled with good people, not with evil, not with death, more death than she could begin to imagine.

She put her notebook back in her purse. She didn't want to go back to Amabel's cottage.

She was afraid.

Why had that poor woman whose screams she'd heard on two different nights been taken prisoner in the first place?

Had she seen something she shouldn't have seen? Had she heard something she shouldn't have heard?

Why had Doc Spiver been murdered? Had he killed the woman and someone else in town found out about it and shot him so there would be a kind of justice?

She tried to empty her mind. She hated to be afraid. She'd been afraid for too long.

TWENTY-EIGHT

She stopped at the World's Greatest Ice Cream Shop. Amabel wasn't there, but Sherry Vorhees was.

"Sally, how good to see you. You here with that cute Mr. Quinlan?"

"Oh, yes. Can I try the banana walnut?"

"It's yummy. We've sold more of this flavor in a week than any other in the history of the store. We have so many repeat customers now—coming in regularly from a fifty-mile radius—that we might have to hire on some of those lazy old codgers out there playing cards around their barrel."

Velma Eisner came in from the back room, which was curtained off from the shop by a lovely blue floral drape. She snorted. "Yeah, Sherry, I can just see those old coots selling ice cream. They'd eat it all and belch at us and try to look pathetic."

She turned to Sally and smiled. "We discussed having the men involved. Of course, they'd grouse and complain and say it was women's work. But we decided to keep them out of it just so we'd be the ones bringing in all the profits."

"You're probably right," Sally said and accepted her ice cream cone. She took a bite and thought her taste buds had gone to heaven. She took another bite and sighed. "This is wonderful. I wonder if Helen would marry me."

The women laughed.

Sherry said, "We've come a long way since we used to store ice cream in Ralph Keaton's caskets, haven't we, Velma?"

Velma smiled as she took $2.60 from Sally.

Sally took another bite. "I went to Amabel's cottage, but nobody's home."

Helen came in from the back room. "Hi, Sally. Amabel went to Port-land."

"For art supplies and shopping," Velma said. "She'll be back in a couple of days, she said. Probably by Friday."

"Oh."

She licked at the ice cream, felt the taste explode in her mouth, and closed her eyes. "This has to be more sinful than eating three eggs a day."

"Well," Helen said, "if you eat only one ice cream cone a week, what does it matter?" She turned to say to Velma, "I saw Sherry eat three cones last Tuesday."

"I did not!"

"I saw you. They were all double dip chocolate."

"That's stupid! I did not."

The three women started sniping at each other. It was obvious they'd been doing this for years. They knew each other's red buttons and were pushing them with abandon. Sally watched, eating her banana walnut ice cream cone. Velma had the last word. Before Sherry or Helen could pipe up, she turned to Sally. "No, we won't let the men get behind the counter. They'd eat everything."

Sally laughed. "I'd be as bad as the men. I'd eat the entire stock in one morning." She finished her cone and patted her stomach. "I don't feel quite so skinny now."

"Stay here, Sally, and you'll look all pillowy and comfortable like us in no time," Sherry Vorhees said.

"I was admiring the town," Sally said. "It's so beautiful, so utterly perfect. And all those flowers, every spring flower that will bloom is out and planted and wonderfully tended. Even the cemetery. The grass is mowed, the headstones are well cared for. I was wondering if you ever forgot anything at all that would make the town look even more perfect?"

"We try to think of everything," Helen said. "We have a town meeting once a week and discuss improvements or things that should be repaired or brought up to date."

"Whatever were you doing in the cemetery?" Velma asked, as she wiped her wet hands on her apron, the same cute blue floral pattern as the drape.

"Oh, just wandering around after I realized that Amabel wasn't at home. I noticed something kind of unusual."

"What was that?" Helen asked.

For a moment, Sally wondered if she shouldn't just keep her mouth shut. But no, these women were sniping at each other about ice cream, for heaven's sake. They knew who had died and when. They'd tell her. Why, not? There was nothing frightening going on here. "Well, there were about thirty graves on the perimeter of the cemetery. All of them were men. There was nothing special on the headstones, only a name and date of birth and death. The older headstones have personal stuff. There was one in particular, just said BILLY. I thought it was strange. Maybe everyone got tired of being personal. So many men died, not a single woman. You must have been surprised at that."

Sherry Vorhees sighed deeply and shook her head. "A terrible thing it was," she said. "Hal was so depressed that we lost so many of the flock in those years. And you're right, Sally, it was all men who died. All different reasons for their deaths, but it still hurt all of us."

Helen Keaton said quickly, "Don't forget that quite a few of those deaths came from folk living in the subdivision. Their relatives thought our cemetery was romantic, set near the cliff as it is, with the sea breezes blowing through. We let them bury their dead here."

"Did that poor woman Mr. Quinlan and I found at the base of the cliffs get buried here?"

"No," Velma Eisner said. "Her husband was a rude young man. He was yelling around that we were somehow responsible. I told him to look at our muscles and do some thinking. As if we could have had something to do with his wife's death. He stormed out of here."

"He didn't even buy an ice cream cone," Helen said. "We had vanilla with fresh blueberries that week. He's never been back."

"Well, that wasn't very nice of him," Sally said. "I've got to go now.

Thank you for the ice cream." She turned at the door. "I didn't see Doc Spiver's grave."

"He isn't there," Velma said. "He wanted to be cremated and sent back to Ohio. He said there was no way he was going to let Ralph Keaton lay him out."

Helen Keaton laughed. "Ralph was put out, I can tell you."

"No, Helen," Sherry said. "Ralph was pissed. Put out is something you are when Ralph doesn't throw his shorts in the hamper."

The women laughed, Sally along with them. She walked straight across the street to Thelma's Bed and Breakfast.

SHERRY Vorhees flipped the curtain back down on the windows of the World's Greatest Ice Cream Shop. She said to the two other women, "There are three FBI agents in town and Sheriff David Mountebank."

"Those big shots should keep everyone safe," Velma said.

"Oh, yes," Helen said, slowly licking a swipe of ice cream off her fingers. "Safe as bugs in a miner's winter blanket."

QUINLAN finally hung up the phone. "It took a while to read out all those names and dates. Savich is on it. Finding out all the stats will be a piece of cake for him. He'll get back to us soon."

Sally said slowly, "I told the women at the World's Greatest Ice Cream Shop that I hadn't seen Doc Spiver's grave. They told me he was cremated and sent back to Ohio."

"Interesting," Quinlan said, and picked up the phone. "Savich? It's Quinlan again. Find out if a Doc Spiver was cremated and sent back to Ohio, okay? No, it isn't as important as the other names, just of interest to Sally and me. Supposedly Doc had no relatives alive. So why would they cremate him and not bury him here in their own cemetery?

"Now, don't say that. It isn't polite. I bet Sally heard that. Yes, she did, and she's shaking her head at your language."

He was grinning, still listening. "Anything else? No? All right, call us as soon as you've got something. We're staying here for dinner and the evening." When he hung up, he was still grinning. He said to Sally, "I love to hear Savich curse. He doesn't do it well, just keeps repeating the same thing over and over. I tried to teach him more vocabulary—you know, some phrases that connected a good number of really bad words, animal parts, metaphysical parts, whatever—but he couldn't get the hang of it." He gave her some examples, adopting a different pose for each example. "Here's the one that Brammer does best, but only when he's really pissed at one of the agents."

She rocked back on the bed, she was laughing so hard. Then she sobered. Laughing?

"Stop it, Sally. It's fine to forget. It's great to hear you laugh. Keep doing it. Now let's go have Martha's cooking."

It was a feast, better than Thanksgiving, Corey Harper said. Martha brought in a huge platter with a pot roast in the center, carrots, potatoes, and onions placed artistically around it. There was a huge Caesar salad with tart dressing, garlic bread that indeed made your teeth snap, and for dessert, an apple crisp. And there was eggplant parmigiana on the side. Thelma hadn't waited. She'd wanted her eggplant at four-thirty.

Martha appeared at precisely the right times to refill their wineglasses with the nicest Cabernet Sauvignon anyone had tasted in a long time.

She clucked primarily around the men, encouraging them to eat, until finally Quinlan dropped his fork, sat back in his chair, and groaned. "Martha, any more and God will strike me down for gluttony. Look at David—his shirt buttons are about to pop off. Even Thomas, who's skinny, would fill out in no time here with you. Since I'm polite, I won't refer to how much the women poked down their gullets."

Sally threw the rest of her garlic bread at him. She turned to a beaming Martha. "You said apple crisp, Martha?"

"Oh, yes, Sally, with lots of Basque vanilla ice cream from the World's Greatest Ice Cream Shop."

They had coffee with Amaretto, a treat from Thelma—who was eating in her room since Quinlan had worn her out earlier with all her talk, or so she claimed according to Martha. Actually, Thelma had to sleep off all that eggplant parmigiana she'd eaten.

After Martha returned to the kitchen, Sally told Thomas Shredder, Corey Harper, and David Mountebank, who had easily been persuaded to return for dinner and another conference, about the cemetery.

Quinlan said, "I called Savich. Knowing how fast he is, I'll probably hear back from him tonight. If it's something weird, I'll wake all of you up."

"I don't know if anyone will be able to wake me up," David said, as he sipped at his coffee. "Forget the coffee as a stimulant. This is the best Amaretto I've ever tasted. I'm already feeling like I want to put on my jammies. I hope my girls don't try to climb up my body when I get home. With luck, Jane will already have them in bed."

Sally didn't say anything. She hated Amaretto, always had. She'd taken one drink, then discreetly poured her coffee into Quinlan's cup while Corey Harper was telling a story about a guy at Quantico who'd arrested some visiting brass by mistake after a bank robbery in Hogan's Alley, the fake USA town set up for training. The biggest of the brass had thought it a great exercise until one of the trainees had clapped handcuffs on him and hauled him off.

Quinlan promised he would call if Savich found out anything urgent. But he couldn't imagine waking up even if the phone rang off the wall.

"I think you're tipsy," he told Sally as he held her up with one arm and unlocked the tower room door with the other.

"I'm tipsy?"

"I think Ms. Lilly would get a kick out of seeing you now."

"Next time I see her, I'll have to tell her that even though I was tipsy I had your pants off you in record time."

She was laughing so hard that when she jumped on him, he wrapped his arms around her back and brought her down to the bed, on top of him. He was kissing her, his breath warm with the tart taste of Amaretto.

"For a small favor I won't tell Martha what you did. You know, pouring your Amaretto in my coffee cup. Now, what's this about getting my pants off?"

She tried to give him a sultry look. He nearly doubled over laughing. Then she touched him and he groaned, his laughter choking in his throat. His eyes closed, his neck muscles convulsed.

He began kissing her, his tongue in her mouth, and she loved the feel of him, the taste of him. His hands were strong, kneading her, pressing her against him. He was hard as the bars on her windows at Beadermeyer's sanitarium. Oh, God, why had she thought that?

She felt a shiver of cold. No, that was only a horrible memory that belonged in the past. It couldn't touch her now. She kissed him again. His mouth was slack. He wasn't so hard now against her belly. He wasn't rubbing his palms over her.

She lifted herself on her elbows and stared down at him, preparing to see him wink at her, preparing to have him toss her over onto her back.

"James?"

He smiled vaguely at her, not moving, not winking, nothing. "I'm tired, Sally," he said, his words soft and slurred. "Aren't you?"

"A bit," she said, leaned down, and kissed him again. Suddenly he closed his eyes, and his head fell to the side.

"James? James!"

Something was wrong. He wasn't teasing her. Something was very wrong. She pressed her fingers to the pulse in his throat. Slow, steady. She flattened her palm over his heart. The beat was solid and slow. She lifted his eyelids and called his name again. She slapped his face.

No response.

He was unconscious. The damned coffee had been drugged. She'd had only a single sip of it, and that's why she was still conscious. There was no other explanation. She tried to pull herself off Quinlan, and she did manage it, but her arms and legs felt soft and wobbly. One drink of that amaretto was doing this to her?

She had to get help. She had to get to Thomas Shredder and Corey Harper. They were staying down the hall. Not far, not far at all. Oh, God, they'd drunk the coffee too. And so had David, and he was driving. She had to see if Thomas and Corey were unconscious. She had to go to their rooms and see. She could make it.

She fell off the bed and rolled. She lay there a moment on her back, staring up at the beautiful molding that ran around the edge of the ceiling. There were even Victorian cherubs at each corner, naked, holding up harps and flowers.

She had to move. She got herself up on her hands and knees. What room was Corey Harper in? She'd told her, but she couldn't remember. Well, it didn't matter, she would find both of them. Their rooms had to be close. She crawled to the door. Not far at all. She managed to stretch up and turn the knob to open the door.

The hallway stretched forever to her left, the lighting dim and shadowy. What if the person who had drugged the coffee was waiting in those shadows, waiting to see if someone didn't succumb to the drug, waiting to kill that person? She shook her head and managed to heave herself to her feet. She made her feet move, one step at a time, that was all she needed to do, one foot in front of the other. She'd find Thomas and Corey. Finally, a door appeared on her left—number 114. She knocked.

There was no answer.

She called out, her voice only a miserable whisper, "Thomas? Corey?"

She knocked again. Still no answer. She turned the knob. To her surprise, the door opened. It opened quickly, and she stumbled into the room, her knees buckling under her. She fell on her side.

She called out, "Thomas? Corey?"

She managed to get onto her hands and knees. There was only a single lamp burning, on top of the bedside table. Thomas Shredder was lying on his back, his arms and legs sprawled out away from his body. He was unconscious. Or he was dead. She tried to scream. She wanted to scream, but only a small cry came out of her mouth.

She heard footsteps behind her. She managed to get herself turned around to face the open doorway. James? Was he all right now? But she didn't call out his name. She was afraid it wasn't him. James had drunk a whole cup of that coffee. It couldn't be him. She was afraid of who it might be.

The light was dim. Shadows filled the room, filled her vision. There was a man standing in the doorway, his hands in his pockets.

"Hello, Sally."

TWENTY-NINE

"No," she said, staring at that shadowy figure, knowing it was him, accepting it, but still she said again, "No, it can't be you."

"Of course it can, dear. You'd know your father anywhere, wouldn't you?"

"No." She was shaking her head back and forth.

"Why can't you get up, Sally?"

"You drugged us. I only drank a little bit, but it must have been very strong."

"Didn't get enough, did you?" He was coming toward her now, quickly, too quickly.

"Dr. Beadermeyer got to try so many new drugs on you. Actually, I was surprised you survived with your brain intact. Well, I'll take care of that."

He leaned down, grabbed the hair at the back of her neck, and yanked her head back. "Here, Sally." He poured liquid down her throat. Then he threw her away from him, and she fell hard onto her back.

She stared up at him, seeing him weave and fade in the dim light. She tried to focus on him, watching him closely, but his features blurred, his mouth moved and grew bigger. His neck stretched out, becoming longer and longer until she could no longer see his head. Surely this was the way Alice in Wonderland must have felt. Off with her head. "Oh, no," she whispered. "Oh, no."

She fell onto her side, the smooth oak boards of the floor cool against her cheek.

* * *

HER father was here. That was her first thought when she woke up.

Her father.

No doubt about it. Her father. He was here. He had drugged her. He would kill her now. She was helpless again, as helpless as she'd been for days upon weeks, weeks upon months.

She couldn't move, couldn't even lift a single finger. She realized her hands were tied in front of her, not all that tightly, but tight enough. She shifted her weight a bit. Her ankles were tied, too. But her mind wasn't fettered. Her mind was clear—thank God for that. If she'd been vague and blurry again, she would simply have folded up on herself and willed herself to die. But no, she could think. She could remember. She could also open her eyes. Did she want to?

James, she thought, and forced her eyes open.

She was lying on a bed. The springs squeaked when she shifted from one side to the other. She tried to make out more detail but couldn't. There was only a dim light coming from a hallway. It looked to be a small bedroom, but she couldn't tell anything more about it.

Where was she? Was she still in The Cove? If so, where?

Where was her father? What would he do?

She saw a shadowy figure walk into the bedroom. The light was too dim for her to make out his face. But she knew. Oh, yes, she knew it was him.

"You," she said, surprised that the word had come from her mouth. It sounded rusty and infinitely sad.

"Hello, Sally."

"It is you. I was praying I'd been wrong. Where am I?"

"It's a bit soon to tell you that."

"Are we still in The Cove? Where's James? And the other two agents?"

"It's a bit soon to tell you that as well."

"I was praying desperately you'd left the country, that, or you were dead. No, actually I was praying that they would catch you and put you in prison for the rest of your miserable life. Where am I?"

"How poor Noelle suffered for years from that tongue of yours. You were always sniping at her, always moralizing, always telling her what she should do. You wanted her to call the police. You wanted her to leave me. The fact is, she didn't want to, Sally. Maybe at first she did, but not later. But you wouldn't stop. You depressed her with all that criticism of yours, with your contempt. That's why she never came to see you in the sanitarium.

She was afraid you'd preach at her some more, even though you were crazy."

"That's bullshit. Naturally you can say anything you want about anybody now. Noelle isn't here to tell you what she really thinks of you. I'll bet you she'll be the happiest woman in Washington once she truly realizes she doesn't have to be your punching bag anymore. I'll bet you she's already wearing short-sleeved dresses and shirts again. No more fear of showing bruises. I'll bet she'll even try two-piece bathing suits this summer. How many years couldn't she wear them? You loved to punch her in the ribs, didn't you? You brutalized her. If there's any justice at all, you'll pay. Too bad you didn't die."

"That's more out of you than I've heard in more than six months. You were blessedly silent most of the time during your too brief stay at the sanitarium. Too bad Dr. Beadermeyer is out of business, thanks to that bastard Quinlan.

"Everything got so complicated, and it was all your fault, Sally. We had a lid on everything until Quinlan got you away from Dr. Beadermeyer again."

"His name's Norman Lipsy. He's a cosmetic surgeon. He's a criminal. He gave that poor man your face, but you're the one who killed him. You're a filthy murderer, not just a wife beater. And a traitor to your country."

"Why do you denounce me only for my more pedestrian deeds? I did one really good thing, something I'm quite proud of that you haven't mentioned.

"I put my darling daughter away for six months. I do believe that was my favorite project in the last few years.

"Putting you away. Having you under my control. Never having to see the contempt and hatred on your face when you happened to see me. How I enjoyed seeing you like a rag doll, your mouth gaping open, looking so stupid and vague it wasn't even much fun watching that pathetic Holland take off your clothes and bathe you and then dress you again like you were his dolly.

"Toward the end there, I didn't even enjoy slapping you to get your attention. You didn't have any to get, and you got too thin. I told Dr. Beadermeyer to feed you more, but he said all he could do was keep you stabilized. Then you escaped by hiding the pills beneath your tongue.

"To see you in my house, in my study, just after I'd shot Jackie. It was a shock."

He struck a pose she'd seen many times in her life. He propped his elbow up on his other arm and cupped his chin in his hand. It was his intellectual, thoughtful look, she supposed. All he needed was Scott's pipe and perhaps Sherlock Holmes's hat.

"There you were, leaning over poor Jackie—that greedy little bugger—then you turned and saw me, saw me as clear as day. I could see the recognition in your eyes. You picked up my gun. I'd put it down to get some papers from my desk. But then you picked it up, and I had no choice but to run. I hid outside and watched you shake your head, clearly disbelieving you'd seen me. I saw Noelle and Scott come running in. I heard her scream. I saw Scott nearly chew through that damned pipe of his.

"Then you ran, Sally. You ran and you threw my prized pistol in the bushes. I couldn't get you then and I'll tell you the truth, I was scared. I had to get my gun first, though, and I did. But I'll tell you, I was worried, and I stayed worried for a long time. So what if you told the world you'd seen me, your father? If you did, even though you were certifiably crazy, they might have insisted on doing a lot more than just an autopsy. But you were so afraid you ran. You ran here, to The Cove, to Amabel.

"I didn't find out for a good four days that you'd blocked it all out. That you ran because you believed that either you'd killed me or dear Noelle had."

She was trying to take it all in, to realize that she'd never been wrong, to at last understand what this man was. She said slowly, "James made me remember. That and re-creating the scene, I guess you'd say. I saw everything then, everything."

"I bet you want to know who the man was who looked like me. He was just a guy I discovered in Baltimore one day when I was meeting one of the Syrian agents. He was broke, looked remarkably like me—same height, nearly the same weight—and then I knew when I saw him, knew that he'd be the one to save me."

Why, she wondered, was he talking so much? Why was he standing there pouring all this out to her? And she realized then that it pleased him to brag about his brilliance to her. To make her realize how truly great he was. After all, she'd been in the dark about everything. Oh, yes, he was enjoying himself.

"Jackie who?"

"You know, I really don't remember his last name. Who cares? He played his role and played it perfectly." Amory St. John laughed. "I promised him a truckload of money if he could impersonate me. I wish you could have heard him practicing my voice tones, my accent. It was pathetic, but both Dr. Beadermeyer and I told him he had a great ear, that he had all my mannerisms, that he could play me to perfection. That's what he believed would happen. He believed he was going to take my place at a big conference. It was his chance to do something, his chance to make a big score. He was a credulous fool."

"Now he's a dead fool."

"Yes."

She began to pull on the ropes ever so slightly as she said, "Dr. Beadermeyer is down, but you already know all that. He'll spend the rest of his miserable life in prison. Holland told the FBI everything. All those people—people like me—will be let out of that prison that you call a sanitarium, like it's a resort where people go to recuperate and rest."

"Yes, but who cares about all those other people? They weren't my problem, only you. I'm sorry that the sanitarium will be closed down. It was such a perfect place for you. Out of the way for good. It all fell into place once I met Jackie. I already knew Dr. Beadermeyer and all about that little racket of his. Nearly seven months ago, it all came together.

"I got you out of the way—with Scott's help, of course. He was so weak and pathetic, afraid he'd get caught, but I'll tell you, he sure liked the money he got from helping me. And, you see, I knew all about his lover. At least I made sure you didn't get AIDS. I threatened Scott that if he made love to you—if he could force himself to do the deed—then he had to use a condom. Dr. Beadermeyer checked your blood. Thanks to me, you're well. But Scott did play his part. Once he was free of you, he spent his money and dallied openly with his lover. He was a good pawn. Where was I? Oh, yes, then Jackie went under the knife, and I finalized my plans. But you had to butt in, didn't you, Sally? I had you all locked away and still you got out. Still you had to try to ruin my plans. Well, no more."

"Do you hate me so much just because I tried to protect my mother from your fists?"

"Actually not. It was natural that I wouldn't like you very much."

"It's because you believed that I'd learned about your illegal arms sales?"

"Did you?"

"No."

"My dealings with other governments had nothing to do with it. Scott was afraid you'd seen something, but I knew you would have acted in a flash if you had. No, that didn't concern me. Fact of the matter is, you're not my daughter. You're nothing but a little bastard. And that, my dear Sally, is why Noelle never left me. She tried once, when you were just a baby. She didn't believe me when I told her she was in this for life. Perhaps she thought she'd test me. She ran back to her rich, snotty parents in Philadelphia, and they acted true to form just as I knew they would. They told her to get back to her husband and stop making up lies about me. After all, I'd saved her bacon. How could she say such things about me, a wonderful man who'd married her when she was pregnant with another man's child?"

He laughed, a long, deep laugh that made her skin crawl. She kept lightly tugging on the ropes. Surely they were a little bit looser now, but she wasn't really thinking about those ropes. She was trying to understand him, to really take in what he was saying. But it was so hard.

He continued, his voice meditative. "When I think about it now, I realize that Noelle really hadn't believed me. She hadn't believed that my price to marry her, other than the five hundred thousand dollars I got from her parents, was that she stay with me forever, or until I didn't want her anymore. When she came dragging back with you—a screaming little brat—I took you away from her and held you over a big fire in the fireplace. The fire was blowing really good. It singed off what little hair you had and your eyebrows. Oh, how she screamed. I told her if she ever tried anything like that again, I'd kill you.

"I meant it, you know. I bet you wonder who your father was."

She felt as though she'd had a ton of drugs pumped into her body. She couldn't grasp what he was saying. She understood his words—he wasn't her father—but she couldn't seem to get it to the core of herself.

"You're not my father," she repeated, staring beyond his left shoulder toward the open door. She wanted to cheer. She didn't have any of this monster's blood. "You kept Noelle with you by threatening to kill me, her only child."

"Yes. My dear wife finally believed me. I can't tell you the pleasure it gave me to beat that rich little bitch. And she had to take it. She had no choice.

"Then you were sixteen and you saw me hit her. Too bad. It changed everything, but then I had good reason to get rid of you. Remember that last time? You came back into the house and I was kicking her and you got on the phone to call for help and she crawled—actually crawled—over to you and begged you not to call? I enjoyed that. I enjoyed watching you simply disconnect from her.

"I kicked her a couple more times after you left. She really moaned delightfully. Then I had sex with her and she cried the whole time.

"After that I was free of you for a long while. Life was really quite good those four years you were out of my house, out of your mother's life. But I wanted to pay you back. I got Scott to marry you. That got you away for a little while, but you didn't want him, did you? You realized he was a phony almost immediately. Well, it didn't matter.

"I just had to bide my time. When I saw Jackie I knew what to do. You see, the feds were closing in. I'm not stupid. I knew it was only a matter of time. I'd gotten very rich, but arms sales to terrorist countries are always risky. Yes, it was just a matter of time. I wanted to pay you back for all the trouble you caused me. Those six months you were in Dr. Beadermeyer's sanitarium were wonderful for me. I loved to have you beneath me, watching me fondle you, fondle myself. I adored hitting you, watching you wince in pain. But then you got away and ruined everything." He leaned down and slapped her, her left cheek, then her right cheek. Once, again, and yet again.

She tasted blood. He'd split her lip.

"You puking coward." She spit at him, but he jerked away from her in time. He slapped her again.

"I never wanted to have sex with you in the sanitarium," he said, close to her face now, "though I could have. I saw you naked enough times, but I never wanted you. Scott wouldn't even look at you. He only came one time because I insisted. Now that little bastard will take the fall because I won't be around. Come on, Sally, spit at me again. I'm not the coward, you are."

She spit at him, and this time she didn't miss. She watched him wipe his mouth and his cheek with the back of his hand. Then he smiled down at her. She had a stark memory of him smiling down at her in the sanitarium. "No," she whispered, but it didn't change anything.

He struck her hard and she fell into blackness. Her last thought was that she was grateful he hadn't given her more drugs.

THIRTY

"This is not good," Quinlan said and meant it, but he wasn't thinking about himself and the other agents, he was thinking about Sally. If she was here in this black hole, she was still unconscious. Or dead.

There was a grunt from Thomas Shredder and a "yeah" from Corey Harper. It was true. This indeed wasn't good. It was also true that it was as black as the bottom of a witch's cauldron in this room where they were being kept.

No, it wasn't a room. It was a shed with a dirt floor—the shed behind Doc Spiver's cottage.

"Look," Thomas said, "Quinlan's right, but we're trained agents. We can get out of this. If we don't, they'll fire us. We'll lose our careers and our federal pensions. I sure don't want to lose my federal health benefits."

Corey Harper laughed despite the cramps in her ankles. Her hands were okay. They hadn't tied them all that tightly, probably because she was a woman. Still, the knots were secure and weren't about to slip or slide.

"That's the funniest thing I've ever heard you say, Thomas."

Quinlan said, as he tugged at the ropes at his wrists, "One of these clowns must have been in the Navy in World War Two. These ropes are very well tied, not a bit of give to them. Anybody want to try hands or teeth?"

"I would," Corey said, "but I'm tied to the wall over here. Yeah, there's a rope around my waist, and I can feel it's wrapped around one of the wall boards. And yes, it's solid. Even with big teeth and a long reach, I couldn't get to you."

"I'm tied too," Thomas said.

"At least everyone's alive," Quinlan said. "I wonder what happened to David?" But he was wondering about Sally. He was afraid to say her name aloud.

"He probably ran off the road," Thomas said matter-of-factly. "He isn't here. Maybe he's already dead."

"Or maybe somebody rescued him," Corey said.

"What do you mean 'already dead'?" Quinlan said, wishing he could see an outline of something, anything. He kept working on the ropes, but they wouldn't budge.

"Do you think they're going to keep us here for the next ten years?"

"I hope not," Quinlan said. "They're all so old they'd be dead themselves by then. I'd hate to be forgotten."

"That was't funny, Quinlan."

"Maybe not, but I'm trying."

"Keep trying," Corey said. "I don't want to fall into a funk. We've got to think. First of all, who did this to us?"

"That's pretty obvious, isn't it?" Thomas said. "That scary old relic. She probably had Martha bring her the Amaretto and she put something into it. I was out like a light the second I lay down on my bed."

"Where's Sally?" Corey asked suddenly.

"I don't know," Quinlan said. "I don't know."

He'd prayed she was locked up with them, still unconscious from the drug. "Everyone stretch your legs out in front of you. Let's see how big this shed is."

Quinlan could barely touch Thomas's toe.

"Now lean to one side and then the other."

Quinlan got a pinch of Corey's blouse.

No Sally.

"Sally isn't in here with us," Quinlan said. "Where'd they take her?" Why had he asked that question aloud? He didn't want to hear what Thomas had to say.

Thomas said, "Good question. Why would they bother to separate us anyway?"

"Because," Quinlan said slowly, "Sally's aunt Amabel is a part of this. Maybe she has Sally. Maybe she'll protect her."

Thomas sighed. To Quinlan's surprise, he said, "Let's pray you're right. My head feels like a drum in a rock band."

"Mine too," Corey said. "But I can still think. Now, Quinlan, you think the whole town is part of a conspiracy? You think the whole bloody town has killed at least sixty people in the past three to four years? For their money? And then they buried all of them in their cemetery?"

"It shows respect," Quinlan said. "Can't you see all those old folk, stroking their chins as they look down at an old couple they've just offed, saying, 'Well, Ralph Keaton can lay 'em out, then we'll bury 'em really nice and Reverend Vorhees can say all the right words.' Yeah, Corey, the whole bloody town. What other possibility is there?"

"This is nuts," Thomas said. "An entire town killing people? No one would believe that in a million years, particularly since most of them are senior citizens."

"I believe it," Quinlan said. "Oh, yeah, I believe it. I'll bet it started with an accident. They got money from that accident. It gave them—or maybe just one of them or a couple of them—an idea of how to save their town. And it grew and grew."

Corey said slowly, "The way they lure victims here is that big advertising sign on the highway."

"Right," Quinlan said. "The World's Greatest Ice Cream Shop. By the way, it is the best ice cream I've ever eaten."

He had to make jokes, he had to or else he'd go nuts. Where was Sally? Could Amabel really be protecting her? He had to doubt it.

"Come in and buy your last ice cream cone," Thomas said. "That's the bottom line."

"What about that woman who was murdered? And Doc Spiver?" Corey said.

Quinlan said, even as he was working furiously on the ropes at his wrists, "The woman must have heard something she shouldn't have heard. They held her prisoner for at least three nights, probably more. She must have gotten her mouth free because Sally heard her screaming that first night she was here in The Cove. Then, two nights later, she heard her screaming again. The next morning Sally and I found her body. My guess is they had to kill her. They didn't want to, but they did. They knew it was either the woman or them. No choice really. They killed her. They must have been pissed—they just threw her off that cliff, didn't bother laying her out or burying her in their precious cemetery."

"What about Doc Spiver?" Thomas said. "These ropes are strong, I can't get even a micron of play in them."

"Keep working on them, everybody," Quinlan said. "Now, Doc Spiver. I don't know. It's possible he was a weak link. That as a physician, all the killing had turned him. Maybe the woman's murder was the last straw. He couldn't stand it anymore. He cracked. They shot him in the mouth, trying to make it look like a suicide. Again, they saw it as they had no choice."

Corey Harper said, "Do you guys know that most FBI agents never get close to the big trouble we're in now? Some of them never even draw their guns. They spend their whole careers interviewing people. I've been told that quite a few agents, when they retire, become psychologists—they're that good at getting information out of people."

Quinlan laughed. "We'll get out of this, Corey. Believe it."

"You think you're so bloody smart, Quinlan. How the hell are we going to get free? And a swarm of little old people are going to show up any minute. Do you think they'll form a firing squad? Or just beat us to death with their canes?"

Corey said quietly, "Don't, Thomas. Let's get loose. There's got to be a way. I don't want to be helpless when someone comes, and you both know they'll come."

"What, dammit?" Thomas shouted. "What can we do? The ropes are too tight. They even tied us to the wall so we couldn't get to each other. We're in the dark. So what are we going to do?"

"There's got to be something," Corey said.

"Maybe there is," Quinlan said.

* * *

SALLY'S jaw hurt. She opened and closed her mouth, working it until the pain eased to a dull throb. She was lying in the dark, the only light coming through the open doorway from the hall.

She was alone. Her hands were still tied in front of her. She lifted her hands to her mouth and began to tug with her teeth on the knot.

She was concentrating so hard that she nearly screamed when a quiet voice said, "It's really no use, Sally. Relax, baby. Don't move. Just relax."

"No," Sally whispered. "Oh, no."

"Don't you recognize where you are, Sally? I thought you'd know right away."

"No, it's too dark in here."

"Look toward the window, dear. Maybe you'll see your dear father's face again."

"I'm in the bedroom down the hall from yours."

"Yes."

"Why, Amabel? What's going on?"

"Oh, Sally, why'd you have to come back? I'd give anything if you hadn't shown up on my doorstep that day. I had to take you in. I really didn't want you involved, but here you are again, and there's nothing I can do."

"Where are James and the other two agents?"

"I don't know. They're probably in that little tool shed behind Doc Spiver's cottage. That's a sturdy prison. They'll never get out."

"What are you going to do to them?"

"It's really not up to me."

"Who is it up to?"

"The town."

For a long moment, Sally couldn't breathe. It was true. The whole bloody town. "How many people has the town killed, Amabel?"

"The first old couple, Harve and Marge Jensen, the ones Quinlan was supposedly here to look for, they were both accidents. Both of them keeled over with heart attacks. We found cash in their Winnebago. Next there was this biker. He started wailing on poor old Hunker, and Purn cracked him over the head with a chair to protect Hunker. It killed him. Another accident.

"Then the biker's girlfriend realized he was dead. Sherry Vorhees had no choice but to kill her. She slammed her over the head with an industrial blender.

"It got easier after that, you know? Someone would spot a likely old couple or someone who looked rich. Or maybe one of the women who was working in the World's Greatest Ice Cream Shop saw a whole lot of cash when the person pulled open his wallet. Then we just did it. Yes, it got easier. It got to be nearly a game, but don't misunderstand me, Sally. We always treated them with greatest respect after they were dead.

"You've told me how beautiful the town is now. Well, it was a rundown mess before. But now, our investments are doing well, everyone is quite comfortable, and many tourists come here not only for the World's Greatest Ice Cream but also to see the town and buy souvenirs and eat at the cafe."

"How wonderful for you. More people to choose from. You could discuss it among yourselves. Did that couple look richer than that one over there? You played Russian roulette with people's lives. That's disgusting."

"I wouldn't put it so crassly, but as we've gotten to be more of a tourist attraction we've been able to be more selective. But we've killed only old people, Sally. They had all had a full life."

"That biker's girlfriend didn't."

Amabel shrugged. "It couldn't be helped."

Sally was shaking her head back and forth on the pillow, believing but still incredulous. "Amabel, you've killed people. Don't you understand that? You've murdered innocent people. It doesn't excuse anything that they were old. You robbed them. You buried them in the cemetery—what? Oh, I see. You buried them two to each grave. Only you used a man's name. Does one of you have a list identifying who's really in each grave?"

"No, but we left identification on the bodies. Don't sound so appalled, Sally. We were dying here. We desperately wanted to survive. We have. We've won."

"No, everything's coming down on your heads now, Amabel. There are three FBI agents here, and Sheriff David Mountebank knows everything they know, maybe more. You kill the agents, and you'll all be in the gas chamber. Don't you understand? The FBI is involved!"

"Oh, Sally, here you are, going on and on about something that really doesn't concern you. What about yourself, baby? What about your father?"

"He's not my father, thank God. At least I found that out."

"Good, there's anger there. I was afraid you were still trying to believe he was a nightmare come back to haunt you."

"You're saying he's here with you, Amabel? You want him here?" She knew the answer. But she didn't want to hear it.

"Of course, Sally."

She stared beyond her aunt to the man illuminated in the doorway. Her father. No, not her father, thank God. It was the bastard who raised her, the bastard who beat her mother and locked her away in Dr. Beadermeyer's sanitarium, the bastard who beat her just because it pleased him to do so.

"So how does our little bastard feel, Ammie?"

Ammie? What was this?

"I'm not the bastard. You are."

"Sally, I hesitate to hit you in front of your aunt. It bothers her, even though she knows what a vicious mouth you have, even though she knows I've got to do it to control you."

"Amabel, why do you have him here with you? He's a murderer. He's a traitor to our country."

Amabel sat down beside her. Her fingertips were light and soft as they drifted over Sally's forehead, pushing her hair behind her ears, lightly smoothing her eyebrows.

"Amabel, please. When I was here before, I knew it was him on the phone to me. He admitted that he'd looked in through the bedroom window."

"Yes, dear."

"Why was he here, Amabel?"

"He had to come here, Sally. He had to take you back to the sanitarium. He hoped to make you doubt your sanity with the phone calls and his face at the window."

"But how could he possibly know I was even here?"

"I called him. He was staying at a small inn in Oklahoma City. He took the next plane to Portland, then drove here. But you knew even as you asked that question, didn't you, Sally?

"Ah, but you didn't doubt your sanity at all. That was due in part to Quinlan. That man. His being here made everything more difficult. Isn't it strange? Quinlan made up that story about coming here to try to find a trace of those old folk? All he wanted was you. He didn't care about any missing old people. Just you. He thought you'd either killed your father or were protecting your mother.

"I've always been amused by the ways of fate. Well, I'm not amused now. There are big problems now."

"Now, Ammie, do you think it was fate that brought all those nice old people here to buy the World's Greatest Ice Cream so you could then kill them and steal all their money?"

Amabel turned and frowned at him. "I don't know, and neither do you, Amory. Now, I don't care what happens to Quinlan and the others, but I don't want Sally hurt."

"He doesn't agree with you, Aunt Amabel," Sally said. "He hates me. You know he's not my father. He has no latent tender feelings for me. As for my mother, did you know that he forced Noelle to stay with him?"

"Why, of course, Sally."

Sally gaped at her. She couldn't help it. On the other hand, why was she so surprised? Her world had flipped and turned more times in the past seven months than she could cope with. It seemed she'd never known who she really was or why things were the way they were. And she'd hated her mother for her weakness. She'd felt contempt for her, wanted to shake her herself for letting her husband knock her around.

"Who's my father?"

"Now she wants to know," Amory St. John said, as he strolled into the small bedroom, his hands in his pants pockets.

"Who?"

"Well, dear," Amabel said, "actually your father was my husband. And yes, he was my husband before he met Noelle and the two of them fell in love—"

"In lust, you mean, Ammie."

"That too. Anyway, Noelle was always rather stupid, and Carl wasn't all that much of this earth himself. Knowing both of them as well as I did, I had difficulty figuring out who got whom into bed. But they must have managed it. She got pregnant. Fortunately she was seeing Amory at the time, and things got worked out to everyone's satisfaction."

"Not to my mother's."

"Oh, yes, she was thrilled that she wouldn't have to abort you, Sally. She would have, of course, if it meant no husband as a cover.

"I brought my Carl out here to The Cove so he could paint and spend the rest of his meaningless little life doing landscape oils that sell at airport shows for twenty dollars, and that includes their vulgar gold-painted frames. Carl never roamed again. In fact, he begged my forgiveness, said he'd do anything if only I wouldn't leave him. I let him do quite a bit before he died twenty years ago."

"You didn't kill him, did you?"

"Oh, no. Amory did that, but Carl was already very ill with lung cancer. He never would stop smoking unfiltered Camels. Yes, it was a blessing for Carl that his brakes failed, and he died so quickly. Thank you, Amory."

"You're welcome, Ammie."

"So how long have you been lovers?"

Amabel laughed softly, turning to look at the man who was standing in the doorway. "A very long time," she said.

"So you don't mind him beating you, Amabel?"

"No, Amory, don't!" Amabel walked quickly to him and put her hand on his arm. She said over her shoulder, "Listen to me, Sally. Don't talk like that. There's no reason to make your father angry—"

"He's not my father."

"Nevertheless, mind your tongue. Of course he doesn't hit me. Just Noelle."

"He hit me too, Amabel."

"You deserved it," Amory said.

Sally looked from one to the other. In the dim light she couldn't see either of them clearly. Amory took Amabel's hand, pulled her closer to his side. The shadows seemed to deepen around them, moving into them, drawing them into one. Sally shivered.

"I thought you loved me, Amabel."

"I do, baby, indeed I do. You're my husband's child and my niece. And I agreed with Amory that you were better off in that nice sanitarium. You weren't doing well. He told me how erratic you'd become, how you were cheating on your husband, how you'd gotten in with the wrong people and were taking drugs.

"He said that Dr. Beadermeyer would help you. I met Dr. Beadermeyer. An excellent doctor, who said you were doing nicely but that you needed complete rest and constant supervision by professionals."

"That was all a lie. Even if you don't want to believe he's such a monster, just think about it. You've read the papers, seen the news. Everyone is looking for him. Everyone knows that many of the patients in Dr. Beadermeyer's sanitarium were prisoners, just like I was."

"Oh, baby, don't do this. I don't want to put a gag in your mouth, but I will. I won't let you talk about him like this."

"All right, but didn't you wonder about how crazy I was when he showed up here, knocked me over the head, and drugged me? When he nearly killed James?"

Amory St. John pulled away from Amabel. He walked to the bed and stood there, staring down at Sally. "In this dim light I can't tell if you're going to be bruised or not."

"You really hit her that hard, Amory?"

"Don't fret, Ammie. She deserved it. She spit on me. Over the years I learned exactly how hard I could hit Noelle to get a certain kind and color of bruise. But everyone's skin is different. We'll have to wait and see, won't we?"

"You're nuts," Sally said. "You're a monster."

"I would have whipped you if you'd ever said that when you lived under my roof."

"It doesn't matter, Amory. She's frightened. She doesn't know what's going to happen to her."

Sally said, "I know exactly what's going to happen to me. He doesn't have Dr. Beadermeyer to hold me prisoner for him anymore. No, he's going to kill me, Amabel. You know that as well, otherwise you wouldn't have admitted everything to me. No, don't deny it. You've already accepted it. But I don't really count. What will bring both of you down is hurting the FBI agents. You try killing James, and all hell will break loose. I know his boss, and you can count on it."

"They're stupid, all of them," Amory said. He shrugged. "I know things will get even more difficult, but we'll deal with it. Actually I've already set things in motion. It's true I didn't count on that damned agent getting you away from Dr. Beadermeyer again. That's what ripped it apart. All my plans, Sally, everything has had to be rearranged. It has put me out. Now I'm no longer dead, thanks to the two of you. Now I'll have to leave the country forever."

"You try it. They'll catch you. With those arms sales to terrorist countries, you've got the feds ready to tear the world apart looking for you."

"I know. Such a pity. But it will be fine. I got most of my money out of the Caymans and Switzerland nearly a year ago. I left a bit in all those foreign accounts to tantalize the feds so they'd realize I knew exactly what I was doing. It will make them crazy, and they won't catch me."

"James will catch you."

"Your James Quinlan isn't going to catch a cold. He won't have time before he's six feet under."

She felt such rage she couldn't stop herself. She heaved up, hitting him in the face with her bound fists. Hard. He cursed, shoving her back, his own fist raised.

She heard Amabel yell, "Don't, Amory!"

But that fist kept coming down, not toward her face but toward her ribs.

THIRTY-ONE

"Sorry, guys," Quinlan said, "but the old codgers were thorough. My army knife is gone. I always taped it to my ankle. Damn."

Thomas said, "Corey, what are you doing? Why are you heaving around like a gutted fish? Why are you making those weird groaning sounds?"

She was breathing hard. "You'll see. I didn't count on Quinlan finding that knife. Wait a moment, I've nearly made it through."

"Made what through?" Quinlan said, desperately straining to see her in the darkness.

"I was a gymnast. I have the dubious honor of being the most flexible agent to go through the program at Quantico. I'm getting my arms beneath my butt and pushing on through and in just a minute— This is tougher than it used to be when I was younger and skinnier—" She stopped, breathing hard, straining. "There."

She was panting, laughing. "I did it!"

"What, Corey?"

"My hands are now tied in front of me, Thomas. Thank heaven they left enough leeway between me and the wall. The rope around my waist was higher than the rope tying my wrists together. Now, I'm going to turn around and untie the rope around my waist. When I'm free, I can do my feet and then get to you guys."

"Corey," Quinlan said, "if you get us out of this, both Thomas and I will recommend that you become the special agent in charge of the Portland field office. Right, Thomas?"

"If she gets us out of this, I'll beg her to marry me."

"Thomas, you're a sexist. I won't ever marry a sexist."

"Corey, how are you doing?" Quinlan said.

"It's coming. The knot at my waist is pretty easy."

"Good. Hurry."

But how much time did they have left before the old folk came for them? Where was Sally? Quinlan hadn't prayed much in his life, but he was praying now. Did Amabel have her?

"Got it! Now let me get my feet."

"I hear something," Thomas said. "Hurry, Corey, hurry!"

"DON'T hit her, Amory!"

Amabel grabbed his arm, jerking it away. It slammed against the bed just an inch from Sally's ribs.

He was panting. He wheeled about, his fist raised. "You shouldn't have done that, Ammie. You shouldn't have done it."

Sally reared up, yelling, "Don't you dare hit her, you cretin!"

But he did, his fist hard against Amabel's jaw, knocking her against the wall. She slid down to the floor.

Sally didn't say a word. She was staring at her aunt, praying she wasn't dead.

"How could you?" She stared up at the man who had to be mad. "You're lovers. She called to tell you I was here so you could come and get me. You hit her just like you hit Noelle."

"Actually," he said, rubbing his knuckles, "it's the first time I've ever had to discipline her. She won't go against me in the future now. I wonder how her skin will bruise."

NO blinding light came through the door as it creaked open—a tiny bit, then wider until all three of them could see the stars and the half-moon.

"You awake in here?" It was an old man's voice. Which one of them? Quinlan wondered. Was there only one of them come to check on their prisoners, or more? He prayed it was just the one old man.

"It ain't quite morning yet, but you should be awake."

"Yeah," Thomas said, "we're awake. What? You hoped you'd killed us?"

"Nah, there weren't enough of that stuff Doc had on hand to put your lights out. It would have been easier that way, though. Now, well, it ain't going to be any fun."

Quinlan nearly jumped out of his skin when he heard Corey whimper. "Oh, please, I don't feel well. Please take me to a bathroom. Please." She was moaning quietly, very effectively.

"Oh, shit," the old man said. "It's just you, little gal?"

"Yes," Corey managed to choke out. "Please, hurry."

"All right. Damn, I didn't expect any of you to be sick. Nobody was ever sick before."

Corey was slumped over, straight ahead of the old guy, against the back wall. The old man opened the door wider as he came into the shed. Quinlan recognized Purn Davies, the old coot who owned the general store. He saw that Corey had her hands behind her back, as if they were still tied there.

"Please hurry," she whispered. She sounded god-awful, like she would puke at any moment.

Quinlan looked at Thomas and shook his head.

Just as Purn Davies passed Quinlan, he whipped up his feet and kicked the old man on his thighs, knocking him right onto Corey's lap.

"Gotcha!" Corey said. When the old man began to struggle, she raised her fists and knocked him cold.

"Well done, Corey," Thomas said. "You sure you won't marry me? What if I promise to change?"

"Ask me again if we get out of this alive," she said. "Okay, guys, I'm going to untie Quinlan's wrists, then yours, Thomas. Keep an eye on the old man."

It took her only about three minutes to untie Quinlan. In another three minutes all of them were free. They rose and stretched and tried to get the blood moving back into their legs and arms. "I think I'll tie him up real good," Corey said and dropped to her knees. "Look, he's got one of our guns."

Quinlan looked outside the shed. "It's near dawn. I don't see a soul. I guess they sent Purn here to make sure we were still alive. Why, I don't know. There's no way they could have afforded to keep us alive, no way at all.

"Ah, look here. The old man brought us some sandwiches. They're out here on a tray. How did he expect us to eat them with our hands tied behind our backs?"

"All done," Corey said, standing behind the two men. "What now, Quinlan?"

"Thomas, bar the shed door. Since they took our cell phone we'll get into Doc Spiver's house and pray the phone's still connected. We can get the cavalry here. Then we'll go find Sally."

"HE'S mad, Amabel, utterly mad."

Amabel was rubbing her jaw. She looked bewildered. "He's never hit me before, never," she said slowly. "He's always caressed me and loved me. He's never hit me. I always thought it was Noelle who brought that out in him, like she made him hit her, like she was sick and needed it."

"No, she hated it. He demeaned her, Amabel, and she stood for it all because he'd threatened to kill me if she didn't stay with him, if she didn't take his abuse. He hasn't hit you because you're not with him all that much and because if he did, you'd probably shoot him or just leave. Noelle couldn't leave. She had to stay to protect me. Now that he's got you, he'll beat you whenever he feels like it."

"No. I'll tell him that if he ever hits me again, I'll leave him."

"You can try it, but I bet he'll find a way to keep you, just like he did your sister."

"You're wrong. You've got to be wrong. We've been intimate for twelve years, Sally. Twelve years. I know him. He loves me. The only reason he hit me tonight is because he's afraid. He's upset and worried that we won't get away. And you pushed. Yes, you made him furious. It's your fault."

"Wake up, Amabel. He's insane."

"Shush, Sally, here he comes."

"Quick, Amabel, untie me. We can escape."

"Now what's this? My two girls conspiring against me?"

"No, dear," Amabel said, rising to go to him. She hugged him, then kissed him on the mouth. "Oh, no. Poor Sally thinks because you hit me this one time you'll do it again and again. I know you won't, will you?"

"Of course not. I'm sorry, Ammie. I've been under so much stress, and you were arguing with me. Please, forgive me. I won't ever touch you again."

"He's lying," Sally said. "If you believe him you're stupid, Amabel. Yeah, come on, you lousy human being, come on over here and hit me again. I'm tied, so I can't hurt you much. You're safe. Come on, you pitiful excuse for a man, come and hit me."

He was heaving with rage, the veins in his neck red and thick. "Shut up, Sally."

"Look at him, Amabel. He wants to kill me. He has no control. He's crazy."

Amory turned to Amabel. "I'll take care of her. I know what to do. I swear I won't kill her."

"What are you going to do?"

"Trust me, Ammie. Can't you trust me? You have for the past twelve years. Trust me now."

"You think he won't kill me, Amabel? He's a filthy liar. Do you want to be an accessory to murder?" Her words swallowed themselves. Amabel was already an accessory to murder maybe sixty times over. Maybe she'd even killed some of the people. Sally shut her mouth.

Amory St. John laughed, low and mean. "I see you understand, Sally.

Ammie belongs with me. We're two of a kind. Now, Ammie, untie her feet. I'm taking her out of here."

She couldn't stand up because her legs were numb. Amabel dropped to her knees and massaged her ankles and calves. "Is that better, Sally?"

"Why didn't you kill me before? Why go through this charade with Amabel?"

"Be quiet, you little bitch."

"You swear you won't hurt her, Amory?"

"I told you," he said, so impatient that Sally wondered how Amabel couldn't hear it, couldn't know that he was ready to strike out. "I won't kill her."

When she could stand and walk, Amory took her arm and pulled her out of the small bedroom. "Stay here, Ammie," he called over his shoulder. "I'll be back shortly and then we'll leave."

Sally said, "While you're waiting, Amabel, call Noelle. Tell her how you let him kill me. Yeah, tell her that, Amabel."

He pulled her out of Amabel's sight, then sent his elbow into her ribs. She doubled over, gasping with the pain. He yanked her back up.

"Keep your mouth shut, Sally, or I'll keep hurting you. Do you want that?"

"What I want," she said when she could finally speak, "is for you to die. Very slowly and very painfully."

"Not in your lifetime, my dear," he said, and laughed.

"They'll get you. There's no way you can escape, not with the FBI after you."

He was still laughing softly, highly amused with her. It made no sense. Then he walked beneath a strong light at the head of the stairs and stopped. He laughed again. "Look, Sally. Look at me."

She did. It wasn't Amory St. John.

THE phone service was still on. Thomas called the Portland office. When he hung up, he said, "They're bringing a helicopter up here. Thirty minutes, tops."

"What about David?" Corey said.

"Here, let me call his wife." David's lovely sweet wife, Jane, who'd taken him in when they cracked him over the head, who'd fed him soup. He prayed David was alive. Please, let him be alive.

Quinlan said, "This is Quinlan. Please tell me David's there. What? Oh, no. I'm sorry. Tell his doctors that he was drugged. That's why he banged himself up. No, no, things are under control here. No, I'm going to call his office and get his three deputies here. Yeah, I'll speak to you soon. Sally? I don't know. We're going to hunt for her now."

He hung up the phone. "David's in a coma. They medivaced him to Portland. His condition's stable so far. Nobody knows anything yet, just that he ran off the road into the only oak tree in his neighborhood. His wife was the first person to get to him. She said the doctors told her that if he hadn't been transported so quickly to the hospital he probably would have died."

"This is a nightmare," Corey said. "The whole town, all of them murderers. I want to get them, Quinlan."

"I sure want them to lose their Social Security," Thomas said. "No means testing."

"That wasn't funny," Corey said, but she laughed.

"It's Shakespearean. You know, comedy mixed with tragedy."

"No," Quinlan said, "it's evil. It didn't start out evil, but they've made it all the way, haven't they? Let's go find my future wife."

IT was Amory St. John, but it wasn't. She blinked up at him. No, the light here was excellent. "Dr. Beadermeyer changed your face, just like he did the man you murdered."

"Yes. I didn't want to be completely different, only different enough that if an old friend happened to see me he wouldn't wonder. He did his nicks and cuts and sutures after we got you back from The Cove that first time." He patted his neck. "Gravity was taking a bit of a toll, but no longer. He tucked that all up, too. Would you go out with me, Sally, a young woman your age?"

She didn't say anything. She was afraid if he hit her again she'd lose consciousness. She couldn't let that happen. Her legs were free. The numbness was nearly gone. Surely she could run now. She had to get away from him. She had to find James and the others. What if they were already dead? No, she wouldn't think like that. They weren't dead. There was still time.

She looked up at him. She hated him more than she believed it possible for one human being to hate another. She wanted to break him. She wanted him to suffer, to realize he'd lost, to realize that he wasn't as smart as he thought he was. "Scott told the FBI everything you'd done. He's cooperating with them, hoping to save his wretched little hide."

"Who cares what the little prick does? Shut up now, and let's get you out of here."

He forced her down the stairs. As if he guessed she would try something, he grabbed her hair and went down behind her.

What to do?

There was a noise at the front door. His hand jerked her hair upward. She didn't even notice. She heard him under his breath. She knew the moment when he drew a gun. "Let's just hope it's one of the old folk."

But it wasn't. The door slowly opened. If only they'd been upstairs no one would have heard anything. She stared at that opening door, mesmerized.

She saw James's face. She didn't think, just acted. She raised her arms, grabbed his hair, and dropped down. Amory stumbled over her head and rolled over and over down the stairs. He landed on his back, panting hard, but still conscious. Quinlan was on him in an instant, the gun pointed at his temple.

"Who the hell are you?"

"It's Amory St. John," Sally said. "Dr. Beadermeyer changed his face like he did that other man's."

Quinlan's SIG pressed harder against St. John's temple. "Sally, are you all right?"

"I'm fine. My aunt's upstairs. He was taking me away, probably to kill me. He told my aunt that he wouldn't, but he's a miserable liar. James, he hit her and she's all ready to forgive him. What's wrong with her?"

"I'll get her," Thomas said. "Don't worry, Sally. I won't hurt her."

Sally got to her feet. She was sore, her scalp hurt, and she felt better than she'd ever felt in her life. "James," she said, "I'm so glad to see you. You, too, Corey. Amabel said the three of you were in that shed behind Doc Spiver's cottage."

"Yeah," Quinlan said, "but we're special agents. We got out. Well, actually, it's Corey who's the hero. You know, Sally, I noticed a gray hair. Let Corey untie your hands."

When she had feeling back in her wrists, she went and stood over the man who'd been her father for so many years, the man she'd hated for so long, the man who hated her. He was on the floor, at her feet.

She got down on her knees. She smiled. "Now it's my chance to tell you what I think of you. You're pathetic. You're nothing. You'll never have a hold over anybody again for as long as you live. I hate you. More than that, I despise you." She drew back her fist and slammed it into his nose.

"I've wanted to do that for such a long time." She rubbed her knuckles.

He was quivering with rage. His nose began to bleed. He quieted only when he felt the gun press still harder against his temple.

"You want to know something else? Noelle is ecstatic that you're gone.

She hates you as much as I do. She's free of you. I'm free of you. Soon you'll be in a cage where you belong."

She stared down at him, at the blood seeping out of his nose, at the rage in his eyes. "God-awful bastard." She rose and kicked him in the ribs, then kicked him two more times.

"You crazy bitch. Hey, you're a cop. Don't let her beat me."

"I'll let her shoot you in the balls if she wants to," Quinlan said. "Sally? Would you like to shoot him?"

"No, not now. Well, not this exact minute. You know what, old man? Noelle looks utterly beautiful. I'll bet she'll be going out again very soon. She'll have any man she wants."

"She won't dare. She knows I'd kill her if she even looked at another man. Yes, I'd kill both of them."

"You aren't going to kill anybody," Sally said, eyes mean and bright, joy in her voice. "You're going to jail for the rest of your miserable life." She patted his face. "You're an old man. Think of how much faster you'll sag and wrinkle in prison."

"I won't go to prison. I'm going to get you. I played with you for six months. I should have strangled you."

"Just try it, you old bastard." She smiled down at him, lifted her foot, and landed it square in his groin.

He screamed, clutching himself.

"Well done, Sally," Quinlan said. "You sure you don't want to shoot him?"

There was a shot from upstairs.

THIRTY-TWO

Quinlan struck Amory St. John hard on his jaw.

One down, he thought, as St. John's head lolled to the side. They had only one weapon—Quinlan' s gun, taken off old Purn Davies, the one that Quinlan had pressed to Amory St. John's temple.

When Thomas had gone upstairs unarmed, Sally hadn't thought, hadn't imagined that her aunt could shoot someone.

Suddenly Corey moved like lightning, throwing herself into the shadowed recess to the side at the base of the stairs.

They watched in silence as Thomas, his arm bleeding rivulets through his fingers, came down the stairs, Amabel behind him with a pistol to the back of his head.

"Throw that gun toward the living room, Mr. Quinlan."

Instead, Quinlan slid it across the highly polished oak floor toward the spot where Corey was crouched.

"You don't have such a good aim, do you? No matter. Now, move away from him. That's right. Go stand by Sally.

"You, sir, keep moving or I'll shoot you in the back of your neck. You wouldn't like that, would you?"

"No," Thomas said, sounding dazed, "I wouldn't like that at all."

"You're bleeding all over my floor. Well, who cares? I doubt we'll ever come back here anyway. Now, Mr. Quinlan, you and Sally take two more steps back. Good. Don't try anything. You're always bragging about FBI agents, but this one's just like you, Mr. Quinlan, he's just a man. Look at all that blood—and it's only a little wound in his arm. He's not whining, I'll say that for him. Now don't move." She looked down. "Amory, you can get up now."

There wasn't a sound from Amory.

"Amory!"

She waved the gun and screamed at Quinlan, "What did you do to him, you bastard?"

"I coldcocked him, Amabel. Real hard. I don't think he'll be coming around anytime soon."

"I should shoot you right now. You've been a pain ever since you set foot in this town, ever since you first saw Sally. No, Sally, keep your mouth shut. My future is with him, and I intend to have it. I know the town will fall, but I won't. No one will catch us, not even your precious FBI."

She shoved Thomas to the bottom step. She must have sensed something because she quickly moved back up two steps. "You try to turn on me, boy, and I'll blow your head off."

"No, ma'am," Thomas said. "I won't do anything. Can I go on down and let Quinlan wrap a handkerchief around my arm? I don't want to bleed to death. I don't want to ruin your pretty floor and carpets."

"Go on, but try anything and you're dead."

Thomas was pale, his mouth drawn thin with pain. He was holding his arm tightly. Blood still dripped slowly between his fingers.

"Come here, Thomas," Quinlan said, motioning him forward with his hand. "You got a handkerchief?"

"Yeah, in my right coat pocket."

Quinlan pulled out a spiffy blue handkerchief with the initials TS in the corner and tied up his arm. "That should do it. Too bad you guys killed Doc Spiver, Amabel. Thomas could use his services right about now."

She had to come down those three remaining steps. She had to. Just three steps. Come on, Amabel, come on.

Sally said suddenly, her voice loud with shock, "There's blood coming from his mouth." She was pointing wildly at Amory St. John. "And something white, oh, my God, I think it's foam. He's foaming!"

"What?" Amabel came down the last three stairs, slowly, trying to keep her attention on the two agents and Sally and see what was wrong with Amory. "All of you, bunch together, there. Sit on the floor. Now."

They all sat.

Come a bit farther, Quinlan said to her silently. Just a bit farther. He saw Corey poised in the shadows, his SIG at the ready.

Amory St. John groaned. He jerked up, then fell back. He groaned again, opened his eyes.

Sally shrieked, "There's blood in his eyes. James, you hit him that hard?"

In those precious seconds when all of Amabel's attention was focused on Amory, Corey leaped from her left side, a lovely training move taught at Quantico, her right fist going right into Amabel's side, her left fist straight into her neck.

Amabel turned, but not in time. The gun went spinning out of her hand.

Corey said, "I'm sorry, Sally," and hit Amabel square in the jaw. She crumpled to the floor.

Amory St. John groaned again.

"Corey," Thomas said, "please say you'll marry me. Like a reformed smoker, I'm now a reformed sexist. I'll become a feminist."

Sally laughed from sheer relief. Quinlan told Thomas to stay where he was on the floor. He rose and shook hands with Corey and hugged Sally to his side. "Now we'll wait for the cavalry to arrive."

"I smell smoke," Thomas said, stiffening as he sniffed the air. "Quinlan, there's smoke coming from under that door."

"It's the kitchen," Sally said, dashing to it.

"No, Sally, don't open it. It'll just suck the flames in here."

Amory St. John moaned again and lurched to his side.

"More flames," Corey said. "Someone's set us on fire. The old folks have set the place on fire!"

"I'll carry St. John. Corey, you get Amabel. Sally, can you help Thomas? Let's get out of here."

"Whoever set the fire will be waiting for us," Sally said. "You know it, James."

"I'd rather risk being shot than burn to death," he said. "Everyone agree? There's no other way out except through the kitchen, and the door's already burning. It's got to be the front door."

"Let's go," Corey said, as she shoved the SIG in her belt. She heaved Amabel over her shoulder.

Quinlan, with St. John over his shoulder in a fireman's carry like Corey's, kicked the cottage door open. The sun was rising, the dawn sky streaked with pink. The air was crisp and clean, the sound of the ocean soft and rhythmic. It was a beautiful morning.

There were at least thirty people standing in front of the cottage, all of them armed.

Reverend Hal Vorhees shouted, "Throw down your gun, Mr. Quinlan, or we'll shoot the women."

At least the old folk hadn't automatically shot them down when they'd come out of Amabel's cottage. All the bravado about preferring a gunshot to a fire—was bullshit. Nobody wanted to die. Now they had some time—at least Quinlan prayed they did.

He nodded to Corey. She threw his SIG right at Reverend Hal Vorhees. It landed close to his feet.

"Good, now lay that madman down, Amabel next to him. We don't care what happens to him. He's evil and a blight. He's nothing more than a filthy traitor. He made Amabel turn on us. Come on now, the four of you come with us."

"We're going to a church service, Reverend?"

"Shut up, Mr. Quinlan," Hunker Dawson said.

"A helicopter will be arriving in about five minutes, Hal," Quinlan said after he'd dropped St. John to the ground, landing him in the middle of Amabel's daffodils.

"We called the FBI office in Portland from Doc Spiver's cottage. Sheriff David Mountebank's deputies will be here soon as well."

Actually the deputies should have been here long ago. Where the devil were they?

"No, we took care of the deputies," Gus Eisner said. "Come now. We don't want to waste any more time. You're lying about that helicopter. Besides, it don't make no difference. You'll be gone by the time the feds arrive."

"You'll never get away with this," Sally said. "Never. Don't you have any idea at all what you're dealing with?"

"Look at us, Sally," Sherry Vorhees said. "Look at all these nice old people. We wouldn't even kill mosquitoes, now would we? Who would deal with us? Why, there's nothing to deal with. I'd invite them all in for some of the World's Greatest Ice Cream."

"It's gone far beyond that now," Sally said, stepping forward.

Reverend Hal Vorhees immediately raised his gun higher. "Listen to me," Sally went on. "Everyone knows that James and the other agents are here. They'll mow you down. Another thing, they'll dig up every grave in the cemetery and they'll find out those are all the missing people reported over the past three years. It's all over. Please, be reasonable about this. Give it up."

"Shut up, Sally," said Hunker Dawson. "All of you, enough of this. Let's go."

"Yes, sure thing, Hunker," Quinlan said. They had more time. How much more, he had no idea. But even one more minute meant hope.

They walked like condemned prisoners in front of the mob. He was aware of the unreality of the whole situation even as he felt fear seeping deep into him.

Quinlan said over his shoulder, "What will you preach on this Sunday, Hal? The rewards of evil? The spiritual high of mass murder? No, I've got it. It'll be the wages of trying to bring justice to people who were brutally murdered for the amount of cash they carried."

Quinlan staggered from the blow on his shoulder.

"That's enough," Gus Eisner said. "Shut up. You're upsetting the ladies."

"I'm not upset," Corey said. "I'd like to pull out all your teeth and listen to you scream."

"I don't have any teeth," Hunker said. "That ain't a good punishment for this group."

What to say to that? Quinlan thought and winked at Corey. She looked furious. Thomas was walking on his own, but Corey was helping him. His arm wasn't bleeding so much now, but the blood loss was taking its toll, that and shock.

Sally was trudging along beside him, looking pale and very thoughtful. He said out of the side of his mouth, real low, so maybe all those old people wouldn't hear him, "Hold up, Sally. We'll figure out something. Hey, I can take at least a dozen of the old guys, no problem. Could you pound the old ladies?"

That made her smile. "Yeah, I could pound them into the dust. But I want to go back and get Amory St. John. They left him and Amabel there, James, both of them. They'll get away. My aunt, well, I don't know, but she's not quite the aunt I'd hoped she was."

An understatement, Quinlan thought. Another blow for her, another person she'd believed she could trust had betrayed her. Thank God her mother had come through for her. He thought he just might come to like Noelle St. John a lot in the future. If he had a future.

Quinlan said, "Maybe the calvary will arrive before St. John and your aunt get their wits back together and can get away. But even if they do escape, we'll get them sooner or later."

To Quinlan's surprise, they were herded up the wide, beautifully painted white steps and into Thelma's Bed and Breakfast. He had thought they'd be taken to the Vorhees house.

"Would you look at that," Quinlan said as he got a poke with a rifle, shoving him into the large drawing room. There was Thelma Nettro, sitting on that chair of hers that looked for all the world like a throne. She was smiling at them. She was wearing a full mouth of false teeth and her pumpkin peach lipstick.

She said, "I wanted to join in the fun, but I don't get around as well as I used to."

There was Purn Davies sitting on one of the sofas, looking white and shriveled. Good, Corey had whacked him hard.

"Why are we here?" Quinlan asked, turning to Reverend Hal Vorhees.

"You're here because I wanted you here. Because I ordered my people to bring you to me. Because, Mr. Quinlan, I'm going to tell you all what we're going to do with you."

They all stared at Martha as she moved from behind Thelma Nettro's chair. There was nothing soft and bosomy about her now. There were no pearls around her neck. Her voice was loud and clear, a commander's voice, not her gentle cook's voice announcing an incredible meal. What was going on here?

"Martha?" Sally said, bewildered. "Oh, no, not you too, Martha?"

"Don't look so surprised."

"I don't understand," Sally said. "You're a wonderful cook, Martha. You go out with poor Ed. You take grief from Thelma. You're nice, damn you. What's going on?"

Quinlan said slowly, "I knew there had to be a ringleader, one person with a vision, one person who could get all the others to fall in line. Aren't I right, Martha?"

"Exactly right, Mr. Quinlan."

"Why didn't you let them elect you mayor?" Sally said. "Why murder innocent people?"

"I'll let that go, Sally," Martha said. "Oh, poor Mr. Shredder. You, Corey, set him down in that chair. Too bad Doc Spiver fell sick of cowardice and remorse. He drew the straw and had to kill that woman who'd overheard a meeting we were having. We caught her on the phone, dialing nine-one-one. Poor bitch. She was different. We didn't know what to do with her. She wasn't like those tourists who came into town for the World's Greatest Ice Cream. No, we wouldn't ever have picked her. She was too young; she had children. But then, we didn't know what to do with her either. We couldn't very well let her go.

"When she got loose that first night and screamed her head off—you heard her, Sally, Amabel told us the next day—we put a guard on her. But then two nights later she got loose again, and that time Amabel was forced to call Hal Vorhees over, because of you, Sally. There was no choice. Since it was Doc's fault that she got loose, since he'd been her guard, we all decided that she had to die. There was simply no other choice. We were sorry about it, but it had to be done, and Doc Spiver had to kill her. But he couldn't stomach it. He was going to call Sheriff Mountebank." She shrugged.

"Fair is fair. We've always been scrupulously fair. Helen Keaton drew the straw. She put the gun in his mouth and pulled the trigger. If it hadn't been for that sheriff and that medical examiner in Portland, it would have been declared suicide. Yes, that was a pity. Amazingly unfair."

It was remarkable, Quinlan was thinking, that every criminal he'd ever known had loved to talk, to brag about how great he was, how he was smarter than everyone else. Even a little old lady.

"Yeah," he said, "a real pity."

Martha was fiddling with her glasses, since she wasn't wearing her pearls, but her voice was calm and assured. "You don't appreciate what we've done, Mr. Quinlan. We turned a squalid little ghost town into a picture postcard village. Everything is pristine. Everything is beautifully planned. We leave nothing to chance. We discuss everything. We even have a gardening service for those who don't enjoy tending flowers. We have a painting service that comes in every week. Of course, we also have a chairperson for each service. We are an intelligent, loyal, industrious group of older citizens. Each of us has a responsibility, each has an assignment."

"Who selects the victims?" Corey asked. She was standing beside Thomas, her hand on his shoulder. He was still conscious, but his face was white as death. She'd wrapped a hand-crocheted afghan around him. It looked as if a grandmother had spent hours putting those soft pastel squares together.

Quinlan stared at that afghan. Then he stared at Martha. He'd be willing to wager she had knitted the afghan. No accounting for grandmothers. Martha was a vicious, cold-blooded killer.

Martha laughed softly. "Who? Why, all of us, Ms. Harper. Our four gentlemen who play gin rummy around their barrel? They look over everyone who drives in for refreshment at the World's Greatest Ice Cream Shop.

"Zeke down at the cafe eyes every tourist from his window in the kitchen. When he's too busy, then Nelda pays attention when folk take out their wallets to pay.

"Sherry and Della run the souvenir shop in that little cottage close to the ocean cliffs. They check out tourists there. As you can imagine, we must make decisions very quickly." She sighed. "Sometimes we've erred. A pity. One couple looked so very affluent, drove a Mercedes even, but we only found three hundred dollars, nothing else of any use. All we could do was send Gus to Portland with the car to sell it. It turned out it was leased. That was close. As I recall, Ralph refused to lay them out, didn't you, Ralph? You said they didn't deserve it. And we all agreed. They weren't honest with us. They lied."

"Exactly right," Ralph Keaton said. "I wrapped them each in a cheap sheet, the dirty liars. Helen wanted the name Shylock on their grave marker, but we knew we couldn't be that obvious so we changed it to Smith, so nondescript it was like they'd never even existed."

"This is amazing," Sally said, looking at each one of those old faces. "Truly amazing. You're all mad. I wonder what they'll do with all of you. Put you all on trial as mass murderers? Or chuck you into an insane asylum?"

"I hear a helicopter," Reverend Hal Vorhees said. "We've got to hurry, Martha."

"You're going to shoot us?" Corey asked, stepping away from Thomas. "You honest to God think you can get away with killing all of us?"

"Of course we can," Purn Davies said, rising from the sofa, looking a bit less pale. He picked up a shotgun from beside him and walked forward. "We've got nothing to lose. Nothing at all. Isn't that right, Martha?"

"Perfectly right, Purn."

"You're all senile and stupid!" Sally screamed.

In that instant, when most attention was focused on Sally, Quinlan grabbed Purn Davies's sawed-off shotgun and leaped at Martha. He took her down and rolled over her. He had his arm around her throat and the gun digging into the small of her back. His right hand was tangled in the chain that secured her glasses.

There was stunned silence. Thelma Nettro slowly turned around in her chair. "Let her go, Mr. Quinlan. If you don't, we'll kill her along with the rest of you. You agree, don't you, Martha?"

There was no choice, none at all. Quinlan knew that. He knew he had to act quickly, with no hesitation. He had to make them believe. He had to scare them down to their old bones. It had to be shocking. It had to punch these old people back to reality, out of the insane world they'd created and inhabited. He had to show them they had no more control.

Quinlan raised the shotgun and shot Purn Davies in the chest. The blast knocked the old man off the floor, against an ancient piano. Blood spewed everywhere. The old man didn't make a sound, just slid onto the floor. There were a dozen screams, curses, and horrified yells.

Quinlan shouted over the din, "I can get at least three more of you before you get me. Want to bet it's not going to be you? Come on, you old geezers, come and try it."

The shotgun was double-barreled. One of them would realize quickly enough that he had only one shot left.

"Corey, grab my gun, quick."

She had it in an instant. Reverend Hal Vorhees raised his pistol. Quinlan shot him cleanly through his right arm. Corey threw Quinlan his SIG.

"Who else?" Quinlan said. "This gun is a semiautomatic. It can take you all down. Anybody else? It will make a bigger, bloodier mess than that wimpy little shotgun did on old Purn. It'll spew your ancient guts all over this room. I'll bet none of you has ever dispatched your victim with a semiautomatic. It ain't a pretty sight. Look at Purn. Yeah, look at him. It could be you."

Silence. Dead silence. He heard someone vomiting. That was amazing. One of them could actually throw up seeing Purn Davies after they'd killed sixty people?

Thelma Nettro said, "You all right, Martha?"

"Oh, yes," Martha said. She flexed her hands. She smiled. She kicked back against Quinlan's groin. He felt searing pain, felt his head swim with dizziness, felt the inevitable nausea. He hit her on the temple with his SIG.

He didn't know if she was dead. He didn't particularly care. He said between gritted teeth as the nausea began to get to him, "Sally, get me Gus's gun. Be sure to stay clear of any hands that could grab you. The rest of you, drop all your weapons. Ease down to the floor. We're going to stay here nice and quiet until my guys arrive."

Thelma Nettro said, "Did you kill her, Mr. Quinlan?"

"I don't know," he said, the pain still roiling through his groin.

"Martha's like a daughter to me. Don't you remember? I told you that once." She raised a pistol from her lap and shot him.

In the next instant, the front door burst open. Sally, who was running to Quinlan, heard a man shout, "Nobody move! FBI!"

THIRTY-THREE

"Agent Quinlan, can you hear me?"

"Yes," he said very clearly. "I can hear you, but I don't want to. Go away. I hurt and I want to hurt alone. My Boy Scout leader told me a long time ago that men didn't whine or moan, except in private."

"You're a trooper, Agent Quinlan. Now, I'll make that hurt go away. How bad is it?"

"On a scale from one to ten, it's a thirteen. Go away. Let me groan in peace."

The nurse smiled over at Sally. "Is he always like this?"

"I don't know. This is the first time I've ever been around him when he's been shot."

"Hopefully that won't happen again."

"It won't," Sally said. "If he ever lets it happen again, I'll kill him."

The nurse injected morphine into his IV drip. "There," she said, lightly rubbing his arm above the elbow, "you won't hurt very soon now. As soon as you have your wits together, you can give yourself pain medication whenever you need it. Ah, here's Dr. Wiggs."

The surgeon was tall, skinny as a post, with the most beautiful black eyes Quinlan had ever seen. "I'm in Portland?"

"Yes, at OHSU, Oregon Health and Sciences University Hospital. I'm Dr. Wiggs. I took that bullet out of your chest. You're doing fine, Agent

Quinlan. I hear you're a very brave man. It's a pleasure to save a brave man."

"I'm going to get even braver soon," Quinlan said, his voice a bit slurred from the morphine. He was feeling fine now. In fact, if he weren't tied to this damned bed with all these hookups in every orifice of his body, he'd want to dance, maybe even play his saxophone. He'd like to call Ms. Lilly, maybe even tell Marvin the Bouncer a joke. He realized his mind wasn't quite on track. He had to remember to ask Fuzz the Bartender to get some decent white wine in stock for Sally.

"Why is that, Agent Quinlan?" the nurse asked.

"Why is what?"

"Why are you going to get even braver?"

He frowned, then smiled as he remembered. He said, his voice as proud and happy as a man's could ever get, "I'm going to marry Sally."

He turned his head and gave her the silliest smile she'd ever seen. "We're going to spend our honeymoon at my cabin in Maryland. On Louise Lynn Lake. It's a beautiful place, with smells that make your senses melt and—"

He was out.

"Good," Dr. Wiggs said. "He needs lots of sleep. Don't worry, Ms. Brainerd. He'll be fine. I was a bit worried for a while in surgery, but he's young and strong and he's got a will to survive that's rare.

"Now, let me just check him over. Why don't you go outside? Agent Shredder and Agent Harper are in the waiting room. Oh, yes, there's a Mr. Marvin Brammer there too and a man who's sitting on the sofa with a computer on his lap."

"Mr. Brammer is James's boss. The guy with the computer—"

"The sexy one."

"Yes, that's Agent Savich. He's also FBI."

"Mr. Brammer's got quite a twinkle in those eyes of his," Dr. Wiggs said. "As for Agent Savich, no matter how gorgeous he is, I don't know if he's even aware of where he is. I heard him say, to no one in particular, 'Eureka!' but nothing else. Go out now, Ms. Brainerd, and leave me alone with my patient."

The waiting room was down the hall. Sally ran into Marvin Brammer's arms. "He's all right," she said over and over. "He'll be fine. He's already complaining. He was talking about his Boy Scout leader telling him that men never whine or moan except when they're alone. He'll be fine. We're going to get married, and I'll make sure he never gets shot again."

"Good," Marvin Brammer said, hugged her tightly, then turned her over to Savich, who gave her a distracted hug and kiss on the cheek. "I've found them, Sally," he said. "I've found that monster who isn't your father."

Marvin Brammer said, "Eureka?"

"That's it. I've got to call the FBI office in Seattle. They're at Sea-Tac Airport. Yeah, the idiot bought two tickets to Budapest, via New York. He used a phony credit card and a phony passport."

"Then how did you get him?" Thomas Shredder said, walking over. His arm was in a sling. He had good color in his cheeks again. "He doesn't look like Amory St. John anymore."

"Not hard," Savich said, patting his laptop. "Me and MAX here and our modem can do anything. Sally's aunt used her own passport. Ain't that a kick? She had to, I guess. I suppose they prayed she'd get through. They should have laid low until they got a phony one for her too. Corey, you and Thomas must have really scared them. They couldn't wait to get out of the country."

"So," Sally said slowly, as Savich phoned the Seattle FBI office, "it's nearly over. What's going to happen to the town, Mr. Brammer?"

"Agents are all over the cemetery. Like the old folk said, they buried all the people they murdered with their identification, so there's been no problem determining who anybody is.

"Mass murder, nothing else to call it, all by a bunch of senior citizens." He shook his head. "I thought I'd seen everything, but this takes the cake.

"Evil," he added, stroking his chin. "Evil can sprout up anyplace. None of the seniors is saying a word. They're loyal to each other, I'll say that for them, even though it doesn't matter. That Martha Crittlan, she'll pull through, although I'll bet she'll wish she hadn't. Imagine, that seemingly sweet lady was the brains and resolution behind the town."

"She's the most wonderful cook," Corey Harper said and sighed. "That last dinner was the most delicious meal I've ever eaten in my life."

"Yeah," Thomas Shredder said, "and it could have been our last meal, since she drugged us."

"You'll survive," Marvin Brammer said. "Oh, yes, one of the agents found a slew of diaries that old Thelma Nettro kept throughout all her time in The Cove."

Sally said, "She always had one with her. Do you know that she had a black circle on her tongue from licking the end of the fountain pen before she wrote?"

"Knowing our people, they'll probably check for that. Old Thelma was very specific about how everything came about. It's probably the best proof and history anyone could have of the entire episode. I mean, she wrote everything, beginning back in the 1950s five or so years after she and her husband came to The Cove.

"It's all the attorney general's problem now. I'll wager they're hating every minute of it. You can't begin to imagine what the media are doing with all this. Well, maybe you can. It's nuts. At least Sheriff Mountebank came out of the coma this morning, that's one good thing. His three deputies are pulling through as well. They were drugged and tied up in that shed where you guys were."

"Amory St. John and my aunt Amabel," Sally said. "Mr. Brammer, what will happen to them when you nab them?"

"He'll be in jail three lifetimes. As for your aunt, Sally, I don't know if they'll toss her in with the other seniors or if they'll add kidnapping charges and conspiracy charges. We'll have to see."

"Eureka again!"

Everyone turned to Savich. He looked up, grinning a bit sheepishly. "I wanted all of you to know that Sally's divorce will be final in six months. Let's make it the middle of October. I've booked Elm Street Presbyterian in D.C. for the fourteenth. Everything's set."

"Will you marry me, Corey?" Thomas Shredder said.

She gave him a sharp look. "You have to prove to me you're no longer a sexist. That could take a good year, even if you try really hard. Don't forget, a condition is that I become the SAC of the Portland office."

"You could always shoot him in the other arm if he backslides," Brammer said. "As to special agent in charge, why, Ms. Harper, I'll do a great deal of thinking about that."

Sally smiled at them all—all of them lifelong friends now—and walked back to James's room.

He would live. As to all the rest of it, well, she wasn't going to think about it until she had to.

Life was all in your perspective, she'd decided during that helicopter ride to Portland, James white as death lying on that stretcher beside her, tubes sticking out of him. She was going to keep her perspective on James's face. A nice face, a sexy face. She couldn't wait for him to get well so they could go to the *Bonhomie Club* and he could play his saxophone.

THE next morning, Quinlan opened the *Oregonian* that a nurse had brought him. The headline was:

ARMORY ST. JOHN KILLED
WHILE FLEEING FBI

Like he didn't deserve it, he thought. "Yeah, poor bugger," he said aloud, and read on. Evidently Amory St. John had tried to run, but he hadn't made it. He'd left Amabel in a flash, jumped onto a baggage truck, knocked out the driver, and driven off, the FBI right behind him. He hadn't gotten far. He'd even been stupid enough to fire on the agents, refusing orders to stop and throw down his weapon.

He was dead. The bastard was finally dead. Sally wouldn't have to go through a trial. She wouldn't ever have to face him again.

What about Amabel?

Apparently the *Oregonian* hadn't known which headline to splash— The Cove murders or Amory St. John. Since The Cove had gotten the big print the day before, he supposed they decided it was Amory's turn.

Amabel Perdy, he read, had pleaded innocent of all charges, both with regard to Amory St. John and with regard to The Cove, saying she had no idea what was going on in either case. She was an artist, she maintained. She helped sell the World's Greatest Ice Cream. That was all she did.

Wait until the media found out about Thelma's diaries, he thought. That would nail her hide but good. All of the seniors' hides. He was tired, his chest hurt real bad, and so he pumped a small dose of morphine into his arm.

Soon, he knew, he would be sleeping like a baby, his mind free of all this crap. He just wished he could see Sally before he went under again.

When she appeared at his bedside, smiling down at him, he knew he must be dreaming.

"You look like an angel."

He heard a laugh and felt her mouth on his, all warm and soft.

"Nice," he said. "More."

"Go to sleep, buster," she said. "I'll be here when you wake up."

"Every morning?"

"Yes. Always."

EPILOGUE

Sally St. John Brainerd and James Railey Quinlan were married on the date Dillon Savich had set for them—October 14. Dillon Savich was Quinlan's best man and Sally's mother was her matron of honor. She attended her daughter's wedding with Senator Matt Montgomery from Iowa, a widower who'd taken one look at Noelle and fallen hard. She had worn a two-piece bathing suit that summer.

There were one hundred and fifty special agents from the FBI, including two special agents from the Portland field office, one of them the newly appointed SAC, or special agent in charge. Every Railey and Quinlan within striking distance arrived at the Elm Street Presbyterian Church in Washington, D.C. Sally was simply enfolded into her new family.

Ms. Lilly, Marvin the Bouncer, and Fuzz the Bartender were in attendance, Ms. Lilly wearing white satin and Marvin announcing to everyone that the chicky looked gorgeous in her wedding dress. Fuzz brought a bottle of Chardonnay for a wedding present. It had a cork.

The media mobbed the wedding, which was expected since the trial of Dr. Beadermeyer—aka Norman Lipsy—had ended the previous week and Sally had been one of the major prosecution witnesses. He'd been found guilty of conspiracy, murder, kidnapping, extortion, and income tax evasion, which, a TV news anchorwoman said, was the most serious of all the charges and would keep him in jail until the twenty-second century.

Scott Brainerd had plea-bargained to a charge of kidnapping and conspiracy, which the government finally agreed to, since the feds could find no solid proof of his activity in arms dealing. He was sentenced to ten years in jail. But Sally knew, she told Quinlan, that Scott would have the best behavior in the entire prison system. She'd bet the little worm would be out in three years, curse him. Quinlan rubbed his hands together and said he couldn't wait.

In the previous June, Sally had become the senior aide to Senator Bob McCain. She had begun showing Quinlan a glitzy Washington, D.C., that was sleazy in a very different way from what he was used to. He said he wasn't certain which Washington was more fascinating. Sally was running every day, usually with James, and in July she began to sing in the shower again.

Amabel Perdy, it had been agreed to in late July, was going to be treated differently from the other fifty members of The Cove. Besides committing eight murders—four by stabbing—she'd also shot a special agent, kidnapped her niece, and aided and abetted the escape of a murder suspect, thus becoming an accessory. Her trial would be held at the end of the year. Neither Quinlan nor Sally was looking forward to it.

All the murders were detailed in Thelma Nettro's diaries—how they had been done, when, and by whom. Thelma Nettro wrote that there was little or no remorse among the townspeople after the twentieth victim had been dispatched. Poison was the favored method, she wrote, because Ralph Keaton didn't like mess when he laid the people out for burial.

She herself had murdered two people, an old couple from Arkansas, she wrote, who'd died quickly, smiling, because they'd eaten slices of Martha's New Jersey cheesecake and hadn't tasted the poison.

It came out that the last two murders of old people who'd had the misfortune to want to try the World's Greatest Ice Cream had occurred two months before Sally Quinlan had arrived for the first time in The Cove to hide at her aunt Amabel's cottage. Reverend Hal Vorhees had drawn the highest number. He'd persuaded an affluent old couple to remain for a special evening spiritual revival service that had been organized that very afternoon.

Thelma had written in her diary that it had been a very pleasant service, with many people rising to give thanks to God for what He'd done for them. There were punch and cookies after the service. Revered Hal hadn't put enough arsenic in the cookies, and the old couple had had to be poisoned again, which distressed everyone, particularly Doc Spiver.

Three books were being written on The Cove, all with a different slant, the biggest best-seller presenting Reverend Hal Vorhees as a crazed messiah who had murdered children in Arizona, then come to The Cove and converted all the townspeople to a form of Satanism.

Since it was obvious that the murders would have continued until either all the townspeople died off or were caught, as was the case, the Justice Department and the lawyers agreed that the old people would be separated, each one sent to a different mental institution in a different state. The attorney general said simply in an interview after the formal sentencing, "We can't trust any two of them together. Look what happened before."

The ACLU objected, but not very strenuously, contending that the ingredients in the World's Greatest Ice Cream (the recipe remained a secret) had induced an irresponsible hysteria in the old people that led them to lose their sense of moral value and judgment. Thus they shouldn't be held answerable for their deeds. When the ACLU lawyer was asked if she would go to The Cove to buy ice cream, she allowed that she would only if she was wearing tattered blue jeans and driving a very old Volkswagen Beetle. Perhaps, one newspaper editorial said, it was a collective sugar high that drove them all to do it.

Thelma Nettro died peacefully in her sleep before the final disposition of her friends. Martha hanged herself in her cell when she was told by a matron in mid-July that young Ed had died of prostate cancer.

As for The Cove and the World's Greatest Ice Cream, both ceased to exist. The sign at the junction of highways 101 and 101A fell down some two years later and lay there until a memorabilia buff hauled it away to treasure it in his basement.

Hikers still visit The Cove now and again. Not much there now, but the view from the cliffs at sunset—with or without a martini—is spectacular.

THE MAZE

ACKNOWLEDGMENTS

Whenever I hear writers brag about how their editors don't require any changes to their manuscripts, I'm honestly floored. It's an editor's job to be the reader's representative and thus make the manuscript better. And believe me, a manuscript can always be made better.

I've got to be the luckiest writer ever. I don't have just one editor, I have a three-person hack-and-maim team, and all three of them give me very timely feedback, all with an eye to making my novels the best they can be. My ongoing thanks to Stacy Creamer, Leslie Gelbman, and Phyllis Grann.

I'd also like to thank my husband, Anton, for getting back into the editing saddle after a ten-year hiatus. He's the Editor from Hell (in the good sense).

And finally, my continuing thanks to Karen Evans with the red Babylonian harlot hair. Without her incredible mental energy, enthusiasm, and support, I would soon find myself in a sorry state.

Life is good.

ONE

It wouldn't stop, ever.

She couldn't breathe. She was dying. She sat upright in her bed wheezing, trying to control the terror. She turned on the lamp beside her bed. There was nothing there. No, there were shadows that kept the corners dark and frightening. But the door was closed. She always closed her bedroom door at night and locked it, then tilted a chair against it so that its back was snug against the doorknob, for good measure.

She stared at that door. It didn't move. It didn't so much as rattle in its frame. The knob did not turn. No one was on the other side trying to get in.

No one this time.

She made herself look over toward the window. She'd wanted to put bars on all the windows when she moved in seven months before, but at the last minute she decided that if she did she would have made herself a prisoner forever. Instead she'd switched to the fourth-floor apartment. There were two floors above her and no balconies. No one could come in through the window. And no one would think she was crazy because she lived on the fourth floor. It was a good move. There was no way she could continue living at home, where Belinda had lived. Where Douglas had lived.

The images were in her mind, always faded, always blurred, but still there and still menacing: bloody, but just beyond her ability to put them in focus. She was in a large dark space, huge; she couldn't see the beginning or the end of it. But there was a light, a narrow focused light, and she heard a voice. And the screams. Loud, right there on her. And there was Belinda, always Belinda.

She was still choking on the fear. She didn't want to get up, but she made herself. She had to go to the bathroom. Thank God the bathroom was off the bedroom. Thank God she didn't have to unlock the bedroom door, pull the chair back from beneath the knob, and open it onto the dark hallway.

She flipped the bathroom light on before she went into the room, then blinked rapidly at the harsh light. She saw movement from the corner of her eye. Her throat clogged with terror. She whirled around: It was only herself in the mirror.

She stared at her reflection. She didn't recognize the wild woman before her. All she saw was fear: the twitching eyes, the sheen of sweat on her forehead, her hair ratty, her sleep shirt damp with perspiration.

She leaned close to the mirror. She stared at the pathetic woman whose face was still tense with fear. She realized in that moment that if she didn't make some serious changes the woman in the mirror would die.

To the woman staring back at her, she said, "Seven months ago I was supposed to go study music at Juilliard. I was the best. I loved making music, all the way from Mozart to John Lennon. I wanted to win the Fletcher competition. But I didn't. Now I'm afraid of everything, including the dark."

She turned slowly away from the mirror and walked back into her bedroom. She walked to the window, turned the three locks that held it firmly in place, and pulled it up. It was difficult. The window hadn't been opened since she'd moved in.

She looked out into the night. There was a quarter moon. There were stars flooding the sky. The air was cool and fresh. She could see Alcatraz, Angel Island beyond it. She could see the few lights in Sausalito, across the bay. The TransAmerica Building was brightly lit, a beacon in downtown San Francisco.

She turned away and walked to the bedroom door. She stood there a very long time. Finally she pulled the chair away and set it where it belonged, in the corner beside a reading light. She unlocked the door. No more, she thought, staring at that door, no more.

She flung it open. She stepped out into the hallway and stopped, every burgeoning whisper of courage in her freezing as she couldn't help but hear the sound of a creaking board not more than twenty feet away. The sound came again. No, it wasn't a creak; it was a lighter sound. It seemed to be coming from the small foyer by the front door. Who could be toying with her this way? Her own breath whooshed out. She was shaking, so frightened she could taste copper in her mouth. Copper? She'd bitten her lip, drawn blood.

How much longer could she live like this?

She dashed forward, turning on every light as she went. There was the sound again, this time like something lightly bumping against a piece of furniture—something that was a lot smaller than she was, something that was afraid of her. Then she saw it scurry into the kitchen. She burst out laughing, then slowly sank to the floor, her hands over her face as she sobbed.

TWO

Seven Years Later
FBI Academy
Quantico, Virginia

She would get to the top of that rope if it killed her. And it just might. She could actually feel each individual muscle in her arms pulling, stretching, feel the burning pain, the rippling cramps that were very close to knotting up on her. If that happened, she'd go sprawling to the mat below. Her brain already felt numb, but that was okay. Her brain wasn't climbing. It had just gotten her into this fix. And this was only the second round. It seemed as if she'd been climbing this rope since she was born.

Just two more feet. She could do it. She heard MacDougal's steady, unhurried breathing beside her. From the corner of her eye she saw his huge fists cover that rope, methodically clamping down one fist over the other, not consuming that rope as he usually did. No, he was keeping pace with her. He wasn't going to leave her. She owed him. This was an important test. This one really mattered.

"I see that pathetic look, Sherlock. You're whining even though you're not saying anything. Get those twerpy arms working. Pull!"

She grabbed that rope three inches above her left hand and pulled with all her strength.

"Come on, Sherlock," Mac said, hanging beside her, grinning at her, the bastard. "Don't wimp out on me now. I've worked with you for two months. You're up to twelve-pound weights. All right, so you can only do ten reps on your biceps, but you can do twenty-five on your triceps. Come on now, do it. Don't just hang there like a girl."

Whine? She didn't have enough breath to whine. He was goading her, doing a good job of it actually. She tried to get annoyed. There wasn't a pissed bone in her body, only pain, deep and burning. Eight more inches, no, more like nine inches. It would take her two years to get those nine inches. She saw her right hand pull free of the rope, grab the bar at the very top of the knotted rope that was surely too far for her to make in one haul, but her right hand closed over that bar and she knew she'd either do it or she wouldn't.

"You can do it, Sherlock. Remember last week in Hogan's Alley when that guy pissed you off? Tried to handcuff you and haul you off as a hostage? You nearly killed him. You wound up having to apologize to him. That took more strength than this. Think mean. Think dead-meat thoughts. Kill the rope. Pull!"

She didn't think of the guy in Hogan's Alley; no, she thought of that monster, focused on a face she'd never seen, focused on the soul-deep misery he'd heaped upon her for seven years. She wasn't even aware when she hauled herself up those final inches.

She hung there, breathing hard, clearing her mind of that horrible time. Mac was laughing beside her, not even out of breath. But he was all brute strength she'd told him many times; he'd been born in a gym, under a pile of free weights.

She'd done it.

Mr. Petterson, their instructor, was standing below them. He was at least two stories below them; she would have sworn to that. He yelled up, "Good going, you two. Come on down now. MacDougal, you could have made it a little faster, like half the time you took. You think you're on vacation?"

Mac shouted down to Petterson since she didn't have a breath in her lungs, "We're coming, sir!" He said to her, grinning so wide she could see the gold filling in a molar, "You did good, Sherlock. You have gotten stronger. Thinking mean thoughts helped, too. Let's get down and let two other mean dudes climb this sucker."

She needed no encouragement. She loved going down. The pain disappeared when her body knew it was almost over. She was down nearly as fast as Mac. Mr. Petterson waved a pencil at them, then scribbled something on his pad. He looked up and nodded. "That was it, Sherlock. You made it within the time limit. As for you, Mac, you were way too slow, but the sheet says you pass so you pass. Next!"

"Piece of cake," Mac said, as he handed her a towel to wipe off her face. "Look at all that sweat on you."

If she'd had the energy, she would have slugged him.

SHE was in Hogan's Alley, the highest-crime-rate city in the United States. She knew just about every inch of every building in this town, certainly better than the actors who were paid eight dollars an hour to play bad guys, better than many of the bureau employees who were witnesses and robbers alike. Hogan's Alley looked like a real town; it even had a mayor and a postmistress, but they didn't live here. Nobody really lived here or really worked here. It was the FBI's own American town, rife with criminals to be caught, situations to be resolved, preferably without killing anyone. Instructors didn't like innocent bystanders to be shot.

Today she and three other trainees were going to catch a bank robber. She hoped. They were told to keep their eyes open, nothing else. It was a parade day in Hogan's Alley. A festive occasion, and that made it all the more dangerous. There was a crowd of people, drinking sodas and eating hot dogs. It wasn't going to be easy. Chances were that the guy was going to be one of the people trying to blend in with the crowd, trying to look as innocent as an everyday guy; she'd stake a claim on that. She would have given anything if they'd gotten a brief glance at the robber, but they hadn't. It was a critical situation, lots of innocent civilians milling about and a bank robber who would probably run out of the bank, a bank robber who was probably very dangerous.

She saw Buzz Alport, an all-night waiter at a truck stop off I-95. He was whistling, looking as if he didn't have a care in the world. No, Buzz wasn't the bad guy today. She knew him too well. His face flushed scarlet when he played the bad guy. She tried to memorize every face, so she'd be able to spot the robber if he suddenly appeared. She slowly worked the crowd, calm and unhurried, the way she'd been trained.

She saw some visitors from the Hill, standing on the sidelines, watching the agents' role-playing simulations. The trainees would have to be careful. It wouldn't look good for the Bureau if any of them killed a visiting congressman.

It began. She and Porter Forge, a southerner from Birmingham who spoke beautiful French without a hint of a drawl, saw a bank employee lurch out of the front doors, yelling at the top of his lungs, waving frantically at a man who had just fled through a side door. They got no more than a brief glimpse. They went after him. The perp dove into the crowd of people and disappeared. Because there were civilians around, they kept their guns holstered. If any one of them hurt a civilian, there'd be hell to pay.

Three minutes later they'd lost him.

It was then she saw Dillon Savich, an FBI agent and computer genius who taught occasional classes here at Quantico, standing next to a man she'd never seen before. Both were wearing sunglasses and blue suits and blue-gray ties.

She'd know Savich anywhere. She wondered what he was doing here at this particular time. Had he just taught a class? She'd never heard about his being at Hogan's Alley. She stared hard at him. Was it possible that he was the suspect the bank employee had been waving at as he'd dashed into the crowd? Maybe. She tried to place him in that brief instant of memory. It was possible. Only thing was that he didn't look at all out of breath, and the bank robber had run out of the bank like a bat out of hell. Savich looked cool and disinterested.

Nah, it couldn't be Savich. Savich wouldn't join in the exercise, would he? Suddenly, she saw a man some distance away from her slowly slip his hand into his jacket. He was going for a gun. She yelled to Porter.

While the other trainees were distracted, Savich moved away from the man he'd been talking to and ducked behind three civilians. Three other civilians who were close to the other guy were yelling and shoving, trying to get out of the way.

What was going on here?

"Sherlock! Where'd he go?"

She began to smile even as other agents were pushing and shoving, trying desperately to sort out who was who. She never lost sight of Savich. She slipped into the crowd. It took her under a minute to come around him from behind.

There was a woman next to him. It was very possibly about to become a hostage situation. She saw Savich slowly reach out his hand toward the woman. She couldn't take the chance. She drew her gun, came right up behind him, and whispered in his ear as she pressed the nose of the 9mm SIG pistol into the small of his back, "Freeze. FBI."

"Ms. Sherlock, I presume?"

She felt a moment of uncertainty, then quashed it. She had the robber. He was just trying to rattle her. "Listen to me, buddy, that's not part of the script. You're not supposed to know me. Now, get your hands behind your back or you're going to be in big trouble."

"I don't think so," he said, and began to turn.

The woman next to them saw the gun, screamed, and yelled, "Oh my God, the robber's a woman! Here she is! She's going to kill a man. She's got a gun! Help!"

"Get your hands behind your back!" But how was she going to get cuffs on him? The woman was still yelling. Other people were looking now, not knowing what to do. She didn't have much time.

"Do it or I'll shoot you."

He moved so quickly she didn't have a chance. He knocked the pistol out of her hand with a chop of his right hand, numbing her entire arm, bulled his head into her stomach and sent her flying backward, wheezing for breath, landing in a mass of petunias in the flower bed beside the Hogan's Alley Post Office.

He was laughing. The bastard was laughing at her. She sucked in air as hard and fast as she could. Her stomach was on fire. He stuck out his hand to pull her up.

"You're under arrest," she said and slipped a small Lady Colt .38 from her ankle holster. She gave him a big grin. "Don't move or I guarantee you'll regret it. Since I climbed that rope, I know I'm capable of just about anything."

His laughter died. He looked at the gun, then at her, up on her elbows in the petunia bed. There were a half dozen men and women standing there watching, holding their breath. She yelled out, "Stay back, all of you. This man's dangerous. He just robbed the bank. I didn't do it, he did. I'm FBI. Stay back!"

"That Colt isn't Bureau issue."

"Shut up. You so much as twitch and I'll shoot you."

He made a very small movement toward her, but she wasn't going to let him get her this time. He was into martial arts, was he? She knew she was smashing the petunias, but she didn't see any way around it. Mrs. Shaw would come after her because the flower beds were her pride and joy, but she was only doing her job. She couldn't let him get the better of her again.

She kept inching away from him, that Colt steady on his chest. She came up slowly, keeping her distance. "Turn around and put your hands behind you."

"I don't think so," he said again. She didn't even see his leg, but she did hear the rip of his pants. The Colt went flying onto the sidewalk.

She was caught off guard. Surely an escaping crook would turn tail and run, not stand there looking at her. He wasn't behaving the way he should. "How'd you do that?"

Where were her partners?

Where was Mrs. Shaw, the postmistress? She'd once caught the designated bank robber by threatening him with a frying pan.

Then he was on her. This time, she moved as quickly as he did. She knew he wouldn't hurt her, just disable her, jerk her onto her face and humiliate her in front of everyone, which would be infinitely worse than being actually hurt. She rolled to the side, came up, saw Porter Forge from the corner of her eye, caught the SIG from him, turned and fired. She got him in midleap.

The red paint spread all over the front of his white shirt, his conservative tie, and his dark blue suit.

He flailed about, managing to keep his balance. He straightened, stared down at her, stared down at his shirt, grunted, and fell onto his back into the flower bed, his arms flung out.

"Sherlock, you idiot, you shot the new coach of Hogan's Alley High School's football team!" It was the mayor of Hogan's Alley and he wasn't happy. He stood over her, yelling. "Didn't you read the paper? Didn't you see his picture? You live here and you don't know what's going on? Coach Savich was hired last week. You just killed an innocent man."

"She also made me rip my pants," Savich said, coming up in a graceful motion. He shook himself, wiping dirt off his hands onto his filthy pants.

"He tried to kill me," she said, rising slowly, still pointing the SIG at him. "Also, he shouldn't be talking. He should be acting dead."

"She's right." Savich sprawled onto his back again, his arms flung out, his eyes closed.

"He was only defending himself," said the woman who'd yelled her head off. "He's the new coach and you killed him."

She knew she wasn't wrong.

"I don't know about that," Porter Forge said, that drawl of his so slow she could have said the same thing at least three times before he'd gotten it out. "Suh," he continued to the mayor who was standing at his elbow, "I believe I saw a wanted poster on this big fella. He's gone and robbed banks all over the South. Yep, that's where I saw his picture, on one of the Atlanta PD posters, suh. Sherlock here did well. She brought down a really bad guy."

It was an excellent lie, one to give her time to do something, anything, to save her hide.

Then she realized what had bothered her about him. His clothes didn't fit him right. She leaned over, reached her hands into Savich's pockets, and pulled out wads of fake one-hundred-dollar bills.

"I believe ya'll find the bank's serial numbers on the bills, suh. Don't you think so, Sherlock?"

"Oh yes, I surely do, Agent Forge."

"Take me away, Ms. Sherlock," Dillon Savich said, came to his feet, and stuck out his hands.

She handed Porter back his SIG. She faced Savich with her hands on her hips, a grin on her face. "Why would I handcuff you now, sir? You're dead. I'll get a body bag."

Savich was laughing when she walked away to the waiting paramedic ambulance.

He said to the mayor of Hogan's Alley, "That was well done. She has a nose for crooks. She sniffed me out and came after me. She didn't try to second-guess herself. I wondered if she'd have guts. She does. Sorry I turned the exercise into a comedy at the end, but the look on her face, I just couldn't help it."

"I don't blame you, but I doubt we can use you again. I have a feeling this story will pass through training classes for a good long while. No future trainees will believe you're both a new coach and a crook."

"It worked once and we saw an excellent result. I'll come up with another totally different exercise." Savich walked away, unaware that his royal blue boxer shorts were on display to a crowd of a good fifty people.

The mayor began to laugh, then the people around him joined in. Soon there was rolling laughter, people pointing. Even a crook who was holding a hostage around the throat, a gun to his ear, at the other end of town looked over at the sudden noise to see what was going on. It was his downfall. Agent Wallace thunked him over the head and laid him flat.

It was a good day for taking a bite out of crime in Hogan's Alley.

THREE

She met with Colin Petty, a supervisor in the Personnel Division, known in the Bureau as the Bald Eagle. He was thin, sported a thick black mustache and a very shiny head. He told her up front that she'd impressed some important people, but that was at Quantico. No one working here in Headquarters was impressed yet. She was going to have to work her butt off. She nodded, knowing where she'd been assigned. It was tough, but she managed to pull out a bit of enthusiasm.

"I'm pleased to be going to the Los Angeles field office," she said, and thought, I don't want anything to do with any bank robberies. She knew they dealt with more bank robberies than any field office in the U.S. She guessed it was better than Montana, but at least there she could go skiing. How long was a usual tour of duty? She had to get back here, somehow.

"L.A. is considered a plum assignment for a new agent right out of the Academy," Mr. Petty said as he flipped through her personnel file. "You originally requested Headquarters, I see here, the Criminal Investigative Division, but they decided to send you to Los Angeles." He looked up at her over his bifocals. "You have a B.S. in Forensic Science and a Master's degree in Criminal Psychology from Berkeley," he continued. "Seems you've got a real interest here. Why didn't you request the Investigative Services Unit? With your background, you would probably have been escorted through the door. I take it you changed your mind?"

She knew there were notes about that in her file. Why was he acting as if he didn't know anything? Of course. He wanted her to talk, get her slant on things, get her innermost thoughts. Good luck to him on that, she thought. It was true it was her own fault that she was being assigned to Los Angeles and there was no secret as to why.

She forced a smile and shrugged. "The fact is I don't have the guts to do what those people do every day of their lives and probably in their dreams as well. You're right that I prepared myself for this career, that I believed it was what I wanted to do with my life, but—" She shrugged again. And swallowed. She'd spent all these years preparing herself, and she'd failed. "It all boils down to no guts."

"You always wanted to be a Profiler?"

"Yes. I read John Douglas's book *Mindhunter* and thought that's what I wanted to do. Actually I've been interested in law enforcement for a very long time, thus my major in college and graduate school." It was a lie, but that didn't matter. She told it easily, with no hesitation. She had practically come to believe it herself over the past several years. "I wanted to help get those monsters out of society. But after the lectures by people from ISU, after seeing what they see on a day-to-day basis for just a week, I knew I wouldn't be able to deal with the horror of it. The Profilers see unspeakable butchery. They live with the results of it. Every one of those monsters leaves a deep mark on them. And the victims, the victims . . ." She drew a deep breath. "I knew I couldn't do it." So now she'd go after bank robbers and he would remain free and she wanted to cry. All this time and commitment and incredibly hard work, and she was going to go after bank robbers. She should have quit, but the truth of the matter was that she didn't have the energy to redefine herself again, and that's what it would mean.

Mr. Petty said only, "I couldn't either. Most folks couldn't. The burnout rate is incredible in the unit. Marriages don't do well either. Now, you did excellently at the Academy. You handle firearms well, particularly in mid-distances, you excel at self-defense, you ran the two miles in under sixteen minutes, and your situation judgment was well above average. There's a little footnote here that says you managed to take down Dillon Savich in a Hogan's Alley exercise, something never before done by a trainee." He looked up, his eyebrows raised. "Is that true?"

She remembered her rage when he'd disarmed her twice. Then, just as suddenly, she remembered her laughter when he'd walked away, his boxer shorts showing through the big rip in his pants. "Yes," she said, "but it was my partner, Porter Forge, who threw me his SIG so I could shoot him. Otherwise I would have died in the line of duty."

"But it was Dillon who bought the big one," Petty said. "I wish I could have seen it." He gave her the most gleeful grin she'd ever seen. Even that bushy mustache of his couldn't hide it. It was irresistible. It made him suddenly very human.

"It also says that you pulled a Lady Colt .38 on him after he'd knocked the SIG out of your hand. Do you still have this gun?"

"Yes, sir. I learned to use it when I was nineteen. I'm very comfortable with it."

"I suppose we can all live with that. Ah, I know everyone must comment on your name, Agent Sherlock."

"Oh yes, sir. No stone left unturned, so to speak, over the years. I'm used to it now."

"Then I won't say anything about offering you a pipe."

"Thank you, sir."

"Let me tell you about your new assignment, Agent Sherlock," Petty said, and she thought, because I don't have any guts, I'm going to be catching jerks who rob banks. He continued, "The criminal you brought down in Hogan's Alley, namely, Dillon Savich, has asked that you be reassigned to his unit."

Her heart started pounding. "Here in Washington?"

"Yes."

In one of those huge rooms filled with computers? Oh God, no. She'd rather have bank robbers. She didn't want to play with computers. She was competent with computer programming, but she was far from an intuitive genius like Savich. The stories about what he could do with a computer were told and retold at the Academy. He was a legend. She couldn't imagine working for a legend. On the other hand, wouldn't he have access to everything? Just maybe—"What is his unit?"

"It's the Criminal Apprehension Unit, or CAU for short. They work with the Investigative Services Unit for background and profiles, get their take on things, that sort of thing. Then they deal directly with local authorities when a criminal takes his show on the road—in other words, when a criminal goes from one state to another. Agent Savich has developed a different approach for apprehending criminals. I'll let him tell you about it. You will be using your academic qualifications, Agent Sherlock. We do try to match up agents' interests and areas of expertise with their assignments.

Although you might have seriously doubted that if you'd gotten sent to Los Angeles."

She wanted to leap over the desk and hug Mr. Petty. She couldn't speak for a moment. She'd thought she'd doomed herself after she'd realized she simply couldn't survive in the ISU as a Profiler. The week she'd spent there had left her so ill she'd endured the old nightmares in blazing, hideous color for well over a week, replete with all the terror, as fresh as it had been seven years before. She just knew, deep down, that she could have never gotten used to it, and the ISU people did admit that many folks couldn't ever deal with it, no matter how hard they tried. No, she wouldn't have been able to survive it, not with the horror of the job combined with the horror of the nightmares.

But now, she felt an incredible surge of excitement. She hadn't known about Savich's unit, which was strange because there was always gossip about everything and everyone at the Academy. And this sort of unit would provide her with an ideal vantage point. At the very least, she would be able to access all the files, all the collected data impossible for her to see otherwise. And no one would wonder at her curiosity, not if she was careful. Oh yes, and she would have free time. She closed her eyes with relief.

She'd never felt as though anyone was looking after her before. It was frightening because she hadn't believed in much of anything since that long ago night seven years ago. She'd had a goal, nothing more, just that goal. And now she had a real chance at realizing it.

"Now, it's two-twenty," Mr. Petty said. "Agent Savich wants to see you in ten minutes. I hope you can deal with this work. It's not profiling, but I don't doubt that it will be difficult at times, depending on the case and how intimately involved you have to become in it. At least you won't be six floors down at Quantico working in a bomb shelter with no windows."

"The people in the ISU deserve a big raise."

"And lots more help as well, which is one of the reasons Agent Savich's unit was formed. Now, I'll let him tell you all about it. Then you can make a decision."

"May I ask, sir, why Agent Savich requested me?"

There was that unholy grin again. "I think he really can't believe that you beat him, Agent Sherlock. Actually, you will have to ask him that."

He rose and walked her to the door of his small office. "I'm joking, of course. The Unit is three turns down this hallway and to the right. Turn left after another four doors and two conference rooms. It's just there on the left. Are you getting used to the Puzzle Palace?"

"No, sir. This place is a maze."

"It's got more than two million square feet. It boggles a normal mind. I still get lost, and my wife tells me I'm not all that normal. Give yourself another ten years, Agent Sherlock."

Mr. Petty shook her hand. "Welcome to the Bureau. I hope you find your work rewarding. Ah, did anyone ever refer to a tweed hat?"

"Yes, sir."

"Sorry, Agent Sherlock."

It was hard not to run out the door of his office. She didn't even stop at the women's room.

SAVICH looked up. "You found me in ten minutes," he said, looking down at his Mickey Mouse wristwatch. "That's good, Sherlock. I understand from Colin Petty that you're wondering why I had you reassigned to my unit."

He was wearing a white shirt rolled up to his elbows, a navy blue tie, and navy slacks. A navy blazer was hanging on a coatrack in the corner of his office. He rose slowly from behind his desk as he spoke. He was big, at least six two, dark, and very muscular. In addition to the martial arts, he clearly worked out regularly. She'd heard some of the trainees call him a regular he-man, not a G-man. She knew just how strong and fast he was, since he'd worked her over in that Hogan's Alley exercise. Her stomach had hurt for three days after that head butt. If she didn't know he was an agent, she would have been terrified of him. He looked hard as nails. He was patiently looking at her. What had he been talking about? Oh yes, why he'd wanted her reassigned to this unit.

She smiled and said, "Yes, sir."

Savich came around his desk and shook her hand. "Sit down and we can discuss it."

There were two chairs facing his desk, clearly FBI issue. On top of the desk was an FBI-issue computer. Beside it was a laptop that was open and humming, definitely not FBI issue. It was slightly slanted toward her, and she could see the green print on the black background, a graph of some kind. Was this little computer the one she'd heard everyone say that Savich made dance?

"Coffee?"

She shook her head.

"Do you know much about computers, Sherlock?" Just Sherlock, no agent in front of it. It sounded fine to her. He was looking at her expectantly. She hated to disappoint him, but there was no choice.

"Not all that much, sir, just enough so I can write reports and hook into the databases I will need to do my job."

To her unspeakable relief, he smiled. "Good, I wouldn't want any real competition in my own unit. I hear you had wanted to be a Profiler but ultimately felt you couldn't deal with the atrocities that flood the unit every moment of every day and well into the night."

"That's right. How did you know that? I just left Mr. Petty less than fifteen minutes ago."

"No telepathy." He pointed to the phone. "It comes in handy, though I much prefer e-mail. I agree with you, actually. I couldn't do it either. The burnout rate for Profilers is pretty high, as I'm sure you've heard. Since they spend so much time focusing on the worst in humanity, they wind up having a difficult time relating to regular folks. They lose perspective on normal life. They don't know their kids. Their marriages go under."

She sat forward a bit in her seat, smoothing her navy blue skirt as she said, "I spent a week with them. I know I saw only a small part of what they do. That's when I knew I didn't have what it took. I felt as if I'd failed."

"What any endeavor takes, Sherlock, is a whole lot of different talents. Because you don't end up profiling doesn't mean you've failed. Actually, I think what we do leaves us more on the normal side of things than not.

"Now, I asked to have you assigned to me because academically you appear to have what I need. Your academic credentials are impressive. I did wonder, though. Why did you take off a year between your sophomore and junior years of college?"

"I was sick. Mononucleosis."

"Okay, yes, here's an entry about that. I don't know why I missed it." She watched him flip through more pages, watched his dark eyes scan the page. He hadn't missed it. She couldn't imagine he'd ever miss a thing. She would have to be careful around him. He read quickly. He frowned once. He looked up at her. "I didn't think mono took a person out for a whole year."

"I don't know about that. I just wasn't worth much for about nine or ten months, run-down, really tired."

He looked down at a page of paper that was faceup on his desktop. "You just turned twenty-seven, I see, and you came directly to the Bureau after completing your Master's degree."

"Yes."

"This is your first job."

"Yes." She knew he wanted more from her in the way of answers, but she wasn't about to comply. Direct question, direct answer; that's all she'd give him. She'd heard about his reputation. He wasn't only smart; he was very good at reading people. She didn't want him reading anything about her that she didn't want read. She was very used to being careful. She wouldn't stop now. She couldn't afford to.

He was frowning at her. He tossed her file onto the desktop. She was wearing a no-nonsense dark blue business suit with a white blouse. Her curly red hair was pulled severely back, held at the base of her neck with a gold clamp. He saw her for a moment after he'd butted her into the petunias in Hogan's Alley. Her hair had been drawn back then, but curls had pulled loose and corkscrewed around her face. She was on the point of being too thin, her cheekbones too prominent. But she'd taken him, not lost her composure, her training. He said, "Do you know what this unit does, Sherlock?"

"Mr. Petty said when a criminal takes his show on the road, we're many times called in by the local police to help catch him."

"Yes. We don't deal in kidnappings. Other folk do that brilliantly. No, primarily we stick to the kinds of monsters who don't stop killing until we stop them. Also, like the ISU, we do deal with local agencies who think an outside eye might see something they missed on a local crime. Usually homicide." He paused and sat back, just looking at her, seeing her yet again on her back in the petunia bed. "Also, like the ISU, we only go in when we're asked. It's our job to be very mental, intuitive, objective. We don't do profiling like the ISU. We're computer-based. We use special programs to help us look at crimes from many different angles. The programs correlate all the data from two or more crimes that seem to have been committed by the same person in order to bring everything possibly relevant, possibly important, into focus. We call the main program the PAP, the Predictive Analogue Program."

"You wrote the programs, didn't you, sir? And that's why you're the head of the unit?"

He grinned at her. "Yeah. I'd been working on prototypes a long time before the unit got started. I like catching the guys who prey on society and, truth be told, the computer, as far as I'm concerned, is the best tool to take them out. But that's all it is, Sherlock, a tool. It can turn up patterns, weird correlations, but we have to put the data in there in order to get the patterns. Then of course we have to see the patterns and read them correctly. It comes down to how we look at the possible outcomes and alternatives the computer gives us; it's how we decide what data we plug into it. You'll see that PAP has an amazing number of protocols. One of my people will teach you the program. With luck, your academic background in forensics and psychology will enable you to come up with more parameters, more protocols, more ways of sniffing out pertinent data and correlating information to look at crimes in different ways, all with the goal of catching the criminals."

She wanted to sign on the dotted line right that minute. She wanted to learn everything in the next five minutes. She wanted, most of all, to ask him when she could have access to everything he did. She managed to keep her mouth shut.

"We do a lot of traveling, Sherlock, often at a moment's notice. It's gotten heavier as more and more cops hear about us and want to see what our analysis has to offer. What kind of home life do you have? I see you're not married, but do you have a boyfriend? Someone you are used to spending time with?"

"No."

He felt as if he were trying to open a can with his fingernails. "Would you like to have your lawyer present?"

She blinked at that. "I don't understand, sir."

"You are short on words, Sherlock. I was being facetious."

"I'm sorry if you don't think I'm talking enough, sir."

He wanted to tell her she'd talk all he wanted her to soon enough. He was good. Actually, he was better with a computer, but he could also loosen a tongue with the best of them in the Bureau. But for now he'd play it her way. Nothing but the facts. He said, "You don't live with anyone?"

"No, sir."

"Where do you live, Agent Sherlock?"

"Nowhere at the moment, sir. I thought I was being assigned to Los Angeles. Since I'll be staying in Washington I'll have to find an apartment."

Three sentences. She was getting positively chatty.

"We'll be able to help you on that. Do you have stuff in storage?"

"Not much, sir."

There was a faint beep. "Just a moment," Savich said and looked at the computer screen on his laptop. He rubbed his jaw as he read. Then he typed quickly, looked at the screen, tapped his fingertips on the desktop, then nodded. He looked up at her. He was grinning like a maniac. "E-mail. Finally, finally, we're going to have a chance to catch the Toaster."

FOUR

Savich looked as if he wanted to jump on his desk and dance. He couldn't stop grinning and rubbing his hands together.

"The Toaster, sir?"

"Oh yes. On this one, I had feelers out with everyone. Excuse me, Agent Sherlock." He pulled out his cell phone and began to punch in numbers, then abruptly punched off. "I forgot. Ellis's wife is having their baby; she went into the hospital an hour ago and so he's not available. No, I won't ask him. He'll insist on coming, but he needs to be with his wife. It's their first kid. But he's going to be really pissed to miss this. No, I just can't. He's gotta be there." He looked down at his hands a moment, then back up at her. He looked just a bit worried. "What do you think of trial by fire?"

Her heartbeat speeded up. She was so new she still squeaked, but he was going to take a chance on her. "I'm ready, sir."

She looked ready to leap out of her chair. He didn't remember being this eager on his first day. He rose. "Good. We're leaving this afternoon for Chicago. Bottom line: We've got a guy who killed a family of four in Des Moines. He did the same thing in St. Louis three months later. After St. Louis, the media dubbed him the Toaster. I'll tell you about it when we're in the air. That was Captain Brady in the Chicago Police Department, homicide, and he believes we might be able to help him. Actually, he's praying we can do something. The media wants a sideshow, and he can't even give them a dancing bear. But we can." He looked at his watch. "I'll meet you at Dulles in two hours. We should be there no more than three days." He rolled down the sleeves of his white shirt and grabbed his jacket. "I really want this guy, Sherlock."

The Toaster. She knew about him as well. She scoured all the major newspapers for monsters like this one. Yes, she already knew the details, at least the ones that had made the papers.

He opened the office door for her. Her eyes were positively glistening, as if she were high on drugs. "You mean you know how to catch him?"

"Yes. We're going to get him this time. Captain Brady said he had some leads, but he needs us to come out. You go ahead and pack. I've got to up-date some people in the unit. Ollie Hamish is in charge when I'm unavail-able."

THEY flew on United in Business Class. "I didn't think the Bureau let its agents fly anything but tourist class."

Savich stowed his briefcase beneath the seat in front of him and sat down. "I upgraded us. You don't mind that I have the aisle?"

"You're the boss, sir."

"Yeah, but now you can call me Dillon or Savich. I answer to either one. What do most people call you?"

"Sherlock, sir. Just plain Sherlock."

"I met your daddy once about five years ago, right after he was ap-pointed to the bench. Everyone in law enforcement was tickled to have him named because he rarely cut a convicted criminal any slack. I remember his selection didn't go over too well with liberals in your home state."

"No," she said looking out the window as the 767 began to taxi down the runway. "It didn't. There were two serious efforts to have him recalled—neither succeeded. The first try was after he upheld the death penalty for a man who'd raped and tortured two little boys, then dumped their bodies in a Dumpster in Palo Alto. The second was when he wouldn't grant bail to an illegal Mexican alien who'd kidnapped and murdered a lo-cal businessman."

"Hard to believe there are people who'd want to rally behind those kinds of killers."

"Oh, there are. Their rationale in the first case was that my father showed no compassion. After all, the man's wife had died of cancer, his lit-tle boy had been killed by a drunk driver. He deserved another chance. He'd been pushed to torture those little boys. He had shown remorse, claimed grief had sent him out of his mind, but Dad said 'bullshit' and up-held the death penalty. As for the illegal Mexican, they claimed Dad was a racist, that there was no proof the man would flee the U.S. Also they claimed that the man had kidnapped the businessman because he had re-fused to give him a job, had threatened to call Immigration if the guy didn't leave the premises. They claimed the man hadn't been treated fairly, that he'd been discriminated against. It didn't matter that the businessman was an immigrant—a legal one. I also seriously doubt he made that threat."

"They didn't succeed in recalling him."

"No, but it was close. You could say that the Bay Area is a fascinating place to grow up. If there's any other possible take on something, some group of locals will latch onto it."

"What does your dad think of your joining the FBI?"

The flight attendant spoke over the PA system, telling them about their seat belts and the oxygen masks. He saw it in her eyes—the wariness, the relief that now she could concentrate on her flotation cushion instead of his questions. She was proving to be a puzzle. He very much appreciated puzzles. A good one fascinated him. He'd get her again with that question. Maybe when she was tired or distracted.

He sat back in his seat and said nothing more. Once in the air, he opened his briefcase and gave her a thick file. "I hope you read quickly. This is everything on the three different crimes. I knew you didn't have a laptop, so I had it downloaded and printed out for you. Read everything and absorb as much as you can. If you have questions, write them down and ask me later." He gently lifted his laptop onto the fold-down tray and got to work.

HE waited until they were served a snack before he spoke again. "Have you finished reading everything?"

"Yes."

"You're fast. Questions? Ideas? Anything that doesn't seem kosher?"

"Yes."

This time he didn't say anything. He just chewed on a carrot stick and waited. He watched her cut a small piece of lettuce from her salad. She didn't eat it, just played with it.

"I already knew about this man from the papers. But there's so much more here." She sounded elated, as if she'd made the insiders' club. He frowned at her. She suddenly cleared her throat, and her voice was nearly expressionless. "I can understand that he has low self-esteem, that he probably isn't very bright, that he probably works at a low-paying job, that he's a loner and doesn't relate well to people—"

He waited, something he was excellent at.

"I always wondered why it killed families. Families of four, exactly."

"You called him 'it.' That's interesting."

She hadn't meant to. She forked down her lettuce and took her time chewing. She had to be more careful. "It was a slip of the tongue."

"No, it wasn't, but we'll let that go for now, Sherlock. This family thing—the people in the ISU, as you've read in their profile, believe he lived on the same block as the first family he killed in Des Moines, knew them, hated them, wanted to obliterate them, which he did. However, they couldn't find anyone in the nearby area of the first murders in Des Moines to fit that description. Everyone figured that the profile wasn't correct in this particular case. When he killed again in St. Louis, everyone was flummoxed. When I spoke to Captain Brady in Chicago, I asked him if the St. Louis police had canvassed the area for a possible suspect. They had, but they still didn't find anybody who looked promising."

"But you had already talked to the police in St. Louis, hadn't you?"

"Oh yes."

"You know a lot, don't you?"

"I've thought about this case, Sherlock, thought and thought and re-created it as best I could. Unlike the cops, I firmly believe the profile is right on target."

"Even though they didn't find anyone in Des Moines or St. Louis to fit the profile?"

"Yeah, that's right."

"You're stringing me along, sir."

"Yes, but I'd like to see what you come up with. Let's see if you're as fast with your brain as with that Lady Colt of yours."

She splayed her fingers, long slender fingers, short buffed nails. "You still kicked it out of my hand. It didn't matter."

"But you made a good catch. I wasn't expecting that move from Porter."

She grinned at him then, momentarily disarmed. "We practiced it. In another exercise, he got taken as a hostage. I threw a gun to him, but he missed it. The robber was so angry, he shot Porter. As you can imagine, we got yelled at by the instructors for winging it." She said again, still grinning, "Practice."

He said slowly, shutting down his laptop, "I got creamed once when I was a trainee at the Academy. I wish I'd learned that move. My partner, James Quinlan, was playing a bank robber in a Hogan's Alley exercise, and the FBI got the drop on him. I had to stand there and watch him get taken away. If I'd thrown him a gun, he might have had a chance. Although God knows what would have happened then." He sighed. "Quinlan turned me in under questioning. I think he expected me to break him out of lockup, and when I didn't, he sang. Although how he expected me to do it, I have no idea. Anyway, they caught me an hour later heading out of town in a stolen car, the mayor's blue Buick."

"Quinlan?"

"Yes." Nothing more, just the yes. Let her chew on nothing for a bit.

"Who is this Quinlan?"

"An agent and longtime friend. Now, Sherlock, what do you think we're going to find in Chicago?"

"You said the Chicago police believed they were close. How close?"

"You read it. A witness said he saw a man running from the victims' house. They've got a description. We'll see how accurate it is."

"What do you know, sir, that's not in the reports?"

"Most of it's surmise," he said, "and some excellent stuff from my computer program." He nodded to the flight attendant to remove his cup of tea. He gently closed his laptop and slipped it into its hard case. "We're nearly at O'Hare," he said, leaned back, and closed his eyes.

She leaned back as well. He hadn't shown her the computer analysis on the case. Maybe he thought she already had enough on her plate, and maybe she did. She hadn't wanted to look at the photos from the crime scenes, but she had. It had been difficult. There hadn't been any photos in the newspapers. The actual photos brought the horror of it right in her face. She couldn't help it; she spoke aloud: "In all three cases, the father and mother were in their late thirties, their two children—always a boy and a girl—were ten and twelve. In each case, the father had been shot through the chest, then in his stomach, the second shot delivered after he was dead, the autopsy reports read. The mother was tied down on the kitchen table, her face beaten, then she was strangled with the cord of the toaster, thus the name the Toaster. The children were tied up, knocked out, their heads stuck in the oven. Like Hansel and Gretel. It's more than creepy. This guy is incredibly sick. I've wondered what he would do if the family didn't have a toaster."

"Yeah, I wondered about that too, at first," he said, not opening his eyes. "Makes you think he must have visited each of the homes to make sure there was one right there in the kitchen before the murders."

"That or he brought the toasters with him."

"That's possible, but I doubt it. Too conspicuous." He brought his seat back into its upright position. "Someone could have seen him carrying something. Another thing, in a lot of houses, kitchen ovens are set up high and built in. In a situation like that, how would he kill the children? In the photos, all of these are the big old-fashioned ovens."

"He had a lot of checking out to do when he visited the families, didn't he?"

She looked at his profile. He didn't say anything. She slowly slid all the photos back into the envelope, each of them marked. She slowly lined up all the pages and carefully placed them back into their folders. He'd given this a whole lot of thought. On the other hand, so had she. She still wanted to see the computer analysis. Then again, she hadn't demanded to see it either.

The flight attendant announced that they were beginning their descent into Chicago and for everyone to put away any electronic equipment. Savich fastened his seat belt. "Oh yes, our guy did a lot of checking."

"How did you even remember my question? It's been five minutes since I asked it."

"I'm FBI. I'm good." He closed his eyes again.

She wanted to kick him. She turned to look out the window. Lights were thick and bright below. Her heart speeded up. Her first assignment. She wanted to do things right.

"You're FBI now too, Sherlock."

It was a bone, not a meaty bone, but a bone nonetheless, and she smiled, accepting that bone gladly.

She fastened her own seat belt. She never once stopped looking down at the lights of Chicago. Hallelujah! She wasn't going after bank robbers.

FIVE

Chicago was overcast and a cool fifty degrees on October 18. Sherlock hadn't been to Chicago since she'd turned twenty-one, following a lead that hadn't gone anywhere, one of the many police departments she'd visited during her year of "mono."

As for Savich, he wasn't even particularly aware that he was in Chicago; he was thinking about the sick little bastard who had brutally murdered three families. Officer Alfonso Ponce picked them up and ushered them to an unmarked light blue Ford Crown Victoria.

"Captain Brady didn't think you'd want to be escorted to the station in a squad car. This one belongs to the captain."

After a forty-five-minute ride weaving in and out of thick traffic, everyone in the radius of five miles honking his horn, he let them off at the Jefferson Park station house, the precinct for what was clearly a nice, middle-class neighborhood. The station house was a boxy, single-story building on West Gale, at the intersection of two major streets, Milwaukee and Higgins. It had a basement, Officer Ponce told them, because it had been built in 1936 and was one of those WPA projects. When there'd been a twister seven years before, everyone had piled into the basement, prisoners and all. One nutcase had tried to escape. There had been little updating since the seventies. There was a small box out front holding a few wilted flowers and a naked flagpole.

Inside, it was as familiar as any station house Savich had ever been in— a beige linoleum floor that had been redone probably in the last ten years, but who knew? It still looked forty years old. He smelled urine wearing an overcoat of floral room spray. There were a dozen or so people shuffling around or sitting on the long bench against the wall, since it was eight o'clock at night. At least half of them were teenage boys. He wondered what they'd done. Drugs, probably.

Savich asked the sergeant on duty where he could find Captain Brady. They were escorted by an officer, turned wary after he'd seen their FBI shields, to a squad room with several offices in the back with glass windows. The room was divided off into modular units, a new addition that nobody liked, the officer told them. There wasn't much noise this time of night, just an occasional ring of the phone. There were about a dozen people in the squad room, all plainclothes.

Captain Brady was a black man of about forty-five with a thick southern drawl. Even though there wasn't a single white hair on his head, he looked older than his years, very tired, lines scored deeply around his mouth. When he saw them, his mouth split into a big smile. He came out from behind his cluttered desk, his hand out.

"Agent Savich?"

"Yes, Captain." The two men shook hands.

"And this is Agent Sherlock."

Captain Brady shook her hand, gave her a lopsided grin, and said, "You're a long way from London, aren't you?"

She grinned back at him. "Yes, sir. I forgot my hat, but my pipe's in my purse."

Savich was studying the computer on the captain's desk.

Captain Brady waved them into two chairs that sat opposite a sofa. The chairs were surprisingly comfortable. Captain Brady took the sofa. He sat forward, his hands clasped between his knees. "Bud Hollis in St. Louis said you had followed this case since the guy killed the first family in Des Moines and the DMPD had asked the FBI to do a profile. He said I should get you here, and that's why I e-mailed you. He, ah, appreciated your ideas even though they didn't get him anywhere. But you already know that. The guy's a mystery. Nothing seems to nail him. It's like he's a ghost."

Captain Brady coughed into his hand, a hacking low cough. "Sorry, I guess I'm getting run-down. My wife chewed me out good this morning." He shrugged. "But what can we do? We've been putting in long hours since the guy killed the family three and a half days ago. He did it right at six o'clock, right at dinnertime, right at the same time he killed the other two families. Sorry, but you already know that. You got all the police reports I sent you yesterday?"

"Oh yes," Savich said. "I was hoping you'd contact me."

The captain nodded. "Bud Hollis also said you had a brain and weren't a glory hound and did your investigating with a computer. I don't understand that, but I'm willing to give it a try.

"I still wasn't sure bringing you here was such a good idea until five minutes before I e-mailed you. Thank you for coming so quickly. I thought I should talk to both of you for a few minutes before I introduce you to the detectives on the case. They're, ah, a bit unhappy that I called you in."

"No problem," Savich said and crossed his legs. "You're right, Captain. Neither Sherlock nor I am into glory. We just want this guy off the streets."

Actually, she wanted him really badly. She wanted him dead.

"Unfortunately we don't have anything more than we did when I e-mailed you this afternoon. The pressure from the mayor's office is pretty intense; everyone's hiding in the men's room because the media's been on a tear since the first night it happened. They haven't let up. Do you know that one station got hold of the crime scene photos, and they splashed them all over the ten P.M. news? Bloody vultures. They know all about Des Moines and St. Louis and that the media there had called the guy the Toaster. Got everyone scared to death. The joke in the squad room is that everyone is throwing out their kitchen appliances. You've read all the files from all the murders, haven't you?"

"Yes. Every one. They were very complete."

"I guess it's time to cut to the chase, Agent Savich. Can you help us?"

"Both Agent Sherlock and I have a few questions. Perhaps we can meet with your people and get the answers. Yes, Captain, there's not a doubt in my mind that we can help you."

Captain Brady gave Savich a dubious smile, but there was a gleam of hope in his tired eyes. "Let's get to it," he said, grabbed a huge folder from his desk, and walked to the door of his office. He yelled out, "Dubrosky! Mason! Get in the conference room on the double." He turned back to them and said, "I hate these modular things. They put them in last year. You can't see a soul, and chances are the guy you want is in the john." He glanced at her. "Well, or the girl, er, female officer you want is in the women's room."

Evidently neither Dubrosky nor Mason had gone to the john. They were already in the conference room, standing stiff and hostile, waiting for the FBI agents. Captain Brady was right about one thing—they weren't happy campers. This was their turf, and the last thing they wanted was to have the FBI stick their noses into their business. Savich was polite and matter-of-fact. They looked at Sherlock, and she could see that they weren't holding out for much help from her. Dubrosky said, "You don't expect us to be your Watsons, do you, Sherlock?"

"Not at all, Detective Dubrosky, unless either of you is a physician."

That brought her a grudging smile.

She wanted to tell all of them, Savich included, that she now knew as much about this guy as they did, maybe even more than the Chicago cops, and she'd thought about him for as long as Savich had, but she kept her mouth closed. She wondered what Savich had up his sleeve. She'd only known him for seven hours, and she would have bet her last buck that he had a whole lot up that sleeve of his. It wouldn't have surprised her if he had the guy's name and address.

They sat in the small conference room, all the files and photos spread over the top of the table. There was a photo of the crime scene faceup at her elbow. It was of Mrs. Lansky, the toaster cord still around her neck. She turned it facedown and looked over at Savich.

He had what she already thought of as the FBI Look. He was studying Dubrosky in a still, thoughtful way. She wondered if he saw more than she did. Poor Dubrosky: he looked so tired he was beyond exhaustion, a man who wasn't smiling, a man who looked as if he'd just lost his best friend. He was wired, probably on too much coffee. He couldn't sit still. His brown suit was rumpled, his brown tie looked like a hangman's noose. He had a thick five-o'clock shadow.

Savich put his elbows on the table, looked directly at the man, and said, "Detective, were there any repairmen in the Lansky household within the past two months?"

Dubrosky reared back, then rocked forward again, banging his fist on the table. "Do you think we're fucking idiots? Of course we checked all that! There was a phone repair guy there three weeks ago, but we talked to him and it was legit. Anyway, the guy was at least fifty years old and had seven kids."

Savich just continued in that same calm voice, "How do you know there weren't other repairmen?"

"There were no records of any expenditures for any repairs in the Lanskys' checkbook, no receipts of any kind, and none of the neighbors knew
of anything needing repairs. We spoke to the family members, even the ones
who live out of town—none of them knew anything about the Lanskys'
having any repairs on anything."

"And there were no strangers in the area the week before the murder?
The day of the murder?"

"Oh sure. There were pizza deliveries, a couple of Seventh-Day Adven-
tists, a guy canvassing for a local political campaign," said Mason, a
younger man who was dressed in a very expensive blue suit and looked as
tired as his partner. Savich imagined that when they took roles, Mason was
the good cop and Dubrosky the bad cop. Mason looked guileless and naïve,
which he probably hadn't been for a very long time.

Mason gave a defeated sigh, spreading his hands on the tabletop. "But
nobody saw anyone at the Lansky house except a woman and her daughter
going door-to-door selling Girl Scout cookies. That was one day before the
murders. That doesn't mean that UPS guys didn't stop there a week ago, but
no one will even admit that's possible. It's a small, close-knit neighborhood.
You know, one of those neighborhoods where everybody minds everybody
else's business. The old lady who lives across the street from the Lanskys
could even describe the woman and the little girl selling the cookies. I can't
imagine any stranger getting in there without that old gal noticing. I wanted
to ask her if she kept a diary of all the comings and goings in the neighborhood, but Dubrosky said she might not be so happy if I did and she just
might close right up on us."

Captain Brady said, "You know, Agent Savich, this whole business
about the guy coming to the house, getting in under false pretenses, actually
coming into the kitchen, checking before he whacked the families to make
sure they had a toaster and a low-set big gas oven didn't really occur to anyone until you told Bud Hollis in St. Louis to check into it. He's the one who
got us talking to every neighbor within a two-block radius. Like Mason
said, there wasn't any stranger, even a florist delivery to the Lansky house.
Everyone is positive. And none of the neighbors seem weird. And we did
look for weird when we interviewed, just in case."

Savich knew this of course, and Captain Brady knew that he knew it,
but he wanted the detectives to think along with him. He accepted a cup of
coffee from Mason that was thicker than Saudi oil. "You are all familiar
with the profile done by the FBI after the first murders in Des Moines. It
said that the killer was a young man between the ages of twenty and thirty,
a loner, and that he lived in the neighborhood or not too far away, probably

with his parents or with a sibling. Also he had a long-standing hatred or grudge or both toward the family in Des Moines, very possibly unknown by the family or friends of the family. Unfortunately this didn't seem to pan out."

Dubrosky said as he tapped a pen on the wooden tabletop, "The Des Moines cops wasted hours and hours going off on that tangent. They dragged in every man in a three-block radius of the house, but there wasn't a single dweeb who could possibly fit the profile. Then it turned out the Toaster wasn't just a little-time killer, he's now a serial killer. Thank God we didn't waste our time going through that exercise. You people aren't infallible." Dubrosky liked that. He looked jovial now. "No, this time you were so far off track that you couldn't even see the train. Like the captain said, we did talk to all the neighbors. Not a weirdo in the bunch."

"Actually, on this case, we're not off track at all," Savich said. "Believe me, it's astounding how often the profiles are right on the money." He was silent a moment, then said, "Now, everyone agrees that the same guy murdered all three families. It makes sense that he had to visit each of the houses to ensure there were both a toaster and a classic full-size stove/oven combo that sat on the kitchen floor. And not an electric stove, a gas one. There were delivery people all over the neighborhoods in both Des Moines and in St. Louis, but the truth is no one is really certain of anything. By the time they acted on the profile theory of the killer living in the neighborhood, there wasn't much certainty anymore about any repairs or deliveries. Nobody remembered seeing anybody."

"Good summary, Savich," said Dubrosky.

"Bear with me, Detective." He looked at the cup of coffee but didn't drink any. "This stuff looks so potent, I bet it breeds little cups of coffee."

There was one small smile, from Sherlock.

Savich said, "You guys have done hours of legwork here and you did it immediately. You've proven that there wasn't a repairperson or a salesman or even a guy whose car broke down and wanted to phone a garage near the Lansky house. So then we come back to the basic question. How then did he get into the Lansky house? Into the kitchen specifically so he could make certain they had all the props he needed?"

Dubrosky made a big show of looking at his watch. "Look, Savich, we thought of all that. We found out that all the houses were older, not just here, but also in Des Moines and St. Louis. To me it means that chances are excellent that you'd have a big low gas oven in the kitchens. And who wouldn't have a toaster? This is all nonsense. Our perp is a transient. He's nuts. None of the shrinks agree on why he did this. Maybe

God told him to strangle every mother with the toaster cord. Maybe God told him that kids are evil, that he was the evil witch out of Hansel and Gretel. Who knows why he's whacking families? Like I said, the yahoo's crazy and he's traveling across the U.S., probably killing at whim, no rhyme or reason."

Mason said, "Buck's right. We don't know why no one saw him in the Lansky neighborhood, why a single dog didn't bark, but maybe he disguised himself as the postman or as that old woman who lives across the street from the Lanskys. In any case, he got lucky. But we'll find him; we've got to. Of course with our luck, he's long gone from Chicago. We'll hear about him again when he murders a family in Kansas."

And that was truly what they believed, Sherlock thought. It was clear on all their faces. They believed the guy was long gone from Chicago, that they didn't have a prayer of ever getting him.

"Let me tell you about the magic of computers, gentlemen," Savich said and smiled. "They do things a whole lot faster than we can. But what's important is what you put into them. It's a matter of picking the right data to go into the mixer before you turn it on to do its thing." He leaned down and picked up his laptop and turned it on. He hit buttons, made the little machine bleep, and all in all, ignored the rest of them.

"I've got to go home, Captain," Dubrosky said. "I've got gas, I need a shower or my wife won't even kiss me, and my kids have forgotten what I look like."

"We're all bushed, Buck. Just be patient. Let's see what Agent Savich's got."

Sherlock realized then that Savich was putting on a little show for them. He had the pages he wanted to show them in his briefcase. But he was going to call up neat-looking stuff on the screen and make them all look at it before he gave them any hard copy. In the next minute, Savich turned the computer around and said, "Take a look at this, Detectives, Captain Brady."

SIX

The three men crowded around the small laptop. It was Detective Dubrosky who said suddenly, "Nah, I don't believe this. It doesn't make any sense."

"Yes, it does." Savich handed out a piece of paper to each of them. Sherlock didn't even glance at the paper. She knew what was on it. In that moment, Savich looked over at her. He grinned. He didn't know how she knew, but he knew that she'd figured it out.

"You tell them, Sherlock."

They were all staring at her now. He'd put her on the spot. But he'd seen the knowledge in her eyes. How, she didn't know. He was giving her a chance to shine.

She cleared her throat. "The FBI Profilers were right. It's a local neighborhood guy who hated the Lansky family. He killed the families in Des Moines and St. Louis because he wanted to practice before he killed the people he hated. He wanted to get it perfect when it most mattered to him. So, the families in Des Moines and St. Louis were random choices. He undoubtedly drove around until he found the family that met his requirements. Then he killed them."

Captain Brady whistled. "My God, you think the profile is correct, but it was meant only for the Lanskys?"

"That's right," Savich said. "The other two families were his dress rehearsal." He turned to Dubrosky and Mason. "I wanted you to be completely certain that there was no stranger around the Lansky household before the killings. Are you both certain?"

"Yes," Mason said. "As certain as we can be."

"Then we go to the Lansky neighborhood and pick up the guy who will fit the profile. He screwed up and now we'll nail him. The computer hit on three possibles, all within walking distance of the Lanskys' house. My money's on Russell Bent. He fits the profile better than the others. Given how well the profile fits this guy and given no strangers, the chances are really good that this wasn't another dress rehearsal. Also, Russell Bent lives with his sister and her husband. She is exactly two years older than he is."

"I don't understand, Agent Savich," Captain Brady said, sitting forward. "What do you mean she's two years older?"

"The boy and girl in all three families," Lacey said. "The girl was twelve and the boy was ten."

"Jesus," Captain Brady said.

"Why didn't you just tell us?" Dubrosky was mad. He felt that Savich had made him look like a fool.

"As I said," Savich said as he rose from his chair, "I wanted you to be certain that no stranger had been near the Lansky home. It was always possible that the guy was having a third dress rehearsal. But he wasn't. This time it was the real thing for him. I wasn't really holding out on you. I just got everything in the computer this morning, once Captain Brady had sent me all your reports. Without the reports I wouldn't have gotten a thing. You would have come back to this. It's just that I always believed the profile and I had the computer."

RUSSELL Bent lived six houses away from the Lanskys' with his sister and her husband and one young son. Bent was twenty-seven years old, didn't date, didn't have many friends, but was pleasant to everyone. He worked as a maintenance man at a large office on Milwaukee Avenue. His only passion was coaching Little League.

The detectives had already spoken to Russell Bent, his sister, and her husband as part of their neighborhood canvassing. They'd never considered him a possible suspect. They were looking for a transient, a serial killer, some hot-eyed madman, not a local, certainly not a shy young guy who was really polite to them.

"One hundred dollars, Sherlock, says they'll break him in twenty minutes," Savich said, grinning down at her.

"It's for certain that none of them looks the least bit tired now," she said. "Do we watch them?"

"No, let's go to Captain Brady's office. I don't want to cramp their style. You know, I bet you that Bent would have killed one more family, in another state, just to confuse everyone thoroughly. Then he wouldn't have killed again."

"You know, I've been wondering why he had to kill the kids like that."

"Well, I've given it a lot of thought, talked to the Profilers and a couple of shrinks. Why did Bent murder these families with two kids, specifically a boy and a girl, and in each case, the kids were two years apart, no more, no less? I guess he was killing himself and his sister."

She stared at him, shivering. "But why? No, don't tell me. You did some checking on Mr. Bent."

"Yep. I told Dubrosky and Mason all about it in the john. They're going to show off now in front of Captain Brady."

"I wish I could have been there."

"Well, probably not. Mason got so excited that he puked. He hadn't eaten anything all day and he'd drunk a gallon of that atomic bomb coffee."

She raised her hand. "No, don't tell me. Let me think about this, sir."

She followed him down the hall and into Captain Brady's office. He lay down on the sofa. It was too short and hard as a rock, but he wouldn't have traded it for anything at the moment. He was coming down. He closed his eyes and saw that pathetic Russell Bent. They'd gotten him. They'd won this time. For the moment it made him forget about the monsters who were still out there killing, the monsters that he and his people had spent hours trying to find, and had failed. But this time they'd gotten the monster. They'd won.

"The mother must have done something."

He cocked open an eye. Sherlock was standing over him, a shock of her red hair falling over to cover the side of her face. He watched her tuck the swatch of hair behind her ear. Nice hair and lots of it. Her eyes were a soft summer blue, a pretty color. "Yes," he said, "Mrs. Bent definitely did something."

"I don't think Mr. Bent did anything. The three fathers Russell Bent shot were clean kills. No, wait, after they were dead, Bent shot them in the stomach."

"The quick death was probably because to Bent, the father didn't count, he wasn't an object of the bone-deep hatred. The belly shot was probably because he thought the father was weak, he was ineffectual, he wasn't a man."

"What did Mrs. Bent do to Russell and his sister?"

"To punish Russell and his sister, or more likely, for the kicks it gave her, Mrs. Bent gagged them both, tied their arms behind them, and locked them in the trunk of the car or in a closet or other terrifying closed-in places. Once they nearly died from carbon monoxide poisoning. The mother didn't take care of them, obviously; she left them to scrounge food for themselves. Social Services didn't get them away from her until they were ten and twelve years old. Some timing, huh?"

"How did you find out this stuff so quickly?"

"I got on the phone before we left to pick up Russell Bent. I even got Social Services down to check their files. It was all there."

"So the toaster cord is a sort of a payback for what she didn't do? Beating her face was retribution?"

"Yeah, maybe. A payback for all eternity."

"And he must have come to believe that even though his mother was a dreadful person, he and his sister still deserved death, only they hadn't died, they'd survived, so it had to be other children just like them?"

"That doesn't make much sense, does it? But it's got to have something to do with Russell Bent feeling worthless, like he didn't deserve to live."

"But why did he pick the Lansky family?"

"I don't know. No one reported any gossip about the family, nothing about physical abuse, or the mother neglecting the children. No unexplained injuries with the kids winding up in the emergency room. But you can take it to the bank that Russell Bent thought the two Lansky kids were enough like him and his sister to merit dying. He thought the mother was enough like his own mother to deserve death. Why exactly did he have to gas the children? God only knows. Your explanation is as good as any. Brady will find out, though, with the help of the psychiatrists."

"Russell Bent coached Little League. The Lansky boy was in Little League. Maybe the Lansky boy got close to Bent; just maybe the Lansky boy told Russell that his mother was horrible." She shrugged. "It really won't matter. You know what they'll do, sir. They'll dress it all up in psychobabble. Do you know what happened to the Bents' parents?"

"Yes," he said. "I know. Sherlock, call me anything but 'sir.' I'm only thirty-three. I only turned thirty-three last month, on the sixth. 'Sir' makes me feel ancient."

The three cops erupted into the office. Captain Brady was rubbing his hands together. There was a bounce to his step. There would be a press conference at midnight. Mason and Dubrosky kept giving each other high fives. Brady had to call the mayor, the police commissioner—the list went on and on. He had to get busy.

It took the CPD only two hours to prove that Bent had traveled to Des Moines and to St. Louis exactly a week before each of those murders had been committed there and back on the exact dates of the murders.

Unfortunately, at least in Sherlock's view, Bent was so crazy, he wouldn't even go to trial. He wouldn't get the death penalty. He would be committed. Would he ever be let out? The last thing she heard as they were leaving the Jefferson Park precinct station was his sobs and the soft, soothing voice of his sister, telling him over and over that it would be all right, that they were in this together. She would take care of him. She had been two years older and she hadn't protected him from their mother. She wondered if the sister knew how lucky she was that her brother hadn't gassed her.

They took a late-morning flight back to Washington, D.C. It didn't occur to Savich until they were already in the air that Sherlock might not have a place to stay.

"I'm staying at the Watergate," she said. "I'm comfortable. I'll stay there until I find an apartment." She smiled at him. "You did very well. You got him. You didn't even need the police. Why didn't you just call Captain Brady and tell him about Bent? Why did you want to go to Chicago?"

"I lied to Brady. I'm a glory hound—even if it's just a crumb, I'm happy. I love praise. Who doesn't?"

"But that's not even part of why you went."

"All right, Sherlock. I wanted to be in at the kill. I wanted to see this guy. If I hadn't seen him, then it would never be finished in my mind. Too, this was your first day. It was important for you to see how I work, how I deal with local cops. Okay, it was a bit of a show. I think I deserved it. You're new. You haven't seen any disappointments yet; you haven't lived through the endless frustration, the wrong turns our unit has suffered since the first murders in Des Moines. You didn't hear all the crap we got about the profile being wrong. All you saw was the victory dance. But I can't ever forget that there was Des Moines and St. Louis and twelve people died because we didn't figure things out quickly enough. Of course Chicago was the key, since that was his focus. As soon as I realized that the neighbors knew one another and watched out for one another, and there hadn't been any strangers at the Lansky house, then I knew our guy lived there. He had to. There wasn't any other answer."

Savich added in a tired voice, "You did just fine, Sherlock."

For the first time in years, she felt something positive, something that made her feel really good wash through her. "Thanks," she said, and stretched out in her seat. "What if I hadn't known the answer when you asked me to explain it?"

"Oh, it was easy to see that you did know. You were about to burst out of your skin. You looked about ready to fly. Yeah, you really did fine."

"Will you tell me about your first big score sometime? Maybe even the second one?"

She thought he must be asleep. Then he said in a slow, slurred voice, "Her name was Joyce Hendricks. She was seventeen and I was fifteen. I'd never seen real live breasts before. She was something. All the guys thought I was the stud of the high school, for at least three days."

She laughed. "Where is Joyce now?"

"She's a big-time tax accountant in New York. We exchange Christmas cards," he mumbled, just before he drifted off to sleep.

SEVEN

Sherlock moved a week later into a quite lovely two-bedroom town house in Georgetown on the corner of Cranford Street and Madison. She had four glasses, two cups, a bed, one set of white sheets, three towels, all different, a microwave, and half a dozen hangers. It was all she'd brought with her from California. She'd given the rest of her stuff to a homeless shelter in San Francisco. When she'd told Savich she didn't have much in storage, she hadn't been exaggerating.

No matter.

The first thing she did was change the locks and install dead bolts and chains. Then she hung up her two dresses, two pairs of jeans, and two pairs of slacks on her hangers. She was whistling, thinking about MacDougal and how she'd miss him. He was on the fifth floor, working in counterterrorism. It had been his goal, he'd told her, since an uncle had been blown out of the sky on the doomed Pan Am Flight 103 that exploded over Lockerbie in the late eighties. He'd gotten his first big assignment. He would go to Saudi Arabia because of a terrorist bombing that had killed at least fifteen American soldiers the previous week.

"I'm outta here, Sherlock," he'd said, grabbed her, and given her a big hug. "They're giving me a chance. Just like Savich gave you. Hey, you really did well with that guy in Chicago."

"The Toaster."

"Yeah. What a moniker. Trust the media to trivialize murder by making it funny. Anything big since then?"

"No, but it's been less than a week. Savich made me take three days off to find an apartment. Listen, no impulsive stuff out of you, okay? You take care of yourself, Mac. Don't go off on a tear just because you're FBI now and think you're invincible."

"This is just training for me, Sherlock. Nothing more. Hey, you're good little-sister material."

"We're the same age."

"Nah, with those skinny little arms of yours, you're a little sister."

He was anxious to be gone. He was bouncing his foot and shifting from one leg to the other. She gave him one more hug. "Send me a postcard with lots of sand on it."

He gave her a salute and was off, whistling, just as she was now, his footsteps fast and solid down the short drive in front of her town house. He turned suddenly and called back, "I hear that Savich is big into country-and-western music. I hear he loves to sing the stuff, that he knows all the words to every song ever written. It can't hurt to brownnose."

Goodness, she thought, country-and-western music? She knew what it was but that was about it. It was twangy stuff that was on radio stations she always turned off immediately. It hadn't ever been in her repertoire—not that she'd had much of a repertoire the past seven years. The last time she'd played the piano was in the bar at the Watergate a week and a half before. The drunks had loved her. She'd played some Gershwin, then quit when she forgot the next line.

She was standing in the middle of her empty living room, hands on hips, wondering where she was going to buy furniture when the doorbell rang.

No one knew she was here.

She froze, hating herself even as she felt her heart begin to pound. She had been safe at Quantico, but here, in Washington, D.C., where she was utterly alone? Her Lady Colt was in the bedroom. No, she wasn't about to dash in there and get it. She drew in a deep breath. It was the paperboy. It was someone selling subscriptions.

The only people she knew were the eight people in the Criminal Apprehension Unit and Savich, and she hadn't given them her address yet. Just Personnel. Would they tell anyone?

The doorbell rang again. She walked to her front door, immediately moving to stand beside it. No one would shoot through the front door and hit her. "Who is it?"

There was a pause, then, "It's me, Lacey. Douglas."

She closed her eyes a moment. Douglas Madigan. She hadn't seen him for nearly five months. The last time had been at her father's house in Pacific Heights the night before she'd left for Quantico. He'd been cold and distant with her. Her mother had wept, then ranted at her for being an ungrateful girl. Douglas had said very little, just sat there on the plush leather couch in her father's library and sipped at very expensive brandy from a very old Waterford snifter. It wasn't an evening she liked to remember.

"Lacey? Are you there, honey?"

She'd called her father the day before. Douglas must have found out where she was from him. She watched her hand unfasten the two chains. She slowly clicked off the dead bolt and opened the door.

"I've got a bottle of champagne, for us." He waved it in her face.

"I don't have any silverware."

"I don't usually drink champagne from a spoon anyway. You nervous to see me, Lacey? Come, honey, all you need is a glass or two."

"Sorry, my brain's a bit scattered. I wasn't expecting you, Douglas. Yes, I've got some cheap glasses. Come in."

He followed her to the empty kitchen. She pulled two glasses from the cupboard. He said as he gently twisted the champagne cork, "I read about you in the *Chronicle*. You just graduated from the Academy and you already nailed a serial killer."

She thought about that pathetic scrap, Russell Bent, who'd murdered twelve people. She hoped the inmates would kill him. He had murdered six children and she knew that prisoners hated child abusers and child killers. She shrugged. "I was just along for the ride, Douglas. It was my boss, Dillon Savich, who had already figured out who the guy was even before we went. It was amazing the way Savich handled everything—all low-key, not really saying anything to anybody. He wanted the local cops to buy in to everything he'd done, then give them the credit. He says it's the best P.R. for the unit. Actually, I'm surprised my name was even mentioned."

She smiled, remembering that the very next day Savich's boss, Deputy Assistant Director Jimmy Maitland came around to congratulate everyone. It had been quite a party. "Savich told me that I arrived just in time for the victory dance. Everyone else had done all the hard work. His main agent on the case was with his wife in the hospital, having a baby, the wife, that is.

And so I went in his place. Savich was right. I didn't do a thing, just watched, listened. I've never seen so many happy people."

"It was a Captain Brady of the Chicago police who thanked the FBI on TV, for all their valuable assistance. He mentioned both your names."

"Oh dear, I bet Savich wasn't very happy about that. I had the impression that he'd asked Captain Brady not to say anything. Oh well, it's still very good press for the FBI. Now everyone knows about his unit."

"Why shouldn't the two of you get the credit? He caught a serial killer, for God's sake."

"You don't understand. The FBI is a group, not an individual. Loyalty is to the Bureau, not any single person."

"You're already brainwashed. Well, here's to you, Lacey. I hope this works out the way you want it to."

Douglas raised his glass and lightly clicked it against hers. She nodded, then took a sip. It was delicious. "Thank you for bringing the champagne."

"You're welcome."

"His wife had the baby at about midnight."

"Whose wife? Oh, the agent who'd done all the work."

"Yeah, I thought he'd cry that he'd missed it, but he was a good sport about it. Why are you here, Douglas? I only called my father yesterday with my new address."

He poured himself some more champagne, sipped it, said with a shrug and a smile, "It was good timing. I had to come to Washington to see a client and decided to put you up front on my itinerary." He moved into the living room. "I like your living room. It'll have lots of afternoon sunlight. It's good sized. Why don't you have any furniture?"

"It wasn't worth it to have all my old stuff trucked across the country. I'll get some new stuff."

They were standing facing each other in the empty living room. Douglas Madigan downed the rest of his champagne and set his empty glass on the oak floor. He straightened, took her glass, and set it next to his. "Lacey," he said, taking her upper arms in his hands, "I've missed you. I wish you had come home for a visit, but you didn't. You didn't write me or call. You left a hole in my life. You're beautiful, you know that? I'll bet all the guys are always telling you that, or staring at you, even with your hair all curly around your face, even with those baggy jeans you're wearing and that ridiculous sweatshirt. What does it say across the back? *Dizzy Dan's Pizza?* What's that all about?"

"Nothing, Douglas, just a local place. And no one seems to have noticed my soul-crushing beauty at all. But you're kind to say so." Actually, she'd gone out of her way at the Academy and now at Headquarters to dress very conservatively, even severely. As for her hair, she'd always worn it pulled back and clipped at the base of her neck. But this was Saturday. She was in jeans and a sweatshirt, her hair loose around her face. Since it wasn't raining and there was next to no humidity, Douglas obviously didn't know what curly was.

"You're looking good, Douglas. But you never change. Maybe you just get better." It was true. He was six feet tall, had a lean runner's body and a thin face with soulful brown eyes. Women loved him, always had. Even her mother had never said a word against Douglas. He charmed easily. He dominated just as easily.

"Thank you." He touched her hair, then sifted it through his fingers. "Beautiful. It's the softest red in this dim light. I'll bet it's like flame in the sun. Ah, you know I didn't want you doing this silly FBI thing. Why? Why did you leave me and do this?"

Leave him? She said in her low, calm voice, the one she'd practiced and practiced at the Academy when she took courses in interviewing, "I always wanted to be in law enforcement, you know that. The FBI is the best, the very best. It's the heart of the whole system."

"The heart? I doubt it. As to your always wanting to be in law enforcement, I don't remember that. You started out as a music major. You play the piano beautifully. You were playing Beethoven sonatas since you were eleven years old. You wanted to go to Juilliard. I remember you dropped out of the Fletcher competition. I always believed you weren't quite of this world. You seemed to live for your music. Of course we all changed after Belinda. It's been a very long time now. Seven long years. Your father didn't appreciate your talent, didn't understand it since he didn't have any at all, but everyone else did. Everyone was worried about you when you sold your Steinway years ago, when you stopped even playing at parties. You even stopped going to parties."

"That was a long time ago, Douglas. Dad isn't particularly disappointed in me now. He hoped I'd finally do something worthwhile. He hoped this was my first step to growing up. He only acted cold to me because I hadn't asked him to help me get in. He was dying to use his pull, and I didn't let him." Actually, she had blackmailed him. When the FBI agents interviewed him after she'd applied, he'd not said much of anything about Belinda or how Lacey had changed. She'd told him straight out that she'd never speak to him again if he did. He'd evidently glossed over everything, and very smoothly. She'd gotten into the FBI, after all.

She still missed her piano, but that missing was buried deep down, so deep she scarcely ever thought of it now. "Yes, I did sell it. It didn't seem important anymore." A piano was nothing compared to what Belinda had lost. Still, though, she would still find herself playing a song on the arm of a chair, playing along with the music in a movie or on the car radio. She could remember when she was nineteen playing on the arm of a young man she was dating.

Douglas said, "I don't remember much from that time, to tell you the truth. It's blurred now, distant, and I'm grateful for it."

"Yes," she said. But she remembered; she had lived it and held it deep and raw inside her since that awful night. He moved closer to her and she knew he would kiss her. She wasn't sure she wanted him to. Douglas had always fascinated her. Seven years. A long time. But still it didn't seem quite right.

He did kiss her, only a light kiss, a touch of his mouth to hers, a brief remembrance, a coming back. His mouth was firm and dry. The kiss was so brief, she didn't get the taste of him, just a whisper of the tart champagne. He immediately dropped his hands and stepped back.

"I've missed you. I had to listen to your father yell and curse that you'd lost it and gone off the deep end when you told him you were changing your major to Forensic Science. 'Fingerprinting, for God's sake,' he told me. 'She'll be wasting herself lifting some goon's damned fingerprints from a dead body!' "

"You know there's lots more to it than that. There are a good dozen specialties in forensics."

"Yes, I know. He wanted you to go to law school, of course. He still thought there was hope after you finished your Master's degree in Criminal Psychology. He said it would be helpful in nailing scum. Your dad, the judge, is always forgetting that I'm a defense attorney."

"I changed my mind, that's all."

"That's what I told the FBI guy who came doing a background check on you. I figured if you wanted to go into the FBI, then I wasn't going to stand in your way."

What did Douglas mean by that? That he could have told the FBI that she was unstable, that she'd gone around the bend seven years ago? Yes, he could have said that. She wondered if anyone had told the FBI that. No, if they had, then she wouldn't have been accepted, would she?

"I know my father was positive when the agents came to interview him."

"Yes, he told me you'd given him no choice. I said good for you, it was your life and he should keep his mouth shut if he ever wanted to see you again. He was pissed at me for a good month."

"Thank you for standing up for me, Douglas." She had assumed at the time that the people doing the check on her background simply hadn't considered it all that important. But they had, evidently, and they'd asked questions. "I had no idea, but I am grateful. No one dredged up anything about that time. Do you know that you haven't changed? You really are looking good." He was thirty-eight now. There were just a few white strands woven into his black hair. He was very probably more handsome now than he had been seven years ago. She remembered that Belinda had loved him more than anything. Anything. She felt the familiar hollowing pain and quickly picked up the champagne bottle. She poured each of them another glass.

"You've changed. You're a woman now, Lacey. You're no longer a silent kid. You still have a dozen locks on your door, but hey, this is D.C. I'd probably have a submachine gun sitting next to the front door. What does the FBI use?"

"A Heckler and Koch MP-5 submachine gun. It's powerful and reliable."

"I have trouble imagining you even near something like that, much less holding it and firing it. Ah, that sounded sexist, didn't it? You spoke of change. As for me, perhaps I haven't changed all that much on the outside, but well, life changes one, regardless, doesn't it?"

"Oh yes." She was the perfect example of what life could do to a person.

"You're on the thin side. Did they work you that hard at the Academy?"

"Yes, but it was a classmate of mine—Ford MacDougal—who worked me the hardest. He swore he'd put some muscle on my skinny little arms."

"Let me see."

He squeezed her upper arm. "Flex."

She did.

"Not bad."

"My boss works out. Don't picture him as a muscle-bound, no-neck bodybuilder. He's very strong and muscular, but he's also into karate, and he's very good. I was on the receiving end of his technique once at the Academy. The other day I saw him eyeing me. I don't think he liked what he saw. I'll bet he'll have me in the gym by next Tuesday."

"Boss? You mean this Savich character?"

"I suppose we're all characters in our own way. He's a genius with computers. One of his programs helped nail Russell Bent. He's the chief of the unit I'm in now. I was very lucky that he asked for me. Otherwise I would have ended up in L.A. chasing bank robbers."

"So may I take you out to lunch to celebrate your first case? How about we have lunch at one of the excellent restaurants you've got in this neighborhood?"

She nodded. "How long will you be here, Douglas?"

"I'm not certain. Perhaps a week. Did you miss me, Lacey?"

"Yes. And I do miss Dad. How is his health?"

"You e-mail him every week, and I know for a fact that he e-mails you back every week. He told me you don't like the telephone. So he has to e-mail. So you know he's fine."

Of course Douglas knew very well why she hated phones. That was how she'd been told about Belinda. "Everybody e-mails now. In my unit you hardly ever hear a phone ring."

"I'll write my e-mail address down for you before I leave. Let's go eat, Lacey."

"You look like a prince and I look like a peasant. Let me change. It'll take me just a minute. Oh yeah, everybody calls me Sherlock."

"I don't like that; I never did. And everybody has to make a stupid remark when they meet you. It doesn't suit you. It's very masculine. Is that what the FBI is all about? Turning you into a man?"

"I hope not. If they did try, I'd flunk the muscle-mass tests."

Actually, she thought, as she changed into a dress in her bedroom, she liked being called Sherlock, just Sherlock. It moved her one step further from the woman she had been seven years ago.

It was at lunch that he told her about this woman who claimed he'd gotten her pregnant.

EIGHT

Savich stopped by her desk Monday morning and said, "Ollie told me you still didn't have any stuff for your apartment. I thought you were going to take care of it this weekend. What happened?"

She looked over at Ollie Hamish and cocked her elbow at him, tapping it with her other hand. He waved back at her, shrugging.

Why should Savich care if she slept in a tent? "A friend from California came into town. I didn't have a chance."

"Okay, take off today and shop yourself to death." Then he frowned. "You don't know where to shop, do you? Listen, I'll call a friend of mine. She knows where to find anything you could possibly invent. Her name's Sally Quinlan."

Lacey had heard all about James Quinlan, presumably this woman's husband. She'd heard about some of his cases, but none of the real details. Maybe when she met Sally Quinlan, she'd find out all the good stuff.

It turned out that Sally Quinlan wasn't free until the following Saturday. They made a date. Sherlock spent the day learning about PAP, the Predictive Analogue Program, and all the procedures in the unit.

That Monday evening, she found two lovely, but small, prints at Bentrells in Georgetown, which would probably look insignificant against that long expanse of white wall in her living room. She bought some clothes at another Georgetown boutique. When she got back to her apartment, there was Douglas waiting for her. He'd been busy Sunday, hadn't even had time to phone her. She said, "I'm starving. Let's go eat."

He nodded and took her to Antonio's, a northern Italian restaurant that wasn't trendy. Over a glass of wine and medallions of veal, he said, "I guess you want to know about this woman, huh?"

"Yeah, you dropped that bomb and then took off." She fingered a bread stick. "If you don't want to tell me, Douglas, that's all right."

"No, you should know. Her name is Candice Addams. She's about your age, so beautiful that men stop in midstride to stare at her, smarter than just about anyone I know." He sighed and pushed away his plate. "She claims I got her pregnant and I suppose that I could have, but I've always been so careful. Living in San Francisco, you're probably the most careful of any American."

"Do you want to marry her?" Odd how it hurt to say the words, but they had to be said. Although she didn't know what she wanted from Douglas, she did realize that she valued him, that he attracted her, that he amused her, that he stood up for her, at least most of the time. And he'd been there for her through it all. She'd been closer to him during those awful months than to her father. Of course no one was really close to her mother. That was impossible.

"No, of course not. She's a local TV reporter. I can't imagine she wants to have a baby at this point."

She felt suddenly impatient with him. "Haven't you spoken about all this with her? Does she want to have the baby? An abortion? Does she want to get married? What, Douglas?"

"Yeah, she says she wants to marry me."

"You said she's smart and beautiful. You said you always wanted to have kids. So marry her."

"Yeah, I guess maybe I'll have to. I wanted to tell you about it in person, Lacey. I don't want to marry her, I'm not lying about that. I'd hoped that someday you and I could, well, that would probably never have happened, would it?"

"I don't know," she said finally, setting down her fork. The medallions of veal looked about as appetizing as buffalo chips. "There's been so much, Douglas, too much. I'm very grateful to you, you know that. I wish I could say that I wanted to be with you—"

"Yeah, I know."

"What will you do?"

"I'd turn her down flat if you'd have me, Lacey."

She wondered in that moment what he'd do if she said yes. She'd thought several times in the last few years that she was a habit to him, someone he was fond of, someone he would protect, but not as a woman, not as a wife. No, she was Belinda's little sister and she probably always would be in his mind. She dredged up a smile for him. "I hope she hasn't given you an ultimatum."

"Oh no, Candice is far too intelligent to do that. I'm hooked, but she isn't pulling at all on the line."

It was his life. He had to forget and move on. It had been seven years. And as for her, well, she would move on as well, toward the goal she'd always had, toward the goal she would pursue until the monster was caught and dead, or she was.

She'd heard that Russell Bent had gotten himself a hotshot lawyer who was claiming police brutality and coercion. The press was speculating that the lawyer might get him off. She wouldn't let that happen to him. Never.

ON Thursday, Savich said, "I don't want you to flab out on me, Sherlock. You don't live more than a mile from me. My gym is right in between. I'll see you there at six o'clock."

"Flab out? I've only been out of the Academy for two weeks. And I've walked every square inch of Georgetown since Monday, shopping until I dropped, just as you ordered me to do. Flab out?"

"Yeah, you haven't been lying around, but your deltoids are losing tone. I'm an expert. I can tell these things. Six o'clock."

He strolled away, singing, *"Like a rock, I was strong as I could be. Like a rock, nothin' ever got to me . . ."* He walked into his glass-enclosed office. That wasn't country-and-western, that was a long-ago commercial. Was it Chevrolet? She couldn't remember. She watched him sit down at his desk and turn immediately to his laptop.

Flabby deltoids, ha. She grinned toward his office. He was just being a good boss; that was it. She was new in town, and he didn't want her to get lonesome. She shook her head and went back to work. She jumped a good six inches when a woman's voice said from behind her, "Don't even consider going after him."

Sherlock blinked up at Hannah Paisley, an agent who'd started with the Unit some six months before. She'd been in the Bureau five years. She was very tall, beautifully shaped, and very smart. She'd seen Hannah do her dumb-blonde act on a witness at the Academy, on video. She'd made the guy feel like the stud of the universe. Then he'd spilled his guts. She was very good, which was why she was loaned out on sting operations. She also seemed to have a sixth sense about killers, which was why she'd joined this unit. Sherlock envied her this ability.

Hannah wanted Dillon Savich? She was jealous because Savich thought Sherlock was flabby? What was all this about? "I wasn't going after him, Hannah. Actually, I was thinking he was a jerk, criticizing my deltoids."

"I know. I was joking. Are you doing work on the Radnich case?"

Lacey nodded. Was Hannah joking? She didn't think so. She didn't need this. Hannah gave her a small salute and went back to her desk and computer.

Lacey was working with Ollie Hamish on the Radnich case. It had flummoxed everyone, including Savich. It wasn't the "who" of it that was driving everybody nuts; it was the "how." Sherlock was feeding in more data they'd just gotten from the various local police reports and the autopsies and the forensic evidence, and in the back of her mind, she was also trying to figure out how this weirdo guy could have gotten into four nursing homes—the count as of today—and strangled old women with no one seeing a single thing. The first nursing home was in Richmond, Virginia, eight months ago. Then four months ago, it happened again in northern Florida, home of the nonagenarian. Norma Radnich was the old woman strangled at the South Banyon Nursing Home in St. Petersburg, Florida. They'd been called in by the SPPD only after this last murder. To date there were no leads, no clues, no guesses that were helpful. The Profilers were working on it now as well. Ollie was committed to this one. He was the lead agent on it, and Sherlock wanted it that way.

She wanted to go digging. She'd figured out how to access everything she needed. Perhaps tonight after Dillon let her leave the gym she would come back here and work. If he didn't kill all her body parts, if she'd still be able to walk once he was through with her.

No one would know. She'd be very careful, do her work for the unit during the day and search at night. She felt her heart speed up at the thought. She'd get him. She had to get him. But he'd lain low for nearly seven years. It would be seven years in three days. An anniversary. Just as the past six years had each been an anniversary. Had he died? Had he simply stopped? She didn't think so. He was a classic psychopath. He would never stop until he was dead or locked away. Cycles, she'd thought many times. He was into cycles and so far it hadn't triggered yet for whatever reason.

The weekly update meeting was at two o'clock. There were nine agents in the conference room: six men, including Savich; three women; one secretary, Claudia, a gum-chewing grandmother with platinum hair and a brain like a razor; and one clerk, Edgar, who would bet on about anything and won the pool on the birth weight of Ellis's baby.

Everyone presented what he or she was doing, the status, what he or she needed.

The status meeting went quickly, no wasted time. All the agents felt free to speak up when another agent wanted advice. Savich moderated.

When it was Ollie's turn, he said, "I'm working the Radnich case with Sherlock. She's up to speed on it now. We got the last pile of stuff today from the Florida cops. Sherlock, you finished inputting all the data, didn't you?" At her nod, he said, "Then we'll push the magic button later."

Savich turned to her. "Sherlock? You got anything to add?"

She sat forward, clasping her hands together. "It's like a locked-room murder mystery. How can this guy just saunter into these three nursing homes in Florida and the one in Richmond at ten o'clock at night and kill these poor old women with nobody seeing or hearing a thing? Naturally, all the old women killed were in single rooms or suites, but that shouldn't matter. This whole thing is nuts. There has to be something we're missing."

"Obviously," said Hannah. "But we'll get there. We usually do."

Savich said, "Actually, Ollie and I are going to St. Petersburg tomorrow morning. I just got another call from Captain Samuels. There's been another murder. That means our guy is going into overdrive. The Profilers don't like it. It means he's losing control. Five murders in eight months, the last two in the past week and a half. Captain Samuels really wants us to go down there and poke around, look at everything with new eyes. So, that's where we'll be for the weekend."

Ollie nearly leaped out of his chair in excitement. "When?"

"Eight A.M. United flight from Dulles."

Suddenly Ollie blanched and raised his eyes heavenward. "I won't get too up for this. No, I'm a fatalist. If I really want to go, then my future mother-in-law will tell Maria that I'm a workaholic and lousy husband material and Maria will dump me. It's the way my life works."

"Don't worry, Ollie," Savich said, closing his folder. "It's no big deal. We'll just go down there to see if there's anything they haven't seen. I think it's time to look the situation over firsthand."

"Do you already know who did it?" Sherlock asked, sitting forward, her hands clasped on the conference table.

Savich heard that utterly serious voice, looked at that too-intense face, at that thick curling red hair trying to break free of the gold clasp at the back of her neck. "Not this time—sorry. Now, Ollie, don't panic. Nothing to it."

Still, Ollie looked doubtful. Sherlock had heard he'd already wagered with at least a dozen other agents that his wedding wouldn't come off because either a terrorist would blow up the church or the preacher would be arrested for stealing out of the collection plates.

"I sure want to catch this creep," Ollie said.

"I do too," Savich said. "Like you and Sherlock and every cop in Florida, I want to know how he keeps pulling off this ghost act." He stood. "Okay. Everyone is cooking along fine. No big problems or breakthroughs. Cogan, see me for a minute. I've got an idea about those murders in Las Vegas."

* * *

AT six o'clock, Lacey walked into the World Gym on Juniper Street wearing shorts, a baggy top, and running shoes, her hair pulled back and up high in a ponytail. She paid her ten dollars and went into the huge mirror-lined room. There was the usual complement of bodybuilders who watched every move they made in the mirrors. She got a kick out of watching them walk. They were overbulked and couldn't really get around normally. They moved like hulks.

There were beautiful young women who were six feet tall, professional women on the StairMasters, looking at their watches every few minutes, probably thinking about their kids and what they were going to cook for dinner and did they have enough time if they did just five more minutes.

And there were quite a few professional men, all ages, all working hard. She didn't see a single slacker. Then she saw Dillon. He was wearing shorts, running shoes, and a sleeveless white cotton tank. He was doing lat pulldowns.

He was slick with sweat, his dark hair plastered to his head. He looked good. Actually, he looked better than good; he looked beautiful. Then she saw him glance over at a clock, do two more slow pulldowns, then release the bar and slowly stand up. He turned, saw her immediately, and waved. Seeing him from the front made her realize that she hadn't seen any male as a man in a very long time. She let herself appreciate the clean definition of his muscles, the smooth contours, then she set him away from her, back into his proper role.

He looked her over as he approached. "I've decided your delts are okay. What you need is karate. I didn't like the fact that despite the SIG and your Lady Colt, I still disarmed you with no sweat. You need to know how to protect yourself, and guns are dangerous. What do you say?"

What could she say? She'd begun karate and then had to stop it because she'd broken her leg skiing. Two years before. She'd gotten pretty good. But two years was a long time to be away from an art like karate. He was offering her another chance. She nodded. What followed was a warm-up, then stretching, then the most grueling hour of her life. Savich realized quickly enough that she'd already had some training. He threw her, hurled her, smashed her, and encouraged her endlessly. After one particularly bouncing toss, she lay on her back staring up at him.

"I'm not getting up. I'm not that much of a masochist. You'll just do it again. I'm tired of hearing how great I am at falling and rolling."

He grinned down at her. "You're doing very well. Don't whine. You took karate before, so it's not at all new to you. Learning how to fall is very important."

"I'm still not going to get up. It's been two years."

He sighed, then offered her his hand. "All right. It can be your turn now. But I didn't do all that just to torture you. If you don't know how to fall properly, you might as well hang it up. Now it's your turn. You get to toss me around."

She grabbed his hand, leaped to her feet, and took the position.

He grinned at her. Her look was intense, as grim as could be. She wanted to kill him. "Never stop thinking, Sherlock. Never stop looking at my eyes. Get your muscles ready, but don't tense. You know how to do it. Okay? Let's go."

He let her throw him, using his own momentum to help her. But she was hooting and shouting that she'd finally gotten him on the mat. "Not bad," he said as he got back to his feet. They went through that single routine for another half hour.

She finally stepped back, bent over, her chest heaving, so exhausted she could barely breathe. "Enough. I'm nearly dead. I've nearly sweated off my eyebrows."

He tossed her a towel. It was perfectly dry. He wasn't even sweating. "Now that you've gotten a renewed taste, what do you think?"

She threw the towel at him. "I've never had so much fun in my life."

He laughed and tossed the towel back to her.

"I've never worked so hard in my life."

"Yeah, but on the other hand, it's you in control and not a gun."

"You can't smack someone from twenty feet, sir. Even I could have blown you away if you hadn't been so close to me."

"True, but I was and if it had been the real thing, then you'd be dead. I don't want that to happen. I'll be spending a lot of time training you. I don't want you to go get yourself shot. Now, there's a class that would be great for you. It's both women and men, and the guy who teaches it is an old buddy of mine. His name's Chico and he's one tough buzzard. He might let you in even if you do have skinny little arms."

She laughed. It was impossible not to. They both showered and changed. He walked her home, gave her a salute, and said, "You get your apartment furnished this weekend, Sherlock. No more excuses. See you at headquarters Monday. Here's Chico's phone number. Oh, Sherlock. You might be kind of sore tomorrow, but nothing too bad. Be sure to take a long hot bath. Maybe a couple of aspirin, too. You might also consider some ice packs first."

He paused a moment, looking at her face, clean of any makeup, her ratty hair, curls straggling around her face. He cocked his head to one side, then just smiled at her. "You did fine, Sherlock, just fine. I plan to overlook all your whining."

She eyed the sidewalk, wondering if she could possibly throw him.

"I'm watching your eyes. I'm seeing right into your twisted mind. Nah, Sherlock, don't try to toss me into the flower bed, not tonight." He waved and walked away.

She stood watching him a moment before she went into the town house. And then she watched him until he turned at the corner, east.

"Is that Savich?"

She was so startled she nearly fell over backward. As she was flailing for balance, he came out from behind a tree. "Oh my heavens, it's you, Douglas. You nearly stopped my heart. Is something the matter? Is everyone all right?"

"Oh yes. I've been waiting for you, Lacey. I came over hoping we could have dinner. But you weren't here."

"No, I was at the gym. Savich beat the stuffing out of me." At his stare, she added, "Karate. I don't know if you remember, but I began taking karate lessons two years ago, then stopped. I'm getting back into it, starting with learning how to fall."

"Why with him?"

"I'll be taking classes with a guy named Chico after tonight. Knowing Savich, he'll want me there every night."

"Is the guy coming on to you, Lacey?"

"Goodness, Douglas, he's my boss. He's the chief of the unit. It's all business."

"Yeah, he's got the best way to get to you."

He was jealous. It was amazing to see this side of him. She smiled up at him and lightly placed her hand on his arm. "Agent Savich is a professional. He has no interest in anybody in his unit, not the kind you're worried about." She thought about Hannah Paisley. Was there something between Savich and Hannah?

Douglas saw the lie in her eyes. Why? He'd never known her to lie, but on the other hand, he hadn't seen her in five months. The damnable FBI had had her in their clutches for sixteen weeks. What more would they do to her? He breathed in deeply. "Why don't we go inside? You can change, then I'll take you to dinner. I've got to go back to San Francisco in the morning."

"That would be nice, Douglas. When you get home, you'll be speaking to Candice Addams, won't you?"

"Yes."

She nodded and preceded him into her empty town house.

NINE

She smiled at the guard and flipped open her black FBI wallet. Her beautiful gold star shone.

"You're Agent Sherlock?" He checked the list in his hand. "You're a new agent?"

"Yes, I would like to go to my office and do some more work."

"Hey, you can't light your pipe here in the building, Sherlock."

"That's too bad. I've got a really nice blend."

"Guess you hear that lots, huh?"

The guard was about her age, black, his head shaved, a real hard jaw. "No," she said, grinning at him, "this was the very first time."

"How about: Do you live on Baker Street?"

"Where's that?"

"All right. But I'll be thinking of a new one you really haven't heard before. You're clean. Sign right here. On your way out, check with me again. Oh, my name's Nick."

She waved back at the guard. She walked to the elevators, the low heels of her shoes loud on the marble floor. If anyone asked, she planned to say that she wanted to do more study on the Radnich case. She exited the elevator at the fifth floor, walked down a long hall, turned right, then left, down another hall. She unlocked the door to the CAU. It was dark. Unfortunately she had to light up the entire area. It was different at night. The absence of people, laughing, talking, just breathing, robbed her of even an illusion of safety. She was alone in this large room. She also had her SIG in her holster.

"Don't be a goon and a wimp." She laughed, a ghostly sound in the room. She hated the overhead fluorescent lights.

She brought up the menu on her computer and checked all the available databases. She found him after only twenty minutes. She would have found him in under two minutes if he'd killed any more women in the past seven years. But he hadn't.

She read the profile, then read it again, cursed. She could have written it. She'd written profiles, dozens of them, during her graduate courses in

Criminal Psychology. She'd even written her Master's thesis on *The Inclusive Psychometry of the Serial Criminal*. She supposedly knew all the ingredients that went into the psychotic mind, co-mingled in endless patterns to produce a monster. The "inclusive" had been her advisor's idea. She still thought it sounded obtuse and pretentious, but her advisor had patted her on the back and told her he knew what the professionals respected. She'd passed, so at least she must have sounded convincing in her defense. In fact, she'd gotten high grades on all the various protocols, tests, and measuring tools she'd developed to predict and judge the depths of contamination in the serial murderer's mind. None of it had helped. He'd gone underground.

But even the FBI profile hadn't provided a clue about where to find him. There was nothing at all that provided a different slant or perspective. Nothing new. Wait. She scrolled up again and reread two sentences. "The subject would never vary in his execution. His mind is locked into performing this single repetitive act again and again."

It made sense. As far as she knew, each of the seven murders had been utterly identical. She slowly went through all the police reports, including Belinda's, then printed them out.

She hated the autopsy reports, but through the courses she'd taken, she'd learned to remove herself from the gruesome details, most of which were couched in medicalese. But the photos were different, tougher. She didn't read Belinda's autopsy report. She knew she'd have to, but not now. No, not now, or tomorrow either. She printed out all of them, including Belinda's.

She had to stop. She'd barely be able to carry out all the papers she'd already printed out.

Nick was smiling, that jaw of his out there, when he saw her. "You got lots of stuff there, Agent Sherlock. You gonna take it all back to two twenty-one B Baker Street now? I just remembered the two twenty-one B part."

"Yep. It's all on Moriarty, you know. I'll catch that villain yet."

"I don't know about this Moriarty. But I did see a Sherlock Holmes movie about that hound. Boy, was that hound mean."

"It was a good one," she agreed as she signed out.

"You'll be working more overtime?"

"Probably. They're all real hardnoses here. They never let up."

When she reached her car, she clicked her security alarm before she reached her Ford Explorer. Everything worked. Lights went on inside. No one had broken in.

When she got to her town house, she checked all the entries, then fastened the dead bolts and the two chains. She turned on the security alarm. She left her bedroom door open.

She read over the reports far into the night. But not Belinda's, not just yet.

"FEAST your eyes on this, Sherlock."

She looked down at a map with dots on it. The computer had connected a number of lines. "It's the Star of David, Ollie. So what?"

He was rubbing his hands together. "Nothing bad happened, Sherlock. Savich and I got there and we talked with everybody. You know Savich, he was cool and low-key and then he showed this to everyone. I thought Captain Samuels—she's with the St. Petersburg Police Department—was going to kiss him. These four dots are where the killer's already hit. Savich just did some extrapolation and voilà!"

"It could be anything, Ollie. A Star of David?" She studied the three dots that represented murder sites. They formed a nearly perfect right-side-up equilateral triangle. The other murder could very well be the beginning of an upside-down equilateral triangle, but who knew? "Well, sure, it could be, but it could also be random."

"We'll soon see," Ollie said. "If you go with Savich's reasoning, then the guy is going to kill right here next." He pointed to the next point.

"That's pretty neat," she said. "But no ideas on how the Ghost gets into the nursing homes and out again without anyone noticing?"

"Not yet. But the surveillance on the next one Savich pinpointed is going to be intense. You know what? The media took up your word. All the papers and TV are screaming about the Ghost murdering their grandmothers."

"Surely not. How would they know about our saying that?"

Ollie looked down at his black wing tips. "Well, I kind of said it to a TV woman who was really pretty and wanted something so badly." Ollie looked up at her and grinned. "I thought Savich was going to deck me."

"Better you than me. He's already thrown me all over that gym of his. I'm still sore, but I don't dare say anything because he'll accuse me of whining."

"Ain't that the truth? He's got you into karate?"

She nodded.

"He told me I was one of the best basketball players in the Bureau. He said I should keep myself in shape playing games with all my nieces and nephews. He said kids kept you honest and in shape out of fear of humiliation."

"Ha. He just said that because he realized he couldn't throw you around, the sexist jerk."

"Nah, he cleaned my clock but good when I asked him about karate. He really flatten you, Sherlock?"

"More times than I can count."

"What's this about a sexist jerk?"

Both she and Ollie turned to see Savich standing behind them, his laptop in one hand, a modem in the other.

"I don't know about any sexist jerk, do you, Ollie?"

"Me? I never even heard the word except from Maria, and she didn't even know what it meant."

Savich grunted at them. "What do you think of the Star of David angle, Sherlock?"

"It's so weird as to have a grain of truth in it. But you know, the murders started in Virginia, not Florida. That could put a monkey wrench in the works."

"Agreed. We'll see soon enough. The local cops are covering the next probable nursing home."

She frowned at him. "I do prefer comparing all the physical evidence, but truth be told there isn't all that much. Actually, this Star of David thing, well, I have this feeling you're right. But I also have the feeling it won't matter. He'll probably kill at the nursing home you picked out but no one will see him."

"She's said what I'm feeling," Ollie said. "It's driving me nuts. I've asked the computer to compare and contrast all sorts of evidence, but we're coming up with nothing."

"We'll get him, Ollie."

"I sure hope so," Sherlock said. She turned to Ollie. "Did your future mother-in-law convince Maria that you're a workaholic since you were gone for the whole weekend?"

"No, I blamed it on the chief. I told her that Agent Savich would kick me into the street if I didn't go with him. Then I'd be blackballed and permanently on unemployment. She backed off."

Savich laughed and walked back to his office. Sherlock saw Hannah Paisley rise quickly and follow him. To her surprise, Ollie was watching Hannah, a frown on his face.

"What's wrong?"

"Nothing really. I wish Hannah would be a little more cool about Savich."

Sherlock didn't say a word; she didn't want to know anything personal about anybody. It was safer that way. But Ollie didn't notice, said thoughtfully, "I heard Savich and Hannah dated before she came to the Unit. Then when she joined the Unit, word was that Savich called it off. I heard him say that no one in the Unit should dip his Bureau quill into Bureau ink."

"Now that was sexist, Ollie. You think Hannah's still interested, then?"

"Oh yeah, look at her. She can't keep her eyes off him. Why don't you talk to her, Sherlock? Maybe she'd listen to you. Savich isn't interested, or if he is, he still wouldn't go near a woman agent in his unit."

Sherlock shook her head as she punched up one of the forensic reports. She didn't care what Savich did with his Bureau quill. Goodness, she thought. She'd just made a joke to herself. It had been a long time. She saw Hannah come out of Savich's office, her face set. She wasn't about to say a word to that formidable woman. She sincerely doubted Hannah Paisley would listen to her opinion on the time of day. She went back to work on the Ghost.

SHERLOCK unfolded the *Boston Globe*, the last large city newspaper in her pile. She was tired of scouring the ten largest city newspapers every day of the week, but she couldn't stop. She'd done it for nearly seven years. It cost a fortune for all the subscriptions, but she had enough money from her trust fund so she'd never have to worry about feeding herself and buying as many subscriptions as she wanted. She knew he was out there. She would never stop.

She couldn't believe it. She nearly dropped her coffee cup. It was on page three. Not a big article, but large enough to immediately catch her eye. She read:

"*Yesterday evening at 6:30, Hillary Ramsgate, 28, a stockbroker with Hameson, Lyle & Obermeyer, was found brutally murdered in an abandoned warehouse on Pier Forty-one. Detective Ralph Budnack of the BPD said that she had apparently been led through a bizarre game that had resulted in her death from multiple stab wounds to her chest and abdomen. A note tied around her neck said that she had lost the game and had to pay the forfeit. At this point, police say they're following leads.*"

He was back. In Boston. He'd begun again. She prayed this poor woman was his first victim of this new cycle, that she hadn't missed others, or that he hadn't murdered women in small towns where the AP wouldn't pick up the story.

Hillary Ramsgate. Poor woman. She reread the newspaper article, then rose from her kitchen table. She had died just as Belinda and six other women in San Francisco had seven years ago. They'd all lost the game.

What the newspaper article didn't say was that her tongue had also been cut out. The police were holding that back. But Sherlock knew all about that. She'd been brutally stabbed and her tongue had been sliced out.

She realized then that yesterday had been the seventh anniversary of the last murder.

Seven years. He'd struck seven years ago to the day. The monster was back.

SHERLOCK was pacing back and forth in front of Savich's office when he came around the corner. He watched her a moment. He said very quietly, so as not to startle her, "Sherlock, it's seven in the morning. What are you doing here? What's wrong?"

When she turned abruptly to face him, he saw more pain on her face than he'd seen in a long time. Then the hollow, despairing look was gone. She'd gotten a grip. She'd hidden the pain again. And left nothing at all.

What was going on here?

"Sherlock? What's wrong?"

She smoothed out her face. What had he seen? She even managed a smile. "I'm sorry to bother you so early, but I have a favor to ask. I need to take a few days off and go to Boston."

He unlocked his office door and waved her in. "Boston?"

"Yes. I have a sick aunt. It's an emergency. I know I've only been in the Unit a couple of weeks, but there's not anyone else to see to this situation."

"Your aunt is elderly?"

"Not really, well, she's got Alzheimer's. She's gotten suddenly worse."

"A relative called you?"

Why was he asking all these questions? Didn't he believe her? "Yes, my cousin called me. He, well, he's not well himself so there's no one but me here on the East Coast."

"I see," he said slowly, not looking at her directly now. She looked pale, scared, and excited—an odd combination, but that's what he saw in her face. Her hair was pulled severely back, held in the same gold clasp at the nape of her neck. It looked like she'd flattened it down with hair spray. She couldn't seem to be still, her fingers now flexing against her purse, one foot tapping. She'd forgotten to put on any makeup. She looked very young. He said slowly, "How long do you think you'll need to be away?"

"Not more than three days, just long enough to see that her care is all locked into place."

"Go, Sherlock. Oh yes, I want you to call me from Boston tonight and tell me what's going on, all right?"

Why did he care what she was doing away from Washington? More lies. She hated lies. She wasn't particularly good at them, but she'd rehearsed this one all the way in. Surely he believed her, surely. "Yes, sir. I'll call you this evening."

He jotted down his cell number on a piece of paper. "If it's late, call me at home." He handed her the folded paper. He said nothing until she was nearly at the outer door, then, "Good luck. Take care."

He turned back to his office only after she was out the door. He listened a moment to the sound of her quick footfalls.

This was odd.

Why was she lying to him?

IT was 10:30 that night when the phone rang. Savich muted the sports talk show and answered the phone.

"Sir, it's Sherlock."

He grinned into the phone. "What's going on?"

"My aunt is fine. I have more details to tie up but I'll be back by Thursday, if that's all right."

He said easily, "I have a good friend at Boston Memorial, a doctor who specializes in geriatrics. Would you like his name so you can speak to him about your aunt?"

"Oh no, sir. Everything's under control."

"That's good, Sherlock. What's the weather like in Boston?"

"It's chilly and raining. Everything looks old and tired."

"About the same here. I'll see you on Thursday. Oh yes, call me again tomorrow night."

There was a pause, then, "Very well, sir, if that's what you want."

"It is. You sound tired, Sherlock. Sleep well. Good night."

"Thank you, sir. You too."

HE watched her from his office. It was nearly one o'clock Thursday afternoon. He'd been in meetings all morning. This was the first time he'd seen her since she'd left for Boston. She looked tired beyond her years. No, it was more than that. She looked flattened, as if she'd lost her best friend, as if someone had pounded her, not physically, but emotionally. He wasn't at all surprised.

She was typing furiously on the keyboard, completely absorbed. He waited for a few more minutes, then strolled to her workstation. He'd spoken to her three nights running, each night at 10:30, each night mirroring the previous one and the next, except that on Wednesday, she hadn't quite been the same. He'd wished he could see her. When he looked at her, her thoughts were clear as the shine Uncle Bob put on his wing tips every Wednesday.

"Sherlock."

She raised her face, her fingers stilling on the computer keyboard. "Good afternoon, sir. You just get here?"

"Yes. Call me Savich. Or Dillon."

"Yes, sir. Dillon."

"Would you please come in my office? In say ten minutes?"

She nodded, nothing more, just a defeated nod she tried to hide from him.

When she walked into his office, he said immediately, "I don't like lies or liars."

She just looked at him hopelessly.

"Your mother's sister lives in San Diego. You have three cousins, none of them older than thirty-five, all living on the West Coast. You don't even have a third cousin in Boston. Also, there's nary a trace of Alzheimer's in anyone in your family."

"No, I guess there isn't."

"Sit down, Sherlock."

She sat.

He watched her pull her skirt to her calves. She sat on the edge of her chair like a child ready to be chastised. Only she wasn't remotely a child.

"Don't you think it's about time you leveled with me?"

"Not until I call Chico and take a dozen or so lessons."

Humor from her. He appreciated it. At least she had her balance, if nothing else. "I could still wipe up the floor with you. I'm an old hand at karate and other things as well. Speaking of hands, I played right into yours when I requested you for my unit, didn't I? You must have thought God was looking out for you when Petty told you you didn't have to go to L.A."

It didn't matter now. He probably knew everything. At least she didn't have to lie anymore. "It's true I wasn't interested in bank robbers. I told you that the day you first interviewed me."

"Oh no, that's for sure. What you wanted was the chance to track down the serial killer who murdered your sister seven years ago. Her name was Belinda, wasn't it?"

TEN

She took the blow, bending slightly inward to absorb the pain of it, the unbearable nakedness of it spoken aloud. She knew she'd blown her chance to hell and gone. It was all over for her now. But maybe it wasn't. He was in Boston. She would simply resign from the FBI and move to Boston. She had no choice.

She didn't stir, just looked at him and said, "They named him the String Killer. Isn't that a stupid name? String! Something hardly thicker than a thread, a piece of skinny hemp he used to torture the women, all seven of them—psychological torture—and the media reduced it to string, to make it sexy and clever."

"Yes, I remember the case well. And now he's struck again after seven years, in Boston this time. In fact, it's seven years to the day."

She sat there, looking at him, and said in that flattened voice of hers, that held no surprise at all, "How do you know?"

"I went into your computer, saw what you'd accessed, and downloaded. I saw that you'd used my password to get into a couple of specialized data banks. Odd, but I never thought one of my own people would steal my password. You looked over my shoulder one day?"

She nodded, didn't say anything, which was smart. He was very angry.

He drew a deep breath, tamping down on the anger. "I checked the security log. You spent three and a half hours here Monday night. You read the paper Tuesday morning and left for Boston the same day. I bought a *Boston Globe*. The story was on the third page."

She rose slowly, like an old woman. "I'll clean out my desk, sir, then go see Mr. Petty."

"And what will you tell Petty?"

"That I lied, that you discovered it, and I've been dismissed. I'm really sorry, sir, but I had no choice."

"I haven't canned you. If you think I intend to let you loose on the Boston Police Department, you're mistaken, Sherlock. But you've already spoken to them, haven't you? They kissed you off, right? No matter, don't tell me just yet. I'll call Ralph Budnack."

She looked as if he'd struck her. Then she gave him the coldest smile he'd ever seen. Her chin went up. "I know how the killer got into the nursing homes in Florida to strangle those old ladies."

He realized in that instant that he admired her brain. Was she trying to bargain with him? Make a deal? Gain some kind of leverage? "I see," he said easily, sitting back in his chair, fiddling with a pen between his fingers. "I give you something and you give me something in return?"

"No. I guess I want to show you that I'm not a complete fool, that I do care about something other than the man who murdered my sister. I really don't want any more old ladies to die. I just wanted to mention it before I forgot and left."

"You wouldn't have forgotten, as you couldn't bring yourself to put your sister's death behind you and go on with your life. Now, I already told you. You're not leaving. Go back to your desk, Sherlock, and write out your ideas on the Ghost. We'll talk later."

She didn't want to talk to him. She wasn't in his league. Her very first attempt at deception, and he'd nailed her but good. She hadn't realized she'd been so obvious. But she had been. He'd seen through everything. His anger was frightening, since he didn't yell. It was cold, so very cold, that anger of his. Why hadn't he fired her? She'd betrayed him.

Why?

He would, soon enough; she was certain of that. She'd fire herself if she were in his shoes. She would pull everything else out of the database and then she would slip away. He would know what she'd done quickly enough, but who cared? She couldn't continue here. He wouldn't allow it; the breach had been too great, her conduct too far beyond the line. No, he wouldn't allow her to stay, no matter what game he was playing with her now.

She'd barely sat down at her desk before Hannah Paisley said from behind her, "You're stupid, Sherlock, or does he call you by your cute little first name, Lacey?"

"I'm not stupid, Hannah, I'm just very tired. Well, maybe I am stupid."

"Why are you so tired? Did Savich keep you up all night? How many times did he fuck you, Sherlock?"

Sherlock flinched at the harshness of Hannah's voice, not the naked word. That naked word conjured up some smutty, frankly silly photos in *Playboy*, showing contorting bodies. Now that she thought about it, they hardly ever showed the men completely naked, only women. Really naked.

"Please, Hannah, there's nothing at all between us. Savich doesn't even like me. In fact—"

"In fact what?"

Sherlock just shook her head. No, let Hannah hear it from Savich. It would happen soon enough.

"Look at me, Hannah. I'm skinny and very plain. You're beautiful—surely you must know that. I'm no threat to you, please believe me. Besides I don't like Savich any more than he likes me. Would you try to believe at least that?"

"No. I spotted what you were the minute you walked into the Unit."

"What am I?"

"You're a manipulative bitch. You saw Savich at the Academy and you got him interested so he'd bring you into the Unit. But you listen to me, you stay away from Savich or I'll take you apart. You know I can. Do you hear me?"

Ollie came walking over, nearly sauntering, whistling, if Sherlock wasn't mistaken, as if he didn't have a care in the world, but she saw his eyes. He recognized what he was seeing and he didn't like it. "Hey, Hannah, what's happening with the Lazarus case? What does the guy use all those Coke bottles for?"

She wasn't shaking because of what Hannah had said—no, Hannah and her ridiculous jealousy meant less than nothing to her. Sherlock had seen other women in Savich's office, young women, nice-looking women. Did Hannah go after all of them as well?

Who cared? Forget Hannah. She turned her back on both Hannah and Ollie and booted up her computer, tapped her fingers while she waited, then punched in Savich's password. Nothing happened.

Then suddenly, there appeared: *Not this time, Sherlock.*

The screen went black. The computer was her enemy. As long as Savich was still breathing, the computer would remain her enemy. She lifted her fingers from the keyboard and laid her hands in her lap.

"Your aunt all right?"

It was Ollie. He pulled up a chair and sat beside her. "You don't look so good, Sherlock."

"Thanks. Yes, my aunt is fine now."

"You look like you're ready to go over the edge."

She'd lived on the edge for seven years; no reason to go over now. She smiled at him. "Not really. I'm tired, and that's what I told Hannah. Thanks for drawing her fire, Ollie. I wish she'd open her eyes and realize that I'm about as much a threat to her as a duck in the sights of a hunter."

"That's an odd thing to say, Sherlock. Savich told me to tell you to come into the conference room. What's it all about?"

"TELL the agents how the Ghost gets into the nursing homes, Sherlock."

She sat forward, her hands clasped together. "The Ghost is disguised as an old woman, a nursing home resident. Ollie showed me how to mix and match report data and plug it into two overlapping protocols. I did it with data from what the witnesses had said after each of the murders. No one found anything unusual in any of these reports—not the witnesses, not the cops, not us. But the computer did." She handed out a piece of paper. "These are direct quotes from the witnesses, just the pertinent parts, naturally, the parts that, once tied together, pull the killer out of the bag."

Savich read aloud: " 'No one around, Lieutenant. Not a single soul. Oh, some patients, of course. They were scared, some of them disoriented. Perfectly natural.' " He raised his head. "This is from a night floor nurse." He read down the page. "This one is from a janitor: 'There wasn't anybody around. Only our old folks and they're everywhere. Scared, they were. I helped several of them back to their rooms.' "

Romero nearly squeaked when he read: " 'There was this one old lady who felt faint. I carried her into the nearest room, the recreation parlor. Poor old doll. She didn't want me to leave her, but I had to.' " Romero had a long narrow face, rather like Prince Charles's. He had thick, black brows that nearly met between his eyes, eyes that were black and mirrored a formidable intelligence. He shook the paper toward Sherlock. "Good going. That last quote was from a cop. A cop! It was there all the time."

Savich was sitting back in his chair, looking at each of the agents, one by one. "So," he said finally, once all of them were looking at him, "do you think this is the answer? Our killer is disguised as an old woman, a patient?"

"Looks good to me," replied George Hanks, a thirty-five-year veteran of the Bureau who had the oldest eyes Lacey had ever seen.

Savich turned to Ollie. "You're the lead on this case. What do you think?"

Ollie was staring at Sherlock. He looked wounded, his mouth pinched. "I didn't know anything about what Sherlock was going to do. It seems fairly straightforward, put like this. Like it's so out there that we were all fools not to catch it. Of course they did already check this once, and we mulled it over too, but I guess none of us went deep enough. The first thing to do is call that cop and ask him who that old lady he carried into the recreation room was."

"Good idea," Savich replied. "That could pretty well clinch it if the cop remembers." He turned to Sherlock. "I don't suppose you know if the killer is Jewish, Sherlock? Or hates Jews? Not necessarily the residents, since only two of the five old ladies who were killed were Jews. The owners, you think? Or have you dismissed the Star of David idea?"

"I don't know, sir, about either. Listen, this idea just came to me, that's all. It was blind luck."

"Yes, I rather suppose it was," Hannah said as she rose, "since you're so new at this."

Ollie was dogging Sherlock's heels out of the conference room. "Why?" he said, lightly touching her arm.

"There honestly wasn't time, Ollie. No, of course there was time. It's just that I, oh damn, this sounds ridiculous, but I really wasn't even thinking about it until it popped right into my head. Surely you've done the same thing."

"Yeah, sure, but then when I find something, the first thing I do is tell my partner. You didn't say a word. You tromped into the conference room and showed everyone how great you were. It wasn't a very nice thing to do, Sherlock."

"No, you're right. It wasn't. I can only say I honestly wasn't thinking about it." It was true. She hadn't known that Savich would put her on the spot in front of the whole Unit, but he had. There'd been no time then to say anything to Ollie. No, there'd been time. She just hadn't thought about it. "Listen, Ollie, what happened was this. When I was on the plane going to Boston, I was pushed into this old woman coming out of the gangway. She turned on me and blasted me with the foulest language I'd ever heard. She looked mean. She looked at me as if she wanted to kill me. She's the one who should get all the credit if this works out."

"How did Savich know that you'd come up with something?"

"I can't tell you that, Ollie. I'd like to, but I can't. I'm sorry. Please. I might not be around much longer. I don't know."

"What's going on?" Even though Ollie was a fatalist, he forgot anger very quickly. He laid his hand on her shoulder. "It's something heavy, isn't it?"

"Yes. Very heavy."

"Sherlock. In my office. Now."

Ollie spun around at Savich's voice. "Would you like to tell me what's wrong?"

"No, this is between the two of us, Ollie. Stop looking like a rottweiler. I'm not going to pound her into the floor—at least not yet, not here. Come along, Sherlock."

But they didn't go to his office. He led her out of the Hoover Building to a small park that was catty-corner to it. "Sit." She sat on the narrow bench. Fortunately, she didn't have to wake up a homeless person and ask him to leave. It was a beautiful day, the sky clear, just a light, cool breeze. The sidewalks were crowded with a batch of fall tourists. There were two families with small kids eating picnic lunches on blankets. It was utterly foreign to her, this family thing. It hadn't been, a long time ago. That was before her mother had become ill. At least before Sherlock had realized how very ill she was.

"I've given this a lot of thought."

"You found me out so quickly, I'm sure that you've had plenty of time to figure out everything."

"Look at me, Sherlock."

She looked. Then suddenly she began to laugh. "You look like Heathcliff: all broody, piercing eyes, and dangerous."

He wanted to smile, but he didn't. He said, "I've reviewed the seven murders this guy did seven years ago. I called Ralph Budnack in Boston and asked if he'd heard of any murders committed with this same M.O. other than the one they'd had the other day. He said they hadn't heard about other murders, but that they'd realized they had a serial killer on their hands, a guy who'd struck in San Francisco seven years ago." He paused a moment, turning at the unearthly cooing of a pigeon.

"I finally managed to get in to see Detective Budnack," Sherlock said. "He wouldn't even talk to me. He said I was a sicko and that they didn't need any help."

"I know. I spoke to him right after he kicked you out of his office."

She wanted to hit him. "That was Tuesday afternoon. You didn't say a damned thing about it when I called you that night!"

"That's right. Why should I?"

"Well, so you really didn't have to, but you knew. You knew all the time what I was trying to do."

"Oh yes. Tell me, Sherlock, what did you do for the other two days?"

"Nothing that got me anywhere. The medical examiner wouldn't talk to me even when I managed to lie my way in. With my background, it wasn't that hard. But he was closemouthed, said he didn't like outsiders poking their noses in his business. I spoke to the main reporter at the *Boston Globe*. His name's Jeb Stuart, of all things. He didn't know much more than was in the paper. I bought him dinner and he spilled his guts, but there wasn't much I could use. Then I came home. To you. To get the ax for being a fool."

Savich looked out over the park. He leaned back, stretching out his arms on the bench back. Horns sounded in the background, the sun slivered through the thick canopy of oak leaves, a father was shouting at his kid. "The Boston police have asked for our help. Why didn't you tell Lieutenant Budnack that you were FBI? Chances are good he would have cooperated."

"I knew that if I did, you'd hear about it and aim your computer toward Boston and you'd find out everything. Of course you did that anyway. I should have shown my shield. Maybe I would have gotten something before Budnack tossed me out on my ear. I was stupid. I didn't think it through. I thought if I pretended to be a member of the Ramsgate family, it would be my best shot at getting information." A pigeon darted close to her feet, then away again. "They're used to being fed," she said, watching the pigeon begin to pace in front of her. "I hope the person who feeds them isn't dead."

"Old Sal usually sits here. She isn't here this afternoon because she's picking up her Social Security check. Her health is better than yours. She has names for all the pigeons. Now, what are you planning to do?"

She stood abruptly and looked down at him, hands on hips. "What do you want from me? I already told you I'd resign."

"Then I suppose you'll hightail it up to Boston and go on a one-woman hunt for the String Killer?"

"Yes. I have to. I've prepared myself. I've waited a very long time for him to strike again."

"Very well. I don't seem to have any choice." He stood up abruptly. He was very big. Inadvertently, she took a step back.

He looked impatient. "You afraid I'll throw you here in the park?"

No, she'd been afraid that he'd kill her. Just as that man had killed Belinda. She tried to shrug it off. "I guess I'm just a bit nervous. Sorry. What don't you have a choice about? You have a choice about everything."

"If you only knew," he said, and plowed his fingers through his hair. "I had you call me every night from Boston because I was afraid you'd get yourself into trouble."

"I'm a trained FBI agent. What trouble? Even if I couldn't get to my gun, I sure know how to fall."

He grinned down at her, raised his hand, then lowered it. "Okay, here's what's going to happen. You know more about this guy than any other living person. Would you say that's accurate?"

"Yes." Her heart began to beat in a slow cadence. "I guess you know I printed out all the police and autopsy reports from the seven murders in San Francisco?"

He nodded, looking toward an old woman who was pulling a grocery cart loaded with bags filled with old clothes, cardboard, empty cola bottles. "It's Old Sal. I'll introduce you, then we need to get back."

Old Sal looked her over with very worldly, bloodshot eyes. She could have been any age from fifty to ninety.

"Get your check, Sal?"

"Yeah, Dillon, I got it. You feed my little birdies?"

"No, Sherlock here wanted to, but I wouldn't let her."

The old eyes turned to her. "You Sherlock?"

"Yes, ma'am. Nice to meet you."

"You be good to my boy here, you get me, young lady?"

"I'm not a young lady, ma'am, I'm an FBI agent."

Savich laughed. "She's right, Sal. I rather think I'll be the one taking care of her."

"You get your problems solved, dear, then you can play with my boy here. He's a good lad."

"I will, ma'am."

"I don't like this ma'am stuff."

"It's okay, Sal. She calls me sir, right to my face, as if I were her father or something even worse."

"How old are you, Sherlock?"

"I'm twenty-seven."

"That's a good age. Dillon is thirty-three. Just turned thirty-three three and a half weeks ago. We had a little party for him here. Me and my birdies. Is Sherlock your first or last name?"

"It's my last name, Sal. My first name's Lacey."

"Huh. I like Sherlock better. It gives you distinction."

"I agree."

"You need anything, Sal?"

"No, Dillon. I just want to sit in this lovely sun, rest my bones, and feed my birdies. I got them a pound of unsalted peanuts. I don't want to harden their little arteries."

Sherlock was still smiling when they went back into the Hoover Building. She wasn't smiling ten minutes later.

ELEVEN

"So he's going to take you to Boston. How'd you manage that, Sherlock?"

Hannah Paisley was leaning over her, her voice low and furious in her ear.

"You shouldn't be going. You're new, you don't know anything. You don't deserve to go. It's because you're sleeping with him, isn't it?"

Sherlock slowly turned in her chair, looked up. "No, Hannah. Stop this. This is all business, nothing else. Why don't you believe me?"

"You're lying, damn you. I've seen women look at him. They all want him."

"Ollie told me Savich doesn't believe in becoming involved with anyone in his unit. That includes all of us, Hannah. If you want him, then I suggest you transfer out. Listen, all I want is to catch this monster in Boston. Actually I did lie. I do want Savich's brain and his expertise. Does that count? Is that brain lust?"

Finally Hannah had left.

Now Sherlock leaned her head back against her new sofa and grabbed one of the fat pillows to hug. She closed her eyes and thought of the woman who had just about everything and wanted more. She was sorry if Hannah loved Savich, but there was nothing either of them could do about it. Hannah had to get a grip. Sherlock was the last woman on earth who was a threat to her. No matter now. She wouldn't worry about it anymore. It was Savich's problem. She leaned over and stared at the phone. She picked up the receiver, stared at it some more, then took a deep breath. She dialed the number very slowly.

It rang once, twice, then, "Hello, Judge Sherlock here."

"Hello, Dad."

"Lacey?"

"Yes, Dad."

"This is a surprise. You usually only e-mail. Is something wrong?"

"No. I just didn't have time to write. How are you? How is Mom?"

"Your mother is the same as ever, as am I. So Douglas tells me you're in this special unit in the FBI and then I read about you and this genius guy catching that murderer in Chicago. You happy now?"

She ignored the sarcasm in his voice, but it was difficult. She'd always hated that awful cutting tone of his that used to annihilate her when she was growing up. In e-mails, she usually missed it, which was one reason why she didn't like to call. "Dad, he's struck again."

"What? Who's struck whom?"

"The monster who murdered Belinda. He's struck again in Boston. He killed a woman exactly the same way he killed the seven women in San Francisco. It's been exactly seven years since he stopped. It's a cycle. He's on a seven-year cycle."

There was no sound, no breathing, nothing.

"Dad? He's begun again. Didn't you understand me?"

"Yes, Lacey, I understand you."

"I'm going to Boston tomorrow morning with my boss, Dillon Savich, who's the chief of the Criminal Apprehension Unit. I'm going to catch this monster, Dad. Finally, I'm going to get him."

She was breathing hard. There was nothing but silence on the other end of the line. She drew a deep breath. She had to calm down. She didn't want to sound like some sort of obsessed nut.

But she was. That monster had taken everything from her and left her with a fear she'd managed to control, but it was there still, deep inside of her. No, it wasn't just for her. She wanted to get this scum off the streets. She wanted to shoot him herself.

"Lacey? What do you mean, you're going to catch him? You're not involved. Leave it to the professionals."

"That's what I am, Dad."

"No," he said, angry now. "No, you're not. You're a scared little girl. I think you should come home now. Listen to me. Your sister's been dead seven years. Seven years, Lacey. Douglas told me what you were doing, but I didn't want to believe it. We all know you've given up the last seven years of your life. It's way beyond time to let go of it. Forget it. Come home. I'll take care of you. You can play the piano again. You enjoyed that, and it sure as hell won't get you killed. I won't say a word about law school. Come home."

Forget it? Forget what that butcher had done to Belinda, to her? She drew a deep breath. "How is Mom?"

"What? Oh, your mother. She had a quiet day. Her nurse, Miss Heinz, told me at dinner that she ate well and she watched television, *The Price Is Right*, I believe it was, with seeming understanding."

"I'm not like my mother."

"No, certainly you're not. But this has got to stop, Lacey."

"Why?"

"Let the police catch that madman."

"I am the police. The highest police in the land."

He was silent for a very long time, then he said quietly, "Your mother began this way."

"I must be going, Dad. I had hoped you'd be pleased that I have a shot at catching this monster."

Her father said nothing at all.

To her shock, a soft whispery voice came on the line. "Is that you, Lacey?"

"Hello, Mom. You sound great. How do you feel?"

"I'm hungry, but Nurse Heinz won't get me anything from the kitchen. I'd like some chocolate chip cookies. You always liked chocolate chip cookies when you were small, I remember."

"I remember too, Mom."

"Don't try to catch the man who murdered Belinda. He's too dangerous. He's insane, he'll kill you and I couldn't bear that. He's—"

The line went dead, then the familiar dial tone.

The phone rang again immediately. It was her father. "I'm sorry, Lacey. I was so agitated that I dropped the phone. Listen, I'm scared. I don't want anything to happen to you."

"I understand, but I must try to catch him. I must."

She heard him sigh. "I know. Be careful."

"I will." She looked at the receiver a moment, then gently laid it back in its cradle. She looked at the lovely Bentrells paintings on the stretch of white wall. Landscapes—rolling hills, some grazing cows, a small boy with a bucket on either end of a pole, carried across his back and balanced over his shoulders. She slowly lowered her face into her hands and cried. She saw her father's face from seven years ago, silent and still, no expression at all, just the silence of the grave, and he'd leaned down and whispered very softly in her ear, just after Belinda's funeral, when she'd been so blank, so hollow, but not quite yet utterly terrified, "It's over, thank the good Lord. You'll survive, Lacey. She was only your half sister; try to remember that."

And she'd stared at him as if he were crazier than her mother. Only her half sister? That was supposed to mean something? It had only been three days later when the first nightmare had come in the deep of the night and her grief had become terror.

When the doorbell rang, she nearly shrieked, memories from the past overlaying the present. It was the doorbell, that was all, only the doorbell. Still, where was her gun? She looked frantically around the living room. There was her purse. She always carried her Lady Colt in her purse, in addition to the holster with her SIG.

She grabbed it, feeling its cold smoothness caress her hand like a lover even as the doorbell sounded again. She moved to stand beside the door.

"Sherlock? You there? Come on, I see the lights. Open the door."

She nearly shuddered with relief as she shucked off the two chains, clicked back the dead bolt, and unlocked the door.

He was standing there in a short-sleeved shirt, jeans, and running shoes. A pale blue sweater was tied in a knot around his neck. She'd seen male models in magazines dressed like that—with the knotted sweater—and thought it looked ridiculous. It didn't on him. He was frowning at her.

He stepped inside, still frowning. "That's quite a display of gadgets you've got on that door. A strong guy, though, could still kick it in."

She hadn't thought of that. She lowered the gun to her side, still saying nothing. She would have to reinforce the door. No, she was being absurd.

He closed the door behind him. "I wanted to see if you were furnished yet," he said, and walked into the living room. He looked around at the very expensive furnishings, then whistled. "The FBI must pay you too much. When did you get all this stuff, Sherlock?"

He was acting as though nothing was wrong. He was acting as though she was normal. She was normal. She gently laid her Lady Colt on the lamp table beside the sofa. "I'm not much of a shopper, and Sally Quinlan had to cancel out on me. I called an interior designer in Georgetown and told him what I wanted and needed in place before my boss found out. He took care of it. Really fast."

He turned slowly to look at her. "As I said, we must pay you too much."

"No, I have a trust fund. Normally I don't ever dip into it. I don't need to, but I wanted this place furnished and I didn't want to take the time to do the shopping myself. I knew you'd keep after me until I at least got a sofa."

"The trust is from your grandmother, right? If I remember correctly, she died four years ago and left you a bundle."

"Yes." She wasn't at all surprised. "Please tell me you have better things to do with your time than memorize my personal history."

"Yeah, I'll tell you about my better things if you tell me why you've been crying."

Her hands went to her face. She'd forgotten. She stared at him, straight in the eye, and said, "I have an allergy."

"Yeah, right. Would you look at all the pollen floating around in the air in here. Come on, who upset you?"

"It's nothing, sir, nothing at all. Now, would you like a cup of coffee? Some tea?"

"Tea would be great."

"Equal in it?"

"Nah, only women use Equal. Make mine plain."

"No chemicals for you?"

He grinned at her as he followed her to the kitchen. A whole row of shiny new appliances, from a blender to a Cuisinart, were lined up on the pale yellow tiles. "No," he said, more to himself than to her, "not all of them are unused. I see you've pushed buttons on the microwave, but nothing else."

"That's right," she said coolly, as she put the teapot spout beneath the water spigot. "However, I've always believed that woman can indeed live by microwave alone," she added, trying to smile at him, which really wasn't all that difficult. She turned on the electric burner. "As for the toaster, that needs bread and I haven't bought any yet."

She said over her shoulder as she set the kettle on the stove, "I'm not packed yet, sir, but I will be ready in time. I will meet you at the airport tomorrow morning."

"I know," he said, staring at the bread maker that looked like a lonely white block at the end of the counter. "You know how to use that thing?"

"No, but a recipe book came with it. The designer said that every modern kitchen needs one."

"Why were you crying, Sherlock?"

She shook her head, went to the cabinet, and got down two teacups and saucers.

"You got any cheap mugs? I don't want to get my pinky fingers near those. They look like they cost more than I make in a week."

"I guess they do. The guy went overboard on some of the things."

"I thought women liked to pick out their own dishes."

"Actually, I thought everyone did, guys included. But I just didn't want to take the time. There's too much happening that's so much more important. I told you."

"Come to think of it, I did pick out my own dishes. They're microwavable."

"So are mine. That was the only criterion on my list, that and not too much fancy stuff."

"Why were you crying?"

"I would appreciate it if you would leave that alone, sir."

"Call me Savich and I might."

"All right, Savich. Old Sal calls you Dillon. I think I like that better."

"What's the guy's name?"

"What guy?"

"The one who made you cry."

She shook her head at him. "Men. You think a woman's world has to revolve around you. When I was young I used to watch the soaps occasionally. A woman couldn't seem to exist by herself, make decisions for herself, simply enjoy being herself. Nope, she was always circling a man. I wonder if they've changed any."

"I hadn't thought of it quite like that before, but yeah, I guess that's about right. What's his name, Sherlock?"

"No man. How about I pour some milk in your tea? Is that manly?"

"Sometimes, but not in tea. Keep it straight."

She wanted to smack him. But he'd made her smile, a good-sized smile. She walked to a pristine white wallboard and ostentatiously wrote Equal on it with a blue washable Magic Marker. "There. All done. You happy?"

"Happy enough. Thanks. You call Chico yet?"

"Things have been happening a bit fast. I haven't had the time."

"If you don't, I'll have to take you back to the gym and throw you around."

"The first dozen or so falls weren't that bad."

"I went easy on you."

"Ollie told me you nearly tromped him into the floor."

"At least Ollie's a guy, so he didn't whine."

She just grinned at him. "This cup is too expensive to waste throwing at you."

"Good. Do you have plain old Lipton's tea bags?"

"Yes."

He watched her pour the hot water over the tea bags. "If it wasn't a guy who made you cry, then what did?"

"I could throw a tea bag at you."

"All right, I'll back off, but I don't like to see my agents upset—well, upset by something else other than me and my big mouth. Now, let's talk about our game plan in Boston. That's why I busted in on you this evening. There's a lot we need to get settled before we descend on the Boston PD."

"You're really not going to fire me?"

"Not yet. I want to get everything out of you, then if I'm still pissed off that you lied to me, that's when I'll boot you out."

"I'm sorry."

"You got what you wanted. How sorry can you be?"

He was right about that. She was a hypocrite. She gave him a big smile. "I'm not sorry at all. I'm so relieved, so grateful, that I'll let you say anything sexist you want, at least for tonight."

"You won't whine about getting up early tomorrow, will you? The flight's at seven-thirty A.M."

She groaned, then toasted him with her teacup. "Thank you, sir . . . Dillon. I won't make you sorry."

"Somehow I can't imagine that you won't."

Savich left at ten o'clock, singing to himself as he left. It had to be a line from a country-and-western song, but of course she'd never heard it before. She grinned as she heard his deep voice drawl, *"A good ole boy Redneck is what I aim to be, nothing more, nothing less will ever do for me. All rigged out in my boots and jeans, my belt buckle wide, my belly lean . . ."*

She closed the door, refastened the chains and clicked the dead bolt into place. That was the third or fourth time she thought she'd heard him singing country-western words. Oddly, her classical leanings weren't offended. What could be wrong with music that made you smile?

They hadn't spoken much about the case after all. No, he'd just checked out her digs and told her she needed a CD player. It was clear what kind of music he preferred.

She packed methodically. She prayed he would help her find the man who had killed her sister.

TWELVE

Savich said to Sherlock, "As I told you last night, Detective Budnack will be meeting us at the station. It's District Six in South Boston. They found Hillary Ramsgate in an abandoned warehouse on Congress Street. Somebody called it in anonymously, either the killer or a homeless person, probably the latter. But they've got the guy's voice on tape so when we catch him, we can make a comparison.

"He'll have all the police reports, the autopsy, the results of any other forensic tests they've done as of today. I'd appreciate it if you'd go over all this stuff. You got all our things?"

"Yes," she said, turning in her seat to face him fully. "Also, I doubt Detective Budnack understood the game. He knew there was a game because of the note saying Hillary Ramsgate lost and had to pay the forfeit, but he didn't understand what it meant."

"No, but it's his first hit with this guy. By the time we get there, he'll have spoken to the police in San Francisco and probably read most of the reports. Tell me your take on his game, Sherlock. I'm sure you've got one."

They accepted tea from the flight attendant, then settled back. It was pretty weak, but it was at least hot. She looked hard at the cup. A lock of hair had come loose from its clamp and dangled along the side of her face, curving along her jawline. He watched her jerk it behind her ear, never looking away from that tea of hers. What was going on here?

She said finally, "I've pictured this in my mind over the years, refined it, changed it here and there, done many profiles on him, and now I think I've got it exactly the way he did it. He knocks the woman on the head and takes her to a deserted building, the bigger the building the better. In three instances, he used abandoned and condemned houses; in one, he used a house whose owners were out of town. He's intimately familiar with the buildings and houses. He's set up all his props and arranged the sets. He's turned them into houses of horror, then, finally, into mazes.

"When the woman regains consciousness, she's alone and unharmed. She isn't in complete darkness, although it's late night outside. There's a faint light, just enough so she can see about a foot or two all around her.

What she does first is call out. She's afraid to have an answer and just as afraid when there's dead silence. Then she's hopeful that he's left her there alone. She yells again.

"Then she gets herself together and tries to find a way out of the building. But there isn't a way out. There are doors, but they're bolted. She's nearly hysterical now. She knows something is very wrong. Then she finds the string lying beside where she'd awakened.

"She doesn't understand the string, but she picks it up and begins to follow it. It leads her through convoluted turns, over obstacles, into mirrors he's set up to scare her when she suddenly comes upon her own image. Then the string runs out. Right at the narrow entrance to this set he's put into place.

"Then perhaps he laughs, calls out to her, tells her she's going to fail and when she fails, he's going to have to punish her and she won't like that. Yes, he will have to punish her because she will lose the game. But he doesn't tell her why he's doing it. Why should he? He's enjoying her ignorance. Maybe he even calls out to her, taunts her, before she walks into the maze. That's possible, too. The note thing. He only did that with the first woman he killed in San Francisco. It's as though he's identified what he's done and the next time and the time after that, it isn't necessary. Everyone will know who he is."

He said slowly, "You are awfully certain of what he does, Sherlock."

"I told you, I've thought and thought about it. The shrinks believe—as do the FBI Profilers—that he watches every move she makes, memorizes every expression on her face, possibly even films her. I'm not so sure about that.

"But I bet he even tells her she can win the game if she runs, if she manages to reach the center of the maze. She does run, hoping, praying he isn't lying, that she can save herself, and she runs right into this maze he's built since there's nowhere else for her to go. There are dead ends in the maze. Finally she finds her way to the center. She's won. She's breathing hard. She's terrified, hopeful, both at the same time. She's made it. She won't be punished.

"He's waiting for her there." She had to stop trembling. She drew a deep breath, took another drink of her now-cold tea, then said with a shrug, "This much was obvious when everything was reconstructed by experts after the fact."

Savich said, "So then he stabs her in the chest and in the abdomen until she's dead. Is everyone you know of certain he does this when she makes it to the center of the maze?"

"Yes. Instead of winning, she loses. He's there, with a knife. He also cuts out her tongue. This fact never appeared in any publicized reports so that any confessions could be easily verified."

"Why does he do that?"

She didn't look at him. "Probably to shut her up forever. He killed only women. He hates them."

"A game," Savich said slowly, looking down at a ragged thumbnail. "A game that leads to certain death. I don't understand why she loses if she manages to find the center of the maze. As you said, usually that means you've won. But not with this guy. You have any ideas about why he kills her when she makes it to the center of the maze?"

"Not a clue."

But she did and he didn't know how she did. "Do you remember the legend of Theseus and the Minotaur?"

"Yes," she said. "I remember that at the center of the cave, Theseus came upon the Minotaur. But Theseus didn't lose. He killed the Minotaur."

"And Ariadne led him out with a string."

"You're thinking that maybe he sees himself as Theseus and that the women are the Minotaur? I don't know. It doesn't make much sense to me."

"But you know that it makes perfect sense to him. How much of a study did you do of the legend?"

"Not all that much really," she said.

"Do it when we get home again."

"But even if I happen to discover more parallels between what the killer does and the Theseus legend, it won't tell us anything about the man's identity, about how to find him. Do you know that he used the same abandoned building for two of his victims in San Francisco? It was down in the China Basin. The very same building! Then the police put a watch on it, but it was too late. He was surely laughing at them, at all of us, because we were helpless."

"It surprises me that no one saw anything. There are usually lots of homeless around those abandoned buildings. And cops do patrol. To set up all the props, he would have had to carry stuff in and out of the buildings, yet no one appeared to see anything. He would have had to transport his props. A truck? He had to make them himself or buy them somewhere."

"Yes, but only once. He took away most of his props after he killed each woman. He left just enough so the police would know what he'd done."

"And still no one saw anything. That boggles the mind."

"Evidently one old man saw him, because he was found strangled near one of the abandoned buildings. It was the same kind of string used to get to the center of the maze. He wanted the cops to know it had been him."

"What did you mean that he was laughing at us?" She had been nineteen years old at the time her sister was murdered. How was she involved? He would find out later. She was shaking her head at him as he said, very quietly, "You're on a cycle too, Sherlock. A seven-year cycle. He's done nothing for seven years, gone about his business, probably stewing inside but not enough to make him snap. As for you, you've given the last seven years of your life to him."

She was stiff, her eyes colder than the ice frozen over her windshield the previous winter. It was what Douglas had said to her, what her father had said: "It's none of your business."

"I suppose your family has told you it isn't very healthy."

"It's none of your business."

"I imagine you couldn't bear to let your sister go, not the way she was removed, like the pawn in a game that she had to lose."

She swallowed. "Yes, that's close enough."

"There's more, isn't there? A whole lot more."

She was very pale, her fingers clutched around the paper cup. "No, there's nothing more."

"You're lying. I wish you wouldn't, but you've lied for a very long time, haven't you?"

"There's nothing more. Please, stop."

"All right. Do you want to shoot this guy once we nab him? You want to put your gun to his head and pull the trigger? Do you want to tell him who you are before you kill him? Do you think killing him will free you?"

"Yes. But that's unlikely to happen. If I can't shoot him then I want him to go to the gas chamber, not be committed the way Russell Bent will be. At least that's what my brother-in-law, Douglas Madigan, told me."

"No one knows yet if Russell Bent will be judged incompetent to stand trial. Don't jump the gun. Life imprisonment without parole isn't good enough?"

"No. I want him dead. I don't want to worry about him escaping and killing more women. I don't want to worry that he might be committed to an institution, then fool the shrinks and be let loose. I don't want him still breathing after he killed seven—no, eight—people. He doesn't deserve to breathe my air. He doesn't deserve to breathe any air."

"I've heard the opinion that since killing a murderer doesn't bring back the victim, then as a society we shouldn't impose the death penalty, that it brings us down to the murderer's level, that it's nothing but institutional revenge and destructive to our values."

"No, of course it doesn't bring the victim back. It's a ridiculous argument. It makes no sense at all. It should be very straightforward: If you take another human life, you don't deserve to go on living. It's society's punishment; it's society's revenge against a person who rips apart society's rules, who tries himself to destroy who we are and what we are. What sort of values do we have if we don't value a life enough to eradicate the one who wantonly takes it?"

"We do condemn, we do imprison, we just don't necessarily believe in killing the killer."

"We should. It's justice for the victim and revenge as well. Both are necessary to protect a society from predators."

"What about the argument that capital punishment isn't a deterrent at all, thus why have it?"

"It certainly wouldn't be a deterrent to me, the way the appeals process works now. The condemned murderer spends the taxpayer's money keeping himself alive for at least another nineteen years—our money, can you begin to imagine?—no, I wouldn't be deterred. That monster, Richard Allen Davis, in California who killed Polly Klaas and was sentenced to death. You can bet you and I will be spending big bucks to keep him alive for a good dozen more years while they play the appeals game. Someone could save him during any appeal in those years. Tell me, if you knew that if you were caught and convicted of killing someone you'd be put to death within say two years maximum, wouldn't it make you think about the consequences of killing? Wouldn't that be something of a deterrent?"

"Yes. And I agree that nearly two decades of appeals is absurd. Our paying for all the appeals is nuts. But revenge, Sherlock, plain old revenge. Wouldn't you have to say that the committed pursuit of it is deadening?"

That's what he'd wanted to say all along. She was very still, looking out the small window down at the scattered towns in New England. "No," she said finally, "I don't think it is. Once it's over you see, once there's justice, there can be a final good-bye to the victim. Then there's life waiting, life without fear, life without guilt, life without shame. It's all those things that are deadening." She said nothing more.

He pulled a computer magazine out of his briefcase and began reading.

He wondered what else had happened to her. Something had, something bad. He wondered if the something bad had happened to her around the time her sister had been killed. It made sense. What was it?

HOMICIDE Detective Ralph Budnack was a cop's cop. He was tall, with a runner's body, a crooked nose that had seen a good half dozen fights, intelligent, a stickler for detail, and didn't ever give up. His front teeth lapped over, making him look mischievous when he smiled. He met them at the District 6 Station and took them in to see his captain, John Dougherty, a man with bags under his tired eyes, bald and overweight, a man who looked like he wanted to retire yesterday.

They reviewed all that they knew, viewed the body in the morgue, and met with the medical examiner. There had been twenty stab wounds in Hillary Ramsgate's body: seven in the chest, thirteen in the abdomen. No sexual assault. Her tongue had been cut out, really very neatly, and there was a bump on her head from the blow to render her unconscious.

"Ralph tells me the guy's on a seven-year cycle and we lucked out that he just happened to be here when the seven years were up. That kind of luck can kill a person." Captain Dougherty chewed on his unlighted cigar. "The mayor called before you came. The governor is next. I sure hope you guys can catch this guy."

"There are many meanings and contexts to the number seven," Savich said, looking up from the autopsy report he was reviewing again. "I don't know if we'll get much out of this, but as soon as we've inputted all the information from Ms. Ramsgate's murder into the program, I'm going to correlate it to any instances of the number seven as working behavior in numerology." He looked over at Sherlock, who was staring blankly at him. "Hey, it's worth a try. There might be something; it might be our guy buys into all that stuff, that it will give us some clues about him."

Captain Dougherty said, "Use a psychic if you think it might help. A trained cat, if you've got one."

Savich laughed, not at all insulted. "I know it sounds weird, but you know as well as I do that people can be loonier than the Mad Hatter."

"I didn't catch your name," Ralph Budnack said, staring at Sherlock, "but I've seen you before. Now I've got it. You came in here claiming to be related to the victim." He turned to Savich, his jaw working. "You want to tell me what's going on here?"

"Calm down, Ralph. It's all very understandable. Her sister was killed seven years ago in San Francisco by this guy. That's why she realized so fast that he'd struck again. That's why she came up here. Thanks to her, we're on to him immediately. Now, you don't have to worry about her. She works for me. I'll have her under control."

Captain Dougherty stared at her, chewed harder on the unlit cigar. "I don't want any vigilante stuff here, Agent Sherlock. You got that? You even tiptoe outside the boundaries and I'll bust you hard. I don't care if you're FBI. I wouldn't care if you were Mueller himself. It appears to me that Savich would bust you too. I wouldn't want to go in the ring with him."

"I understand, sir." Why did Dillon have to tell them the truth? She could have lied her way out of it. She caught his eye and realized he knew exactly what she was thinking. He didn't want her to lie anymore. Well, bully for him. It hadn't been his sister who'd been butchered; it hadn't been him to have nightmares horrible enough to wake you up wheezing, knowing that you were dying, that someone was close, really close, nearly close enough to kill you. She wanted to throw him through the window, although it looked as though it had been painted shut.

Now Budnack would tell the other cops who she was and what she'd done, and no one would trust her as far as the corner.

"I hope we'll find out something about this seven-year thing," Savich said. "It also occurred to me that he knows how to build sets and props. Not just build them, but he has to transport them to the buildings where he intends to commit the murders. They must be constructed to fold pretty small to fit in a car trunk or in a van. That means he has to be proficient at least at minimal construction.

"Also, surely a truck would have been remarked upon. And he must do it in the middle of the night to cut way down on the chance of being seen. It's possible that the seven business will correlate to building things. Who knows?"

"Like a propman in the theater," Sherlock said slowly, hope soaring.

"Could be," Savich said. "Let's get the rest of the goodies in the program, then see what we come up with. He stood. "Gentlemen, anything else?"

"Yes," Ralph Budnack said. "I want to help you input into this magic program of yours."

"You got it," Savich said and shook his hand.

The three of them took turns until late in the afternoon. Savich said, "There, that about takes care of it. Now let me tell MAX to stretch his brain and see what he can find for us. I inputted every instance of the number seven I could find. For example, two of the murders were committed on the seventh day of the week. Another murder was committed in the seventh month of the year. Sounds pretty far-out, but we'll see. The real key is the seven-year cycle and the fact that he killed seven women. MAX has more to work with here than he's ever had before. Also I gave MAX another bone—the construction angle." His fingers moved quickly over the keys. Then he grinned up at Sherlock and pressed ENTER.

"That computer your kid?" Ralph Budnack asked.

"You'd think so," Savich said. "But no, MAX is a partner, and by no means a silent one." He patted the keyboard very lightly. "Nope, I'll have some real kids one of these days."

"You married?"

"No. Ah, here we go. MAX's first effort. Let me print it out."

There were only two pages.

Savich grinned at them. "Take a look, guys."

THIRTEEN

"The Pleiades?"

Ralph Budnack looked ready to cry. "We spent four hours inputting stuff and we get the Pleiades? What the hell are the Pleiades?"

"The seven daughters of Atlas and Pleione," Sherlock read. "They're a group of stars, put in the sky by Zeus. Orion is behind them, chasing them."

"This is nuts," Ralph said.

"Keep reading," Savich said. "Keep reading."

Sherlock looked up, her face shining. "He's an astronomer, he's got to be. That or he's an astrologer or into numerology, with astronomy as a hobby."

Ralph Budnack said, "Maybe he's a college professor, teaching mythology. He builds furniture on the side, as a hobby."

"At least there appears to be something in the seven scenario," Savich said, laying down page two. "We've got some leads. I've got a couple of other ideas, but Ralph, you and your guys can start checking this all out. Chances are, according to the Profilers, that the guy has been here at least six months, but less than a year. Enough time, in other words, for him to scout out all the places he's going to take his victims."

"Good point," Budnack said, rubbing his hands together. "My other team members are interviewing everyone they can scrape up from the Congress Street area. I'll pull them off to do this."

When Sherlock and Savich were alone, she said, "You're having a problem with all this, aren't you?"

"This whole business with the seven sisters of the Pleiades, it seems too easy, too obvious."

"Why? It took MAX to come up with it. The SFPD didn't come up with it. The Profilers didn't either. Also, it's a seven-year interval between killings. He kills seven women at each cycle. Two sevens is a goodly number of sevens."

Savich stood up and stretched, he scratched his stomach. "You're probably right. I'm dragged down because MAX got it and we didn't. But you know, I've got this itch in my belly. Whenever I've gotten this itch in the past, there's been something I've missed.

"I need to go to the gym. Working out clears my brain. You want to come along? I won't tromp you this time. In fact, I'll start work on your deltoids."

"I didn't bring any workout stuff. Besides, I plan to protect my deltoids with my life."

THE cops tracked down four possible suspects within the next twenty-four hours—two of them astrologers who'd come to Boston during the past year, two of them numerologists. Both the numerologists had come during the past year from southern California. They didn't arrest any of them. Budnack, Savich, and Sherlock met later that day in Captain Dougherty's office.

"No big deal about that," Ralph Budnack said, frowning. "All the nuts come from southern California."

"So does Julia Roberts," Savich said.

"Point taken," Budnack said and grinned. "So what do you think, Savich? It just doesn't feel right with any of these guys. Plus two of them have pretty good alibis. We found a homeless guy, Mr. Rick, he's called, who said he saw a guy going in and out of the warehouse on Congress. He said he was all bundled up and he wondered about that since it was really warm that night, said it was so warm he didn't even have to sleep in his box. Said he hadn't seen him before."

"Any more specifics about the man?" Lacey asked. "Anything about what he looked like?"

"Just that he looked kind of scrawny, a direct quote from Mr. Rick. Whatever that means. Mr. Rick is pretty big. Scrawny just might mean anything smaller than six foot. I might add that only one of the four guys we picked up could be called scrawny, and he's got the strongest alibi."

Savich had wandered away. He was pacing, head down, seemingly staring at the linoleum floor.

"He's thinking," she said in answer to Captain Dougherty's unasked question.

"Your sister was really offed by this guy?"

"Yes. It's been seven years. But you never forget."

"Is that why you got into the FBI?"

"I didn't know what else to do. I went to school and learned a bit about all the areas in forensics, then I focused on how the criminal mind works. Actually I'd planned to be a Profiler, but I couldn't live what they do every day. So here I am. Thank God for Savich's new unit."

"You even learn about blood-spattering patterns?"

"Yeah, some of the examples of that were pretty gruesome. I'm not an expert, but at least I learned enough so that I'd know what to do, where to find out more, who to contact."

Captain Dougherty said, "Everyone thinks profiling is so sexy. Remember that show on TV about a Profiler?"

"Yeah, the one with ESP. Now that was something, wasn't it? Why bother with profiling? A waste of time. Just tune into the guy and you've got him."

He grinned and she distracted him with another question about one of the men they'd hauled in for questioning.

IT was at midnight when Savich sat up in bed, drew a very deep breath, and said softly, "Gotcha."

He worked at the computer until three o'clock in the morning. He called Ralph Budnack at seven A.M. and told him what he needed.

"You got something, Savich?"

"I might," he said slowly. "I might. On the other hand, I might be off plucking daisies in that big flower market in the sky. Keep doing what you're doing." He then called Sherlock's room.

"I need you," he said. "Come to my room and we'll order room service."

The fax was humming out page after page from Budnack. "Yeah," Savich was saying, "this will help."

"You won't tell me what you're homing in on?"

"Nope, not until I know there's a slight chance I'm on the right track."

"I was thinking far into the night," she said, and although it wasn't at all cold in the room, she was rubbing her hands over her arms. She looked tired, pinched. "I couldn't get this seven business out of my mind." She drew a deep breath. "We banked everything on seven, and so we got the Pleiades and all that numerology stuff. But what if it doesn't have anything to do with seven at all? What if there was just the one instance of seven and that was merely the time lag before he started killing again? What if he killed more than seven women? Eight women or even nine?" She looked nearly desperate, standing there, rubbing her arms. "Not much of a big lead there. I think you're right, it's too pat, and too confining. But if there's nothing there, then what else is there?"

"You're perfectly right. You've got a good brain, Sherlock. My brain was working in tandem with yours—"

She laughed, some of the tension easing out of her. "Which means that you've got a good brain too."

"Me and MAX together have a top-drawer brain. All right, let me tell you where I'm heading and if you think I'm off the wall, then you can haul me back. I've been thinking that we've gotten too fancy here, exactly what you said—it's too complicated out there. It assumes our killer is a really deep, profound fellow with lots of esoteric literary or astrological underpinnings. That he probably builds designer furniture on the side. I woke up at midnight and thought: Give me a break. This is nothing but a headache theory. It's time to get back to basics.

"I knew then that our guy isn't any of those things. I think the answer might lie with the obvious. I've been asking MAX to come up with other alternatives or new options based on new factoring data I've put in." He drew a deep breath. "Remember, Sherlock, this still might not lead anywhere."

"What's obvious?"

"A psychopath who knows how to build props, make them fold up small, and make them portable. I know that they checked into this in San Francisco—they went to all the theaters, interviewed a dozen prop designers and builders. I went back in to see exactly what they did find—and where they'd looked, what kind of suspects they'd turned up.

"Not much, as it turns out. So, I'm having MAX look where they didn't look. I've inputted everything I can think of into the program so we've got a prayer of turning up something helpful."

She didn't say anything, just looked at him. She felt hope well up, but she was afraid to nourish it. She saw he was rubbing his neck.

"What's wrong with you?"

"I worked out too hard last night after you left and then spent too much time hunched over MAX. No big deal."

"If you're not too macho, you might consider some aspirin. On the other hand, I hesitate to say anything at all now, given that you and MAX together are such a great team and MAX has got the bit between his teeth."

"Yeah, he's got a great byte."

"That was funny, Dillon, if you spelled it right."

"Trust me. I did."

"You look like you're ready to burst out of your skin and you can still be funny."

"You're not laughing."

"I'm too scared." And it was the truth. She was terrified he would kill again, terrified that he would escape and there would never be justice.

He watched her walk away from him across to the far windows that looked down eight floors to the street below.

"You want to tell me what else happened seven years ago?"

She actually flinched as if he'd struck her. He rose slowly and walked to her. He reached out his hand, looked at it, then dropped his arm back to his side. He said only, "Sherlock."

She didn't turn, shook her head.

MAX beeped. Savich pressed the PRINT button. After a moment, he picked out one sheet of paper from the printer. He began to laugh. "MAX says our person may be in building supplies."

She whipped around so fast she nearly fell. "As in a lumberyard?"

"Yes. He says that odds are good that with all the building materials the killer left behind, the type of hardware the killer used, the type of nails, the wood, the kinds of corkboard, the brackets, etcetera, that our guy works in lumber. Of course, the cops in the SFPD looked at every prop he left behind at every murder. It turns out that the wood wasn't traceable, that all the brackets, hinges, and screws were common and sold everywhere. They came up dry. Now, they never specifically went after men who worked in lumberyards. MAX thinks that's exactly where we should look."

Her eyes were sparkling. "MAX is the greatest. It's brilliant."

"We'll see. Now in addition to a guy who works in lumber, we've also got a psychopath who hates women and cuts out their tongues. Why? Because he himself has taken grief from them or seen other men take the grief?"

She said slowly, not meeting his eyes, "Maybe he cuts out their tongues because he knows they bad-mouth their husbands and curse a whole lot. Maybe he doesn't believe women should curse. Maybe that's how he picks out the women to kill."

She'd known that all along, he thought, but how? It was driving him crazy, but he let it go for now. He knew she was right on the money. It felt right to his gut—no, it felt perfect. He said easily, "That sounds possible. Weren't there some profiles drawing that conclusion?"

"Yes, certainly there were. The guy's not in the theater or anything sexy like that?"

"Nope. I'll called Ralph. He can check to see who's arrived during the past year in Boston who works for a lumberyard." Now that he thought about it, perhaps he had seen some speculation about that in some of the reports and profiles he'd read. Still, there was a whole lot more to all this. He looked at her. She looked away. Trust was a funny thing. It took time.

MARLIN Jones was the assistant manager at the Appletree Home Supplies and Mill Yard in Newton Center. He was in conversation with his manager, Dude Crosby, when a pretty young woman with thick, curly red hair came up to him, a piece of plywood in her hand. There was something familiar about her.

He smiled at her, his eyes on that foot-long piece of plywood. He said before she could explain, "The problem is that the plywood's too cheap. You tried to put a nail through it and it shredded the plywood. If you'll come over here, I'll show you some better pieces that won't fall apart on you. Have we met before?"

"Thank you, er, Mr. Jones," she said, looking at his name tag. "No, we haven't met before."

"I'm not very good at remembering faces, but well, you're so pretty, maybe that's why I thought I'd met you before." She followed him out into the lumberyard. "What are you doing with the plywood, ma'am?"

"I'm building props for my son's school play, and that's why I need to use plywood, not hardwood. They're doing *Oklahoma!* and I've got to put together a couple of rooms that can be easily disassembled then put back up. So I'll need some brackets and some screws too."

"Then why'd you pound a nail through it?"

"That was just experimentation. My husband, that miserable dick head, won't help me, drinks all the time, won't take part in raising our son, won't show me any affection at all, well, so I've got to do it all myself."

Marlin Jones stared at her, as if mesmerized. He cleared his throat. "I can help you with this, Mrs.—?"

"Marty Bramfort." She shook his hand. "I live on Commonwealth. I had to take a bus out here because that bastard husband of mine won't fix the car. Next thing I know, that damned car will be sitting on blocks in the front yard and the neighbors will call the cops."

"Mrs. Bramfort, if you could maybe draw what you need to build, then I could gather all the stuff together for you."

"I don't suppose you'll help me put it all together?"

"Well, ma'am, I'm awfully busy."

"No, never mind. That's my jerk husband's job, or it should be. It's not yours. But I would appreciate your advice. I already made some drawings. Here they are."

She laid them out on top of a large sheet of plywood. Marlin Jones leaned over to study them. "Not bad," he said after a few minutes. "You won't have much trouble doing this. I'll cut all the wood for you and show you how to use the brackets. You want to be able to break all the stuff down quickly, though. I know just how to do that."

She left the Appletree Home Supplies and Mill Yard an hour later. Marlin Jones would deliver the twelve cut pieces of plywood to the grade school gymnasium, along with brackets and screws, hinges, paint, and whatever else he thought she'd need.

Before she left him, she placed her hand lightly on his forearm. "Thank you, Mr. Jones." She looked at him looking at her hand on his forearm. "I bet you're not a lazy son of a bitch like my husband is. I bet you do stuff for your wife without her begging you."

"I'm not married, Mrs. Bramfort."

"Too bad," she said, and grinned up at him. "But hey, I bet lots of ladies would like to have you around, no matter if they're married or not." When she walked away from him, she was swinging her hips outrageously. "Who knows what building props can lead to?" she called out over her shoulder and winked at him.

SHE whistled to herself as she walked from where she'd parked her car toward the Josephine Bentley Grade School gymnasium. It was Ralph Budnack's car, a 1992 Honda Accord that drove like a Sherman tank. Toby, the temporary school janitor and a black cop for the Sixth Division, opened the door for her.

His voice carried as he said, "Jest about done, Mrs. Bramfort?"

"Oh yes, very nearly done now. You going home, Toby?"

"Yep, just waiting to let you in. Don't forget to lock up now, Mrs. Bramfort."

"I won't."

She was alone in the gymnasium, a vast room that resounded with her breathing, with every step she took, filling the empty air with echoes. All the nearly built props were neatly stacked in the corner. She'd been doing this a good five evenings in a row now. She unstacked all of them, laying them out side by side. Not much more to do.

She began work, her right hand turning the screwdriver again and again, digging in new holes through the plywood. Some of them were L shaped, most flat. The brackets were just to support the two pieces of plywood. She didn't have all the lights on; just the corner where she worked had lighting. It wasn't much. There were deepening shadows all around her, growing blacker as the minutes passed. Soon it would be nine o'clock. Dark outside. Darker inside.

It was the fifth night.

There wasn't much more to do now except paint. Everything he'd sent over she'd used. She rose and dusted her hands on her jeans. She'd been to see Marlin Jones several times. He was always polite, always eager to help her, seemed to like it when she flirted with him. He had dark, dark eyes, almost opaque, as if no light ever shined behind them. He had dark brows, a thin nose, and full lips. He was good-looking, built well, if a bit on the thin side. He wasn't all that tall, so perhaps then he could be called scrawny. After each time she saw him, she thought that he was just a plain man who earned his living cutting wood.

"There," she said aloud, wishing something would happen soon, praying it would happen, knowing she wasn't going to like being conked on the head, but not caring. A drop of pain behind her ear, a headache, were nothing compared to what he was going to get. "Done. Now let's see how easy it is to undo all this stuff."

"It's real easy, Marty."

It was his voice, Marlin's voice. He was right behind her. She'd never heard him come in. She wanted to leap for joy. Finally, he'd come.

Her heart pounding, she whirled about, a gasp coming out of her mouth. "Oh goodness gracious, Marlin, you scared the stuffing out of me. Oh yeah, you scared me shitless."

"Hi, Marty. I came by to see how you were doing with the props. You know, you really shouldn't curse like that. Ladies shouldn't. It doesn't sound right."

"Everyone does, Marlin, everyone. You should hear that scum bucket husband of mine cut loose. Look at this. I'm all done. I need to paint, but I forgot which colors go on which piece so I'll have to go home and get the drawings."

"Not bad," he said after a couple of minutes. He had run his fingers over the brackets, frowning when they weren't straight, frowning even more when the screws weren't all the way in.

He turned to smile down at her. "How's your husband?"

"That asshole? I left him drinking Bud in front of the television. I'm going to leave that jerk, anytime now, I'm going to tell him to haul his saggy butt out of there and—"

It came so fast, she didn't have time to do a single thing, even be frightened, even to prepare herself for it. The lights went out. At nearly the same instant, she felt a shock of heavy pain behind her left ear. She wanted to cry out, but there wasn't any sound in her throat, nothing at all, and she simply collapsed where she stood. She realized before the blackness took over everything that she hadn't hit the floor. No, Marlin was holding her. Where was Toby? Well hidden, she hoped. Please, don't let him freak out and ruin the plan. No, he wouldn't. Everyone knew she had to take a hit.

She'd begged for it.

FOURTEEN

She woke up to dull, thudding pain behind her left ear. She'd never been hit in the head before. She'd only known what to expect in theory. The reality of it was that it wasn't all that bad. Marlin knew what he was doing. He didn't want her incapacitated. He wanted her up soon, panicked, scared, and begging. He didn't want her crawling around puking up her guts from nausea.

She held perfectly still until the pain lifted. She knew this time that she was lying on the floor, a raw-plank floor that smelled like old rotted wood, decades of dust and dirt embedded deep, and ancient carcasses, withered and stale, probably rats.

It should have been pitch black, but it wasn't. She knew what was going to happen and still she felt such terror she doubted she could even get enough saliva in her mouth to yell. She thought briefly of the other women—of Belinda—the terror of waking alone, head pounding, knowing something was desperately wrong, and it was made all that much worse because it was unknown. She was scared to her very soul even though she knew what would happen.

She wanted to kill Marlin Jones very badly.

It seemed there were some hidden lights giving off enough light so she could see about a foot around her. She knew she was in a big deserted building. She also knew she wasn't alone. Marlin Jones was here, somewhere, watching her. With infrared glasses? Maybe so.

She rose slowly to her feet, rubbing the back of her head. She had a slight headache, nothing more now. Oh yes, Marlin was good at what he did. She wondered how long he'd keep quiet. She called out, her voice credibly shaky, rife with rising panic, "Is anyone there? Please, where am I? What do you want? Who are you?"

Hysteria bubbled up, making her voice shrill now, raw in that silent air. "Who's there? You cowardly little bastard, show yourself!"

There was no answer. There was no sound of any kind except for her hard breathing. She didn't bother checking the boundaries of the building. Let him be disappointed that she was shortening the play, shortening his fun. She looked down to see the string lying where her hand had lain. It disappeared into the distance. She leaned down and picked it up. Skinny, strong string, leading her to the maze. It was fastened to something a goodly distance away. She slowly began to follow it. As she walked, the dim light behind her disappeared and the darkness ahead of her became shadowy light. Slowly, so slowly, breathing hard, she walked.

Suddenly a light snapped on overhead, fiercely white, blinding her momentarily. Then she saw a woman staring at her, a woman whose mouth was hanging open, a wild-looking woman, pale as death, her hair tangled around her face. She screamed at her own image in the mirror staring back at her, frozen for an instant in time and terror.

Slowly she backed away from the mirror, one short step, then one more. She saw that there were walls, props, really, some fastened together with hinges, others with brackets, not amateurish like the ones she'd made. No, Marlin's props were professional all the way.

Then the bright light snapped off as suddenly as it had come on, and she was left again in the narrow dim light.

It was then she heard breathing. Soft, steady breathing, just to her right. She whirled to face it. "Who's there?"

Just the breathing, no voice, no answer. An amplifier of some kind. She whimpered, just for him, then again, making it louder, hugging herself, then started following the string again. Suddenly the string ran out. She was standing in front of a narrow opening that had no door. She couldn't see beyond the opening.

"Hello, Marty. Come in. I've been waiting for you."

His voice. Marlin Jones.

"Oh God, Marlin, is it really you? How did I get here? You've come to save me?"

"I don't think so, Marty. No, I'm the one who brought you here. I brought you here for me."

She felt rage pour through her. She pictured Belinda standing here, not knowing what was happening or why, so frightened she could scarcely breathe, and here that maniac was talking to her in a voice as smooth and gentle as a parish priest's.

"What do you want, you pathetic bastard?"

He was silent. She'd taken him by surprise. He was expecting tears, pleading. She yelled, "Well, you fucking slug? What do you want? You too scared to talk to me?"

She heard him actually draw in his breath. Finally he said, his voice not quite as smooth as it had been, but calm enough now, "You were fast coming here. I expected you to search around, to check for a way out of the building, but you didn't. You looked down, saw the string, and followed it."

"What the hell is the damned string for? Some sick joke? Or are you the only sick joke in this silly place, Marlin?"

His breath speeded up; she could hear it. His breath was wheezing with anger. Push him. She wanted to push him. Let Savich curse her, let all of them curse her, it didn't matter. She had to push him to the edge; she had to defeat him, then obliterate him. "Well, you fucking little pervert? What is it for? Something to excite your sick little brain?"

"Now, Marty, don't mouth off at me. I hate it when a woman has a foul mouth. I thought you were so sweet and helpless when you first came to me, but then you talked filth. You opened your pretty mouth and filth spewed out. And your poor husband. No wonder he drinks—anything to escape that horrible language. And you put him down; you tell the world how horrible he is just because he was unlucky enough to marry you."

"I might spew out bad words, but at least I'm not a fucking psycho like you. What do you want, Marlin? What is this string bit?"

His voice was now a soft singsong, a gentle monotone, as if he were seeing himself as an omniscient god and she as a child gone astray, to be led back. Led back to hell. "I'll tell you everything when you find the center of the maze, Marty. I build props like you do only I'm better because I've done it more. I want you to come in now, Marty. You'll win when you find the center of the maze. Even though you say bad things, you'll still win if you find the center. I'll be timing you, Marty. Time's always important. You can't forget about the time. Come along, now. You've got to come in or else I'll have to punish you right now. Find the center, Marty, or you won't like what I'll do to you."

"How much time do I have to get to the center of the maze so you won't punish me?"

The gentle monotone was now tinged with impatience. "You ask too many questions, Marty."

"I'll find the center if you'll tell me why the string bit."

"How else am I supposed to get you to come here? I didn't want to paint signs. That would have been too obvious. FOLLOW THE ARROWS. That's tacky. The string is neat. It's tantalizing. Now my patience is running out, Marty. Come into the maze."

There was sudden anger now, cold and hard. "Marty? What are you doing?"

"My sneaker was untied. I was tying it. I don't want to trip over myself."

"It didn't look to me like you were tying your sneaker. Come on now or I'll have to do something you won't like at all."

"I'm coming." She walked through the small entrance into a narrow corridor of six-foot-high sheets of plywood, painted green to simulate yew bushes. She came to an intersection. Four choices. She took the far-left turn. It led her to a dead end.

He laughed. "Wrong choice, Marty. Maybe if you didn't curse so much, God would have let you find the right way to go. Maybe if you weren't so mean to your poor husband, God wouldn't have brought you to me. Try again. I'm getting impatient."

But he wasn't at all impatient; she realized it in that instant. He was relishing every moment. The longer it took her to get to the center, the more he enjoyed himself.

"You're slow, Marty. You'd best hurry. Don't forget about the time. I told you that time was important."

She could hear the excitement in his voice, unleashed now, feel the stirring of his excitement in the air around her. It nauseated her. She couldn't wait to see him.

She backtracked and took another turn. This one also led to a dead end. On the third try, she picked the right path. There was only a small pool of light around her, never varying, never growing brighter or dimmer. She hit another dead end off a wrong turn. She heard his breathing quicken; his excitement was peaking. She was close to the center of the maze now.

She stopped and called out, "Why a maze, Marlin? Why do you want me to find the center of a maze?"

His voice trembled, he was so excited. No one had asked him this before. He was bursting to tell her. "It's like finding your way to your own soul, Marty. There are lots of wrong turns and dead ends, but if you're good enough, if you try hard enough, you'll eventually come to the center of your soul and then you'll know the truth of who and what you are."

"That's very poetic, Marlin, for a stupid psychopath. Who let you out of the asylum?"

"I'll have to punish you for that, Marty. I'm not your husband. You've no right to insult me."

She yelled, "Why the fuck not, you puny, pathetic little bastard?"

"Stop it! Yes, keep quiet, that's better. Now, I'm waiting, Marty, I'm waiting for you. You're running out of time. You'd better stop mouthing off at me and run."

She did, no wrong turns now, just right to the center, no hesitation at all.

He was there, standing right in the center of the maze, wearing goggles. In the next moment, he'd pressed a button and a pool of light flooded down where they stood. He was dressed in camouflage fatigues with black army boots laced up to the top. He pulled off the infrared goggles. He looked as white as a death mask in the eerie light. Now he did look scrawny. He gave her a big smile. "You made it here real fast when you tried, Marty. I scared you enough so that you knew if you didn't hurry, I'd have to hurt you really bad."

"Scare me? You stupid moron, you wouldn't scare a dead chicken. Did I beat your time limit, you worthless little shit?"

His smile dropped away. He looked more confused than angry. "Why aren't you afraid? Why aren't you begging me to let you go now? You know it makes me crazy when you say bad words, when—"

"You're already so crazy I don't have to say anything, you stupid prick."

"Shut up! I hate to hear a woman curse, hate it, hate it, hate it! You didn't make the center in time, Marty. I've got to punish you now."

"Just how will you do that, you little creep?"

"Damn you, shut up!" He pulled a hunting knife out of the sheath at his waist. It was a foot long—sharp, cold silver. It gleamed in that dead white light.

"Why a maze, Marlin? Before you punish me, tell me about why you use a maze?"

"It's special for you, Marty, just for you." He was playing with the knife now, lightly running the pad of his thumb over the blade. "It's real sharp, Marty, real sharp."

"Of course it is. It's a knife, you idiot. Not only are you pathetic, you're also a liar. You didn't build this maze just for me. Your little game isn't at all special. You aren't capable of any originality at all. Nope, the same thing over and over. Every one of the women you've killed had to find her way to the center of your maze. Why the maze, Marlin? Or are you too afraid to tell me?"

He took a step closer, then stopped. "How do you know about all the other women?"

"I'm psychic, you toad. I can read that miserable little brain of yours without trying. Yeah, I'm psychic, as opposed to a psychopath, which is what you are. Why the maze, Marlin? You're afraid to tell me, aren't you? I knew it: you're nothing but a pathetic little coward."

"Damn you, shut up! I'll tell you, then I'll cut out that filthy tongue of yours and I'll make you eat it before I slice you like a stalk of celery." He was panting, he was breathing so hard, as if he'd sprinted a good hundred yards. "My father loved mazes. He said they were a work of art when done well. He taught me how to build mazes. We lived in the desert outside Yuma. There weren't any nice thick green bushes, so we had to build our own bushes. Then we had so many, we made them into mazes." He shook his head, frowned at her. "You got me off track. You made me change my lines. I've never done that before. I've got to punish you for that now, Marty."

"I sure hope your father isn't alive. He sounds as sick as you. You said the other women didn't make you change your lines. Why did you punish them? What'd they do to you?"

"Damn you, shut up! Don't you dare talk about my dad! And I won't tell you anything!"

"Bad language, Marlin. You're not a very good role model. Did the women you butchered always use bad language? Or was it because they insulted their husbands?"

"Bitch! Shut up!"

She shook her head at him. "I can't believe you called me that, Marlin. I hate bad language, too. It makes me crazy, did I tell you that? I'll have to punish you as well. Who goes first?"

He yelled, running at her, jerking the knife over his head.

Savich yelled, "Down!"

At the same instant, full lights came on. Marlin stumbled, blinded by the sudden lights. So was she, but she knew what to do.

She was already rolling as she jerked her Lady Colt from her ankle holster and came up onto her elbows.

Marlin Jones was yelling, bringing the knife down, slicing it through the air again and again, yelling and yelling. Then he saw her, lying there, the gun pointed at him.

Captain Dougherty's voice came out of the darkness. "It's the police, Marlin. Throw down the knife and back away from her! Do it now or you're dead."

"NO!"

"I want to kill you, Marlin," she whispered, aimed the gun at his belly, "but I won't if you put that knife down." Her finger was stroking the trigger. She wanted to squeeze it so badly she felt nausea rise in her belly.

Marlin stopped in his tracks. He stared down at her, at that gun she was training on him. "Who are you?"

'I'll tell you that in court, Marlin, or I'll wire it to you in hell. How many times did you stab all those women, Marlin? Was it always the same number of times? Didn't you ever vary anything? No, you didn't. You stabbed them and then cut out their tongues. How many times, Marlin? The same number as Hillary Ramsgate? Twenty stabs? Keep coming to me now, Marlin, if you want a bullet through your gut. I want to kill you, but I won't, not unless you force me to."

He was shaking his head back and forth, his jaw working madly as he took one step back, then another. Then, suddenly, in a move so fast it blurred before her, he aimed the knife and released it.

She heard Savich yell even as she jerked to the right. She felt the knife slice through her upper arm. It didn't hit the bone. "Thanks, Marlin," she said, and fired the Lady Colt. The impact sent him staggering back, his arms clutched around his belly.

Savich yelled, "He's down! Hold your fire! Don't shoot!"

He wasn't in time. Sporadic rounds of fire burst from a dozen weapons, lighting up the warehouse with dim points of light. Savich yelled out again, "He's down! Stop!"

The guns of the dozen police officers surrounding the maze fell silent one by one. They stared at the ripped-up rotted flooring. Incredibly, they hadn't hit Marlin Jones. The closest shot had ricocheted off the side of one of his army boots.

Then the silence was abrupt and heavy.

"Sherlock, damn your eyes, I'm going to throw you from here to Buffalo!"

She was lying on her back, grinning up at him even as he dropped to his knees beside her, ripping the sleeve off his own shirt. The knife was sticking obscenely out of her upper arm. "Hold still now, and don't move a muscle. This just might hurt a bit." He pulled out the knife.

She didn't yell until she saw it in his hand, her blood covering the blade.

"Don't whine. It barely nicked you. Hold still now." He bound her arm with his shirtsleeve. "I can't believe you did that. I'm going to kill you once you're okay again. I'm going to tromp you into the mat three dozen times before I even consider letting up on you. Then I'm going to work your deltoids so hard you won't be able to move for a week. Then I'll kill you again for doing this."

"Is he dead, Dillon?"

Savich turned to look at Ralph, who was applying pressure to Marlin's stomach. "Nope, but it will be close," Ralph said. "You got him in the belly. The ambulances are real close now. You did good, Sherlock, but I agree with Savich. You nearly got yourself killed. After Savich is done with you, I think I should take you to my boat in the harbor, go a bit out into the ocean, and drown you."

She smiled up at Savich. "I sure hope he bites the big one. If he doesn't die, he'll prove he's mad, which he is, and if he gets a liberal judge and easy shrinks then he could be pronounced cured and let out to do it all again in another seven years and then he—You pulled that knife out of me. It sort of hurts really bad now. Goodness, look at all that blood."

Her eyes simply drifted closed, her head lolling to the side.

"Damnation," Savich said, and pressed harder on the wound.

He heard two men and a woman calling out, "Let us through. Paramedics! Let us through!"

Savich took the Lady Colt from her slack fingers, stared down at the little gun that could so easily kill a human being, shook his head, and pocketed it. He didn't touch the bloody knife.

FIFTEEN

She woke up in the ambulance, flat on her back, an IV dripping into her arm, two blankets pulled up to her chin. A female paramedic was sitting at her feet. Savich was sitting beside her, his face an inch from hers.

He said the moment her eyes opened, "It's all right, Sherlock. Mrs. Jameson here redid the bandage on your arm, applied a little pressure, and the wound is only bleeding lightly. You're going to have to be checked for any arterial damage, then have some stitches when we get to the hospital, and antibiotics, but you deserve it. I'm going to tell the doctor not to anesthetize you at all and use a big needle. The IV in your arm is water and some salts, nothing for you to worry about. I told you, the knife just nicked you, no big deal."

Her arm burned so hot she was vaguely surprised that it didn't burst into flame. She managed to smile. "So I'm not to whine?"

"Right."

Mrs. Jameson said, "You've got great veins. How do you feel, Agent Sherlock?"

"Really good actually," she said and nearly groaned.

"She's lying. It hurts bad. Listen to me, Sherlock. When Marlin threw the knife at you, if you hadn't already been moving away, it would have gone right through your heart and none of us would have been able to stop it. What you did really makes me mad. I never should have trusted you, never. I was sure you knew what you were doing, but you didn't. You turned those blue eyes of yours on me and that super-sincere FBI voice, and I bought everything you told me. I knew I shouldn't have, but I did, so it's my fault too. You lost it and you didn't even care. You pushed him and pushed him. He could have forgotten all about his act. He could have just killed you without following his script. That was stupid. That really pisses me off, Sherlock."

"It hurts, doesn't it?" said Mrs. Jameson, drawing Savich off. "But I can't give you any pain medication. We'll have to let the doctor decide on that. Your blood pressure's fine. Now, hang in there. We'll be there in a few minutes."

At that moment, when she thought her arm would burn off her body, she said, "I'm sorry, Dillon, but I had to."

"Why did you shoot him in the gut? Why didn't you go for his chest?"

Her eyes were vague, filled with blurred shadows, but she knew there were no more ghosts to weave in and out of her mind, tormenting her. No, everything was all right now. His voice seemed farther away than just an instant before. What had Dillon wanted to know? Oh yes. She licked her lips and whispered, "I wanted him to suffer. Through the heart would have been too easy on him."

"Finish it, Sherlock."

"All right, the truth. He hasn't told us everything. If I could have gotten all of it out of him, then I would have shot him clean. Well, maybe. Yes, we have to get him to tell us everything, then I'll shoot him in the chest, I promise."

She was utterly serious. On the other hand, she was woozy from pain and shock. He said slowly, smiling at her, "Actually, if you hadn't shot him at all, if the bullet hadn't thrown him a good three feet backward in the same instant, he would have had at least thirty rounds pumped into him. So, Sherlock, the bottom line is that you really saved his life."

"Well, damn," she said, then smiled back up at him.

"If he pulls through, you can question him and get everything you want out of him. We'll do it together. Don't worry now. Despite the fact that I'm going to throw you across the gym when you're okay again, you still got the monster. Another win for the good guys." But it had been close, far too close, unnecessarily so. She'd totally disobeyed orders. She'd been a loose cannon. On the other hand, he doubted she'd have ever done that if it hadn't been the psycho who had killed her sister. He'd chew her up some more when she was well again. He hoped it would be soon. She could have died so easily.

She said, "Thank you, Dillon. Give me a while before we go to the gym and you tromp me into the floor. I don't feel so good right now."

She leaned up and vomited into a basin quickly put under her face by Mrs. Jameson.

"YOU'LL do, Agent Sherlock. Hey, you're not related to Mohammad Sherlock, that famous Middle Eastern sleuth?"

She wanted to shriek at him for the ghastly pain of those six stitches in her upper arm, but she wasn't about to make a peep. He'd given her a pain shot before he'd ever touched her with that needle, but it hadn't helped all that much. Savich was sitting in a chair by the small cubicle door, his legs crossed, his hands folded across his chest, looking at her, daring her to wuss out on him. She said between gritted teeth, "That's one of the best ones I've heard yet, Dr. Ashad."

He swiftly knotted off the thread. "I pride myself on not being too trite. There, all done. Now, let's pour some stuff on this, sorry, but it'll really sting, then give you three more shots in the butt—tetanus, an antibiotic, and another pain med. Then you'll be out of here. Do go see your doctor down in Washington in a couple of days. The stitches will resorb. You can forget about them. A great detective like you, I don't suppose you want anything for the pain?"

"I still have the strength to give you a good kick, Doctor. If you don't give me a shot, I'll do it."

"I thought for sure that local would be strong enough for a big FBI agent, particularly one with such a flamboyant name."

"I'm a new agent. It'll take a while to get to full pain-absorbing capacity, like that guy over there who could have his head kicked in and still sing and crack jokes."

Savich laughed. "Yeah, go ahead and give her a shot of something to knock her out. Otherwise she's so hyped up she won't shut up until I gag her."

Dr. Ashad, thin, dark-skinned, yellowish teeth from too much smoking, said as he prepared three needles, "Are you really a new agent, or is that a joke? Come on, you guys have worked together for a long time, haven't you?"

"No, I never saw her before in my life until a month ago. Now I'm going to kill her as soon as she's fit again, so our total acquaintance will have been very short in cosmic terms."

"You're funny, Agent Savich."

"No, I'm not."

"Drop your pants, Agent Sherlock."

"In the arm, please, Dr. Ashad."

"No can do. In the butt, Agent."

"Not until he leaves the room."

Savich stood right outside the door. He smiled grimly when he heard her yell. Then she yelled again. Two shots. Another yell. There, that was all of them. That should fix her up. She'd nearly died. He should have known that she'd lose it and do what she'd probably planned to do for the last seven years. He looked up to see Ralph Budnack and Captain Dougherty walking toward him.

"How is she?"

"Fine. Back to being mean again."

"That woman likes to dance right up to the edge," Captain Dougherty said. "You need to talk to her about that, Savich." Then he smiled. "Got him," he said, and rubbed his hands together. He didn't look at all old or worn out tonight. Indeed, there was a bounce to his step. As for Ralph, he couldn't hold still, jumped from one foot to the other, his hands talking faster than his mouth moved.

There was another yelp.

"Four shots," Savich said. "In the butt. She deserves all the jabs the doctor gives her. I wonder what that last one was for? Maybe part of her punishment."

A few minutes later, Sherlock came out of the small cubicle tucking in her blouse with one hand since her other arm was in a dark blue sling. "He's a sadist," she said to Savich before she saw the two cops. "He's not trite, but he is a sadist. I think I might invite him to dinner so I can poison his food."

"You look pretty fit, Agent Sherlock," Captain Dougherty told her, and patted her good shoulder with a beefy hand. "We thought maybe you guys wanted to come upstairs to see about Marlin Jones's condition."

"As of now I'm officially discharged and I wouldn't miss it," Sherlock said, then looked up at Savich. "What about you, sir? Are you feeling better too? Not quite as violent as you were five minutes ago?"

He wanted to wrap his hands around her skinny neck and squeeze. But it would have to wait. "Allow me the courtesy of processing my violent thoughts without further comment from you, Sherlock. Trust me, it's to your benefit."

"Yes, sir."

"You're not going to collapse or anything, are you, Agent Sherlock?"

"No, Ralph, I promise. I'm fine." She lasted until they got to the OR waiting room. No one could tell them anything. Jones was still in surgery. They settled in, Savich sitting next to Sherlock. She crashed two minutes later.

"I think she's out," Savich said. "Tell you what, I'll take her back to the hotel. Call me in the morning with Jones's condition and when the doctors think we'll be able to talk to him. Sherlock will be mad to miss anything, but I doubt the dead could rouse her right now."

Ralph Budnack reached back and lightly shook her shoulder. She fell more onto Savich.

"Yeah, she's out like a light. Keep an eye on her, Savich. She scared the bejesus out of every cop in that warehouse, but she sure got the job done.

Funny thing how her shooting him saved his life. If you hadn't called a quick halt, the cops would have turned him into a pincushion. Hey, we'll call tomorrow. Oh yeah, we got a lot on film."

Savich carried her into the hotel, over one wimpy protest. At least it was late and only one old guy thought Savich was a pervert, from the way he was licking his chops. Because Savich was worried about leaving her alone, he took her to his room, pulled off her shoes, and tucked her into his bed. He turned the light on low over by the desk by the windows. He called his boss, Jimmy Maitland, to tell him they'd caught the String Killer. He wasn't about to tell his boss yet that Agent Sherlock had nearly gotten herself killed because she'd lost all sense and turned into a cowboy, something the Bureau ferociously discouraged.

SHERLOCK slept through the night. She came abruptly awake early the next morning. Her eyes flew open, she realized her arm felt on fire, and yelped.

"Good morning. You're alive, I see."

She frowned up at him, trying to piece things together. "Oh, I'm in your room."

"No one should croak alone," he said. "I got your clothes from your room. If you feel up to it, go bathe and change. When you come out, breakfast should be here. Lots of protein, lots of iron, lots of orange juice."

"What's the orange juice for?"

"To keep you from coming down with a cold."

He watched her swing her legs over the side of the bed. That hair of hers had come loose from the clasp and was rioting around her face. She looked totally different. He backed up a step. "I even put out some female stuff on the counter for you. If you need to shave your legs, forget it. I've only got one razor."

He was distracting her from the pain in her arm.

"Oh yeah, Sherlock, before you go haring off to catch another killer, hold on a second." He disappeared into the bathroom, then came out a few moments later. "Here, take two pills. Doctor's orders."

She knew the little blue one would take the wretched cutting pain away. Then maybe she could attack that breakfast Savich was talking about.

"You're eyeing those pills the way the cannibal would the sailor in the cooking pot." He handed her the pills and a glass of water. She was fast getting them down.

"Why don't you just sit there until the meds kick in. I'll call room service."

Forty-five minutes later, wrapped in a robe, bathed as well as she could with just one hand, Lacey was seated opposite Savich, a fork piled with scrambled eggs very nearly to her mouth. She sighed as she swallowed.

He let her eat for three minutes, then said, "I didn't tell Mr. Maitland that you're an idiot, that in your first situation you didn't follow orders, you taunted the suspect until he threw the knife at you, that you nearly got yourself whacked because of this obsession you have."

"Thank you, sir."

"Cut the 'sir' stuff. He'll find out soon enough. I still might kick your butt out of the Bureau. That was the stupidest thing I've ever seen, Sherlock." He'd said it all the previous night, but she might have been too dazed to get it all. He needed to pound it in.

"I wanted to push him to the edge. I wanted him to tell me everything— the why of everything. I don't know if I believe that maze story he told me about his father."

"It's a fact easily checked. I'll bet you Ralph has already got in calls to Yuma, Arizona. Tell me, Sherlock, is the obsession gone now that you took out the monster? Was your revenge sweet?"

"Is he still alive?"

"Yes. They operated on him three straight hours. Chances are he'll make it."

"There's still a chance he'll croak after we get it all out of him. Do you think that's possible?"

"I don't plan to let you near him with a weapon."

She sat back in her chair and sighed. "The pain medicine's worked really well. The breakfast was excellent. Are you going to tell Mr. Maitland that I should be suspended or disciplined or cut off without pay, or what?"

"I told you, I'm still chewing on that. But it just occurred to me this was the only reason you came into the Bureau in the first place, wasn't it?"

She nodded, chewing on a piece of toast.

"And your undergraduate degree in Forensic Sciences and your Master's degree in Criminal Psychology, these were all for this one moment— the very slim chance that you'd get to confront this crazy?"

"Yes. I never really believed I'd get him, not deep down, but I knew if I didn't try, then I couldn't live with myself. I wouldn't have even had the chance at him if it hadn't been for you. You made it possible. I thank you, sir."

"I don't like you very much at this moment, Sherlock, so cut the 'sir.' If I had known what I was doing, I wouldn't have done it. What would I have done if you'd bought the farm?"

"I guess you would have had to call my dad. That wouldn't have been much fun. Thank you for—"

"If you thank me one more time for letting you play bait, I'll wrap that sling around your throat and strangle you with it."

"What's going to happen now?"

"You're going back to Washington and I'll handle things here."

She turned into a stone. "No," she said at last. "No, you wouldn't do that." She sat forward. "Please, you've got to let me see this through to the end. You've got to let me talk to Marlin Jones. I've got to know why he killed my sister, why he killed all the other women. You told me I could talk to him."

"I'd be nuts to let you keep on with this case."

"Please, be nuts for a little while longer."

He looked at her with a good deal of dislike. Actually he'd had no intention of pulling her out now. He tossed his napkin on the table and pushed back his chair. "Oh, why not? At least now he can't hurt you and you can't hurt him. You won't try to shoot him, will you, Sherlock?"

"Certainly not."

"I'm an idiot to believe you. Tell you what. I'll take you to the hospital. We'll see if you can keep yourself from ripping the guy's throat out."

"I only want to know. No, I've got to know. Why did he kill Belinda?"

"Did she have a salty tongue?"

"She cursed, but nothing that would shock anybody, except my father and mother. Her husband loved her very much. Douglas will be pleased this guy has been caught. As for my father, since he's a judge, it's one more criminal off the streets. But you know, Dad never really liked her because she wasn't his real daughter. She's my half sister, you see. My mother's daughter from her first marriage. She was twelve years older than I."

"Did she ever bad-mouth her husband?"

"No. Well, I don't think so. But I can't be sure. Twelve years make a big difference. She married her husband when I was sixteen. What difference does that make?"

"So she'd only been married three years when she was killed?"

"Yes. She'd just had her thirty-first birthday."

"If she didn't curse or bad-mouth her husband in public, then Marlin wouldn't have had any reason to go after her. You remember that he wouldn't have touched you if you hadn't let loose with all those curse words. Then you added the bad-mouth of your mythical husband for frosting on the cake. So it only makes sense that your sister did something to make him go after her. Either she really lost it and cursed up a storm within his hearing, or she put down her husband in his hearing. One or the other, Sherlock. What's the most likely?"

"I don't know. That's why I've got to talk to Marlin. He's got to tell me."

"If he refuses to talk to you at all?"

She was silent, staring down at a forkful of scrambled eggs that she'd sprinkled too much pepper on. "It's odd. All the other women, no one admitted that they'd ever cursed a word in their lives or bad-mouthed their husbands. But they must have. You saw how Marlin came after me."

"You shocked my socks off when I listened to you let loose on Marlin in that hardware store."

"Good, because I knew you'd be the toughest to convince."

"As for the other women, evidently the family and friends were just trying to protect the good name of the dead. It happens all the time, and that makes it even more difficult for the cops."

"He's got to tell me."

He said very gently, "You've got to bring it to a close, Sherlock."

She hated him for the gentleness, the kindness. He had no idea. He couldn't begin to understand. She jerked up to look at him across the table. Her voice was as cold as Albany in January as she said, "Would you like another bagel?"

He sat back, folding his arms over his chest. "You're tough, Sherlock, but you still aren't in my league. If you put cream cheese on the bagel, I'll eat it."

SIXTEEN

Both Captain Dougherty and Ralph Budnack were standing outside Room 423 when Savich and Sherlock arrived at Boston Memorial Hospital.

"You don't look too bad," Ralph said, peering down at her. "On the other hand, Savich doesn't look too good. You haven't been a pain in the butt, have you?"

She rolled her eyes. "Why do you guys always stick together? I'm the one injured here, not Savich."

"Yeah, but Savich had to make sure you didn't croak it at the hotel. He deserves combat pay."

"I slept all the way through, didn't moan or whine or anything to disturb His Highness. All he did was order room service. How about Marlin Jones? Can we see him now?"

Dr. Raymond Otherton, wearing surgical scrubs dotted with blood, said from behind her, "Not more than three at a time. He still isn't all that stable. You the one who shot him?" At her nod, he said, "Well, you blew a big hole in his gut. Either you're a bad shot, or you didn't want to kill him."

"I didn't want to kill him. Not yet."

"If that's true, then go easy now, all right?"

Marlin Jones was pasty white, his lips bluish. His eyes were closed. She could see purple veins beneath the thin flesh under his eyes. There was an IV going in each arm, a tube in his nose, and he was hooked up to a monitor. A police officer sat in a chair beside his bed, and another officer sat in a chair outside the hospital room.

He was awake. Sherlock saw his eyelashes flutter—dark, thick lashes.

Captain Dougherty looked at Sherlock, frowned a moment, then said quietly, "You worked him; it's only fair that you talk to him first. We've Mirandized him. He said he didn't want a lawyer yet. I really pressed him on that, even taped it. So, everything's aboveboard."

She looked at Savich. He gave her a long emotionless look, then slowly nodded.

She felt her blood pound, a delicious feeling, her arm began to throb and that made her feel even better as she leaned down, and said, "Hello, Marlin. It's me, Marty Bramfort."

He moaned.

"Come on, Marlin, don't be a coward. Open your eyes and look at me. You'll be pleased to see that my left arm is in a sling. You did punish me, don't you want to see it?"

He opened his eyes and stared at that sling. "I've thrown a knife since I was a boy. It should have gone through your heart. You moved too fast."

"Yes."

"You didn't kill me either."

"I didn't want to. I thought a gut shot would make you feel really bad, make you suffer for a good long time. I want you to suffer until you yell with it. Are you suffering, Marlin?"

"Yeah, it hurts like bloody hell. You're not a nice woman, Marty."

"Maybe not. On the other hand, you're not at all a nice man. Tell me, would you have murdered another five women if you'd managed to kill me?"

He blinked rapidly. "I don't know what you mean."

"You killed Hillary Ramsgate. If I hadn't been a cop, then you would have killed me too. Would you have killed another five women and stopped again at seven?"

The pain seemed to bank in his eyes. He looked off into something she couldn't see, that no one could see, or begin to fathom, his eyes tender and vague, as if he were looking at someone or something behind a veil. His voice was soft with the radiance of worship when he finally said, "Who knows? Boston has rich pickings. Lots of women here need to be punished. I knew that long before I came here. Men have let them get away with foul language, with putting them down, insulting them. I don't know if I ever would have stopped."

"But you stopped your killing in San Francisco at seven."

"Did I? I don't remember. I don't like it that you're standing up and I'm not. I like women on their knees, begging me, or on their backs, watching that knife come down and down. You should be dead." Incredibly, he tried to spit at her, but he didn't have the strength to raise his head. His eyes closed, his head lolled to the side away from them.

She felt Savich's hand on her arm. "Let him rest, Sherlock. You can see him again later. Yes, I'll let you talk to him again. I'm sure Captain Dougherty will agree as well, even though I think he'd like to pin back your ears nearly as much as I did."

She didn't want to leave until she knew every single detail, but she nodded and followed them out. The little psycho was probably faking it. She wouldn't put it past him.

Marlin Jones opened his eyes as the door closed. Who was that woman? How had she known so much? Was she really a cop? No, he didn't believe that. There was more to her than that. Bunches more. There was lots of deep wormy stuff inside her. He recognized the blackness, had felt it reaching out to him. Pain burned in his gut. He wished he had a knife, wished the cop sitting next to him were dead, wished he were strong enough, then he'd gut her but good. He needed to think before he spoke to her again. He knew she'd come back. He knew.

"THAT wasn't bad for a first interview, Sherlock."

"Thank you, Captain Dougherty. But it wasn't enough time. He was faking it."

"I think you're right, but it doesn't matter."

"No," Savich agreed. "It doesn't. We'll come back later, Sherlock. I wanted to go back to Washington today, but I don't dare take a chance of leaving you here alone. You'd probably smile at the captain here, wink at Ralph, cajole in your FBI voice, and they'd agree to anything you wanted."

"Not true," Ralph Budnack said. "I'm the toughest cop in Boston. Nobody ever winks at me and gets away with it."

She laughed, actually laughed, enjoyed the sweetness of it for a moment, then punched him in the arm. "I won't try it, I promise. As for you, sir, I really don't think you need to stay unless you really want to."

"Stow it, Sherlock. We'll both go home tomorrow. What I want to do now is go over those reports again and have MAX correlate how many times anyone said the murdered women might have even occasionally cursed or even bad-mouthed their husbands just one time."

"I told you that no one did. Remember about not wanting to say bad things about the dead? It was just that there couldn't have been any other reason to cut out their tongues."

"Yeah, you said that, didn't you? However, somebody had to have said something sometime."

"He's anal, ain't he?" Ralph said, and Sherlock laughed.

"Thank God the cursing was right on," Captain Dougherty said. "You nailed him good with that, Sherlock. My people told us that you really surprised him when you let out with the curses the first time at the lumberyard. They thought Savich was going to fall over with shock. Well, not really, but you didn't do badly."

"Thank you, I think."

"I'm sure glad we weren't wrong about the cursing being the red button for Marlin Jones. And talking back to the husbands. I guess we have to score a big one for the Profilers. Of course it made sense, since old Marlin had cut out their tongues."

She knew, Savich realized, looking at that sudden brightness in her eyes. She knew without question that was what pushed Marlin Jones into violence. But how? There was something else that had happened seven years ago. It drove him nuts to not know what it was. If MAX couldn't find anything in any of the interviews of the other murdered women, then that meant that Sherlock had based everything on the Profilers' reports, that, or, well, something else had to have happened. But how could she have possibly known something that no one else did?

*　*　*

IT was just past lunchtime in San Francisco when Sherlock got through to Douglas Madigan at his law office.

"Lacey, that really you? What's happening? Are you all right? It was all over the TV on the early news about that guy being caught. You were in on it, weren't you?"

"Yes, I was, and yes, I'm fine, Douglas. We've got him. I've already spoken to him once. I'll find out everything from him, Douglas, everything."

"But what more is there to know?"

"I want to know why he killed Belinda. You know she never cursed all that much. She worshiped you, you told me that, so she wouldn't have ever cursed you out in front of any strangers."

"That's right, but so what?"

She drew a deep breath. "The reason he picked each of the women is because he knew she cursed and bad-mouthed her husband or boyfriend. If that's not true in Belinda's case, then there has to be another reason. I just want to know, Douglas. I have to know."

"Were you the police decoy?"

"Yes, but please don't publicize it. I was the best one for the job. I know him better than anyone else."

"My God, that was nuts, Lacey." It was his turn to calm down. She heard his breathing become slower. He was an excellent lawyer.

"I'm going to call Dad."

"No, let me do it, although I bet he already knows about it and that you were involved. He'll be relieved you weren't injured."

Her arm started throbbing. She needed another pain pill. "Oh no, I'm fine. What have you done about Candice Addams?"

"I married her last weekend. Funny thing was she got her period on our wedding night."

"She wasn't pregnant?"

"She told me that she had had a miscarriage two days before but she loved me so much she was afraid to tell me. She believed I wouldn't have married her if I'd known there wasn't a baby involved."

"Would you have?"

"Married her? No, of course not. I don't love her, you know that."

"What a mess, Douglas." She was very thankful she was three thousand miles away at that moment. "What are you going to do?"

"I haven't decided yet."

"Do you think she really loves you?"

"She claims she does. I don't know. I wish you were here. I wish I could see you, touch you, kiss you. I miss you, Lacey. So do your father and your sweet mother. Both of them hoped we'd marry, you know."

"No, I didn't know. No one ever said a word to me about that. You were my sister's husband. Nothing could ever change that."

"No, maybe not." He sighed. "Here's my lovely wife, standing here in the open doorway of my office." She heard him say to her, "How long have you been there, Candice?"

She heard a woman's voice but couldn't make out what she said, but that voice was shrill and angry. Douglas came back on the line. "I'm sorry, Lacey. I've got to go now. Will you come home now that you've gotten rid of your nightmare?"

"I don't know, Douglas. I really don't know."

Slowly, she placed the phone back into its cradle. She looked up to see Savich standing there, a cup of tea in each hand. How long had he been there? As long as she imagined Candice Addams Madigan had been standing in Douglas's office?

He handed her the cup. "Drink your tea. Then we'll go to the hospital again. I want to get this wrapped up, Sherlock."

"Yes, sir."

"Call me by my name or I'll tell Chico to wrap your karate belt around your neck."

"Yes, Dillon."

"Here's to catching the String Killer and ridding you of all your baggage. Is your brother-in-law to be considered baggage?"

She took a long drink of the hot tea. It was wonderful. She still needed another pain pill. She said finally, shrugging, "He's just Douglas. I never really realized the way he felt, until he was here in Washington a couple of weeks ago. But he's remarried now."

"Lucky for you, I'd say. I can't see that guy giving up all that easily."

"How would you know that?"

"I know everything. I'm a Special Agent."

He probably did, she thought, and excused herself to take another pill.

RAIN splattered against the hospital window. The officer in the chair was sitting forward. Lacey leaned over the bed and said in a soft voice, "Hello, Marlin. Do you remember me? I'm the woman you bashed on the head, took to your little playhouse, and forced through your little house of horrors. But I really won and you lost big-time."

"What's your name?"

"Lacey Sherlock."

"No one's named that. That's stupid. That's out of some dumb detective story. What's your real name?"

"It's Sherlock, Marlin. Didn't I track you down? Didn't I bring you in? Wouldn't you say I've earned the name?"

"I don't like you, Marty."

"It's Lacey."

"I like you even less now than I did before."

"Do you mind if I turn on the tape recorder again, Marlin?"

"No, go ahead. Turn it on. I like to hear myself talk. I'm a real good talker. Mr. Caine, he's the guy who owns the Appletree Home Supplies and Mill Yard, he begged me to be his assistant manager. He knew I could sell anybody anything, and he knew that I was an expert on everything to do with building."

"Yeah, you're really great, Marlin. But a question. Tell me why you refused to say a word to the police. Why?"

"I only want to talk to you, Marty. I'm going to kill you one of these days, and I want to get to know you better."

"If it makes you feel good, you keep holding on to that thought, Marlin. You want to talk? Tell me why you killed Hillary Ramsgate. She wasn't married. All the other women you've killed were married."

"I knew her boyfriend. Well I didn't really know him, but I saw him a bunch of times. He told a group of guys she was a ball buster and once he had her married, he was going to teach her a lesson."

"Where was this, Marlin?"

"At a bar, the Glad Rags, in Newton Center. He was there a whole lot. He'd sleep with her, let her tell him what a jerk he was, then come to the bar and let it all out. I told him he should punish her, that she deserved it."

"Did you go into the Glad Rags a lot?"

"Oh yeah. I wanted to see this Hillary woman. He brought her in one night. They had a big argument right there. She even threw a beer in his face. She cursed him up one side and down the other. She even called him a motherfucker. Most women, even bad ones like you, they don't say that word. That's a word for real bad guys. Well, all the other guys were laughing, but I wasn't. I knew she had to be punished and that he wasn't ever going to do it right. No, if anything, he'd just smack her around a little bit. You know that while she was tearing him down, that guy laughed, he took it. I would have sliced her up right there."

"Maybe her boyfriend liked exactly the way things were between them. Did you ever think of that?"

"No, that's impossible. She was bad. He was weak and stupid."

"Did you go to lots of bars, Marlin?"

"Oh yes. I like bars. You can sit there in the dark and watch people. No one hassles you. I saw lots of women who needed to be punished."

"How many different bars?"

He shrugged, then winced, lightly touching his fingertips to his stomach. "About a half dozen, I guess. Lots more in San Francisco. You should have been sliced up too, Marty. But you don't cuss, do you? Not really. I'll bet you're not married either. You're just a cop. You said all those bad words to trap me."

"I didn't trap you, Marlin. All I did was give you a woman you could relate to. Nothing more, nothing less."

"I never should have believed you. You just fell into my lap. You're still wearing the sling. I like that."

"Yeah, but I'm not lying flat on my back with my gut burning through my back."

He tried to lurch up. The cop beside the bed was up in an instant, his hand on his gun. Sherlock smiled at him and shook her head. "Marlin doesn't have a knife now, Officer Rambling. He's like an old man without his teeth."

"I sure would like to kill you," Marlin said and fell back against the pillow, breathing hard.

"Not in this lifetime, Marlin. Now, you're so good at talking, you like to do it so much, why don't you tell me about the women you killed in San Francisco? I know each of them was married. Did you hear them all bad-mouthing their husbands?"

"Why should I tell you anything? You don't like me. You shot me in the belly. It still hurts real bad. I might want a lawyer now."

"Fine. Do you have any money or shall I call the public defender?"

"I can get the best and you know it. Those guys don't care if I have a dime or not, they just want their faces in the news. Yeah, get me a phone book and let me pick out the highest-priced one of the lot."

"I could connect you to the ocean bottom, if you like."

"That was funny, Marty. Lawyers and bottom feeders, yeah, that was pretty funny."

"Thanks. It's Agent Sherlock. I'm with the FBI. You want to call a lawyer now, Marlin? Or would you like to answer a few more of my questions?"

"I'll call a lawyer later. Sure, I can answer anything you ask. I can always take it back. I read all about the Toaster. He'll get off because he's crazy, and it won't cost him a dime. I'll get off too, you'll see, and then I'll come after you, Marty."

She felt a shock of rage, but no fear. She should have killed him right there in the warehouse to ensure there'd be justice. She was a fool to want all her questions answered. Besides, he could lie to her as easily as he could tell her the truth. Her face was flushed red with her fury. She'd been a fool. At that moment, she heard Dillon singing quietly from beside the door, "*I always played it cool when I was young, always swam when I wanted to sink, always laughed when I wanted to cry, always held my cards tight when I wanted to fold . . .*"

He hadn't said a single word until now. She jerked, then turned to look at him. His expression was unreadable. He was just singing those words. They weren't great lyrics, but it worked. She grinned; she couldn't help herself. Talk about finding words to fit the situation. She thought briefly of her classical music training. Mozart would have cast her out of the classical club if he knew she was smiling over some god-awful country-and-western music. Her rage fell away.

"We'll see about that," she said, turning back to Marlin, calm as anything now. "Hey, you look as if you're getting tired, Marlin. You'll want to take a nap really soon now. Why don't you just tell me why you killed seven women in San Francisco—not more, not less? Exactly seven, and then you stopped."

"Seven?" He fell silent. She watched him tick off his fingers. The psycho was counting on his fingers the number of women he'd butchered. She'd bet anything he remembered every name, every face. She wanted to kill him right that instant.

"No," Marlin said. "I didn't kill no seven women in San Francisco."

So the number seven had no relevance whatsoever. Thank God for Savich's brain. Dear God, how many more women had he butchered?

"How many then?"

"Six. I killed just six ladies. They all deserved it big-time. Then I was tired. I remember I slept for three days and then I was told to go to Las Vegas."

"Told? Who told you to go to Las Vegas?"

"Why the voices, of course. The Devil, sometimes his buddies. Sometimes a black cat if I see one."

"You're making that up. You're practicing on me so the judge will find you nuts and you won't have to stand trial."

"Yeah. I'm good, don't you think? But I am crazy, Marty, real crazy."

"Six women? You're certain? Not seven?"

"You think I'm stupid as well as crazy?" Then he proceeded to count them off again on his fingers, this time with their names. *Lauren O'Shay, Patricia Mullens, Danielle Potts, Ann Patrini, Donna Gabrielle, and Constance Black.*

When he finished, he looked over at her and smiled.

She felt like Lot's wife: nothing more than a pillar of salt, unmoving.

He hadn't said Belinda's name.

Why? Just a simple omission. He'd killed seven women. He was lying. The little bastard was lying.

She stood up, wanting to strangle him. He flinched, seeing the rage in her eyes. "You're stupid, Marlin. You can't even count right. Either that or you're a liar. That's what you are, a liar. I'll bet my next paycheck on that."

He was whimpering, holding himself so stiff against the backboard of the hospital bed, he looked frozen. "You want to kill me, don't you, Marty?"

"Oh yes, Marlin. When the time comes, I'd like to throw the switch on you and watch you fry."

She heard his voice from behind her, felt his hand on her good arm, his blunt fingers lightly stroking her skin. "Let's go, Sherlock. I'll make you a deal: you can talk to him one last time. Tomorrow, all right?"

"Yes, all right. Thank you. See you mañana, Marlin. Don't choke on your soup, will you?"

"I'll have my big-time lawyer here tomorrow, Marty. We'll see what he has to say to a dumb cop like you. Hey, I like that guy with you. He's got a real good voice. Do you happen to know that song, "Sing Me Home Again Before I Die"?

SEVENTEEN

"Yes, I'll be home for a few days, Father, when I can get away. I want to see both you and Mother."

"You're satisfied now, Lacey?" The sarcasm was deep and rich in his voice. She felt the familiar churning in her stomach. She had caught the man who'd killed Belinda. Why wasn't he pleased?

Be calm, be calm. The training academy taught you that. "Yes. I truly never dreamed that I would ever catch him. I've even interviewed him twice now. But there is one thing that bothers me."

"What is that?"

"He claims he killed only six women here in San Francisco."

"He's a crazy little psychopath. They're liars all the way to their genes. I know, I've sentenced enough of them."

"Yes, I agree. I don't know why I mentioned it, really. But it's curious— he listed the names of the women he killed. He left out Belinda."

"So he forgot her name."

"Possibly. But why didn't he forget one of the others? You know I'll be doing all sorts of checking now to make certain he did kill Belinda." She realized what she'd just said but had no time to apologize. Her father said in his low, controlled voice, "What are you saying, young lady? You think it's possible some other man killed Belinda? Someone who copycatted this Jones guy? Who, for God's sake?"

"I didn't mean that, Dad. I know Marlin Jones killed her, that he's just playing some sort of twisted game with me. But what game? Why leave out her name specifically? Why not one of the others? It doesn't make any sense at all."

"Enough of this bullshit, Lacey. And that's all it is. He could have left out any name. Who cares? Will you come home this weekend?"

"I'll try, but I want to speak to Marlin Jones at least one more time. But, Dad, when I come home, it will just be for a few days." She drew a deep breath and closed her eyes, exhaling slowly. "I'm going to stay in the FBI. I want to keep doing what I'm doing. I can make a real difference."

There was silence. Sherlock didn't like herself for it, but she couldn't help it. She started fidgeting. Finally, her father said, "Douglas has made a stupid error."

He was letting it go, at least for now. "Well, he's married, if that's what you mean."

"Yes, that's exactly what I mean. The woman went after him, then lied about being pregnant. Douglas has always been very careful about taking precautions. I tried to tell him to have blood tests, get positive proof that the child was his, but he said there was no reason for her to lie. He was wrong, of course. The bitch got him. He told me he wanted a kid, that it was time. She wasn't even pregnant. Douglas was a fool."

"Didn't Douglas want kids with Belinda?"

Her father gave a hoarse laugh. He didn't laugh often. It sounded strange and rusty, and a bit frightening. Her fingers tightened around the phone. "Remember who her mother is, Lacey. Naturally he wouldn't want to take the risk of any child being as crazy as Belinda's mother."

"I can't believe he told you that."

"He didn't, but I'm not stupid."

She hated this. Usually he was sly in his insults to his wife, but not now. "She's my mother as well."

"Yes, well, that's different. I am your father. There's nothing crazy in you."

Hadn't he told her not two weeks before that her obsession reminded him of her mother's early illness? She shook her head, wanting to hang up, and knowing she wouldn't. "I never met Belinda's father."

Her father said coolly, "That's because we've never mentioned him to you; there was no need. Indeed, Belinda didn't even know what happened to him. Again, there was no reason to be cruel about it."

"Is he still alive? Who is he?"

"His name's Conal Francis. I can't see that it matters now if you know the truth. He's in San Quentin; at least he was the last time I heard."

"He's in prison?" Sherlock couldn't believe it. Neither he nor her mother had ever said a thing about Belinda's father being in jail.

"What did he do?"

"He tried to murder me. Instead he killed a friend of mine, Lucas Bennett. It was a long time ago, Lacey, before you were born, before your mother and I married. He was a big Irish bully, a gambler, worked for the mob. He must be at least sixty by now. He's four years older than I. Which is why Belinda was cursed. Her genes ruined her. Despite the fact that I raised her, she still would have turned bad. It was already beginning even before she died. A pity, but there it is."

"But Belinda knew about him, didn't she?"

"She only knew that he'd left her and her mother when she was eight or nine years old. We never told her anything different. There was no point. Look, Lacey, that was a long time ago. You've caught the man who killed her. Belinda's madness died with her. Now the man who killed her will die as well. Forget it. Forget all of it."

She hoped he would prove to be right about that. No, she didn't want to forget Belinda. But at least now that Marlin Jones was in custody, that helpless feeling was gone.

Except for the fact he'd claimed he hadn't killed Belinda.

"Come home soon, Lacey." There was a pause, then, "Do you want to speak to your mother?"

"Oh yes, please, Dad. How is she today?"

"Much the same as always. She's downstairs with me in the library. Here she is."

Her fingers tightened on the receiver. Her father had spoken about her first husband and Belinda like that in front of her? Savich had come into the room, but it was too late for her to hang up. "Mom? How are you?"

"I miss you, dearest. I'm glad you caught that bad man. Now you can come home and stay. You always were so pretty, dear, so sweet and pretty. And how well you played the piano. Everyone told me how talented you were. Why, you could teach little children in a kindergarten, couldn't you? You're so suited to something like that. Your grandmother was a pianist, you remember?"

"Yes, Mom, I remember. I'll be home to visit you soon. Not long now and we'll be together for a couple of days."

"No, Lacey, I want you to stay here, with me and your father. I have your piano tuned by Joshua Mueller every six months. Remember how much you admired him?"

"Look, Mom, I've got to get back to work now. I love you. Please take care."

"I always do, Lacey, since your father tried to run me down with that black BMW of his."

"What? Dad tried to run you down with his BMW?"

"Lacey? It's your father. Your mother is having one of her spells."

"What did she mean that you tried to run her down?"

"I haven't the foggiest idea." He sighed deeply. "Your mother does have good days. This is not one of them. I have never harmed your mother or tried to harm her. Forget what she said, Lacey."

But how could she? She stared at the phone as if it were a snake about to bite her. She could swear she heard her mother crying in the background.

Savich was looking at her. Her face was white. She looked to be in shock—yes, that was it.

When Savich took the phone from her, she didn't resist. She heard him say in his calm deep voice, "Judge Sherlock? My name is Dillon Savich. I'm also with the FBI. I'm the head of the Criminal Apprehension Unit. Your daughter works for me. I hope you don't mind, but Lacey is a bit over-whelmed by all that's happened." He paused, listening to her father. "Yes, I understand that her mother isn't well. But you must realize her mother's words shocked her deeply."

She walked across the room, rubbing her arms with her hands. She heard him say in that firm, calm voice, "Yes, I will see that she takes care of herself, sir. No, she'll be just fine. Good-bye."

Savich turned to look at her—nothing more, just to look. Then he said very slowly, "What in the name of heaven is going on with your family?"

Her laugh was on the shaky side, but it was a laugh. "I feel like Alice in Wonderland. I've just fallen down the rabbit hole. No, it's always like that, but this is the first time the hole is deeper than I am tall."

He smiled. "That's good, Sherlock. You've got some color back. I'd appreciate it if you wouldn't scare me again like that."

"You shouldn't have stayed in the room."

"Actually, I brought you a message from Marlin Jones. He wants to talk to you again, with his lawyer present. He got Big John Bullock, a hotshot shark from New York who does really well with insanity pleas. I recommend that you don't go. He's doubtless set this up so his lawyer can humiliate you. He won't let you get to first base with Jones anymore."

He would have wagered his next paycheck that she'd still insist on seeing Marlin Jones. To his surprise, she said, "You're right. The police and the D.A. can get the rest of the pertinent information from him. There's nothing more for me to say to him. Can we go home now?"

He nodded slowly. He wondered what she was thinking.

THE taxi stopped in front of her town house at ten o'clock that night. She felt more tired than she could ever remember in her life. But it wasn't the peaceful, good sort of tired she would have expected, now that Belinda's killer had been caught.

She hadn't said much to Savich on the flight from Boston or on the ride in the taxi from Dulles to Georgetown. He walked her to the door, saying, "Sleep late, Sherlock. I don't want to see you before noon tomorrow, you got that? You've had more happen to you in the past three days than in the past five years. Sleep, it's the best thing for you, all right?"

She didn't have any words. How could he know that her brain was on meltdown? "Would you sing me just one more outrageous country-and-western line before you leave?"

He grinned down at her, set her suitcase down on the front step of her town house, and sang in a soft tenor whine, "I told her I had oceanfront property in Arizona. She nodded sweetly and I told her to buy it, that I'd throw in the Golden Gate for free. She thanked me oh so sweetly so I told her that I loved her and that I'd be true for all time. Sweetly, sweetly, she kissed me so sweetly and bought every word I said."

"Thank you, Dillon. That was amazing. That was also very coldhearted and cynical."

"Anytime, Sherlock. Not until noon now. Hey, that's just a silly song, sung by a lonely man who's not going anywhere. All he can do is dream that he's a winner, which he's not, and he knows it deep down. See ya tomorrow, Sherlock."

She watched him until he turned the far corner. It was as it had been before, Douglas's voice coming out from behind her, low, angry. Even as he spoke, she was leaning down to pull her Lady Colt from her ankle holster. She straightened back up slowly. She was so tired of angry voices. "I wish you wouldn't keep seeing that guy, Lacey. He's such a loser. What was that nonsense he was singing to you?"

"You startled me, Douglas. Please don't wait for me like this again. I could have shot you."

"You're a musician. You play the piano brilliantly. At least you used to. You wouldn't shoot anybody. What were you doing with him?"

She almost shouted at him that she wasn't that soft, pathetic girl anymore, hadn't been for seven long years, that two days ago she'd belly-shot the psychopath who'd killed her sister. She managed to hold it back. "We just got back from Boston. He brought me home, that's all. I'd hardly call him a loser, Douglas. Because of him, we got the guy who killed your wife. It would seem to me that you'd want to give him a medal. Now, what are you doing here?"

"I had to see you. I had to know what you thought about my marrying Candice. She lied to me, Lacey. What am I going to do?" It was then he noticed the sling on her arm. "What happened to you? You didn't tell your father you'd gotten hurt. Who did this? That man you were with?"

"Come into the house and we'll talk."

Five minutes later she placed a snifter of brandy into his hand. "There, that will make you feel better."

He drank slowly, looking around her living room. "This is nice. Finally, you've decorated the way you should."

"Thank you. Now, what do you want to tell me about I don't already know?"

She sat opposite him on a pale yellow silk love seat. While she'd been in Boston, her designer had had soft recessed lights installed. It made the room very warm and cozy. Intimate. She didn't like that at all. She pressed herself against the sofa back.

"First tell me how you got hurt."

"It's a small wound. I'll take the sling off in another couple of days. It's no big deal, Douglas, don't worry. Now tell me about Candice."

"I'm going to divorce her."

"You've been married less than a week. What are you talking about?"

"She crossed the line, Lacey. She overheard us talking on the phone, I told you that. Well, the minute I hung up she started in on me, accused me of sleeping with you, yelled that I'd slept with both you and Belinda at the same time, that you were a slut and she'd get you. I can't take the chance she'll hurt you, Lacey."

"Douglas, calm down. She was angry. I don't blame her. You were newly married and saying things to me that shouldn't have ever been said. I would have yelled too. Forget it. Didn't you discuss everything with her?"

"What was there to say? She lied to me. Your dad thinks I should divorce her. So does your mom."

"My mother and father have nothing to do with you now. It's your life, Douglas. Do what you want to do, not what someone else wants."

"So wise, Lacey. You were always so gentle and wise. I remember sitting on the sofa in your father's house listening to you play those Chopin preludes. Your playing moved me, made me feel more than what I was."

"It's kind of you to say that, Douglas. Would you like some more brandy?"

At his nod, she returned to the kitchen. She heard him moving about the living room. Then she didn't hear his footsteps. She frowned, walking slowly out of the kitchen. He wasn't in the living room. He wasn't in the bathroom. She stood in her bedroom doorway watching him look at the framed photos on her dresser. There were three of them, two of Belinda by herself, and one with both of them smiling at the camera.

"You were seventeen when I took that picture of you and Belinda at Fisherman's Wharf. Do you remember that day? It was one of the few perfectly clear sunny days and you guys took me to Pier Thirty-nine. We bought walnut fudge and ate some horrible fast food. I believe it was Mexican."

She remembered, vaguely. His details astounded her.

"I remember everything. You were so beautiful, Lacey, so full of fun, so innocent."

"So was Belinda, only she was always far prettier than I. She could have been a supermodel, you know that. She was very close to making it when she met you. She gave it all up because you wanted her to be there only for you. Come into the living room, Douglas."

When they were seated again, she said, "I can't help you with your wife. However, I do think you and Candice should discuss things thoroughly."

"She bores me."

Lacey sighed. She was exhausted. She wanted him to leave, just leave and go back to San Francisco. It was odd, but since they'd caught Marlin Jones, she'd felt herself withdrawing from Douglas. It was as if Belinda's murder had somehow bound them together, but not anymore. "You know one thing still disturbs me," she said slowly, lightly stroking her fingertips over the yellow silk arm of the sofa. "I suppose Dad told you Marlin Jones denied killing Belinda."

"Yes, he told me that. What do you think?"

"I agree with Father. He's a psychopath. He probably skips a woman's name every time he recites them. Why did he happen not to recite Belinda's name? I don't know. Random chance? He probably doesn't know either. It has to be coincidence. There's simply no other explanation." She sat forward, clasping her hands between her knees. "But you know me, Douglas, I'm going to have to check to make triple certain that he did kill Belinda."

"Of course he killed her, Lacey. There's absolutely no other choice."

"You're right, of course, it's just that—" She broke off and dredged up a smile for a very nice man she'd known for nearly twelve years. "I'm sorry. It's still so painful for you as well. How long are you staying in Washington?"

He shrugged and rose when she did. "Drop it all now, Lacey. Don't do any more searching. That kook killed all those poor women. Let him rot for what he did." He walked to her, his smile deep, his eyes intent.

She took a step back, turning quickly out of the living room into the small front hallway. He followed her.

"Will you let it all go now, Lacey?"

She took another step toward the front door. "It is all gone. Only details now, Douglas, nothing more than silly details. Shall we have dinner tomorrow night? Maybe you'll have made some decisions about Candice." Were they going to perform this same act every couple of weeks? Would he leave after tomorrow night? She hoped so. She hoped he'd leave for good. She was exhausted.

He brightened at that and took her hands between his. "It's good to see you again, Lacey. I wish I could see you all the time, but—"

"Yes, 'but,'" she agreed and stepped back. "I'll see you here about seven tomorrow night."

*   *   *

JIMMY Maitland nodded to Sherlock but said to Savich, "I heard from Captain Dougherty that Sherlock here didn't do what she was told to do, that she wrote her own script. He let some of it drop, then I pried the rest of it out of him. John Dougherty and I go way back. He's a good man, fair and hard."

Savich didn't change expression, merely cocked his head to one side in question. "She got the job done, sir."

"I don't like having my agents knifed, Savich. What the hell did she do?"

"I can answer that, sir."

Both men turned to look at her.

"It better be good, Agent Sherlock," Jimmy Maitland said, and broke a pencil between two fingers. Maitland had been a Special Agent for twenty-five years. He was bald, built like a bull, and held a black belt in karate. His wife was five foot nothing, blond, and punched her husband whenever she wanted to. They had four boys, all over six foot three. She punched them whenever she wanted to as well.

She shrugged. "Really, sir, the perpetrator took us a bit by surprise, that's all, but nothing we couldn't handle. Dillon yelled out. I shot Marlin Jones at practically the same instant he threw the knife. I was already down and rolling when he released it. It's just a minor wound."

"That's exactly what Savich said. Did you two rehearse this?"

"No, sir, certainly not."

Maitland raised an eyebrow at Savich, then said quickly, "Fine. Okay. You're excused, Agent Sherlock. Savich, you stay a moment. There's been another murder in Florida. It wasn't a nursing home on the Star of David matrix MAX generated. As for the perp disguised as an old woman, that doesn't look good anymore. They talked to every old woman in the nursing home. All of them longtime residents. Tell MAX he's got to do better."

"Agreed," Savich said. "I'll get Sherlock back on the Radnich case with Ollie. I'll see you later."

EIGHTEEN

She prayed her involvement in the String Killer case would be kept under wraps, and it had been, at least so far. She knew Savich had spoken privately with Captain Dougherty and Ralph Budnack. If anyone blew the whistle on her, it wouldn't be one of them. So far no one in the media knew anything about her relationship to one of the victims of the String Killer. It would be a nightmare if anyone found out.

So far the FBI had gotten lots of good publicity: always a welcome circumstance for the continually besieged Bureau. Savich and his new FBI unit had brought down two killers in weeks. Reporters wanted to interview him, but he wasn't having any of it. No one was to speak to any reporters. Director Mueller held a press conference, praising the work of the new Criminal Apprehension Unit. Savich had asked not to attend. Mueller had wanted him there but hadn't insisted.

She avoided Hannah Paisley, worked closely with Ollie to get back into the Radnich case. She wasn't looking forward to the evening with Douglas, but it couldn't be helped.

Sherlock dressed up that evening, wearing her hair loose, pulled back with two small gold combs, gold hoops in her ears that her mother had given her for her twenty-fifth birthday, a nice black dress that was classic enough to be two years old and still pass as current style, and three-inch heels. She felt strange in her different plumage and a bit exposed. But good. She felt really good. She realized at the last moment that Douglas could take it wrong. But there wasn't time to change.

The first thing Douglas said when he walked in was "The sling looks awful with that dress" and grinned at her. "Don't you have several styles and colors to match different outfits?"

The evening was lighthearted and amusing until near dessert, when Douglas dropped his good humor and said, "You've gotten what you wanted, Lacey. I want you to quit the FBI and come home. Surely you see that it's finally over, that it's your music that is important now. You nailed the guy who killed Belinda. Come home. Do what Belinda did. Come stay with me. I'll take care of you."

She looked at him across the candlelit table, at the pure lines and angles of his face, and said simply, "No."

He drew back as if she'd punched him. "I plan to divorce Candice. It will be done quickly, perhaps I can even get an annulment. It can be you and me, Lacey, as I always wanted. Give us time together, once I'm rid of Candice."

He'd always wanted her? He'd never said a word to her until she'd joined the FBI and finished her training. Had he somehow gotten turned on because she was now a law officer? It didn't make sense to her. She was shaking her head even as she said again, "No. I'm sorry, Douglas, but no."

He said nothing more about it. When they were once again in her living room an hour later, she held out her hand to him, desperate for him to leave. "Douglas, I had a lovely time tonight. Will I see you tomorrow?"

He didn't say anything, just jerked her against him. He kissed her hard, hurting her arm. She pushed at his chest but couldn't move him. "Douglas," she said against his mouth and felt his tongue push against her front teeth.

The doorbell rang. He still didn't release her, just kept grinding his mouth into hers. Her knee was almost in motion when she managed to jerk her head back far enough to call out, "Who's there?"

"Let me in, Miss Sherlock."

A woman. Who could she be?

Suddenly Douglas was two feet away from her, standing there looking bewildered, wiping his mouth with the back of his hand. "It's Candice," he said blankly, then walked to the door and opened it.

The woman standing there was no older than Sherlock, with long honey-blond hair, nearly as tall as Douglas, with very high cheekbones that had to be a cameraman's dream. But it was her eyes that riveted Sherlock. Dark, dark eyes that held fury, malice, and even more fury this instant than just the moment before. She looked ready to kill.

"Candice! What the hell are you doing here?"

"I followed you, Douglas. And you came here just like a little trained pigeon. I knew you'd come to her, even though I prayed you wouldn't. Damn you, I'd hoped our marriage meant something to you. You let her kiss you. You've got her lipstick on your mouth. Damn you, you smell like her."

"Why should our marriage mean anything to me? You lied to me. You weren't pregnant."

"We'll have children, Douglas. I'm just not ready yet. I'm hitting my stride with my career. I could make it to one of the nationals, but not if

I take off now. In another year, we can have a dozen kids if that's what you want."

"That doesn't jibe with what you told me before we got married. Then you said you'd had a miscarriage and you were so upset. Now you don't want to get pregnant. You know what? I don't think you were ever pregnant at all." Douglas turned to Lacey, waving a languid hand toward his wife. "This is Candice Addams."

"I'm your *wife*, Douglas. I'm Candice *Madigan*. She is your dead wife's sister. No, half sister. Nothing more. What are you doing here with her?"

He changed from one moment to the next. His bewilderment, his frustration, all were gone. He was standing tall and arrogant, a stance Sherlock recognized, a stance that was second nature to him. It held power and control, and the control was of himself and of the situation. He was in a courtroom, in front of a jury, knowing he could manipulate, knowing he could convince, knowing he would win.

"Candice," he said very patiently, as if speaking to an idiot witness, "Lacey is part of my family. Just because Belinda died, I didn't cut her out of my life."

"I saw you kissing her through the window, Douglas."

"Yes," he said quite calmly, "I did. She's very innocent. She doesn't kiss well and I like that."

It was another rabbit hole. Only this time, she wasn't going to slide in. "I didn't want you to kiss me, Douglas. I wasn't kissing you at all." Sherlock turned to Candice. "Mrs. Madigan, I think you and Douglas should go discuss your problems. I have no part in any of it. Honestly, I don't."

Candice smiled at her, stepped quickly around Douglas, and slapped her hard, whipping her head back.

A deep voice came from behind them. "This appears to be very interesting, but I really can't allow anyone to smack my agents, ma'am. Don't do it again or I'll have to arrest you for hitting an officer."

Sherlock looked up to see Dillon standing in the open doorway. This was all she needed. Did he have to show up whenever her life seemed to be flying out of control? It wasn't fair. She rubbed her hand over her face, then took a step back to stop herself from hurling herself on Candice. She was sorely tempted even though she doubted she could take her down, not with her arm in a sling. But she wanted to try.

"Sir," she said, although she wanted to say "Dillon." No way was she going to use his first name in front of Douglas. It would be waving a red flag. "What are you doing here? No, don't tell me. I've been elected the recreation meeting center for the evening. Do come in and close the door, sir, before a neighbor calls the cops."

"I am the cops, ma'am."

"Very well. Would anyone care for a cup of tea? A game of bingo?"

Douglas plowed his fingers through his hair. "No, nothing, Lacey." He turned to his wife. "We have to talk, Candice. I am upset with you. I don't care at all for your behavior. Come along, now."

Sherlock and Savich watched them leave, their voices raised before they even reached the end of the driveway.

"I'll take some tea now," Savich said.

Ten minutes later, she and Dillon were drinking tea in the now blessedly empty living room.

"What are you doing here?"

"I was out running when I came by here. You had a hard day. I wanted to make sure you were all right. The front door was open and I heard this woman yelling. How's your cheek?"

Lacey massaged her jaw. "She's a strong woman. Actually it's a good thing you came in or else I might have jumped her. Then she might really have beaten me up, what with my broken wing. I'll call Chico tomorrow."

"You called me 'sir' again."

"Yes, I did. On purpose. Douglas is jealous of you. If I'd called you 'Dillon,' it might have pushed him over the edge. Then you might have had to fight him. You could have messed up all my beautiful new furniture."

That gave him pause. He grinned, toasted her with his teacup, then said finally, "This was the man who was married to Belinda?" At her nod, he said, "And this is his new wife. Tell me about this, Sherlock. I love family messes."

"I'll say only that Douglas thinks he might like me a bit too much. As for Candice, his wife, she told him she was pregnant with his child, he married her, and then it turns out she wasn't pregnant. He's angry and wants a divorce. She blames me. That's all there is to it, not a mess really, at least it doesn't involve me." She sighed. "All right, when I was talking to Douglas on the phone, he said some things he shouldn't have said and she overheard them. She was upset. She probably wants to kill me more than Marlin Jones does."

"Do you realize you're speaking to me in nice full sentences? That I no longer have to pry basic stuff out of you?"

"I guess maybe I was a bit on guard when I first came to you. On the other hand, you were a criminal in Hogan's Alley and kicked two guns out of my hand before I overcame overwhelming and vicious odds and killed you."

"Yes, you were wary. Still, it didn't take too long to break you in. You've been spilling your guts for a good long time now. As for my day as the bank robber, you didn't do too badly, Sherlock. No, not badly at all." He raised his hand and lightly stroked his fingers over her cheek. "She walloped you pretty good, but I don't think you're going to bruise too much. Makeup should take care of it."

Suddenly his cheekbones flushed. He dropped his hand and stood up. He was wearing gray sweatpants and a blue sweatshirt that read ACHY BREAKY COP. He looked big, strong, and harassed. His fingers had been very warm. They'd felt good against her cheek.

"Go to bed, Sherlock. Try to avoid any more trouble. I can't always guarantee to drop by when you're butt-deep in trouble."

"I've really never had so many difficulties in such a short time before in my life. I'm sorry. But you know, I could have dealt with this all by myself."

He grunted in her general direction and was gone. Just plain out of there, fast.

She touched her own fingers to her face, saw his dark eyes staring at her with antagonism and something else, and walked slowly to the front door. She fastened the chain, clicked the dead bolt in place, and turned the key in the lock. What would have happened if Savich hadn't shown up? She shuddered.

She'd caught Belinda's killer and her life seemed messier than ever. What had her mother meant, ". . . since your father tried to run me down?"

SHE walked out of the doctor's building the following afternoon, trying to put up her umbrella in the face of a sharp whipping wind and swirling rain—hard, heavy rain that got you wet no matter what you did. It was cold and getting colder by the minute. She got the umbrella up finally, but it was difficult because her arm was still very sore. She stepped off the curb, trying to keep herself covered, and started toward her car, parked down the block on the opposite side of Union Street.

Suddenly she heard a shout, then a scream. She whipped about, the wind nearly knocking her over, her umbrella sucked out of her hand. The car was right on her, a big black car with dark tinted windows, a congressman's car, no, probably a lobbyist's car, so many of them in Washington. What was the fool doing?

She froze in that blank instant, then hurled herself back onto the sidewalk, her sore arm slamming into a parking meter.

She felt the whoosh of hot air even as she went down half into the street, half on the sidewalk. She twisted around to see the black car accelerate and take the next corner in a screech of tires. She lay there staring blankly after the car. Why hadn't he stopped to see if she was all right? No, naturally, the driver wouldn't have stopped—he'd probably be arrested for drunk driving. Slowly, she pulled herself to her feet. Her panty hose were ruined, as were her shoes and clothes. Her hair was plastered to her head and over her face. As for her healing arm, it was throbbing big-time now. Her shoulder began to hurt, as did her left leg. At least she was alive. At least she hadn't been farther out into the street. If she had been, she wouldn't have stood a chance.

She'd gotten three letters of the license plate—PRD. Now that she thought of it, it hadn't been a government license.

People were all around her now, helping her to straighten up, holding umbrellas over her. One gray-haired woman was fussing, patting her here and there, as if she were her baby. She managed to smile at the woman. "Thank you. I'm all right."

"That driver was an idiot, a maniac. The man over there called the cops on his cell phone."

A businessman said, "Miss, do you want an ambulance? That guy could have killed you!"

She held up her hands. The rain pounded down on her. "No, no ambulance, please. I'm all right."

The cops were coming soon; she didn't have much time. She was on her cell phone dialing Savich's number. He wasn't there. Hannah answered. Where was Marcy, Savich's secretary? She didn't need Hannah, not now, but there was no choice.

"Hannah, I need to know where Dillon is. Do you know? Do you have a number for him?"

"No. Even if I did, I wouldn't tell you."

"Hannah, listen to me. Someone just tried to run me down. Please tell me how I can get hold of him."

Suddenly Ollie was on the line. "What happened, Sherlock? Marcy's down in the lunchroom. Hannah and I are covering Savich's phone. Someone tried to run you down? What happened?"

"I'm all right, just really dirty and wet. I'm right in front of Dr. Pratt's building. Dillon knows the location, since that's his doctor, too. Please tell him where I am. Oh dear, the police are here."

It was nearly an hour before Savich strode up and knocked on the window of her Explorer. He was very wet. He looked very angry, which wasn't right. He didn't have any right to be angry yet.

"I'm sorry," she said immediately, as she opened the passenger door, "I didn't know who else to call. The cops left about twenty minutes ago. My car wouldn't start."

He slid into the passenger side. "Good thing this is leather or the cloth would stay wet for weeks. Now tell me what happened."

She did, saying finally, "It sounds pitiful. I think whoever was driving lost it. Maybe he was drunk. When he realized he could have killed me, he didn't want to hang around."

"I don't like it."

"Well, no, I don't either. The police are certain it was a hit-and-run. I did see the first three letters of the license plate—PRD. They said they'd check it out. They laughed when I showed them my FBI shield, just laughed and laughed."

"Who knew you were going to see Dr. Pratt?"

"Everyone in the office. It wasn't a secret. I even met Mr. Maitland in the hall, three clerks, and two secretaries. All of them asked about it. Oh no, you don't think it was on purpose, do you?"

He shrugged. "I don't know anything. I really like this car. I'm glad you didn't let your little designer buy it for you. He'd have gotten you one of those dainty little Miatas. How's your arm?"

"Fine. I just banged it against a parking meter. I went back up to see Dr. Pratt and he checked it out."

"What did he say?"

"Not much, shook his head and suggested I might consider another line of work. He said being president was a lot safer than what I did. He put the sling back on for another couple of days. Why won't my car start?"

"If it stops raining, I'll take a look." He crossed his arms over his chest and leaned back. "As I said, I don't know anything or think anything particular at the moment. If someone tried to kill you, then you've brought me into another mess. And don't call me 'sir' or I'll pull off that sling and strangle you with it."

She was much calmer now, her breath steady, the deadening shock nearly gone. "All right, Dillon. No one would have any reason to hurt me. It was an accident, a drunk driving a big black car."

"What about Douglas's wife?"

"All right, so I did think about her, but that's silly. She was angry, but surely not angry enough to kill me. If she wanted to kill somebody, she would pick Douglas, not me. The cops pushed me on it and I did give them her name, but no specific circumstances. I noticed those faint white lines on your finger pads. What are they from?"

"I whittle. Sometimes the knife slips and you cut yourself. No big deal. Now, that's really good. A jealous wife would really make them laugh. It's not raining as much. Let me see what's wrong with the Explorer."

Nothing was wrong. She'd flooded it.

"I should have thought of that," she said, annoyed and embarrassed.

"You're excused this time."

"So it was an accident. I was scared that you'd find the distributor cap missing or the oil line cut."

"It doesn't have to have been an accident. It's possible it was on purpose and if it was, you know what the guy intended, don't you?"

"Yes, to obliterate me."

Savich tapped his fingers on the dashboard. "I've always thought that trying to hit someone with a car wasn't the smartest or most efficient way of whacking your enemy. On the other hand, it's a dandy way to scare someone. Yeah, that sounds about right. If, on the other hand, someone did want to kill you, then I wonder why the car came at you when you'd just stepped off the curb and into the street. Why didn't the guy wait until you were nearly to your own car? You'd have been a perfect target then. That doesn't sound too professional. All the planning was in place, but the execution was way off." He shrugged. "As of this point in time, we haven't the foggiest notion. I'll run those three letters of the license plate through MAXINE and see what she can dredge up."

"MAXINE? You got another computer?"

"No. MAXINE used to be MAX. Every six months or so there's a sex change. I've had to accept the fact that my machine is a transsexual. Pretty soon, she'll start insisting that I compliment her when I'm working with her."

"That's crazy. I like it."

"Now, back to the accident—"

"It was an accident, Dillon. That's what the police think."

"On the other hand, they don't know you. Now, see if this wonderful ski-hauling four-by-four will start."

She turned the key and the Explorer fired right up. "Go back to the Bureau, Sherlock, and drink some of Marcy's tea. That'll fix you up. Oh yeah—stay away from Douglas Madigan and his wife. Don't you call him. I will. Where is he staying?"

* * *

SHE sat propped up against pillows in bed, the TV on low, just for background noise, reading the police and autopsy reports on Belinda. She didn't realize she was crying until the tears hit the back of her hand. She laid down all the pages and let herself cry. It had been so long; the tears had been clogged deep inside her, dammed up, until now.

Finally, the tears slowed. She sniffed, then returned to the reports. Tomorrow she would consult with MAXINE to see if there were any differences, no matter how slight, between Belinda's killing and all the others. She prayed with all her might that there wouldn't be a smidgen of difference. Now that she'd studied the reports, she hoped to be able to see things more clearly.

On the edge of sleep, she wondered if indeed Candice had tried to run her down. Just as her father had tried to run down her mother? No, that was ridiculous. Her mother was ill, had been for a very long time. Or maybe her mother had said that because of what her husband had said so casually about Belinda and her father. It had come out of left field. Who knew?

Of course Douglas had called her, furious that she'd given Dillon his cell number. It took her ten minutes to talk him out of coming over to her town house. He said he'd spoken to Candice, who'd been visited by the police. He was outraged that anyone would believe she had tried to run down Lacey. It had been an accident.

"I wouldn't be leaving unless I was certain it was an accident, Lacey. I want you to be certain, though, that it wasn't Candice."

"I'm certain, Douglas." She'd have said her tongue was purple to get him off the phone. "Don't worry. I'm fine. Everything is fine. Go home."

"Yes, I am. I'm taking Candice home too."

Now that sounded interesting, but she was too tired to ask him to explain.

THE next morning, Big John Bullock, Marlin Jones's lawyer, was on FOX, telling the interviewer, a drop-dead gorgeous guy who looked like a model right out of *GQ*, that the FBI and the Boston police had forced Marlin to confess, that he hadn't known what he was doing because he'd been in so much pain. He would have said anything so they'd give him more medication. Any judge would throw out a confession made under those circumstances.

Was Marlin guilty? the gorgeous young hunk asked, giving the audience a winning smile even as he said the words.

Big John shrugged and said that wasn't the point. That was for a jury to decide. The point was the police harassment of the poor man, who wasn't well either mentally or physically. Sherlock knew then that if the judge didn't suppress the confession, Big John would go for an insanity plea. The evidence was overwhelming. Sherlock knew that when the lawyer saw all the evidence against Marlin, he'd have no choice but to go for an insanity plea.

Sherlock stared at the TV screen, at that model interviewer whose big smile was the last thing on the screen before the program skipped to a toothpaste commercial. She'd been a fool. She should have shot Marlin straight through the heart. She would have saved the taxpayers thousands upon thousands of dollars. It would have been justice and revenge for all the women he'd butchered.

By the next afternoon, MAXINE hadn't come up with a thing. There were no differences at all in Belinda's killing versus the other women's. Only tiny variations, nothing at all significant.

She felt better. Belinda would finally find justice, if the little psycho ever made it to trial. A psychopath wasn't crazy, necessarily, even not usually. But who else knew that? Then she pictured him with Russell Bent of Chicago, both of them playing cards in the rec room of the state mental institution, both of them smiling at each other, joking about the idiot liberal judges and dumb-ass shrinks who believed they weren't responsible for their savagery because they'd had bad childhoods.

She had to stop it. There was nothing more she could do. Her father was right. Douglas was right. It was over. It was time to get on with her life.

NINETEEN

"It had to be Marlin Jones."

"It seems likely, but you don't sound as if you're really satisfied."

"I'm not, but MAX—oh, I forgot, he's in drag—MAXINE—didn't turn up a single variation in the way Belinda was murdered as opposed to the other women. Marlin killed them all; he had to have." She sighed. "But why did he leave out Belinda in particular; It makes no sense."

"I'm glad you're not satisfied. I'm glad you have that itch in your gut," Savich said slowly, tapping his pencil on his desktop, deliberately. "You've inputted all the physical data and run endless comparisons, but there are other aspects you need to take into account. Now you've got to finish it."

She was frowning ferociously. A long, curling piece of hair flopped into her face. She shoved it behind her ear, not even aware of what she was doing.

He smiled as he said, "MAXINE and I have been doing a little work. It's her opinion that we need to go back to the props. Okay, think now about how he killed the women. Think about what he used to kill them and where he killed them."

"A knife."

"What else?"

"He killed them in warehouses and in a couple of houses. He obviously prefers warehouses; there aren't as many people around at night."

"What did he use?"

"He built props."

"Just the way Marty Bramfort was building props for her kid's school play in Boston. Think about what you had to do to build those props."

She just stared at him, then leaped to her feet, her hands splayed on his desktop, her chair nearly falling over backward. Her face was alight with excitement. "Goodness, Dillon, he had to buy lumber, but the SFPD said they couldn't trace it, it was too common. But you know a better question: Is it possible to know if the same lumber was used in all the killings, that is, was all the lumber bought in the same place? Okay. He had to screw all those boards together, right? They couldn't trace all the brackets and hinges and screws, but is there any way of knowing if someone screws in a screw differently from someone else? If the slant is different? The amount of force? Is this possible? Can you tell if some lumber matches other lumber from the same yard? The same screws?"

He grinned at her. "I don't see why not. You've got it now, Sherlock. Now we've got to pray that the San Francisco police haven't thrown away the killer's props from each murder. Actually, I'd be willing to bet they've got it all. They're good.

"Say they still have everything. Unfortunately MAXINE can't help us here; not even using the most sophisticated visual scanners would work. We've got to have the human touch. I know this guy in Los Angeles who's a genius at looking at the way, for example, a person hammers in a nail. You wondered if this was possible. It is. Not too many people know how to do it, but this guy does. You could show him a half dozen different nails in boards and Wild Burt could tell you how many different people did the hammering. Now we'll test him about not only hammering nails but screwing in the brackets and hinges. Now go find out if you've still got a match."

THREE days went by. It was hard, but Savich kept his distance. He'd given her Burt York's number—Wild Burt—nicknamed ten years before when a suspect in a murder case had tried to kill him for testifying and Burt had saved himself with a hammer. Unexpectedly, the suspect had survived. He was now serving life in San Quentin. Savich had heard there was still a dent in his head.

No, he'd keep his mouth shut, at least for another day. To do anything active would be undue interference, and he knew she wouldn't appreciate it. If she had questions, she'd ask; he knew her well enough to know that she didn't have a big ego. He forced himself not to call Wild Burt to see what was going on. He knew, of course, that the SFPD hadn't done any comparisons of this sort, simply because they'd never had any doubts that all the murders had been committed by the same person. Also, this kind of evidence wasn't yet accepted in a court of law. He found himself worrying. As for Sherlock, she didn't come near him. He knew from the security logs that she had worked until after midnight for the past two nights. He was really beginning to grind his teeth when she knocked on his office door three days later at two o'clock in the afternoon. She stood in his doorway, saying nothing. He arched an eyebrow, ready to wait her out. She silently handed him a piece of paper.

It was a letter from Burt. He read: "Agent Sherlock, the tests I ran included: 1) type of drill used, 2) drilling and hammering technique, 3) type and grade of lumber, and 4) origin of lumber.

"The drill used in all the San Francisco murders except #4 was identical. However, the drill used in murder #4 was too close in particulars for me to even try to convince the D.A. that it wasn't identical. As to the drilling and hammering technique, it is odd, but I believe some was done by the same person and others were not. They were utterly different. No explanation for that. Perhaps it's as simple as the murderer had hurt his right hand and was having to use his left, or that he was in a different mood, or even that he couldn't see as well in this particular instance The lumber wasn't identical, and it did not come from the Bosman Lumber Mill, South San Francisco. Again, it doesn't really prove anything one way or the other, it is merely of note, although again, I wonder why only murder #4 had lumber from a different lumberyard.

"This was an interesting comparison. I've spoken to the police in San Francisco. The San Francisco D.A. is speaking with the Boston D.A. They will doubtless have comparisons made between the props used in the San Francisco murders and the props used in Boston. I don't doubt that even though the lumber can't be identical, the technique will be, and thus perhaps the presiding judge will allow it to be used as evidence in Marlin Jones's trial, if and when the man stands trial.

"So, the bottom-line results of my test are inconclusive. There are differences, aberrations. I must tell you that I have seen it happen before, and for no logical reason.

"I hope this is of assistance to you, but given the reason for your request I doubt that you are overjoyed. My best to Savich."

Savich said nothing, merely took in her pallor, the stark disappointment in her eyes, the hopelessness that seemed to be draining her. He wished it could be different, but it wasn't. He said finally, "Burt said it himself. Inconclusive. It doesn't nail down the coffin lid, Sherlock."

"I know," she said and didn't sound as though she believed it. "He didn't write this in his letter, but Mr. York said on the phone a few minutes ago that all the same particulars with the other murder props were completely identical. It was only with murder number four where there were inconsistencies."

"That's something," Savich said. "Look, Sherlock, either Marlin did it or he didn't. As to Marlin claiming he killed only six women in San Francisco, Belinda not included, then someone else did. You're not happy, are you?"

She shook her head. "I wanted to be certain once and for all and it's still not proven, either way. Can you think of anything else to do?" But she didn't look at him, just stared down at her low-heeled navy pumps.

"Not at the moment, but I'll think about it some more. Now let's get back to the Radnich case." He wished he could let her mull over her sister's murder, but there were too many demands on the Unit. He needed her.

"Yes. Thank you for giving me all this time. Ollie also said there was a new murder spree, a couple of black guys killing Asian people in Alabama and Mississippi."

"Yes. We'll talk about it in the meeting this afternoon." He watched her leave his office. He tapped his pen on the desktop. She'd lost weight she couldn't afford to lose. He didn't like it. Even though he saw the results of it in the families of victims, he still couldn't begin to imagine what it must feel like to have lost someone you loved in such a horrible way. He shook himself. He turned to MAXINE and typed in a brief note to his friend James Quinlan, pressed send.

Sherlock stopped outside his office, leaned against the wall. It was too much and not nearly enough. She had to go to Boston again. She had to speak to Marlin Jones one more time. She had to make him tell her the truth. She had to. She looked up to see Hannah staring at her. "Why are you so pale? You look like someone's punched you. Actually, you look like you're coming down with the flu."

She shook her head. "I'm fine. It's the case I'm working on. Things are inconclusive and I hate that."

Hannah said, "Yes, that's always a bitch, isn't it? How's your arm?"

"What? Oh, my arm's fine."

"How are you feeling after that hit-and-run driver nearly hit you the other day? That must have been pretty bad."

"It was, but not as bad as this. I think it was an accident, some drunk guy who probably was so scared that he nearly hit someone that he couldn't wait to roar away from me. The cops said the three numbers I saw on the license plate didn't lead anywhere. Too many possibilities. It could have happened to anybody. I was just the lucky one."

"Did you hurt your arm again?"

"Banged it up a bit more, no big deal."

"Dillon isn't busy now, is he?"

"I don't know." She walked away, thinking about who had had access to all the crime details in San Francisco.

She sat at her desk and stared at the blank computer screen. She heard a sound and turned to see Hannah standing by the water cooler, frowning at her. It was more than a frown, and Sherlock felt a brief burst of cold run through her. She forced herself back to the Radnich case, but there was nothing new there. Another murder and her old-woman theory hadn't washed. The afternoon meeting was canceled because Savich had an emergency meeting with Jimmy Maitland. She was still puzzling over the newest developments in the Mississippi/Alabama cases, when she heard Savich behind her. "It's after six. It's time for you to hang it up. Let's go work out."

She stared up at him blankly. "Work out?"

"Yeah, I bet you haven't moved from that desk since this afternoon. Come along. I won't throw you around because you have this wimp excuse about your arm."

SHE could barely walk. Nor could she talk. She was still using all her breath to pull oxygen into her lungs. It was just as well because Hannah Paisley turned up before they were ready to leave. She looked fit and strong, and every guy in the gym was staring at her. She was wearing a hot-pink leotard with a black top and black thong.

Savich gave Hannah a salute as he said, "Come on, Sherlock. I told you you've got to work on your breathing. More breath or you'll collapse on me the way you're almost doing now."

She eyed him and gasped out, "I'm going to kill you."

"Good. An entire sentence. You're getting it together again. You want to go shower?"

"I'd drown. I'd fall down, plug the drain, and that would be the end of it."

"Then let's walk home. A nice walk dries all the sweat."

"I want to be carried. These legs aren't going anywhere on their own."

Hannah was standing behind Savich. She lightly touched her fingers to his bare arm. His skin glistened with sweat.

"Hello, Dillon, Sherlock."

Lacey only nodded. She was still breathing hard.

"You're looking good, Hannah," Savich said. Sherlock realized at that moment how clear it was to her that they'd slept together. They were both magnificently made, beautiful specimens. She could imagine how they'd look together, naked, all over each other. She forced herself to smile. To look the way the two of them did, they had to sweat a lot to build those sleek muscles. Sherlock wasn't too fond of sweating. She watched Dillon squeeze Hannah's biceps. "Not bad. Look at poor Sherlock here. She's threatening to collapse on me all because she got her arm hurt and we had to spend the time on her legs."

"She does look a bit on the edge. While she rests up, could you come coach me a minute on my bench presses?"

"Sorry, not tonight, Hannah. Sherlock has to get home, and I promised I'd drop her off."

Hannah nodded, smiled at both of them, and walked off, every man's eyes, except Dillon's, on her butt.

"She's very beautiful," Sherlock said, pleased she could talk without wondering if she was having a heart attack.

"Yes, I guess so," Savich said. "Let's go."

They stopped for a half-veggie, half-sausage pizza at Dizzy Dan's on Clayton Street.

"You only left me two slices," Savich said, picking up one slice quickly. "You're a pig, Sherlock."

Cheese was dripping down her chin. She was so hungry, she was pleased she hadn't started chewing on the red-and-white checkered table-cloth. She quickly grabbed the last slice. It was still hot enough so that the cheese pulled loose and dripped down the sides of the slice. She couldn't wait to get it into her mouth. "Order another one," she said, her mouth full.

He did, and this garden delight pizza he ate himself. She was so full she didn't want to move, didn't even want to raise her hand from the tabletop.

"You stuffed?"

"To the gills." She sighed, sat back in her chair, and crossed her arms over her stomach. "I didn't realize I was so hungry."

"If Marlin didn't kill Belinda, then someone else did. Who was it, Sherlock?"

"I don't know, truly, I don't."

"But you've been thinking about it a whole lot, ever since Marlin told you he didn't kill her. Who had access, Sherlock? Who?"

"Why don't we talk about Florida instead? Or Mississippi?"

"Fine, but you're going to have to face up to it soon. I do have some new information from Florida for you. The latest murder wasn't on the projected map matrix, as you already know. MAXINE is trying to come up with something else. We poor humans are trying too. This time the police made an effort to question everyone in sight. They herded all the residents into the rec room. They wanted to catch your old woman in disguise. The initial word I got back, and what you heard, was that it wasn't someone disguised as an old woman. However, I found out before we left this afternoon that a new cop had had two of the old folks get sick on him because of the murder and he'd let them go. One was an old woman, one an old man. Was one of them the murderer? No one knows.

"As for the new young cop being able to identify the two old people, we can forget it. All old people look alike to him. He remembers that one was an old man and he fainted; the other was an old lady and she puked. You can bet your life that he got his ears pinned back, probably worse.

"So, it's still unclear whether or not your theory is right. You know, the likeliest person to kill a wife is the husband."

He'd steered so smoothly back on course that the words spilled out of her mouth: "No, Dillon, Douglas loved Belinda. All right, for argument's sake, let's say that I'm wrong and he hated her. He would simply have divorced her. There's no reason he would have killed her. He's not stupid, nor, I doubt strongly, is he a murderer. There was no reason for him to kill her, none at all."

"No, not that you know of. But one thing, Sherlock, he does seem to think too much of you, his sister-in-law. How long has he been looking at you, licking his chops?"

"I'm sure that's recent. And I think he's over it now." She remembered him staring at hers and Belinda's photos in her bedroom—all that he'd remembered, all that he'd said about her innocence. She felt a knot of coldness settle deep into her. She was shaking her head even as she added, "No, not Douglas."

"Your daddy's a judge, but he wasn't a judge seven years ago. He couldn't have had access to everything on the String Killer case."

She wondered only briefly how he knew that, but then wanted to laugh at herself. That was easy stuff. Actually she wouldn't be surprised if Savich knew what the president's next speech would be about. She had complete faith that MAXINE could access anything Savich wanted. "No, impossible. Don't lie to me. I'll bet you know my father did have access to everything. He came out of the D.A.'s office. He knew everyone. He could have accessed anything he wanted. But Dillon, how could a man kill his own daughter? And so brutally?"

"It's been done more times than I can remember. Your dad's not all that straightforward a guy, Sherlock, and Belinda wasn't his daughter. He appears to have this mean streak in him. He didn't much like Belinda, did he? He thought she was nuts, like his wife, who claimed that he'd tried to run her down in his BMW."

She scooted out of the booth, the tablecloth snagging on her purse strap. His two remaining slices of pizza nearly slid off the table.

"Then there's Mama. Does she have mental problems, Sherlock? What did she think of Belinda?"

He was standing there in front of her, very close, and she couldn't stand it. "I'm going home. You don't have to see me there."

"Yeah, I do. You've got to do some thinking. You know very well Burt York has sent his findings to the SFPD. They might reopen Belinda's case or they might not. No way of telling yet. At the very least though, everything we're talking about they'll be talking about too. Douglas could be in some warm water, Sherlock, no matter how you slice it. Daddy too."

"Since everything is so inconclusive, it's very possible the San Francisco police won't do a thing. I think once they talk to Boston, they'll know it was Marlin. They won't have any doubts. They'll shake their heads at Burt's report."

"I think they will pay some attention. We're all the law. We're all supposed to try to catch the bad guys, even if it might mean opening a can of worms."

"I've got to call Douglas, warn him. This can't be right, it can't. I never meant for this to happen."

He rolled his eyes. "Maybe I'll understand you in another thirty years, Sherlock. Do what you must. Come on. I've got things to do tonight."

"Like what?"

"My friend James Quinlan plays the sax at the Bonhomie Club on Houtton Street, owned by a Ms. Lily, a super-endowed black lady who admires his butt and his soulful eyes as much as his playing. He tries to be there at least once or twice a week. Sally, his wife, loves the place. Marvin, the bouncer, calls her Chicky. Come to think of it, he calls every female Chicky. But Sally to him is a really nice Chicky. I'll never forget that Fuzz the bartender gave them a bottle of wine for a wedding present. It had a cork. A first. Amazing."

Now all this was strange. She said slowly, willing, happy to be distracted, even if only for a moment, "So you go to support him?"

He looked suddenly embarrassed. He didn't meet her eyes. He cleared his throat and said, "Yeah."

He was lying. She cocked her head to one side. "Maybe I could go with you sometime? I wouldn't mind supporting him either. Also, I've never gotten together with Sally Quinlan. I heard she's an aide to a senator."

"Yeah. Okay, sure. Maybe. We'll see."

She didn't say a word. They were nearly at her town house. There was a quarter moon showing through gothic clouds—all thin and wispy, floating past, making sinister images. It was only eight-thirty in the evening, cool with only a slight breeze. "You should keep a light on."

"The FBI doesn't pay me all that well, Dillon. It would cost a fortune."

"Do you have an alarm system?"

"No. Why? All of a sudden you're worried? You were mocking all my locks just a while ago."

"Yeah, and I wondered why someone who faced down Marlin like a first-class warrior would need to have more locks in her house than the president has guards."

"They're two very different things."

"I figured that. I don't suppose you'll tell me about it, will you?"

"There's nothing to tell. Now, what's all this about an alarm system?"

"Someone tried to run you down. That changes things, big-time."

They were back to that. "It was an accident."

"Possibly."

"Good night, Dillon."

TWENTY

Lacey unlocked the front door and stepped into the small foyer. She reached for the light switch and turned it on. It flickered, and then the light strengthened. She turned to lock the front door—the dead bolt, the two chains. From habit, she looked into the living room, the kitchen, before she went to her bedroom. Everything was as it should be.

She stopped suddenly. Slowly, she lowered the gym shoe she'd just pulled off to the floor. She turned, silent as stone now, and listened. Nothing.

She was losing it. She remembered that long-ago night in her fourth-floor apartment when she'd awakened to hear noises and nearly heaved up her guts with terror. Then she'd gotten a grip and gone out to see what or who was there. It had been a mouse. A silly little mouse, so scared he didn't know where to run when he saw her. And that had been the night she'd changed.

She took off the rest of her gym clothes and went into the bathroom. Just before she stepped into the shower, she turned the lock on the door, laughing aloud at herself while she did it. "You're an idiot," she said, unlocked the door, then stepped into the shower.

Hot, hot water. It felt like heaven. Dillon had nearly killed her, but the hot water was soaking in. She could feel her shrieking leg muscles groan in relief. He'd told her that working out kept his stress level down. It also gave him a gorgeous body, but she didn't tell him that. She was beginning to wonder if he didn't have something about bringing down the stress. For the hour they'd exercised, she hadn't given a single thought to Marlin Jones or to the inconclusive report from Wild Burt York.

She finally stepped out of the shower some ten minutes later and into the fog-heavy bathroom. She wrapped a thick Egyptian-cotton towel around her head, then used the corner of her other towel to wipe the mirror.

She stared into the masked face right behind her.

A yell clogged in her throat. She froze. She realized she wasn't breathing, couldn't breathe, until air whooshed out of her mouth.

The man said in a soft, low voice that feathered warm air on the back of her neck, "Don't move now, little girl. I expected you to come home a bit later. You seemed well ensconced at that pizza place with that big guy. What's the matter, didn't the guy push hard enough to sleep with you? I could tell he wanted to, just the way he was looking at you. You told him no, didn't you? Yeah, you're here a little earlier than I expected, but no matter. I had a chance to settle in, get to know you a bit."

His mask was black. His breathing was quiet, his voice so very soft, unalarming. She felt the gun pressing lightly against the small of her back. She was naked, no weapon, nothing except a ridiculous towel wrapped around her head.

"That's right. You're holding perfectly still. Are you afraid I'll rape you?"

"I don't know. Will you?"

"I hadn't thought to, but seeing you all buck naked, well, you're good-looking, you know? It turned me on to hear you singing that country-western song in the shower. What was it?"

" 'King of the Road.' "

"I like those words—but they fit me, not you. You're just a little girl playing cop. The king of the road goes to Maine when he's all done, right? That's where I might go once I'm through with you."

Slowly, very slowly, she brought the towel down in front of her. "May I please wrap the towel around me?"

"No, I like looking at you. Drop it on the floor. Leave the one wrapped around your head. I like that too. It makes you look exotic. It turns me on."

She dropped the towel. She felt the gun pressing cold and hard against her spine. She'd had training, but what could she do? She was naked, without a weapon, in her bathroom. What could she possibly do? Talk to him; that was her best chance, for the moment. "What do you want?"

"I want to talk you into going back to him, all the way back to San Francisco."

"Did you try to run me down?"

He laughed, actually laughed. "Do you think I could have done something like that, little girl? Though you ain't all that little, are you?" The hand holding the gun came around and stroked the dull silver barrel over her right breast.

She flinched, leaning back, only to feel him against her back, his groin against her hips.

"Now that's nice, isn't it?" He continued to press the cold metal against her breast, then downward to her belly. She was quivering, she couldn't stop it, her flesh trying to flinch from him. Fear was full-blown now, and she didn't know if she could hold herself together. She gasped out, "Why do you want me to leave Washington?"

The gun stopped. He drew his hand away. "Your mama and daddy need you at home. It's time you went back there and took care of your responsibilities. They don't want you here, involved in conspiracies and shooting people, the way the FBI does. Yeah, they want you home. I'm here to encourage you to go."

"I'll tell you why I can't go back yet. You see, there's this murderer, his name is Marlin Jones, and he killed this woman in Boston. He's a serial killer. I can't leave yet. I'll tell you more but it could take a while. Can't I put on some clothes? We can go in the kitchen, and I'll make some coffee?"

"Hard-nosed little girl, aren't you? It doesn't bother you at all with my dick pressing against your butt."

"It bothers me."

He stepped back. He waved the gun toward the bedroom. "Go put yourself in a bathrobe. I can always take it off you if I want."

He followed at a distance, not getting close enough for her to kick out at him. She didn't look at him again until she had the terry-cloth robe belted tightly around her waist.

"Take the turban off your head and comb out your hair. I want to see it."

She pulled off the towel and began combing her fingers through her hair. Had he moved closer? Could she get him with her foot? It would require speed, and she'd have to be accurate or he'd kill her.

"Use that brush."

She shook her head, picked up the brush, and brushed her hair until he finally said, "That's enough." He reached out his hand and touched the damp hair. He grunted.

Keep calm. She had to keep herself calm, but it was hard to do, really hard. She wanted to see his face, to make him human, and real, to look hard at his eyes. The black ski mask made him a monster, faceless, terrifying. He was dressed in black too, down to the black running shoes on his feet. Big feet. He was a big man, big arms, long, but his belly was flabby. He wasn't all that young, then. His voice was low, sort of raspy, as if he'd smoked too much for a long time. Keep thinking like this, she told herself over and over as she walked into the kitchen. Keep calm.

She watched him from the corner of her eye. He was leaning against the counter, the gun—a small .22—still pointed at her, as if someone had told him that she'd had some training, that he shouldn't just assume that because she was a woman she had no chance against him.

"Who are you?"

He laughed. "Call me Sam. You like that? Yeah, that's me—Sam. My pa was named Sam too. Hey, I'm the son of Sam."

"Someone hired you. Who?"

"Too many questions, little girl. Get that coffee on. Now start talking to me about this Marlin Jones. Tell me why you're so important to this case."

Nothing she told him about Marlin Jones would make any difference that she could see, and it would buy her time. "I was the one who was the bait to catch him in Boston. FBI agents do this sort of thing. There was nothing unusual about it. I was the bait because he'd killed my sister seven years ago in San Francisco. He was called the String Killer. I begged the cops to let me bring him down. They let me and I did bring him down, but it's not over yet. I can't go back home yet."

He pushed off the counter, walked to her, and very calmly, very slowly, pulled back his arm and brought the gun sharply against the side of her head. Not hard enough to knock her unconscious, but hard enough to knock her silly. Pain flooded through her. She cried out, grabbed her head, and lurched against the stove.

"I know a lie when I hear it," he said in that low, soft voice of his and quickly stepped back out of her reach. "This guy butcher your sister? Yeah, sure. Hey, you're bleeding. Scalp wounds bleed like stink, but you'll be okay. Tell me the truth, tell me why you really want to stay here or I'll hit you again."

She suddenly heard an accent. No, her brains were scrambled, she was imagining it. No, wait, the way he'd said "bleed like stink." It was faintly southern; yes, that was it. And wasn't that phrase southern as well?

He raised his arm. She said quickly, "I'm not lying. Belinda Madigan, the fourth victim of the San Francisco String Killer, was my sister."

He didn't say anything, but she saw the gun waver. Hadn't he known? No, if he didn't know, why else would he be here? He said finally, "Keep going."

"Marlin Jones said he didn't kill her. That's why I've got to stay. I've got to find out the truth. Then I can go home."

"But he did kill her, didn't he?"

"Yes, he did. I wondered and wondered, then I even had some tests done on the wooden props used in all the murders in San Francisco, the hammering and screwing techniques, stuff like that. There's an expert in Los Angeles who's really good at that sort of thing. But his results were inconclusive. Marlin Jones killed her. He must have realized who I was and lied to me, to torture me. Who are you? Why do you care?"

"Hey, I'm a journalist." He laughed again. He was big into laughter, this guy. She felt blood dripping off her hair onto her face. She wiped it away with the back of her hand.

"Yeah, I'm a journalist and I like to know the inside scoop. You guys are so closemouthed that none of us know what's going on. Yeah, I'm with the *Washington Post*. My name's Garfield." He laughed. He was really enjoying himself.

Then just as suddenly, he straightened, and she knew that if he weren't wearing that mask, she'd see that his eyes had gone cold and dead. "Is that all, little girl?"

"Yes, that's all," she said now, her voice shaking with fear. No, she thought, it wasn't enough. More shaking, more show of fear. "But why do you care whether or not I go home? Or does the person who sent you want me to leave? Why? I'm no threat to anyone." Marlin Jones was in her mind. Was he somehow behind this?

The man was silent for a moment, and she knew he was studying her, weighing his options. Who was he?

He said finally, reaching out his hand to touch a clump of bloody hair, "You know what I think? I think that maybe old Marlin didn't kill your sister. You're like a little terrier, yanking and jerking and pulling, but you won't find anything.

"Now I believe that's all I need to know. I'll tell you one last time. Leave Washington. Stay with the FBI if you want to, but transfer. Go home, little girl. Now, let's have us a good time."

He walked toward her, the gun aimed right at her chest. "I want you to march your little butt to the bedroom. I want you to stretch out all pretty-like on the bed. Then we'll see."

She knew pleading wouldn't gain her anything. She turned and walked out of the kitchen. He was going to rape her. Then would he kill her as well? Probably. But the rape, she wouldn't take the rape, she couldn't. He'd have to kill her before she'd let him rape her. Who had hired him?

What to do? He didn't think Marlin had killed Belinda? Why did he care? What was going on here?

"Please, who are you?"

He motioned the gun toward the bed.

She was standing now beside her bed, not wanting to lie down, hating the thought of him being over her, of him in control.

"Take off that bathrobe."

Her hands were fists at her sides. He raised the gun. She took off the bathrobe.

"Now lie down and open those legs real wide for me."

"Why don't you think Marlin killed my sister?"

"Business is over. It's party time. Lie down, little girl, or I'll have to hurt you real bad."

She couldn't do it. She couldn't.

He took a step toward her, the gun raised. He was going to hit her with the butt again, probably break her jaw this time. She had to do something.

The phone rang.

Both of them stared at it.

It rang again.

"It might be my boss," she said, praying harder than she'd ever prayed in her life. "He knows I'm home. He said he might call. There was an assignment he wanted to talk to me about."

"That big guy who brought you here? That's your boss?"

She nodded and wished again that she could see his face, see his expression.

Another ring.

"Answer it. But you be careful what you say or you're dead where you stand."

She picked up the phone and said quietly, "Hello?"

"That you, Sherlock?"

"Yes, sir, it's me, sir."

He was silent a moment. She was praying, hard.

"I wanted to tell you that Sally asked to meet you. She wants you to come to the Bonhomie Club tomorrow night. Quinlan's going to be playing both nights."

"That sounds nice, sir, but you know that I never mix any business with pleasure. It's a rule I always stick to, sir."

He was mouthing at her, "Get rid of him!"

"I've got to go, sir. Tell Sally I'm sorry, sir. That assignment you wanted to talk to me about, sir, I'll be in early tomorrow. I've got to go now."

The gun was pressing at her temple. She gulped, then gently hung up the phone.

"I heard what the guy said. You're lucky you didn't blow it, little girl. Now."

He pulled some slender nylon rope from his pocket. "Put those arms up over your head."

He was going to tie her down. Then he could do anything he wanted to with her.

Slowly, slowly, she raised her arms. Why had she wanted a brass bed with a slatted brass headboard? He was coming over to her; soon now, soon, and she would have a chance.

He leaned down, the rope in one hand, the gun in the other. He seemed uncertain what to do with the gun. Put it down, she said in her mind, over and over, as she looked up at him. Put it down. I'm skinny. You can take me. Don't be afraid.

He made up his mind. He backed off. "Turn on your stomach."

She stared at him.

"Do it now or I'll make you really sorry."

She couldn't do it. She just couldn't. Without thought, without hesitation, she lurched up and rammed her head into his belly. At the same time, she flung out both fists against his forearms. She heard him cursing, heard the pain in his voice, and kept hitting him. Quickly she threw herself to the floor, rolling onto her back. He was heaving hard, over her now, the gun up, and she kicked with all her strength, her foot hitting his hand.

The gun went flying.

He threw himself down on her. His fist landed hard against her jaw, then he raised her head, grabbed fistfuls of damp hair, and slammed her head against the floor once, twice, three times. She heard a yell and a moan. The sounds were from her. She tried to bring her legs up to kick him but couldn't manage it. She felt numbness, then knifing pain shot through her head. She vaguely heard his curses from above her, and they grew more distant. She thought she heard the phone ring again. She thought she heard him breathing hard over her. Then she didn't know about anything. She fell into blackness.

HE was scared spitless. The front door stood wide open. Savich forced himself to be careful, to go slowly, but what he wanted to do was roar in there.

He drew his gun and eased inside the town house. Slowly, he reached for the light switch and flipped it on. He was in a crouch in the next instant, sweeping his SIG around him in a wide arc.

No one.

"Sherlock?"

Nothing.

He didn't even pause now. He ran into the living room, switching on lights as he went. She wasn't there. Nor was she in the kitchen.

He was in the hallway when he heard a moan.

She was lying on the floor next to the bed, naked. Blood streaked down the side of her face.

He was on his knees beside her, his fingers pressed against the pulse in her neck. Slow and steady.

"Sherlock! Wake up!"

She moaned again, low and deep in her throat. She tried to bring up her hand to her head, but couldn't do it. Her hand fell. He caught it before it hit the floor. He laid her hand over her belly.

He leaned close over her, an inch from her face. "Sherlock, wake up. You're scaring the bejesus out of me. Wake up!"

She heard his voice. He sounded incredibly angry—no, not angry, but really worried. She had to open her eyes, but she knew any movement at all would hurt really badly.

"Talk to me. Come on, you can do it. Talk to me."

She managed to open her eyes. He was blurry, but his voice was low and deep and eminently sane. She was so grateful, so relieved. She whispered over the pain, "You came. I knew the multiple *sirs* would get to you."

"They did. The first time you said it, I wanted to trim your sails but good, but then you said it again. I knew something was wrong. Where'd he hit you?"

"My head, with the butt of his gun."

He didn't want to ask, but he had to. "Did he rape you?"

"He would have tried, but I couldn't let him do it. He wanted me to lie down on my stomach. When he moved in I attacked him and got off the bed. That's when he started banging my head against the floor. It kind of hurts, Dillon."

"Did he hit you anywhere else?"

"Just a fist in the jaw."

"Let me get you up on the bed."

"He's gone? You're sure he's gone? I don't want him to sneak back and hurt you."

Hurt him? Blood was trickling down the side of her face and she was worried about him? "I'll go lock the front door in a minute." While he spoke, he slid his hands beneath her and lifted her. She didn't weigh much. He laid her on the bed, then very quickly drew a blanket over her.

"Don't move," he said, turned, and went back to the front door. He looked around outside, then came back into the house and locked the door.

When he was seated beside her again on the side of the bed, he said quietly, "No one's about now. I'm going to call the paramedics and get you to the hospital."

Her hand shot up. "No, no hospital. I'm all right. I've got a very hard head. Maybe a concussion, but there's nothing they can do for that, just time. I've got time here. Please, no hospital. I hate hospitals. They'll give me more shots in the butt. That's awful."

He looked down at her, then turned to the phone. He dialed a number, then said, "It's Savich. Sorry to bother you, Ned, but could you come to this address and check out one of my agents for me? The guy who attacked her hit her pretty hard in the head. I don't know if she'll need stitches. No, no hospital. Yeah, thanks."

When he hung up the phone, she said, "A doctor who makes house calls? That's got to be rarer than the great auk."

"Ned Breaker owes me. I got his kid away from kidnappers last year. He's a good guy. We became friends. Now, enough of that. It'll take him a good thirty minutes to get here. Do you feel well enough to tell me what happened?"

"After you left, I took a shower. When I got out, he was standing behind me when I wiped the fog off the bathroom mirror. He was wearing a black ski mask and carrying a cheap .22. He wanted me to leave town. Then I talked about Marlin Jones, and he seemed interested in that. I don't know whether or not the person who sent him meant for him to rape me. Maybe, like that almost hit-and-run, he was trying to scare me, which he did.

"Really, though, the bottom line was that I should go home to my family. When I asked him if he was the one who tried to run me down, he didn't answer me. I think he could have been. He had a slight accent, from Alabama, maybe."

"What did you tell him about Marlin Jones?"

"The truth. There was no reason not to. I think somehow Marlin Jones had to have sent him. He tried not to be too interested in Marlin, but he was. He wanted me to believe Marlin was innocent."

"You sure about that?"

"Yes, but again, I think his mission was to scare me to death, scare me enough to make me run. Then he said business was over. He said he wanted to rape me."

Her eyes were vague, her voice slowing down, her words slurring. He shook her shoulders. "Sherlock, wake up. Come on, you can do it." He lightly slapped her cheek, then cupped her jaw in the palm of his hand. "Wake up."

She blinked, trying hard. She wanted to tell him that his hand on her jaw hurt, but all she said was, "Probably a concussion. I'll stay awake, I promise. He was going to tie my hands above my head, to the slats of the bed, but he knew I'd attack if he dropped the gun, so he told me to lie on my stomach. I couldn't do that, Dillon, I couldn't. That's when—" Curtains, black curtains were swinging down over her eyes, over her mind. She couldn't see anything.

"Wake up, Sherlock!"

"I'm awake. Don't yell at me, it hurts. I won't konk out on you, I promise. But I can't see."

"Your eyes are closed."

"That's not it."

In the next moment, she was unconscious, her head lolling to the side. He'd never dialed 911 so fast in his life.

TWENTY-ONE

The heat burned straight into her head. It was hotter than anything she could have imagined. Any second now she'd go up in flames. No, it was a light, a real light, not some monster that her brain had dredged up. It was too bright, too strong, too hot. It burned beneath her eyelids. She tried to turn away from the light, but it hurt too much to move her head.

"Sherlock? Can you hear me? Open your eyes."

Of course she could hear him. He was using that deep voice of his that made her nerve endings quiver, but she couldn't say anything, her mouth was too dry. She tried to form the words, but no sound came out.

A woman said, "Give her some water."

Someone raised her head. She felt cold water on her lips and opened her mouth. She choked, slowed down. She drank and drank until finally the water was dribbling down her chin.

"Now can you talk to me?"

"The light," she whispered. "Please, the light."

The same woman's voice said, "It must be hurting her."

The light was gone in the next instant and it was now shadowy and dim. She sighed with relief. "That's better. Where's Dillon?"

"I'm right here. You scared me out of a good year at the gym. We were both doing fine until you had the nerve to pass out on me."

"I didn't mean to do that. It was weak and unnecessary. I'm sorry. Does my health coverage take care of the paramedics and the emergency room?"

"I doubt it. I think it will come out of your pay. Now, here's Dr. Breaker. He got to your house just as the paramedics were pulling out, claims he was speeding to get there. Turns out he has admitting privileges here at Washington Memorial."

"Your voice made me quiver—all dark and soft, like falling into a deep, deep well. If I were a criminal, I'd say anything you wanted to keep you talking to me like that. It's a wonderful voice. Plummy—that's how a writer would describe your voice."

"Thank you."

"Agent Sherlock. I'm Dr. Breaker."

He shined a penlight in her eyes, felt the bumps on her head, and said over his shoulder to Dillon, "She's not going to need any stitches, just some of my magic tape. Scalp wounds tend to really bleed."

"They bleed like stink."

"Yes, that's right. Interesting way of saying it."

"It's what the man said. And he said it in a southern way. He drawled out stink into two syllables."

She'd already told him that, but he said, "That's good, Sherlock. Anything else?"

"Not yet, Savich. Hold off a bit. Let me clean her up, then you can talk her ear off." He cleared his throat. "She wasn't raped, was she?"

"No, I wasn't. I'm not dead, Dr. Breaker. You can speak to me."

"Well, you see, Agent, I owe everything to Savich here and nothing at all to you. If he wants me to report to him, he's got it."

"I report to him. You report to him. Soon the president will report to him. Maybe that's not such a bad idea. My head hurts."

"I'll bet it does. Lie still now. When you first came in, we did a CT scan. Not to worry, it was normal. We always do a CT scan when there's a head injury, to check for evidence of bleeding. You didn't have any. What happened to your arm? What's this sling for?"

"A knife wound," Savich said. "It's nearly well now. Happened a couple of weeks ago."

"Why don't you let her heal before you send her into the arena with the monsters again?"

She laughed. There was nothing else to do.

THE next time she heard anything, it was a strange man speaking.

"When you roared out of the club like a bat out of its belfry, I thought Sally was going to have Marvin tackle you. You scared us, Dillon. This is Sherlock?"

"Yes, that's her in all her glory."

"She looks like a little mummy."

She realized that there was a huge bandage over the cut in her scalp. She raised her hand to touch it, but to her disgust, she didn't have the strength. Dr. Breaker was right. It wasn't fair that she had to be hurt again before she'd healed completely from the other time. Her hand fell, only again Dillon caught it and laid it gently at her side.

"You alive, Sherlock?"

"Yes, thank you. I'm really tired of this, sir. At least last time in that Boston hospital I was sitting up the whole time."

"Don't whine. You'll live."

"She calls you 'sir'? Do you require that all your people call you sir?"

"No, only the women. It makes me feel powerful."

"He's lying," she said, cracking open her eyes. To her relief, the light in the room was dim. "He takes all the women to the gym and stomps them into the floor. The 'sir' stuff is my idea. I hope it makes him feel responsible, and guilty."

"I don't feel guilty. I walked you home. You want me to believe I should have taken you inside? Checked all your closets and looked under the bed? Well, maybe from now on I will. You attract trouble, Sherlock, too much of it." But he sounded guilty, really guilty. She wanted to tell him not to be ridiculous, but he said quickly, "This is Special Agent James Quinlan. We go way back together."

"You make it sound like we're nearly to retirement, Savich. Hi, Agent Sherlock." He took her hand in his, a strong hand, with calluses on his thumbs. She'd seen a web of scars on Dillon's fingers and hands: fine, pale white scars. He'd told her he whittled. Whittled what?

"You call him Savich, not Dillon."

"Yeah, I always thought Dillon sounded too wussy, too soft, so to toughen him up I never called him that. Hey, what's in a name?"

"He was with you at that place called The Cove?"

"Nah, he just came in on the deal when most of the fun was over."

"That's a lie. I saved Sally."

"That's true, he did help. A little bit. Dillon's always there to back me up."

She said, "You're Sally's husband?"

"Yes, she's mine. I've got to tell you, Agent Sherlock, I don't like any of this. You're a target and we've got to find out why."

"None of us likes it, Quinlan," Savich said. "Don't act proprietary. She's not in your unit. I will get to the bottom of this. Hey, Sherlock, you do look like a mummy. You want some more water before I start grilling you again? I'll use my special voice."

Neither man said anything until she'd drunk her fill. Then Quinlan laughed when Savich said to her, "Having you suck on a straw is better than trying to balance you on the edge of the cup. You don't drool so much."

"Because you tried to dump the entire glass of water down my throat that first time—" she broke off, gave him a silly grin.

Quinlan said, "Not just yet, Agent Sherlock. Er, did you know that Sally and I were married a year last month—in October? Savich here found us the wedding date and the church."

"Why did he do that?"

"Well, I was kind of out of it at the time and Sally was so worried about me that she didn't even think about marrying me. So Savich had to take care of it."

"What he means to say is that he had a bullet in his heart and couldn't do much but press more morphine into his vein. As for Sally, she probably only agreed to marry him because she felt sorry for him."

She smiled at that, and thankfully, it didn't hurt. "Oh goodness. Have I gotten into the wrong career?"

"You're off to a good start," Quinlan said. "Wounded twice and you've been out of training only what? A month? Hey, don't worry. I've made it to thirty-three, same as Savich here."

They heard voices outside. Quinlan raised an eyebrow and said, "I think my whirlwind of a wife has just blown in. The guard you've got out there doesn't stand a chance."

"No indeed," said a very pretty young woman about Lacey's own age as she came into the room. She had dusty blond hair, clasped with barrettes behind her ears, and blue eyes that looked soft and tender, and had seen too much. "Don't blame Agent Crammer. He knows me. He helped me barbecue those half a dozen corn on the cob last month, remember, James?"

"Our venture into vegetarian barbecuing," James Quinlan said with disgust and poked Savich's arm. "Just for you I had to barbecue corn on the cob."

Savich said, "Hey, Sally, this is Sherlock. She's the one who needed your decorating help until she had it done herself. She called up one of those expensive designers and the guy tripped all over himself to please her."

Lacey felt a soft hand lightly stroke her forearm. "You certainly scared the sense out of Dillon here. I was watching him on the phone, and he turned white, threw the phone down, and ran out of the club. Ms. Lily thought he was so horny he couldn't hold himself back another second. As for Fuzz the bartender, he shook his head and said Savich should have a beer occasionally, it would make him more mellow. Marvin the bouncer, said he was glad Savich didn't drink. He never wanted to have to try to bounce him."

Sherlock said, "I'd like to meet these people. Dillon said he went there to support Agent Quinlan."

"Oh, sure, but it's not just that, he—"

"Now, Sally," Savich interrupted her without apology, "Sherlock here is looking as though she's ready to fall through the railing. Let's leave her alone. She needs to rest. Ah, here's Dr. Breaker. Ned, your patient is looking glassy-eyed."

"Out," Dr. Breaker said, not looking at any of them. When they were alone, he said quietly as he took her pulse, "I didn't intend for you to begin partying so soon, Agent Sherlock. Hey, where'd you get that neat name?"

"My dad. He's a judge. I understand that lawyers hate to be in his courtroom. They say it scares their clients to death, being up in front of a guy named Judge Sherlock." She smiled up at him, then closed her eyes, her head falling to the side.

Dr. Breaker gently laid her hand on the bed. He checked her eyes. He stood quietly and studied her face. Then he nodded. Everything was fine. She would recover. He had only one foot out her door when Savich was in his face, saying, "Well?"

"No 'well' about it, Savich. She'll be fine. She's out now and should stay out until morning, with the medication she's had. Nasty business. The guy could have killed her pounding her head on the floor the way he did, to say nothing of hitting her head with the butt of a gun."

Savich sighed, looking down at his clasped hands. "Thanks again for coming so quickly. How long will she be in here?"

"Another day, I'd say. As I told you, the CT scan was normal. No bleeding, no abnormalities that any of the radiologists could see. I'll reevaluate her again in the morning. Now I'm home to bed."

When Dr. Breaker disappeared into the elevator, Quinlan said, "This is a strange business, Savich. You want to tell me about it now?"

Savich looked at two of his best friends and said slowly, "I'm in deep trouble."

"What does that mean?" Sally said, sitting on the bench beside him.

Savich shook his head. "Listen, you guys, thanks for coming down. I think I'll stay here. One of the nurses offered me a bed. I'd feel better with Crammer out here and me inside her room. She'd really be safe then."

"You've got no idea who's behind all this?"

"It could be someone involved with Marlin Jones; that makes the most sense. But who? He's a real loner from what we know. And why would Marlin care if she left town or not? Other than Marlin, there's no one else out there waving a flag. Well, there is someone else. We'll see." To Savich's relief, neither Sally nor Quinlan asked him more questions.

An hour later, he was lying on his back on a very hard cot, listening to her even breathing. She moaned once, sending him to his feet in an instant and to her bedside, only to see that she was still asleep. He stood there, looking down at her, white and bandaged, an IV in her arm. She twitched, her hand clenching into a fist, then relaxing again. He didn't like any of this. Why did that guy want to hear what she knew about Marlin Jones? It made no sense. If someone else had killed Belinda, one of her family, then it would make sense that they'd want her out of the way. But then why would he or she hire that man to tell Sherlock that Marlin was innocent? Surely if he thought enough about it, examined every little detail, he would find an answer. But all he could think about now was listening carefully to her breathing. He lightly touched his fingertips to her jaw. It was a khaki green. He stepped back.

He lay back down, felt the smooth cold of his gun next to his hand, and kept listening to her until finally, after what seemed an interminable amount of time, he fell asleep.

"I want to go home."

"Now, Agent Sherlock, I think another full day would be just the thing for you. The medical staff likes having FBI agents in here. It makes them feel important. Ah, and a bit on the superior side since they're still on their feet and you, an agent, aren't."

"You've got to be making that up. The nurse this morning was very sweet when she poked me with a needle. And it wasn't in the rear end, thank God. Listen, Dr. Breaker, it's already four o'clock in the afternoon. I've been counting sheep since nine o'clock this morning. I'm fine. My head hurts just a bit, but nothing else, not even the cut on my head. Please, Dr. Breaker, I want to go home."

"Let's talk about it a bit more," he said, backing away from the bed.

She swung her legs over and sat up. "I need some clothes, Dr. Breaker."

"Keep your socks on. I've got clothes for you, Sherlock. Ned told me you'd probably demand to take off."

She looked down at her bare foot. "I don't even have any socks, just this flimsy hospital gown that's open in the back."

Savich grinned at her. "Well, Ned, shall I take her off your hands?"

"She's yours, Savich. She'll be fine. She needs another day taking it easy and these pills for any pain." He handed Savich the bottle of pills.

"Good-bye, Agent Sherlock. That's a weird name. If I were you, I'd have it changed. How about Jane Sherlock?"

"That wasn't funny, Ned," Savich said, but Dr. Breaker was chuckling. "I've never before had the chance to say that. It's an old joke, you know."

"Yes," Sherlock said. "I know."

"Heard it, huh?"

"I've heard all of them. Thank you, Dr. Breaker. Dillon, give me my clothes and see Dr. Breaker out."

"Yes, ma'am."

Savich stayed out until she opened the door. He was talking to Agent Crammer, a ruddy-faced, barrel-chested young man who had a degree in accounting from the University of Pennsylvania.

She eyed them. When Savich looked up, he took in her outfit and grinned. "Not bad, huh? You won't be arrested by the fashion police."

He'd brought her a dark green silk blouse and a pair of blue jeans, a blue blazer and a pair of low-heeled boots that she'd only worn one time. She liked the outfit but would never have picked it out. It made her look too—

"You look real sharp, Agent Sherlock," Crammer said.

"Yeah," Savich added, "real sharp. Cute even."

"A Special Agent shouldn't look anything but competent and trustworthy. I'll go home and change."

"With that bandage on your head, you're not going to make it into the competence hall of fame. Best settle for cute. At least it's only a big Band-Aid now."

"I want to go home."

"Crammer, thanks for keeping watch."

They made her ride downstairs in a wheelchair.

"You ready?"

She stared at a sexy red Porsche. "That's yours?"

"Yes, it's mine."

"How do you fit into it?"

Whatever he'd expected her to say, evidently that wasn't it, because he chuckled. "I fit," he said only and opened the door for her.

He did fit. "This is wonderful. Douglas drives a black 1990 Porsche 911. Every time I drove that dratted car, I got a speeding ticket."

"They do that to you if you don't watch it. Now, Sherlock, you aren't going home yet."

"I have to go home. I have plants to water—"

"Quinlan will water your plants. He's magic with plants. He'll probably even sing to them. Sally says she expects those African violets of his to try to get into bed with them. Don't worry about your plants."

"Where do you want me to go? A safe house?"

"No. You're coming home with me."

TWENTY-TWO

"No one followed us, and yes, I saw you looking too. Forget the baddies for the moment. What do you think of my humble abode?"

"I forgot about anybody following us the moment I stepped in here. I've never seen anything quite like it." She raised her face and splayed her fingers in front of her. "It's filled with light."

It wasn't a simple two-story open town house. There were soaring pale-beamed ceilings with huge skylights, all the walls painted a soft cream. The furnishings were beige, gold, and a dozen shades of brown. The oak floors were dotted with Persian carpets, the colors soft, mellow, old. A winding oak stairway covered with a running Tabriz carpet in multiple blues went up the stairs. There was a richly carved wooden oak railing running the perimeter of the landing.

"Dillon," she said slowly, turning to look at him for the first time since she'd stepped into this magic place, "my house is to this as a stable is to Versailles. This place is incredible; I've never seen anything like it. You have unplumbed depths. Oh dear, I'm not feeling so good."

She wasn't nauseous, thank goodness, but she did collapse into one of his big, soft, buttery brown leather chairs, close her eyes, and swallow several times. He put her feet on a matching leather hassock.

"You need to eat. No, you need to rest. But first I'll get you some water. How about some saltine crackers? My aunt Faye always fed saltines to my pregnant female relatives. What do you think?"

She cocked open an eye. She sighed and swallowed again. "Maybe a saltine wouldn't be a bad idea."

He covered her with a rich gold chenille afghan, tucking it around her feet on the leather hassock, and took off to the kitchen. She hadn't seen the kitchen. She wondered if its ceiling went up two stories like the rest of the house.

After she ate a saltine and drank some water, she said, "I think the FBI pays you too much money. You could open this place to the public and charge admission."

"I'm poor, Sherlock. I inherited this house and a bit on the side from my grandmother. She was an artist—watercolors and acrylics."

"Was she a professional? What was her name?"

"Sarah Elliott."

She stared at him, one eyebrow arched, chewing another saltine cracker. "You're kidding," she said finally. "You're telling me *the* Sarah Elliott was your grandmother?"

"Yes, my mother's mom. A great old lady. She died five years ago when she was eighty-four. I remember she told me it was time for her to go because the arthritis had gotten really bad in her hands. She couldn't hold her paintbrushes anymore. I told her that her talent wasn't in her hands, it was in her mind. I told her to stop bitching and to hold the paintbrushes between her teeth." He paused a moment, smiling toward a painting of an orchid just beginning to bloom. "I thought at first that she would slug me, then she started laughing. She had this really deep, full laugh. She lived for another year, holding the paintbrushes between her dentures." He would never forget the first time he'd seen her with that paintbrush sticking out of her mouth, smiling when she saw him, nearly dropping the brush. It had been one of the happiest moments of his life.

"And you were Sarah Elliott's favorite grandchild? That's why she left you this beautiful house in the middle of Georgetown?"

"Well, she was worried since I'd chosen the FBI and computer shenanigans for a career."

"Shenanigans? I like that. But what exactly was she worried about?" She pulled the afghan higher up on her chest. A headache was slowly building behind her left ear. She hated it. Even her arm ached where Marlin Jones had knifed her weeks before.

"She was afraid that my artistic side would stultify, what with the demands of my job and with my constant computer fiddling."

"Ah, so this place is to inspire you? Get you in touch with your artistic genes?"

"Yes. You look green, Sherlock. I think it's time you took a nap. Do you have to puke?"

"Not really. May I stay here for a while? It's very comfortable. I'm a bit on the thready side."

"No wonder," he said, and watched her head loll to the side. She was out. The chair was oversized, so he wasn't worried that she'd wake up stiff as a pretzel. He unfolded another afghan over her, one his mother had knitted, this one so soft it spilled through the fingers. He stroked it as he gently tucked it around her shoulders. She'd French-braided her hair, but it really wasn't long enough, and so red curls stuck up here and there, curled around her face. The big Band-Aid looked absurd plastered over the shaved spot on her temple, faintly pathetic really, since she was so pale.

All she needed was a little rest. She'd be fine. He lightly stroked his fingertips over her eyebrows.

He saw she had a spray of freckles over the bridge of her nose.

She didn't have any freckles anywhere else. And he'd looked. He hadn't meant to, but he had. He really liked the freckles on her nose.

No doubt about it. He was in deep trouble.

SHE woke up to the smell of garlic, onion, and tomatoes. Her mouth started watering even before her brain fully registered food. Her stomach growled. She felt fine, no more nausea.

"Good, you're awake."

"What are you cooking?"

"Penne pasta with sun-dried tomatoes, pesto, onions, and garlic. And some garlic toast. You're drooling, Sherlock. You've got an appetite, I hope."

"I could eat this afghan."

"Not that one, please. It's my favorite. The nurses told me you hadn't eaten much all day. Time to stuff yourself. First, here's a couple of pills for you to take."

She took them without asking what they were.

"No wine. How about some cider?"

He put a tray over her legs and watched her take her first bite of Savich pesto pasta. She closed her eyes as she slowly, very slowly, chewed, and chewed some more until there was nothing left in her mouth but the lingering burst of pesto and garlic. She licked her lips. Finally, she opened her eyes, stared at him for a very long time, then said, "You'll make a fantastic husband, Dillon. I've never tasted anything so delicious in my life."

"It's my mom's recipe. She taught me how to make the pasta when I was eighteen and headed off to MIT. She'd told me she'd heard the only thing they ate up there was Boston beans. She said guys and beans didn't mix well so I needed to know how to make something else. You really like it better than the pizza you devoured a couple of nights ago?"

"Goodness, it was just two nights ago, wasn't it? It seems like a decade. Actually, I like it better than anything I can ever remember eating. Do you make pizza too?"

"Sure. You want some for breakfast?"

"You cook it anytime you want, I'll consume it." They didn't say anything more for a good seven minutes. Savich's tray was on the coffee table, close enough to keep a good eye on her. She stopped halfway through and stared down at the rest of her pasta. He thought she was going to cry. "It's so good. There's no more room."

"If you get hungry later, we can heat it up."

She was fiddling with her fork, building little structures with the pasta, watching the emerging patterns with great concentration. She didn't look up as she said, "I didn't know there were men like you."

He studied his fingernails, saw a hangnail on his thumb, and frowned. He didn't look up either, said, "What does that mean?"

"Well, you live in a beautiful house, and I can't see a speck of mess or dust. In other words, you're not a pig. But that's extraneous stuff, important, sure, but not a deal breaker. You have a big heart, Dillon. And you're a great cook."

"Sherlock, I've lived alone for four years. Man cannot live by pizza at Dizzy Dan's alone. Also, I don't like squalor. There are lots of men like me. Quinlan, for example. Ask Sally, she'll say his heart is bigger than the Montana sky."

"What do you mean you lived alone for four years? You didn't live alone before that?"

"Your FBI training in action. Very good. I was married once upon a time."

"Somehow I can't see you married. You seem so self-sufficient. Are you divorced?"

"No, Claire didn't divorce me. She died of leukemia."

"I'm sorry, Dillon."

"It's been even more than four years now. I'm sorry that Claire never got to live in this wonderful house. She died three months before my grandmother."

"How long were you together?"

"Four years. She was only twenty-seven when she died. It was strange what happened. She'd read that old book by Erich Segal—*Love Story*. She was diagnosed with leukemia weeks later. There was a certain irony in that, I suppose, only I didn't recognize it for a very long time. I've watched the movie several times over the years. Claire's death wasn't serene and poignantly tragic like the young wife's death in the movie or the book, believe me. She fought with everything in her. It wasn't enough. Nothing was enough."

He hadn't spoken of Claire this much since her death. It rocked him. He rose abruptly and walked over to the fireplace, leaned his shoulders against the mantel.

"I'm sorry."

"Yes."

"Do you still miss her?"

He looked toward one of his grandmother's paintings, given to him on his graduation from MIT, an acrylic of a bent old man haggling in a French market, in the small village near Cannes where his grandmother had lived for several years back in the sixties. Then he looked at Lacey, his expression faintly puzzled. "It's odd, but you know, I can't quite picture Claire's face in my mind anymore. It's all blurry and faded, like a very old photograph. I know the pain is there, but it's soft now, far away, and I can't really grasp it. Yes, I miss her. Sometimes I'll still look up from reading a book and start to say something to her, or expect her to yell at me when I go nuts over a football play. She was an ice skater. Very good, but she never made the cut to the Olympics."

"That's how Belinda is now to me. At first I never wanted the pain to lessen, but it did anyway, without my permission. It's almost as if Belinda wanted me to let her go. When I see a photo of her now, it seems like she was someone I knew and loved in another place, another time, maybe the person who loved her was another me as well. Sometimes when I'm in a crowd, I think I hear her call out to me. She's never there, of course."

He swallowed, feeling tears of bittersweet memory he hadn't felt in years. Maybe the tears were for both of them.

Her eyes were clear and calm as she said, "You know, I'd fight too. Never would I go quietly into that good night, just sort of winking out and isn't that too bad, and wasn't she a nice person? No, I'd be kicking and yelling all the way."

He laughed, then immediately sobered. Guilt because he'd spoken about Claire, then laughed? Suddenly, he laughed again. "I would too. Thanks, Sherlock."

She smiled at him. "My head doesn't hurt anymore. One of those magic pills?"

"Yeah. Now, would you like to watch the news while I clean up the kitchen?"

"No dessert?"

"You didn't clean your plate and you're demanding dessert?"

"Dessert's for a completely different stomach compartment, and my dessert compartment is empty. I know I smelled cheesecake."

She ate his New York cheesecake while he cleaned up the dishes. She watched the national news. More trouble with North Korea. More trouble in Iraq. Then, suddenly, there was Big John Bullock, Marlin Jones's lawyer, full of bluff and good nature for the reporters, flinging out answers as they pursued him from the Boston courthouse to his huge black limousine.

"Will Marlin Jones go to trial?"

"No comment."

"Is Marlin crazy?"

"You know the ruling." He rolled his eyes and shrugged his massive shoulders.

"Will you plead him not guilty?"

"No comment."

"Is it true you told everyone that he had a bad childhood, a mother who beat him up, and an uncle who sexually abused him?"

"Public records are public records."

"But there's a confession."

"It won't be admissible. The cops and the FBI made him confess."

"But what about that FBI agent? Your client knocked her cold and took her to that warehouse to kill her. They've got everything on tape and on film."

Big John gave an explosive wave of his arms. "Pure and simple entrapment. There wasn't a thought of killing her in his mind."

"I heard he even knifed the agent."

Big John just shook his head. "No more. Just remember, it was entrapment. It was all a setup. It won't be admissible, you'll see."

And one woman newscaster said, "Oh, so you're saying if he'd killed the FBI agent then it wouldn't have been entrapment?"

Lots of laughter. And a lot of faces looking hard at Big John Bullock.

"No more questions, folks. Talk to you later."

A commercial came on for Bud Light.

She felt Savich behind her. She said quietly, "I'm going back to Boston. I've got to see Marlin Jones again."

"They won't let you see him, Sherlock."

"I've got to try." She turned slowly and looked up at him. "You see that, don't you? I've got to try. I can't just sit around waiting for some maniac to come after me again. If you tell them to let me in, they will."

"He's not the maniac who's after you now. Besides, you go talk to him again, and it could all come out that Belinda was your sister."

"No, I wouldn't tell him any of that. I wouldn't tell anyone about that."

"It's still a risk. Trust me on this: You can't begin to imagine what the media would do if they found out you were the sister of one of the murdered women and finding Marlin has been your obsession for seven years. You think the way I said it sounds hard. Wait until the media got hold of it. Big John would certainly squawk about entrapment then.

"I think a more worthwhile trip would be to San Francisco. Why don't I call the San Francisco office and have a couple of agents go talk to Douglas, your father, and your mother?"

She shook her head.

"As for Marlin, maybe, after you've rested a couple of days. Look, it's Sunday. I want you to take it easy until Tuesday. You promise?"

She stroked the gold chenille afghan. "I guess I could use a good night's sleep."

"Two days, Sherlock. I want your promise that you'll lie low for two days. Then we'll talk about it."

She was silent, and he felt a good dollop of anger.

"You're an FBI agent, Sherlock. That means you do what I tell you to do. You carry out assignments that I instruct you to carry out. You don't go surfing any wave that catches your fancy. You got that?"

"You're nearly yelling. How could I not get it?"

He stepped forward, then stopped. "I've got a nice guest room upstairs. I also packed you a suitcase. It's still in the trunk of the car. I'll take you up, then bring it in."

She didn't think about her underwear until she was standing in the Victorian bathroom with its highly polished walnut floor, its claw-feet tub, pedestal washbowl, and plush pale yellow Egyptian towels with small flowers on them. She'd stripped down to her bra and panties, turned and seen herself in the mirror and stared. He'd picked out the softest peach silk set she owned. What had he thought when he picked them out of the drawer? Without thinking, she ran her hand over her belly, the silk smooth and slithery against her palm. What had he thought? No, she wouldn't think about that.

They were just a bra and drawers, no matter how exquisite, how potentially sexy. He probably hadn't even thought a thing, just grabbed them up. She loved pretty underwear. This set she'd bought herself for her last birthday. So expensive. Soft and flimsy and wicked. She took off the bra and rubbed the smooth lace against her cheek. She hadn't worn it in months. Dillon had picked it out.

"Sherlock."

TWENTY-THREE

She quickly wrapped a towel around herself and looked around the bathroom door. He was standing in the middle of the bedroom, a suitcase in his hand.

"On the bed, please, Dillon."

He thought she looked beyond tired. He probably should have left her at the hospital, tied to the hospital bed. He looked again. He'd never before realized a towel could look so sexy wrapped around someone. "You need any help?"

That made her smile. "No, sir. I can brush my teeth without you holding my arm up."

"Then I'll see you in the morning. There's no reason for you to wake up early. Sleep in. When you wake up, holler, and I'll bring you breakfast. Don't forget, Sherlock, you promised to stay put."

She hadn't, but she nodded. "Thank you, Dillon."

"Oh, another thing. I need to run a couple of errands tomorrow morning. While I'm gone, I want you to leave the doors locked and don't open up for anybody; I don't care who anyone says they are. There's lots of food, even some pesto left over for you. You don't need to go out. You open it only for me, you got that?"

"I got that."

"Your SIG is downstairs in my office. Your Lady Colt is in the drawer by your bed. Now, let me decide what we'll do about this mess. I'll tell you tomorrow."

"What are your errands?"

He frowned at her. "Not your business. I won't be gone more than a couple of hours."

"Would you sing me a couple of lines before you go?"

"You want something down-home?"

"Yeah, real down-home."

His rich deep baritone filled the room, sounding really twangy this time. *"She ain't Rose but she ain't bad. She ain't easy, but she can be had. So am I when she whispers in my ear. She ain't Rose, and Rose ain't here."*

"Who's Rose?"

He grinned at her, gave her a salute, then left, closing her bedroom door behind him.

It was dawn when he shot straight up in his bed. He hit the floor running when another scream rent the silence.

SHE was wheezing, her arms wrapped around herself. She struggled to sit up in bed.

"Sherlock. You're awake? What's wrong?"

She was still sucking air into her lungs. It was as if someone had tried to suffocate her. He sat down beside her and pulled her against him. He began rubbing her back. "It's all right now. Did you have a nightmare?"

Slowly, so very slowly, her breathing began to steady, but it still hurt to breathe, as if someone had clouted her in the ribs. She couldn't talk yet, didn't want to talk. "That's it, relax. I'm here. Nothing's going to hurt you, nothing."

Her face was buried in his shoulder, her arms limp at her sides. Then, suddenly, she put her arms around his back and held on tight.

"Yeah, I'm real and I'm solid and I'm mean. No one's going to hurt you. It's okay."

He could feel her harsh breathing against his flesh, then she said, "Yes, I know. I'm all right now."

He tried to pull away from her but she still held on tight. He could feel her shivering. "It's really okay, Sherlock," he said again. "I'm not going anywhere. You can let go now."

"I don't think I want to. Give me a few more minutes." She tightened her grip around him.

She was still shivering. "Sorry, but I seem to have packed you the wrong kind of nightgown. You must be freezing."

"You're a man. You picked it out because it's sexy and sheer, like my underwear."

"Well, yes, I suppose you could be right. It feels really soft and nice. Sorry, but my hormones must have gotten the better of me. Listen now. Let me go, Sherlock, and lie back."

If anything, she gripped him tighter.

He laughed. "I promise you everything's okay now. Listen, you've got to let me go. Come on now."

"No."

He laughed again. He sounded like he was in pain. "Okay, tell you what. I'm cold too. Why don't we both lie back and I'll keep holding you until we both warm up."

He knew it wasn't a good idea, but he was worried about her. Truth be told, he didn't want to think about his motives. He was wearing boxer shorts, nothing else. No, this was definitely not a good idea.

He got under the covers with her, lay on his back, and pulled her against him. She settled her face on his shoulder, her hand on his bare chest. He pulled the covers as high as her ears.

She was stiff. "It's okay," he said, hugged her against him hard, then eased up. "You want to tell me about it?"

He felt her jerk, her breath fan over his skin. She was still afraid. He waited. He began to stroke her back—long, even strokes. Finally, she said,

"It was a nightmare, a stupid nightmare. Talking about Belinda probably brought it on again."

"What do you mean 'again'? You've had this dream before?"

She was quiet for a very long time. At least she wasn't shuddering anymore. He was hoping she'd keep talking. Getting her to open up was turning out to be one of his toughest assignments. And he was beginning to seriously doubt his strategy for calming her down. In the silence he noticed how uneven his own breathing had become. He began breathing deeply. "Tell me about the dream, Sherlock."

It was near dark, she was cocooned in blankets against him, she was safe, her mind wasn't on alert, and so she said, her breath warm and light against his skin, "I was the one in the warehouse, or I was with Belinda, or somehow a part of her. I don't know. But in the dream it's as if I'm the one who was there, I was the one in his maze, the one he was supposed to kill, not Belinda. Then I went through the whole thing in Boston. I truly believed it would bring me full circle, but it didn't."

"I'm not understanding all of this."

"No wonder. Sometimes I think I'm mad."

"Talk to me." He kissed the top of her head. It wasn't a good move. "Talk to me," he said again, his voice lower this time, deeper, because he was aware of her woman's body against him, aware of her scent, aware of her hair on his shoulder, tickling his cheek.

"Every time I've had the dream in the past, it's gone a bit further. He hasn't yet killed me, but this time I woke up just as he raised the knife."

He waited, held her, and waited. He could feel her tensing, feel her heart speeding up. "Say it, just say it, Sherlock. What is it?"

"I know, Dillon, I know that when that knife comes down I'll die."

It was no longer dark in the bedroom. It was a soft pearly gray, yet dark enough so that it was still two people sharing confidences in the night. He knew she had to tell him all of it now or she might never tell him. She was vulnerable now. He didn't know how much longer it would last. Probably not long.

"The dream began just after Belinda was murdered?"

"Yes. I've thought about it and thought about it over the years. It's as I said before—if I'm not the one who's there, then it's as if I'm actually following her same path, feeling the terror she felt." Her fingers clutched the hair on his chest and he jerked a bit.

"Sorry, Dillon. Oh my, you're not wearing any clothes. I'm sorry. I hadn't realized before."

"It's all right. I'm wearing boxer shorts. Ignore it. How long since you've had the nightmare?"

"Well over a year. This time I went through it all the way to the center of the maze and he was there, only it was so dark I couldn't see him, but I saw the silver arc of his knife. Then I screamed and it woke me up."

"Do you think what you did in Boston brought the dream back?"

"I don't know. Probably."

He was silent for a moment, then said very quietly, "So this was why you were so sure exactly what Marlin was going to do. It wasn't the Profilers' reports, it wasn't all the study you've done during the past seven years, all the thought you've given to it. You knew every step. Because of the dream, you knew each move to make, each move he would make."

"Yes. But it still doesn't make any sense, does it?"

"Not at this moment, but it will sooner or later."

"I have studied him. The Profilers had it right—he hates women who curse, and that's why he cuts out their tongues. What they couldn't have been certain about was that the women also bad-mouthed their husbands. But I knew it was true. That's why I had to be the bait—I knew exactly how to get him to come after me, I knew which buttons to push. He didn't have to doubt for a second that I was the best candidate for punishment around.

"But there was a difference that I realized now. In my dream, when the murderer raised the knife, it wasn't the same way that Marlin raised his knife in the center of the maze in Boston. It wasn't so vicious in the dream. It was as if he—"

"As if what?"

"As if he wasn't really serious, but I knew he was and I was scared to death. I'm sorry. That doesn't make a lick of sense."

He thought about that a moment, then said, "But in Boston, you'd put him on the defensive. He wasn't facing a terrified, helpless woman. That could make the difference." He tightened his arm around her again. "Listen to me. Even if that dream does continue on some night in the future, even if he does stick a knife into you, you can't die. It's only a dream. You've got to believe that. As real as it seems, it still isn't. It never will be."

She shuddered, then was quiet against him. Her hand had been fisted on his chest. He'd managed to ignore it, but now her hand was lower, nearly to his belly. His breathing speeded up.

"What do you think it all means?"

He thought about that a long time. It took him longer than usual because he was hard, his heart was pounding fast and strong, and he was having a good deal of difficulty concentrating. His brain no longer had any control. He wanted to pull that beautiful soft peach nightgown over her head and—

"I don't know. It's almost as if you have some connection with Belinda. No, that sounds like psychic nonsense. But regardless, there's got to be something there. Something that happened that you don't remember. Don't you think?"

Her hand was now a fist on his belly. "I don't know. What could have happened? Why wouldn't I remember? I was never hurt at that time. No trauma or head wound of any kind."

He laid his own hand over hers, pressing down until her fingers splayed over him, her palm soft and flat against his flesh. "Just relax. Everything will be all right. I know a woman who could help take you back to what really happened. There's got to be something from seven years ago, something that triggered this, something you've blocked out that's resurfacing. Yes, if anyone can get to the bottom of this, she can. But don't worry about it anymore right now."

"You really think she'll help us?"

"I really think so. Since this all started, I knew there was something you were keeping from me. You promise this is all of it?"

"Yes." The terror was gone. She didn't even care that this woman he was talking about was probably a shrink. She could see him in the dull morning light; she could feel the strength of him, the deep smooth muscles, the texture of his flesh. She didn't feel anything remotely close to terror now. She felt something she didn't think she'd ever felt in her life. The feel of him beneath her palm, beneath her fingers, it made her so alive her body was thrumming with the power of it.

"Dillon?"

"Hmmm?" He didn't know if he had any more words available to him. His brain was all in his groin, need for her was raging through him, making him shake, and it took everything in him to keep control.

"I feel really warm, but warmer in some places than in others. My shoulders feel really cool, but not other parts of me, like my chest."

She was seducing him? No, that couldn't be right. He prayed that it was, then cursed himself. He had to get out of there. He should be back in his own bedroom, with two doors closed between them. He cleared his throat. "Talking would help, but if you can't talk, then I'll go back to my own room. That would be the smart thing to do. Going back to my room this very instant would be the very smartest thing to do."

"I know." She sighed deeply, leaned her face into his shoulder, and lightly bit him. She then licked where she'd bitten. "You're probably right. But I have to tell you those warmer places have gotten even warmer. Hot nearly."

"Sherlock, stop now. This isn't good. I knew it wasn't good when I got in bed with you. Now I know it's maybe one of the stupidest things I've done in a good long while." He thought if he moved now, he was in for seven years of bad luck, because he'd crack into a billion pieces, just like a mirror.

She pulled her hand away from beneath his. He sucked in his breath in disappointment. "I'm sorry. Ollie told me you didn't ever get involved with your people."

Why had Ollie told her that? He had dated Hannah before she'd joined the Unit, but then he'd called a halt when she'd come on board. Well, yeah, at least at one time Ollie had been right. Actually, until an hour ago, he would have bet the farm on it. Maybe even ten minutes ago he would have bet a second farm on it. "No, I don't get involved with any of my people. At least I haven't. It seems that's shot now, though. And don't say you're sorry again. If you do, I'll do something unsuave."

"What?"

"Sherlock, I'm outta here. I'm not about to take advantage of a nightmare. You're vulnerable and afraid and I happen to be convenient. But you don't need me now. You're okay, right?"

She didn't say a word. He thought he'd been punched in the gut when he felt her tears against his chest.

He hauled her on top of him, and kissed her. All light, feathery kisses, and between the kisses he was saying, "Don't cry. I'm trying to be noble. It's a battle and I'm losing. You've got to help me with this. I want you a whole lot, but this isn't the way, surely. Actually, I want you whole again, I just said it wrong. Does that make any sense to you?"

Her palm smoothed over his thigh, upward. She said against his ear, "That must be what it is then."

He didn't know what she was talking about. All he was thinking about was kissing her.

"I've got to stop," he said between another round of kisses, "or if I don't, then I'm going to be on top of you and that nightgown is going to end up on the floor."

She lurched away from him, taking him completely by surprise. "Let me be plain about this," she said, smiling down at him. He wanted to weep until he realized what she was doing. "Let me be straightforward. I don't want you to have any doubts where I stand on this."

He watched her pull the gown over her head and throw it across the room. She was sitting over him, naked, staring down at him, and she looked defiant and determined.

Oddly enough, it calmed him. He wanted to put his hands on her, but no, not just yet. "What do you want me to do, Sherlock?"

"I want to make love with you, that is, if you'll make an exception for me."

"I've made an exception for you since I kicked you into the bushes in Hogan's Alley. Why do you look scared to death if you're so certain about all this?"

"I'm not scared. It's just the morning light."

"Yeah, right." But he was more than willing to believe it.

She had lovely breasts, all high and smooth and round, just the right size for his hands, his mouth, any other part of him that wanted to touch her there. And he wanted to. He couldn't remember ever wanting anything so much in his life.

Then he remembered that he'd wanted more than anything to be an FBI agent. That sure put a crimp in things.

TWENTY-FOUR

Nah. In the scheme of things, that had been very shortsighted of him. This woman sitting naked on top of him was, he figured, about the most important milestone in his life. She was what was real, what was urgent, more urgent to him than anything else in his life. He wanted her, right now, he wanted all of her. Slowly, he lifted his right hand and lightly touched his fingertips to her breast.

She drew back, as if surprised.

He cupped her breasts in his palms. Lovely, a perfect fit. Again, she flinched.

"What's wrong? You don't like me holding you?"

"Dillon, I should tell you something."

He couldn't take his eyes off her, but he did manage to drop his hands, for the moment, although his fingers itched like mad. But he knew he had to pay attention. Something wasn't quite right here. Now he was looking at her ribs, at her stomach, at the smooth expanse of thigh.

"Dillon?"

"Yes? Keep talking, I'll try to pay attention, but I can't help but look at you, Sherlock. You're really quite nice to look at."

She sucked in her breath, then blurted it out. "I've only done this once. When I was nineteen. It was in the backseat of Bobby Wellman's yellow Jaguar. It was really cramped and no fun at all. Actually it was messy and horrible, but I was philosophical about it, really. After all, it was the backseat of a car. But then, well, after Belinda's death, I couldn't stand to have any men around me."

"Once? In your whole life? In a Jaguar? Surely not an XJ6? That would be practically impossible."

"That's the truth, but Bobby managed somehow. It wasn't at all pleasant, as I said, and I didn't realize how bony he was, all knees and elbows, even his chin was sharp. I guess if anybody was looking, they'd have laughed their heads off. Bobby loved that car. I remember that the leather was really smooth and slick because he was always oiling it. Then he'd leer and say he used his mother's extra-virgin olive oil."

"What a jerk. Now that I think back on it, I did something similar to that when I was seventeen and eighteen. But you're twenty-seven, Sherlock."

"Yes. When I was nineteen, after Belinda was murdered, I shut down. I've never even been interested in another man since that time with Bobby. Not even remotely. Until you. Do you mind?"

"I don't think so. Never Douglas, then?"

"No. Once, a couple of weeks ago, he kissed me, but that's all there was to it. No, it's just you."

"Just me." That sounded incredibly fine. Actually, he thought, as he eased her down on top of him, if he didn't suffer from sensory overload first, he would give her pleasure if it killed him.

And when she cried out, her back arching, her fists on his shoulders, he knew that he was the luckiest man on the earth.

He wanted to bring her pleasure again, but he knew he simply couldn't take it any longer. "Sherlock," he said. Looking into her eyes he came into her fast and deep, his powerful arms shaking with his effort to control himself, to keep his weight off her.

When she came again he let himself go.

And it was just fine, all of it.

"LACEY, close your eyes, that's right, and lean your head back. Let your shoulders drop. Good. No, don't stiffen up. Now, breathe very deeply. Deeper, let go. Good. Yes, that's fine."

Dr. Lauren Bowers, a conservative congresswoman from Maryland and one of the best hypnotists Savich knew, raised her head and grinned at him. "People like Agent Sherlock here," she said in her normal tone of voice, "are usually the easiest to get under. Once you get past her defenses, she's an open book, all the pages ruffling in the wind; that sharp brain of hers invites you right in. Now, Savich, you've written down your questions."

She took the sheet of paper from him and scanned it. "Did I ever tell you you are really quite good? Of course you know you are; you've been trained by the best."

Dr. Bowers turned back to the young woman who looked flaccid and pale, as if something had been sapping her from deep inside for far too long a time.

"Lacey? Can you hear me?"

"Of course, Dr. Bowers. I'm not deaf."

Dr. Bowers laughed. "That's very good. Now, I want you to go back, Lacey, back to the last time you saw Belinda. Do you remember when that was?"

"It was April thirteenth, three days before Belinda was killed." Lacey suddenly lurched forward, then flopped back. She was shaking her head frantically, back and forth. "No!"

"Lacey, it's all right. Just breathe in deeply."

"I want Dillon."

Without pause, he was lightly stroking her hand. "I'm here, Sherlock. I won't leave you. Let's go back together, all right? You're going to have to do something for me. You're going to have to paint that day to me in words, so I can see it as you see it. Can you do that? Can you tell me where you are? What you see?"

Her expression changed, softening, and incredibly, she looked like a girl again, a teenager. She sighed, then smiled. "It's very sunny, crisp and cool, a low fog swirling in over and through the Golden Gate Bridge. I love days like that, watching the sailboats on the Bay, seeing the Marin Head-lands through open patches in the fog, all bleak and barren, but still green from the winter rains."

Dr. Bowers nodded to Savich to keep going. He said in his low, deep voice, "What are you doing?"

"I'm sitting out on the deck off the living room."

"Are you alone?"

"Yes. My mother's in her room napping. My father is at the courthouse. He is prosecuting a big drug case, and he wants to make sure the defense is sticking to the sitting judge's gag order. He said if they weren't, he was go-ing to skin them alive."

"Where is Belinda?"

Her mouth tightened, her eyebrows drew together. She wasn't smiling anymore. She started to shake her head, back and forth.

"It's okay," Savich said easily. "Where is Douglas?"

"I thought he was at work."

"But he wasn't?"

"No, he's here, in the house. He is with Belinda, upstairs in their suite. They're out on the balcony above me."

"What are they doing?"

For an instant she looked incredibly angry, then her face smoothed out and her voice was smooth, unworried. "They're making love."

He hadn't expected that. "You understand what's happening, right? It doesn't freak you out?"

"No. It's embarrassing. Douglas is saying lots of really dirty things."

"Then what happened?"

"Belinda cries out."

"Is she having a climax?"

"I don't think so. She rolls off the chaise onto the brick balcony. I hear her crying, then she stops."

"Why?"

"Douglas tells her that if she cries anymore someone might hear her and he won't like that at all. In fact, if she keeps whining, he just might throw her off the balcony."

"Then what happened?"

"Nothing. Belinda's quiet. After a few minutes, they make love again. Douglas tells her she'd better moan because if she doesn't moan, he won't believe she really loves him. She moans really loudly then and he says more really dirty things to her. He keeps telling her that she owes him, owes him but good."

"Do you know what he means by that?"

She shook her head.

"What happened then?"

"Douglas goes out, and I go to their bedroom and call out her name. She wants me to go away but I refuse. I walk in. She's standing in the middle of the room, naked. She grabs for her jeans and puts them in front of her. I ask her if Douglas hit her and she says no, that's ridiculous. Douglas wouldn't hit anybody. But I don't believe her. I think I saw a bruise below her ribs when she raised her hand to wave me away. But I don't leave. I can't."

"Had this happened before, to your knowledge?"

She was shaking her head. "Oh no. I'm certain. I thought they loved each other. Douglas was always so light and caressing with her, so tender. They were always laughing and hugging, kissing when they didn't think anyone was looking. But not now. She can't stand up straight. I want to kill him. But she says no, if anyone kills him it'll be her. She tells me to go away, that she doesn't want to see me, I'm a pain in the butt. She had a miscarriage that night."

"You never told anyone about this? Not even the police after she was murdered?"

She didn't say anything. She was frowning again. "She must have had a miscarriage because Douglas hit her. I'd forgotten all about that." Suddenly, her eyes opened and she stared blankly ahead of her. She looked bewildered, then frightened. He began to massage her hand, closing his fingers over hers. "It's all right, Sherlock. I'm here. Nothing bad is going to happen."

She started to cry. She stared at him, made no sound, but tears streaked down her pale cheeks. Her lips were chapped.

Dr. Bowers wiped the tears away with a Kleenex. "Now, Lacey, that's enough. I want you to wake up now. I'm going to count to three. On three, you'll be awake, smile at Dillon here, and remember everything we talked about."

On three, Sherlock, her eyes still open, came back into herself. "Why am I crying?"

She rubbed her fingers over her eyes. "Oh, I remember now. It was—"

"It's okay," Savich said, pulled her against him, and began stroking his big hands up and down her back. "You don't have to talk about it right this minute."

She grew very still in his arms. Her heart was against his. He could feel the slow, steady beat. He kissed her hair. "You okay?"

She nodded against his shoulder. "I miss Belinda so much. She was more my mother than our real mother was. Our real mother stayed in her room all the time. She loved to eat Godiva chocolates. And she was so beautiful—both Belinda and my mother. I was the plain one, but neither of them held it against me; well, maybe Belinda didn't like me so much when I was older. I don't know why.

"I know Douglas had never hit her before; she told me he hadn't. I asked her why he'd hit her this time, why he'd humiliated her."

"What'd she say?"

"She wouldn't tell me. She stood there, shaking her head. She told me I wouldn't understand. That it had nothing to do with me, that I was to forget it.

"I was confused, then angry. I told her I was nineteen, that I wasn't a kid anymore, that I could play the piano and she couldn't. She laughed at that, but it hurt her rib to laugh, so she stopped really fast. She told me to forget this, that it wasn't important in the scheme of things. She told me to go away. I went to Napa Valley with some friends. I never saw Belinda again."

"How did you know that Belinda had a miscarriage?"

"I don't remember. Someone must have told me. But no one seemed to know about it. It isn't in the medical reports or the autopsy report. I don't remember."

"But somehow you followed her through the warehouse, followed her to her death, saw everything she saw, felt her terror, felt her die."

Dr. Bowers looked as if she wanted to leap on Savich, but he shook his head. Sherlock was stiff now, withdrawn from him, but he didn't say anything more, just held her, rocking her slightly, back and forth.

"How could I have possibly been there? It doesn't make any sense. I was in St. Helena when my father called me. I left San Francisco that very day I'd spoken to Belinda."

"What did your father say when he called you?"

"He said that Belinda had been killed by the String Killer. He told me to come home. I went. There wasn't anything more."

"Did your father tell you about her miscarriage?"

"I don't remember."

"When did you have the first dream?"

"Six weeks later. He was stalking me, and I knew he was there, only there was nothing I could do about it. I couldn't get away from him. I yelled at him, 'Why are you here? What do you want?' He didn't say anything. He just kept coming closer and closer. I knew he would hit me on the head but it didn't matter. I couldn't get away from him. I felt helpless, and I was. He was right there, over me. The dream ended."

"When did you come to realize that he picked women because they cursed and put down their husbands?"

"The dreams got longer, more detailed. Later, he told me, told me over and over. That began maybe three months later. He said in my ear just after he struck me, 'You're a filthy-mouthed little bitch, aren't you? You curse and say all those bad things you shouldn't be saying and you blame your husband and call him bad names. I've got to punish you.'

"I'll never forget that, never. The dreams continued, got more and more involved until the one last night when I woke up just the instant before he killed me. I honestly don't know how much effect the profiling papers influenced me, and all my studies. There was a lot of gruesome stuff in the courses and I thought about him all the time, read all the big-city newspapers, studied other serial killers. But I don't understand where this dream came from."

"It's there, Lacey. We'll get it all out. It will take a bit of time."

"Dr. Bowers is right. It's all there in that magnificent brain of yours, somewhere. We'll unlock all of it, but no more today." He kissed the top of her head, then said in that calm unhurried voice, "Do you remember if it was Marlin Jones speaking?"

He held his breath. She was perfectly silent, perfectly still. Finally, she said in a voice muffled by his shirt, "No, I can't be certain."

Or she couldn't bear to remember. It was enough for now, more than enough. He said aloud, "I think we should pack it in for today. What do you say, Lauren? Has she had enough of the wringer?"

"I'd say so. Go watch the Redskins play ball. Eat popcorn. Forget it, at least for today. She's still recovering. She needs rest. We'll get at the rest of it in a couple of days."

TWENTY-FIVE

Jimmy Maitland chewed on an unlit cigar, wrote two words in his small black book, then looked back at Agent Sherlock, who was sitting on the edge of Savich's sofa, looking pale as death. Savich was across from her in his favorite leather chair, his legs crossed at the ankles. He was, as far as Maitland could tell, looking at Sherlock's hands. He hadn't said a word. Jimmy Maitland, who'd known Savich since he'd become a special agent eight years before, said, "I don't like any of this, Savich. I got a call from Crammer's section supervisor, telling me Sherlock here had been attacked and that Crammer had stayed outside her hospital room. I'd like to know why you didn't bother to tell me about this."

Sherlock looked up. Her eyes were very bright and very blue. "It's Sunday, sir, and we were going to watch the Redskins game. I'd prefer the San Francisco 49ers but you don't show them here unless they're playing on Monday Night Football."

Before Jimmy Maitland could leap on Sherlock, Savich said, "I wanted her to rest today, sir. I'd planned to speak to you about it tomorrow. However, it's kind of you to have driven all the way over here."

"Why is she here?"

"She was attacked in her town house. I didn't think it was safe for her to remain there."

Maitland grunted at that. "So what's going on here? It's about Marlin Jones, isn't it?"

She knew if she told him she had no idea what it was about, he'd probably have a coronary, so she said simply, "Yes, sir. I don't think our job is quite done yet. I'm going back to Boston to talk to him again. There are some loose ends, some things that don't fit together. The last thing we want is any uncertainty. Remember Richard Jewell and the Atlanta Olympic bombing? We looked like secretive, cover-your-behind boobs in that deal. We were heavy-handed, let the media in on everything before we had anything conclusive, and then we left the guy twisting in the wind. We took his reputation, his good name. Sir, we even took his Tupperware. Let me finish properly with Marlin Jones. Just this week, sir. That's all I need, just this week."

Reference to the long ago Richard Jewell fiasco made Jimmy Maitland nearly chew clean through his cigar. "You mean we could get burned in this?"

"It's possible, sir. As I said, I'll be going up on Tuesday and get everything settled. Maybe stay until the end of the week. Please, sir."

"Who tried to whack you, Agent Sherlock?"

She should have known he would home in on that. Mr. Maitland was a very tenacious man. "I don't believe it was a whack job, sir, more like a threat, but it is one of the loose ends."

"I don't like my agents getting whacked, Agent Sherlock."

"No, sir." As the whackee, she hadn't liked it either, but she didn't think Mr. Maitland would laugh if she said that. She moved even closer to the edge of her seat. Her head was aching. Her shoulder throbbed. She felt mildly light-headed. She wanted Dillon to kiss her. She saw him naked over her and choked on the sip of water she'd just taken.

"You okay, Sherlock?" Savich half rose in his chair, then at her look, he sat down again. What would he have done anyway? Hugged her? Yeah, that would have been a real treat for Maitland. He might have stroked out on the spot. Savich prayed he wouldn't ask any more questions about her attacker. He didn't have any convincing answers made up yet.

She said, "Yes, sir, I'm fine."

She was red in the face; she wouldn't look at him. She was staring at the black toes on her Bally loafers. If his boss hadn't been sitting six feet from him, he might have thrown her over his shoulder and carried her upstairs. He smiled really big at his boss. "I'll go with her to Boston. We'll get it all wrapped up."

"Marlin Jones is in jail. Who attacked Agent Sherlock? Why?"

"We don't know yet, sir, but we're betting the answer lies with Marlin Jones."

"You don't know that, Savich. It might be entirely unrelated." No one said a word. Jimmy Maitland sighed and pulled himself to his feet. He was tired. He'd had too much beer to drink the night before at a retirement party for Stu Hendricks, an old New York agent who'd been a terror in his day. Even the Mob had sent him a gold watch. He wanted to go home and watch the Redskins too. He said, "Go on to Boston, then. I see you don't want to tell me you really have no idea if Marlin Jones is connected with this attack on Sherlock. There is one thing though, Savich. The young cop who messed up and let two of the old people go in that Florida nursing home murder—he has no idea. We were right—all old people look the same to him. Oh yeah, there's been a spate of murders in South Dakota, right in Elk Point, then the guy went over the border into Iowa. Nasty business. The police chief in Sioux City is frantic."

"I'll deal with it tomorrow, sir." Savich rose and walked Jimmy Maitland to the front door.

"This place," Maitland said, taking one last sweeping look. "I remember one night when your grandmother came down those stairs wearing this lemon yellow chiffon gown. Lord, she must have been at least seventy-five then but she was a queen. You've done well with it, Savich. Your brother the artist still pissed at you that she gave you the house?"

"Not too pissed now. He got over it."

"I hate that modern stuff. Tell Ryan to go Impressionist, can't go wrong there. As for that dolphin of yours I bought, I still like it. Nice work. Oh yeah, take care of Sherlock." He paused a moment, carefully wrapped his unlit cigar in a handkerchief and slid it into his jacket pocket, then walked to the front door. He lowered his voice. "I suppose you know what you're doing." He nodded toward the living room where Sherlock was sitting still as a stone, still staring down at her shoes.

"I sure hope so."

"It's been what? Five years since Claire died?"

"Nearly."

"Sherlock is getting high marks in the Bureau."

"She deserves them. I'm glad I was bright enough to latch onto her right out of Quantico. She's a plus to the Unit."

"I imagine she's also other things to you, but that's none of my business. Make sure it remains none of my business. You take care of her, all right, Savich? And yourself. And call when you need backup."

"Yes, sir, I will." Savich paused just a moment, then turned, smiled, and strolled back into the living room, whistling.

She said immediately, "What dolphin was Mr. Maitland talking about?"

"I told you I whittled. The dolphin was a piece my sister stole out of here and put on consignment in the Lampton Gallery. She was all over me to quit the FBI when the piece sold. I didn't have the heart to tell her that my boss bought it."

"I see," she said slowly. "Do you happen, by any chance, to have any more whittled pieces around here?"

"A couple."

He was clearly uncomfortable. She smiled at him. "Have you ever carved teak?"

"Oh yes, but my favorite is maple."

"You've been doing it a long time. Some of the scars on your hands look very old."

"Since I was a kid."

She said nothing more.

IT was chilly in Boston, the sky a dull gray, the clouds fat with rain. The buildings looked old and tired, ready to fold in on themselves. Sherlock shivered in the small interrogation room, waiting for them to bring in Marlin Jones. She would have given about anything to be in San Francisco at that moment, where everything was at least two hundred years newer and the chances were really good it was sunny. Then she remembered what was in Boston and shook her head. Where was Marlin Jones? Naturally his lawyer, Big John Bullock, would be with him. She hoped she could talk him into leaving her alone with Marlin. Five minutes; that's all she wanted. Dillon was close by, speaking with the two homicide detectives in charge of Marlin Jones's case. Lots of people behind the two-way mirror would be watching and listening.

She heard leg shackles pounding hard. She looked up. Marlin stood in the doorway. He looked hard and tough, all gentle edges carved off him. He stared at her for a very long time, not moving, not saying a word. Then, finally, terrifyingly, he smiled. He lifted his shackled hands and waved his fingers at her. "Hey, Marty, how's your arm? I remember how that felt, throwing that knife at you, watching it hit you, dig right into your skin. It went in so easy. Still hurt from my knife, Marty?"

"No, Marlin, I'm just fine. How's your belly? Can you stand up straight yet? You got a big scar to show for my bullet?"

He grew utterly still. The vicious light in his eyes went out, leaving them dark and opaque. "You've still got that smart mouth on you, Marty. That wasn't an act you put on for me. You need a man to teach you how to behave."

"Be quiet, Marlin," Big John said, lightly touching his fingertips to Marlin's forearm. Marlin shook him off.

Big John never stopped looking at her. "Forget it, Agent Sherlock. There's no way I'll leave you alone with him." He sat down.

"You sit down now too," a sergeant said, shoving Marlin into a chair.

"Don't move or I'll shackle you to the arms. I'm standing right behind you, boy. Just keep your hands on the tabletop. Don't even let your hair grow, you got that?"

Marlin didn't say a word. "He's got it," said Big John. "Don't worry, Officer."

"You and I did a lot of dancing when I was last in Boston, Marlin. You remember our last tango through your little maze, don't you?"

"I thought you were so pretty, so precious, but then you started saying those bad things. But you don't even have a husband, do you?"

"Nope, no husband." She was holding her ballpoint pen, lightly tapping it on the tabletop. She said, "You never saw me before I came into the lumber store, did you, Marlin?"

"Me? See you?" He paused a moment, then smiled at her. "You think maybe that's possible?" Then he shrugged and looked down at his dirty fingernails, ignoring her.

"I don't think I ever would have dated you, Marlin. You want to know why? Even though you look pretty interesting on the outside, you look dead on the inside, really dead, like you've been dead for a very long time."

"I'll ask you that question on the witness stand, Agent Sherlock," Big John said as he laced his fingers over his stomach. "Good stuff. To think I nearly refused to let Marlin say anything to you. Do keep talking. No juror will convict this poor fellow. Talk about not responsible—"

She ignored Big John. She sat forward, laid down the pen, and clasped her hands on the table in front of her. It was Formica, scarred, stained. She wondered briefly when it had last been cleaned. "Have you ever seen me before, Marlin?"

He was staring at her. At that moment, she felt she could see his dead eyes looking through her skin down to her bones, looking at the blood pulsing through her veins. For an instant, she saw him dip his hands into her blood. She jumped, then forced herself to stillness again. He was scary with those eyes of his, but she was the one making him into more than he was. He was a monster, but she was making him into the Devil. Just let him stare. There was nothing he could do to her. He'd already tried and she'd won. She had to remember that. "Did you, Marlin? Ever see me before Boston?"

Slowly, he shook his head. "Nah. Maybe, but who cares? I still don't like you even though you're pretty. You're a real bitch, Marty."

"I'd like you to tell me something, Marlin."

"If I feel like it."

"Remember when you were in the hospital I asked you to list the women you'd killed in San Francisco?"

"I remember."

"You left out a woman named Belinda Madigan. Why? Why did you leave out her name?"

"Did she curse?"

"No. I've never cursed either, Marlin. Why did you leave out Belinda Madigan's name?"

He shrugged, his eyes narrowing now, and she saw into him, clearly. He knew he could play her, knew he was in control, knew he could string her until—until what? Had he ever seen her before? In San Francisco? Did he know who she was? Something was awfully wrong. She knew he was playing mind games with her, but she couldn't stop.

He grinned, showing all his beautiful straight white teeth. "I got trouble remembering sometimes, you know?"

"Maybe my father prosecuted you? He was an assistant D.A. in San Francisco seven years ago. His name is Corman Sherlock. Was that it, Marlin?"

"I heard about your daddy, heard he was a mean son of a bitch, heard he never cut anybody any slack, but I never met him."

"Why did you kill Belinda Madigan?"

Big John roared out of his chair, knocking it over. The sergeant grabbed his arm, his gun out. The door to the interrogation room burst open, and three armed officers rushed into the room.

Sherlock stood up slowly. "It's all right, gentlemen. Mr. Bullock got a bit riled, didn't you, sir?"

"You've got no right to ask him questions like that, Agent Sherlock. If you do it again, Marlin won't say another word, the interview will be over, and there'll never be another one. You got that?"

"I got it." She saw Dillon standing in the doorway, his expression set, his eyes hard. They'd argued about this, but in the end, he'd given in, allowing her to see Marlin alone. She knew he'd seen her desperation. He said nothing now, merely looked at her. She smiled, gave him a slight nod, then sat down again. "I'll be careful with my questions, Mr. Bullock," she said. "Please sit down, sir. If you feel like bounding around like that again, please don't. I'd just as soon not get shot by accident."

"You watch yourself, little lady."

"I'm Special Agent Sherlock," she said mildly, admiring his tactic.

He wasn't stupid. He merely shrugged and sat back in his chair, crossing his arms over his chest.

She turned to Marlin, who hadn't moved or spoken throughout the ruckus. "Did I entrap you, Marlin?"

"I don't know what that means, Marty. I just knew I had to punish you. God sent me to punish his weak vessels, to purify them, to make them whole again."

"As in to make them dead, Marlin?"

"Don't answer that, Marlin. Watch yourself, Agent Sherlock."

"Why did you leave out Belinda Madigan's name?"

He gave her that superior smile again, disregarding her question. "Belinda who? I don't know any Belinda. That's a pretty name, old-fashioned. What's she to you, Marty?"

"Do you think I look much like her, Marlin?"

"No, I think you're prettier, I always—"

Big John Bullock's mouth was working. He didn't know what was going on, but he soon would. He wasn't stupid.

Sherlock sat back in her chair and drew in a very deep breath.

Big John said finally, "Who's Belinda?"

"She was one of the women in San Francisco that Marlin had to purify. It was seven years ago. He purified seven women in San Francisco. It was seven, wasn't it, Marlin?"

He was shaking his head. "No, not seven. I don't do seven. My pa always told me that seven was a bad number, that it was even worse than thirteen. He'd always laugh at the hotels that didn't have a thirteenth floor, told me that the fools on the fourteenth floor were on the thirteenth really, but they were too stupid to realize it. No, I never did seven, did six, like my pa told me."

"All right. The six women you purified in San Francisco, all of them cursed and bad-mouthed their husbands?"

He nodded. Big John didn't say anything, which Sherlock considered a gift.

"Did you date any of them, Marlin? You're a good-looking guy, I bet it wouldn't have been hard for you to get a date with almost any woman, right?"

He nodded again. "Ladies like me," he said, and studied his thumbnail. "They tell me I'm a great lover."

She nearly gagged. "You date Belinda?"

"I told you, Marty, she wasn't one of the women I had to purify. Why are you so interested in her anyway?"

"I like the name. It's unusual."

"I don't like the name, but I like yours, Marty. It sounds kind of like a boy's name. It was close, you know? Once I thought God wanted me to purify little boys, to correct them if they'd gotten a bad start, put them on the right path, but then I realized it wasn't boys, it was girls. Women who'd had their chance to straighten out, but hadn't. Women who'd married good men and turned on them. I slept with them, you know, to make sure they were the ones to take out. All six of them cheated on their husbands, told me what jerks they were, so then I was sure they had to walk the walk through my maze."

"Marlin," Big John said very quietly, "shut up."

"Yeah, well, purify, then. That's it, purify. I wish I'd gone to college. I could have learned more pretty words like *purify*."

She was riveted. She imagined all the people listening to Marlin were riveted. She wondered what Savich was thinking.

"You didn't ask me out when I came to the hardware store."

"I know. That was weird. I slept with Hillary. She was good. She sucked me off really well. Do you know that she said bad things while I fucked her?"

She would push back. "Why didn't you try to fuck me, Marlin?"

She watched him actually flinch. None of it was an act. "Don't, Marty. That sounds so crazy coming from you. Don't talk like that, okay?"

"Okay. But why didn't you want to be intimate with me, Marlin?"

He shrugged. "You came on so strong, talking about your poor husband like you did, and then there was your foul mouth. You said all those bad words right in front of me." He sighed. "But you know, I was in a hurry. I couldn't take the time to ask you out, to see if you'd sleep with me."

"Why the hurry, Marlin?"

"Because God wanted me to go to Toronto. I couldn't until I'd taken care of six women here in Boston. Yeah, I was in a hurry. I'm sorry, Marty. Do you wish I'd made love to you?"

"I don't think so, Marlin. I do find your claim hard to believe. No one reported seeing any of the women in San Francisco with you. No one saw you with Hillary here in Boston. Why do you think that's so?"

"I knew I had to be careful. After Denver, I was real cautious, not that I could do everything I wanted to there. Only two women and then it was too dangerous. I'd been seen with both women. I had to leave. God saved me there, but he told me I had to be smarter and so I was in San Francisco. The women all loved the mystery, the secrets I shared with them, the dark little places I took them to. They all loved how I smelled, you know, like fresh-cut wood, real fresh. They all thought I was dangerous and wonderful. With two of them I didn't even have to hit them on the head. I asked if they wanted to play the maze game with me, and they couldn't wait. They both loved it. Until the end. Until I told them what I had to do. I think they forgot I was a good lover then."

"Marlin, shut up!"

TWENTY-SIX

She wondered what would happen if she threw up on the Formica table. Would anyone even know?

"But not Belinda? She wouldn't sleep with you, would she, Marlin? She thought you were sick. She thought you were disgusting. She didn't want to have anything to do with you. She wanted her husband, nobody else, only her husband."

His hands were fists. "I don't know what you're talking about."

The sergeant was away from the wall in an instant, gun up.

Sherlock shook her head. "You know what I'm talking about. God wouldn't want you to lie. Tell the truth. Belinda didn't want you. She probably laughed at you, told you you were pathetic. That's why you ki—purified her, isn't it? She didn't want you, plain and simple. She didn't curse. She didn't bad-mouth her husband. She didn't fit the mold of the other women. You know she didn't. Why, Marlin, why did you kill her?"

"This is over," said Big John, rising slowly from his chair, one beefy hand on Marlin's shoulder. "Don't say anything, Marlin, nothing more for these folks."

"What makes you believe I didn't have Belinda?" Marlin said in a low whisper, leaning toward her. "You really think a woman could laugh at me? Turn me down? No way, Marty. Yeah, I had Belinda. I don't want you, Marty. You're cynical. You probably hate men, you probably don't ever—"

"Marlin, dammit, let it go. Listen, you moron. I told you to shut up."

It took only an instant of time, just the barest instant, for the violence to erupt. Marlin raised his chained hands, clasped them together into fists, and brought them down with all his strength on John Bullock's left temple. Big John groaned very softly in his throat and slumped back into his chair, his head falling forward to hit the Formica tabletop. He was out. A trickle of blood snaked out of his right nostril.

The sergeant was all over Marlin. The door burst open again, and three cops surged in. She wondered why they didn't shoot him. It would save the taxpayers millions of dollars. But they didn't shoot him. She wanted to yell at them that he was filth, that he'd probably go to an institution and maybe get out in twenty years and begin it all again. She managed to keep her rage to herself.

"They'd send me to jail for sure if I did," Dillon said close to her ear. "Sorry but I can't, Sherlock." It was then she realized that she'd whispered aloud what she was thinking. Only Dillon had heard her, thank God. No one was paying any attention to her at all. They were all over Marlin, dragging him out of the room. She heard someone yell out, "Get an ambulance in here! The guy cracked his own lawyer's head!"

Marlin turned very slightly and smiled back at her. "She was good, Marty, really good. That punk husband of hers was a monster, not me. I cared about them, cared about their souls. But he was real bad. She wanted me, Marty, not the other way around, I swear. You know something? I miss Belinda."

And then he was gone, surrounded by cops, shuffling forward, the leg shackles clanking against the linoleum of the hallway.

"What is going on here?" Savich said, his hand tightly around her wrist.

"Nothing makes any sense, nothing." They walked out of the station. She remained silent for three blocks, then stopped and said, "He was playing me, Dillon. The minute I said Belinda's name, he began his game. You heard all those questions I asked. I was trying to learn the truth, but now things are muddier than ever."

"That's why Big John let you go on and on with Marlin with just a bit of his famous bluster. He wanted to muddy the waters."

"He succeeded. Do you think Marlin was intimate with Belinda?"

Savich frowned at her, then shook his head.

THAT evening, on Newbury Street, coming out of Fien Nang Mandarin Restaurant with its red paper lanterns swinging in the evening breeze, Savich was speaking to Sherlock, his hand raised to flag down a taxi. He never saw the car that came around the corner, skidding loudly on two tires, heading right toward them, until it was too late.

He threw her to the sidewalk just before the car struck him, flinging him onto the hood of an old Buick Riviera.

* * *

"NO doctor, Sherlock. No hospital, no paramedics. Forget it. We can't afford the time. No, it's not the time. Imagine the police reports, the investigation, the questions, it would take too long. No doctor."

He was right, but she worried. He was holding his arm, limping slightly. She knew every step hurt him. The elevator door opened onto their floor. He leaned on her heavily. "No, don't say anything. I'm all right. I've had enough injuries over my thirty-three years to know when it's serious and when I'm banged up. You promise me you're okay? I threw you pretty hard."

"I'm a little bruised on my left side, nothing more."

She unlocked the hotel room door. "If I'd been the one struck by the car, what would you have done?"

He stopped in the middle of the room. He had the audacity to grin at her. "You'd be strapped to a gurney on your way to the Emergency Room."

She shut the door very quietly and locked it. She slid the chain home.

"I see. But you, the big he-man, can take anything anybody dishes out."

"Yep, that's about the size of it. Now, I need to make a phone call."

She got ice and wrapped it in a towel. He was on the phone when she handed it to him. He lifted his shirt and pressed it against his ribs. So, it was his ribs, not his arm.

"Quinlan? I need your help. Yeah, some ugly-ass trouble here in Boston. Can Sherlock and I visit your parents' cabin on Louise Lynn Lake for a couple of days? No, I'm not at my best at the moment. A car got me. I need a few days to get myself together again. No, nothing to Maitland. He's not expecting anything in any case. That gives me a little leeway. Yeah, all right."

He hung up the phone and lay back, closing his eyes. "That feels good. Thank you."

"Take the aspirin." She handed him three pills and a glass of water. He took the pills. "What's this cabin on Louise Lynn Lake?"

"It's a nice lake in Maryland where Quinlan's parents have a small home. You and I are driving there tomorrow. Rent us a nice big comfortable car, Sherlock. I'd like to get out of here early tomorrow morning."

"The wounded animal going to his lair?"

"That's about it. Quinlan's lair. I need to get one for myself. This hurts, but it's not serious." He opened his eyes and looked at her standing beside the bed, her legs spread, her hands on her hips. She didn't look happy.

"You look pretty bad. I saw you limping. You sprain your ankle?"

He tried to grin at her, but it hurt. "Only a minor sprain. No big deal. Hey, I didn't hurt my pretty face, did I?"

"Yes, a bit. Lie there and I'll clean you up. Are all your teeth still in there?"

"Teeth are fine." He watched her walk to the bathroom. She was stiff, holding on to her control. He was grateful for that. He'd already had a strip taken off him. He didn't need her to take off another one. He heard the water running. She would bring him a cold compress for his aching head. The ice sure felt good over his ribs.

She was taking this well. He sighed with relief and closed his eyes again. After she cleaned off his face and wrapped ice in a towel around his ankle, she stood there, looking down at him. "I hope you know what you're doing. If you don't, I'm going to hurt you."

He gave her a big smile. He slept until two o'clock in the morning. She was there with three more aspirin.

At six o'clock A.M. they'd checked out of the hotel and were on the road fifteen minutes later in a good-sized Ford. Savich's seat was tilted back as far as it would go. His eyes were closed. He looked bruised, wrung out. Sherlock gave him a long look before turning off onto I-95 South. It would take them a good six to eight hours to get to Maryland. At least they had a full bottle of aspirin and blankets.

Louise Lynn Lake was in southern Maryland. It took them nine hours to get there. She was so wired from all the coffee she'd drunk, she couldn't keep still. She was tapping her foot on the accelerator, drumming her fingers on the steering wheel. She was too nervous to listen to music or talk radio. "You're feeling all right, Dillon? You promise?"

"Yes. Stop worrying. You want me to drive?"

She gave him a look. He closed his eyes and leaned back against the seat. Thirty minutes later, he was tapping his own fingers and looking for landmarks. He said, "Turn here. Yes, this is it. Around this bend. We're here. You did really well, Sherlock. Nice place, huh?"

"There's someone already here," she said. "Damn, we'll have to keep going. I don't want to take any chances, not with you in such bad shape. If there's more than two of them, I might not be able to protect you."

He arched a black eyebrow at that. "I could maybe take on one, Sherlock, if he was a little guy."

"No, we'll keep going. I'll drop you off at a motel and then come back and check things out."

"No, wait, Sherlock, it's Quinlan."

She watched James Quinlan come loping toward the car. She rolled down the window, giving him a big smile.

"I am so glad it's you. We've had enough bad guys for a while."

"Nope, I'm a hero, ask my wife. Hey, Savich looks like he lost the fight, Sherlock. Did he get fresh with you? Did you have to pound him?"

"No, he was hit by a car. I'll smash him when he's feeling better. No doctors. He's a fool. Help me get him inside."

Sally Quinlan met them at the door. Behind her was a black man dressed all in Calvin Klein. He was huge, ugly as sin, and had a Marine haircut.

"Oh, this is Marvin the bouncer from Ms. Lily's Bonhomie Club. He didn't think James could take care of all the possible trouble and insisted on coming. Marvin, this is Lacey Sherlock."

"She a nice chicky?"

"I think so."

"She's got a weird name."

"Lacey isn't at all weird." Where had the attempt at humor come from?

"Hey, maybe you're not a bad chicky after all. Oh my God. You're looking beyond ripe, Savich. Ms. Lily wondered if you and Quinlan were tough enough to do this stuff." Marvin was out the door in that moment, racing down the porch steps. Lacey saw him, a giant of a man, help Dillon into the weathered porched house.

"You do look like dirt-shit, boy," Marvin told Savich as he laid him down on the long sofa. "Don't you move now. Let Marvin check out those ribs of yours. Good thing I had nine brothers. I've bandaged some ribs in my day. But you know, I don't bandage anymore. I've stayed up with med- ical strides. Nope, don't do anything now except to tell you to take it easy. They're not broken, Savich, but you sure got some cracks in there. My third brother, Tomalas, now that boy had broken ribs. We used to tell him jokes just to see him laugh and groan at the same time."

Savich's eyes were closed. He didn't say a word, just listened quietly to Marvin's rich, low voice drawling out his words until you thought the sen- tence would never end. He suffered Marvin, who appeared to be surpris- ingly gentle, his big black hands moving slowly and expertly over Savich's chest.

"Nothing's broken, Marvin. I'm bruised, that's all. I'm glad you're here. Is Ms. Lily all right?"

"Ms. Lily is always all right. She won five hundred dollars last night in a poker game off this black smart-ass goon from Cleveland. Yeah, she's real happy. You look like Ms. Lily got pissed at you and smacked you but good. She smacked me once and I was laid out like you are now. Took me damned near three days to pull myself together again."

"Ms. Lily owns the Bonhomie Club," Sally said to Sherlock. "I've got a painkiller for him, Marvin. What do you think?"

Savich said without opening his eyes, "Sally, give me whatever you've got and I'll kill dragons for you."

"My hero," Sally Quinlan said and disappeared into the small kitchen.

"Don't be so loose with that," Quinlan called after her. "I'm your main hero, remember?"

Sherlock watched Marvin's big hands move over Savich's body, pulling slightly here and there, kneading, pressing. Finally, he rose, crossed his arms over his chest, and said, "You'll live, boy, but I don't like this at all. You and Quinlan, you two shouldn't have such dangerous day jobs. You boys are just too soft, too trusting. There are lots of mean fuckers out there. I should know, I bounce them out of the club nearly every night."

"It was a brown Ford Taurus, license number 429JRD, a 2001, I think."

Savich opened his eyes at that. "You sure, Sherlock? All I got was the RD. Hey, that's really good. Why didn't you tell me before?"

"You jerk, I was worried about you."

"I'll run it now," Quinlan said and went to the phone. Sally returned with a pill and a glass of water.

Ten minutes later, Savich's eyes were shut. Sally covered him with a blanket. Marvin took off his shoes.

"He's got nice feet," Sally said.

"What he's got is big feet," Marvin said. "Look at these suckers, Chicky, they're size twelve."

Both women looked up. Marvin looked from one to the other. "Well, ain't this a kick? I've never had this problem before."

Sally said to Sherlock, "Marvin calls every female Chicky, except for Ms. Lily of course. How about your mother, Marvin?"

"She's the Big Chicky. Nobody screws with the Big Chicky, even my dad. You can go to Sally now, but she's still Chicky."

"I don't mind at all."

"Chicky Savich," Dillon said slowly, relishing the sound. "Talk about strange. I don't know if I can deal with that. But you know, it's not as bad as Chicky Sherlock."

"We thought you were asleep. How do you feel, Dillon?" Sherlock leaned over him, her fingertips lightly touching his dark eyebrows, the bruise on his cheek.

"Alive."

"Yes, that's good. You're kind of out of it, aren't you, Dillon?"

"No, not at all. I hurt enough still to keep me out of the ether."

"You don't know what you just said, do you?"

"Yeah, I know what I just said. It does sound strange, don't you agree?"

"I think," Sherlock said very slowly, staring down at the man who'd become more important to her than anything or anyone in her life, "that I could get used to it, until Marvin gets to know me well enough to call me Sherlock."

"Good," Savich said. "I hadn't really meant to bring it up here, at this particular moment. It lacks suavity and timing. It just came out of my mouth. How about I try it again later, when three people aren't staring at us?"

"Yes, I think that would be an excellent idea."

His head fell to the side. He was out cold this time.

"Chicky Sherlock Savich," Marvin said slowly. "Yeah, that's so funny it would make Fuzz's mouth split from laughing so hard."

"I prefer Sherlock Savich," Sally said. "That's unforgettable. With a name like that maybe they'd make you director one day."

Some minutes later, Quinlan said from across the room as he dropped his phone back in his shirt pocket, "The car was rented to a Marlin Jones. Paid for in cash, but he presented them with a credit card with his name on it, and a driver's license."

"I don't like this," Sherlock said, her face washed of color. "I really don't like this at all. But wait, the picture couldn't have matched, could it?"

James Quinlan said, "The guy said the picture was real fuzzy, but since the name was the same, the guy's age was about right, what the hell? So who knows?"

"Jones. Marlin Jones? Hey, that's the serial killer, isn't it?" Marvin the Bouncer asked as he set an old issue of the Economist magazine back down on the coffee table. "I thought he was in the can, in Boston."

"He is," Sherlock said. "I spoke to him yesterday. He's in the can, probably in maximum security. He brought his fists down on his lawyer's temple. Knocked him out cold. Actually, as we were driving here, the news reported the first thing Big John Bullock said when he regained consciousness was, 'I'm going to get that little bastard off so I can kill him.' Then he passed out again. The doctors think it's a concussion."

"The guy's a real comedian," Quinlan said.

"I don't think he was concussed," Sherlock said. "I know Big John meant every word."

"I was hoping it would be one less lawyer," Sally said from the kitchen. "James, come out and help me. Everyone needs to have some dinner. It's nearly five o'clock."

"I'll go catch us some bass," Marvin said. "Where's the rods, Quinlan?"

"Why'd the guy hit his lawyer?" Sally asked Sherlock, looking up from the carrot she was alternately cutting and eating.

"He told him to shut the fuck up because he'd admitted to me that he'd killed the women in San Francisco. Marlin went nuts. Evidently he doesn't like bad language from men either. I wish the cops had shot him then and there." She sighed, her hands clasped between her knees. She rose slowly. "I guess I'd better call Mr. Maitland. I'm afraid he's going to be really upset about this."

SAVICH was mending. All he had to do was lie quietly, not breathe deeply, keep his eyes either closed or focused on Sherlock, and he'd be fine. Sherlock Savich. Boy, that had a real ring to it. He couldn't wait to get her alone and kiss her. Then he could ask her to marry him again, only this time it would be properly done.

The pain in his ribs and hip and ankle came in waves, not really big surfing kind of waves, just small ones that were rhythmic, steady, and relentless.

He felt her hand on his cheek. "I have another pain pill for you. Open up."

He did. Soon the pain was nothing but an annoying throb that didn't even touch his mind. "Good stuff," he said.

"The best," Quinlan said. "It's from our favorite doctor."

"Ah, Dr. Ned Breaker."

"He said give him a call if you need him to drive up and check you out."

"Let's call him," Sally said. "Savich, you really don't look so hot."

"I'm feeling better by the minute," Savich said. "Really. I'm not stupid. Everything's okay."

"You ready for something to eat? Marvin caught three bass, good-size suckers. I gutted them and Sally fried them."

Savich thought he'd puke right there. The thought of anything fried went right to his belly and turned nasty.

"No, I don't think so," said, lightly cupping his cheek in her hand. "We'll have the good stuff and Dillon here can have some soup. Got any chicken noodle, Sally?"

Sherlock didn't want to leave him alone. She slept beside the sofa on three blankets, close enough to hear him breathing.

THE next morning, she came into the house to see Dillon standing at the small bar that separated the kitchen from the living room. He was drinking a cup of tea. He needed to shave.

"You're not dead."

He grinned at her over the rim of his cup. "Nope, but I appreciate you sleeping guard beside me all night. You know what might be fun, Sherlock? We could strip naked and have a bruise-off contest. I might be catching up with you. How's your left side?"

"Hardly any bruising at all. How could Marlin Jones have rented the car, Dillon?"

"Obviously someone else did, using his name. You and I are going to California tomorrow, okay?"

"No, not until you're back to your full strength. I'm not going to take any more chances with you."

"That sounds nice."

She walked to him, lightly kissed his mouth, then pulled up his shirt. "I'll be objective. Now, I think my ribs looked more like the Italian flag than yours do." He felt her fingers on his flesh, light, so light, not hurting him at all, skimming over his flesh, and to his own blessed wonder, he got hard. He didn't mean to say it, but the words just came right out of his mouth. "Do you think you could go a bit lower?"

Her fingers stopped cold. Then, she laughed. "Dillon, I'm going to fly us First Class, all right?"

"Yeah, that's fine. I'll be okay by day after tomorrow, I swear it. We'll have a day to make some plans with Quinlan." He sucked in his breath and stared at her.

Her fingers had gone beneath the waistband of his slacks, way beneath. He didn't know about this, didn't know if he was going to start crying or shouting or moaning, and not from any pain in his ribs. He was going to die, lose it, be premature, the whole thing. But then it was academic. Marvin came into the house, singing at the top of his lungs.

"Sorry," Sherlock said and kissed his ear.

He sighed deeply. "Do you think maybe I did something really bad in a former lifetime?"

"You're breathing awfully hard, Dillon."

"Hey, Chicky, what'd you do to our boy here?"

"I was just checking him out. Just like you did, Marvin."

"I doubt that, Chicky. I surely doubt that. More like you tortured the poor man but good."

TWENTY-SEVEN

Sherlock stared at the doorbell for a long time before she rang it. Savich didn't say a word, just looked beyond the Art Deco three-story mansion to the incredible view of Alcatraz, the Golden Gate, and the stark Marin Headlands in the distance. The day was sunny and cool, so clear and vivid it made your eyes sting. There were dozens of sailboats on the Bay. The air was crisp and sharp.

A middle-aged black woman, plump, very pretty, her eyes bright with intelligence, opened the door, gasped, and grabbed Sherlock into her arms. "My baby, it's you, it's really you. Thank God you're home. They've been telling me for weeks that you'd come home and now you're here. But I'd begun to believe that you'd finally turned your back."

Sherlock hugged her back. Isabelle had been more her mother than the woman upstairs in her elegant bedroom had ever been. She'd been the Sherlock housekeeper and cook since before Lacey was born. "It's good to see you, Isabelle. You all right? Your kids okay?"

Sherlock drew back and looked carefully at the fine-boned face, a beloved face that radiated warmth and humor.

"Things are fine with my family, but they aren't too good here, Lacey, no, not too good at all. Your daddy's all quiet and keeps to himself. Your mama never comes out of her room now, stays there and looks at those ridiculous talk shows, best I can tell. She says she wants to write a book and send it to Oprah so Oprah will recommend it and your mama will become really rich and leave your papa. Hey, who's this guy with you?"

"This is Agent Dillon Savich. He's also with the FBI, and my boss.

Dillon, this is Isabelle Tanner. She's the one who told me how wicked boys were just after my sixteenth birthday. She's the one who told me to keep out of Bobby Wellman's Jaguar."

"You should have listened to her."

"Oh, Lordie. You mean you let that boy crawl all over you in that little Jaguar, Lacey? Oh goodness, I thought I'd won that one."

Savich shook her hand. "Ms. Isabelle, I promise you that Sherlock here hasn't gotten into any more cars since the Jaguar. You taught her well."

"You call her Sherlock," said Isabelle, clasping her arms beneath her ample breasts. "That sounds funny, but cute too. Well, come on in. I'll get you some fine tea and some scones that just came out of the oven."

"Who is it, Isabelle?"

Isabelle's face grew very still. Slowly, she turned and called out, "It's your daughter, Mrs. Sherlock."

"No, Belinda's dead. Don't do that to me, Isabelle. You're cruel."

"It's Miss Lacey, not Belinda."

"Lacey? Oh. She said she was coming back but I didn't believe her."

Isabelle said quickly, "Don't look like that, Lacey. It's just a bad day for her, that's all. Besides, you haven't been around in a long time."

"Neither has Belinda."

Isabelle waved away her words. "Come into the living room, honey." She turned to the stairs that wound up to the second-floor landing. "Mrs. Sherlock, will you be coming down?"

"Naturally. I'll be there in a moment. I must brush my teeth first."

The house looked like a museum, Savich thought, staring around the living room. Everything was pristine, thanks probably to Isabelle, but stiff and formal and colder than a Minnesota night. "No one ever sits in here," Sherlock said to him. "Goodness, it's uninviting, isn't it? And stultifying. I'd forgotten how bad it was. Why don't we go into my father's study instead. That's where I always used to hang out."

Judge Sherlock's study was a masculine stronghold that was also warm, lived-in, and cluttered, stacks of magazines and books, both paperback and hardcover, on every surface. The furniture was severe—heavy, dark brown leather—but the look was mitigated by warm-toned afghans thrown everywhere. There were lots of ferns in front of the wide bay window that looked out onto the Bay in the distance. There was a telescope aimed toward Tiburon. This wasn't at all what he'd expected. What he had expected, he wasn't certain, but it wasn't this warm, very human room that had obviously been nurtured and loved and lived in. Savich took a deep breath. "What a wonderful room."

"Yes, it is." She pulled away and walked to the bay windows. "This is the most beautiful view from any place in San Francisco." She broke off to smile at Isabelle who was carrying a well-shined silver tray. "Oh, Isabelle, those scones smell delicious. It's been too long."

Savich had a mouthful of scone with a dab of clotted cream on top when the door opened and one of the most beautiful women he'd ever seen in his life walked in with all the grace of a born princess. She was, pure and simply, a stunner, as his father used to say about a knockout woman. She also didn't look a thing like Sherlock. Where Sherlock had lovely curly red hair, her mother had blond hair as soft and smooth and rich as pale silk. Sherlock's eyes were a warm blue; her mother's, a brilliant green. Sherlock wasn't tall, but she wasn't fragile, fine-boned, not more than five foot three inches tall, like her mother. Sherlock was wearing a dark blue wool suit with a cream turtleneck sweater, all business. Her mother was wearing a soft peach silk dress, her glorious hair pulled back and held with a gold clip at the nape of her neck. There was nothing overtly expensive about her jewelry or clothing, but she looked well-bred, rich, and used to it. There were very few lines on her face. She had to be in her late fifties, but Savich would have said forty-five if he hadn't known that she'd had a daughter who'd be in her late thirties now, if she hadn't been murdered.

"So you're Dillon Savich," Mrs. Sherlock said, not moving into the room. "You're the man who spoke to her father on the phone after I said to Lacey that he'd tried to run me down with his BMW."

"Yes, ma'am." He walked to her and extended his hand. "I'm Dillon Savich. Like your daughter, I'm with the FBI."

Finally, after so long that Sherlock thought she'd die from not breathing, her mother took Dillon's hand.

"You're too good-looking," Mrs. Sherlock said, peering up at him for the longest time. "I've never trusted good-looking men. Her father is good-looking and look what's come of that. Also I imagine that you are built splendidly. Are you sleeping with my daughter?"

Savich said in that smooth interview voice of his, "Mrs. Sherlock, won't you have a cup of tea? It's rich; Indian, I believe. As for the scones, I'm certain you'll enjoy those. They're delicious. Isabelle is a wonderful cook. You're very fortunate to have her."

"Hello, Mother."

"I wish you hadn't come, Lacey, but your father will be pleased." Her voice was plaintive, slightly reproachful, but her beautiful face was expressionless. Did she never show anger, joy? Anything to change the look of hers?

"I thought you wanted me to come home."

"I changed my mind. Things aren't right here, just not right. But now that you're here, I suppose you'll insist on remaining."

"For a few days, Mother. Would you mind if Dillon stayed here as well?"

"He's too handsome," Mrs. Sherlock said, "but again I suppose I have no choice. There are at least four empty bedrooms upstairs. He can have one of them. I hope you're not sleeping with him, Lacey. There are so many diseases, and men carry all of them, did you know that? It's been proven now at least, but I always knew it. That's why I stopped sleeping with your father. I didn't want him to give me any of those horrible diseases."

"A cup of tea, ma'am?"

Mrs. Sherlock took the fine china saucer from Savich and sat down on the very edge of one of her husband's rich brown leather chairs. She looked around her. "I hate this room," she said, then sipped at her tea. "I always have. It's the living room I love. I decorated the living room, did Lacey tell you, Mr. Savich?"

Savich felt as though he'd fallen down the rabbit hole; but Sherlock just looked tired. She looked used to this. It came to him then that Mrs. Sherlock was acting a great deal like his great-aunt Mimi—in short, outrageous. She always made it known that she was fragile, whatever that meant, so she could get away with saying whatever she wanted, so that she could be the center of attention. Savich didn't doubt that Mrs. Sherlock did suffer from some mental illness, but how much was real and how much was of her own creation?

"I forgot to tell him, Mother," she said. "But as rooms go, this one really isn't that bad. There are so many books."

"I dislike clutter. It's the sign of a chaotic mind. Your father is going to sell that BMW of his. I believe he's going to buy a Mercedes. What model, I don't know. If it's a big car, I'll have to be really careful not to be outside when he's driving. But, you know, if you're standing in the driveway, those tall bushes make it impossible to see if someone is coming. That's how he nearly got me last time."

"Mother, when did Dad try to run you down? Was it recently?"

"Oh no, it was some time last spring." She paused, sipped some more tea, and frowned down at the beautiful Tabriz carpet beneath her feet. It was a frown, but it wasn't obvious. There were no frown lines on that perfect forehead. She waved a smooth white hand. "Maybe it was this past summer. It's hard to remember. But once I remember things, they stay with me."

"Yes, Mother, I know."

Savich said, "Perhaps your husband will buy a little Mercedes, ma'am."

"Yes, or perhaps a Porsche," Mrs. Sherlock said, looking thoughtfully at Savich.

"I own one. They are very nice. I've never tried to run anybody down in my 911. It could hurt the car. I'd get caught. No, a Porsche is a good choice."

"Actually, I've been thinking about a Porsche."

Savich was on his feet in an instant to face a very handsome middle-aged aristocrat standing in the doorway. He had a fine head of silver hair, Sherlock's soft blue eyes, beautiful, wide, luminous eyes, and was taller than he was and as lean as a runner. He was looking at his wife, and the look reflected both irritation and amusement, in about equal amounts.

"I'm Judge Sherlock. Hello, Lacey."

She was on her feet as well, walking slowly to her father. She held out her hands to him. "Hello, Dad. We just got here. Do you mind if we stay with you for a while?"

"Not at all. We've plenty of room. It will be nice to have different voices to listen to. My dear," he continued to his wife as he walked to the beautiful woman who was sitting there staring at him, her eyes large and intent. "How was your day?"

"I want to know if she's sleeping with him, Corman, but she wouldn't tell me. He's too good-looking and you know how I feel about that. Why, look at what Douglas did, just because he's a man and doesn't have any sense. He married that tramp and Belinda barely in her grave."

"Belinda's been dead for seven years, Evelyn. It was time for Douglas to marry again." He shot Savich a quick look from the corner of his eye that said, *Look, isn't she a fool?* Savich drew back.

"That's a good point," Evelyn Sherlock said, her beautiful expressionless face turned away from her husband. "But they shouldn't be married. Can't you get Douglas to divorce her, Corman?"

"No, I don't do that sort of thing, you know that. Or don't you remember?"

"When I remember something I never forget it. That's what I was telling Lacey and Mr. Savich before you came in. Will you buy a Porsche so I'll be safe?"

"Perhaps I will, Evelyn, perhaps I will. Mr. Savich spoke about a classic 911. I like that car. Lacey, may I have a cup of tea, please? Mr. Savich, rather Agent Savich, I'm delighted to finally meet you. I understand you're my daughter's boss at the FBI."

"Yes, sir. I head up the new Criminal Apprehension Unit."

"I think your approach is a fine idea. Why not use technology to predict what psychopaths will do? Why are you here with her in San Francisco?"

"We're working on the Marlin Jones case."

"Why here? Marlin Jones is in Boston."

"That's true, but there are loose ends. We're here to check things out."

"I see." Judge Corman Sherlock sat down in the beautiful rosewood chair behind his rosewood desk. The desk was piled with books and magazines. There were at least a dozen pens scattered haphazardly over the surface as well as a telephone and computer. It was a working place for him, Dillon realized. Not just pleasure in here. The man spent hours here working.

"I heard on the news that Marlin Jones hit his own lawyer, knocked him out. Everyone in the courthouse was talking about it. You were there, weren't you, Lacey?"

She nodded. "Yes, we both were. I believe everyone was cheering because there would be one less lawyer—" She broke off and smiled at her father. "Forgive me, but I never think of you as a lawyer since you're a judge and a former prosecutor. You put criminals away, not defend them."

"True enough. Big John Bullock has quite a reputation. Your Marlin might escape any punishment at all when he goes to trial. Big John is magic with juries. If this Marlin character doesn't already have a pitiful, tragic childhood, then Big John will manufacture one for him and the jury might believe everything he says."

"People aren't stupid, Dad. They can look at Marlin Jones and see he's a psychopath. He's crazy but he's not insane. He knows exactly what he's doing and he has no remorse, no conscience. He's admitted to all the killings. Besides, even if he's acquitted in Boston, he'll be sent here to be tried. He also admitted he'd murdered two women in Denver. He'll go down. In one of those places, he has to go down."

"Ah, Lacey, people can be swayed, they can be manipulated, they can see gray when there's nothing really but black. I've seen it happen again and again. Juries will see what they want to see—if they want to free a defendant, no matter what the evidence, they'll do it. It's that simple, and many times that tragic."

"I hope Marlin Jones does come to California to stand trial. At least here we've got the death penalty."

"If he got the death penalty, I think the electric chair would be too easy and quick. I think all the families of the women he killed should be able to kill him, over and over."

"That's very unliberal of you, Lacey."

"Why? It's only right. It's justice."

"It's vengeance."

"Yes, it is. What's wrong with that?"

"Not a thing. Now, my dear child, Agent Savich probably wonders if you and I go on and on like this. Let's take a short time out. Tell me about these loose ends you're here to tie up."

Evelyn Sherlock smiled, but again, it seemed to Savich that her face still remained without expression. It was as if she'd trained herself not to move any muscles in her face that would ruin the perfect mask. She said, "They probably think you murdered Belinda, Corman, isn't that right, Agent Savich?"

Now that was a kicker. It was Savich's turn not to change expression. He said, bland as chicken broth, "Actually, no, ma'am."

"Well, you should. I guess you're not as smart as you are handsome. He tried to run me down. No reason why he wouldn't kill Belinda. He didn't like her, hated her, in fact, since her father is in San Quentin. He said Belinda would be as crazy as her father and me. That's an awful thing to say, isn't it, Agent Savich?"

"It's certainly not what I'd say, Mrs. Sherlock, but everyone is different. Now," he continued, turning back to Judge Sherlock, "I wonder, sir, if you would mind telling us if you ever had Marlin Jones in your courtroom."

"No."

"You're very certain?"

"Yes, naturally. I remember every man and woman who's ever stood before my bench. Marlin Jones wasn't one of them."

"Before you became a judge, did you ever prosecute him?"

"I would have remembered, Mr. Savich. The answer is still no."

Savich opened his briefcase and pulled out a black-and-white five-by-seven photo. "You've never seen this man?"

He handed Judge Sherlock Marlin's photograph, taken the previous week.

"No, I've never seen him in my courtroom. It's Marlin Jones, of course. Lacey, you're right. He does look like a classic psychopath, which is to say, he looks perfectly normal."

Savich handed him another photo.

"I'll be damned. It's Marlin Jones but you've doctored this photo, haven't you?"

"The FBI labs are the very best. I asked them to render me photos with various disguises a man could use effectively."

"It's a mustache, the sideburns longer, the hair combed over as if the guy wants to cover a bald spot—it's amazing. Sorry, but I've never seen this man either."

Savich gave him a third photograph.

Judge Sherlock sucked in his breath. "I don't believe this. I prosecuted this guy years ago, but I remember him. He was a hippie sort, up on marijuana charges. Look at that bushy beard and the thick bottle-cap glasses. Hunched shoulders, but he was still tall, as tall as I am. I remember that he looked at me as if he wanted to spit on me. What was his name, anyway?"

He fell silent, staring down at the photo, tapping his fingers on the arm of the leather chair. Then he sighed and said, "I'll have to look it up. I guess I'm getting old. No, wait a minute. It was a weird name. Erasmus. That's it. His name was Erasmus something, I don't remember his last name, but it was a common name. It was at least fifteen years ago. I managed to plea-bargain him into three years even though it was his first offense. He himself was so offensive I didn't even hesitate to push the public defender. He had no respect. Yes, it was three years. This is Marlin Jones?"

Sherlock took the photo from her father. Dillon hadn't told her about this. She stared at the photo, then at her father. "It's possible, then, that because you gave him that three-year sentence, he wanted revenge. It's possible when he got out, then, that he killed Belinda, to get his revenge on you."

"There's a problem here," Savich said.

Both Judge Sherlock and his daughter looked at him, their left eyebrows arched in an identical way.

"Look again at the photo, Judge Sherlock."

"Yes, all right. What?"

"Marlin Jones would have been twenty-three years old fifteen years ago. This man is older, maybe fifty or fifty-five."

"Well, yes, you're right, he is. It's hard to tell with all that hair and the glasses. Oh, I see what you mean. It isn't Marlin, is it?"

"It's his father," Sherlock said slowly. "This man, Erasmus, the man Dad prosecuted, is Marlin's father. And this is an old picture of him, isn't it?"

"Yes. The FBI field office in Phoenix got hold of this photo of him from an old driver's license. Our lab people worked on it. I didn't tell you about it, Sherlock, because I didn't really think it would lead to anything."

"Is the man still alive?"

"He is as far as we know. He hasn't been back to Yuma in years. That's where he raised Marlin. Marlin left at eighteen. Erasmus drifted in and out for a few years, then disappeared. He'd be about sixty-four now. Where is he? No one knows."

"Let me see the man," said Mrs. Sherlock.

Lacey handed her mother the photo.

"He's scruffy. I remember his sort; they were all over San Francisco back in the sixties and seventies. But he was in court in the late eighties, Corman?"

"Yes, some fifteen years ago."

"I think he would be handsome without those glasses and all that hair and beard."

"His son is handsome, Mother, very handsome. Here's his photo. But you know, he's got dead eyes."

Mrs. Sherlock looked at Marlin Jones's photo, stared toward her husband, and fainted, sliding out of the chair and onto the carpet before anyone could catch her.

TWENTY-EIGHT

"What do you want?" Douglas stared at Dillon Savich. He laid down the papers he'd been reading and rose slowly, splaying his fingers on the desktop.

"It's okay, Marge. Let him in. He's FBI. Ah, you're here too, Lacey. Why is he with you? You know I don't like him. He's corrupted you, changed you."

"He's my boss. He has to be with me."

"Madigan," Savich said, barely nodding.

Douglas said nothing. He sat back down in his chair. He crossed his hands over his stomach.

"How are you doing, Douglas?"

"I'm very angry at the moment, but you don't care about that. Why are you here with him?"

Savich said easily as he sat down in one of the plush client chairs opposite Douglas Madigan's large high-tech chrome-and-glass desk, "It appears Belinda had an affair with Marlin Jones. Did you know about it?"

"No. I don't like your jokes, Agent Savich."

"No joke, Mr. Madigan. As far as we know it's a distinct possibility—that Belinda slept with Marlin Jones seven years ago."

Lacey was watching his face. There was no sign of pain, of anger, of remembered betrayal. Nothing.

"So you're saying you know why he killed her?"

"No, that's not what we're saying. I'm sorry, Douglas," Lacey said, sitting forward, extending her hand to lightly touch his forearm. "It seems there were some things about Belinda none of us knew. Mother saw a photo of Marlin Jones and fainted. She'd seen him, she said, seen him kissing Belinda in the driveway. At least that's what she told us. You know Mother. One can never be quite certain if the flag is going to be flying high or hanging at half-mast."

"That crazy old bitch is probably right about this. Belinda was a gold-plated faithless bitch."

They all turned to see Candice Addams Madigan standing in the doorway, a flustered Marge behind her, waving her hands. Douglas smiled and said, "It's all right, Marge. Tell you what, anyone else comes, wave them on in. Hello, Candice."

Candice walked into the office, head high, beautifully dressed in a pale blue wool suit and a Hermès scarf. "She was a bitch and she did cheat on you."

"But was the man Marlin Jones? I doubt it. Where could she have met him?"

Candice gave her husband a scornful look. "Belinda had low tastes. I've heard that she went to dives, to real low-class places. That's where she would have met this killer. Yes, I'll bet she did sleep with him. She slept with everyone. Why don't you ask *her*?" She turned and gave Lacey a vicious look. "Yes, ask the little princess here. She probably went with her sister. She might have slept with him too."

Sherlock had blood in her eye. Her heart was pounding; she was ready to kill. It was Savich who grabbed her wrist and kept her in her place. "Ignore her," he said low, only for her hearing. "She's miserable she's so jealous. Let it be. Let's listen. Consider this a bad play. Let's see if we can't figure out the theme of the play."

She tried to pull away from him. She couldn't take any more from this miserable woman. "Okay, then, Agent Sherlock, this is an order from your superior. Don't move and be quiet."

She tried to calm her breathing, but it was hard. "That's different, then, but I still want to pound her."

"I know, but later. Now let's listen."

"What are you two talking about?"

Savich smiled at Candice Madigan. "I was telling Sherlock that you looked pregnant to me. She insists you're not, that you look too slender. But I can tell your stomach is out there. Who's right?"

Candice immediately sucked in her stomach, taking two steps away from Savich. Then she realized what he'd done to her. She dropped her hands to her sides, straightened really tall, and shot a look toward her husband. He merely smiled at her. "Go ahead, Candice. After all, I don't have a client for another twenty minutes. Feel free to talk about whatever."

Candice Madigan walked to her husband, kissed him on the mouth, then turned to say to Sherlock, "I'm not pregnant but I will be soon. You keep away from my husband, do you hear me? You haven't seen mean until you've seen me mean."

"Yes, I hear you," Sherlock said. Then she smiled. "You and Douglas planning a baby, then?"

"We will be soon. It's none of your business. You're a little gold-digging tart, just like your sister. Stay away from Douglas."

"Oh, she will," Savich said. "Now, Candice, how do you know so much about Belinda? She was killed seven years ago. You weren't even around then."

"I'm an investigative reporter. I looked up everything. I spoke to people who'd known her. She betrayed Douglas, over and over again. All the women in your crowd knew about it. With this Marlin Jones character? Why not? Again, it wouldn't have been a problem for her to run into him at any one of the low-class bars she frequented."

Savich pulled out his little black notebook and his ballpoint pen. "Could you give me some names, please?"

She turned stiller than Lot's wife. "I did this last year. I don't remember now."

"Give Mr. Savich two names, Candice. Just two."

"All right. Lancing Corruthers and Dorthea McDowell. They're both rich and idle and know everything about everyone. They live right here in the city."

Savich wrote down the names. "Thank you. Actually, I'm pleased you could come up with even one name. I'm impressed."

"I am too," Douglas said.

"They knew all about her too," she added, nodding toward Sherlock.

"That should prove to be interesting," Savich said, again taking hold of Lacey's wrist. "You see, I'm hoping she'll agree to marry me, once I ask her properly." He paused a moment, then looked very worried. "I sure do hope they won't tell me things that will change my mind about asking you. Were you a loose teenager, Sherlock? Will you corrupt me if I marry you?"

"I don't think that Bobby Wellman could count as loose, do you?"

"Who's Bobby Wellman?" Douglas asked.

Savich shook his head.

"No one will say anything remotely questionable about Lacey," Douglas said. "Look Candice, Lacey was only nineteen when Belinda died. She was even a bit on the backward side for her age. All she did was play the piano. I don't think she ever even saw other people. She just saw her music. Now, tell me that was all a joke about you marrying him, Lacey."

"He still has to ask me right and proper."

"No!" Douglas stood now, leaning toward Lacey, and said, his voice rough and low, "Listen to me, Lacey. I've known you for a very long time. I don't think you should marry this man. You can't. It's a very bad idea."

"Why, Douglas?"

"Yes, Douglas, why?" Candice asked.

"I know his kind. He doesn't care about you, Lacey. You'd just be another notch on his belt."

Savich started whistling.

Everyone turned to stare at him. Sherlock wanted to laugh, but she held it back.

"Sherlock Savich," Savich said slowly, looking up at the ceiling, rolling the words on his tongue. "It has quite a ring to it, doesn't it?"

"Dammit, no, you can't marry him, Lacey. You can't. Look at him; he's one of those stupid bodybuilder types you see at the gym who are always staring at themselves in the mirror. Their biceps and pecs are all pumped up but their brains are the size of peas."

Lacey said mildly, "Douglas, you need a reality check here. You need to get a grip."

"All right. So he can play with computers, that's no big deal. He's a nerd with big arms. You can't marry him."

"Well she can't marry you, Douglas; you're already married to me." Candice took one step toward Sherlock, then pulled up when she saw the look on Savich's face.

"Congratulations," Candice said, stepping back. "I do mean that. Marry him."

"This is getting us nowhere fast," Savich said. "Now, Candice, Sherlock and I are here to speak to Douglas about Belinda. Would you like to stay or go?"

"Why? Belinda's been dead for seven years. Her killer is in jail, in Boston. I've even given you two names, women who knew her, who knew what she was like. Why are you talking to Douglas? He doesn't know anything."

"There are all sorts of loose ends, ma'am," Savich said. "Tell you what, why don't we come back after you and your husband bond or kill each other or eat lunch or whatever else you'd like to do?" Savich rose as he spoke, his hand out to Sherlock. She looked at that big strong hand and smiled. She still wanted to belt Candice.

"No, wait," Douglas called out, but Savich shook his head and waved.

She said as they walked from Douglas's office, "What will we do now?"

"Let's duck around the corner for a minute. Douglas's door is still open; Marge isn't at her desk. Who knows? Maybe we'll hear something we shouldn't."

They moved as close to the open door as they could, pressing back against the wall.

"You can't still want her, Douglas. Didn't you see what she was wearing? By God, she even chews her thumbnail!"

Sherlock looked at her thumbs. Sure enough, one thumbnail was nearly down to the quick. How had that happened?

"That's enough, Candice," Douglas said. He sounded incredibly tired. "That's really quite enough. She shouldn't marry him. I'll have to think about this, then write down all the good sound reasons why it wouldn't work. This shouldn't be happening."

"No, what shouldn't be happening is that you still lust after her. Are you blind? What's there to lust over? Get over it, Douglas. Buy some glasses."

Douglas didn't appear to have heard her—that or he was ignoring her. He said, "They're back here because of Belinda. There must be something going on with Marlin Jones. Savich called them loose ends, but I don't trust him. Mrs. Sherlock claimed she saw Marlin Jones kissing Belinda in the driveway. You say it's likely Marlin had slept with Belinda, but you're just jealous, Candice. You didn't know Belinda. It's all nuts. I don't understand any of it, but I think they must doubt that Marlin Jones killed Belinda. Maybe they think I killed her and that's why they're here."

"That's crazy, Douglas. They don't have a clue. They're here fishing around. Keep your mouth shut. Now, take me to lunch. I have to be back at the station at two o'clock."

"We're outta here," Savich said. They were in the elevator and on their way down from the twentieth floor of the Malcolm Building within a minute.

DINNER had been quiet; that is, no one had had much to say about anything, which to Savich, was a relief. Evelyn Sherlock ate delicately, gave Savich disapproving looks, and said again that he was too good-looking and not to be trusted. She said nothing at all to her husband, except over a dessert of apple pie, she finally said, not looking at him, but down at her pie, "I spoke to one of your law clerks—Danny Elbright. He said he needed to speak to you but I told him you'd gone to the gas station. I asked him if I could help him and he said no, it was something really confidential. Even your wife couldn't know."

"It was probably about a current case," Judge Sherlock said and forked down another bite of pie. He closed his eyes for a moment. "This is delicious. I need to give Isabelle another raise," he said.

"No, she makes too much already," said Evelyn Sherlock. "I think she bought the pie. She's rarely here except when she knows you'll be here. I don't like her, Corman, I never have."

"How is your companion, Mother?" Sherlock said. "Her name is Mrs. Arch, isn't it?"

"She's fine. She never says anything, only nods or shakes her head. She's very boring, but harmless. She's younger than I am and looks the way my mother would look if she were still alive. She doesn't try to seduce your father and that's a relief."

"Mrs. Arch," the judge said, "is not younger than you are, Evelyn. She must be all of sixty-five years old. She's got blue hair and is a good size sixteen. Believe me, your mother never looked like Mrs. Arch."

"So? She's not dead yet," said Mrs. Sherlock. "You've slept with every size and age of woman. Did you think I didn't know? I remember everything once I'm reminded."

"Yes, dear."

It was an hour later in Judge Sherlock's library that Savich finally said, "Sherlock didn't realize until recently that Belinda had had a miscarriage. Why didn't this come out?"

Judge Sherlock was stuffing a pipe. The smell of this particular tobacco was wonderful—rich and dark and delicious. He didn't answer until the pipe was lit and he'd sucked in three or four times. The scent was like a forest. Savich found himself breathing in deeply. Finally, Judge Sherlock said, "I didn't want any more publicity. What difference did it make? Not a bit. What do you mean Lacey didn't remember?"

"Evidently she'd blocked it out, for some reason neither of us can figure out. She remembered under hypnosis. Do you know why she'd block it out, sir?"

"No, no reason to as far as I can see. It was seven years ago. It no longer matters," Judge Sherlock said and sucked on his pipe. The library was filled with the delicious, rich smell. Savich took another drink of his tea.

Sherlock took a deep breath. "Do you know if Douglas was the father?"

"Look, Lacey, Mr. Savich, Belinda shouldn't have been pregnant in the first place. I told you, Lacey, that Douglas knew they shouldn't ever have children because of her defective genes. Look at her mother. Her father is even worse. Yes, I keep tabs on him. He'll be out one of these days, despite my efforts to the contrary. I don't want that crazy man coming here."

"But she was pregnant," Savich said.

"Yes, evidently, but not very far along, not more than six or seven weeks. That's what the doctor said. After the autopsy, they knew, naturally, that she'd just miscarried, but since it wasn't relevant to anything, they didn't mention it. The press never got hold of it, thank God. It would have caused more pain. Was Douglas the father? I've never had reason to suspect he wasn't."

"It would have also caused more outrage," Sherlock said.

"No, not unless they led the public to think the miscarriage was tied to her murder, and it wasn't."

But Sherlock wasn't so certain. Actually, as she told Dillon later as she walked him to the guest room where he was staying, "There are more than simple loose ends here. There are ends that don't seem to have any beginning." She sighed, staring down at her navy pumps. Candice was right. She looked dowdy and uninteresting. How then could she be a slut at the same time?

Savich pulled her against him, lightly pressing her face against his shoulder. "I know what you mean. It's infuriating. Everything that comes out of your mother's mouth makes Alice's Wonderland look like MIT. How long has she been like this, Sherlock?"

"As long as I can remember. She's more so now, I think. But I don't see her all that often anymore."

"Do you think she could be doing some of this to gain your father's attention?"

"Oh yes. But how much of it is real and how much is her own playacting? I don't know."

"I don't either."

"And my father?"

"I don't know," he said slowly, leaned down and kissed her left ear. "I just don't know. He's slippery, hard for me to read. But you know, Sherlock, it's tough not to like him."

"I like him too, most of the time," Lacey said and looked up at his mouth. "Do you really want to marry me now that you've met my mother and father?"

"Unfair. But you haven't met my family yet. Now there's a scary bunch. Actually, they're going to be so grateful that you're taking me on that they'll probably try really hard not to be weird around you, at least until after we're married. Then, no guarantees. Oh yes, Sherlock, we're all alone here in the corridor. I think now's the time. Will you marry me?"

"Yes, I will."

He kissed her. It was sweet and warm and he tried very hard not to overwhelm her with his need, which was growing by leaps and bounds. But then she pushed him against the wall, pressing herself up tight against him. "You feel delicious," she said into his mouth, her breath warm and dark from the espresso. "You taste even better. Dillon, are you sure you want to marry me? We haven't known each other all that long. We've been stressed-out since we met. Nothing's been normal or natural."

"Sure it has. I kicked your butt in Hogan's Alley and at the gym. What's more natural than that? I've cooked my pasta for you. I've fed you pizza at Dizzy Dan's. You've slept in my house. I think we've got great experience going into this. Besides, the sex isn't bad either, except it's been so long that I'm having a tough time remembering all the details, any of the details, actually."

She kissed his chin, his jaw, lightly bit his earlobe. "I don't understand how you've managed to stay footloose for four whole years."

"I run fast and I don't chase too well. Actually, I guess I was waiting for you. Nobody else, just you. I'm more surprised that no one snapped you up."

"I was so locked in the past, locked into only one path, all of it focused on Belinda. What will we do?"

He said as he slowly traced the buttons of her blouse, "I have this inescapable feeling that everything revolves around Belinda, not Marlin, not Douglas, not anybody else, just Belinda. I don't think anyone ever really knew who she was. I'd like to see pictures of her around the time she was killed. Do you have any albums?"

"Yes. I hope Mother didn't throw them away. Would you like to see them now?"

"Nope. We're still on East Coast time, so it feels like three hours later than it is. I want to get some sleep. Actually I want to sleep with you, but that wouldn't be right, not in your parents' house. Besides, your mother is so worried that we're shacking up, she just might go on patrol tonight to make certain we're separated."

She laughed. "Mother is a hoot, isn't she? You never know what will come out of her mouth. But it seems she's gone even more around the bend lately. Lots of it might be an act. Who knows? She's not going to change. But it still scares me because some of what she says just might be true. Did my father really try to kill her? Run her down in his BMW?"

"If he did, at least he knows she's told us about it. Your father isn't stupid. If he did do it deliberately, it won't happen again."

"I don't want my mother to die, Dillon."

He brought her close. "She won't. Everything will be all right. I'll even have a chat with your father, to make sure he understands completely."

Much later, when Sherlock was on the edge of sleep, she thought, *Who were you, Belinda?*

TWENTY-NINE

It was dawn, the bedroom a soft, vague gray, and chilly. She woke up slowly. Someone was shaking her arm, someone speaking to her. "Sherlock, we've got a problem. Come on, wake up."

He was lightly caressing her upper arms, then lightly tapped her face. She blinked up at him. "Dillon? I'm so glad it's you. I thought it was someone else, another nightmare. What's wrong? Did Mother try to run you off the property?"

He sat down beside her and she reached for him. He took her hands in his and held them tightly. "No, that I could have handled. Listen to me, Sherlock. It's Marlin Jones. Brace yourself—he's escaped."

She stared up at him, slowly shaking her head on the pillow. "No, that's impossible. A prisoner doesn't escape nowadays, except in the movies. There's no way Marlin could have gotten away. There were cops all over him. He even went to the bathroom with a cop on either side of him. Besides, he was wearing more shackles than an Alabama chain gang. This has to be an early-morning joke, right, Dillon?"

"I'm sorry, Sherlock, he's gone. The court had ordered him taken to the Massachusetts State Institute for more psychological testing. The doctors there blew fits when they saw the guards and all the restraints—he had full leg shackles. They complained they'd never get anything meaningful out of him, that they'd never gain any true and accurate testing results unless Marlin could trust them, the doctors. The cops refused, naturally. The doctors called the judge who'd dictated more testing. The judge ordered the cops to remove the shackles, even the handcuffs. The cops were even ordered to wait outside the room. The long and the short of it—Marlin hit two doctors over the head, smashed an orderly's jaw, knocked him unconscious, and got out through a bathroom window that was right off the office. They haven't recaptured him yet. They didn't know he'd escaped until the orderly re gained consciousness and staggered out to tell them."

She was fully awake now, sitting up, rubbing her arms with her hands. "How did you find out?"

"Mr. Maitland called me about thirty minutes ago, said the cops called him, but it had been on TV even before they bothered to telephone. He got hold of the FBI in Boston and put them on it big-time. He made it sound like everything was in complete disarray."

"Do you think maybe that judge who ordered Marlin Jones released will now be under the bench instead of sitting on it?"

"There'll be big-time fallout. Hopefully that nitwit judge will either swear he's seen the light or he'll go down, which is what he deserves. Get on your robe and let's get downstairs. Isabelle's made us some tea and warmed up some rolls."

Ten minutes later they were downstairs in Judge Sherlock's lair watching TV. They'd just turned on the big set when a news bulletin flashed on. A big black-and-white photo of Marlin Jones filled the screen. A newswoman's voice said, ". . . The manhunt has extended in all directions now. The FBI, state and local police are all trying to find the alleged killer of more than eight women." The picture then flashed to the newsroom. A beautiful blond woman, not more than twenty-eight, was beaming at the camera, saying in her happy, perfect voice, "It's just been learned that the FBI agent, Lacey Sherlock, who was instrumental in catching Marlin Jones in Boston, is the sister of one of the women he allegedly murdered in San Francisco seven years ago. What this means isn't exactly clear, but John

Bullock, Marlin Jones's lawyer, has said his client was entrapped all along by the FBI."

"It's out," Savich said, and sighed. "I wonder who told them."

"Oh no." A photo of Sherlock appeared on the TV screen. The newswoman was saying, "Agent Sherlock has been with the FBI for only five months now. It's said that the reason she joined was to catch her sister's killer." The newswoman gave a dazzling smile to the people watching her. "It appears she succeeded, but now, no one can say what will happen once Marlin Jones is recaptured. Let's switch to Ned Bramlock, our affiliate in Boston. Ned?"

They watched in silence as the cops in the Boston PD stood in stiff and angry silence. The local FBI representative stood behind the small group, saying nothing.

Ned Bramlock, who wore Italian tasseled loafers and had a full head of beautiful chestnut hair, said as he managed to furrow his brow in concern, "We've tried to speak to Judge Sedgewick who issued the order to the police officers to release Marlin Jones, but he's refusing comment at this time." They switched to an ACLU lawyer, who claimed what the judge did was exactly correct since to have refused to allow the alleged killer privacy for the testing would have been a violation of his civil rights. They switched to another judge, this one retired, who said flatly that Judge Sedgewick was an idiot without a lick of judgment or sense.

Savich turned off the TV set. He stretched. "Let's go work out."

She rose. "Yes, let's go. There's a World Gym just two blocks from here, down on Union Street. It's open at six A.M. It's nearly seven-thirty now."

By the time they'd finished, Lacey was so exhausted, even her rage was dampened somewhat, at least until she could breathe normally again. They walked home, holding hands.

"It's going to be a beautiful day."

"It usually is in San Francisco," she said. "Even when the fog comes rolling through the Golden Gate, it's breathtaking. The fog makes it more lovely." She fell silent.

"They'll catch him. He's got no money, no transportation. Everyone is looking for him. His photo is all over the TV. Someone will see him and they'll call the cops. Don't worry, Sherlock."

She was thinking about Judge Sedgewick and what she'd like to do to the guy as they walked back to her parents' home. As they turned onto Broadway, she spotted three local TV station vans and a good dozen people equipped with cameras and microphones parked in her parents' front yard. They heard Isabelle yelling, "Get out of here, you vultures, go! Scat!"

"Come on, ma'am, tell Agent Sherlock we're here. We need to talk to her for a little while."

"Yeah, the public's got a right to know."

"Hey, did you know her sister, Belinda Madigan? Is it true that Lacey joined the FBI just to bring down Marlin Jones?"

"Is it true she entrapped Jones?"

Isabelle looked ready to kill. She raised her hands, palms out. To Sherlock's surprise, the rowdy group quieted down instantly. She said in a voice that carried to the end of the block, "Go talk to that moronic judge who made the police remove Marlin Jones's restraints. Maybe he can take that killer's place until he's caught again."

"Good for her," Savich said.

Sherlock pulled out her cell and called her parents' house.

"Sherlock residence."

"Isabelle? It's Lacey. We saw them all in time. You did great, told the reporters the truth. Is Dad there?"

"Yes, just a moment, Lacey. I'm glad you're out of here. The reporters are planning to camp out here, I think. How did they know you were here?"

Hannah, she thought with sudden insight. Hannah hated her guts. She'd do anything to hurt her. "We'll find out, Isabelle. Get Dad for me."

Twenty minutes later they were picked up by Danny Elbright, one of Judge Sherlock's clerks. He had their luggage in the trunk. "Isabelle carried everything out the back and I swung around to pick up the luggage.

"Judge Sherlock called the airline and got you on a flight leaving at ten o'clock A.M. Is this all right?"

"That's great," Savich said. He stretched out, leaned back his head, and closed his eyes. "What a day and it's only nine o'clock in the morning. I hope the media aren't smart enough to call the airlines yet."

"Don't worry about me, Lacey," Danny Elbright said, looking at her in the rearview mirror. "I know if I ever opened my mouth your daddy would send me up the big river. I won't say a word. I want you to catch this creep. Wasn't Isabelle a kick? I'll bet she'll be all over the news."

Lacey said, "Thanks, Danny. Hey, maybe Marlin's been caught as we speak."

"Let's see." Danny turned on the radio and began station surfing.

By the time their plane left San Francisco International, Marlin Jones was still on the loose. He'd been free for five hours and twenty minutes. There were two seats left in First Class, and Judge Sherlock had snagged them. Both Savich and Sherlock were relieved when no one recognized them at the airport.

"You'll be staying with me," Savich said as he took a glass of orange juice from a flight attendant. "We're not going to take any chances."

"All right," she said, and stared down at where Yosemite would be if only they had been sitting on the right side of the airplane instead of the left.

"I know you're scared. Don't be."

"Actually I'm furious, not scared. There's no reason why Marlin would come after me. You know he's not crazy, and he'd have to be totally off the deep end to fixate on getting back at me.

"What I can't believe is that a judge—a person who's supposed to have a tad of common sense—would even listen to those idiot shrinks and their ridiculous demands."

"Well, I'll bet you no judge is going to pull that kind of stunt again anytime soon. This was an aberration, Sherlock, an unfortunate blip. Everyone will raise hell and the ACLU will look like idiots for defending the judge's ruling.

"Also, it turns out one of the doctors might not make it. The other doctor has a severe concussion, according to the news. As for the orderly, his jaw's broken and he has a lump over his left ear the size of a hockey puck. You can bet next week's paycheck that restraints will be left on prisoners in the future. If that doctor dies, the hole Marlin's in will be so deep he'll never see the sunshine again."

Savich took her hand. "We'll see. I do wonder where Marlin's daddy is. I have this feeling he's still out there, still kicking around. What's he doing, I wonder? Does Marlin know where he is? Is Marlin going to see him? Could Erasmus have been the one to come after you in Washington? Could he have been the one to hit me in Boston? Have Marlin and his daddy possibly been in contact and maybe even now are in cahoots?"

She sucked in her breath. "I was thinking the same thing. But as to the father-and-son-duo idea, I don't know if it's another seemingly random piece to the puzzle or a major gluing piece."

"I think it says a lot about how well we're suited that I understand exactly what you just said." He picked up her hand and kissed her fingers. He looked deep into her eyes. He tucked a piece of hair behind her ear. His fingers lightly caressed her ear. "Hey, gorgeous, what do you want from this gourmet lunch menu?"

* * *

MARLIN Jones was still free when they arrived at Savich's house at seven-thirty that evening.

There were no reporters waiting for them.

"If they're anywhere, it's at your town house. Another excellent reason for staying here with me."

"Yes," she said and followed him in. "I hope Hannah doesn't tell them where I probably am."

"I'm going to call Mr. Maitland and let him know we're back. And Ollie. Yeah, I think I'll give Hannah a ring. I think you're right. She's probably behind the leak. I'm beginning to think this might be a good time for her to transfer to another section. She'd better keep her mouth shut from now on or she'll be out of the Bureau."

"Maybe she's not the one who talked."

"We'll see. You unpack and then relax. We'll have dinner in. I've got some great spinach lasagna in the freezer that I made a while back. You'll love it."

"I think I'd rather have Dizzy Dan's pizza. Do they deliver?"

"They will for me." He frowned at her, then strode back to her, grabbed her, and pulled her tightly against him. "It's going to be all right. We'll get through this. Marlin will be in jail again by tomorrow morning, you'll see. All the FBI's in on this, big-time. I don't think I've ever seen Mr. Maitland so pissed. Marlin doesn't stand a chance."

But she didn't know if she agreed. Marlin Jones was out there. She nodded though, saying nothing, and laid her cheek against his shoulder.

HER clothes went into his closet, her shoes on the floor beside his size-twelve wing tips and gym shoes. Her underwear went in the second drawer of the dresser. And when he was kissing his way down her body, his mouth against her, she forgot everything but him and what he was making her feel. She yelled and arced upward and told him between gasping breaths, "I love you, Dillon. Just in case you didn't hear me the first time, I'll marry you. You're the best."

"Good. Don't forget it," he said, staring down at her, and came into her.

It was nearly morning when Savich came slowly awake, aware that something strange was happening, something that was probably better than any pesto pasta he'd ever made, better even than having won a huge bet off one of his relatives. The something strange suddenly intensified and he lurched up, gasping. She was leaning over him, her tangled hair covering his belly, her mouth on him.

All he could do was moan and clutch her hair. And when he kissed her mouth, she said, "If you could do that to me, surely you had to like it too. It only makes sense, doesn't it? I've never done that before. Did I do okay?"

"It was okay," he said. "Yeah, I think maybe it was okay. Really not bad for your first time." She slid down his chest again. Then it was all over for him.

OLLIE said, "Mr. Maitland has a representative speaking to the media downstairs. Sherlock, don't worry, they'll lay off, that was the deal he struck with them."

"Good," Savich said.

"But there's lots of gossip, lots of innuendo," Hannah said, tapping her pen against the conference table. "Marlin Jones's lawyer is making hay with Sherlock here being one of the murdered women's sisters."

"That's true," Savich said. "Does anyone know how the media found out about that?"

No one said a word.

"Hannah?" Savich said, looking at her.

She looked right at Lacey. "No, certainly not. But I don't think it's bad that the media found out what she did. It's possible the case against Jones could be tossed out as entrapment." She shrugged. "You knew it was going to come out anyway. At least now there's time to get the media through chewing on it by the time Marlin Jones is recaptured."

She was lying, but how could he prove it? Savich smiled at her, a smile cold enough to freeze water. He said, his voice so gentle it made the hair rise on the back of Sherlock's neck, "I wonder that it didn't occur to the one who told the press that Sherlock wasn't the one who made the decision? That both the Bureau and the local cops all discussed her as bait for Marlin and okayed it?"

"I bet you talked him into it," Hannah said to Sherlock. The other agents were squirming, looking off, wishing, Savich knew, that they were anywhere but seated here at the conference table.

Savich raised his hands. "All right, that's enough. As most of you know, Sherlock is at my place. Not a word about this to anybody outside this room. Okay, we'll have our regular status meeting tomorrow. I wanted everyone up to speed on this debacle. Hannah, I'd like to see you in my office."

The meeting broke up. Ollie collared Sherlock. "I've been working through MAXINE's protocols using a different slant with the Florida nursing home killings. Come and see where I'm at. I'd like your input. Besides, it'll get your mind off Marlin Jones. You're looking hunted."

She wanted to go after Savich and Hannah. Then Hannah turned around and looked at her. Sherlock changed her mind. She didn't want to get within spitting distance of Hannah.

In Savich's office, he waved his hand to a chair facing his desk. "Sit down, Hannah."

She sat. He said nothing at all for a very long time, just looked at her, his head cocked to the left.

"You wanted to speak to me, Dillon?"

"Oh yes. I know it was you who told the media about Sherlock's connection to one of the San Francisco murders. I'd like you to tell me why you did it."

THIRTY

She said in a low voice that was hard as nails, "I told you already that I didn't do it."

"You're lying. Understand this, Hannah. It wasn't Sherlock's decision to be used as bait. Sure, she wanted to do it, very badly, but it wasn't her decision. You're the last person who should have opened your mouth. The fact of the matter is that you talked to the press to cause trouble. That's unprofessional and unacceptable behavior in a Special Agent."

"I didn't do it. You can't prove that I did. Don't forget it was a judge who ordered the removal of Marlin Jones's shackles. Why wouldn't a judge throw this out as well?"

"Because of the bloody evidence, that's why. Look, Hannah, I don't want you in this unit. I think a transfer is in order. You're a good agent, but not here, not in my unit."

"That dowdy little prig is that good in bed?"

"Special Agents don't talk about other Special Agents that way. It's sexist. It's not acceptable. I won't have it."

Hannah rose slowly, bent over toward Savich, splayed her hands on his desk, and said in a low voice, "Tell me what you see in her, just tell me so I'll understand. You swore to me that you'd never allow yourself to become serious over anyone who worked in your unit, yet you saw little miss prim and fell all over yourself."

He rose to face her. "Listen to me, let it go. Sherlock's never done anything to you. If you want a target, I'm right here, really big, right in front of you. Take your best shot. Leave Sherlock alone. Oh yeah, I know too that you called the media in San Francisco and told them where Sherlock lived.

"You have compromised this case, Hannah; you've muddied the waters because of your stupid jealousy. Now, if you want to stay in the Bureau, you'd best be very careful from here on out. I'll call Colin Petty in Personnel. You can discuss transfer options with him right now."

"Tell me why. Why her?"

Sherlock's face was vivid in his mind's eye. He looked bemused as he said slowly, "You know, I really can't answer that. Lots of things, I guess. Good day, Agent. I'll be calling Personnel right now."

She called him a shit, but it was low enough so he could ignore it. At least he hoped he was the shit and not Sherlock. He'd never meant to hurt Hannah, never meant to do anything to encourage her. He called Colin Petty, then buzzed Hannah to go see him.

He sighed, turned on MAXINE, and was soon in another world, one that he controlled, one that answered only to his siren's song, one that never let him down. He reviewed everything on Marlin Jones.

Where was he? Hiding? On the run? Was he alone?

MAXINE brought up the driver's license photo of Marlin's father, Erasmus Jones. Were they together? Did Erasmus play any role at all in any of the murders in Denver or San Francisco or Boston? Was it actually he who rented the Ford Taurus? If he had, then they were probably together.

He reviewed the reports, completely immersed until Jimmy Maitland said from the open doorway, "Maitland to Savich and MAXINE. Are you two hovering anywhere close?"

Savich blinked, forcing himself to look up. He rose. "Hello, sir. What can I do for you? Have they caught Marlin Jones?"

Jimmy Maitland shook his head mournfully. "No, not yet, but it won't be much longer. All the major corridors out of Boston are covered with agents and locals. Oh yeah, Big John Bullock is hassling the Bureau office in Boston big-time. He wants to see Agent Sherlock. He wants what he's calling a predeposition. He wants to make some hay now before the cops have Marlin in custody again. What do you suggest we do?"

Savich sat back in his chair. Jimmy Maitland lowered himself into one of the chairs facing Savich's desk. "This isn't easy, is it? That opportunistic jerk, I wish Marlin had hit him harder."

"Too late. Come on, Savich, do you think Big John will make hash out of Sherlock?"

"No. Besides, we'll have a person from Justice with us. I think Sherlock is incidental. What he wants is to have the media crawling all over her, making her look guilty, and thus exonerating Marlin Jones, which is impossible. The guy's spitting in the wind."

"And if that doctor dies, it's more than impossible. They might launch him into space. Last I heard, it's still too close to call."

"If the doctor dies, I can see Big John going for manslaughter or murder two. No premeditation, an act of passion by an insane man, a man out of control, a man terrified about what was going to happen to him." Suddenly Savich sat upright in his chair, his hands clasped in front of him. "Let's do it. I think Sherlock can handle herself fine. Let's face that bastard down. Who knows? We might get something out of it."

Jimmy Maitland said very slowly, "You think maybe Marlin will find out about her being in Boston? He'll try to get to her?"

Savich was very still. "Yeah, bottom line, that's why I think we should go."

"It's a real long shot. Next to impossible."

"Yeah, but even if there's a remote chance it'd be worth it. But it's not my decision to make. I'll speak to Sherlock. But you know something? I don't think Marlin would even find out about her going to Boston—unless we let it loose to the media. Also, even if he does find out, he'd really have to be crazy to come after her."

"Maybe, but I don't know. Big John will leak it to the media, count on it. I will too. But you're right, it's got to be Sherlock's decision. But you already know the answer, don't you, Savich?"

"Oh yes."

"THE media are out in force, thicker than fleas on a one-eared dock rat," Jimmy Maitland said, blew his nose, then stuffed the handkerchief back into his coat pocket. He drew away from the window in the twenty-third-floor office of Big John Bullock. He wasn't happy with all this, but he knew that with the leak, there was no way Marlin Jones didn't know about Sherlock being here in Boston. He wouldn't be surprised if Sherlock had called the media. She really wanted Marlin Jones, badly.

Buzz O'Farrell, the SAC of the Bureau field office, was shaking his head. "It amazes me how they don't send one reporter, no, it's four dozen with eight dozen mikes, enough cameras to film World War II, and everybody screaming. I wanted to shoot that damned judge, but the media? A nice deadly virus might be the answer for them."

"They ain't got no manners, that's for sure," Savich said, grinning down at Sherlock, who looked both stoic and furious, an interesting combination he would have liked to explore with her in private. Which, unfortunately, wouldn't be an option this morning.

"Big John leaked it," Jimmy Maitland said, "we didn't. Actually, we decided to keep our noses clean. And yes, we know he leaked it. He's still counting on coming out smelling like a rose in all this and that's why he did it."

"If he hadn't, then I probably would have," Sherlock said. "Sorry, sir, but there it is. Anything to give us another shot at Marlin Jones."

"Well, good morning to all you good law enforcement representatives," Big John Bullock said, walking into the immense walnut-paneled conference room in his law offices. He homed in immediately on Sherlock. "Good to see you again," he said.

She smiled at him. "I must say you're looking a bit more fit than the last time I saw you. Marlin sure did a number on your head, didn't he?"

"Poor boy, he was frantic to get out of that torture chamber. Shall we get down to business now?"

"That's fine with us," Savich said, all calm and cool, in that FBI voice of his.

"Do tell us exactly what you want," Georgina Simms, the attorney for the Justice Department said, sitting forward. "This is on the unusual side. But we certainly want to cooperate all we can."

"Well, I really wanted to know what Agent Sherlock has to say about all her unethical behavior in the case to date."

Savich rose. He walked slowly up to Big John and said not two inches from his face, "Agent Sherlock doesn't have anything to say. Now, if you can't come up with something worth our while, then we're out of here. You heard Ms. Simms. We've got a murderer to catch. Maybe you think it's funny that at least eight women were brutally murdered and a doctor is hanging on for his life as we speak, but we don't."

Big John sobered immediately, nodding to the stenographer to begin as he sat down and opened a thick file. "All right, then. Agent Sherlock, here's the problem you've created for the state. Your sister is one of the women allegedly killed by my client. Is this true?"

"Yes."

"So the reason you became an FBI agent was to get in on the inside so you'd have a better chance of catching him?"

"Yes, initially."

"Was it your idea, your plan, that resulted in the capture of Marlin Jones?"

"It was a plan developed by the local BPD and the FBI. It was also a plan approved by the local BPD and the FBI. I was merely the bait."

"Why?"

"Because I knew his profile very well. I knew better than any other female officer or agent exactly how to play him, how to work him. I was simple bait, Mr. Bullock. All he had to do was ignore me. There was no entrapment."

"That will be up to the judge, won't it?"

Georgina Simms, said, her voice easy and slow, "This is all a waste of time, Mr. Bullock. If you have a point, make it now or we're leaving."

"My point is, exactly how did you know how to 'play' Marlin Jones so well, Agent Sherlock?"

She didn't pause. She saw Dillon tense up, then consciously relax. He was worried. Well, she wasn't. She'd thought about this a whole lot. "I've studied everything about the killer for the past seven years, Mr. Bullock. I felt that I knew him. He cut out the women's tongues, thus it was assumed that the women he'd picked to walk the walk through his maze needed to be punished in his mind. His first marker was cursing. If he heard a woman using language unbecoming to a woman—and of course he was the judge of how bad the language was—that was half of his decision. The other half was whether or not she bad-mouthed her husband. This one was more iffy, but again, I felt I knew Marlin Jones; I'd studied him so closely for seven years and through my course work in undergraduate and in graduate school. As you know, he's now claimed that he slept with most of the women he murdered, though we don't have any confirmation on that. It's really very straightforward. That's all there is to it, Mr. Bullock."

"So your sister cursed and bad-mouthed her husband. Did your sister also sleep with her killer, Agent Sherlock?"

"Since she's been dead for seven years, stabbed many times, her tongue cut out, I don't think we have much hope of getting the answer."

Savich could have kissed her. It had been a question meant to inflame, meant to incite rage and thus to gain an untempered response. She'd held firm. He could tell Jimmy Maitland was impressed as well.

"That sounded all rehearsed, Agent Sherlock."

She merely shrugged.

Big John said, "It sounds to me like you're one obsessed little lady, excuse me, one obsessed little Special Agent. I would have thought that the FBI interviewers and psychologists would have spotted all this and not given you the time of day. That's scary."

"No, sir, what's scary is a judge who presents Marlin Jones, a vicious murderer, with a perfect chance to escape." She sat forward in her chair. "And you're scary, Mr. Bullock. You're doing this all to enhance your career—in other words, for fame and profit. If I am obsessed or have ever been obsessed, sir, then you are unethical, another word for basic slime."

Big John roared to his feet. "You can't talk to me like that, Agent Sherlock."

"Why not, sir?"

Georgina Simms smiled. "It's a good question, an excellent point actually, but we'll let it go. Anything else you wanted to know, Mr. Bullock?"

"No judge is going to accept that she was only another well-trained agent doing a job. She taints the case. She's a self-interested participant, not an objective law officer."

"We're gone," Savich said, rose, and nodded to Sherlock. "See you in court, Mr. Bullock, if the cops can't manage to bring down Marlin when he resists arrest, which you know he will."

Sherlock smiled over her shoulder at him. "Perhaps you shouldn't be spending so much time on Marlin Jones now, Mr. Bullock. You know Agent Savich is right. Marlin will resist arrest. The chance of your getting to eviscerate the law with your tactics isn't likely to happen. Seems to me you're wasting your time, which is worth lots of money, right?"

She felt Savich's palm beneath her elbow. He said close to her ear, "We're out of here. You did well."

"We'll go out the back way," Jimmy Maitland said in the elevator. "I've already scoped it out."

"That was interesting, Agent Sherlock," Georgina Simms said. "I don't understand either how you got into the FBI in the first place."

"Actually, Ms. Simms, I was surprised too. Don't get me wrong; finding Marlin Jones was a big part of my motivation for joining, but then I realized that this was what I wanted to do with my life. You know, before

Agent Savich brought me to his unit, I could have ended up chasing bank robbers in Los Angeles. And that was the bottom line. I would have caught as many bank robbers as I could."

"I rather think a judge might buy that," Georgina Simms said. "But as I said, however did you manage to even get accepted with this in your background?"

"I guess nobody made a big deal out of it."

"I guess not."

Before they all parted in the underground parking lot, Jimmy Maitland said to Savich, "Simms buys it because it sounds good and it is true, for the most part. However, what she doesn't know is that you've got the hots for Sherlock. What are you going to do about that? Are you two going to get married, or what?"

"Yes, but as they say, timing is everything."

"But the point is, why did you ask for her for the Criminal Apprehension Unit in the first place?"

Savich didn't hesitate. "Because she was so damned good in Hogan's Alley. No, I didn't have the hots for her then, sir. I simply thought that she'd be one of the best I could get my hands on. I found out she'd turned down profiling because she said she couldn't stomach it, but she had all this great training and knowledge in forensics. No, sir, at that time, there was no lust scrambling my brains."

Jimmy Maitland grunted. "Timing," he said. "You're right. All of this will have to be controlled very tightly. You took care of the leak out of your unit?"

"All gone," Savich said.

"I don't suppose you're going to tell me about it?"

"I would appreciate your not asking, sir, since there's no solid proof."

THIRTY-ONE

They spent the rest of the day with local field office agents and police, seeing exactly what was going on with the manhunt. "It looks like everything's being done right," Savich said to one of the cops on the newly formed task force. "And there's zero hint or word that Marlin Jones could have met up with someone?"

"Not an echo of a word," Officer Drummond said. "My feet hurt. I think I've walked from one end of the zone to the other a good dozen times. I've spoken to every informant who's ever migrated to Boston or was born here."

By eight o'clock that evening, Marlin Jones was still at large.

They decided to eat again at the Chinese restaurant on Newbury and walked there.

"I doubt he'll show, Sherlock."

"I know. At least we're giving him every opportunity to make a move."

"Okay. We'll keep walking everywhere and when the media catches up to us, we'll wave to our mothers and smile really big. Speaking of mothers, do you think your mother really saw Marlin kissing Belinda in the driveway?"

"Actually, I have no idea what she saw or if she even saw anything. I think you're right about the attention bids. My father was there and she wanted him to focus on her. It was an excellent way to go about it."

"So you don't believe your father would ever try to run her down?"

"I don't know. But I think she loves him. I could be wrong. It's nuts, isn't it? Maybe she did see someone perhaps speak to Belinda in the driveway, but Marlin?"

"Do you think your father prosecuted Erasmus Jones fifteen years ago?"

"Oh yes. My father's firmly planted in the here-and-now, no matter how unpleasant it can get. He doesn't make stuff up. If he said Erasmus Jones was in his courtroom, then he was. The question is—Is it possible that Erasmus Jones has anything to do with this?"

Savich said slowly, "There's a tremendous resemblance between father and son. Is it possible that maybe your mother saw Erasmus with Belinda, not Marlin?"

"I have no idea. But she didn't have any reaction at all to Erasmus Jones's photograph."

"No, she didn't."

Over egg rolls and fried wonton, half with meat and half vegetarian, Savich said, releasing her hand, "Your fingers are cold."

"All of me is cold."

"Next summer we'll go to Louise Lynn Lake with Quinlan and Sally. I want to see you in a bikini. A blue one. I want to buy it for you. I want to put it on you and take it off."

Next summer, she thought: a lifetime away from a Chinese restaurant in Boston where, she prayed, Marlin Jones was lurking somewhere, waiting for her to come out. Cops were stationed at short intervals all around the restaurant.

She gave Dillon a huge smile. "Thank you," she said, stood on her tiptoes, and kissed his mouth. Then she sat down again, took a huge forkful of garlic pork, and chewed while Savich sat there, staring at her, bemused.

Princess prawns and garlic eggplant arrived. While Savich was spooning rice onto his plate, he said, "What do you think about Douglas?"

"I really don't want to think about him right now. I just want to eat." She sighed as she speared a princess prawn on her fork. "Everyone is accusing everyone else of killing Belinda. We go down one passageway, then another." She waved her fork, flinging rice onto the table. "The only thing I am sure about is that Isabelle didn't do it. My money would be on Candice if she'd only been around seven years ago."

"I find myself still going back and back yet again to your nightmare, to your experiencing exactly what happened to Belinda."

"I try not to anymore. It's too scary. It makes me sweat. Do you think we could go work out after dinner?"

He grinned at her over a forkful of garlic eggplant, which had been nicely prepared. "My soul mate," he said. "Your delts still need work. Your thighs are really nice, though. Those triceps of yours make me hard."

"I love it when you talk gym to me."

THEY didn't fly back to Washington until the next afternoon. Not a single sign of Marlin Jones. He was still at large.

They stopped off to see Captain Dougherty at the station on their way to Logan International. "It seems to me that someone has to be helping him," Savich said.

"Yeah," said Captain Dougherty. "Everyone is coming to that conclusion now. There haven't been any murders or robberies that haven't checked out. Since Marlin didn't have any money, he would have to get some if he remained alone. He didn't so far as we know. So, someone must be helping him. Someone's hiding him, a someone who has enough money to keep him out of sight. But who? We've checked with the people at the lumberyard where he worked. He didn't have any close friends that they knew of, at least no one close enough to go out on this long a limb for him."

Sherlock handed Captain Dougherty the eight-by-ten photo of Erasmus Jones. "This is his father. You might want to distribute this photo."

"They sure do look alike. You think his old man might really be in on this thing? Do you think he's the one helping Marlin?"

"We have no idea. We don't even know if he's dead or alive. It's just an idea, something we can sink our teeth into." They rose. "We're going back home, Captain. Keep us informed and good luck."

"DOUGLAS told me he's being followed. Damn you, this has got to stop."

Candice Madigan spoke angrily from behind them as Savich was unlocking his front door.

Sherlock's hand was already on her Lady Colt. Savich was already in a crouch. He took a deep breath. "I suggest you never do anything like that again, ma'am. Sherlock could have shot you and I could have broken your neck. May I inquire what you're doing here?"

"Waiting for you."

"How did you know I'd be here?" Sherlock asked, stepping directly under the porch light.

Savich unlocked the door and shoved it open. "Everyone might as well come inside. You first, Mrs. Madigan. I'd as soon keep you in front of me." He said over his shoulder, "I hope you have frequent flier miles. What is this? Your second or third trip to Washington?"

"Of course I have frequent flier miles," she said. "Do you think I'm a fool?"

If Candice was blown away by the inside of Savich's house, she didn't show it. Her eyes never left Sherlock. "Did you hear me, Lacey? I know it's not the San Francisco cops. Judge Sherlock found that out for me. So it has to be the FBI following him. It's your doing, isn't it? No, you don't have that kind of authority." She turned on Savich. "You'd do anything for little miss sweetness, wouldn't you? Even have my husband followed. Are you trying to blame Douglas for Belinda's murder? Stop it; he's going nuts. I won't have it."

"You know," Savich said easily, waving Candice into the living room, "when you pause to think a bit, Douglas had a very good motive for killing Belinda. He wanted out of the marriage but she wouldn't give him a divorce. He knew if he tried to get one that Judge Sherlock would have ruined him. He was trapped. So he used the String Killer's M.O. and killed her. What do you think? Sound good?"

Candice lunged at him.

He caught her wrists and held her away from him. She kicked at him. He quickly turned to the side. Then he began shaking her, saying in his low calm voice, "Stop it, Mrs. Madigan. For a woman of some sophistication, you're not playing the part."

"Give her to me," Sherlock said. "I'm sick of you, Candice. You want to fight, then come here. I'd love to take you down."

"You'd wreck my living room," Savich said, looking at a red-faced Sherlock, and smiled. "Will you try to keep some control, Mrs. Madigan? I'll protect you from Sherlock if you'll mind your manners. Will you?" Slowly, she nodded. Savich let her go. She stood there, rubbing her wrists. Then, slowly, she turned to face Sherlock, but she said over her shoulder to Savich, "Did it ever occur to you that she killed Belinda? Talk about crazy, look at her family. Every gene coursing through her is nuts, just plain nuts."

There was dead silence except for Candice's heavy breathing.

"Well? What do you have to say to that?"

Sherlock smiled, an awesome feat she told Dillon later, but she managed it. "Candice, why are you really here?"

"I told you, someone's following Douglas. It's got to be the FBI. I want it stopped. So I came to make you do it."

Sherlock said, "Why didn't you just call? It sure would have been cheaper. No answer to that? Maybe you wanted to hire that guy again to terrorize me? Maybe you wanted to try to run me down again?"

"I don't know what you're talking about. As for you," she continued, looking at Savich, "you're blind. Douglas was too, but for only a little while. Now he realizes what she is." Candice gave them a triumphant smile and sat down on the beautiful sofa. "Well?"

"Well what, Mrs. Madigan?"

"Will you have the FBI stop following my husband?"

Savich sighed. "Sure, Mrs. Madigan. The thing is, though, we have an agent following him in order to keep him safe. Marlin Jones is still on the loose. It's possible he plans to go back to California. It's possible that he would want to see Douglas, maybe even kill him. That's why we have an agent on him, to protect him."

"That's crazy," Candice said slowly. "There's no reason in the world why Douglas would be in any danger from Marlin Jones."

"Oh? Are you really so sure about that? Didn't Douglas tell you about Mrs. Sherlock seeing Marlin kissing Belinda in front of the house? Who knows what's going on in Marlin Jones's mind these days? But who cares, when all's said and done? Sure, I'll call off the FBI. Douglas can be on his own, no problem." Savich calmly pulled his cell out of his jacket pocket and punched in numbers.

"Do you really think he could be in danger?"

Savich ignored her, waiting. Then he said, "This is Dillon Savich. Please connect me with James Maitland. Thank you."

"What if this creep is after him? What if he does manage to get to San Francisco? Douglas needs help. You can't leave him alone like this. It's inhuman."

"Sir, Savich here. Yes, we need to call off the protection on Douglas Madigan in San Francisco. Yes, I'm sure. There's no more need."

"No, don't call it off! What if this Marlin Jones goes after Douglas? No, don't!"

"Yes, that's right. No need any longer. Thank you."

Savich hung up the phone in time to block Candice Madigan from shoving him into the fireplace.

"That's it," Sherlock said. She roared toward Candice, grabbing her arm and pulling her around. She sent her fist into Candice's jaw.

"Ow! That hurts, you mean little bitch!"

Sherlock hit her again, then groaned herself at the pain in her knuckles.

Candice looked at her, astonishment written clearly on her face, and slumped to the floor.

"Are you all right, Dillon?"

She was standing there rubbing her knuckles, asking him if he was all right. He could only shake his head. "Thank you for protecting me," he said, laughing.

She'd rushed in to protect him. Life with Sherlock would never be boring. He hoped she hadn't hurt her hand.

"Could you come and kiss me, Sherlock? I'm feeling a little shaky."

"Sure," she said, smiling sweetly at him. She kissed his chin, ran her fingertips over his eyebrows, kissed his nose. "You're better now?"

"Getting there," he said, and kept kissing her.

They stopped only when they heard Candice say from the floor, "If the two of you make out in front of me, I'm going to call the police. Then you'll both be arrested."

Sherlock began to laugh; she couldn't help it. Savich said, "Would you like a cup of coffee before you leave, Mrs. Madigan?"

"What I want is for the FBI to protect my husband."

"But you flew all the way here to get us off him."

"Look, I know I haven't been really nice to either of you, but Douglas, he's different. He needs me. Please, if you truly believe he's in danger, protect him."

Savich pulled out his cell again, punched in numbers, and said, "Reinstate the surveillance on Douglas Madigan. Yes, that's right. Thank you." He hung up, then turned to Candice. "It's done."

"Thank you," she said. "Really, thank you very much." Then she turned to Sherlock. "As for you, you're nothing but trouble. You're going to bring trouble to this very nice man who doesn't know you at all. Stay away from Douglas!"

With that, she was gone.

Savich stood there, looking toward the front door. "I guess she didn't want coffee."

"Did you really have surveillance on Douglas?"

"Oh yes."

"Did you take it off then put it back on?"

"Nope. Douglas is a suspect. I want an eye kept on him. Hey, if it protects him as well, so be it."

"She loves him," Lacey said. "She really truly loves him."

"The two of them deserve each other. I hope they live happily ever after. Now, if you're ready for bed, I'll race you."

She'd been so depressed, then she'd wanted to shoot Candice, but now, looking at Dillon Savich, she felt relief and something wild and wonderful pour through her. "Let's go."

THIRTY-TWO

Marlin Jones was still free on Thursday at noon. His photo was shown on TV special bulletins throughout the day and evening. Hundreds of sightings from Boca Raton to Anchorage had flooded in.

Savich tried to work, tried to concentrate on the killings in South Dakota and Iowa, but it was tough. He called everyone together Thursday afternoon to announce that Hannah Paisley had been reassigned. He would let everyone know where she would be going when it was decided. No one was particularly sorry to see her go.

As for Sherlock, she felt as if a hundred-pound weight had been lifted off her back.

An hour later, there was a resolution to the nursing home murders in Florida. Savich, Ollie, and Sherlock were hooting when they walked into the conference room, giving everyone high fives.

Savich, grinning from ear to ear, rubbing his hands, said, "Good news. Great news. It turns out our murderer is an old man—Benjamin Potter from

Cincinnati who's been a magician for thirty years. He's a master of disguise, which all of you know. Also, he's never done a bad thing in his life. He easily entered the nursing homes as just another old person in need of round-the-clock attention. Sometimes he passed himself off as an old woman, other times, an old man. Because he was in basic good health, no nurse ever saw him without his clothes on, important since he could have been play-acting an old woman. He never had difficulty escaping after each murder, because he didn't. Nope, he always stayed on until a 'relative' came to take him home to his family. He paid the 'relative' fifty bucks for this service." Savich turned to Ollie.

Ollie said, "The cops found the 'relative' in Atlanta. He denied knowing anything about the murders. He said only that the old man was a kick and it was easy money." He nodded to Lacey.

"Benjamin Potter wouldn't have been caught after the sixth murder except that he happened to trip on a used syringe on his way out of the victim's room and suffered a heart attack. He died before he could tell anyone why he'd killed six old women."

Ollie picked it up. "Yep, the relative is my part. He said he had no clue. The old man always seemed happy and well adjusted to him. So go figure."

They all tried to figure it out, but no one could come up with anything that sounded like the perfect fit. Although Savich said that MAXINE thought it might be that the old man had always wanted to be an old woman and he was killing off his competition.

"A real big one down," Savich said. "Everybody to the gym for celebrations."

There was groaning from around the table.

Sherlock was still on a high when she went to the women's room in the middle of the afternoon, a redone men's room that looked it. When workmen had removed the urinals, they hadn't patched the wall tile very well. The big room was always dank and smelled like Pine Sol.

Sherlock was washing her hands when she looked up to see Hannah in the mirror, standing behind her. She didn't say anything, just looked at her reflection.

"Your lover didn't want to take the chance I'd slap him with a sexual harassment complaint so he couldn't fire me."

"I thought you denied leaking my relationship to a murder victim to the press."

"I did deny it."

"Then how could Savich have fired you without proof? Oh enough, Hannah. Say what you have to say and go about your business."

"You're really cute, you know that? Tell me, Sherlock, did you set your sights on Savich while you were still at Quantico?"

"No."

"He'll screw your eyes out but he won't marry you. Has he made love to you in the shower? He loves that."

"Hannah, it's none of your business what either of us does. Please, let it go. Forget him. You know I'm irrelevant in all this. Even if I weren't here, Savich still wouldn't be going out with you."

"Maybe, maybe not."

"Good-bye, Hannah."

Ollie was waiting outside for her. He said only, "I didn't want her to shoot you."

"So you were waiting out here to see if a gun went off?"

"Something like that."

"I'm fine, Ollie. Any word yet on Marlin Jones?"

"Nope, nothing. Oh yeah, your father called, asked that you phone him back. He said it was really important."

She didn't want to pick up that phone. She didn't want to, but she did. She felt an urgency that she'd never felt before. Even as she was dialing her parents' home number, she was terrified.

"Isabelle? It's Lacey."

"Oh God, Lacey, it's your mama. Let me get your daddy on the phone. You just caught him in time. He's leaving now for the hospital."

"The hospital? What happened to Mother?" But Isabelle had already hit the hold button. "Father?"

"Lacey? Come home, my dear, it's your mother. There was an accident. She's in the hospital. It doesn't look good, Lacey. Can you get some time off?"

"What kind of accident? What is her exact condition?"

"I was backing out of the driveway. She darted out from the bushes that line the street. I hit her. It was an accident. I swear it was an accident. There was even a passerby who saw the whole thing. She's not dead, Lacey, but her spleen is ruptured and they're taking it out as we speak. I feel terrible. I don't know what's going to happen. I think you should come home now."

Before she could say anything, he hung up. She stared down at the receiver, hearing the loud dial tone. What more could happen?

AT nine o'clock the next morning she was on a nonstop flight to San Francisco. Dillon took the Dulles shuttle with her to the terminal to catch her United flight, using his FBI identification to get through security. "You'll call me," he said, kissing her hair, just holding her against him, his hands stroking down her back. "It will be all right. We'll get through it. Remember in the Bible how God kept testing Job? Well, these are our tests. Call me, okay?" And he kissed her again. He watched at the huge windows until her plane took off.

He didn't like her to go alone but he couldn't pick up and leave, not now. Everything was coming to a head, he knew it. More important, she knew it. It was just a matter of time. Actually he was rather relieved that she'd be three thousand miles away, although he'd never tell her that. She'd blow a fuse because he wanted to protect her and she was a professional and could take care of herself.

He stepped back onto the shuttle, realizing, as he stared blankly at a businessman with a very packed briefcase, that she would be justified smacking him but good if he'd said that to her. He had to remember she was well trained. She was a professional. Even if his guts twisted whenever he thought of her going into the field, he'd have to get used to it.

He shook his head as he walked to his Porsche. Could her father have deliberately hit her mother?

FOR the first time that Sherlock could remember, her mother looked all sixty-one of her years. Her flesh seemed loose, her cheeks sunken in. And so white and waxy, tubes everywhere. Mrs. Arch, her mother's ten-year companion, was there, as was Lacey's father, both standing beside her bed.

"Don't worry," her father said. "The operation went well. They took out her spleen and stopped the internal bleeding. There's lots of bruising and she'll have some sore ribs, but she'll be all right, Lacey."

She looked over at her father. "I know. I spoke to the nurse outside. Where were you, Mrs. Arch, when this happened?"

"Your mother got by me, Lacey. One minute she was there watching a game show on TV, the next minute she was gone. I'd gone down to the kitchen for a cup of tea."

She looked at her father. He seemed remote, watching the woman who had been his wife for nearly thirty years. What was he thinking? Did he expect her to say something against him when she regained consciousness? "Father, tell me what happened."

"I was backing out of the driveway to go to the courthouse. I heard this loud bump. I'd hit your mother. I never saw her. The first thing was to get her to the hospital; then I called the police. It was a Sergeant Dollan who found a witness to the whole thing. His name's Murdock."

"What did he tell them?"

"That she ran out into the driveway. He said he couldn't figure out why she'd do such a stupid thing."

She had to go talk to this Mr. Murdock herself.

"You don't believe your mother's crazy tale that I tried to run her down, do you?"

"No. You're not stupid."

He'd been tense before but now he relaxed. He even smiled. "No, I'm not stupid. Why did she do that?"

"Probably to get your attention."

"Now that's nuts, Lacey."

"Maybe more of your attention would be a good thing."

She looked down at her mother. She was so still. Here she was lying in a hospital bed with a squirrelly brain and no spleen.

"I'll think about what you said. Where are you going?"

"To talk to Mr. Murdock. No, Dad, I don't doubt you. I need to hear him tell it. Maybe it will help us both understand her a bit better."

Sherlock left her mother's hospital room and stopped again at the nurse's station.

"Mrs. Sherlock will be fine," Nurse Blackburn said. "Really. She'll be asleep for another three or four hours. Come back to see her later, about dinnertime."

Sherlock called the precinct station. Ten minutes later, she was driving to a Mr. Murdock's house, three doors down from her parents' home on Broadway. It was a fog-laden afternoon, and very chilly. She felt cold to the marrow of her bones.

It wasn't nearly dark yet, but a light was shining in the front windows of his house. A desiccated old man, stooped nearly double, answered the door just when she was ready to give up. Standing next to him was a huge bulldog. Mr. Murdock nodded to the dog. "I walk him at least six times a day," he said first thing. "Bad bladder," Mr. Murdock added, patting the dog's head. "He needs more potty time than I do." He didn't invite her in, not that she wanted to step into that dark hallway behind him that smelled too much like dog and dirty socks.

"You saw an accident, Mr. Murdock? A man in a car struck a woman?"

"Eh? Oh that. Yes, I did see the whole thing. It happened yesterday afternoon. This real pretty woman I've known by sight for years is standing kind of bent over in the thick oleanders. I start to call out to her, you know, I thought she must have some kind of problem, when she suddenly steps out into the driveway. I hear a car hit her. It was weird. The whole thing was weird. That's what my nephew said too when I called him about it. What do you want,

Butchie? You got bladder needs again? All right. Go get your rope. Sorry, little lady, but that's all I know. Either the woman ran out into the car's path on purpose or she didn't, and that makes it an accident, plain and simple."

Lacey walked slowly back to her rental car. Why had her mother done such a ridiculous thing? Was it really that she wanted more attention from her husband? That was far too simple, but maybe it was a place to start. She hadn't understood her mother for nearly all her life. Why should she begin understanding her now?

HER father came back to the hospital at seven o'clock that evening.

"She's the same," Sherlock said.

He said nothing, walked to the bed and looked down at his wife.

He said, "Did that old man tell you that I didn't try to kill your mother?"

"Yeah, he did. Look, Dad, you know I had to go talk to him, hear everything in his own words."

"You're my kid. I can understand that. I called a new psychiatrist to come talk to your mother tomorrow. I told her what had happened, what you thought. We'll see. I'm glad you didn't think I was stupid enough to try something like that."

"Oh no."

"I've found myself wondering if I could have done it. Maybe, if it had been dark and we'd been in the Andes with no possible witnesses who spoke English."

"You're joking."

"Yes, I'm joking." He looked at his watch. "I've got to be in court early tomorrow. I'll see you at lunchtime, Lacey." He paused in the doorway. "You know, it's easy to fall into certain ways of thinking, of behaving. You know that your mother could irritate a saint into wickedness. We'll see."

She spent the night in her mother's hospital room on a cot an orderly brought in for her. She lay there, listening to her mother breathing, thinking about Dillon, and wondering, always wondering where Marlin was.

She got a call from Dillon at nearly eleven o'clock, which made it two o'clock A.M. his time.

"I was going to leave you be, at least for tonight, but I couldn't. How's your mom?"

"She'll make it. I personally interviewed a witness who told me that my mother appeared to be hiding in some bushes, then dashed out when my father was backing out of the driveway. I had a good talk with my dad. He's bringing in a new psychiatrist to see her tomorrow. I mentioned that maybe she was trying to get his attention. Should I have opened my mouth? What do you think?"

"I still think it sounds like your mother really wants something she's not getting from your father. You're the daughter. Of course you should say what you think. You know, she might really be mentally unstable."

"As my dad said, 'we'll see.'"

"You hanging in there?"

"Yes, don't worry about me. Any word on Marlin Jones?"

"No. It's driving everybody crazy. It's as though he's just disappeared off the face of the earth. Oh yeah, Hannah called me about an hour ago. She wanted to come over and talk. When I said no, she told me how you'd attacked her in the women's room this afternoon. She told me you'd accused her of blackmailing me so I wouldn't fire her. She said you were furious that we'd slept together."

The last thing she needed in this crazy mix was Hannah. "I don't think so, Dillon. But that's a thought. Let me consider it. I don't know, she's pretty strong. It's possible she could take me down."

He grunted. "Yeah, she probably could. Call me at the Bureau tomorrow with an update. Sherlock?"

"Yes?"

"I miss you really badly. I had to go to the gym by myself. It used to be just fine—in fact, I used to like going by myself—but now all I could do was one lat pulldown before I was looking around for you."

At least she was smiling when she gently punched off her cell.

WHEN a shaft of light from the hospital corridor flashed across her face, Sherlock was awake in an instant, not moving, frozen, readying herself. It had to be a nurse, but she knew it wasn't. She smelled Douglas's distinctive cologne, a deep musky scent that was very sexy. She remembered that scent from the age of fifteen when he'd first come into their lives.

She lay very still. She watched him walk slowly to her mother's bed. He stood there for the longest time in the dim light sent in through the window, staring down at her mother.

She saw him lean down and kiss her mother. She heard him say quietly, "Evelyn, why did you do this stupid thing? You know he's a bastard. You know, surely, he'll always be a bastard. What did you expect to prove by running out like that behind his car?"

Her mother made no sound.

Douglas lightly caressed her face with his cupped palm. Then he straightened and turned. He froze in his tracks, staring down at Sherlock.

"Lacey, what are you doing here?"

"I wanted to stay with my mother," she said, very slowly coming up onto her knees, her back against the wall. She was wearing one of her favorite Lanz flannel nightgowns that came up high on her neck and covered her feet. "Didn't my father tell you I was staying with her? No, I guess not. What are you doing here, Douglas?"

He shrugged. "I was naturally worried about her. I wanted to make sure she was all right. I wanted to see her when I knew your father wouldn't be here."

"Visiting hours were over a long time ago. How did you get in?"

"Not a problem. I know the nurse, Lorette. She let me in. Seeing you is a surprise. I didn't know you'd come. That Marlin Jones jerk is still free. I didn't think you'd ever leave the hunt."

"Why were you kissing my mother?"

"I've known your mother for many years, Lacey. She's a good woman, almost like a mother to me."

"That kiss didn't look at all filial."

He ignored that, saying, "I don't want anything to happen to her, anything more, that is."

"That's hard to believe, Douglas. You were kissing her like she was a lover."

"No, Lacey, you're way off base. Why are you looking toward the door?"

"I'm waiting for Candice to burst in here. She always seems to show up when you're with me."

"I left her sleeping. She isn't coming here." Then he laughed. "But she'll hate herself that she missed such an opportunity. Here you are in your nightgown in the same room with me. Yeah, she'd go wild."

"Well, I'm not up to anything wild tonight. Are you certain she's home asleep?"

"I hope so."

Lacey stood up, her nightgown like a red-patterned tent around her. There was sweet lace around the wrists and the neck. "I think you should leave now, Douglas. I don't want her disturbed. I need to get some sleep. Oh yes, my father would never hurt her. She ran out behind his car on purpose."

"That makes no sense."

She had to smile at that. It seemed to be everyone's litany recently.

She closed the door after Douglas had left. She took a deep breath once she was in the blessed darkness again. She heard her mother's even breathing. She burrowed under the three hospital blankets. It still took her a long time to get warm.

Why had Douglas spoken to her unconscious mother as if she were his lover? Or had she imagined it?

Her head began to pound. She wanted nothing more at the moment than to go home, to Dillon.

THIRTY-THREE

"I didn't run into the driveway. Your father saw me pruning some oleander bushes. He called out to me, told me he wanted to talk to me about something. When I walked onto the driveway, he gunned his BMW and deliberately ran into me."

Lacey said very quietly, "Mother, there was a witness. He's an old man who lives down the block from you. He claims you were hiding, then ran out so that Father could run into you."

"Old man Murdock," her mother said, her voice deep with anger. Then she winced at the pain. "That old liar. He wanted me to have an affair with him, years ago, after his poor wife died of breast cancer. I told him where to shove it. So this is his revenge. The malicious old moron."

"It's all right, Mom. Relax. That's better. Breathe deeply. You can push that button if you want pain medication."

"How do you know what to do?"

"When I was hurt, that's what they told me. It helped. Please, Mom, help me understand what this is all about. Why would Dad want to kill you?"

"To get my money, of course, so he can marry that bimbo lawyer clerk of his."

"What money? What clerk? Danny Elbright is his law clerk."

"I don't know her name. She's new, works with Danny. I don't really care."

Judge Sherlock came into the room. "Ah," he said from across the room, "you're awake, Evelyn. How are you feeling?"

In a querulous old-woman's voice, Evelyn Sherlock said, "What are you doing here? You're always at the courthouse this time of the morning. What do you want, Corman?"

"This isn't exactly a day to have business as usual. I'm here to see how you're doing, naturally."

"I'll live, no thanks to you. I'll be pressing charges, you can count on that. Oh my, my head feels all soft. What's on TV, Lacey? I always watch *Oprah*. Is she on yet?"

"*Oprah* is on in the afternoon," Judge Sherlock said. "Get a grip, Evelyn."

"Oh, then it's *The Price Is Right*. That's a great show. I can guess the amounts of money better than those stupid contestants. Do turn it on, Lacey."

It was down the rabbit hole, Sherlock thought as she switched on the TV, then handed her mother the remote.

"You can leave now, Lacey. I'm not going to die. Your father didn't hit me hard enough. I guess he couldn't build up enough speed to get it done once and for all."

"All right," Sherlock said. She leaned down and kissed her mother's white cheek. "You take it easy, okay?"

"What? Oh yes, certainly. I'll bet that powerboat with all that stuff on it costs exactly thirty-three thousand five hundred dollars."

As Lacey walked from the room, she heard Bob Barker call out, "It's thirty-four thousand!"

She wasn't aware her father was there until he stepped into the elevator with her.

"I'll see that she's well taken care of. I've decided Mrs. Arch isn't keeping good enough control. She never should have let her get away like that. Also, after the new shrink sees her this afternoon, I'll call and let you know what she says. I'll tell you one thing, though. Right now she certainly doesn't sound as if she wants any attention from me. She sounds as if she wants me hung up by my balls."

"As you said, we'll see." She looked up at her handsome father, at the uncertainty and confusion in his eyes, at that stern set of his jaw. She lightly laid her hand on his forearm. "Take care, Dad. You don't really think she'll try to press charges?"

"Probably not. She'll forget all about it by this afternoon. If she doesn't, the cops will treat her gently and ask me to see that she has better care."

"Dad, does Mother have money of her own?"

"Yes, something in the neighborhood of four hundred thousand. It's safely invested, has been for years. She's never had to touch it. Why do you ask? Oh, I know. Your mother's been claiming I married her for her money again. Not likely, Lacey."

On a hunch, she called San Quentin from the airport. Belinda's father, her mother's first husband, Conal Francis, had been out of jail since the previous Monday. She pressed her forehead against her fisted hand. Where was Belinda's father? Was he as crazy as her father had said he was?

She called Dillon from the plane and got his answering machine. He was probably at the gym. She'd surprise him. She could see him walking through the front door all sweaty and so beautiful she'd have to try to touch all of him at once, which was great fun but impossible. Suddenly, in her mind's eye she saw him and Hannah in the shower. The jealous rage surprised her. She was breathing hard, wanting to yell, but the person seated next to her on the plane probably wouldn't understand. It was in the past. Every woman he'd ever had sex with was in the past, just as Bobby Wellman and his yellow Jaguar were in her past. That made her smile.

It was raining hard in Washington, cold, creeping down into the forties, and utterly miserable. She couldn't wait to get home. Home, she thought. It wasn't her own town house, it was Dillon's wonderful house, with the skylights that gave onto heaven. She got into the taxi at the head of the line and gave the black middle-aged driver directions.

"Bad night," the driver said, giving her a huge white-toothed smile in the rearview mirror.

"I'm hoping the night is going to be a lot better than the day was," she said.

"Pretty little gal like you, I hope it's a hot date?"

"Yes, it is," she said, grinning back. "In fact, I'm going to marry him."

"This guy get lucky or what?"

"Oh yes." She leaned back and closed her eyes. When the taxi pulled up in front of Dillon's red brick house, she was asleep. The driver got out of the cab and walked to the front door. When Savich answered, the driver gave him a big grin.

"I've got a nice little present for you, but she's asleep in the back of my cab. I guess you're her hot date, huh? And the guy who's going to marry her?"

"She told you that, did she? That's a really good sign."

"Women always tell me everything," the driver said, walking back to the taxi.

Savich couldn't wait to get her inside the house.

*　*　*

"DILLON?"

"Yes, it's me. Go back to sleep, Sherlock. You're home now. But I'm not going to let you sleep very long. That all right with you?" He leaned down and kissed her nose.

"Okay," she said, and bit his earlobe.

She giggled. He thought it was the sweetest sound he'd ever heard in his life.

The phone was ringing as he laid her on the bed.

"She lay on her back, looking over at him, listening to his deep voice, his very short answers. When he punched off, she said, "Have they caught him?"

Savich shook his head. "No, but it might be really soon. That was Mr. Maitland. A call came through from this woman in southern Ohio claiming to have seen both Marlin and Erasmus in a restaurant off the turnpike. It sounds like it's for real. They're going to check. They'll get back to us when they know one way or the other. Nothing to do now but wait."

"Is this the first time both Erasmus and Marlin have been reported being seen together?"

He nodded as he pulled his navy blue sweater over his head. He smiled at her as he unfastened his jeans.

Sometime later, she whispered in his mouth, "Please sing to me."

His rich baritone filled the air. *"You're my gateway to heaven, all tied up in a bow. Let me at your hinges and I'll oil them really slow."*

The bedroom phone rang. He held her close as he rolled to his side. "Savich here."

"We think it's Erasmus and Marlin," said Jimmy Maitland, more excitement in his voice than Savich had heard in three months. "So it looks like they're in Ohio. I'll get back to you when I hear any more."

"That's a relief," Savich said and slowly hung up the phone. He turned back to her, saw that the sated vague look was long gone now, and there was fear there, haunting fear. "No, no, Sherlock, Mr. Maitland thinks it was Erasmus and Marlin. They're way off in Ohio someplace, far away from us. It's okay. They'll catch them." Still, the fear didn't leave her eyes. He said nothing more, just came over her again.

He didn't ease his hold on her until he was certain she was asleep. He kissed her temple. He wondered what had happened in San Francisco. Then he wondered if they'd caught Marlin yet and if they'd dispatched him to hell.

*   *   *

SHERLOCK was feeling mellow as she sipped Dillon's famous home-brewed tea. Morning sunlight poured through the kitchen windows. She was leaning against the refrigerator.

Dillon took her cup and kissed her until she was ready to jump him. Then he gave it back to her. It took another three long drinks of coffee and a distance of three feet from him before she could function again. He grinned at her.

When she had her wits together, finally, she told him about her parents, about Douglas. "Douglas was treating my mother like she was his lover. He kissed her, caressed her face, called her by her first name. I'm not wrong about this even though he denied it, denied it quite believably."

He nearly dropped his spoon. "You're kidding me. No? Well, I guess I shouldn't be surprised. When it comes to your family, I'm willing to believe about anything. Do you think it's possible Douglas was sleeping not only with his wife but also with his wife's mother?"

She took a bite of toast, added another dollop of strawberry spread. "I have no idea. Maybe he wanted all the Sherlock women. After all, he wanted to sleep with me too." She sighed, rubbed her stomach, knew she was going to have to relax or she'd get an ulcer. "It's as if I know them but they're strangers to me in the most basic ways. I found out that Belinda's father, my mother's first husband—his name is Conal Francis—was released from San Quentin a short time ago."

"Interesting. He's the one your father told you tried to kill him? That he was nuts?"

"Yes. My father told me that was why Belinda shouldn't have kids. She had too many crazy genes in her. My father also told me Belinda was already well on her way to being as nuts as her father. I think I'll call the shrinks at San Quentin and see what they have to say about it."

He rose. "Go ahead and call San Quentin. That's a good idea. You want to ride downtown with me?"

OLLIE greeted her with a hug and began talking immediately about a string of kidnappings and murders in Missouri. "It's the same perps, that's pretty well established. They kidnap a rich couple's child, get a huge ransom, then kill the kid. Actually, it's likely that they kill the kid immediately, then string the parents along. There have been three of them, the most recent one in Hannibal, you know, the birthplace of Mark Twain. These folk are real monsters, Sherlock."

She took a deep breath. After all, monsters were their business.

She understood that, she accepted it, and wanted to get them put away, that or get them on death row. But children. That was more than monstrous. Once they had Marlin and Erasmus, she wanted to concentrate on the kidnappers. No, they were murderers; the kidnapping really didn't count.

She went back to her desk and booted up her computer. Dillon had put a lion on her screen, and he roared at her out of the small speakers on either side of the console. She heard two agents shouting at each other. She heard a woman laugh, saw a Coke can go flying past her desk, heard the agent shout his thanks. She heard the hum of the Xerox, someone cursing the fax machine, heard an agent speak in that deep, rich FBI voice on the phone. Everything was back to normal chaos. Only it wasn't, not for her, at least not yet.

Marlin Jones was still free. Belinda's killer, whoever that was, was still out there. She prayed that both Marlin and Erasmus were in Ohio, with the state police getting really close. She hoped the police would take both of them out.

She looked up to see Ollie stretching. "Anything new on Missouri?"

Ollie shook his head. "Nothing, *nada*, zippo. But you know, I got this funny feeling in my gut. I know we're going to get the perps. Despite MAXINE being really stumped on this one, I know it's going to come to an end soon now."

She sighed. "I hope so." But what she was thinking about was smoke and mirrors. Her life seemed filled with smoke and mirrors. Everyone looked back at her, but their faces weren't real, and she wondered if they were looking at her or at someone they thought was she. No one seemed as he really was. Except for Dillon.

"You haven't called Chico for a karate lesson," Dillon said as he revved up the engine of his 911 just after six o'clock that evening in the parking garage.

"Tomorrow. I swear I'll call this madman of yours tomorrow."

"You'll like Chico. He's skinny as a lizard and can take out guys twice his size. It will be good training for you."

"Hey, can he take you out?"

"Are you crazy? Naturally not." He gave her a fat smile. "Chico and I respect each other."

"You going to tromp me into the ground tonight?"

"Sure. Be my pleasure. Let's swing by your place and pack up some more things for you." Actually, he wanted all of her things at his house. He never wanted her to move back to her town house, but he held his tongue. It was too soon.

But it was Sherlock who swung by her own town house, Dillon having gotten a call on his cell. He dropped her off at home for her car, then headed back to headquarters. "An hour, no longer. There's this senator who wants to stick his nose into the kidnappings in Missouri. I've got to give an update."

"What about Ollie?"

"Mr. Maitland couldn't get hold of him. It's okay. I'll see you at the gym in an hour and a half, tops. You be careful." He kissed her, patted her cheek, and watched her walk to her own car. He watched her lock the car doors, then wave at him.

The night was seamless black, no stars showing, only a sliver of moon. It was cold. Sherlock turned on the car heater and the radio to a country-western station. She found herself humming to "Mama, Don't Let Your Babies Grow Up to Be Cowboys."

She'd have to ask Dillon to sing that one to her. Her town house was dark. She frowned. She was certain she'd left on the foyer light that lit up the front-door area. Well, maybe not. It seemed as though she'd been gone for much longer than a week. She supposed she might as well rent the place out, furnished. She'd have to call some realtors to see how much would be appropriate to ask. Why had Douglas been leaning over her mother, kissing her, talking to her as if she were his lover?

She knew this was one question she'd never be able to ask her mother. And Douglas had denied it was true. She wondered if all families were as odd as hers. No, that wasn't possible. Not all families had had a child murdered.

She wasn't humming when she slid the key into the dead bolt and turned it. She was wishing she were at the gym. She wished he were throwing her to the mat when she turned the lock and pushed the front door open. She felt for the foyer light, flipped it on. Nothing happened.

No wonder. The miserable lightbulb had burned out. It had been one of those suckers guaranteed for seven years. She had replacement lightbulbs in the kitchen. She walked through the arch into the living room and found the light switch.

Nothing happened.

Her breathing hitched. No, that was ridiculous. It had to be the circuit breaker and that was in the utility closet off the kitchen, with more of those seven-year-guaranteed lightbulbs. She walked slowly toward the kitchen, past the dining area, bumping into a chair she'd forgotten about, then felt the cool kitchen tile beneath her feet. She reached automatically for the light switch.

Nothing happened. Of course.

Little light slipped in through the large kitchen window. A black night, that's what it was. Seldom was it so black.

"Technology," she said, making her way across the kitchen. "Miserable, unreliable technology."

"Yeah, ain't it a bitch?"

She was immobile with terror for a fraction of a second until she realized that she'd been trained not to freeze, that freezing could get you killed, and she whipped around, her fist aimed at the man's throat. But he was shorter than she was used to. Her fist glanced off his cheek. He grunted, then backhanded her, sending her against the kitchen counter. She felt pain surge through her chest. She was reaching for her SIG even as she was falling.

"Don't even think about doing something that stupid," the man said. "It's real dark in here for you but not for me. I've been used to the dark for a real long time. You just slide on down to the floor and don't move or else I'll just have to blow off that head of yours and all that pretty red hair will get soaked with brains."

He kicked the SIG out of her hand. A sharp kick, a well-aimed kick, a trained kick. She still had her Lady Colt strapped to her ankle. She eased down, slowly, very slowly. A thief, a robber, maybe a rapist. At least he hadn't killed her yet.

"Boy, turn on the lights."

In the next moment the house was flooded with light. She stared at the old man who stood a good three feet away from her, a carving knife held in his right hand. He was well dressed, shaved, clean. He was short and thin, like the knife he was holding.

He was Erasmus Jones.

The boy came into her vision. It was Marlin.

They weren't in Ohio. They were both right there, in her kitchen.

THIRTY-FOUR

"Hi, Marty. Hey, aren't you looking so scared you wanna puke?"

Dillon would miss her in another forty minutes, maybe thirty-five minutes. He'd be worried. It would be an unspecified worry, but worry he would. He might wait another five minutes, then he'd come here. She looked from father to son. She smiled, praying that only she realized it was a smile filled with unspoken terror. "Hey, Marlin. How long have you and your dad been squatters in my house?"

Erasmus Jones answered as he hunkered down to her eye level. "Three days now. That's how long it took us to get from Boston to here. We had to be real careful, you know?"

"I would imagine so. Lucky I wasn't here."

"Oh no," Marlin said. "I wanted you to be here. I wanted you, Marty, but you'd gone. Were you with that cop? Savich is his name, right? You sleeping with him?" He said to his father, "He's a big fella, real big, lots of muscles, and he fights mean."

"I bet he ain't as mean as your mama were," Erasmus said and poked the tip of the knife into the sole of Lacey's shoe. It was so sharp that it sliced through the sole and nicked her foot. She winced, but kept quiet.

"Mama was a bitch, Pa. I remember her. She was a bitch, always cussing and back-talking you, always had a bottle in her hand, swigging it even while she was hitting me in the face."

"Yep, Lucile were a mean one. She's dead now, did I tell you that?"

Another rabbit hole, Lacey thought. Forty minutes, max. Dillon would come over here in no more than forty minutes now. Then what? He wouldn't be expecting trouble; there was no reason for him to. Erasmus and Marlin were supposed to be in Ohio. So he'd think she needed help moving stuff. He'd be vulnerable. She wouldn't let them hurt him. No, she had her Lady Colt. She'd do something. She wouldn't, couldn't, let anything happen to Dillon.

"Ma's dead?" Marlin asked as he sat down on one of Lacey's kitchen chairs.

"Yeah."

His father was telling him this now?

Marlin said, "No, you didn't tell me that, Pa. What happened?"

"Nothin' much. I just carved her up like that Thanksgiving turkey she didn't make me."

"Oh, well, that's all right, then. She deserved it. She never was a good wife or mother."

"Yeah, she was like all those women who walked the walk for you, Marlin. That maze of yours, I sure do like that. You got that from that game we used to play in the desert."

"Yes, Pa."

"Well, we got this gal here now. Let's off her and then get out of here. There's no more food anyways."

"No," Marlin said, and his voice was suddenly different—strong and determined, not like the deferential tone he'd used with his father since he'd come in. "Marty's going to walk the walk. She's got to be punished. She shot me in the belly. It hurt real bad. It still hurts. I got this ugly scar that's all puckered and red. It's her turn now."

Erasmus said, "I want to kill her now. It ain't smart to hang around here."

"I know, but I got my maze all fixed up for her. She'll like it. She already knows the drill. Only this time when she hits the center, she'll have a big surprise."

Thirty minutes, no more.

"You fix up another warehouse, Marlin?"

"Hey, Marty, I fixed it up real good. You'll like it. I had lots of time so it's really prime."

"Why would I walk the walk when you get me there, Marlin? I know you'll be at the center waiting to kill me. I'd be a fool to go into the maze."

"Well, you see, Marty, you'll do anything I ask you to. I got myself a little leverage here."

Dillon. No, not Dillon. Who?

"Let me go get my little sweet chops," Erasmus said and rose slowly. He stretched that skinny body of his. His legs were slightly bowed. He was wearing cowboy boots. Without boots he'd be no more than five foot six inches. "You keep a good eye on her, boy. She's tricky. Look at her eyes—lots of tricks buried in there. I bet you the FBI taught her all sorts of things to do to a man."

Marlin calmly pulled a .44 Magnum out of his belt. "I like this better than your FBI gun, Marty, although I'll take it with me, as a souvenir. This baby will blow a foot-wide hole out of your back if I shoot you in the chest.

I don't think you would survive that, Marty." He assumed a serious pose, rubbing his chin with his hand. "You're real tough, but you couldn't live through this, could you?"

"No," she said, studying his face, his eyes, trying to figure out what to do. "No one could." Should she try to disarm him now?

It was academic. There was Erasmus in the door. He was grinning. "She gave me a mite of trouble so I had to smash her head." He dragged in Hannah Paisley by the hair. She was wearing a charcoal gray running suit, running shoes on her feet. She was unconscious.

"You know her, don't you, gal? Don't lie to me, I can see it writ all over your face."

"Yes, she's a Special Agent. How did you get her?"

"Easy as skinnin' a skunk. She was out running. I stole her fanny pack, saw she was with the FBI, and took her down. Nary a whimper from her. I'm real pleased you know her, personal like. That's gotta make a difference. You don't want me to kill her, now do you?"

"How did you know I knew her?" Out of ten thousand FBI agents he had to get Hannah Paisley? No, it was too much of a coincidence.

"Oh, I was watching you come out of that huge ugly Hoover Building. There was this one, standing there, waving at you, but you didn't see her, you kept walking. I knew I had the one I needed right then. Yep, she knew you."

Hannah groaned. Sherlock saw her hands were lashed together behind her back and her ankles were tied tightly together.

"Don't hurt her. She didn't do anything to you."

Marlin laughed. "No, but I knew you wouldn't cooperate unless we got someone. Pa followed her. He figured she was FBI and he was right. Now, Marty, you ready to come to the warehouse with me and walk the walk?"

Twenty minutes, no more than twenty minutes. There would be no way Dillon would find her if they left, no way at all. She looked around then. They had trashed the kitchen, the living room. He would come in and he would know that she was taken, but he wouldn't know where. For the first time she smelled spoiled food, saw the dishes strewn over the counters and the table. There were a good dozen empty beer cans, some of them on the floor.

"Where is this warehouse, Marlin?"

"Why do you care, Marty? It won't make any difference to you where you croak it."

"Sure it will. Tell me. Oh yes, my name's Lacey, not Marty. Belinda

Madigan was my sister. You having trouble with your memory, Marlin?"

His breathing hitched, his hand jerked up. She didn't drop her eyes from his face.

"Don't piss me off, Marty. You want to know where we're going? Off to that real bad-ass part of Washington between Calvert and Williams Streets. When I was going in and out down there no one even looked at me. They were all dope dealers, addicts, and drunks. Nope, no one cared what I was doing. And you know something else? When they find you, no one will care about that either.

"Every night I got there, I had to kick out the druggies. I'll have to do it one more time. I wonder if they'll report finding you or wait until a cop comes along. Yeah, I'll flush out all the druggies. They're piled high around there, filthy slugs."

"My boy never did drugs," Erasmus said, looking over at Sherlock. She nearly vomited when she saw that he was stroking his gnarled hand over Hannah's breasts, the other hand still tangled in her hair. "Marlin ain't stupid. He only likes gals, too, knows how to use 'em real good. I taught him. Whenever he found his way to the center of the maze I built, why I took him off to Yuma and bought him a whore."

Fifteen minutes.

"I've got to go to the bathroom, Marlin."

"You really gotta pee, gal? You're not shittin' Marlin?"

"I really do. Can I get up? Really slow?"

Marlin nodded. He'd straightened, the gun pointed right at her chest. "I'll go with you, Marty. No, I won't watch you pee, but I'll be right outside the door. You do anything stupid and I'll let my pa cut up that pretty face of yours."

"No, Marlin, I'll cut up this gal's pretty face. First I'll cut off all her hair, scrape my knife over her scalp so she looks like a billiard ball. Then I'll do a picture on her face. You got that, gal?"

"I got it." Ten minutes. Calvert and Williams Streets. She wasn't familiar with them, but Dillon would be.

Her downstairs bathroom was disgusting. It stank of urine, of dirty towels, of dirty underwear, and there were spots on the mirror. "Did anyone ever tell you you were a pig, Marlin?"

She wished she'd kept her mouth closed. He punched her hard in the kidney. The pain sent her to her knees.

"I might be a pig, Marty, but you'll be dead. Not long now and you'll be dead and rotting and my pa and I will be driving into Virginia. There's some real pretty mountains there and lots of places to hide out. Do your business now, Marty. We've got to get out of here. Hey, you gotta pee because you're so scared, right?"

"That's right, Marlin." She closed the door on his grinning face, heard him lean against it, knew he was listening. She knew she didn't have much time.

He banged on the door as she flushed the toilet. "That's long enough, Marty."

When she walked out, he shoved her back in. He looked around. "I'm not the pig. It's my pa. He never learned how to do things 'cause his ma never taught him anything, left him lying in his own shit when he was just a little tyke, made him lie in his own shit when he was older, to punish him. She wasn't nice, my grandma."

"She doesn't sound nice," Lacey said. "Why'd you come here, Marlin? Why do you want to kill me? It's a really big risk you're taking. Why?"

He looked thoughtful for a long moment, but the gun never wavered from the center of her back. "I knew I had to take you out," he said finally. "No one can beat me and get away with it. I thought and thought about how I could get out of the cage in Boston and then that judge handed me a golden key. Those idiot shrinks were a piece of cake. I acted all scared, even cried a little bit. Yes, it was all so easy. There was my pa, sent me a message in prison, and I knew where he was waiting. All I had to do was get in Brainerd to the Glover Motel at the western edge of town. There he was, had clothes for me, everything, a car with a full tank of gas. I knew then that I could get you, take you out, and then I'd be free. Actually, it was Pa who hit that guy in Boston, nearly sent him off to hell where he belongs."

"I know. Your pa used your driver's license. We got the license plate."

Marlin wasn't expecting that. "Well, I told Pa to be careful. He was sure he'd knocked the FBI guy from here to next Sunday, but he didn't. He really got the plate, huh? No matter. Everything's back on track now. I wish that the FBI guy had gotten his."

Hannah moaned from the kitchen.

"Now, let me see if you tried to leave any message for that muscle boy you're sleeping with."

She didn't move, barely breathed. And waited. He poked around a bit, then straightened. "You're smart, Marty. You didn't try anything. That's good."

Hannah moaned again. They heard Erasmus say something to her. They heard a sharp cry. The bastard, he'd hit her again.

"You'll come, won't you, Marty? You'll come to me at the center of the maze? My pa will kill her slow if you refuse. It sounds like he's already got started. You got the picture now, don't you?"

To die for Hannah Paisley, perhaps there was a dose of irony there. No, she'd die anyway. Lacey seriously doubted Hannah would survive this either. But Sherlock had no choice, none at all. "I'll come."

Ten minutes.

"Let me see if Hannah's all right."

"A real buddy, is she? That's excellent. No shit from you then, Marty, or Pa will make her real sorry. Then it'll be my turn to make you even sorrier."

"No shit from me, Marlin."

"Ladies shouldn't say that word, Marty."

She wanted to laugh, realized it was hysteria bubbling in her throat, and kept her mouth shut. When she walked into the kitchen, Hannah was sitting on the floor, her back against the wall.

"I'm sorry, Hannah. Are you all right?"

Hannah's eyes weren't focused, but she was trying. She probably had a concussion. "Sherlock, is that you?"

"Yes."

"Where is this place? Who are these animals?"

Erasmus kicked her.

Hannah didn't make a sound, but her body seemed to ripple with the shock of the pain.

"This is my place. These men are Marlin Jones and his father, Erasmus."

She saw Hannah realized the consequences in that single instant. She also knew she was going to die. Both of them would die. Sherlock saw her trying to loosen the knots on her wrists.

"Gentlemen," Hannah said, looking from one to the other. "Can I have a glass of water?"

"Then you'll probably have to go pee, like Marty here," Marlin said.

"Marty? Her name is Sherlock."

Marlin kicked Hannah, the way his father had. "Shut your mouth. I hate women who haven't got the brains to keep their lips sewn together. I might do that someday. Get myself a little sewing kit. I could use different colored thread for each woman. No water. Let's get out of here. Who knows who's going to show up?"

Five minutes, but it didn't matter now. Sherlock was bound and gagged, lying on her side in the backseat of her own car, a blanket thrown over her. Hannah was behind her in the storage space.

One of them was driving a stolen car she'd seen briefly, a gray Honda Civic. Then she heard her Explorer revved up but didn't know which one of them was driving. She guessed they'd leave her car at the warehouse.

Sherlock closed her eyes and prayed harder than she'd ever prayed in her life. If Marlin left her hands tied behind her, then there would be no way she could get to the Lady Colt strapped around her ankle.

SAVICH stretched his back, then his hamstrings. He heard a woman's voice from the front of the gym and started to call out.

But it wasn't Sherlock.

It had been an hour and twenty minutes. In that instant he knew something was very wrong. He called her cell. No answer. He and Quinlan both had this gut thing. Neither of them ever ignored it. He immediately called Jimmy Maitland.

"It's dinnertime, Savich. This better be good."

"There's no word about Marlin Jones, is there?"

"No, none yet. Why?"

"I haven't seen Sherlock in over an hour. She was supposed to meet me at the gym. She hasn't shown. I called her cell. No answer. I know that Marlin and his father are here. I know it. I know they've got Sherlock."

"How do you know that? What's going on, Savich?"

"My gut. You've never before mistrusted my gut, sir. Don't mistrust it now. I'm out of here and on my way to her house. She was going there to get more stuff. We made a firm time date. She isn't here. Sherlock's always on time. Something's happened and I know it's Marlin and Erasmus. Put out an APB on her car, Ford Explorer, license SHER 123. Can you get a call out to everyone to look for her?"

"You got it."

Savich was at her house within ten minutes. It was dark. Her car wasn't in the driveway. Jesus, he prayed he'd been wrong. Maybe she was at his place, maybe she wanted to unpack her stuff before she came to the gym. No, she wouldn't do that. He went to the front door and tried the doorknob.

It opened.

He had his SIG out as he pushed the door fully open.

He turned on the light switch. He saw the trashed living room. Furniture overturned, lamps hurled against the wall, her lovely prints slashed, beer cans and empty Chinese cartons and pizza boxes on the floor. One piece of molding cheese pizza lay halfway out of the box onto a lovely Tabriz carpet.

The kitchen was a disaster area. It was weird, but he could smell Sherlock's scent over the stench of rotted food. She'd been here. Recently. Then he saw her fanny pack on the floor under the table. He opened it but saw it wasn't Sherlock's. It was Hannah Paisley's. They had both women. How did they get Hannah? How did they *know* to get Hannah?

And why had they taken her?

Of course he knew the answer to that. Marlin knew he'd have to have some leverage, something to make Sherlock do what he told her to do. And that would be? To walk the maze, to get to the center, where he'd kill her, to pay her back for scamming him, for shooting him, for beating him.

So he and his father would have taken the women to some warehouse nearby. But where? There were lots of likely places in Washington, D.C. Sherlock would know that he'd realize what had happened. She'd have left him something, if she'd had the chance. He looked around the kitchen but didn't see anything.

He was on the cell phone to the cops when he walked into the small bathroom off the downstairs hallway. He nearly gagged at the stench. He pulled open the drawers below the sink. Nothing. He pulled aside the shower curtain. There was Sherlock's purse on the floor of the shower stall, open.

"Give me Lieutenant Jacobs, please. I imagine he's gone home. What's his phone number? Listen, this is Dillon Savich, FBI. We've got a real problem here and I need help fast."

Savich was on the phone to Jacobs even as he was bending down to pick up Sherlock's purse. It was a big black leather shoulder bag. He'd kidded her about carrying a full week's change of clothes and running shoes in there.

"Is Lieutenant Jacobs there, please?"

He carefully pulled out each item. It was when he got to her small cosmetic bag that he went really slowly. He unzipped it a little bit at a time, holding it upright.

"Is this you, Lewis? Savich here. I've got a huge problem. You know all about Marlin and Erasmus Jones? Well, they're here in Washington and they've got two of my agents—Agent Sherlock and Agent Paisley. Hold a second." Slowly Savich turned the cosmetic bag inside out. There written in eyebrow pencil was: *Calvert & Williams, wareh—*.

She was good. "Lewis, she managed to leave me a message. There's a warehouse at Calvert and Williams. He's going to make Sherlock go through a maze, Lewis, and Marlin will be at the center. He'll kill her. Do a silent approach, all right? I'll see you there in ten minutes."

He couldn't believe it. His Porsche wouldn't start. He tried again, then raised the hood. Nothing obvious, not that he was a genius with cars. He kicked the right front tire and ran into the street. A motorist nearly ran him down, slammed down on his brakes, and weaved around him. Savich stood in the middle, waving his arms.

A taxi pulled up. A grinning black face peered out at him. "Well, if it isn't the lucky man who's going to marry that pretty little gal."

THIRTY-FIVE

There was no time. No time at all.

She didn't want to die, didn't want to lose her life to this crazy yahoo who was grinning at her like the madman he was. No, he wasn't mad, he knew exactly what he was doing, and he knew it was wrong. He enjoyed it. Remorse was alien to him. Being really human, in all its complexity and simplicity, was alien to him.

She looked at Hannah, who was standing with her back against one of Marlin's props, her head down. At first Sherlock thought she was numb with fear, but then she realized she wasn't terrified senseless, which Marlin and Erasmus probably thought. No, it was an act. Hannah was getting her bearings, thinking, figuring odds.

Good. Let them think she was broken. Sherlock called out, her voice filled with false concern she was sure Hannah would see right through, "Hannah, are you all right?"

"Yes, but for how long?" Hannah didn't look at her, kept breathing deeply, staring at the filthy wooden floor. "I don't suppose there's a chance that Savich will get here?"

"I don't know."

"Shut up, both of you bitches!"

"Really nice language from your daddy, Marlin."

"He can say whatever he wants, Marty. You know that. He's a man."

"Him? A man?" It was Hannah, her voice hoarse because Erasmus had choked her when she'd tried to get away from him. "He's a worm, a cowardly worm who raised you to be a rabid murderer."

Hannah didn't even have time to ready herself before Erasmus hit her hard on the head with the butt of Sherlock's SIG.

"I'll enjoy cutting her throat," Erasmus said, standing over an unconscious Hannah. She was drawn up in the fetal position. There was a trickle of blood from her nose.

"So you will kill her," Sherlock said, and smiled at Marlin. "I'm not going into your maze. There's no reason to. She isn't leverage. You're going to kill her too. You heard your sweet daddy."

Erasmus raised his hand to strike her, but Marlin grabbed his wrist. "Marty's mine. I'll handle her. Lookee here, Pa, a little druggie. You want to take care of her?"

A young black girl, dressed in ragged filthy jeans and an old Washington Redskins jersey with holes in the elbows, was crouched by the door of the warehouse, her eyes huge, knowing she was in the wrong place and knowing too there was nothing she could do about it. Erasmus walked to the girl, took her by the neck, and shook her like a chicken. Sherlock heard the girl's neck snap. It was unbearable. She closed her eyes but not before she saw Erasmus toss the girl aside like so much garbage.

"I'll see if there are any more scum inside," Erasmus said and slid through the narrow opening into the huge derelict building. The area was godforsaken, bleak, an air of complete hopelessness about it. All the buildings had been abandoned by people who had given up. All were in various stages of dilapidation. There were old tires lying about, cardboard boxes stacked carefully together to cover a homeless person. It was the nation's capital and it looked like the remains of Bosnian cities Sherlock had seen on TV a while back.

Marlin took her chin in his palm and forced her face up. "Guess what, Marty?"

"My name's Lacey."

"No, you're Marty to me. That was how you came on to me in Boston. That's how you'll go out. Guess what I found?"

She stared at him.

He pulled her Lady Colt out of his pocket. "I remembered this little number. This is the gun you shot me with in Boston. You were hoping I'd forget, weren't you? You wanted to blast me again, didn't you? Well you aren't going to do anything now. I win, Marty. I win everything."

"You won't win a thing, you slug. I'm not going to walk into your maze."

"What if I promise you I'll let her go?"

She laughed. "Your daddy's the one who's going to kill her, Marlin, not you."

"All right, then. I have another idea." Marlin twisted her chin, slapped her. "Come on, Marty, Show Time."

Erasmus came out of the warehouse, dragging a ragged old man by his filthy jacket collar. "Only one, Marlin—this poor old heap of bones. He's gone to his reward. I bet he'd thank me for releasing him if he had any breath left."

Erasmus lowered the old man to the rotted wooden planks outside the warehouse, kicked him next to a stack of tires. "Take your girlie, Marlin, and have her walk the walk. I want to get out of this damned city. It's unfriendly, you know? And look around you. People ain't got no pride here. Ain't nothing but devastation. Don't our government have any pride in their capital?"

Marlin smiled down at Sherlock, raised the .44 Magnum, and brought it down on the side of her head. She was unconscious before she hit the ground.

"Now, I've got to do this just so," Marlin said to his father as he leaned down over Hannah. "Yes, just so. I can't wait to see her face when she finally comes to the center of the maze, when she finally comes to me."

FOUR local police cars cruised in silently, all of them parked a good block from the warehouse. Men and women quietly emerged from the cars, Lewis Jacobs bringing them to where Savich had just arrived in a taxi, a tall middle-aged black man next to him.

"Jimmy Maitland will be here soon, along with about fifteen Special Agents," Savich said quietly. "Now, here's what we're going to do."

SHERLOCK awoke slowly, nausea thick in the back of her throat, her head pounding. She tried to raise her head, just a bit, but the dizziness brought her down. She closed her eyes. Marlin had struck her with a gun over her left ear, harder this time than in Boston. He'd probably laughed when she was unconscious at his feet. She lay silently, waiting, swallowing convulsively, praying that Dillon had found her message, but knowing in her gut that she had to depend on herself, not on some rescue. Where was Hannah?

It was dead silent in the huge gloomy warehouse, except for the sound of an occasional scurrying rat. The air was thick and smelled faintly rotten, as if things had died here and been left where they'd fallen. Her nausea increased. She swallowed, willing herself not to vomit. There was a small pool of light in front of her, thanks to Marlin.

There was also a ball of string.

Think. He had both her guns. She looked around slowly, wondering if he or Erasmus could see her. There was nothing she could see to use as a weapon, nothing at all.

Except the string. She came up slowly onto her knees. She still felt light-headed, but the dizziness was better. A few more moments. At least he'd removed the ropes from her hands and feet. At least she was free.

She heard Marlin's eerie voice coming from out of the darkness. "Hey, you're awake. Good. It took you long enough, but my daddy said I was too excited to be patient. Marty, listen to this."

Hannah's scream ripped through the silence.

"I've got her here, Marty, at the center of the maze. This was just a little demonstration. Don't panic on me. I only hurt her a little bit. She must have a real low threshold of pain to scream when I just jerked her arm up. Now, if you don't get here, she won't be quite whole real soon. You start moving now or I'll start cutting off her fingers, then her nose, then her toes. Hey, that rhymes. I'm good. Now, I'll work up from there, Marty, and you'll get to hear her scream every time I take my knife to her. I won't cut her tongue out until last. You'll hear everything I do to her."

She stood up, the string in her hand. "I'm coming, Marlin. Don't hurt her. You promise?"

There was silence. She knew he was talking to Erasmus. Good, they were together. She didn't have to worry about Erasmus watching her from a different vantage point.

"She'll be fine as long as I know you're on your way. Move, Marty. That's right. I can see you now."

But he couldn't, at least not all of the time, just at those intervals where he'd managed to place mirrors. She began wrapping the string around her hand. No, this wouldn't do it. She had to double the string and knot it every couple of inches. She redid it as she walked, clumsy at first, gaining in proficiency and speed as she tied it again and again. She was nearly to the beginning of the maze and the string would run out. She prayed she'd have enough.

"I'm coming, Marlin. Don't touch Hannah."

"I'm not hurting her now, Marty, you keep walking toward my voice. That's right. You using the string, Marty? That's part of the game—you've got to use the string."

"I'm using the string."

"Good. You're a smart little bitch, aren't you?"

She drew a deep breath, called out, "Oh yes, Marlin, you stupid prick, I'm so smart I'm going to kill you. Count on it. And no one will miss you. Everyone will be glad you're in hell where you belong." She stepped into the maze.

"Don't you talk to my boy like that, gal, or I'll take a whack at you myself after he's through."

She heard them talking but couldn't make out any words.

Marlin said, "I told my daddy I was right. Yes, I was right all along. You have a dirty mouth. He heard that bad word you said. You deserve my kind of punishment." He laughed, a full, deep laugh, but there was something in it, something that sounded vaguely like fear. Was that really fear she heard? She'd hurt him once, surely he hadn't forgotten that, but she couldn't imagine why he'd be even faintly afraid now. She was alone. She didn't have a weapon. Still, she had no other options. She decided to push. "Remember how it felt to have a bullet in your gut, Marlin? Remember all those tubes and needles they stuck into you at the hospital? You even had one in your cock. You remember that? Remember how you lay there whimpering, all gray in the face? You looked so pathetic. You looked like a beat-up little boy. I looked at you and I was really glad I'd shot you. I hoped you'd die, but you didn't. You'll die this time, Marlin. You're crazy and stupid, you know that?"

"I'm not! I'll pay you back for that, Marty."

"You couldn't pay back anything. You're a coward, Marlin, and you're afraid of me. Aren't you? I can hear it in your voice. It's shaking. You're worthless, Marlin. You're nothing but a loser. Your mama should have strangled you at birth."

"No!" He was heaving now, she could hear him, heaving from rage. "I'll kill you, Marty, and I'll enjoy every minute of it. You deserve to die, more than any of the others."

"Let me take her out, boy."

"No! She's mine, and this one too. I want both of them. You know this other one cusses all the time. Yes, I want both of them. You wait and see how well I slice them up. You'll be proud of me, Pa."

He was screaming and pleading with his father, both at the same time. He was really close to the edge. "I'm the best slicer in the world, not you! I'm the best!"

Lacey walked very quietly, the knotted string wrapped around her hand. He'd built the maze very well. She hit two dead ends and had to retrace her steps.

She called out, "Marlin, it looks like you finally learned how to build a proper maze. I just hit the second dead end. Too bad you're so stupid that your daddy didn't teach you how to build a really good maze way back when you were young. It took you long enough to learn, didn't it, you pathetic little slug?"

"Damn you, bitch, shut up! Don't you talk like that! I know you're doing it on purpose to make me mad, to try to make me lose control, but I won't. I know you don't talk like that all the time. Do you? Damn you, bitch, answer me."

"That's right, you little jerk. It's all just for you, Marlin, you miserable stupid fuck."

"Shut up! SHUT UP!"

His voice was trembling. She could imagine him nearly frothing at the mouth with rage. Good.

Her voice rang out cold and calm. "Why the fuck should I?"

"I'll kill you now, Marty. I've got my Magnum right here, all ready to go. You walk faster or Hannah's going to lose her pinky finger."

"I'm coming, Marlin. I told you I would. Unlike you, I keep my word. Only a coward would hurt her and you've been swearing to me you aren't a coward, right?"

He was breathing real hard now. She was close enough to hear his rage, nearly taste it. It smelled sweet, coppery, like human blood. "No, I won't hurt her. Not yet anyway. You're first, Marty, you. I want you, then I might be satisfied."

She walked into a narrow pool of light. She carefully held the string at her side. "Where's your daddy, Marlin? Is he lurking around one of the corners of the maze? He's a coward too. You got it all from that precious father of yours, didn't you?"

"I ain't lurking no place, girlie," Erasmus shouted out. "I'm just letting my boy do what will make him happy. You do what he wants, and I won't skin you."

"Did you skin your wife, Erasmus? After you slit her throat or before?"

"Ain't none of your business, girlie. You come along now, you hear me? I want to get out of this place; it ain't comfortable. It makes my skin crawl."

"Yes, I hear you." He was on her left, some thirty feet away. Marlin was only about ten to twelve feet away, at about ten o'clock. Imagine anything making Erasmus's skin crawl.

She'd wrapped about six lengths of string around her hand. String, she thought. All she had was a handful of string to take out two killers with three guns. She loosened the string, making it into a large enough circle so she could loop it over Marlin's head. No, it had to be even bigger. It took time.

She felt bile in her throat and swallowed. She couldn't, wouldn't give up until he killed her. She thought of Dillon. He'd go nuts if Marlin killed her.

He'd already had one woman he loved leave him.

She wasn't about to let Marlin kill her.

THIRTY-SIX

The light was steady now, becoming brighter with each step she took. It was from a narrow beam of light he'd strung some eight feet overhead. She was nearly to the center of the maze now. She heard Hannah moan. She heard Marlin's breathing. Hannah moaned louder. The moans weren't from pain. Hannah was giving her directions. Yes, both she and Marlin were at about ten o'clock. She could picture him standing over Hannah, the Magnum in his hand, a big smile on his face. Waiting for her. He couldn't wait. Where was Erasmus? Had he moved at all?

"Hannah? Can you hear me? Are you all right?"

"I'm all right, Sherlock." Then she moaned again, a nice lusty moan. "The bastard kicked me."

"Hang in there, please, hang in there."

And she knew that Hannah was thinking frantically. She knew whatever she tried, Hannah would help her if she could.

There was no sound now except for Marlin's jerky deep breathing.

Had Dillon found her message? Had he even gone to her house yet? Of course he had. She swallowed. Nearly there. Nearly to Marlin.

She stepped into bright light, two spotlights shining directly into her face. She shaded her eyes with her right hand. In her left hand was the string, ready now, if only he didn't see it, if only she had time and opportunity.

"Hello, Marty," he said, nearly gasping with pleasure. "You're here."

He was standing beside Hannah, his chest puffed out, looking very proud of himself. He looked happy. His eyes were dead and glittered. He was grinning at her.

She grinned back at him. "Hi, you little fucker. How's tricks? Have you killed any more women since you escaped that madhouse in Boston?"

He lurched, as if she'd gut-punched him. "It wasn't a madhouse!"

"Sure it was. It was the state madhouse."

"I was just there to talk to some shrinks, nothing else. I was visiting for a little while."

"If that judge hadn't been such an idiot, they'd have you right now in a padded cell. You know what else? They'd shackle your legs together and walk you right out of your padded cell to the electric chair. Then they'd fry you. It will still happen, Marlin. Can you imagine the pain, Marlin?"

"Damn you, shut up! Be quiet! Show some respect for me. I won, damn you, I won! Not you. You're standing there, nothing going for you this time. I'm the big winner. You're nothing, Marty, nothing at all."

"That's right, Marlin, you've won. Even though you haven't had any women walk to the center of your maze since your escape, you've still managed to kill very dangerous and very heavily armed homeless people and teenagers. That's real brave of you, Marlin. Real manly. You make me puke."

"No, that was my pa!"

"Same difference. You're his very image."

He was panting now, trying to hold himself back, and she pushed harder. "You know what, Marlin? I once thought you were pretty good-looking. You know what you look like now? You look like you're ready to drip saliva from your mouth. Is that true? Are you ready to froth at the mouth, Marlin? I've never seen a sorrier excuse for a man in my life."

He snapped, ran at her, the knife raised. Hannah jerked from her left to her right side, whipped up her bound legs and tripped him. He went sprawling, sliding on his stomach almost to Sherlock's feet. She was on him in an instant, looping the thick knotted string around his throat. She had her knee in the small of his back, pulling back on the string, bringing his face off the wooden floor. She knew it was cutting deep into his neck.

"Hannah, where's his gun?"

"Hannah can't get it, Marty."

She turned slowly to see Erasmus holding Hannah's head back at an impossible angle. He had her hair wrapped around his left hand. His right hand held a twelve-inch hunting knife to her throat. "Let my boy go, Marty."

"I will if you release Hannah. Now, Erasmus."

He shook his head slowly. The knife point punched into Hannah's skin. A drop of blood welled up and trickled down to disappear into her running top. Lacey saw no fear on her face; what she saw was some kind of message in her eyes. What?

"You release him real slow, Marty, or the knife goes all the way in."

"The knife goes all the way in, Erasmus, and your sweet boy here is dead." She twisted the string. Marlin gurgled. His face was darkening. She jerked back his head so his daddy could see him. He thrashed with his arms and legs, but he couldn't dislodge her.

Erasmus screamed, "You bitch! Loosen the knot! You're choking him, he's turning blue!"

Suddenly, Hannah sent her elbow back with all her strength into Erasmus's stomach.

He yelled, loosened his grip just a bit, just enough so Hannah could roll away from him and that hunting knife.

There was a single shot, loud and hot in the heavy silent air. Erasmus took the bullet in the middle of his forehead. He stared toward Sherlock, surprise widening his eyes even in his own death. Slowly, so very slowly, he fell forward. Hannah rolled out of his way. He landed on his face. They heard his nose break, loud and obscene in the silence.

"Pa! Damn you, you killed my pa!"

Marlin jerked back, grabbed Sherlock's wrists and pulled her over his head. She landed on her back, winded. Marlin was on her, sitting on her chest, leaning into her face, his knife right under her nose.

"I've got you now, bitch. You killed my pa and now I'll kill you and then that other bitch."

"No, you won't cut me, Marlin. It's too late. The cops are here. One of them shot your pa."

Marlin jerked up and brought down the knife.

"Sherlock, flatten!"

She pressed as hard as she could into the floor even as she heard the gun crack, loud in her ears. It was a very hard shot to make without hitting her in the process. Marlin had been so close to her, they'd had to hold off until they got a better angle. She felt Marlin jerk over her. She knocked him off her, sending him onto his back. The bullet hit him in the back of the neck.

She rolled and came up on her elbows next to him. He was looking up at her. "Tell me how you did it."

"I left him a message. In my purse, in the floor of the shower. I wrote it in eyebrow pencil on the inside of my makeup bag." She looked up. "Dillon, keep everyone away. I've got to talk to him. Just for a moment."

She leaned right into Marlin's face. "Did you kill Belinda?"

He grinned up at her. Blood flowed from his nose and mouth. But he didn't look to be in any pain.

"Did you, Marlin? Did you kill Belinda?"

"Why should I tell you anything?"

"So I can judge which of you is the better man, Marlin, you or your daddy. I can't really until you tell me about Belinda. Did you kill her?"

He looked away from her, upward, but the ceiling was dark, impenetrable. What was he looking at? "You want to know what she did, Marty?"

"What did she do?"

"She killed my kid. Oh yeah, she tried to tell me it was a miscarriage, but I know she killed the kid because she was scared it would be all crazy even before it was born. She told me about her pa being a loony. She told me she'd have to be nuts herself to have a kid I fathered. That's why she killed my kid. She told me she wanted the kid, she didn't care if it was crazy, but then she went and she killed it."

His eyes were vague and wide. She leaned close. "Listen to me, Marlin. Belinda didn't abort your baby. Her husband hit her and she miscarried. It wasn't her fault. It was Douglas's fault. He probably found out the baby wasn't his and he hit her."

"I knew I should have killed that jerk. He couldn't father a kid, at least he hadn't been able to with her. Belinda told me he had this real low sperm count."

"You knew I was Belinda's sister, didn't you, Marlin?"

"Not at first. I recognized you when you came to the hospital. Then I knew who you were."

"But how?"

"You were just a teenager then, but we did have fun with you. I took Belinda to see my maze, made her promise she'd scream and groan and carry on, all for your benefit, to punish you for hiding in the trunk, for spying on us. You really pissed Belinda off."

He closed his eyes and sucked in air. Blood trickled out of his mouth as he whispered, "We drove to the warehouse and Belinda pulled you out of the trunk, told you that you'd been captured and you'd have to walk the walk with her. She told you she was going to die, die because of you, but she prayed that you'd survive. You were sobbing and pleading with me, but Belinda pulled you into the warehouse and kept you with her. She screamed real good for you, then she even let me pretend to knife her when you got to the center of the maze, and you saw it all. You collapsed then. Nobody touched you. You just fell over. Belinda got scared but I told her you were a nosy teenager and you'd get over it. When we got back to Belinda's house, you were still unconscious.

"Belinda told me later you never remembered a thing. She felt guilty about doing that to you. Even though you were a sneak, she loved you. She realized you admired Douglas and were afraid she'd leave him for me. But then she killed my kid. Then I had to kill her. I had no choice at all. She had to die. She betrayed me."

"It was a miscarriage. You killed her and she didn't deserve it. You made a big mistake, Marlin."

"I believed she'd betrayed me. I had to kill her but I didn't really want to."

"She didn't betray you."

He opened his mouth again and a fountain of blood spurted out. Blood flowed from his nose.

Sherlock positioned his head back, then leaned really close to his face. "It's over now, Marlin. You've destroyed quite enough. Yes, Marlin, die now."

He tried to raise his hand, but couldn't. He whispered, his voice liquid with his blood, "You sure are pretty, Marty. Not as pretty as Belinda, but still pretty."

His head fell to the side, his eyes still open, a small smile on his mouth.

She looked up to see Dillon standing not two feet away from them. There were at least twenty other police officers and special agents in a circle around the center of the maze. No one was moving. No one said a word.

She smiled up at him. "No more questions. No more mysteries. He killed Belinda. He told me so and he told me why." All this time—seven long years—she'd driven herself, felt consumed with guilt. All this time she hadn't remembered that Belinda had forced her into Marlin's maze.

She couldn't dredge up a single memory of that night, even after being told what had happened. She wondered if she'd ever remember, even under hypnosis. Well, it didn't matter. Belinda had been dead for seven years. Her murderer was dead. Lacey's life was her own again. And she had Dillon. She had a future.

"Yes," Dillon said. "We all heard him confess. It's over, Sherlock."

"Who shot Marlin?"

A grizzled old cop raised his hand. "Sorry I had to wait so long but I couldn't get a clean shot."

"You did perfectly." She looked at Hannah. "Are you all right?"

"I'm fine now." She was standing beside Dillon, leaning against him.

Lacey looked at her. "Thanks for tripping Marlin. That was really well done. I wasn't quite sure how to get him low enough to loop him. I knew you'd be ready. You'd best stand up straight now, Hannah. I don't want you leaning against Dillon ever again. You got me?"

Hannah laughed, a raw ugly sound that was quite beautiful. "I hear you, Sherlock. I hear you really well. I thought you might be mean once it occurred to you. Good going."

Sherlock slowly stood up. Marlin's blood was all over her. She looked around at the circle of faces.

She was alive.

She gave them all a huge smile. "Thank you all for saving our lives. Mr. Maitland, sir, we finally got him."

"No shit, Sherlock," Jimmy Maitland said, then punched Lewis Jacobs and laughed. Soon everyone was laughing, even as they held their weapons in their hands, their relief, their triumph, made them shout with laughter.

Jimmy Maitland said, "I wanted to say that since I first saw your name among the new trainees. I love it. Does anyone know where that line's from?"

THIRTY-SEVEN

Dr. Lauren Bowers said very quietly, "Lacey, do you remember getting into the trunk of Marlin's car?"

Lacey moaned, her head turning from side to side.

"It's all right. I'm here. Dillon is here. You're safe. This was a long time ago. Marlin's dead. He can't hurt you. You're remembering this for you, Lacey. Now, open your mind. Relax. Did you get into the trunk?"

"Yes. I wanted to be sure Belinda was betraying Douglas. I'd overheard her talking to him an hour before. I heard them make a date. I followed her and this guy. I didn't know she knew I was there. I heard her talking to Marlin but I couldn't make out what they were saying. When we got to the warehouse and they dragged me out of the trunk, I'd never been so terrified in my life. Then Marlin made me walk to the center of the maze with Belinda.

"I believed she was as terrified as I was, but she wasn't, at least she wasn't that night. But I believed she was. I walked every step beside her. Once she even handed me the string. Every few feet Marlin would call out to us, tell Belinda how he'd have to punish her if she didn't get to the center of the maze. I remember being so afraid, feeling so helpless."

"Yes, that's all right, Lacey. You were just nineteen. What happened next?"

"When we finally got to the center of the maze, Marlin was there and he was smiling. He smiled even when I thought he knifed Belinda. I thought he'd kill me next. I can remember screaming, running to where Belinda was lying. The horror of it shut me down. That's all I remember."

"And you just refused to remember it later," Dr. Lauren Bowers said to Savich. "Anything else?"

"Did Marlin tell Belinda he had to punish her because she cursed too much? Because she bad-mouthed her husband?"

"I think so. Wait, yes, he did."

"I think we know everything she needs to let go of the past." Dillon was silent a moment, then he said quietly, "Before you bring her back, ask her what she wanted to do with her life before Belinda's murder. Oh yes, tell her not to recall it."

When Lacey awoke she looked at Dillon and said, "The answer was there all the time, locked in my brain. I guess that's why I had the horrible nightmares for months and months after Belinda's murder, why I was terrified that someone would get to me and murder me. That's why I had the nightmare at your house, Dillon. It was coming too close. The dream helped me keep it under wraps."

"That's right, Lacey. But it's gone now."

Savich asked her later as they walked to the car, "Will you tell Douglas that Belinda did indeed have an affair with Marlin, that it was his child she carried?"

"I think he already knew. I don't think he knew it was Marlin, but he sure had to know that it wasn't his kid."

"Belinda wouldn't have ever had an abortion. She wanted that baby. Douglas must have known he had a low sperm count, even then he must have known. And that's why he hit her: he was furious."

"Yet he married Candice when she told him she was pregnant. Guess he wanted to believe that despite a low sperm count, he'd scored. Who knows?

Now maybe he and Candice have a good shot at making it. If he can't sire a kid and she doesn't want one, well, then, all problems are solved."

"Now that I can remember, I can see that Belinda's life was out of control. I don't think she was difficult, like our mother, which is what my father told me, but she was over the edge. And I was a bratty teenager, bugging her, spying on her."

"Yes, you're probably right. And that's the answer to the differences Wild Burt York found in all the physical comparisons he did of the murders. Marlin killed Belinda for different reasons and the differences show up in how he built the props. You know something else, Sherlock?"

She cocked her head to the side in that unique way she had. He patted her cheek. "It's all over now. Every shred of it, every scintilla. There'll be the media, but you can handle that. Mr. Maitland will try to protect you from the vultures as much as he can. Oh yeah, there's one other detail." He paused a moment, frowning down at his shoes. "Hannah hired a hood, one of her informants, to go after you in that car, and the same guy broke into your house. She claims he didn't follow orders. She never told him to rape you, just scare you. She says she's really sorry, Sherlock, claims she never meant to hurt you. She's been asked to leave the Bureau. It's up to you if you want her prosecuted."

"Did she tell you why she did it?"

"She claims she lost it. She was crazy jealous. She thought she could scare you off, make you pack up and go back to California."

"If we get the guy she hired, then she'd have to take a fall too, wouldn't she?"

He nodded, then said, "Yes. If they catch the guy, she'd be prosecuted."

"Let me think about it."

HE helped her into his Porsche, then walked around to the driver's side. He gave the left front tire a good kick. "I can't believe it wouldn't start that night. If Luke hadn't come along, we might have been in deep trouble."

"Luke's coming to the wedding?"

"Oh yes." He leaned over and kissed her. "Fasten your seat belt. I'm feeling like a wild and crazy guy."

"I'm feeling kind of wild and crazy too. Tell you what. Why don't we go home and watch old movies and eat popcorn?"

"Why don't we go home and make our own movies? Popcorn is optional."

"But you don't have a movie camera, do you?"

"Let's call this a dress rehearsal."

She gave him a slow, sweet smile. "You promise to make me a star?"

EPILOGUE

"I don't believe this," Sherlock said as she took a glass of chardonnay from Fuzz the bartender.

"He never told you, never let on?" Sally Quinlan asked, saluting her with her own glass of chardonnay.

"Never a word. Sure, he would sing me country-and-western songs. But this? I had no idea. Doesn't he look beautiful up there, wearing those boots and that belt with the silver buckle?"

The two women sat back as Ms. Lily, draped in a white silk dress that made her look as epic as Cleopatra, said from the small square stage, "Now listen up, brothers and sisters, even you yahoos we've got here tonight. I've got a special treat for you. We finally got our Savich back. He and Quinlan have agreed to play for us. Take it away, boys."

"This ought to be great," said Marvin the bouncer, at Lacey's shoulder. "You sit back and enjoy, Chicky."

Dillon's beautiful baritone filled the smoky bar, his guitar a mellow background, Quinlan's sax running a harmony with the melody. His voice was deep and rich and sexy, carrying clearly to every darkened corner of the club.

> *What's a man without love?*
> *What's his night without passion?*
> *What's his morning without her smile?*
> *What's his day without her in his mind?*
>
> *Bring her love to my nights.*
> *Bring her smile to my mornings.*
> *Bring her mind to fill my days.*
> *Just bring her back to me.*

What's a man without his mate?
What's his life without her laughter?
What's his soul without her joy?
What's a man without his mate?

Bring her love to my nights.
Bring her smile to my mornings.
Bring her joy to my days.
Just bring her back to me.

Sherlock was crying. She hadn't meant to, didn't even realize she was doing it. Not making a sound, just letting the tears gather and trickle down her cheeks. When the sax and guitar faded out, there was absolute silence in the Bonhomie Club. A woman sighed. A man said, "Ah, shit."

Then the applause came on, really soft and light at first, then gathering momentum. The women were clapping louder than the men.

"It's his cute butt, Sally," Ms. Lily said, leaning over to pat Sherlock. "Well, actually, it's both their cute butts. Now, little gal, when are you and my Savich going to get married? I don't allow any gal shacking up with him. He's innocent. I don't want him taken advantage of, you got me?"

"You'll get the invitation next week, Ms. Lily."

"Good. Maybe Fuzz will bring another bottle of chardonnay that has a real live cork, like he did for Sally and Quinlan. Your Dillon's real talented, honey. You let him sing to you and bring him down here once a week. It's good for my soul to hear him wail out his songs. Also, no crooks dare come near the club when the two supercops are playing here.

"Now he's looking at you and he's got that wicked smile on his face. Imagine an FBI agent who could smile at a woman like that. Goes to show you, doesn't it?

"Well, I'm off to win myself some money in a little poker game. Don't tell my boys about it, will you? Their cop genes might get scrambled and we don't want them to feel like they're in any moral dilemma."

Quinlan announced from the stage, "Savich here is going to get himself married, just like I did. It's about time. Now, we have this song for you that celebrates his short number of bachelor days left. It's called 'Love Surfin'.' "

Moved myself to the bright blue sea.
Knew the change would be good for me.
Made enough money in the old rat race,

> *Sure to die if I kept my pace.*
> *Now I'm lying in the warm, soft sand.*
> *Checking all the girls showing lots of tan.*
> *All these girls—what's a guy to do?*
> *I want them all, think I'll surf right through.*
>
> *Going love surfin',*
> *Gonna love them all*
> *Love surfin'*
> *Heading for a fall.*
> *Love surfin'*
> *Such a greedy man.*
> *Love surfin'*
> *Getting all I can.*

Sherlock was laughing so hard that when she threw her purse at him, it bounced off Quinlan instead.

Ms. Lily was standing outside of her open office door. She yelled out, "You taking your life in your hands, Savich, what with your chicky being an FBI agent."

Savich was beaming at Sherlock. He said into the mike, "My sister wrote that one. I just came up with the music."

"I'll be speaking to your sister," Sherlock called out.

"I heard you got an offer on your town house."

"Yes. A very good offer. It's a done deal. I'm here to stay now, Dillon."

"Good. Let's get married on Friday."

"That would be nice but I don't think we've got the time to pull it off. How about next month? I promised Ms. Lily that she'd get an invitation. Actually I told her she'd get one next week. Also, my friend Ford MacDougal from the Academy just got back from the desert. I want him to come."

"You mean a big wedding? All my family? Your family? Even Douglas and Candice? Even your mother and father and the BMW? A ton of people? All with fistfuls of rice?"

"I guess we have to. You once told me that family was family and there was nothing you could do about it. You made the best of it and went about your business. Hopefully Mom and Dad will try to act normal for the day; hopefully Douglas won't start screaming at Candice and then go slaver over my mother. Oh yeah, there's Conal Francis, Belinda's father, my mother's first husband. He's called my mother. My father is livid."

"Families are grand. Any idea what's going to happen there?"

"Not a clue, but it should be fun to see it played out. I don't think I'll invite him, though. My shot at trying to keep the peace. You know, Sally Quinlan said a big wedding was great sport. You don't want to?"

"Oh—let's go for it." He kissed her nose, her chin.

"We don't have to worry about the BMW. Dad just bought a fire-engine red Corvette. He said even Mom on her worst days couldn't possibly think he'd want to hit her driving that beauty. He laughed then. He said her new shrink is making progress. He's even had sessions with her. Also, Mom's on some new medication."

"Families. Ain't they great?"

She kissed his shoulder.

"Oh yeah, I've got another piece of good news for you. They caught the guys who were murdering those abducted kids in Missouri. Ollie's gut was right. It happened really fast. Turns out it was three young males, all twenty-one, who were reported to a local FBI agent by one of the girl-friends who was angry because her boyfriend kicked her out for another babe." He laughed. "I heard she skipped bail and took off for Mexico City with all the money."

She laughed with him. "I'll bet Ollie is pleased."

"Yep, but he wanted to be the one to make the arrest. Oh yeah," he added, raising his face above hers, "your wedding present from me is arriving tomorrow. You took the day off to see your doc so I set up the delivery."

She grabbed his arms, hugged him, then shook him. "What is it? Tell me, Dillon, what did you get me?"

"I ain't talkin', honey. You'll have to wait, but I sure want to hear something out of you when I come in tomorrow night."

"You won't even give me a hint?"

"Not a single one. I want you to wallow in anticipation, Sherlock."

She sighed, then punched his arm. "All right, but I'll probably be too excited with all this anticipation to sleep. Would you sing me just one line?"

He blinked, then raised his head and sang, *"I don't know nothin' better than a spur that's got its boot."*

"All right, that's not enough. More."

He kissed her ear, then her throat. *"I don't know nothin' better than a barb that's got its wire."*

She laughed and snuggled closer. "More."

"I don't know nothin' better than a poke that's got his cow."

"And the last line?"

"No, I don't know nothin' better than a man who's got his mate."

"Oh, Dillon, that's the greatest."

"Goodness, you're easy." He kissed her mouth. "No, my sister didn't write that one, I did. You like that? You're not putting me on, are you? You appreciate the finer points of my music?"

"Oh yes," she said. "Oh yes."

"I wrote it for you."

She gave him a radiant smile. "I just thought of another verse."

An eyebrow went up.

She sang in an easy western twang, *"I don't know nothin' better than a fetlock with its horse."*

"A team," he said. "We make a great team. What's a fetlock anyway?"

She grinned up at him. He stroked his fingers over her soft skin. He began kissing her and didn't stop for a very long time. When he was finally on the edge of sleep, he wondered what she'd play for him first on the new Steinway grand piano that was being delivered tomorrow.